THE GEEK'S (

WIZARDING

MASTERY

IN ONE EPIC TOME

THE COMPLETE TALE OF BRYANT ADAMS

MEGAN O'RUSSELL

Ink Worlds Press

Visit our website at www.MeganORussell.com

The Geek's Guide to Wizarding Mastery in One Epic Tome: The Complete Tale of Bryant Adams

Cover Art by Sleepy Fox Studio (https://www.sleepyfoxstudio.net/)

Editing by Christopher Russell

Interior Design by Christopher Russell

Printed in the United States of America

DEDICATION

For all the accidental heroes of the world

HOW I MAGICALLY MESSED UP MY LIFE IN FOUR FREAKIN' DAYS

BOOK ONE

1

Monsters poured out the windows that surrounded Times Square. Dark angels with glistening black wings stretched their shadows across the afternoon sky. A ruby red-scaled dragon climbed onto the perch reserved for the New Year's Eve ball drop. Women and children fled as flames licked the sidewalk. There was no help to be seen, no savior to conquer the savage beasts destroying the best tourist trap man had ever created. But as the horde with their gleaming black armor and talons that dragged along the ground, dripping with sizzling ooze, streamed out of the hotel lobby, one boy among the throng was brave enough to stand up and fight. One boy to—

"Ouch!" I choked as something caught me hard around the neck, yanking me backwards.

"Sweetie"—an older black woman had me by the back of the hoodie and was dragging me back onto the sidewalk—"I don't know what you're daydreaming about, but you're about to get yourself killed. And no one wants to see a scrawny little white boy smeared on the street. You better watch out." Shaking her head, she walked away, shopping bag in tow.

"Thank you!" I called after her, rubbing the sore part of my neck and muttering under my breath, "I'm not *that* scrawny," as she disappeared into the crowd.

"I don't know how scrawny you think you're not"—Devon patted my shoulder—"but you still can't stand up to a cab. Seriously, man, you shouldn't be allowed to cross the street. That's, what, three times some old lady has saved your ass this month?"

Devon was right. Old ladies were my guardian angels in New York. I think they formed a league when I was little. The *Keep Bryant Jameson Adams Alive League*. They'd done pretty well so far. I mean, I had made it to sixteen without ever riding in an ambulance. I don't know why they couldn't have formed a *Get Bryant Jameson Adams a Girlfriend League*, or I'd even take a *Make Bryant Jameson Adams Mysteriously Cool League*.

But, beggars, choosers...whatever. I duly acknowledged my begrudging gratitude for the growing bruise on my neck and got on with my afternoon.

We crossed the street, and Devon chose our post for the next few hours. We sat at one of the café tables in the middle of what used to be Broadway before they blocked the road off so tourists could spend their money without worrying about little things like people needing to drive anywhere that might actually matter.

Devon took off his coat and draped it over the back of his chair. He struck a casual pose, turning his face to the sun. "How do I look?"

"Ridiculous," I muttered.

"Don't be jealous of my swagger." Devon twinkled.

He looked like one of those male models plastered on the buildings, glowering down on us.

"Saying 'swagger' automatically makes you ridiculous. And why do we have to come here anyway? We're New Yorkers. It's our obligation to avoid Times Square like our lives depend on it."

"With the way you walk, yours might." Devon winked at a group of girls passing by, sending them all into fits of giggles.

That was Devon's game. Go to Times Square looking like a stereotypical New Yorker—head to toe in black, sleek shoes no sane person would ever want to walk in, requisite coffee in hand—then flirt with all the tourist girls. On a bad day, he'd get winks and giggles. On a good day, he'd ditch me and strut away with a girl on each arm, ready to be their personal tour guide.

I tried my best not to be jealous. After all, it wasn't Devon's fault he was born a naturally muscular, racially ambiguous chick magnet. He couldn't be blamed for that any more than I could be blamed for being a pale string bean with scrawny arms and plain brown hair. I wish I had been born with red hair. Then at least I could blame my pastiness on being a ginger.

I pulled a book out of my school bag. Just because I was lounging in Times Square with Devon didn't mean I needed to watch his attempts at becoming the teen demigod of New York.

"Doing homework isn't cool, Bry." Devon slid the book away from me.

"Neither is failing history."

"Failing is counterproductive," Devon said, giving a slight nod to a passing woman.

"Aw come on, man." I pulled the book onto my lap. "That one was pushing thirty."

"And I just made her day." Devon smiled, sinking back into his well-practiced casualness.

It took two hours for Devon to get his fill of smiling and winking. I finished all my homework before he decided he wasn't going to get lucky that day.

"You know, no one makes you come with me," Devon said as we walked home, interrupting me as I tried to keep my mind on watching for cars.

"Ah"—I shook my head—"but then when one of those out-of-towners you pick up turns out to be a—"

"Harpy?" Devon raised one black eyebrow.

"I was going to say serial killer," I growled, "but harpy works fine. Mythical cause or not, if you go missing, I want to be able to identify which girl you wandered away with so I can help the cops find your body."

"Thanks?"

"I want you to have a proper funeral." I shrugged. "I mean, that's what friends are for, right?"

"Make sure there's plenty of girls crying around my casket, and you've got it covered." Devon smacked me on the back and grinned as I failed to hide that he had made me stumble.

"Tomorrow is pizza and game night at Le Chateau?" Devon asked as we stopped at my door.

"Sure thing." I put the outside door key in the lock. "See you in Chem."

Devon waved goodnight and kept walking. Having a best friend that cool sucked. But when he's your only real friend, you can't be too picky.

The outside door banged shut behind me with its familiar *creak*. Before I could get out the key for the inside door, Mrs. Fortner, the super's wife, waddled out, cramming herself into the tiny safety space between the corridor and the streets of Manhattan.

"Hello, Bryant," she said in her thick accent as her giant boobs knocked into my arms. "Getting home late again? Your mama will worry."

"She knew I was going to stay out," I grunted as Mrs. Fortner squished me into the fake marble wall.

"Mamas always worry." Mrs. Fortner pushed herself past me toward the exit.

I just managed to catch the inside door with my foot and scurried into the hall, escaping before Mrs. Fortner could pin me in for a talk on why mamas are always right.

The hallways smelled like the same stale Chinese food they had for the last thirteen years. It probably smelled like old takeout before that, too, but we hadn't moved in until then, so I couldn't say for sure.

I ran up the grooved stairs, which matched the fake marble walls, two at a time until I reached the top floor. A fifth floor walk-up might not seem too glamorous, but it was home. And at least my mom had always been able to make rent.

The door flew open as I reached the landing, and my mother's head appeared. I inherited her dark brown eyes and brown hair. On her, the colors looked beautiful and gentle. On me, they looked like someone had spread dog poop on my head.

"Hey, Mom," I called up, knowing exactly how the conversation would go. "School was good. Devon didn't get murdered by a Scandinavian spy masquerading as a hottie tourist. Yes, I finished my homework, and whatever you already made for dinner sounds perfect."

As soon as I reached the door, she pulled me into a hug, ruffling my hair. "Very funny, sir. And we need to get—"

"My hair cut. I know, Mom." I walked through the door, tossing my bag onto the nearest chair, which scared Mrs. Mops, sending her skidding under the kitchen table crammed into the corner of the living room. The apartment smelled like lasagna and cake. My two favorite things. *Not* a good sign.

"Anything else fun or interesting happen today?" my mom asked as she crawled under the table to coo to the shaggy, gray, obese cat, comforting it after my faux pas.

I debated telling her about almost getting hit by another car. But I already had the daydreaming lecture memorized, so I didn't really see the point.

It's not that Mom thought daydreaming was bad. That would have been really rich coming from a lady sitting under a table talking to a cat. No, she believed in *directed daydreaming*, like writing books or drawing or being an actor. Things I'm not good at. I might have walked around thinking about dragons bursting into school and freeing all us helpless students from boredom, but I wasn't going to go writing a book about it. I already had it bad enough. I didn't need to be designated any more the artsy kid than I already had been. Especially since I don't actually have any artistic talent.

I turned to go to my room.

"Oh, sweetie," my mom said, at her most suspiciously casual, "I know you have a lot of schoolwork, but I volunteered you for the set crew for *Pippin*."

"Mom, I hate—"

"*Hate* is a strong word, sir." She slinked out from under the table and toward the oven. "Besides, you need to be more involved, and Elizabeth will be there, too. She's in the show, so maybe you could talk to her, ask her out for coffee."

"Not gonna happen, Mom." I shook my head, stifling a sigh. "Never gonna happen."

I walked into my room and closed the door behind me, resting my forehead against the cold, smooth wood.

I don't know what's worst—having a mom who runs the drama department at your school, having a mom who reads you well enough to know which girl you've been crushing on for the last three years, or having a mom who's cool enough to try and set you up with said girl and delusional enough to think this beautiful and perfect girl would ever give you the time of day without the threat of a nuclear apocalypse looming over her head.

Whichever way it landed, I was going to be stuck holding a paint brush and trying not to look like a total ass in front of Elizabeth.

"Why, why, why?" I groaned, punctuating each *why* with a thump of my forehead.

"Sweetie," Mom's gentle voice came from the living room, "if you bang your head against the door, you'll end up with a flat forehead."

"Thanks, Mom."

2

——————

"You ready for tonight?" Devon asked me twelve times before lunch.

That was one of the benefits of having a mom on faculty. You could swing it so your best friend was in all your classes. Bonus: you're less likely to get beat up with your super cool best friend around all the time. Extreme drawback: no girl will ever notice you with your super cool, über chick magnet friend around all the damn time. It's fine though. Maybe I'll get a girlfriend when I'm thirty. Or in the nursing home. Either way, it's bound to happen eventually, right?

"So the plans are all set?" Devon asked again as we left school.

I turned to him to ask what the hell plans he thought I should have made, but at that very second, Elizabeth waltzed out the school door and onto the sidewalk in front of us. I don't want to sound stupid or lovesick or anything, but I swear when Elizabeth walks, she glides on the air. Some guardian angel hauls around a giant fan to make Elizabeth's blond, perfect, curly hair blow gently behind her. Her eyes sparkle like she klepto'd stars and uses them as contacts. Except she would never steal anything because she's the kind of girl who saves puppies, runs fundraisers for the theatre department, and helps lost tourists get out of Hell's Kitchen.

Elizabeth Wick is perfection.

"Close your mouth, man." Devon pushed my jaw shut. "Girls don't dig mouth-breathers."

"It doesn't matter what I do." I shook my head, running my hands through my hair, which really did need cutting. "Elizabeth will never think I'm anything more than her favorite teacher's dorky son."

One of the basketball players was chatting up Elizabeth by the fence that covered the school's ground floor windows, his hand on the metal bars, leaning over her like she was his lunchbox. For an umpteenth time, I wished I was...say, a basketball player with a weird-looking letterman jacket who was cool enough to talk to Elizabeth Wick without tripping over himself while managing to say words that could be recognized as a part of the English language.

"Bryant," Devon enunciated, none too subtly indicating he had been trying to get my attention. "Are the *plans* all set for tonight? For Le Chateau?"

"What? Yes. The *plans*. The plans are all set."

"Awesome!" Devon strolled around the corner from school and headed downtown. I trotted to catch up.

We walked in silence for two blocks, cutting south and then east. Away from where all the other kids from school would be heading. It was the rule I set up three years ago when I finally let Devon in on the big secret.

When we got far enough away, Devon hailed a cab. I told the driver the address. As soon as the door closed, Devon launched into his weekly spiel. It was kind of annoyingly endearing. With more annoying than endearing. But what d'you do? It was tradition.

"Man, this one is going to be epic! Are you sure everything we need is going to be there?"

"I put in all the orders online." I watched Central Park whiz by. "Drake is going to have everything we want."

It only took about five minutes in the cab. We could have walked, but it was against the rules. Cabs only when going to Le Chateau.

The cabbie pulled over and let us out. I tossed him the cash for the fare and a hefty tip—because why not—and we headed to the door.

There was a new doorman that night. All dressed up and shiny. "Good evening, Mr. Adams," he said formally even though I had never seen him before. It was kind of funny to think of doorman training involving learning to recognize my face.

"Good evening, Mr. Adams," Drake said from behind his desk as soon as we walked in. "Mr. Rhodes," he added, nodding to Devon.

"Drake." Devon nodded back, looking all stiff. Like any *normal* person, the only time he'd be caught dead in a building like this is when he came here with me.

"I have your order." Drake pulled three pizzas, two bottles of soda, and a bag from behind the desk.

I took the pizzas and sodas while Devon opened the bag.

"Sweet! I told you it would be epic!" He brandished the new video game we had picked for this week.

"Thanks, Drake." I kicked Devon in the ankles to make him move to the elevator.

Le Chateau looked out onto Central Park from the top floor of the building. Well, really, it *was* the top floor of the building. As soon as the elevator doors opened, I saw me. Well, me from two years ago in a portrait of me and my dad he had commissioned for some unknown reason.

"Hey, Dad," I muttered to the portrait. "Good to see you again."

"Go do your rounds, Bry, and let's get started," Devon called as he flicked on the giant TV that sat in front of the big leather couch.

"Yep," I called back before walking to the kitchen.

It was my job to check the apartment every week. My dad's place. He travels all over the world for work, so I'm lucky if I get to have coffee with him once a month. But he kept this monstrosity in New York so I could have a home with him. And since I'm a minor who shouldn't be staying in an apartment alone, I got paid for "weekly chores." I don't know how much. It's all a business disbursement, but the financial advisor he sent me to last Christmas said from the funds I got deposited in my housesitting account, I could get a few doctorates and never eat Ramen.

I walked through the kitchen, checked the empty fridge. Then all three of the bathrooms for water damage. Looked over the guest rooms, my dad's room, my room. I mean, he designated it my room, but really, I only ever slept there the day after my birthday every year, so I don't know why he didn't let other people stay there. He could have made a killing as an Airbnb. Not that he needed more money.

I finished my rounds and headed back to the living room. Devon had already opened the first pizza.

"All good in Le Chateau?"

"All good." I picked up my controller, ready for battle.

3

W e played for a few hours until the pizza was gone and we knew Devon's dad might freak if we were out much longer. We always had to be really careful not to push it too far. If Devon's parents said he couldn't come with me anymore, I would be stuck hanging out at my dad's all by myself once a week. No one else from school really knew about Dad. Well, I guess they knew I must have one *somewhere*, but no one but Devon knew my dad was super rich. When you're already the dorky outcast, the last thing you want is to be the rich dorky outcast. I mean, sure, more people might be nice to you, but only because they'd want you to buy them stupid things and take them to fancy parties.

Devon was the only one I trusted to know my dad picked me up in a helicopter to take me upstate for Thanksgiving lunch last year without treating me like a human piggy bank.

So, reluctantly, Devon and I went downstairs to catch a cab home. It felt like throwing money away to travel fifteen blocks, but Dad insisted and paid, so I guess it didn't really matter.

There were no cabs lurking out front, and since it was October, it was a little cold to be standing around waiting.

"Let's start walking," I said, and Devon nodded, shoving his hands into his pockets.

"I can arrange for a cab if you'll only wait inside, Mr. Adams," the new doorman said, but I darted past like I hadn't heard him. I don't know if I'll ever feel like a *Mr. Adams*, and I definitely didn't want some dude with polished brass buttons pretending he actually knew who I was.

As soon as we got a block down, Devon and I started hailing cabs. A couple sped past. One slowed down, realized we were teenagers, and pulled away. Devon reached all the way to the back of his vocabulary to cuss out the driver.

"Keep walking, Devon," I said as rain fell in a cold mist.

"We should have waited for the new doorman to call a cab." Devon popped his collar.

"Somebody will stop." I raised my hand again without looking back at the street.

It was like a cue in a play. As soon as I held my hand up, a cab stopped, letting out a guy, who stepped gingerly into the rain as though it offended his sensibilities.

The ex-passenger couldn't have been much older than twenty, but he wore a black suit with a black bowtie and white shirt. His hair was darker than his tie, and his skin an even paler white than mine. He stared right at Devon and me for a second. His eyes were dark, too. The dude seriously looked straight out of a black and white picture. There was no color to him at all.

Devon climbed into the cab while the guy stumbled away.

"Bryant," Devon shouted, "stop watching the drunk dude, and let's go!"

The guy looked back at us for a minute, glowering like he was about to say something. I hopped into the cab and shut the door behind me, giving the cabbie Devon's address. We pulled away as the guy stumbled into a restaurant with a shining purple awning.

"Somebody's having a good night," I muttered.

"Maybe not," Devon said quietly enough to not be heard over the blaring country radio. He flipped his palm to show a phone.

"Everything okay back there?" the cabbie asked.

"Fine." I took the phone from Devon and shoved it into my pocket.

Now, I know what you're thinking. *What about lost and found? Why didn't you turn the phone in?* I've lost enough things in cabs to know that once they go into that logbook in the front of the cab, no rightful owner ever sees any of them again. And, even if the photocopy guy was about to get into a screaming match with me on Central Park West, losing a phone in Manhattan sucks, and I do my best to be a good Samaritan.

But if I had known what that stupid cellphone would lead me to, I would have thrown it out the window of the speeding cab and into the nearest gutter. Not even a rate-jacking, country-blasting, onion soup-smelling cab driver deserved the hell my life was about to turn into.

4

To be honest with you, I didn't actually think about the phone that night. By the time I got home and past the mom monster, I had completely forgotten about its existence. And I don't mean like, *Ahh! My mom sprouted tentacles from her head and tried to feed me to a God from the underworld!* We're still in the part of my life that was completely boring and normal. What I mean by *mom monster* is whenever I get home from Dad's, Mom gets all clingy for the rest of the night. Like she needs to prove that even though she can't dump ungodly amounts of money into my college fund in a questionable way, she still loves me and I should keep living with her in Hell's Kitchen instead of moving to Central Park West. Not that living on Central Park West was ever really an option. I mean, I'm sixteen, but I'm still a minor. And it would kill my mom if I tried it.

So, I let her stuff me full of even more food and talk about all the things we used to do together when I was little and make plans for family bonding time for the weekend. Which in this case meant me painting sets for hours while she directed at the school. Not really my idea of fun, but whatever.

I didn't really think about the phone again until the next day after school when I was elbow deep in a failed art project.

Our school had a giant set shop next to the stage, which was one of the big perks for our theater program. We used to have students build sets in school with like Stage Craft class and all that. And I really do mean all of that in past tense. The set shop is not so much there anymore. Unless you count a smoldering hole in the wall as a set shop. But at least it was a nice set shop while it lasted.

My mom was doing her thing with the students on stage. Elizabeth was the lead. I mean, of course she was. She was perfect and brilliant and freakishly talented... and perfect.

While I was reduced to painting a giant ring of fire onto a set piece, trying to make it look like the flames hadn't been designed by a four-year-old. As I said before, I'm *not* good at painting.

Something weird was going on onstage. But I was too deep in my pre-school art to pay attention. I'd be watching the show all weekend anyway, so I didn't really need to see a cleaning rehearsal.

Mom called a five, and soon I heard quiet crying and that firm yet comforting tone she always used with hysterical actors.

I swung around. Sure enough, in the far corner, Mom had her hands on Elizabeth's shoulders, talking her off the ledge. Not a real one.

I turned back to my painting. Why did Elizabeth have to look so freaking appealing even when she cried? Not that I'd be caught dead staring. I mean, you don't get much creepier than that. But what if there was something I could do? What if she needed money to pay a loan shark? I could find a way to outsmart the shark and corner him in an alley. I mean really, getting the money would probably be easier. But if I had to find a way to sneak into a loan shark's office under an overpass in the Meat-packing District—

A tap on my shoulder made me drop my brush, leaving a big splotch of orange in the middle of the red flames. I cursed, and Mom stage-whispered, "Bryant Jameson Adams, not in school."

Fine, but did she *have* to use my full name?

"Sorry, Mom," I said before noticing the still-soggy Elizabeth and immediately growing tongue-tied.

"Elizabeth, you know Bryant," my mother said, not bothering to ask if I knew Elizabeth.

The girl of my dreams nodded. "Hey, Bryant."

"Elizabeth is in your Pre-Calc class," my mom said.

"Really?" I ran a hand through my hair, trying to play it cool, before realizing my hand was covered in orange paint, which was now in my hair.

"I sit next to you," Elizabeth said. "I have all year."

"Oh, right, yeah you do."

My mom raised an eyebrow at me. "Elizabeth." Mom gestured for her to step forward.

"So," my one-and-only began, "your mom says you're top of our math class."

I shot my mom a quick glare. Why did she have to make me look like more of a geek than I already managed all on my own?

"I shouldn't even be taking that class. I'm not a math person." Elizabeth shook her head. "My dad made me do it. He said I couldn't do art all the time. But I have a *C* in the class, and if I don't get an *A* on the test on Tuesday, the school is going to pull me out of the show."

"Oh." I nodded.

Tears started to stream down Elizabeth's cheeks again. "I'm trying, I really am, but I don't get it. And your mom said maybe you could help?" Elizabeth's porcelain face turned pink. "You could tutor me this weekend during tech?"

I gawked at her, wanting to say, *Hell, I'll take the test for you if it will make you smile at me.* Or even, *I promise I will find a way for you to ace that test.* But she was standing there all pretty, and words seemed too hard.

"Bryant?" my mom said.

"Uhh, yeah." I stumbled over the words. "I can help. Let me see your homework and tests and then I can figure out—"

"Thank you!" Elizabeth threw her arms around my neck. Her arms. Around my neck. Just to repeat for clarity.

"Take a minute, and then come back onstage," Mom said quietly, winking as she walked away.

"You have no idea how much this show means to me," Elizabeth sighed, stepping back.

I should have hugged her back, but I couldn't figure out how arms were supposed to work, and my hands were covered in paint anyway.

"It's okay." I tried to sound as though spending time teaching her math wasn't going to be the best thing that had ever happened in my life.

"Maybe we can meet right after rehearsal tonight?" she asked. "I mean, if you have time."

"I can work it out," I said.

Devon would just have to return the phone on his own. I didn't think he would mind under the circumstances. But as soon as I thought about it, my pocket started to ring.

It wasn't a normal ringtone. It sounded like a song I had never heard before but somehow knew the melody of. I froze for a minute. What if the vampire guy was calling his phone?

I pulled it from my pocket with my less painty hand.

But as soon as it saw the light, the ringing stopped.

"Sorry. I made you miss a call," Elizabeth said.

"Not even my phone." I pushed the button on the bottom to try and see the caller ID. But when I held my thumb to it, the phone unlocked.

"I thought you said it wasn't your phone." Elizabeth frowned.

"It's not."

I studied the home screen, trying to go to the missed calls section, but there was no phone icon. Or email icon. There were no weird little games with jewels or freaky llamas.

Only tiny little symbols I had never seen before. One looked like an old book, one like fire, a dragon, and some weird stuff I couldn't begin to venture a guess on.

"Huh," I muttered.

"What?" Elizabeth leaned over to look at the phone. Her hair smelled like sunshine.

"I, umm, the OS is weird." I tapped the fire button, stupidly thinking it might be some sort of emergency call button. A picture of flames appeared on the screen, along with a level bar.

"Is it a game?" Elizabeth asked.

"Maybe." I slid my finger along the bar, making it tip to one side. The flames started to crackle.

"Weird game," Elizabeth said. "Is the phone making that smell?"

She was right. It had started to smell like smoke. And the crackling didn't sound like it was coming from the phone. And it was getting hot. Really hot.

I looked down at the flat I had been painting with grade school style fire just in time to see it burst into real flames.

"Oh, God!" Elizabeth leapt back.

"It's okay," I shouted, sprinting for the fire extinguisher by the stage door and popping the pin like a boss. She stood behind me while I pointed the foam at the base of the flames, calmly sweeping the tube back and forth. It wasn't as good as fighting a dragon, but it was almost like showing off. My years of battling my mother's kitchen fires had finally come in handy.

The only problem was the fire wasn't going out. It was like it was eating the foam, feeding on it to make itself grow.

"We need to get out." I grabbed Elizabeth's hand, towing her toward the stage and pulling the little fire lever on my way past. Instantly, red lights flashed and sirens started to beep.

"Everybody out!" I shouted over the din. "There's a fire in the shop!"

People screamed, running for the door.

"Bryant! Come on!" Cool under literal fire, Mom herded students toward the door, ordering them to leave their bags. "Bryant, go!" She yanked on her stage manager, who was trying to save the lighting board, and dragged him toward the exit.

I pulled Elizabeth along, her hand clasped tightly in mine. Once we broke out onto the sidewalk, the sirens of the fire trucks blared at us as they sped toward the school.

But over the sirens and the screaming, I still heard Elizabeth when she turned to me with panic in her eyes.

"How?"

5

We were stuck out on the sidewalk for forever. First, we did the whole huddle together and look on in horror thing. Elizabeth held my hand, and we watched the flames grow. I don't think she was really holding my hand on purpose. We both just kind of forgot how to let go. Too soon, she melted into the crowd of crying actors when they moved us all back as the firemen swarmed the scene. They kept shouting and radioing back and forth about how the flames weren't going out as quickly as they should. And then there was the fact that the fire was in a theatre with big heavy lights that were hung by not-so-competent students that could fall on the firefighters any minute.

Mom was being interrogated by the guys at the blockade. They asked questions about everything, and she kept manically counting all the students, making sure she really had gotten all of us out of harm's way. Every few minutes, she would run back and squeeze me hard before talking to the fire dudes again.

About a whole hour later, Devon showed up, pushing his way toward me through the throng.

"Shit, Bry!" He ran his hand through his hair, making it actually not look perfect for once. "Your poor mom."

"She's over there." I pointed to where she was flapping her hands at some guy with a clipboard.

"I mean, I know she made it out." Devon shook his head. "But that theatre was like her *life*."

It was kind of true. I mean, other than me, my mom's whole world was going up in flames. She had been working to build that theatre department since I hit kindergarten.

"She'll be okay." Devon slapped me hard on the back. "We'll figure something out. The school's got to have insurance."

An ear-splitting screech came from inside, and one of the lighting booms crashed down, sending the firefighters running for the door.

"Or maybe your dad can buy a new theatre." Devon shrugged.

I didn't mention that my mom would rather perform for the mole people who live under the subway tunnels than take any help from my dad.

"We need that damn fire to stop!" I pushed the heels of my hands into my eyes so hard, little white spots began to blink in the blackness. "We could lose a lot more than the theatre if it doesn't."

I didn't want to be sent to a different school to spend the rest of my pre-college career someplace strange. Dad would probably try and send me to some fancy boarding school upstate. It's what he had been campaigning for for years. I tried to picture myself wearing a bowtie and living in a dorm. Maybe I could convince him to spring for Devon to come with. Then at least I would have one friend in a hellhole of brats with way too much money.

"Bryant?" Mom put her hand on my shoulder. She looked exhausted, but she was holding it together. She was a trooper.

Elizabeth stood two steps behind Mom, her face all pink from crying.

How could anyone look that pretty after crying for an hour?

"This is the fire marshal." My mom pointed to the clipboard guy. "He wants to ask you and Elizabeth some questions. I'm going to go talk to the principal. I'll be right back."

Out by the fire trucks, the principal was busy glaring at the firemen like she was going to give them in-school suspension if they didn't get those flames put out soon. Like an hour ago.

The fire marshal led us away from the other students who were all still loitering in the middle of the street watching the theatre burn.

He was shorter than me. Stocky and sweaty with black little eyes like a mole.

"So, you two were the first to notice the fire?" he asked without introducing himself.

Elizabeth looked silently to me.

"Yes," I said, "we were."

"And what happened?" the marshal asked.

"We were talking, and then it smelled like smoke," I said, wondering if I was ever not going to smell like smoke again. "We looked down, and the set piece I had been painting was on fire."

"And you were only *talking*?" the marshal asked.

"Yes." I nodded, not missing his so-thin-it-was-practically-invisible-eyebrow creeping up his face. And I do mean eyebrow, not brows. I'd never seen such a pale, thin unibrow in my life.

He turned said unibrow to Elizabeth. "You weren't playing with any tools? No soldering, no sanders left on."

"I had been painting," I said. "I never even plugged anything in."

"We were looking at a cellphone." Elizabeth's voice shook. "Neither of us was touching anything but the phone, and then...." She shot me a weird look. Granted, this was a weird day. But still.

"I don't know if somebody else left something plugged in or what," I said, needing the marshal to stop glaring at Elizabeth with his little mole eyes. "But neither of us touched anything."

"Figures." The man took more notes on his clipboard. "Theatres are death-traps. Why anyone in their right mind would want one in a school..." He handed Elizabeth and me cards. "If you think of anything, give me a call." He waded back into the crowd.

I looked back up at the school. The fire was finally settling down. It was just a lot of smoke now. You couldn't see the flames anymore.

"We were playing with that phone." Elizabeth's voice still shook.

"I know," I said. And for some miraculous reason, I reached out and touched her arm. Just kind of laid my hand on her shoulder like I was comforting her. And she seemed to sort of take it like I was trying to comfort her and didn't tell me I was a loser and to never touch her again.

"We shouldn't have been playing with that phone," Elizabeth said.

"I don't think it would have made a difference." I shrugged. "I mean, even if we had noticed the fire a few seconds earlier, I don't think we could have stopped it. I tried the fire extinguisher—"

"That phone started the fire," Elizabeth whispered, stepping close so no one but me could hear. "You opened the fire app, and then that fire! *We* burned down the theatre."

"That's not possible. It's just a phone." I pulled it back out of my pocket and held it out to her. "See?" I tried to pass it to her, but she backed away like she really was scared.

"I don't care what's possible. I don't care if you don't see it." Elizabeth shook her head. "There is something wrong with that phone."

"It's fine." I pressed my thumb to the button, and the phone unlocked. The fire app was still pulled up. And the setting was still on high. The flames on the screen danced around like the Yule Log channel.

"Bryant, don't touch it," Elizabeth said, but I was already scrolling my finger along the bar, pulling the fire setting all the way down. The logs on the screen turned black as the fire disappeared.

"See? No big deal." I held the phone out to Elizabeth.

But she was pointing up at the school. The smoke was gone. And I don't mean it dissipated a little bit. It was gone. There was still a burned hole in the school where the stage used to be. But there was no more smoke, no fire at all.

"Get rid of it." Elizabeth's face was sheet white. "I don't know what the hell that thing is, but throw it into the river. Get rid of it Bryant, please."

I wanted to throw it into the river right then on the off chance she might say thank you or hug me again. Call me stupid, but I didn't really think there was anything weird about the phone. I thought it was a crazy coincidence. Or fate. Or the school board wanting to collect the insurance money. It really seemed more likely that Zeus had decided to smite my pathetic paint job than a cellphone had magically burned a giant hole in our school.

But I didn't care. Elizabeth was looking at me with her sparkly eyes, and I would have done whatever she wanted, even if I didn't buy the whole demon phone thing. I was going to be really daring and ask Elizabeth if she wanted to walk with me to the river right then so she could watch me toss it into the Hudson. But my mom pushed her way back over to us.

"The marshal said he's done with both of you," she said with her *I would rather stick my foot up his butt than listen to anything he has to say* voice. "So you should both go. You're going to have a lot of studying to do tomorrow, and you need your rest."

"Studying?" I asked.

"You are going to help Elizabeth study for the calculus test, she will get an A, and we will open *Pippin* next weekend." My mom switched to her freakishly determined tone she usually saved for customer service people. "The show must go on, and I will be damned if fires or math tests stop us. Go home and rest up, both of you. Bryant will meet you at the library at ten." She turned to Elizabeth, who looked like she wasn't quite sure what to say.

Elizabeth nodded, which was probably her best bet anyway.

"This is going to be one hell of a week, so we had better all be ready for it."

My mom stalked away, ready and willing to rally each and every theatre student.

"She's a little scary sometimes," Elizabeth said.

"Sometimes?"

Devon was pushing his way through the crowd toward me.

"I have to go." Elizabeth turned to look at the building. "I don't think I have a math book anymore."

"We can figure something out," I said, wondering how much of the inside of the school was actually left.

"Okay." She nodded. "I'll meet you in the morning. Just...get rid of it." She turned and walked away.

"Did you just have a conversation with Elizabeth Wick?" Devon asked.

"Yep. I'm her new math tutor."

"And she doesn't want you to get rid of the idea that you should ever talk to her again? Or yourself in general?"

"Nope." I shook my head, watching Elizabeth disappear down the street.

"Then what was she talking about?" Devon asked.

I held up the little black cellphone.

6

We walked uptown toward my dad's. I don't know if it was instinct, habit, or the fact that my keys to Mom's place had been melted by a fire. Either way, Le Chateau seemed like the best bet.

A cab would have been faster, but since I smelled like a barbeque gone wrong, I figured it was better to walk.

Devon started by giving me a blow-by-blow of what the firemen had been doing: running in and out and a lot of hauling hoses mostly. "And then Linda May, sweet little Linda May, was so terrified she needed comfort, and of course she ran to me. I'm telling you man, the fire made 8th Ave crazy."

"You do remember I was there, right?" I asked, trying not to sound snarky even though I was tired enough to curl up on a subway grate and sleep. "I was the one who saw the fire start and pulled the alarm to get everyone out."

"Really?" Devon asked, looking surprised for a second but trying to cover up his shock by punching me in the arm. "Good for you, man! Elizabeth must think you're a hero. This could be the break you've been waiting for. Did you ask her out?"

"What? No, I didn't ask her out!" I ran my hands through my hair. It was gritty from the smoke and orange paint.

Devon grimaced and shook his head, looking down at the sidewalk.

"What?" I asked again, trying not to get angry. "What did you want me to do? Was I supposed to look down, see a fire, and stop on the way to the alarm to ask Elizabeth to be my girlfriend?"

"I mean, *girlfriend* might have been pushing it, but it would have been better than nothing," Devon said.

"Sorry, I was trying to make sure everyone didn't burn to death."

"What about when you two were talking once everyone was out of the theatre then?" Devon said, nodding and winking at a random dog walker.

The poor girl had two mastiffs, three Chihuahuas, and one drooling pug. Their leashes had all gotten tangled, and one of the Chihuahuas was dangling over the bigger mastiff's back. Being a dog walker was on my top ten list for jobs I never wanted in Manhattan.

"I don't know how many more chances you can hope to get with Elizabeth."

"I've never had a single chance," I said as we turned onto Central Park West, "and now she probably thinks I'm a freak, so...." I was screwed. There was something about knowing she thought I had magically started a fire with a cellphone and was now afraid of me that made it seem more true than years of her never speaking to me ever had. My stomach felt heavy and gross.

"Why does she think you're a freak?" Devon asked. "I mean, you just saved the whole theatre class."

I pulled the little black demon out of my pocket.

"She's thinks you're a freak because you forgot to return the phone? Which, by the way, is not cool, man. You don't leave a guy phoneless in Manhattan."

"If you remember, before you *had* to tell me all about how you made out with Linda May while our school was on fire, Elizabeth wants me to get rid of the phone." I slid it back into my pocket. Somehow having it out in my hand made me feel exposed, like a big eye in a creepy tower was watching me as I ran toward a pit of lava.

"So then let's get rid of the phone," Devon said. "We'll take it to the purple restaurant and make it their problem to find the vampire dude, and you can tell her you did what she wanted."

"She doesn't want me to return the phone," I sighed, knowing full well Devon was going to laugh at me. "She wants me to throw it into the Hudson to destroy it. She thinks the phone started the fire."

I started counting to three in my head. Before I got past two, Devon had tossed his head back and roared with laughter. People stared as they walked by.

It took Devon a full minute to speak. "I'm sorry." He wiped the tears from his eyes. "Was there a stray ray of sunlight you reflected off the screen to ignite the mounds of dried grass in the set shop?"

"No." I pushed Devon in the back to make him start walking again, and he promptly skidded on sidewalk goop. "There's an app on the phone, and she thinks I started the fire with it."

"An app. She thinks you started a fire with an app on a phone you can't even open?"

"I did open the phone," I said, "and a fire app thing."

"How did you open the phone? It should have a password." Devon turned to me, his laughter fading a little. "Do you have like post-traumatic stress or something from the fire? Because I mean, we could call your mom."

"I don't have traumatic stress." I pulled Devon into the shade of a coffee shop awning. The place smelled like vegan food and almond milk. "And I didn't use a password." I glanced around before pulling the phone back out of my pocket. I didn't know what I was looking for. No one seemed to care about the two teenagers hanging out by the vegan coffee shop. But I still couldn't shake the feeling that someone was following me. Or that the evil eye was gazing down at me from the Empire State building. "I used my thumbprint." I pressed my thumb to the button, and the phone opened, showing the same funny symbols as before.

"Whoa!" Devon took it from me, but as soon as it left my hands, the thing turned back off. "Aw, come on." He pressed his thumb to the sensor, but the screen stayed dark. "Damn. Battery must have died."

I took the phone back and pressed my thumb back on the button. The screen popped back up. Devon grabbed the phone again, and it was the same thing. Him—phone off. Me—phone on.

"Bryant." Devon's voice was barely above a whisper. "Did you buy a phone and rig it to do that to freak me out? Because I mean, good for you, but that's a lot of trouble for a prank."

"You found this in the cab. And I would never prank you. I know better." And really I did. Devon would take any reason to punk you. If you were five minutes late when you were supposed to meet him, you had to spend the next week wondering what his revenge would be. Pulling a prank on him would be the worst idea anyone in Hell's Kitchen had ever had. Except maybe the next thing I did. That may have been the worst idea anyone in New York had ever had.

Devon was still giving me the *I don't believe you* stare with his eyebrows raised and his arms crossed. And Elizabeth thought I had a possessed phone, and my mom's theatre had burned down, and I had sort of had enough.

"Fine." I dragged him over to a trashcan by the side of the street, then tapped on the app that showed the picture of the fire. There it was—the still flames with the bar below balancing perfectly centered. I held the phone out like I was going to take a picture of the can and tapped the bar, tipping it all the way to the right.

Big mistake.

Flames shot out of the can and flew ten feet into the air like the sanitation department had decided collecting trash was too hard and installing a giant blowtorch was a better use of resources.

People behind us started to scream. Devon cursed and backed away. I stood there, frozen by the sudden heat. I couldn't move. I mean, I know I had gone to the fire app to prove to Devon that I wasn't wandering the city in some PTSD haze. But finding myself in front of a ten-foot-tall pillar of fire, holding a possessed cellphone in my hands, I sort of felt like maybe I had lost my mind. Maybe this wasn't even New York and I was locked in a cell. Or even better, and less scary maybe, I was still in bed, and this whole thing was a dream. I hadn't even gotten out of bed yet, and soon I would wake up with cat ass on my face.

I squeezed my eyes tightly shut and opened them again. There was still a fire right in front of me. No padded white room. No stinky cat ass.

I tapped the left side of the bar and pulled it all the way down. Just like it had sprung up without warning, in an instant, the fire disappeared with nothing but a melted trashcan to show for itself. Well, that and the sour, nose hair-burning stench of flaming crap.

I turned to Devon who stared, petrified, at where the flames had been.

"See? Not a prank."

"What the hell?" he muttered. "Not okay. That is definitely not okay. Burning trashcans is not okay."

The rubberneckers behind us chattered noisily. One woman shouted into her cellphone, "The fire's gone out, but I think it's a gas line!" She paused for a second. "Back away. 9-1-1 says everybody back away."

People immediately scurried down the street or hugged next to the building, still transfixed in fascinated horror.

"You need to move, boys!" the cellphone lady shouted at us as sirens echoed between the buildings.

"Go!" I pushed Devon so hard his feet finally started to work again. I grabbed his arm and dragged him onto a side street out of view of the fire trucks as they pulled up to the melted trashcan.

Two run-ins with the fire department in one day is not a good thing. Especially not when you might have caused the fires. Even if it was by accident.

We cut back around the block and to my dad's building. The fire trucks had parked down the street, but from here we couldn't even see what all the firemen were staring at.

Drake was behind the desk like always. "Mr. Adams." He smiled. "I wasn't expecting to see you here today."

"Yeah." I tried to put my thoughts into an order that didn't involve a possessed demon phone with the ability to make things spontaneously combust that was currently burning a hole in my back pocket. Not literally. I hoped. "There was a fire at school. Everybody's okay, but I lost my house key, so I'm gonna hang out here until my mom gets home." If my mom still had a house key.

"Of course, Mr. Adams." Drake unlocked the safe beneath the desk. "I would be more than happy to let you into the apartment. I am so relieved you're safe. Have you called your father?"

Drake led us to the elevator and turned the key to go up.

"No." It hadn't occurred to me to call my dad. I mean, how could he be worried about me when he didn't even know my school had been on fire? Never mind the fact that the more time passed, the more convinced I was that I had caused the fire in the first place. But Drake was still looking at me all concerned, so I said, "Not yet. I'm going to call before I shower." And I did need to shower. Even though the elevator was a big one, it was still small enough to trap in the horrible smoke and burning trash smell that was stuck to me.

The door opened to my dad's apartment, and Drake waved us in. "Shall I call for a pizza?"

"Two." Devon half-stumbled into the apartment.

"Very well." Drake closed the elevator doors and was gone.

Devon walked into the living room and collapsed onto the couch. I followed him, a little afraid he might be panicked enough to start throwing up onto the carpet. And having to call the cleaning lady to tell her you got puke in the carpet was never a fun time.

I sat on the metal rim of the glass coffee table and stared at Devon, waiting for him to speak. If he could still speak. I wasn't too sure about that.

"The fire," Devon said finally, his hands shaking as he dragged them over his face. "The phone started the fire."

Elizabeth had been right. She had seen it right away.

"Both fires. And the one at school didn't go out till I put it out with the app."

Devon scrunched his face and let out the longest string of muttered curses I had ever heard. "We have to get rid of it."

"Same thing Elizabeth said. I can take it down to the restaurant and leave it with them."

"No way in *Hell*!" Devon shook his head, looking as pale as I had ever seen him. "You just burned down half the school with that thing. You can't keep it. It's arson evidence, Bry."

"So we give it—"

"We are not giving the damn phone to people who might want to do more damage with it than you've already done! That guy we saw looked evil. He looked like a vampire or demon or something. We can't give an evil dude something this dangerous. What if he lights us on fire? Or decides to take out Times Square. I can't have that on my head, man."

"So, we do what Elizabeth said and dump it into the Hudson," I said, wondering if I could convince Drake to find a guy to take the phone to the river.

No, it couldn't be trusted to a courier. I mean, who wouldn't want to open a package they had been hired to dump into a river. We'd have to do it ourselves.

I turned my wrist over, making my watch blink on. Nearly seven PM. "If we head to the water in a few hours, we should be able to find a place to dump it without getting noticed."

"No way." Devon pushed himself to sit up. "The river's way too risky. What if it washes up and someone finds it?"

"It's a phone. It'll be dead from the water."

"A demon phone that starts fires, and you think water is going to hurt it?" Devon stood up, color coming back into his determined face. "We have to destroy it ourselves. It's the only way to make sure it's done."

M y dad isn't exactly the type to keep a hammer around. If something breaks, he tells Drake, and Drake calls a guy to get it fixed. Since we didn't have a hammer to smash the phone with, like a normal person bent on destroying the Devil's cellular device, we tried all the other heavy objects in the apartment.

First, we tried stomping on it. Then we hit it with the huge frying pan I don't think my dad has ever used. We dumped it in water and let it sit for twenty minutes while we ate the two pizzas Drake had sent up.

After the pizza was gone and I felt sick from the combination of pounding a whole large pie, accidentally burning down half my school, and the sense that something weird was paying me an even weirder amount of attention, Devon fished the phone out of the water. It looked blank.

He held it out to me. "Do your worst."

I pressed my finger to the scanner. My heart flipped for a split second while the screen stayed black. Yeah, but not so much. The phone blinked on. Creepy apps and all.

"It's just not fair." Devon ran his hands over his face. "I drop my phone two feet, and the screen cracks. We spend an hour trying to kill this thing, and nothing."

"I guess a phone that can make fire can protect itself." My mind raced. I mean, I couldn't turn the damned thing in to the police. They would think I was crazy and maybe arrest me for arson, too. I couldn't tell my mom I had burned down her theatre. My dad was halfway around the world. I thought about asking Drake, but I didn't know if evil demon phone destruction was really in his job description.

"Your dad lets you get away with anything, right?" Hope filled Devon's voice in a scary way.

"I mean, define *anything*."

"If there was a little damage done"—Devon stood—"he wouldn't like cut you off or have you killed or something?"

"We're not gonna pitch it out the window!" I shook my head for emphasis. "It could kill someone, and a murder rap would definitely piss my dad off."

"No one's gonna get hurt." Devon grabbed the phone from my hand and bolted to the kitchen. Before I could catch up, he'd tossed it into the microwave and pressed the popcorn button.

"Devon, no!" I shouted.

Too late.

Tiny little lightning bolts leapt around the inside of the microwave. Smoke drifted out through the edges of the door, accompanied by weird tinny *cracks*. I didn't reach out to try and stop it. I mean, if this would destroy the phone, I would hand out flyers in Times Square to earn enough money to buy my dad his fancy replacement. It took less than a minute for the microwave to give one last pathetic hiss and go black.

I reached for the door and pulled it open. A horrible stink of burned plastic made the already burnt hair on the inside of my nose die a final death.

"Don't touch it! It's hot!" Devon shouted as I picked up the phone.

But the thing was, it wasn't hot. Or cracked, burned, melted. Nothing. The microwave had been reduced to a warped pile of stink, but the phone was fine.

My thumb shook as I pressed it to the button. The phone flashed on even faster than when we had tried to drown it.

"It's the Rasputin of phones," Devon murmured. "It can never die."

"We're screwed." I sank down onto the kitchen floor. "Utterly screwed."

Just when I thought things couldn't get worse, the little fire alarm overhead started to beep.

The callbox by the elevator buzzed. It would be Drake calling up before dialing 9-1-1.

"Tell him everything is fine, we burned something in the microwave." I ran to my dad's room, threw myself onto his closet floor, and popped open the fake air conditioning vent at the bottom of the wall. Six inches back was the safe. Dad had given me the combination years ago in case I needed emergency money, but I had never actually opened the thing. Barely even noticing the stacks of cash, I tossed the phone in and slammed the door shut, then slipped the grate back into place so it looked like an air vent again. I was back to the living room in less than a minute.

Devon was still standing next to the intercom, looking dazed.

"Is he sending people up?" I asked.

"No." He shook his head. "I told him we accidentally nuked a spoon."

"Then it's fine." I sighed. "He'll tell my dad, but it's a good story. I'll email him and say I'm sorry. It'll be okay."

"Bryant." Devon's voice quaked like it was very much not okay. Somehow, seeing that crack in Devon's customary coolness made the immortality of the demon device even scarier than anything else had managed to. "We put the phone in the *microwave*, and it didn't kill it! What are we supposed to do?"

"Go home and think of something else." I pressed the elevator button. I didn't even have a backpack to grab. "The phone'll be safe here for the night, and we'll come up with a new plan tomorrow."

I looked down at my real phone. Mom had been texting for an hour.

At home but I don't have keys. Are you upstairs?

Never mind. Found Mr. Fortner, he let me in.

Please call so I know you're okay.

Don't forget you have to meet Elizabeth at ten tomorrow. Do you have math books in your room?

I hit my head on the elevator wall.

"What?" Devon asked.

"I'm meeting Elizabeth tomorrow at ten," I said.

"Well, at least there's a beautiful blond light at the end of the tunnel." Devon patted me on the back.

"Sorry for the alarm," I said to Drake as we passed to go out onto the street.

I don't remember his response. I was in too much of a daze. Devon was telling me how to put the moves on Elizabeth while teaching her about cosines. Oh, and there was an evil phone hidden at my dad's. And I had no idea what to do about any of it.

"Sorry," I muttered as I shoulder-checked a guy dressed in black who was heading into the building. I wasn't even a good New Yorker. I ran into someone on a mostly abandoned street.

I hope you never have a day where you feel like as big a screw up as I did on that walk home.

But things got even worse. So much worse.

My mom didn't let me go to bed till late that night. We were up sitting on the floor, trying to think of anyone we knew with theatre access who might owe somebody we knew a favor. Finally, I said we could ask my dad to rent her a stage for a day. I knew I shouldn't have said it, but I was tired and knew it would end the conversation so I could go to bed. I mean, he would have rented her a stage if she asked. But she'd never ask so...gotta love parents who won't speak to each other.

She woke me up at eight the next morning, and I guess she wasn't mad about my mentioning Dad buying her out of the theatre problem because she made normal Saturday breakfast: bacon, waffles, and homemade whipped cream. It was sort of our thing.

"Do you have everything ready to meet Elizabeth?" For an actor, Mom was really bad at sounding casual.

"I have my math book from last year." I shrugged. "This year's got burned."

"I'm sure you'll be able to help her," my mom said. "She is such a smart and talented girl."

I really didn't need my mom to explain to me how the girl of my dreams was the most brilliant person to ever walk the earth.

I *mmmhmm*ed a response.

"I'm sure you'll be good friends once you spend a little time getting to know each other."

"Mom," I said, trying to act like my stomach wasn't being shaken by a monkey with cymbals, "you do know how weird it is to make your son tutor a girl to try and set him up with her?"

"Tutoring is a great way to spend time with someone," my mom said blithely.

"So they say. Gotta go, Mom." I stood, leaving my half-eaten waffle on my plate. The monkey with the cymbals that lives in the pit of my stomach and likes to practice for his band concerts when I get nervous was working on the *1812 Overture*. His percussion was winning the war against my desire to eat.

I ran out the door and down the steps, thinking up murder scenarios for the poltergeist phone rather than let my stupid brain psych itself out about my non-date.

The library was two blocks away, so I was there before I could try and come up with anything more creative than putting it on the subway tracks, which could kill people. And I had already gotten way too close to that for comfort.

Elizabeth was sitting outside the library, bag in her lap, and long blond braid draped over her shoulder.

"Hi, Bryant." She stood and smiled at me. Her eyes were all sparkly and perfect.

I opened my mouth to say hi, but somehow "*heyaaii*" came out.

She bit her lips together. It was nice of her not to laugh.

"Crazy day yesterday," she said.

"Yep," I managed, which was a recognizable word, so at least I was heading in the right direction.

"But it's done, right?" Elizabeth's sparkly eyes dimmed for a second. "I mean," her voice dropped, "you got rid of it?"

"I, umm..." I took a breath. This was too important to stammer. "I tried. Devon and I both did."

"What do you mean *tried*?" Elizabeth took my hand and dragged me away from the door. Her hand was so soft and delicate in mine. Like a little butterfly hand. "Bryant!"

"I mean, we smashed it, drowned it, *and* nuked it. Nada." I glanced around at the passersby. Even talking about the phone made it feel like that stupid giant eye was back being a creeper.

"Why didn't you throw it into the river?" Elizabeth asked.

"Because," I said, "we didn't want it to turn into another remake of the *Jumanji* movie. If the thing can't drown and it washed up on shore, what if someone who wanted to cause fires found it?" I didn't mention that Devon had thought of it. Elizabeth didn't need to know he was the one who was actually capable of functionally thinking under pressure.

"So where is it?" Elizabeth asked after a few seconds, taking a step back as though she thought I might have the thing in my backpack.

"Someplace safe," I said.

"Take me there."

"What? Why? There's no point," I said. "It's fine where it is until we figure out what to do with it."

"That thing tried to burn me to death," Elizabeth growled. "If you and Devon can't figure out how to break a damn phone, maybe I can. I'm not stupid."

"I—I know you're not," I sighed, rubbing my hands over my face. "It's at my dad's."

"Lead the way." Elizabeth linked her arm through mine.

Now, I know we were on our way to my rich dad's place that I hated when people knew about, to try and do something I had already failed to do, that could quite possibly do a lot more damage than simply wrecking my dad's microwave. But walking down the street with Elizabeth on my arm felt nice. Like we were on an old-fashioned date. She smelled like flowers, and the scent cut through the usual homeless pee stink of the city.

People looked at me differently. I mean, mostly they were noticing Elizabeth, because how could you miss her? But once they saw her, they looked at me differently, too. Like, *Oh, that dude must have some redeeming quality to have a girl so exquisitely perfect walking with him without a knife to her back.* And it made me feel a little bit better, even if they guy winking at me didn't know Elizabeth was only interested in destroying a dangerous cellphone.

"So, here's the thing," I said as we turned toward the park. "My dad's place is different."

"You mean he's like a painter or something?" Elizabeth raised a blond eyebrow at me.

"Not exactly."

"He lives with a man?" Elizabeth stopped in her tracks. "Because there's nothing wrong with having two dads."

"No, not two dads." I know I might seem a little bit crazy to be so shy about having a super-rich dad. But the only thing worse than having Elizabeth walking arm in arm with me because there's a cellphone that might try to destroy the world, would be having her walk with me because my dad plays golf with former presidents. I can deal with being a dork who only has one friend who only likes me because I've been around for so long he hasn't really figured out guys like him aren't supposed to hang out with guys like me. Having a bunch of fake friends who only pretend to like me so I'll spend money on them would be way worse than having no friends at all. Or even no girlfriend at all.

"So what is it then?" Elizabeth asked after a few awkward minutes. "Does he live in the projects?"

She turned to go down the steps to the subway, but I pulled her to walk along Central Park West.

"My dad lives in a penthouse. He makes more money having lunch with someone than a lot of people make in a year. His doorman gets me whatever I want, and I get paid to check in on his empty apartment. When we couldn't break the phone, I locked it in his hidden safe where he keeps a boatload of cash in case I need it and he's not in the country."

Elizabeth stopped as though her feet had been glued to the pavement. "You're joking."

"Nope." I had to look down at my shoes. Her blinking her sparkly eyes at me all confused like that was too much for me to take.

"But you live with your mom in a walkup."

"Yep," I said. Why did I have to sound so lame?

"You go to a public school. A crappy public school."

"Yep."

"You could be going to a private school in Scarsdale. You could already be at an Ivy League college with how smart you are."

"My mom wanted me to go to her school." I glanced back at Elizabeth, vaguely insulted. "She didn't want me to turn into a yuppie rich brat who doesn't appreciate anything. I'll go to an Ivy League after I've applied like everyone else. That was the deal—my mom picked the high school, my dad picks the college."

Elizabeth narrowed her eyes at me. "The deal, huh? So, what do *you* get to pick?"

I opened my mouth to say, I don't know, something about how I got to pick lots of things in my life. But that was a lie. I had been so happy my parents weren't yelling across the lawyer's desk, I had just said everything sounded great. I had been agreeing to everything that might keep the peace for years.

"I might get to pick my major," I said lamely.

"Well, after we destroy the phone, maybe we can look up some state schools. Who knows?" She took my arm. "You already burned down a theatre, maybe there's a bit of rebel in you yet."

"The school thing was an accident," I huffed.

She held my arm closer now, not so stiffly. "I know. But you got everyone out, and that makes you pretty badass."

"Thanks?"

"*Thanks* is right." Elizabeth smirked, shaking her head.

We were at my dad's building now, with its big carved marble front and the awning that reached all the way to the curb so people could get out of their cars without getting wet.

"Wow," Elizabeth murmured as I led her inside, walking quickly past the doorman as he launched into his, "Good morning, Mr. Adams."

That's the thing about living in Manhattan. You know people have lots of money. You see all the limos and furs. You walk past Tiffany's and Cartier and all the super fancy shops. But it's not until you walk into the swanky building where the rich people live that you really think about rich people having bedrooms and toilets. I mean, my dad lived there, but it still creeped me out. Normal people aren't supposed to have marble floors.

"Hey Drake," I said as I walked up to the desk. He looked at me for a second like he couldn't quite figure out who I was. His eyes were bloodshot, and his face drawn and gray. Worse, his shirt front had a wrinkle in it. I know it might sound awkward, but even one wrinkle was like way weird for Drake. "You okay?" I asked. When was the last time he had had a day off? Did he get days off? Or sleep?

"Fine, Mr. Adams." Drake's words were a little slurred, almost like Mr. Klein's, my old chem teacher's, had been before he was fired for keeping straight vodka in his water bottle. "You're back again, I see." His eyes drifted slowly over to Elizabeth. "With a new friend. Is Mr. Rhodes not feeling well?"

"Devon's fine," I said, "but I'm tutoring Elizabeth, and we needed a quiet place to work."

"I understand, Mr. Adams." Drake still looked a little confused. "Would you like me to have a pizza sent up?"

"No thanks," I said, instantly regretting it. Having possession of a thing that could spontaneously combust at any second was making me hungry. "But I still don't have a key, so..."

"Of course." Drake peeked below the desk, and his brow furrowed. "Strange."

"What's strange?" I glanced over the high edge of the desk. Papers were scattered across the shining wooden surface, and the lockbox that held all the extra keys hung open.

"Nothing," Drake said, his voice getting bright again as he stood, the penthouse key in hand. "Nothing at all. Rearranging things this morning."

He led Elizabeth and me to the elevator and put the key in the penthouse hole. He turned it, and as we all stood there silently, the elevator *whooshed* up. I didn't know why, but something still felt off. I thought maybe it was Drake being mad because I ruined my dad's microwave and now he was in trouble with the HOA for letting kids run wild. Or maybe he could only take being nice to me once a week. Or maybe it was bringing Elizabeth to my dad's.

The elevator stopped at my dad's, and the door opened up into his apartment.

"Thanks, Drake." I pulled Elizabeth out of the elevator.

Drake nodded silently as the doors closed.

"Was he all right?" Elizabeth whispered.

"Probably." I shrugged. "Drake's a cool guy." I don't know how *cool guy* was supposed to mean nothing was wrong with him, but it didn't matter. Elizabeth had taken a few steps forward and was staring into the living room. I glanced at the coffee table. Someone had cleaned up the pizza boxes Devon and I had left behind. Maybe that was why Drake was mad.

"The park." Elizabeth pointed out the window.

I looked out, expecting to see our landmark on fire. But Central Park was there, looking fine.

"Yeah," I said, not really sure what she was talking about.

"Your dad has a penthouse view of Central Park," Elizabeth clarified.

"Thanksgiving is the only time my mom comes here. We watch the parade from the window. I mean, my dad's not here or anything..."

But Elizabeth had drifted away. "Chandeliers?"

I looked up. There was a big chandelier in the living room and another in the dining room through the door. I never really looked at them anymore. They were just sort of what turned on with the light switch.

"They're a bit much, I guess," I said.

"You bring the same backpack to school you've had since freshman year." Elizabeth moved through the dining room to the kitchen.

"You kept track of my backpack?" I asked, following her.

She ran her hands over the freakishly prefect countertops. They were some kind of fancy something or other, and Elizabeth walked her fingers between the sparkly patches.

"I sit next to you two classes a day." She turned to me, her blond eyebrows squeezed together. "I thought you had noticed."

"I did," I said too quickly. "I mean, I know we have classes together, but I didn't think you'd noticed me."

"I did, and the bright red backpack."

"My mom got it for me," I said. "And there's nothing wrong with a red backpack."

"But you could get a new Gucci bag every day."

"I don't want them." I tipped my chin up. Since when was not wanting to spend money on backpacks a bad thing?

Elizabeth took a step forward, looking straight into my eyes.

"What now? I should have designer eyes? Is brown not good enough for a rich kid?"

"No." She retreated. "I was thinking there might be more to you than a geek with a cool mom." She sounded annoyed now. "Where's the phone? Let's get this over with."

Why did I have to snap at her? That, right there, is why I had never had a girlfriend. The second a girl looked at me not as a walking calculator and was willing to stand within a foot of me, I turned into a dickwad.

"Look, I'm sorry," I said, feeling stupid as my face got hot, and I knew it was turning pink.

"Let's just get the phone."

I led Elizabeth back through the master bedroom and into the closet.

"Wow," she breathed. I didn't have to ask what she was talking about. I mean, my dad's closet was bigger than a lot of bedrooms in Manhattan.

I knelt and pulled out the back grate.

"If your dad has passports and foreign currency in there..." Elizabeth said as I opened the safe.

"Nope. Just a ton of American money." I pulled the phone out of the safe and locked it back up, sliding the grate in place. "Here ya go."

"I don't want it!" She backed into my dad's arranged-by-color suits. "I can't even open the damned thing."

"And I can't break it." I pressed my finger onto the button. The screen flashed instantly to life. I tossed it on the closet floor and stomped on it. "See? Nothing." I picked it up and bashed it against the metal piping the clothes were hanging from. "Not a crack." I held the phone out to Elizabeth. "It's perfect. I can't break it, so if you want to try, you're going to have to touch it."

At that second, a ding echoed through the apartment.

"What was that?" Elizabeth asked, her voice quiet like we were hiding from something.

"It's the elevator," I said. "Drake must be coming up for something."

"Maybe because you're alone with a strange girl in your dad's empty apartment," Elizabeth whispered. "Did you think he was really going to buy the tutoring thing?"

"But it's true," I said. "My mom wants us to—"

Right then, the elevator doors whooshed open. I reached over and shut off the closet light, pulling Elizabeth into the shadows. I don't know why, but something felt weird. Like Drake was going to have me banned from my dad's house for bringing a girl up here. A few footsteps carried from the living room.

My brain was telling me to call out and tell Drake where we were, hiding was only going to make everything worse. But my gut kept me pinned to the shadows.

More footsteps, and a man came into view. A man who made me instantly decide never to doubt my gut again. The evil vampire who owned the cell-phone from Hell was standing in my dad's living room, large as life and twice as pale.

9

He looked just like he had when he had gotten out of his cab. Dressed in an all-black suit, black shiny hair, unsettlingly white skin.

"Who is that?" Elizabeth breathed in my ear so softly, I could barely hear the words.

"The phone guy," I whispered back, turning to her. We were nose to nose in the closet. I had her pinned to the wall, her heartbeat pounding against my chest. The man's eyes flicked our way, and both our hearts stopped for an instant.

He glanced down at his wrist before walking farther into the living room and out of sight.

"We've got to get out of here," I said.

"He's next to the elevator," Elizabeth pointed out with her trademark, if badly shaken, reasonableness.

"Another way." I took her hand in mine, pulling her out of the closet and into my dad's room as the man's footsteps echoed from somewhere around the kitchen.

I led Elizabeth down the hall to my room. It was on the river side of the apartment even though all you could see from my window was a sea of buildings. There were four doors—one to the hall, the bathroom, the closet, and our way out.

We had gotten to the far side of the bed when a voice called out from the hall.

"Bryant."

I froze in place, but Elizabeth yanked me down to the floor behind the bed.

"Is that your name? Bryant?" The voice sounded angry and also younger than I had thought an evil demon vampire's would. He sounded like the condescending college kids who think they have dibs on every coffee shop in my neighborhood.

"Well, *Bryant*"—he kept inching toward the door—"you have something of mine." The footsteps stopped. "A phone you stole from me, actually. It's as silly as that. Whether you took the thing to pawn it or to try and earn your wretched way in the world, I don't really care. The only thing that matters is that it's useless to you and priceless to me. The only way you can possibly hope to survive long enough to leave this apartment is to give me what I want. So toss the phone out to me, and I'll be on my way. And you and your girlfriend can get back to...whatever it is you were up to."

My stomach purred. He thought Elizabeth was my girlfriend. But then I remembered *he* was an evil man in my dad's apartment, and, even though Elizabeth smelled like sunshine and flowers, the purring disappeared.

"Are you going to give me back my phone, Bryant?" the intruder asked. "Or am I going to have to take it from you?"

"Don't do it," Elizabeth mouthed.

"Any ideas?" I mouthed back.

Elizabeth held the phone up to my face.

I pressed my thumb to the reader, and the light blinked on. There was the fire app, but I didn't really want to risk setting a building full of people on fire...again.

I looked at the different squares, trying to sort through what each of them might do.

"I'll give you to eight," the man said.

"I don't know what to do," I whispered.

"Aren't you supposed to make it ten?" Elizabeth shouted.

I looked at her, but she pointed to the phone. She was trying to buy me time. She was so smart, and bold, and beautiful, if I hadn't been terrified of us being murdered, I wouldn't have been able to look away from her.

"They speak!" the man said. "At least the girl does. I'm surprised you're letting her do the talking for you, Bryant. Is she more of a man than you?"

I tried to ignore him as I scanned through the symbols. There were the ones with letters I didn't recognize. A purple ball of light, promising.

I scrolled to the next screen, and there was a red square with the letters FF emblazoned in white.

"You really think men are braver?" Elizabeth asked. "What century are you from? And what kind of freak breaks into an apartment looking for a phone? What are you anyway?"

"I'm no thief," the man snarled, "and as for *what* I am, I don't think that's any of your concern."

Something in my gut told me to click the red box, and since I had just decided that maybe my gut was the smartest part of me, I did it.

Four choices popped up on the red screen. *Offensive at a Glance, Defensive at a Glance, Quick Escape, Last Resorts.*

I clicked on *Quick Escape.*

"I think it is if you want your phone back," Elizabeth said.

"Funny for a girl hiding behind a bed to press her luck like that," the man shot back.

"Fine then," Elizabeth said. "What's your name?"

The man chortled. "Eric Deldridge. What's yours, blondie?"

"Not going to tell you," Elizabeth growled.

There was a list of words I had never seen before. Each of them had a link next to it, but I didn't have time to look at descriptions.

"Then I'm done with you, in three—"

There was a note in bold at the top of the list that said, *Remember to speak clearly.*

"Two."

Aarantha was the first word on the list.

I heard Eric begin to say "one" and beat him with, "*Aarantha.*"

A weird wind whooshed through the apartment before Eric shouted, "What did you say?"

"*Aarantha!*"

It was like Dad's place had become a tornado, and I was stuck in the eye. The pictures flew off the walls and swirled around the room. The bed ground along the floor, making a terrible *shriek* I could barely hear over the wind. I sat and stared for a minute, but as sparks flew from the ceiling when the chandelier pulled loose, Elizabeth screamed, and I came back to my senses.

I yanked her toward the fourth door in my room.

There was a lock in the door handle, a dead bolt on top, and a stop peg on the bottom.

I started fumbling with the locks, my hands shaking so badly I couldn't grip the bolt. Eric screamed at me, but I couldn't make him out over the wind. I looked behind. He was holding onto the doorway with his fingers, his feet streaming behind like some sort of a creepy human windsock.

The eye of the storm had followed me to the door, but the wind still raged. Eric was glaring at me, looking like he wanted nothing in the world more than me dead.

"Let's go!" Elizabeth shouted. She had undone the locks while I had been staring stupidly at Eric.

I grabbed the door and swung it open an inch, but then it slammed shut like a giant hand had pushed it. Elizabeth and I both pulled together, but the door wouldn't budge.

I glanced back at Eric. His lips were moving like he was muttering something.

"He's blocking the door!" I screamed.

Elizabeth looked terrified, and I mean, who wouldn't be, trapped in a whirlwind that was now ripping chunks of drywall the size of my head from my bedroom walls?

I checked the phone again, the handy *Defensive at a Glance* tab. *Abalata* was the first word my eyes landed on.

I went with it.

For a split second, the wind stopped, and I thought I had done something stupid. I had killed the only thing that was keeping evil Eric from murdering us!

But then my hand tingled like I had touched a lamp with a short in it. I looked down, and saw myself holding a cloud of black.

"You!" Eric pushed himself to his feet. "Who are—"

I didn't let him finish. I threw the black cloud with all my might, and somehow I managed to hit him square in the chest. But the blackness didn't leave my hand. It stretched as it pushed Eric away. He flew backward down the hall and toward the living room window. He was going to fly out the window. I moved to run after him to do I don't know what, but it only accelerated the inevitable. Right before he hit the glass, he screamed something and stopped. I could feel him pushing against my hand, fighting to move.

He screamed something else, and a wave of purple flames streaked toward me.

"*Aarantha!*" I screamed when the fire was a foot from my face. The wind swept the inferno away, sending it crackling to the walls.

"Bryant!" Elizabeth pulled on my sleeve, spinning me to the door. The flames covered the handle, but as I reached for the knob, the wind pushed them out of the way. I yanked the door open, then let it shut behind us once Elizabeth and I were through.

I looked around the stairwell. Plain concrete stairs. I couldn't even hear the fire or the wind. It was deceptively normal. I wanted to curl up and catch my breath or wait for my mom to come and get me.

"Mom!" I yelped as Elizabeth broke the glass over the fire axe and shoved the metal handle against the doorknob, blocking Eric's path. "That freak knows my name. He'll be able to find my mom."

"We have to go." Elizabeth motioned toward the stairs. "Bryant, let's move!"

The apartment was on the fiftieth floor and going down that many stairs is no quick thing. We ran as fast as we could, not saying anything. Just running. I kept waiting for the fire alarm to go off. Or for Eric to come chasing us down.

My mind raced. How had he found me? Would he go after my mom?

"He knew my name," I panted, my words jostling in my chest as we ran. "How the hell did he know my name?"

"You really don't look properly, do you?" Elizabeth said. "Your doorman was acting all weird, his papers were tossed around like someone had searched through them, and then an evil dude walks into your dad's place knowing your name."

"You think Drake gave out my name?"

"*Gave out* might be the wrong term," Elizabeth puffed. "Try and keep up."

When we got to about the tenth floor, the red lights started flashing. There was no way it had taken the fire alarm that long to go off. Except maybe purple fire doesn't smoke as much as the normal kind?

"Slow down," Elizabeth hissed, still holding my hand and slowing to a trot as other residents started moving out onto the staircase.

They were all murmuring angrily like someone had interrupted their pinochle game with a stupid question about Go Fish. I kept glancing up the staircase, waiting for Eric to shower some horrible thing down on us from above.

Soon, we were out in the lobby. Drake stood outside the window, looking up in horror. The brass button doorman shook next to him.

"Stay calm," Elizabeth whispered as I pushed through the crowd to get outside to see whatever it was that was freaking Drake out.

My pulse pounded in my neck as we waddled out onto the pavement. Seriously, I have never seen people move so slowly while alarms blared. Rich people are weird.

As we made it onto the sidewalk, everyone stopped and stared up at the same place Drake did. There was barely any room to stand.

"Watch out!" I shouted at the fat sweaty man trying to shove through us.

The man's face turned the shade of red exclusive to angry New Yorkers, and for a second I thought I was going to be screamed at while being packed in like a sardine with people who didn't have the sense to keep moving away from the burning building. But right after he opened his nasty, garlicky mouth, the woman behind him screamed, "Jared, look!" and fat Jared turned to gawp up at the building.

I followed his gaze, and judging by her gasp and the fact that her hand slipped into mine, I guess Elizabeth had, too. Flames leapt out of the top floor of the building. Right out my dad's front window. But the flames weren't red or orange. They were purple. The same purple Evil Eric had shot at me. Only from down here, they didn't look dangerous at all. They looked beautiful. Inviting.

There were sirens wailing up the street again, but I almost liked their weird song. It sounded calming and strangely normal. Someone stomped hard on my foot, and I looked around. Elizabeth was glaring at me and trying to drag me sideways through the crowd.

"We have to go," she growled.

"But it's not spreading." I wanted to look back at the purple fire. The strangeness of it was magnificent, a shock of brightness breaking through the posh dullness of the Upper West Side skyline.

"We have to warn your mom." Elizabeth stomped hard on my foot again. "Remember your mom? The one you were so worried about?"

I cursed so loudly, fat Jared's lady friend gasped and opened her mouth to berate me. But the enchantment was broken.

I pulled out my phone. My real phone, not the evil devil cellphone that had destroyed my dad's apartment. I dialed my mom as Elizabeth steered me past the fire trucks and down a side street.

"Give me the phone, Bryant." Elizabeth held out her hand. I didn't need to ask to know she meant Eric's. The disgust in her voice made it clear, but the fear was tamped down by purpose.

She pressed her thumb to the print reader. The thing stayed dark.

"Open it." she ordered.

I pressed my thumb to the button, and the phone flashed on. She touched the screen, and it went dark again.

"You'll have to do it." She passed the phone back to me.

"I need to call my mom."

"This first," she said so firmly, I didn't dare argue.

I unlocked the phone. It was still open to the list of defensive spells.

"Go back to the home screen," she said.

I flipped back to the page with all the strange squares.

"Go to settings."

"Settings?"

"Just do it." Elizabeth steered me by the elbow down side streets and through breezeways between buildings.

I scrolled through the icons, fairly certain *this* phone wouldn't have a settings button. But sure enough, there was the little square of cogs looking annoyingly normal.

"Found it," I said.

Elizabeth led me into a bodega and paused for a moment, looking really interested in the Twinkies before shaking her head regretfully and whispering, "Turn off the *find my phone* feature."

"What?" I asked, but before I could say the demon phone didn't have said feature, I noticed the little green toggle and pushed it over to red.

Elizabeth glanced at the phone before lacing her fingers through mine and leading me back out onto the street, then through a hotel lobby and catty-corner from where we had been, toward the park.

"How did you know?" I stumbled on random goo as I stared at her.

"He was looking at his watch," Elizabeth murmured. "He had a smart-watch. He was tracking the phone."

"So, when I pulled it out of the safe," I said, feeling stupid and numb, or stupidly numb, whichever.

"He found us," Elizabeth said. "Now call your mom."

I put the black phone away and pulled out my scratched, non-homicidal model. It had a tiny chip in the corner and a geeky Doctor Who case my mom had bought me for Christmas. I had never appreciated how normal and important my non-fire-starting phone was until that very instant.

Mom answered on the second ring.

"Bryant honey, how's the studying going?" she said in a voice I knew meant that wasn't the question she really wanted to ask.

"Not now, Mom. Where are you?"

"I'm out looking for a theatre space—"

"I'm invoking Family Agreement, Article Seventeen. You can't go home, Mom."

There was silence on the other end of the line.

"Bryant honey—"

"Article Seventeen states that in a true emergency no questions will be asked and no punishment given if the son approaches the mother with a genuine fear," I quoted the thirty-page document we kept in the kitchen drawer. "You can't go home, Mom. It's not safe. Go to Aunt Tina's and stay there. No looking for theatres, no going to school."

"Bryant, what's going on?" My mom's voice was crisp with fear.

"Article Seventeen. There's something weird going on, and I don't really know what. You can't go home, Mom." The reality of it sunk in as I said the words, the weight nearly crushing my chest. "Neither of us can."

"Bryant, meet me at Tina's," my mom whispered, "if someone is after you."

"No," I said. "I'm safe where I am. You go to Tina's and stay there. I'll call when I can." I hung up without waiting for her to argue. I wish I hadn't, but as Elizabeth dragged me across the street and into Central Park, it seemed like the right thing to do.

10

The air in Central Park felt different from the air on the street. It was like all the relaxing things New Yorkers had done on its grass over the years had created a permanent cloud of calm. I wanted to sit and rest. But if I squinted up the street, I could still see the purple flames wafting out of my dad's apartment. I took the lead toward the castle, pulling Elizabeth along since she had taken out her bright purple phone and started texting one-handed.

"No, go south," she said, without looking up.

I didn't argue. She had saved my life twice within the last hour. Arguing seemed like a dumb idea. Instead, I focused on trying to look like I wasn't running away from someone who had tried to kill us by esoteric means. Really, if you had added in some ice cream, you could call it a date.

We slowed down a bit when we hit the paths that led south. Elizabeth shoved her phone back in her bag. We were still outpacing the tourists, who plodded along like walking had never been used to get anywhere and was meant more as an exercise in slowly shifting your weight from one leg to the other while trying to see how little you could move.

"What's Article Seventeen?" Elizabeth said as we skirted a tourist who stopped in the middle of the path to tie his shoe.

"Oh," I said, feeling stupid. "I—I decided we needed a constitution after the first time I got grounded. I didn't think it was fair that she had punished me for doing something that had never been expressly forbidden, so we locked ourselves in the apartment for the weekend and wrote up the articles."

"And one of them was in case your life is in danger, you can tell your mom to run, no questions asked?"

"Not running per se." I shrugged. Mom had insisted on the rule in case I was stuck at a party that got crazy. I had never been to a party that got crazy. "Dangerous life-saving trust in general."

"Bet you didn't think you'd need it for a magic phone and an evil wizard," Elizabeth snorted, dropping her bag by a fountain and sitting on the stone ledge. Her gaze swept over the throng.

"The phone isn't magic." My words came out strangled and small. "It's some kind of super advanced technology. Or something."

"Bryant"—Elizabeth took my face in her hands and stared deeply into my poop-brown eyes with her sparkly perfect ones—"you read a spell off of a magic cellphone and made a tornado that saved us from a magical purple fire that is probably still burning in your dad's luxury penthouse."

"But—"

"Bryant." She leaned in. "It's magic. Wielded by you. And a wizard named Eric. You're supposed to be smart, so please catch up on this."

She was close. So close. Her breath tickled my cheeks. If I moved forward an inch, I would be kissing Elizabeth Wick.

"Okay?" she said.

My mind raced back to the purple fire and the list of defensive spells at a glance.

"Magic." My throat instantly dried out.

"Bryant!" a voice shouted from the sidewalk as Devon waved high above the crowd.

"He *has* to shout," Elizabeth growled, dragging me to my feet. She was a lot stronger than she looked.

"Devon, what are you doing here?" I asked as my BFF looked not so slyly at Elizabeth's hand holding mine.

"I texted him." Elizabeth stepped forward to throw her arms around Devon's neck.

My heart sank. Actually no, it didn't sink. My heart turned to ice, then sank, hit my kidney, and shattered.

"Hey, you okay?" Devon asked, looking over Elizabeth's head.

I opened my mouth to shout that no, I wasn't okay, my best friend was hugging the girl I'd been desperately in love with for three years, but Elizabeth was already talking.

"That phone is magic. I went with Bryant to his dad's to try and get rid of it, but the owner showed up—"

"The vampire?" Devon asked.

"He's not a vampire. He was out in daylight," Elizabeth said without hesitation. "He's a wizard, and he was going to kill us. So Bryant used a spell from the phone to save us, but it caught his dad's apartment on fire. And now we're on the run from Eric Deldridge the murderous wizard, and quite possibly the police for setting another building on fire."

Devon took a step back and bent double, running his hands over his face. "Okay." He stood up. "What do we do now?"

"We?" I burst out, lower and angrier than I had meant to. "Why are you even here?"

"I told you, I texted him," Elizabeth said.

"Why? He wasn't there. Why should he get involved?" I growled. "And why do you even have his number?"

"I've had his number since I've had a phone," Elizabeth's voice hardened. "Not that I see how it's any of your business. And I thought Devon was your best friend, not to mention a guy who knows more places to legally lay low than anyone else I know. So since someone is trying to kill us and probably your mom, too, I thought your good ole bestie here would be able to help." She turned to Devon. "Unless you want to go home and pretend you've never met Bryant, which I wouldn't blame you for."

Devon turned to me without skipping a beat. "Your mom? How is your mom involved?"

"Evil Eric—"

"Evil *Wizard* Eric," Elizabeth corrected.

"Evil *Wizard* Eric found my name. It won't be hard to find our address." I ran my hands through my hair so hard it hurt. "I told her to stay away from the apartment, and she will. Maybe."

"Article Seventeen." Devon nodded. "So Ms. Miller is safe. Do you still have—"

I patted my pocket.

"And the wizard owner who set your dad's apartment on fire is going to be coming after it?"

"Yes."

"Right." Devon glanced at Elizabeth, his face losing its default devil-may-care confidence for half-a-second. "I don't know how you want me to help. Not that I'm being a chickenshit, but I have no wizard-fighting experience. I only found out about wizards two minutes ago."

"We need a quiet place to think where Eric can't find us," I said. It felt like every person walking past was a threat.

"Quiet hidey-hole out of the way in Central Park." Devon smiled. "I've got you covered."

He led the way back up and deeper into the park, Elizabeth next to him, and me taking the rear, trying to feel grateful and pretending I didn't want to punch Devon in the back of the head. We were being chased by a murderous wizard. Betrayal-by-best-friend would have to take a backseat to possible death.

Finally, Elizabeth pulled out her purple phone and speed-dialed, grimacing at Devon as it rang. "Hey Dad, a bunch of theatre kids are going to try and help Ms. Miller wrangle a space for the show next weekend, can I camp out for the night and help?" She paused for a moment as Devon led us off toward a clump of food carts. "Yes, I'll study, and yes it's only girls. Well, mostly. Besides it's a theatre group, Dad, nothing to worry about on the boy front."

Devon scowled and pulled out his own phone, texting someone before slipping it back into his pocket.

"Love you too, Dad," Elizabeth said before hanging up.

"Did you have to insult the masculinity of theatre in order to make an excuse for staying out?" Devon asked as he passed a twenty to the hotdog cart guy, who seemed to wordlessly know exactly what Devon wanted.

"If he knew I was with you," Elizabeth said, "he'd never let me stay out after dark, and I feel like it might take more than a few hours to stop the evil wizard from, you know, triple homicide."

"Touché." Devon grinned.

The hot dog man chortled and shook his head like running from wizards was some kind of hip slang with the wacky youth. It was a true chortle, too. I wished I could have filmed it for my mom to show her students. Pain shot through my stomach at the thought of her running scared to Aunt Tina's.

"What about your parents?" Elizabeth asked as the man handed us ten hotdogs and some sodas.

"I texted and said Bryant was having an existential crisis and needed me there." Devon shrugged as he led us off the path and through a thick stand of trees.

"I suppose realizing you can use magic counts as an existential crisis," Elizabeth said as Devon lifted a branch out of the way so she could climb under. He let go of the branch, and it hit me smack in the face. Somehow it felt like the tree knew how my day was going and just wanted to emphasize the point.

I've never been one to wander the wilds of Central Park. I have a well-instilled fear of finding a dead body in the bushes. Or of becoming the dead body in the bushes. Devon, not so much. Judging by the way he wove through the unmarked trees, he'd been here a lot. Probably with girls. Bile rose in my throat. Hopefully not with Elizabeth.

He stopped at a tiny clearing barely big enough for all of us to sit comfortably around the giant mound of hotdogs.

Elizabeth grabbed the first one and took a huge bite. "So," she said, after downing the entire hotdog in less than a minute, "we have the phone. Eric wants the phone."

"If we give Eric the phone," Devon mumbled between mouthfuls, "he could use it to kill us or destroy Manhattan like a bad movie scene."

"If we don't give him the phone"—I took a bite of my own dog. It was mostly cold and a little rubbery, but somehow running for our lives made it taste good anyway—"he'll chase me and my mom. And since he knows where I go to school and he's seen both of you...."

"He'll be after all of us." Elizabeth lay back on the grass and stared up through the trees.

"We could call the cops," I said lamely. "*Hello, NYPD? I have a magical phone that starts fires, and I think someone may be trying to kill me to get it back.*" No one laughed. Not even me.

"We need a plan that's daring but won't get us killed," Devon said.

Elizabeth nodded. "Why do you think I texted you, Dev?"

Dev? No one called Devon *Dev*. My stomach squirmed.

"Don't you specialize in stupid without getting killed?" Elizabeth asked *Dev* with a smile.

"Just about." Devon grinned stupidly with his stupid face before turning back to his tray of stupid hotdogs.

We sat in silence for a minute.

"The restaurant with the purple awning," Devon said finally.

"The one Eric went into?" My stomach tightened at the thought of finding the phone. I should have let the cabbie hock it. I set down the third hotdog I had been lifting to my mouth.

"I say we go case the place."

"*Case the place,*" Elizabeth said, mocking Devon's tone. "What are we, jewel thieves?"

"And how do we *case the place*?" I looked away as Devon playfully swatted her ear.

"We find different clothes so Eric won't recognize the geek and the blond in the dress. Then find the purple awning, see who's coming and going—"

"And if anyone is pigmentally-challenged, we follow them," I finished for him.

"Stalk albino wizards, and hope they don't figure it out." Elizabeth rested her arms over her face. "Sounds great. Wake me up when it's time for the shopping trip."

11

I watched Elizabeth lying on the grass. Her breathing went steady, and her arms relaxed as she fell asleep in the fall sun.

"You okay, man?" Devon asked after we had been sitting silently for a few minutes.

"Fine." My voice came out all weird and high like it always does when I'm lying. This is why I never did well in acting classes.

"We'll figure it out, Bry." Devon sounded cool and confident like always. It made me want to punch him in the face.

"I said I'm fine." I pulled out the black phone. More for something to look at that didn't make me want to scream than because I actually wanted to play with it.

"I don't know if that's a good idea," Devon said. "I mean, I really like this spot."

"I won't light it on fire." I pressed my thumb to the button.

The screen blinked on, and I flipped back to *Defensive Spells at a Glance*. I thumbed down, rolling all the strange syllables on my tongue. I had only ever taken Spanish, but I knew about roots of words and none of these looked like any language I had ever seen.

I tapped on one of the words. *Pentceena*. A new screen popped up.

Pentceena—A spell that will cause water to boil and explode. When done properly, the boiling water can be directed at your opponent for maximum damage.

WARNING! Water will boil and explode from ALL nearby sources, and directing the stream may be difficult. Proceed with caution and concentration.

I swiped my thumb and went back to the list of spells. All of them were underlined and led to descriptions.

Calimarta dropped things onto your opponent's head. *Dothranta* made everything go black. There was even a note under it, advising the user to be sure to know their way out before attempting the incantation. Too bad I hadn't seen that one at my dad's place. Then maybe my dad would still have a place.

"Let me see." Devon sidled up next to me, reaching for the phone.

"It won't work." I handed it to him and watched the screen go immediately black.

Devon tried to turn it on before handing it back and shaking his head. "Weird."

"Yep." I turned the screen back on and scrolled through the different icons.

"So, does this make you"—Devon paused, scanning the trees—"like, a witch or something?"

"No." I snickered for a split second before stopping. "I mean, I *can't* be a witch. I'm from Hell's Kitchen, and my mom is a drama teacher."

"But you did magic, dude," Devon whispered.

"The evil phone did," I said, feeling a lot defensive and, I hate to admit it, a little afraid. "I just have a thumbprint it likes."

"Do a spell." Devon pointed to the phone.

"I thought you said you didn't want me to burn down your little corner of Central Park?"

"It's an experiment. Just don't pick a fire spell."

There was a glow in his eyes. The one that meant I should say no to whatever he was suggesting. But I wanted to see if I could do another spell. And I wanted to show Devon maybe there was something I could do that he couldn't.

"Fine," I said, choosing the most innocent looking icon I saw. It looked like a teeny tiny forest. The whole picture was in shades of green, and the longer I stared at it, the more variety jumped out at me. Light green, dark green, puke green, greens I'm sure there were fancy names for but I couldn't tell you what they were. After a few more seconds, the trees started to look like they were moving, swaying with a wind that existed only inside the phone.

I tapped on the picture to make the motion stop. It looked like the inside of the *At a Glance* App, but this time there were pictures on the tabs. A rock, a stream, a tree, and a little white rabbit.

"Cute bunny." Devon laughed. "Can you pull it out of a hat?"

I shrugged and tapped on the bunny.

A list popped up with more words I didn't understand, but this time I couldn't tap on the word to get more information. "I don't know what they do."

"Just try it. Come on *witch man*, make the bunnies happen."

I looked down the list.

Eruntulia. I mouthed the word silently. I liked the way it rolled around in my mouth. It didn't feel hard or scary like the other two spells.

"Do it," Devon whispered.

"*Eruntulia,*" I said softly. I waited for something to happen. For the trees to burst into flames or some other kind of scary death to come chasing us. But instead, my eyes fixed on some silver vapor. It was like breathing mist in winter, but the vapor pouring out of my mouth was thicker and shinier. As it floated away from me, it narrowed into a thin strand that hovered in the air for few seconds, twisting around itself like it was looking for something, before separating into three threads and diving off silently into the trees.

Part of me wanted to chase it to see what it would do, but Devon had already punched me in the arm. "It's okay to have a dud spell. Try another one."

I wanted to throw the phone at him and tell *him* to 'try another one' if he didn't think my witch-ness was good enough. Except, and it was a big *except*, by every reasonable standard I could think up with my mind racing so fast it felt like I had pounded three espressos before gym class, I had just done magic. Deliberately and somewhat successfully, I had done magic.

I looked back at the phone, to the little picture of the water. "*Stilgarna,*" I whispered.

A warning sort of gurgle came from right underneath me. I jumped to my feet just as water bubbled up from the ground where my butt had been only a second before.

Devon rolled to his side, laughing silently. "You made a magical bidet. Let me try one." He leaned over my shoulder to look at the phone. "Pull up a cool one."

I flicked to the flower screen as the water trickled downhill only about a foot away from the sleeping Elizabeth.

"A flower, dude?" Devon snickered.

"You want to try one or not?"

"Okay, okay." Devon took a deep breath and pointed dramatically at a tiny blue flower by my feet. "*Milkawa.*"

My heart leapt to my throat as he said the word. I don't know if I was more afraid that it would work, or that it wouldn't. I didn't have time to figure it out because Devon started gagging in my ear.

"The demon phone is cursed," Devon coughed. "That word tastes like shit."

"Words don't taste." It was my turn to laugh.

"*You* try it." Devon swished his mouth out with soda and spat it on the grass.

"*Milkawa.*" I tried to keep my voice clear and firm like it had said to do with the *At a Glance* spells as I glared at the tiny flower Devon had been pointing to, which remained completely ordinary. "The word doesn't taste like anything. You've lost it."

"Close the phone and try it again," Devon said. "Maybe you have to be holding—" He never finished his thought.

The tiny wildflower by my feet had started to twitch and squirm. Devon and I bent down to look at it. I squinted to try and see what the leaves were doing, but suddenly the leaves were easier to see. So, I stopped squinting and almost fell over in the grass. My eyes hadn't gotten better. The flower had grown. A lot. In less than a minute, it was up to my knee.

"Umm, Bryant?" Devon pointed to the ground around the flower. The grass had started to grow too. Shooting up like the flower had. Devon dragged me back as the stalks under our feet started to writhe as they tried to grow under our shoes.

"Elizabeth!" I screamed as the flower pushed her head up in its inexorable upward momentum.

She sat up, gazing around with a look of fright on her face. "What did you do?" she shrieked as the grass swallowed her legs.

I dove forward, grabbing Elizabeth under both arms and dragging her to her feet. But even after her legs were free from the grass, she kept screaming. There were words. I know she was screaming words at me. It was something about a death wish. Or me wanting to kill her. But I couldn't listen. I was too busy staring at the flower.

The tiny flower that had started out no bigger than my little finger was as big as me. Bigger than me. A linebacker version of me. And it showed no signs of stopping.

Devon grabbed my arm and spun me around, dragging me back through the trees, Elizabeth leading the way. I could still catch words like *dumb* and *maniac*. I was about to shout something back, but I looked behind. Huge mistake. The flower now towered over the trees.

All I could think of was Jack and his magic beans. My mom had directed *Into the Woods* for a summer program a few years ago, and here was this flower, with its giant blue petals, looking way better than the flat she had made me paint that no amount of fancy stage lights could really make look like it was touching the sky.

Devon pulled me onto the sidewalk, and we weren't the only people running. Everyone was running. Women in business dress and men who owned hotdog carts. Nannies and dog walkers and their respective charges. Running for their lives. Terrified of the deadly blue flower.

We didn't stop until we reached the very bottom of the park. Tourists lined the sidewalk, packed thick like the flower was some sort of fancy show Central Park was putting on just for them.

Elizabeth caught onto Devon's hand that didn't have a death grip on my wrist as we waded through the crowd.

Soon, we were out by the department stores. Devon dragged us across to the Plaza as more cop cars raced up the street. The NYPD was probably having the strangest day on record, and it was all my fault. I felt myself cackling before I heard the sound or even knew I'd decided a flower looming over Central Park causing 9-1-1 calls was funny.

Soon my sides ached I was laughing so hard. Devon was still dragging me down the street. A tug on my arm spun me right before Elizabeth slapped me hard across the face. I stopped laughing as I rubbed my stinging cheek.

"Look, I know you're a crazy person," Elizabeth hissed, "but I would really appreciate it if you could keep the hysteria in check. You turned Central Park into *Jumanji*—"

"I love *Jumanji*," I said softly.

"Do you really think Eric isn't going to know that was us?"

Devon turned to look at her, his eyes wide with fear.

"We need to get out of sight. We find new clothes, and then we follow Devon's plan." She set off down 5th Avenue before rounding on us again. "Because at least Devon has the sense not to try and get us killed."

I looked at Devon. I thought he would tell her he had said we should try another spell. Or at least say I hadn't meant for anything like this to happen. But he was already trotting next to Elizabeth, not defending what we both had done or even checking to make sure I followed.

Lagging ten steps behind, I cut through the oblivious tourists all transfixed by the park and to the revolving door of a department store. Elizabeth and *Dev* were out on the other side of the door before I had even made it into the glass circle of doom.

It was different inside the store than it had been on the sidewalk. Everyone was calm and quiet. Clearly, they hadn't noticed anything or even heard the sirens over the music pumping in through the speakers.

"We're looking for black and cool." Elizabeth rounded on me. "Not burglar chic." She turned away for a minute to locate the escalator before looking back. "And you're paying."

I felt my pockets. My wallet was still there. And in it would be the black credit card my dad had given me on my twelfth birthday in case there was ever an emergency. I had never tried to use it. I knew it wasn't expired, but I didn't know if it would actually work. I didn't mention that small fact as Elizabeth stepped off on her floor and headed toward the girls' section.

"Meet you in fifteen," Devon called after her before turning toward the guys'.

I hated shopping. Even under the best of circumstances. Shopping to stalk a deadly wizard was even worse. Devon tossed some clothes at me, not asking for my opinion or size. I trudged after him into the fitting room, locking the door behind me and not looking in the mirror as I pulled on the dark jeans and button up shirt.

I didn't want to see myself. I had done magic. I should look cool. Weird cool. But what if my face had gone white like Evil Eric's? Or I was all normal and poop brown like I always was? Either way, I didn't want to know.

"You okay?" Devon called over the door.

I opened the sliding lock.

Devon looked even cooler than usual in a brand new dark ensemble with tags still dangling off the individual pieces like a new round of fawning admirers desperate to cling to the glory that was Devon Rhodes.

"You look good, bro." He smiled. "Very non-magical and ready to blend into the night. Elizabeth's gonna dig it."

Heat and anger bubbled in my stomach, and I wanted to punch Devon. Not in the arm, in the face. Hard enough to break his racially ambiguous nose.

"I don't think she'll care." I backed into the dressing room.

"You gotta look good for the ladies, Bryant." Devon examined himself in the mirror.

"*You* gotta look good for the ladies," I snapped. "*I* have to be ignored by them. And the only person who's going to give a shit how I look is also trying to kill me."

"Elizabeth isn't trying to kill you."

"Elizabeth doesn't care if I'm alive or dead." Blood pounded in my ears.

"The only part of me she cares about is the evil cellphone that's trying to destroy Central Park."

"You had her in your dad's penthouse," Devon said. "You can't tell me that didn't do some good."

"What does it matter, *Dev?*" I shouted, enjoying hearing my voice echo through the empty dressing rooms. "Hasn't she been to your apartment before, *Dev?* And how am I supposed to compete with the great Devon Rhodes? Money? Magic? They're nothing compared to his raw animal magnetism."

"What the hell are you tal—"

"She texted you!" I shouted. "The girl I've been in love with since we started high school texted you to tell you we were being chased by an evil guy from Hell! And how did she get your cell number? Been hooking up with her after school? I mean, we spend so much time together, it must have been quite a feat for you to find time to make out with your best friend's dream girl!"

Devon stood staring at me as I panted, glaring at him, waiting for him to tell me the truth that would end our friendship forever.

"I never hit on Elizabeth," Devon half-growled, half-whispered after a minute had passed. "I never made out with her. I never chased her. Because she's the one girl my best friend wants. She has my number because we've done scene work together before, and she's terrified of your mom. She texts me when she thinks your mom hates her, and I tell her your mom doesn't think she's a talentless hack who will never go anywhere.

"And do you know why I've never hit on her?" Devon took a step in so he was really close enough for me to clock him. "Because my best friend is in love with her. And I would never do anything to hurt my best friend. Even if he is a total moron who has a tendency to destroy things. And by the way, jealousy because a girl texted a guy *friend* is a real dick move, Bry."

Devon stared into my eyes, daring me to punch him.

My chest crumpled as my heart disappeared into oblivion. "It's not about her texting a guy. It's about her texting my best friend. The one guy I thought I didn't have to try and compete with. I thought you were on my side, but who the hell was I kidding? She would take you over me any day even if you're not trying. You're the coolest guy in school. You even have a rockstar name. Every girl in school wants you. And Elizabeth—"

"Is off limits," Devon said. "Always has been. And you're a better catch than you give yourself credit for. I would have tried to set you up with her last year if I thought you could have formed a sentence in front of her, but now you're all magical *and* capable of real English speech. You've got it made, brother." Devon shook me by both shoulders. "We're stopping an evil wizard and getting you the girl, Bryant. Because that's the sort of best friend you have." He hit me on the shoulder harder than usual and turned back to his dressing room, disappearing behind the shutter.

I huffed out a half-guilty, half-relieved breath. Maybe going Goth and stalking wizards wouldn't be a total deadly waste of time after all.

12

Elizabeth waited for us by the register, wearing new clothes. The salesgirl was glaring at her. Maybe because she was wearing clothes she hasn't paid for yet. Probably because Elizabeth looked gorgeous. She wasn't wrapped up in a fancy dress. Just dark pants and a flowy, black top, complete with a floppy knitted hat and big sunglasses.

"You do know the sun will eventually go down, right?" Devon pointed to Elizabeth's sunglasses as I stepped forward with my black credit card in hand.

"I'm paying," I said. The shop girl raised her eyebrows as we all started pulling the tags off our clothes.

"For the record," Elizabeth whispered over the quiet *deeping* of the scanner, "I know it's going to get dark. I also know Eric has seen my face, and I really don't fancy having to tell my parents they need to evacuate our apartment. We don't have articles of confederation in my house."

"It's constitution," I muttered.

I tried not to listen when the girl jabbered out the total. I still had to explain to my dad how I magically burned down his Central Park West penthouse. Well, not me, but a magic guy who wanted to kill me, which didn't seem to make the whole *no more Le Chateau* thing feel any better. A few hundred dollars on a credit card couldn't really make things too much worse.

When we got on the escalator to go back to the first floor, Devon managed to sidestep so Elizabeth and I were riding together.

I looked back at him, and he winked.

I should say something.

I knew I should say something. This was my time to say something cool about being a witch, or how I would protect her, or hey, even *wow Elizabeth, you look awesome!* But no. I walked next to her out of the building and onto the sidewalk, not saying a word. Because that's the sort of loser I am.

We turned to go north, and I stopped. Devon walked into me. But I was too stunned to even stumble forward. The damned flower towered over Central Park.

News vans lined the sidewalk. Every face on the street was turned to look up at the blue mammoth. It was like a disaster scene in a movie or even on the news where everyone is stuck, not knowing what to do or how to process something crazy.

"Let's go." I finally pushed the words through my dry throat. I grabbed Elizabeth's and Devon's hands, weaving them through the frozen crowd. When we got up to the news vans, I overheard the reporters talking into their microphones.

"It's been a day filled with strange, dare I say, impossible occurrences here in midtown," a young woman with long dark hair spoke earnestly into the camera. "We began this morning with a shuddering halt to our metro system after two trains were nearly shaken off their tracks by seismic activity scientists are still struggling to explain. Then came the fire on Central Park West. The fire chief has told News 1 exclusively that, although the fire has been contained, the firemen at the scene have yet to find a way to douse or even approach the strange purple flames that can still be seen flaring from the side of the building.

"And now the latest development. A flower has taken over Central Park. Yes, you heard that right, folks. Over the last hour, this flower has grown more than one-hundred feet, towering over the trees that usually dominate the park. The rangers have yet to make a statement on the cause of this plant's incredible growth. Rumors on the street are explaining what has been dubbed *Big Blue* as everything from miracle of God to biogenic terrorist attack. We can only hope the source of these disturbances can be determined quickly so our park, and our city, can be safe once again. Stay tuned to News 1 as I interview eyewitnesses, coming up next." The reporter's eyes swept the horde.

I led Devon and Elizabeth away as the woman's eyes locked onto Devon. He certainly looked the part, and his eyewitness account of the birth of Big Blue would make her career. Not that the reporter knew that. And there was no way I was going to let her find out. We cut to Central Park West and headed uptown, examining every awning, searching for the something shiny and purple.

Devon and I muttered back and forth, "You sure it was purple?"

"Yes, it was purple. Neither of us is color blind."

"You sure we were still on Park?"

"For God's sake!" Elizabeth stopped in the middle of the sidewalk. "Neither of you even knows where the hell this place is or if it exists, or if you'd even know it if you saw it?" Elizabeth's voice came out as a whispering shriek.

"We'll find it." I took a step forward. "I promise."

"Because you're so good at keeping your word. Like how you weren't going to try and use the magic that, I don't know, might get us noticed?" Elizabeth batted my hand away as I reached for her. "This isn't a game, Bryant."

She turned and cut through the crowd, finding a seat on a bench with her back to Big Blue. Her face was in her hands. She had every warning sign. Red cheeks, shaking hands, tense shoulders. She was girl angry. Girl angry is way worse than guy angry. Guy angry might get you shoved into a locker or punched in the face. Girl angry could get your soul ripped out and your spirit broken beyond repair.

"You should talk to her." I nudged Devon forward. "Tell her we're sorry for playing with the phone."

Playing with the phone sounded better than using magic that had all of New York panicking.

"You're the one who's desperately in love with her," Devon said. "You go talk to her. You're never going to have a girlfriend if you run away every time a girl gets pissed." He planted both hands on my back and shoved me forward. "This is for your own good."

I balled my hands into tight fists and sidled up to Elizabeth. I could do this. Maybe there was a spell in the phone for dealing with angry girls.

The second I thought it, she looked up at me, glowering, like she had heard me think about using the phone.

Even though she looked like she might kill me as soon as speak to me, her eyes were still all sparkly, and she was still beautiful.

"Elizabeth." And there it went, my face traitorously turning red as my voice shook on the one word I had managed to say. "I'm sorry. I shouldn't have been, you know...with the phone."

"We shouldn't be involved in any of this," Elizabeth said. "All I needed was a freaking math tutor, and now I'm looking for a purple awning to try and find a guy who wants to kill us before he manages to get to my favorite teacher."

"We won't let him get to my mom." I swallowed hard as my stomach crawled at the thought of Eric being within ten blocks of my mother.

"I'm sorry!" Elizabeth clamped a hand over her mouth. "That was terrible. I know she means more to you than she ever could—"

"It's fine," I said.

Elizabeth stood up and took both my hands in hers. "It's *not* fine. None of this is fine. But if I'm going to help you, you can't decide to do dumb things behind my back. I'm not following you around Manhattan to be your cheerleader. I could go hide out at a friend's place and wait this whole thing out. But you need me. I can help. I may suck at calculus, but I'm not stupid."

Her eyes had gotten extra glisteny. I could see tears forming in the corners.

"You're not stupid," I said as a tear slid down her cheek. And something happened. I don't know if it was human instinct or reckless abandon from almost being killed that morning. But I reached up and brushed the tear away with my thumb. Her skin was soft, and she didn't back away or wince when I touched her. It even made her smile a little. I stood silently for a second, trying to figure out what I had been saying. "You're the one who realized how Eric found us. You're the one who figured out what the phone was doing. You saw it right away. If I had believed you then—"

"Then Eric would have the phone by now," Elizabeth said, "and we could be looking at something a lot worse than Big Blue. But we're a team, all right? All three of us together."

"A team." I nodded.

She smiled, threading her fingers through mine, and towed me back to Devon. Her palm was pressed into mine. Not like before, when she had been holding my hand like I might as well have been her grandma or a kid she was babysitting.

She and Devon were talking about something. But I couldn't pay attention to anything but Elizabeth's hand held tightly in mine.

"Sound good, Bryant?" Elizabeth asked.

"Yes," I said, not sure what I was agreeing to.

"Then lead the way," Elizabeth said.

"I, uh..." I gave Devon the look that said, *by the Bro Code, you must save me from whatever I just walked into.*

"I'll lead the way." Devon punched me in the arm a little harder than necessary. "Bryant here has never been good with directions. Now, I know we walked south and we didn't go more than six or seven blocks."

"But that means we should have found it by now," Elizabeth said. "You said it was packed in with other restaurants?"

"It's there." I pointed before I really realized I had seen it.

Elizabeth grabbed my arm and lowered it for me while I stared at the awning.

"No, that one's black," Devon said.

And it was. The awning was made out of weird, shining fabric like extra shimmery silk. And in sunlight, it looked black. But walking past it, it had seemed purple. Except, if I squinted and tipped my head a little...

"Squint at it," I told Devon and Elizabeth.

They both bunched up their eyes.

"It's purple," Elizabeth said after a few seconds. "Or at least it would be under street lights."

"I still don't see it." Devon shrugged. "But if you think it's right, you can stay here and watch this place while I go look around a little more."

"No," Elizabeth said. "We stay together. Right, Bryant?" She looked at me.

"Right." I nodded. I swear Devon smiled for a split second before he sighed.

"Fine, we wait at the *black* awning and see if it turns purple or if any creepy, pigmentally-impaired people show up. And look, there's even a nice place for coffee." Devon pointed to a bistro two doors down from the purple/black awning.

He was right. We would be able to see the door to the awning place from there.

As I stared at it, thinking of the black credit card sitting in my pocket that was about to get used again, I noticed faint letters glimmering on the silk.

The Consortium.

It sounded like something out of Star Trek.

"The Consortium." I tasted the word in my mouth. It felt dark and powerful.

"Huh?" Devon asked as we played Frogger with cars that didn't seem to care about the stoplight or the crosswalk. The drivers were all too busy gaping at Big Blue.

"The Consortium is the name of the restaurant," I whispered as we sat down at a café table, pretending to stare at Big Blue while really watching for people walking toward the purply-black/blackly-purple awning.

"How do you know?" Elizabeth asked quietly, trying to read the menu and watch the street at the same time.

"It says it on the awning," I said. "But I could barely read it."

"The *black* awning didn't say anything." Devon's face transformed into his signature grin as the waitress approached. She was probably twenty-five, but when did that stop him?

Elizabeth stared at me while we all ordered and didn't look away once the waitress left.

"What?" I asked, finally turning to her.

"I think there might be something wrong with you." She leaned in close to me.

"Wrong with me?" I managed to say. I wanted to be offended, but somehow I couldn't get away from the feeling that Elizabeth was right.

"I mean different," Elizabeth corrected.

Devon snorted.

"You can make the phone work," Elizabeth said after a *thump* came from under the table that I'm pretty sure meant she had kicked Devon in the shin judging by his grimace. "You can read words on the awning neither of us can see. I don't think it's just that the phone likes your thumbprint. What if you're a witch and just never knew it?"

"You have always been weird," Devon agreed.

"It's just the phone," I said as the waitress brought out our food. "Nothing to do with me."

We all sat and ate, falling in and out of silence as Big Blue crept higher into the sky. When the food was gone, we ordered more coffee. And then more coffee again after that. My hands were beginning to shake. I'm not sure if it was from the enormous amount of caffeine I had consumed, or if I was getting twitchy from being still for too long.

"There," Elizabeth said, not pointing but looking directly at a woman trotting down the street, her gaze fixed on The Consortium.

The woman's skin was stark white, but unlike Evil Eric, her hair was white, too. And since I couldn't see any trace of eyebrows on her face, I could only assume they were white as well. The woman wasn't old enough to have white hair. She looked younger than my mom. It was like someone had dunked her in a vat of bleach.

"Well"—Devon took a sip from his coffee—"either the place is a meeting hall for Pasty Folks Anonymous, or that lady is into the whole weird—"

"Magic," Elizabeth inserted.

"*Magic* thing, too," Devon finished.

"But what can we do about it?" I dragged my fingers across the lattice of metal holes in the tabletop. "Should I walk in there and say, *Hey, your friend Eric tried to kill me this morning, and I have his cellphone that's rapidly destroying*

New York. I would give it back to him, but then he might kill me even faster. Got any ideas that don't end with us dying?"

Elizabeth bit her lips together as she studied her fingers. I knew that look. It was how she looked when we were working on math problems in class.

"Never fear." Devon patted the table, making my coffee slosh. "I'll take care of everything."

"What do you mean *take care of*?" Elizabeth asked before I could say anything.

"For all we know, Eric is in there right now. I'm the only one he hasn't gotten a really good look at, so I'll go in, see what the deal is." Devon grinned.

"See what the deal is?" I asked, trying to convince myself I should feel incredulous even though I knew he was serious as Shakespeare.

"See how many children of the corn are in there." Devon swiveled to the café window to fix his hair in the reflection. "See what the hell that place is for. The usual."

"And when they figure out you're snooping and turn you into a toad?" Elizabeth's eyes narrowed.

"Not gonna happen," Devon said. "Remember, I'm the best actor in school."

It was true. Devon couldn't sing or dance to save his life, but he could play a role that would rip even the evil lunch lady's heart out.

"How will we know if something's gone wrong?" Elizabeth asked.

"I'm assuming the building will catch on fire," Devon said, "but I'll call you, put my phone on speaker, and you dolts stay on mute."

"You saw that in a movie, didn't you?" I asked as Devon stood up.

"Sure did." Devon smiled. "And it worked, too."

"This isn't a movie, Devon," I said. "You can't just pretend to be some big hero. You could get"—he was already too far away to hear me without shouting—"hurt," I muttered as my phone rang right before Devon disappeared into The Consortium.

13

It was Devon's number on the screen. I opened my mouth to tell him to stop being an idiot, but voices were coming from the other end of the line.

"May I help you?" It was a woman speaking. If she was surprised to have a random teenager show up, I couldn't hear it in her voice.

Elizabeth leaned in close to listen, our faces a breath away from touching.

"Just wanted to check the place out," Devon said in his *I'm so cool, I only listened to half of what you said* voice.

"Are you interested in a meal?" the woman asked.

"No." The sound of fabric rubbing on the microphone distorted a few of the words. "...creepy guy, and I was hoping he'd be here."

"I don't know whom you're speaking of." The woman's voice was decidedly tenser now.

"Funny," Devon said, "because I saw him come in here a few nights ago. I was looking for him because he lost something. And what with the weird fires and that"—there was a sound like tapping on glass—"giant flower outside your window, I thought maybe it had something to do with Mr. I-like-to-leave-things-in-cabs Eric Deldridge. But if you don't know him, I guess I'm in the wrong place."

"What did he lose?" A different woman spoke this time, her voice high, thin, and angry.

"Don't suppose it matters since you don't know the guy anyway," Devon said.

"Perhaps I was mistaken," the first woman spoke. "We do have so many customers."

There was a pause. "Really? It looks pretty dead in here to me."

Silence again.

My heart leapt into my throat. Did Devon *have* to insult their business savvy?

"Our clientele come and go at all hours," the first woman said.

Elizabeth leaned in closer to me, her cheek pressed into mine.

"Any idea when Eric might be coming back?" Devon asked. "Or where I could find him, maybe?"

"None," the high-voiced lady said. "But if you leave whatever he lost here—"

"Naw. If you don't know when he'll be back or how to get a hold of him, I probably shouldn't leave his phone here."

The sound of glass smashing was followed by a low chuckle. "Did the glass piss you off, ma'am?" Devon said. "Anyway, I'll just have to find Eric some other way."

"Leave the phone here," the high-pitched voice growled. "It doesn't belong to you."

"You either." If I hadn't known Devon since forever, I wouldn't have been able to hear the fear in his voice.

"You have no idea the lengths to which Thaden will go to retrieve his property," the first woman spoke. "Be a smart boy. Give us the phone."

"Wouldn't even if I could." Fabric whooshed against his cell again. "Besides, don't have it on me anyway." There was silence for a few seconds. "Mind if I grab a takeout menu? Your kitchen smells amazing."

"Thaden will find you," the high-pitched woman warned.

"Well, have him bring along some takeout," Devon said.

The door under the purple awning swung open, and he stepped out onto the street.

I started to lower the phone from my ear. "Well then," Devon said, louder than he had been speaking in the restaurant, "better head down to my bro's name place. Wouldn't want to miss such an awesome evening."

I glanced down to see the screen flash on as Devon ended the call. I stared at the phone for a second before looking up, just in time to watch him turn the corner and swagger out of sight, a woman almost spilling out of The Consortium on his heels.

"She's following him!" Elizabeth sounded like someone was strangling her.

"He knows." I scribbled my name on the bill before leading her in the opposite direction of where Devon had disappeared.

"We...we can't!" She tried to pull me back. "We have to help him. What if..."

"I know where he's going." I dragged her to the curb, raising my arm to hail a cab.

"What? How?" She stepped in front of me and signaled as well. The first cab that passed skidded to a stop in front of her. Not surprising.

"His bro's name place." My stomach sank as I crawled into the cab. "Bryant Park," I called up to the driver. "We have to get to Bryant Park."

14

Three sets of clothes, dinner for three, and a cab ride through midtown traffic. That wasn't too bad. Right?

While the horns honked as the cabbie tried to take us down Broadway, I played out the conversation in my head.

Hey, Dad, how's wherever it is you are?

Fine, son. Have you decided between Harvard and Yale yet? Both are fine institutions, and I have good friends on both acceptance boards.

No. Sorry, Dad. I didn't have time to think about my future today. I was too busy fighting an evil magic dude who was trying to kill me and the girl I'm desperately in love with who thinks I'm an idiot. And I kind of trashed your apartment, so you might want to reconsider the whole paying my way through college thing.

How did my only son get involved with the dark deeds of...witches?

I found a phone and decided to do my best impression of a pyromaniac. And I've gone on a spending spree with the emergency credit card, and I don't see it ending any time soon since Mom is now on the lam. Oh, and a state college sounds good. If we make it through this alive.

I tried to imagine my dad getting mad at me. Maybe yelling at me for destroying part of Central Park. But I didn't really know him well enough to know what him mad would look like.

"You okay?" Elizabeth asked.

I nodded.

"Do you think Devon's okay?"

"He's spent more time chasing girls and then giving them the slip than any other sixteen-year-old in the city." I sighed as the cabbie pulled over. "He's got it covered." My voice sounded confident, but my stomach was still a heavy, squirming mass of terrified worms.

I let the cabbie run the black card and turned to the park. There was no movie or concert on the lawn that night, but even still, people had spread out their blankets and were sitting under the streetlights enjoying the cool night breeze.

We found an empty bench under a tree. I scanned the crowd, searching for Devon or Eric. Or anyone else with creepy bleached skin.

Couples dotted the grass. Some eating food, some kissing. Kind of a lot of kissing.

"Are you really named after the park?" Elizabeth asked.

"Me?" I asked stupidly like there was someone else she could be talking to. "Yeah. I am."

Elizabeth stared at me for a few seconds. "Why?"

"Oh, my parents met in Bryant Park. Mom was performing here, and Dad thought she was amazing. When she was done, he asked her to share his picnic blanket." I smiled, looking out at the park. They had fallen in love here. Which meant they must have been happy in this park. "Anyway, she was going to say no. But he had a bottle of Jameson, so...."

"And that's where the middle name comes from?" Elizabeth grinned.

"You know my middle name?"

"Your mom always uses your full name when she's mad at you in rehearsal," Elizabeth said. "And I'm really good at memorizing. So..."

"Buttons." I laughed. "Lots of button sewing tonight." It's what my mom would have said. It was her favorite line when her students started an excuse with "so...." I tried to think of an excuse I might be able to give her for this whole mess. My brain immediately fizzled, so I went back to scanning the park instead. I kind of needed my neurons in working order.

The streetlights glowed overhead, casting the whole place into shadows. But somehow the park's shadows didn't seem scary like the ones in my bedroom that had given me nightmares when I was little. If the shadows in my room were filled with monsters, the shadows here were filled with possibilities. A thousand different paths hidden just out of sight. You only had to be brave enough to step into one and find out what was there.

"When did your parents split up?" Elizabeth asked, pulling me back to the present.

"When I was three." Maybe I should have felt sad about it, but I never had.

"Dad had been on a *corporate is evil* kick when he and my mom met. But then she had me, and all he wanted was money. For things like Harvard and private schools. She didn't like that all he did was work. He didn't like that she didn't care about money. And then it was over."

"Sad," Elizabeth whispered. "Sad that stupid money broke them up."

"More ideals than money." I ran my hands over my hair. God, I wanted a shower. Catching things on fire and running for your life really makes you long for creature comforts.

"Still sad," Elizabeth sighed. She turned to me, looking into my eyes. And, I know this is going to sound crazy, but it felt like, for the first time, she was seeing *me*. Not my mom's son. Or the smart kid who sat next to her. *Me*. The product of a dark park, a bottle of Jameson, and a divorce. The guy whose parents can't stand each other and who doesn't know enough to care. Me who catches his dad's place on fire with magic but thinks the most amazing thing that's happened this year is sitting on a park bench with Elizabeth Wick. We stayed like that for a moment.

I hated the word *moment* until that bench.

It had always seemed too indifferent. Too romantic. Like you were confusing a measure of time with a state of being and trying to make something quantifiable. But once you have a moment, you understand what a moment is. Because the world stops, and magic doesn't matter. And you're not afraid to be alone with Elizabeth, or of Eric, or magic, or even of the moment passing and never coming back again. Time freezes, and there you are, drinking in the most beautiful girl who's ever lived. And that moment is perfect.

"Am I interrupting?"

I gasped as Devon stood above us, his hands on his hips, his face showing his judgment. "Because if I'm interrupting, I can go. I mean, it's not like I raced across town to lose my tail from Un Café du Magic. Or found out vital information about the evil cellphone that is bent on destroying Manhattan. So I'll just go. Let you two kids go back to staring into each other's eyes."

Heat rose to my cheeks, and I was glad the streetlights wouldn't show their color. I tried to think of something witty to say and had finally settled on, *Glad you're not dead, dude,* when Elizabeth spoke.

"You're sure you weren't followed?"

Because of course even after our moment in the park, she'd be all practical like that.

"Triple sure." Devon nodded.

Elizabeth stood up and threw her arms around his neck—then hauled off and punched him hard in the shoulder. "Don't you ever go all rogue like that again! You could have gotten yourself killed. You could have gotten all of us killed, and for what?"

"I will tell you *for what*." Devon rubbed his arm. "We learned three very important things. First, the ladies of The Consortium didn't know that Eric had lost his magic mobile. Second, Eric's missing phone really scares them. And third, some dude named Thaden is probably going to kill all of us for even knowing about the phone."

"Kill us?" Elizabeth choked.

"This may be hard to believe, but I tell you, when I mentioned the phone, the white chicks got even whiter," Devon said. "Whoever this Thaden guy is, I think he might be the boss. Or at least the creeper the boss is scared of."

I looked up at the sky. Somewhere high above the skyscraper lights were stars. Hidden by the ambient light, but always there. And the way out of this mess was like the stars. There and possible to reach, if you could only see beyond the immediate. Good God, one moment in the park, and my brain had turned into romantic mush. Not that Elizabeth was really interested in me. I mean, maybe. But no. No way ever.

"So, we find Thaden," Elizabeth was saying when I finished giving myself a mental beating for being a romantic sap.

"And if he's the guy who wants the phone," Elizabeth said, "I say we give it to him. We tell him Eric is a nutbag, and if Thaden promises to make Eric leave us alone, aren't we golden?"

Devon shook his head slowly. "I don't think so. The way those ladies were talking about him...Eric is stupid. Thaden is evil."

"How do you know?" Elizabeth tipped her head to the side, narrowing her eyes.

"Because beneath this charming exterior lies a deep and very perceptive soul," Devon said seriously. "Well, that, and I've spent tons of time studying people for acting class."

"I thought you were girl trawling?" I said.

Devon smiled. "Same thing. Either way you swing it, anyone who can make the magic albinos that scared is not a dude we should be trying to make deals with."

"So we're back at the beginning." Frustration seeped into Elizabeth's voice.

"No," I said, and did something brave and stupid. I took Elizabeth's hand in one of mine and brushed the perfect blond hair away from her face with the other. It was like being in a movie. Sitting in the dark romantic park with my dream girl, being all strong and comforting as danger crept closer. But in the movie I was supposed to have a plan. And right then, I had nothing. "We'll... we'll figure this out," I said, trying to sound like that was actually a promising thing.

"Okay." Elizabeth squared her shoulders, her perfect eyes becoming hard and bright, like diamonds. "Then we find a way to tell Eric we know about Thaden. He's got to be getting desperate. We make a deal for the phone, tell him if he doesn't agree, we go straight to Thaden."

"We don't know how to find Thaden," I pointed out.

"Eric doesn't know that." Devon grinned.

"It's the best we've got." Elizabeth shrugged.

"But it's not good enough. It still has Evil Eric ending up with the phone." My mind raced, trying to find an option that didn't involve trying to find the guy who was trying to find us. "I say we go to The Consortium, explain everything, and let them deal with their problem child."

"Unless they tell Eric to take care of us, and then we won't know he's coming," Devon spoke over me.

Elizabeth held her arms up between Devon and me to silence us. "We need to try and find out more about The Consortium and go from there."

"We can't wait!" Devon ran a hand over his face. "This is the time for action."

"We have to find out what the hell is going on. It's not just about getting rid of the phone. It's about making sure no one gets hurt, including us!" I ended in a whispered shout.

"How long do you want to camp out in the park, Bryant? Weeks? Years? Is being homeless a part of this plan, too?" Devon whispered. "You can't sit around and wait for life to get safe, Bry."

"Devon, if you would try and think for a minute—" I wanted to shake my best friend until he realized that maybe being the coolest kid in school wasn't going to keep us from being killed.

But I never finished the sentence because the phone rang. I looked down at my pants, terrified. But it was a normal ringtone. The geek chic one I had picked out for my phone.

The phone screen said *Mom* in big, bright letters.

"Maybe we should ask her to come up with a plan," Devon said. "Maybe she—"

I tapped the screen, fed up with Devon's ideas. "Hey, Mom. Are you at Aunt Tina's yet?"

"No, she isn't at Aunt Tina's," a voice lilted from the other end of the line, freezing my insides at the first word. "Your mother is at home. And, Bryant, you had better hurry. Crazy day today, never know what might happen."

"Leave her alone," I growled, sprinting toward the street. The pounding of footsteps followed me until I stopped at the curb.

"Gladly," Eric said. "I want nothing to do with your mother or your tiny apartment. You're the thief, remember? Give me back what's mine, and your mother won't even need to know what her son has become scrambled up in."

There was a pause on the other end before Mom's terrified voice screamed, "Bryant honey, call the police! Don't come here!"

"Don't call the police," Eric said, and I could hear the sneer in his voice. "We both know the police can't help you. The only way to fix this—"

"Fine," I said as a taxi pulled up and the cabbie eyed me out the window. "I'll be there in a half-hour. Don't hurt her."

"Don't worry," Eric said. "I, unlike you, am an honest man. But be careful, Bryant. I may cross the line if you push me."

Mom shouted something else before the line went dead. I wrenched open the taxi door and three of us piled into the back of the car.

"Where to, kid?" the cabbie asked, supremely unconcerned with the less than savory topic of my conversation. Clearly, this was a lifelong New Yorker.

"10th and 57th," I said, watching the cars speed by as the cab nosed out into traffic.

"I can get you there in ten," the cabbie said happily. "I thought this was going to be a long trip."

"No, sir." I pulled the black phone out of my pocket. "Just needed to buy myself a little time."

15

It only took us ten blocks in traffic to work out a plan. It wasn't the best plan, but I had never been a part of a magical hostage situation before. Devon and Elizabeth agreed with everything I said. I don't know if it was because I had suddenly formed a commanding personality, or if I just looked that close to the edge.

"Neither of you has to do this," I whispered when the cab was only a block from where I asked the driver to stop.

Elizabeth said, "We know," at the same time as Devon said, "Yeah, we do."

"We're not letting you go in there without backup, Bry," Devon said.

"And we're too far in this thing to back out now," Elizabeth murmured as the cab stopped.

I let the man swipe the black card. He kept it in hand until the others climbed out. "Listen, kid," he said, "I don't know what you're into, and I don't want to know. But it sounds like you're in over your heads. I know the cops have a bad rap sometimes, but"—the man paused, shaking his head—"it's better to ask for help, while help is still possible."

I really looked at him for the first time. He was old enough to be my grandfather. His eyes were filled with concern, and somehow that made everything feel so much worse. I wanted to stay in the back of the stranger's cab and tell him everything. Make him come up with a plan and save the day. But even the most concerned stranger wouldn't believe everything that had happened. And curling up in a ball wouldn't save my mom.

"Thanks, sir." I pasted a smile on my face. "But it's not that bad. Honest." I took the card from his hand and slid out onto the street, then watched the cab edge back out into traffic.

"You got the plan?" Devon asked.

"I came up with the plan." My voice faltered in my throat.

"See you up there." Elizabeth kissed me on the cheek. Like she really was worried. And like maybe she really did want to see me upstairs. Maybe it wasn't love. But she wanted me to not die. My chest began to feel all warm and glowey.

"Be careful, Bryant." Devon punched me on the shoulder in lieu of a kiss and, together with Elizabeth, disappeared around the corner while I walked up the two blocks to my apartment.

I almost strode. I was Don Quixote. A demented knight walking into a dragon's lair with a stupid black phone instead of a sword and shield. Mom's artistic soul would like that.

Cliaxo, cliaxo, cliaxo. I thought the word through a few times to make sure I had it right before saying it out loud.

"*Cliaxo*," I said firmly, watching the keyhole on the outside door of my building. The lock twisted around like I had inserted and turned an invisible key.

For once, Mrs. Fortner wasn't there to try and squish past me in the tiny vestibule. I ran up the grooved steps two at a time, only slowing when I reached the last flight before the stairs that led to the roof. My stop.

The door looked normal. No weird shimmering words. No purple flames. Just home. My lungs ached as I took the biggest breath I could manage.

Should I knock? Should I do the spell and walk in?

Screw him. It's my house. I'm not knocking.

"*Cliaxo*." The lock turned, and I walked into the apartment. At first glance, all I noticed was the mess. Like my mom had decided to have all her students over for a post-show pizza party. But then I saw her standing in the corner, her face sheet white and Mrs. Mops growling in her arms.

"Bryant!" Her voice sounded far away like I was underwater and she was trying to yell at me for not getting out of the pool. She raised a finger, pointing behind the door to the chair.

"Hello, Eric." I swung the door halfway shut. He lounged in the chair, still all in black, his pasty skin incongruous against the vibrant colors of my apartment. "Glad you've made yourself at home."

"At home," Eric sneered. "This place is filled with unnecessary clutter. I would never deem such mundane environs my home."

"Then I'm sure you won't mind leaving," I growled.

"As soon as I have what's mine," Eric said, "we can begin to discuss my departure."

Departure. I didn't like the way he said the word. It sounded permanent.

"Fine." There was a stack of books on the floor. I pushed them to the door with my foot, propping it open, and stepped farther into the room, closer to my mom. "But before we discuss anything, you let her go."

"That isn't the way this works." Eric stood up. He looked taller now than he had when he had tried to kill me in my dad's apartment. "You give me what I want, and then I see how generous I'm feeling toward the thief."

"I never stole anything," I shot back. "And I'm not giving you anything until you give me my mom back."

Eric smiled. "*Conorvo.*"

My mom screamed. The air around her shimmered and contracted, pushing her tightly into the corner. Mrs. Mops yowled as she was crushed into my mother's chest.

"How small do you think I can make their cage?" Eric said. "*Conor—*"

"You think because you can do magic, you make the rules, is that it?" I shouted, cutting off Eric's spell.

"That's *exactly* it." Eric smiled. "I'm glad you're catching on so quickly."

"But you see, I don't agree with you." I inched over to my mom. "See? I'm the one with prize." I pulled the black case out of my pocket.

"Give it to me!" Eric took a step forward.

"Maybe," I said. "But maybe I don't want to."

"You don't have a choice."

"Sure I do." I forced out a laugh. "I can take it to Thaden, see if he'll give me a better deal."

Eric's face turned pink as he glanced toward the door. "You know Thaden?"

"Yep." I smiled broadly, sticking my hands in my pockets and tucking that which must not be named safely back in place. "And I don't think he's too happy about you losing the phone."

"I didn't lose it," Eric spat. "You stole it, and now you're trying to frame me."

"Like I said before, I never stole anything. You left it in a cab like an idiot when you stumbled drunk into The Consortium. All I wanted was to return the damn thing." I stood up straight, puffing my chest out as much as I could. "But how can I return a magic phone to a guy who's trying to kill me?"

"It doesn't matter anymore." Fear shook his voice. "If Thaden knows you've seen the phone, we're all done for. He won't make a deal. Not with you, not with me. We're all dead. It's only a matter of time."

"But—"

"Give me the phone. If I have it, I can make a run for it, maybe lead him away."

"You just said it would only be a matter of time before Thaden killed us."

"I could buy myself a few good days of happiness." Eric took a step forward, his arm outstretched. "You can barely form a spell. You can't hide from Thaden, not for an hour."

"I managed to get away from you, didn't I?" I said. "And Thaden might want to hear me out. So, I think I'll take my chances with him." I crossed my arms and watched Eric's mind race.

"Fine," Eric said. "I'll let your mother out. Then you give me the phone. Tell Thaden I lost it. Tell him I stole it from you and ran. Tell him whatever story you like. Just give me the phone."

"Sounds good." I smiled even though my stomach was still trembling. A door creaked open somewhere outside the apartment. The pink that had crept into Eric's face disappeared as he glanced toward the hall.

"*Vanexo*," Eric said.

I spun around in time to see my mother stumble out of the corner and the cat yowl and dart off under the table.

"Now your end of the bargain." Eric reached for me.

"Sure thing." I pulled the phone from my pocket and tossed it to him.

He glanced up at me, and for a second, I thought the plan had gone horribly wrong. Eric was going to murder my mom, me, and Mrs. Mops right there in our tiny living room.

But instead he murmured, "Best of luck, fool," and hightailed for the door. He disappeared into the hall right before a dull *thunk* and a heavy *thud* carried into the apartment.

"Got him!" Devon called as I turned to my mom.

"Are you okay?" I asked as she half-collapsed, half-sat on the floor.

"I know I promised not to ask questions," my mom said, shaking her head, "but Article Seventeen or not, I need to know what the hell you have gotten yourself into, Bryant Jameson Adams."

The sound of my mother using my full name was almost as terrifying as Elizabeth and Devon dragging the unconscious Eric through the door.

"Nice hit," I said to Devon as he kicked the door shut behind him.

"Thank you," Elizabeth said. "I think I did a pretty good job."

"*You* hit him?" I grunted as I helped Devon hoist Eric into a chair.

"Well, he did try to kill me this morning." Elizabeth shrugged. "So, I figured I had first right to *bashing the bastard over the head* duty."

Devon pulled the blue-covered cellphone from his pocket and tossed it to me. I pressed my finger to the button and watched the screen flash on. All the funny square icons were still there.

"He didn't even bother to make sure you gave him the right one?" Elizabeth gave Eric a sharp kick in the shins. "Dolt just sees a phone in a black case and thinks it's his. You so had him pegged."

"I'm sorry," Mom said from behind me, "but I've been pinned to a wall, my son was negotiating with a crazy person from a black and white film, and now it looks like that same crazy person is my son's prisoner. I'm really going to need someone to do some significant explaining."

"How about we make a cup of tea and I'll fill you in, Ms. Miller?" Devon took my mother's elbow, gently leading her to the side of the living room that served as the kitchen.

"It's bad enough for a cup of tea?" she asked faintly.

"Afraid so." Devon patted her on the back.

"Should I find rope?" I asked Elizabeth while we stared at the unconscious Eric. His head lolled onto his chest, his arms dangled limply at his sides. "He isn't dead. Is he?"

"I don't think so." Elizabeth cocked her head to the side. "But if he is, well, he *was* trying to kill us..."

I tried hard not to think about finding a place to hide a murdered witch in Manhattan. I suppose I could have made another flower to hide the body.

"The phone," I whispered more to myself than anyone else as I pressed my thumb to the button and tapped my way to the list of *Offensive Spells at a Glance*. "There has to be some sort of trapping spell here." I spent a minute working my way down the list, clicking on the different spells.

"He's going to wake up before you decide what to do with him," Elizabeth said.

"Well, then hit him on the head again." My eyes flicked up to Elizabeth's face.

She grinned. "I guess I can do that."

"Bryant Jameson Adams, you destroyed my theatre, your father's apartment, and grew the alien flower in Central Park?" my mother half-shrieked from her seat on top of the kitchen counter.

"Yes, but only the flower was really my fault," I said. "Consider it a science project on new plant species."

"Bryant." My mother's voice was low and dangerous.

I clicked through the list of spells faster.

"Sip the tea, Ms. Miller," Devon said. "It probably feels way worse to you right now than it really is."

"No, I think she has about the right level of panic, confusion, and anger," Elizabeth said.

"You're not helping," I grumbled as I clicked on *Parapus.*

Parapus—A spell to bind one's opponent. May be used on multiple subjects if they are all touching when the spell is cast.

Note—The opponent must be stationary at the time of casting.

Note—Parapus is not a permanent spell. Your opponent will break free in time.

Counter Spell—Xorus.

"Well, that sounds a little useless," Elizabeth said as she finished reading over my shoulder.

"Yet oddly applicable." *Parapus.* I mouthed the word, testing out how it should sound out loud. "*Parapus.*" Long, thin bands formed in the air in front of me, like the lines on a piece of notebook paper. They hovered for a moment, then shot off toward Eric so fast, they *whooshed* before hitting him with a dull *clang* like metal on metal.

I took a deep breath, trying not to look afraid of what I had just done. Slowly, I stepped forward. My heart raced in my chest, like I was walking up to a lion to see if it really was asleep and not interested in chomping my head off.

The thin, black lines that had hovered in the air were draped across Eric. But they didn't seem insubstantial anymore. They looked hard and rigid. I reached out to touch one. My hand shook and my head told me not to do it, but there went my hand, reaching out to poke the guy who wanted me dead. The line felt like cold iron molded perfectly to fit, pinning his arms to his sides and binding his legs to the chair.

"I never thought I would need to ban magic in my home," my mother said faintly from behind my shoulder. "No candy from strangers, don't play with matches, always follow the crosswalk signs. It never even crossed my mind to tell you not to use magic on home invaders."

"I'm sorry, Mom," I said.

"Are you two..." My mom turned to Devon and Elizabeth who stood huddled together in the corner.

"I told you, Ms. Miller," Devon said. "It all sort of spiraled."

"But both of you have been using magic?" My mom said *magic* like it was a street term for cocaine or meth.

"Neither of us can." Elizabeth shook her head. "The phone will only open for Bryant."

"And Eric apparently." My mom turned to our uninvited guest. "We had better wake him up and find out exactly who this Thaden is who's supposed to be killing us within the hour."

I looked down at the phone. A wake up spell probably wouldn't be in the *At a Glance* list, but there should be one somewhere.

Smack!

My mom hit Eric hard around the face. With a squeaky grunt, he woke up, struggling wildly to break free from the metal lines.

"Or you could hit him," I mumbled as my mother took a step back.

"Now listen, you," she said in a tone that resembled nothing less than an angry lioness. "I don't care if you think my son stole your damn phone. I don't care who the hell wants you dead because you can't keep track of a stinking thing I have to pry from the hands of my students like it is their damn prized possession every day. The only thing I care about is that you broke into my home. You held me prisoner, and you threatened my son. Now you are going to tell him everything he wants to know, or, magic cellphones aside, I will kill you and dump you into the Hudson."

My mom stalked to the kitchen and pulled out the biggest knife from the kitchen drawer. The blade glinted in the light as she walked back over to Eric and sat down cross-legged on the couch, the tip of the knife only inches from his face. "All right, Bryant. Why don't you ask him your questions so I can get this filth out of my home?"

Every once in a while, I forget my mom was raised in the Bronx. Watching her calmly pointing a knife at a guy who had tried to kill us without her hand so much as shaking made me appreciate my New York heritage. Truly, we're a species unto ourselves.

"Well." My voice came out small. Mom raised an eyebrow at me, and I started again. "First things first. Who is Thaden?"

"You know Thaden," Eric said. "You know exactly what he is."

"Sorry, that was a little bit of a fib," Devon said. "I went to The Consortium, poked around a bit. They mentioned Thaden. We've never met the guy."

"You lied?" Eric said, his face melting from relief to anger in a second. "Then there might still be time. Who did you talk to?"

"I'm the one asking the questions," I said, "and I want to know why Thaden would care enough about a phone you lost to try and kill us."

Eric glared at me, and I held his gaze. I could feel him sizing me up, looking for a chink in my shoddy armor. "Because it's his." He sighed, sort of deflating. "He gave it to me to test out. No one was supposed to see it. Not until he was sure it would work. There have been rumors, but he didn't want anyone to know the prototype was ready for beta-testers. He trusted me above all the others. And I failed him." Eric's eyes went wide with fear. "You only get to fail Thaden once."

"Let me get this straight," Devon said. "A deadly guy gives you something he'll kill you for losing, so you lose it?"

Eric dipped his head low. "I never meant for that to happen. It seems as though fate is conspiring against me. For the thing to fall out of my pocket, and for someone like you"—Eric looked up at me, his eyes boring holes into mine—"to find it."

"Someone like me?" My heart pounded like it was determined to sprint out of my chest. Blood tingled in my fingertips.

"Not just anyone could open that phone," Eric said, his eyes still creepy intense. "Not just anyone could use *parapus* on me. Surely you've realized you are not like your associates."

"You mean," I said, trying to push past the sudden dryness that was making my tongue feel four times its normal size, "I'm a witch?"

Eric tipped his head back and laughed, speaking to the ceiling. "I've been captured by an idiot. No, you're a wizard. Unless you wish to identify as female within The Consortium, which is acceptable, of course. Not that you'll live long enough to become a real wizard as I sincerely doubt any of us will make it through the night."

"I'm sorry. You're saying Bryant's a wizard?" My mom stepped in front of me. "I know my family, and I've met his father's parents. I can assure you, you rude little fear monger, that my son is charming, intelligent, and lovely. He also has nothing to do with this *Consortium* business, and quite frankly, if this murdering Thaden wants you dead for being an idiot who can't do a simple thing like hold onto a dangerous device without letting it fall into the hands of teenagers, then I say let him have you. We'll leave you tied up next to the giant flower in Central Park with a sign that says *free to an evil killer* and call it a night!" She was puffing with rage. I hadn't seen her yell like that since the last time my dad sent me my birthday present two months late.

"You can leave me in the park," Eric said, "but that won't keep your son alive. Thaden will kill anyone who's seen the phone."

"And how do you think he'll find us?" I said. "You think we'll leave a return address?"

Even as the words slipped from my mouth, the apartment grew cold. It was as though the air conditioner had turned on full blast, minus the noise. And the cold didn't invade all at once. It crept up my ankles, tingling my calves, making me shake before I knew I was afraid.

16

"They're here," Eric said, his voice wispy and terrified.

"Thaden." My chest iced up, like the magic in the air had imbued the very name with danger.

"The Ladies of the Consortium." Eric glared up at Devon. "You spoke to them. You told them about the phone."

"I lost them on the subway!" Devon shook his head, backing up into the corner.

"And you thought the Ladies wouldn't sniff you out?" Eric whispered as the mist around my feet stretched and thickened into billowing clouds.

"Guys, take my mom and Mrs. Mops and run!" I slid open the window that led to our ancient fire escape. I had never even been tempted to play on the rusted steps, but now they seemed safer than the mist that had crawled up to my knees.

"I'm not leaving you, Bryant." Mom took my shoulder.

"Neither are we," Elizabeth said.

"None of you can help," Eric said. "The best thing you can do is run. You could outlive him by a few hours if you go now."

"No!" my mother growled. "I will not leave my son!"

The door to the hall rattled on its hinges.

"Too late," Eric breathed as the door burst open. There was a blinding flash of blue light. I saw it coming for me, but my mother knocked me to the ground. I heard her grunt before she fell to the floor.

"Mom!" I screamed. But there were footsteps coming up the stairs. Slow, creeping footsteps. "Mom!"

"Stop them, Bryant!" Eric commanded, still bound to the paint-chipped chair. "Say *abalata*!"

"You say it!"

"You've tied me to a chair, Bryant. *Abalata* requires use of your hands," Eric explained with this false sort of calm that was scarier than his shouting had been.

I turned to the hall. There were shapes in the mist. White shapes with arms and faces.

"Now, Bryant!" Eric hollered.

"*Abalata*!" I shouted back so loudly, the word tore at my throat.

The black sprung out of my palm and stretched toward the mist. I thought it would pass straight through the white, but it made contact with something hard that shrieked as it tumbled backwards.

"She's breathing." Devon knelt by my mom.

"You two," Eric said to Devon and Elizabeth, "take Ms. Miller out of here."

"But those things..." Elizabeth's perfect face was nearly as white as the mist.

"Go the way you came in," I said, helping lift my mother into Devon's arms. He was so big, and she looked so tiny, lying still in his arms. "Get to the roof and then head for the street."

"What about you?" Elizabeth asked.

"We'll find you." I shoved them out the doors and to the roof steps, while the terrible feeling settled deep in my chest that I would never see them again.

Please let my mom be okay. If I can only have one thing, let her be okay.

"Block their path so the Ladies can't follow," Eric said.

"I don't know how." I shook my head. The mist was creeping up in the apartment again, this time churning like a stormy sea. And somehow I knew that meant the Ladies were angry. Like it was a fact written in a science book. The Ladies wanted me dead.

"Are they through?" Eric asked.

I nodded, unable to think of words to express, *yes, I've just sent my unconscious mother away.*

"*Portundo*." The air shook with Eric's command.

I gasped and blinked at the place where Mom, Devon, and Elizabeth had disappeared only seconds before. Where there should have been a rusty door complete with broken alarm, there was nothing but solid wall.

"Let me out," Eric said as the mist turned cold again. "I've helped you. Now free me so I can fight. I will not die strapped to a chair."

"How do I know you won't run off and let the mist get me?" The words came out strangled, like my body was trying to keep the vapor from contaminating my lungs. "How do I know you won't just try and buy yourself a *few good days of happiness*?"

"There is a rather large difference between abandoning enemies and allies, however unwilling the allies might be."

"I let you go, we get out of this together, and you don't leave me here with them."

"I give you my oath as a wizard." Eric's words rung in the air as though he had shouted into an empty cavern.

"*Xorus*." As soon as I said the word, the black lines around Eric dissolved, and in a second, he was standing. "We should go out the fire escape." I moved back toward the window.

"Never leave yourself hanging when the Ladies are coming for you." Eric sneered at the door.

"Then what do we do?" I asked as the shapes reformed in the mist.

"We fight our way out." Eric raised his hands, pressing his palms against the swirling white. "You know what, six spells?"

My mind raced. "Three that might be useful."

"Wonderful." Eric's voice turned strangely businesslike as fingers joined onto hands growing out of the mist. "Use them however you think won't end up getting either one of us killed."

"Right." I nodded as a face peered right at me from inside the haze. "*Abalata!*" The black sprung from my hand, but two other shouts echoed over mine as the black hit the white with a clang that echoed through the hall. The black ricocheted, striking the wall and crumbling the fake marble façade. A shriek of pain blared from within the mist as it clenched around me, pinning my legs together and drawing my arms to my sides.

"*Erunca*," Eric shouted, and lightning struck from the ceiling.

"*Tudina*," a high voice wailed from the mist.

"Duck!" Eric shouted.

A whooshing, whirring sound buzzed over my head as I ducked, screaming, "*Calimarta!*" before I even looked up.

A *crack* shook the hall like a bomb blast. And then everything was still for a moment. Like all of us had frozen, waiting to see what the noise could mean. But before I could take a breath, the ceiling crumbled on the stairs in front of me. Screams of pain and fear far more human than any sounds that had come from the mist before carried over the *crash* of falling debris.

I covered my head as dust and ceiling stuff fell. But a hand closed around my arm, dragging me forward and onto the rubble that had been the stairs to my home. We clambered as fast as we could over the bits of concrete and drywall. The lights of the skyscrapers beamed down on us from above. There was no more roof to keep Manhattan out of the building.

Mrs. Fortner is going to kill me. The irrational thought echoed through my head as we made it down the stairs to the landing.

Something white reached out of the thick chunks of concrete. An alabaster hand that curled its fingers in the air as though grasping for help. Or a fellow victim to drag down with it.

"Run faster!" Eric shouted, pulling me down another flight of stairs and then another. We were almost to the ground floor.

"Bryant Adams!" The voice shook the hall as we reached the lobby. "What in Hell's hot blazes were you doing on the top floor?" Mrs. Fortner took up most of the hall in a nightdress that looked more like a circus tent than a garment meant for a human. The bright red and yellow stripes added to the illusion. Hysteria bubbled up into my throat, and I was laughing. Not chuckling or giggling. Guffawing, like this was a funniest comedy shtick ever.

"Not now," Eric growled.

"Don't you walk out that door," Mrs. Fortner called after us. "You and your mother have been tenants for years, but I won't allow teenage shenanigans to ruin this building! I don't care if you always pay your rent two days early!"

Eric pulled me through the inside door. The lock clicked loudly behind us. But he had committed a cardinal Hell's Kitchen sin. He hadn't looked through the outside door before trapping us in the tiny vestibule. Waiting on the street was the woman we had seen walk into The Consortium. Her skin shone white in the orange of the streetlights. Mist flowed from her hair. And she was smiling as she stared at us through the glass.

I turned to the door behind us. Of course, the keys might have been handy.

"*Cliaxo!*" I shouted, but even as I did, the metal frame of the door melded into the walls. There was no more lock for me to jimmy. I turned to Eric. His eyes were trained on the woman outside.

"Why would you cross The Consortium?" Her voice filled the vestibule as though she were crammed in with us right behind my shoulder.

"I have crossed no one," Eric said.

"Thaden's device." The woman's mouth was moving even as she projected her voice. "He seeks to destroy The Consortium. And you aid him. You assist in his blasphemy."

"The Consortium is built upon knowledge," Eric said. "The phone would bring it to the masses."

"Masses for Thaden to control." The woman tipped her head to the side. "Masses that would rise up against The Consortium. That would bury in darkness the Ladies who have protected our kind for so long. Is that what you wish, Eric Deldridge? To have the Ladies sink into the earth? After all we have sacrificed to protect Magic and all its practitioners, you would draw the craft out of the shadows to destroy us?"

"I know nothing of Thaden's plans." Eric's voice was frighteningly even. "I would never cross The Consortium or the Ladies. Knowledge is my only pursuit."

"Then pursue it you shall. To the grave."

The back of my neck tingled as a high wispy voice filled the vestibule. I spun around. There was another Lady in the hall, this one older, her face sagging and ancient, her skin so white, it defied definition.

"You should have known better than to cross The Consortium, foolish child," agreed the sidewalk Lady. I looked back and forth between the two. We were trapped in my own doorway.

"May your eternal rest be filled with the peace of the darkness," both Ladies intoned as mist poured into the vestibule like water into a tank, sloshing around our ankles. A scent of fresh wild flowers drifted into my nose. If this was death, it wasn't so bad. Warmth and sleep.

"I didn't even think we'd make it down the stairs," Eric sighed, taking in a deep breath of the mist.

The stairs. I had sent my mother up the stairs. My mother, Elizabeth, Devon. The Ladies had scented out Devon. They would...

"*No!*" My scream echoed in the tiny space, making my ears ring. "I won't let you find them! *Aarantha!*"

Obediently, a cyclone formed, like the one in my dad's apartment, only smaller, much smaller. The mist swirled inches from my face, the wind grabbing the oxygen from my lungs. I didn't want it near me. I didn't want any of it near me.

I screamed in rage and fear, pressing my hands into the whirlwind. And the cyclone spread out. I gasped in clean air and kept pushing, the tornado whirling away, even when my fingers could no longer reach it. Right through the walls of the vestibule. Onto the street. The Ladies screamed as the tempest caught them. The mist in the wind thickened as though it had substance of its own.

"We need to get out of here!" Eric shouted over the clamor. He swung open the outer door, and I moved with him, keeping both of us in the eye of the cyclone. Together, we sprinted out into the night, the Ladies' shrieks morphing into howls of anger.

"Now what?" I asked.

"You drop the spell, and we run like hell," Eric said. "Follow me on three!"

"One."

I was going to chase a wizard into the night in Hell's Kitchen.

"Two."

There were probably worse choices I could make at night in Hell's Kitchen.

"Three!"

17

I dropped my hands as he said the word. Part of me expected the storm to keep blowing, for us to stay trapped by my own stupid magic. But the spell dissolved, and the mist shrunk into the night as I launched down 10th Avenue after Eric.

The people on the sidewalks stared at us as we ran. Stared behind us, too, so I chanced a glance back at my building. The façade was...well, kind of missing. The place looked like an open-front dollhouse. Mrs. O'Leery who lived on the second floor was in her giant underpants and pink hair curlers, staring out at the street below her, looking more annoyed than frightened. I caught a glimpse of Mrs. Mops glaring at me from what had been my living room before Eric dragged me around the corner and out of sight.

"We need to find Devon and Elizabeth," I puffed as we pelted toward the water. I wanted to say I needed to make sure my mother wasn't dead, but even thinking that felt like tempting fate.

"Where are they?" Eric asked, breathing easily even as we ran.

"No idea."

"Call them," Eric said as he led me through a creepy alley.

I reached into my pocket and pulled out my phone. Then forgot to breathe until I heard Devon's voice on the other end of the line.

"Are you alive?" he asked.

"No, I'm calling from beyond the grave," I snarked. "Is ah...everyone with you?"

We were running through a dirty hotel lobby now. Eric turned left and cut through the kitchen. The staff swore at us as we tore past.

"Elizabeth is here," Devon said, "and we have your mom. She's still breathing, but I can't wake her up."

Breathing was good. Breathing meant alive.

"Don't let them take her to a hospital," Eric said as we erupted onto the street, and I dutifully panted out the message.

"Yeah, okay," Devon said. "Tell Mr. Obvious we may not be able to use the stinkin' phone, but we're not stupid."

I relayed that, too, as we burst into a butcher shop and paused for a moment, backing out before the man chopping meat could tell us he was closed for the day.

"We need to meet them in a safe place," Eric said.

"And where would that be?" I asked as we sprinted down the street.

"Tell them to meet us at the waterline. Level with 40th," Eric said.

"Presumably with no further explanation from tall, scatterbrained, and pasty?" Devon growled on receiving *that* message. "Fine, bro. You do what you gotta do. The girls and I'll get there."

The phone beeped as he hung up.

It's not that I'm out of shape. I mean, I've never been an athlete, but I do gym and even tap class when my mother makes me feel guilty for having no theatrical talent. But chasing Eric through Midtown at night was on a whole new level. My legs seized up. My lungs burned. I thought I was going to throw up on my shoes. And still Eric ran, weaving circles toward the water. Uptown then downtown, inching around dumpsters.

If it weren't for the fact that at the end of this parkour session I would get to see the very three people in the world I actually cared about seeing, I would have sprawled out on the sidewalk and laid there until morning. Or until the Ladies got me. But I had to get to them. So I ran. And ran. And when I thought there was no way I could run anymore, we started running next to the water, and then Devon and Elizabeth came into sight, flanking a bench, and made all the running worth it.

"Where have you guys been?" Devon demanded as soon as we reached the pool of streetlamp light around the bench where my mom lay unconscious.

"Going around in circles," I puffed, but Elizabeth threw her arms around my neck before I could catch my breath enough to continue with, *because Eric is a sadist who wants to kill me.*

Elizabeth held me tightly. She smelled like heaven and didn't seem to mind that I was sweating worse than a kosher Jew holding cheese-covered bacon. "I thought you were dead," she whispered before Eric cut in, and no, he didn't sound out of breath at all.

"We were laying a trail for the Ladies to follow. If they scent every step we took, it should be long after the sun rises before they ever get here."

"Mom," I breathed, disengaging from Elizabeth to kneel next to her. She looked like she was sleeping. Like she was the cleanest, best dressed homeless person to call a park bench her bed. "What happened to her?"

"The Ladies tried to stop your heart." Eric squinted at my mom. "The spell didn't hit her properly. If we can get her to someone who can care for her, she should theoretically survive."

Theoretically.

"Okay, where are we going?" I lifted Mom into my arms. My muscles shook, and my legs burned like they would give out after the endless running.

"How sweet that you think you will carry her to safety," Eric said. "But that's no way to escape the Ladies."

"So, you run us all over town just so we get to live until morning and then get snuffed out by evil death-shooting mist?" Devon stepped in so he was close enough to punch Eric. "Wait and see if Ms. Miller gets to feeling better in this refreshing Hudson River night air? You know, I think I misjudged you, Eric. You're not only a murdering witch, you're also an optimist."

"I have never murdered anyone—" Eric began.

"So you're a failure, too," Devon said. "Well, keep trying, you might get it right." He didn't even flinch when I kicked him.

"And I have no intention," Eric continued, "of any of us waiting around for the Ladies to find us."

"So then, what do you have in mind?" I asked.

"We're going somewhere the Ladies can't scent us. You carry your mother, and I'll worry about the lot of us living until sunrise." Without a backwards glance, Eric turned and strode to the water's edge.

He stood squinting for a moment at the Hudson, as though trying to make out something in the reflection of the city lights. After a minute, when my arms were really starting to shake from holding my mom, he bent down and picked up a handful of pebbles. One at a time, aiming carefully, he threw them into the river.

"Can I ask why you're throwing stones into the river?" I grunted after another minute.

Eric worked his way south, moving one torturous step at a time. "To save all our lives," Eric said quietly, not stopping whatever passed for his progress.

"Are they magic stones?" Devon lifted Mom easily from my arms. "Do they smell like you? Are they leading *the Ladies* off our scent?"

"No," Eric said, supremely unbothered by the snide tone. "I left myself an escape route a few years ago, and quite frankly, this whole park looks the same, so it can be difficult to find things you've hidden."

Devon opened his mouth to snark at Eric again, but I socked him in the arm, carefully avoiding Mom's head.

We walked for another minute, listening to the tiny splashes barely audible over the nighttime hum of the city and the lapping of the river.

But then, when I was finally sure the shadows under the park benches would rise up and go for our throats, Eric threw a stone and there was no tiny *splash*. Instead there was a dull *thud*.

Eric's face split into a smile. He threw another, bigger rock, and there was another, bigger *thud*. Then the rock disappeared. No ripple in the water. No hovering in midair. It was gone.

"Perfect," Eric said. "*Todunis elarus promotus.*"

His voice rang strangely in the night, and before I could shake the tingle from my spine, a boat wove itself into existence in front of us. Not like a canoe or a yacht. It was one of those little sailboats that have just enough room on them for a bed and a sink below deck. The ones people claim to live on, even though they're smaller than the tiniest New York apartment.

"Wow," Elizabeth breathed.

"If you don't mind," Eric said, gesturing to the boat, "I think we should all get aboard. Right now." He stomped twice on the bank, and a slat of wood appeared, making a gangplank.

"And what's to guarantee you don't throw us overboard and watch us drown?" Devon asked, his voice shaking so slightly I could barely hear it as he glanced between the open water and Eric.

Eric tipped his head to the side, examining Devon. "Well, I suppose you could go for mutual benefit. The exquisitely correct *the enemy of my enemy is my friend.* There are two different groups who would like us indiscriminately eradicated, and survival is seemingly in all of our best interests. But then there is the cold, hard truth." Eric turned to me. "Bryant saved my life. He could have left me for the Ladies to kill, but he didn't. A debt like that has to be paid. I always honor my debts."

"We're supposed to believe you're a good guy now because Bryant didn't leave you to die?" Elizabeth asked.

"I never said I was good." Eric pinned me with his creepy, blue eyes. "I said I always honor my debts. I know enough to understand that if I let the Ladies hurt you, the world will exact a far greater payment than my trying to keep you alive will cost me."

"And if we all die together in your boat?" Elizabeth asked.

"Then I will die with a clean slate." Eric turned and walked onto the boat, his shoes making an odd, hollow sound as he crossed the plank. "Better that than to live owing fate." He didn't turn around until he was on the deck of the boat. "We're in this together, whether we like it or not. Now, shall we idle in the dark, waiting for the Ladies to follow our trail, or attempt to survive?"

Devon and Elizabeth both looked at me like they were waiting for me to make a decision. My mom was unconscious in Devon's arms, and there were mist Ladies coming to kill us. Taking a deep breath and hoping I looked brave, I stepped out onto the plank and crossed onto the wooden sailboat floating in the Hudson.

18

As soon as I was onboard, Devon followed, and then Elizabeth. She didn't take her eyes off Eric as she walked onto the boat. It was like she was daring him to drop her into the water.

I helped Devon lay my mom down on the deck, moving rocks and garbage out of the way.

"Typical New Yorkers," Eric said, punting the beer cans and burger wrappers overboard, "tossing things into the river and not worrying about what the river will do to them in return." He grabbed a rope I hadn't noticed before, leading from the bow to the shore before disappearing into nothingness.

"But didn't you just kick garbage into the river?" Elizabeth took off her bag and knelt, wedging it under Mom's head as a pillow.

Tears burned in the corners of my eyes.

"Occasionally, when one is fleeing for one's life"—Eric gave the rope a giant tug, pulling it free from the rocks on the shore. The rope hit the Hudson with a *splash*—"concerns like properly preserving one's environment must be left behind. As excellently demonstrated by Bryant when he destroyed both his parents' homes today."

I wanted to say something about how it was all his fault any of it had happened in the first place, but I couldn't move past the rope he was hauling onto the boat. It was at least fifteen feet long, even though only six feet of it had been visible a minute before, and it was landing on the deck bone-dry and clean.

"Creepy," I muttered as Eric grabbed the rudder and steered us out onto the open river, no sail catching the stinking wind or whirring motor pushing us forward.

"The Ladies can't find us out here?" Devon asked. "Does mist hate water or something?"

"The Ladies track by scent," Eric said. "You can't scent on the water."

He looked antique standing on the stern, the rudder in hand, the wind blowing his coat and hair around like he was some kind of hero.

"So, we going someplace?" Devon asked, crossing his arms and glaring at Eric. "Fun as this is, we can't stay out here forever."

"We're going someplace they can fix my mom." My voice sounded low and hollow even to my own ears. "Someone can fix her, right?"

"There is a place," Eric said, not unkindly. "It might not be pleasant, but she should be able to help your mother, and The Ladies would have to be desperate to enter there."

I nodded. I wanted to say thanks or something about how if they couldn't fix my mom, I would kill him, but all that came out was, "It's not fair. She wasn't supposed to be in the apartment. She wasn't supposed to have anything to do with this."

Elizabeth wrapped her arms around me, laying her head on my chest. Somehow that made me feel even more helpless.

"Life isn't fair." Eric's voice was barely loud enough to carry over the lapping of the river against the boat. "Magic isn't fair, and fate has definitely never been called fair."

"Fate?" Devon pushed out an angry laugh. "It's got nothing to do with fate. It has to do with you holding Ms. Miller hostage."

"I thought her son was a thief." Eric shrugged. "I was mistaken. But your mother going back for the cat. The Ladies showing up just as we might have come to a peaceful understanding. The strings of fate will draw the things you need close to you at the right moment and pull safety from you just when you think it is near. It's that way in all the world, but the strings are wound tighter when you walk in the world of magic."

"So this sort of thing happens to you all the time?" I asked, too upset to even worry that my voice went all crackly. "You get chased around and blow things up and try to get yourself killed? This is a normal Saturday night for you?"

Eric smiled, suddenly looking younger, like he was barely out of high school. "Exactly."

"This is crazy," I said.

"Crazier than figuring out you're a wizard because you found a phone in a taxi cab?" Eric raised one black eyebrow. It was freaky how the other one didn't even move. "Sometimes the most absurd things in life are the most valid."

We were out in the middle of the river now. It was bright where we were, the lights of New York City on one side and Jersey City on the other.

"So a magic cellphone that destroyed my life is the most valid thing in the world? That's great, just great." I squeezed my head in my hands, wanting to squeeze the past two days right out of existence. Or, just for the pounding in my head to stop, I wasn't picky.

"No, it's valid that the phone found you so you could find your magic," Eric said, sounding like he was explaining to me that morning was when it got bright out.

"To destroy my life, more like." I pulled the solid black culprit out of my pocket. "I could throw it overboard. I should have done that in the beginning, damn piece of magic crap."

"Perhaps." Eric shrugged. "But it's far too late now. The Ladies know we have it, and getting rid of it will only leave us one less card in hand. And by the way, the phone's not magic."

"Is too." I pressed my thumb to the button and watching the screen light up.

"How very mature." Eric snorted as he steered us south toward the tip of Manhattan. "Be that as it may, you are a wizard. *You* possess magic. The phone recognizes it, so it can turn on."

"I am not a wizard!" I shouted, making Eric raise one black eyebrow at me again. "I'm not magical. I'm Bryant Jameson Adams from Hell's Kitchen, and there is nothing extraordinary about my life. Or at least there wasn't until you dragged fate and this magical cellphone freak show into it, and made it all...freaky!"

"You are a wizard." Eric spoke calmly as though I hadn't been screaming at all. "And you were born a wizard. Magic always pounded through your veins, but you never had the cause to feel it. Many are born with magic—fate simply never asks them to use it."

"But my parents are normal." I tried to shout again, but it came out more like a whimper. "I mean, really weird, but normal. I'm not magical."

"You are, Bryant," Elizabeth whispered. "Listen to him."

"Listen to him say what? That the evil lunch lady could be a witch if life had only given her a shove in that direction?"

"I've never met your lunch lady, but yes, that does seem to be the right idea." Eric nodded.

"And when the lunch lady accidentally uses magic to light the cafeteria on fire?' I squeaked.

"If that were to happen, I would assume it would mean she had figured it out." Eric shrugged, like burning down another chunk of my school would be no big deal.

"Wouldn't it be better for you to, I don't know, warn people they have magic superpowers before it turns their lives into flaming death holes?" Devon asked.

"Not at all," Eric said. "At least not for those of us who already live in the mystery that is magic. No one has time to hunt down everyone who might one day produce a spell or two, and the overcrowding would be terrible."

"So burning your way into magic it is," Devon said.

Eric pursed his lips. "I prefer the term *trial by fire*."

"So if you hadn't been an asshat who lost his phone, I could have lived my life as a perfectly normal, completely invisible guy who no one cares about enough to kill." I reached over and touched my mom's hand. She always hated it when I called myself *normal*.

"If by normal you mean toiled in anonymity, yes," Eric said. "But you still would have held magic inside of you, and if fate wants you to leap in blindly now, it probably would have happened even if I had chosen to walk to The Consortium that night. Fate will have its way. The phone just so happened to be the stone that got thrown into your path. Extraordinary though it may be, you are the one who wields it. What's inside the phone is nothing more than a digital library with a few bells and whistles—"

"And by whistles you mean tornados that destroy penthouses." Elizabeth held my mom's other hand.

My heart swelled a little, and my throat got tight.

"Cyclones, yes, and fire," Eric said, blithely ignoring the whole *destroyed my dad's place with a twister worthy of Oz* part. "There's also a section for potions. Using digital ingredients, of course. I must admit, I never really got around to testing that portion. I've never really been one for potions myself."

"And you put all sorts of spells, and"—I forced myself to say the word—"potion things on a pyromaniac's dream device? Who thought that was a good idea?"

"Thaden," Eric said simply.

As he spoke the name, a cold breeze blew across the deck of the boat.

"Why does that keep happening?" I asked as a shiver ran down my spine.

"Please don't say fate," Devon interrupted as Eric opened his mouth.

Eric shrugged and stayed silent.

"Why would Thaden—" I waited for the gust of wind, but there was nothing more than the constant airstream over the river. Maybe I wasn't important enough for fate to send breezes at. "Why would he want to put all that on a cellphone?"

"That's a very long and complicated tale, which involves a bit of sordid history of wizard-dom, and years of a quietly waged war filled with shadows and deeply hidden magic," Eric said.

"We seem to have time while we run for our lives from the mist sisters." Devon leaned back on his arms. "Please, do tell," he added in a formal tone, mimicking how Eric spoke. If I hadn't been terrified and tired, it might have been funny.

"Their preferred term is the Ladies." Eric twisted the rudder, correcting the course toward Manhattan. "And I'm afraid we don't have time, as we're nearing our destination, and I'm sure Bryant will want to get his mother into Lola's care as quickly as possible."

"Who's Lola?"

Eric didn't answer my question as he ran up the nose of the boat and lifted the long, coiled line. I looked back at the rudder. It was moving like Eric was still holding it, steering us toward the shore.

"This is too damn weird," Devon muttered as he followed my gaze.

There was a grunt from the bow as, with a giant heave, Eric tossed the rope to shore, where it connected to the giant stone blocks as though pulled by a magnet, and began to haul us in. But the rope didn't get slack or coil up. The rock absorbed the rope, sucking it in like a kid slurping spaghetti.

"Too damn weird." I nodded to Devon.

With a hollow *thunk*, the boat knocked into the stones.

"If one of you wouldn't mind carrying Ms. Miller." Eric stomped on the deck and the plank appeared, making a way for us to climb ashore. He was on land in two quick strides, and stood, his arms behind his back, studying the night, not bothering to make sure we'd followed.

"I really don't like that guy," Devon said as he picked my mom up and carried her off.

I had always sort of hated Devon a little for having an awkwardly gangly stage that lasted approximately seventeen days during July of the summer before 7th grade. But having a best friend who could easily cart around your unconscious mother was bound to come in handy eventually.

It wasn't until I had followed Elizabeth onto solid ground that I really looked around at where we were. I guess I was expecting a wharf or a dock or something. But we were near an overpass. The stink of the river and the stench of rotting trash were mingling together in a horrible combo that made me want to add eau de vomit to the mix.

"This way." Eric started along the water toward the overpass while his boat disappeared.

Cardboard boxes, old shipping palates, and torn up tents had been turned into shelters flanking the concrete wall, which rose up to form one of the supports for the road twenty feet overhead.

Eric led us toward the tent city, not slowing at all when the residents started inching out of their sad shelters. A dozen dirty faces stared at us.

When we neared the first tent, the people rose up, all silently facing us like something out of a horror movie. Elizabeth gasped, and I reached out without thinking, taking her trembling hand in mine.

The big man closest to us raised an arm, blocking Eric's path, glaring silently.

"I'm here to see Lola." Eric's voice sounded calm, steady, but I wished I could see his face to know if he really wasn't afraid as the tent dwellers all walked toward us.

I slid sideways a few inches, trying to hide Elizabeth behind me.

"We've met many times, remember? Lola is an old friend. I'm having a rather trying evening, and this woman"—Eric gestured to my mom—"is in need of Lola's help. Tell her Eric Deldridge would love to pay her a call and see if she is up to company. I'm happy to wait."

The big guy nodded to a kid behind him, and the boy shimmied up the slope of the concrete wall like it was nothing. At the top of the wall, he blended into the shadows.

We waited silently, the homeless staring at us, us staring at them.

The big guy was probably about the same age as my mom, but he wasn't the oldest person by a long shot. There was a shriveled old lady whose skin sagged away from her tiny frame. I think the youngest was probably the kid who had run up the wall. He couldn't have been more than ten.

I wanted to say something like *I can look up a food pantry for you.* Or better yet, *when my mom's better, she'll make you all dinner.* But somehow it felt like talking might break the spell that was the silent truce Eric had made with them.

It seemed like forever but was probably only a few minutes before the boy sprinted back down the wall, right to where the big guy could see him, and silently nodded. The man nodded back, and as though he had given an order, the people all crawled back into their sad homes. In less than a minute, we were standing alone in the tent city.

"What was that?" I whispered as soon as I figured out how to talk again.

"Lola's guard." Eric started forward, walking the same path the boy had run.

"Those people are her guards?" Devon whispered.

Elizabeth gripped my hand like she was terrified she'd get dragged into one of the tents.

"Those weren't people," Eric said.

"Just because they're homeless—" Devon started.

"I mean they aren't human." Eric threw over his shoulder as he leapt onto the steep wall.

"What are they?" I looked back at the still tents.

"Some of Lola's secrets are best not spoken of in darkness." Eric reached the top of the wall near the shadow.

I took two steps up to get above Devon so I could help him carry my mom, but climbing here wasn't like climbing at all. I took another step forward. My eyes told me I was scaling a nearly vertical wall, but my legs and my balance told me I was on a flat surface.

"Whoa," Devon murmured behind me.

I wanted to turn around to make sure he was okay, but this really was like navigating a funhouse tunnel. It was all I could do just to stay upright and slog one foot in front of the other.

With a sudden movement that made my head spin, Elizabeth let go of my hand and ran past me. I looked up to the top of the wall, and she was standing there next to Eric. I swayed trying to look up/out at them.

"Take it at a run," Elizabeth said. "It's a lot better at a run."

Devon took her at her word.

I took a deep breath and thumped after him. Elizabeth was right, faster was better. My feet didn't have time to notice they weren't where my eyes thought they should be. And before I could freak out about how weird the whole thing was, I was on the ledge at the top, between Eric and Elizabeth.

"Well done." Eric's gaze searched Elizabeth's eyes before he turned and walked off into darkness.

"Allons-y!" I plunged into shadows after him. Unable to see an inch past my nose, I held my hands out, expecting metal or concrete. But there was nothing.

"Bryant," Elizabeth whispered behind me.

I reached back and squeezed her fingers, still forcing myself forward, my free hand stretched out, looking for solid wall.

After a few more steps, my heart jumped up into my throat. This was a trap. Eric had tricked us, and now we were going to be stuck wandering in the darkness forever.

"Don't worry, love," a light voice with a deep resonance purred right in front of me. I stopped and felt Devon smack into my back. "Two more steps, and you'll be out of the dark."

Reaching my toe out in front of me to make sure there was solid ground, I edged forward.

The voice laughed lightly at me.

Taking a deep breath and squaring my shoulders, I forced myself toward the voice.

19

Light filled my eyes, revealing a space so strange, I had to blink for a few seconds to make sure I was properly seeing what was around me.

There were no windows in the room. All the light came from six mismatched lanterns hung from the ceiling, their flickering flames casting the place in a warm glow. Not that it really needed a warm glow. Every surface was colorful. The table in the middle was draped in purple cloth, which looked soft enough to curl up on and sleep right between the steaming pot of tea and the bowl of skittles that sat out like an interrupted midnight snack.

There were big armchairs and fainting couches scattered around the room in no order I could see. Long strips of fabric in every jewel tone I had ever heard of covered the walls, leaving no trace of a door to anywhere else.

I turned to look for Devon and Elizabeth. They were both behind me, Devon still carrying my mother. And staring down into my mother's face was a very...striking woman.

She had dark skin and high cheekbones to go with her angular jaw. Her long black eyelashes fanned out like flying butterflies when she blinked, and shimmering eye shadow reached gracefully up to her perfectly shaped brows. Her lips were painted on like a showgirl's, and she wore a turban on her head with a jeweled clip attached to the front.

The woman reached out to touch my mom's face with her long, deep-purple nails.

"Don't touch her," I spat automatically, shouldering forward.

"Now, love," the woman said, smiling gently at me, "how on earth am I supposed to heal your mother without touchin' her?" She raised one highly arched eyebrow.

Was that like a thing with magic people? Did they go to eyebrow raising school? *Lesson one—How to control magical fire. Lesson two—How to do a perfect skeptical/creepy eyebrow raise.*

"You'll have to forgive Bryant, Lola." Eric stepped in, though I hadn't seen him in the room before. "He's only been a part of our little circle for two days now and has had rather a rough time of it."

"Looks like it," Lola said. "Anyone who ends up finding a way to see me this quick is clearly fated for somethin'." She started toward the table in the center of the room before looking back at me. "I'm not sayin' what that somethin' is, but I don't think you'll ever have to worry about your life being boring. Good Lord, I should've known this day was going to be long when Beville started shakin' badly enough for the folks topside to notice."

I wanted to ask what Beville was, why it was shaking, and what that had to do with my mom. Not to mention if I didn't have to worry about being bored because I was suddenly going to become ridiculously cool and have awesome adventures or because I was going to be killed by the Ladies come morning, but something in the air made me afraid to ask.

"Lay the poor mama down." Lola patted one of the fainting couches.

Devon looked at me, and I nodded. He walked over and carefully laid my mom down. When he stood up, Lola caught his chin in her hand.

She stood for a moment, staring deep into his eyes. "Well, now, that is a twist. Haven't seen one like him in ages." She turned back to my mother, leaving Devon looking stunned.

"It always is the mama," Lola said like she hadn't done anything weird. But then maybe to her, calling my friend a twist was normal. "I know it's because they all love their babies so much, they would do anything to protect them. But then if the kids manage to survive whatever the mama was trying to protect them from, they come dump a dying mama on my sofa."

"She's not dying," I growled, quivering with an almost physical need to run to my mom and shake her, make her wake up and tell Lola to stop being creepy.

"Oh, this mama's not, love," Lola said. "But if you keep her tangled up in your mess, it's only a matter of time before you haul her back here with a problem I can't fix. Mamas with no magic don't last long when fate pushes their babies around in the world. A mama's love is strong, but there is nothing as strong as fate."

"So, you can fix her?" Elizabeth asked. I was grateful she said it. My head was spinning too fast to make words other than *Fix* and *now*.

"This time, sugar." Lola walked to the table and started pouring cups of tea. "You all want cream and sugar?"

"Can't we have tea after you fix Ms. Miller?" Devon said.

Lola turned to examine him again.

"Sweetie, I think I like you. But there are some types of magic I prefer only to play with when the sun shines. So we might as well have a nice cuppa and a snack while we wait for sunrise."

It wasn't until Lola mentioned food that I realized how desperately hungry I was. Right on cue, my stomach made a horrible, embarrassing grumbling sound.

"Next time you take people on the run"—Lola rounded on Eric—"you should pack some snacks. I swear you are going to end up eating me right out of house and home."

"Why pack snacks when your food is better?" Eric winked.

Lola smiled and walked over to the emerald green curtain and disappeared through it. And I don't mean pushed it aside. She walked through it like it wasn't there.

"What is she?" I whispered, staring at the fabric, which hung motionless though a person had just disappeared through it.

"Lola is..." Eric sat down in one of the comfy chairs, rubbing his chin. "Well, since you're completely unaware of how the hierarchy of magic works..."

"Thanks," I grumbled.

"It would be easiest to classify her as a seer, a bit of a black market healer, and a witch, of course," Eric said. "She's never quite fit into the binary mold, has excellent taste is cheese, and is also one of the finest people I know."

"Then why is she living like a bridge troll?" Elizabeth asked.

"I'm the most fabulous troll I've ever heard of," Lola said from right behind my shoulder.

I spun around and nearly knocked the tray out of her hands.

"I-I'm sorry," Elizabeth sputtered, "I meant no disrespect."

"Sugar," Lola laughed, setting down the tray and taking Elizabeth's face in her hands, "don't you ever be sorry for seeing things in this world for what they really are. Some folks will hate you for it, but the truth that lies underneath always comes out in the end. I should know. I've paid my fair share for seeing the truth."

"For being a psychic?" Devon asked.

"Psychic?" Lola quirked that eyebrow of hers. "The things those city folks stuff in their children's heads! I don't see the future. That would be like trying to read a book the author hasn't finished yet. I see what hides in the shadows. In the deep tunnels under the city and in the darkest places of a man's heart." Lola's eyes pinned Eric's for a long moment before she turned to me. "And sometimes people who are scared of what they want to keep hidden, they try to hide you. But exile isn't so bad."

Lola went back to the table and poured herself a cup of tea before settling down in a blood-red armchair.

Elizabeth, Devon, and I all stood still, watching her take slow sips.

"I thought you lot were hungry?" she said after a minute. "Eat, my little refugees, eat."

I glanced at the silver tray. There were still the skittles and the tea, but it was also now laid out with cheese, meat, and olives.

"Some things never change." Eric snagged a few cubes of cheese. "Not that I would ever want them to."

I poured myself a cup and covered the saucer with bits of cheese and meat, then plopped down at my mom's feet. Even though she was unconscious, it felt better to be near her, like somehow she could keep me safe from whatever hid beyond the drapes on Lola's walls.

We sat quietly for a few minutes, me wishing there was a clock ticking nearby if only to make the silence less complete.

"You were banished?" Elizabeth asked, staring down at the untouched cup she had balanced on her lap.

"I was," Lola said.

"Is that why," Elizabeth said slowly, like she was testing waters, "you're so... colorful? I mean not"—she glanced at Eric—"bleached out like this guy. And the Ladies."

Lola tipped her head back and laughed. "Oh sugar, you are smart. I have never allowed myself to turn into one of those color-challenged witches, not even before I was banned. But my darlin' Eric likes to wrap himself up so deep in magic, it pulls bits of him away, starting with color."

"I used to have freckles." Eric made a little moue, whether of regret or disgust I couldn't say.

Lola took a long sip of tea. "And those Ladies hell-bent on killing all you hold dear, love"—she looked right at me, her eyes boring holes into mine—"they've pushed magic further than it was ever meant to go. So white mist is all that's left of them."

"So using magic steals the color out of you?" Devon asked, an olive paused half-way to his mouth.

"The black, the white, hell, my fabulous lair, it's only an outward sign of the magic within. Like playing with finger paint too long, some of it is bound to get stuck to your skin."

"Am I going to change like that?" I said, relieved that for once my voice didn't wobble.

"You'd have to live through the weekend first." Eric grimaced, and Lola tossed a green skittle that hit him right in the temple.

"You would never get all scary white like the Ladies, love." Lola squinted at me appraisingly. "But if things go well, that charming brown hair of yours might darken up a bit. Don't worry though, you'll still be a handsome little thing. Now eat, eat! I lay out food for the famished masses, and everyone is talking instead of gobbling it up. Explaining the whole colorful spectrum that is magic, my, that would take days, and we do not have that kind of time."

Silence filled the room again. I munched on cheese and meat, waiting for it to be okay with Lola to speak again. She didn't say anything until the whole silver tray was empty.

"All right, now that everyone has been fed, and we all feel like good ole friends, darling, how about you tell me what sort of shit storm you dragged through my front door." Lola turned to Eric. "I've got a damaged mama, a boy who's just figured out he's got magic in him, one that fate just can't wait to get its hands on, and one that will change the way fate works. I'm feeding very confused teenagers who don't know which end is up and which end gets them dead. You know I love you, darlin', but this one is going to take some explainin'."

Eric took a deep breath and put his cup down on the table.

"Do you remember—"

"When your *friend* Keadred Thaden asked you for a little favor?" Lola said. "I remember telling you to steer clear of the hurricane that man is trying to stir up."

I waited for the ominous wind or creepy goosebumps which usually accompanied Thaden's name, but just my luck, there was nothing. Still, Lola pointed to me.

"Even little love new wizard here knows enough to be scared of Thaden. You should learn from the new kid, darling. At this point he might outlive you."

"There wasn't any creepy wind that time," I said.

"You invoke an evil man, and yes, darling"—she glanced over at

Eric—"Keadred Thaden is evil, but saying his name isn't going to get you a big movie style *dun-dun-bwa-na*," Lola sang. "It *will* invite some bad strings into the web of fate. You aren't going to feel all creepy every time you mention the evil unmentionable, 'cause that fate has already crept in the back door. He doesn't need to announce himself again."

"If Thaden is so evil"—Elizabeth leaned forward to swipe more skittles from the bowl, which didn't seem to have emptied at all—"why would anyone want to get involved with him?"

"I would love to hear the answer to that question." Lola leaned back in her chair and crossed her legs, staring at Eric.

"Can't you see the answer?" Eric smiled, but it looked like he didn't mean the smile. Like he was trying hard to be suave but it wasn't worth the effort.

"What I see and what you believe don't always line up, darling. If it did, you wouldn't be in this mess." Lola took a sip of her tea and waited, her gaze fixed on Eric.

"Just because Thaden is evil doesn't mean he's the worst thing in this city," he said with a hint of pleading in his voice. "Thaden may be dangerous and heartless, but at least he believes in freedom. The way things are now, we all live in shadow, constantly afraid to stick a toe out of line. In Beville, no one even dares to speak against the system. Anyone who is deemed other—"

"Gets a nice taste of banishment?" Lola's eyebrow rose again. "Darling, I know."

"Precisely!" The entreaty in Eric's voice morphed into anger. "We should be free to live our lives away from The Consortium's rules. Magic shouldn't be doled out based on favor."

"And we should all ride unicorns in Times Square." Lola sighed. "Darling, even if The Consortium didn't control the pages, someone else would step in with a system we would all grow to hate just as much. And some of those someones would leave us with an even bloodier mess than we're already stuck in. There is no such thing as a true Utopia. I've read the book. It had *slaves*."

"I'm sorry." My head spun. Maybe it was because I was tired. Maybe it was because I had no idea what they were talking about. "Can someone please take me through why the evil dude who wants to kill us is better than the evil Ladies who want to kill us? It sounds sexist, but I don't think that's what you're talking about."

Lola waved a hand at Eric. He leaned forward in his chair and locked his creepy, blue eyes on mine.

"Magic is controlled by The Consortium. That restaurant your friend so brazenly walked into is the only outpost of magic aboveground in New York.

The Ladies control The Consortium. The Consortium controls all the spell books, and with them all knowledge of magic. If you want a spell to do something, you have to petition the Ladies for it. And they dole out spells in the most perverse and miserly way. It keeps us under their thumbs. Experimenting is banned by penalty of death. Searching for lost knowledge is banned by penalty of banishment. So, we all exist by The Consortium's will.

"Except Thaden. He's buried himself so far in the darkness, even the Ladies won't follow him. He doesn't want The Consortium to lord over all of us, hiding that which is essentially our birthright. So, he came up with the idea of the phone. The entire contents of The Consortium's archives on one, normal-looking portable without any of the rules of impartment the Ladies have forced upon us. The knowledge of centuries right in your pocket. Freedom. Gaining the spells from the Ladies was…difficult."

"You mean stealin' the spells, darling—"

"And creating a way around impartment was worse," Eric pressed on. "But Thaden created the phone. His greatest weapon, a way to equip the wizard masses to fight the Ladies."

"And those masses end up beholden to Thaden," Lola finished. "Which made this *such* a grand idea you agreed to help him with it?"

"I thought I was helping us all." Eric pinched the bridge of his nose, scrunching his eyes. "I thought I was standing at the front of a fight for all our freedoms. But the phones were only ever meant for those who would serve as his henchmen, helping him build an army that wouldn't be offering anything but a new name for oppression. I wasn't serving freedom, only darkness."

"And it took getting wasted and losing the item of doom to figure out you weren't exactly working with the angels?" Devon asked. "Great, just great."

"First, I have never pretended to be a hero," Eric said flatly. "Second, not that it's any of your business, but it wasn't until I had gained his confidence, to whatever extent, that I quite realized the endgame."

"Did you really think you would come out of this in one breathing piece?" Lola asked.

"Better to die free than to live oppressed. No matter the face of the oppressor," Eric said, "and with friends like you, Lola, perhaps I stand a chance."

"You're not going to have friends long if you get everyone who likes you even a little killed, darling. You come to me lookin' for miracles, and I only deal in magic." Lola sighed. "Darling, you took a shiny piece of forbidden skittles from a monster, and you lost the damn pack. I can't save you from this one."

Elizabeth froze with her hand halfway to her mouth with another batch of skittles.

"I was talking metaphorical skittles." Lola turned to Elizabeth even though she couldn't have seen her freeze. "I don't believe in enchanting food. A world where you aren't even safe to eat something sweet? That's a world I don't want to live in, sugar."

Elizabeth turned bright red as she popped the skittles into her mouth. Somehow her blushing made her even more beautiful. "Thanks."

"So, now that you made friends with the hornet and went and kicked in the side of his nest, what exactly do you plan on doing, darling?" Lola confronted Eric again.

"Not dying was really where I was starting from." Eric took a slow sip of tea. "And considering we all made it here, I'd say we're doing pretty well so far."

"Don't say things like that, darling." Lola looked to the bit of fabric we had all entered through. "You don't want fate to decide she needs to prove you wrong."

"And what do you think we should do?" Eric asked. "You know more about everything in this city than I ever could hope to."

"And you know flattery will get you just about anywhere with Lola." She rolled her eyes and walked over to the nearest lamp.

I hadn't noticed until then that she was wearing glittering, six-inch heels. They were blue, green, purple, red, and as she moved, the way the colors danced was mesmerizing. Even when she stopped, I couldn't look away until she spoke.

"Thaden is buried deep in the darkest places where the mist doesn't go." She was staring into the flames of one of the lanterns. It was like she was reading the fire as it danced. "He doesn't want to come up to the light, the Ladies don't want to go down to the dark."

"So, I should stay in the middle?" Eric joined Lola by the lamp, staring into the flames over her shoulder. But somehow the way he looked at them was different than the way she did. With him, it was like he was puzzling out a book in a language he couldn't read.

"The middle—where it ends." Lola's voice dropped two octaves. The glorious woman had been replaced by a sad and ancient man. "The middle is where you get penned in. Trapped like a pig for slaughter."

The room was silent for a moment. Funeral silent.

"The only way forward is down," Lola murmured. "Go into the dark and drag the light down after you. You can't fight in the city where the light rules, or down in the pits where Thaden reigns. But if you fight in the middle, even the shadows don't know what will happen." A tear rolled down Lola's cheek.

"A chance is better than death." Eric smiled.

"Not for the ones left waiting and banished," Lola whispered.

Eric reached out and took her hand. "You know I've always been good at fighting. It's one of my better features."

"Most people don't consider their better feature something that's likely to get them killed every other month." Lola and Eric stood silently for a moment.

Part of me wanted to leave them to...whatever this was, but my mother was unconscious on the couch, and I didn't know how to get out of the room without going back through the non-human, homeless guards anyway.

"Now then, everybody's had a snack, you might as well get a little sleep," Lola said, all traces of fear and sadness gone. "I won't be able to get to work on mama for a few hours, and rest is exactly what Lola's ordered. Come on, littlelings." She nodded toward the right wall, the one opposite where she had gone for the snacks. "You walk right through the blue strip, you'll find a nice, cozy place to sleep. Mama can rest on the couch till sunrise."

I stood up and walked over to the blue cloth. The color was somewhere between sapphire and the dusky shade of the ocean at sunset. I checked to make sure Elizabeth and Devon were behind me before girding my loins.

"I'll wake y'all up in the morning," Lola called after me as I stepped through the curtain.

20

It felt more like pushing through a cobweb than anything else. The fabric dragged along my face, but it didn't stop me or cling. It was just there, a light thing caught on my nose. Then I took another step, and it was gone. Everything had gone dim for a moment while I walked through the curtain, but once I was past, I was in another room.

There was one light that looked like a giant, glittering chandelier in the middle. Tiny candles burned all over it. But instead of there being clear, diamond-ish hangings, this chandelier was hung with reds, blues, purples, and greens that threw off dancing reflections on the walls as the flames flickered through the crystals.

"Wow," I breathed. It was like Fourth of July fireworks made babies with a laser show.

"I call right side," Devon said from behind me.

It took me a minute to realize what he was talking about. The only furniture in the room was a king-size bed.

"What?" Devon asked when I spun to look at him. "I always sleep on my right so I can see my alarm clock."

"Whatever makes you happy," Elizabeth mumbled, almost falling on the left side of the bed. "As long as no one tries to light me on fire, chase me, or kill me with mist, I'm good."

Which left me to crawl up the middle.

I kicked off my shoes and scrambled up from the foot of the bed, trying not to make it bounce too much since Devon and Elizabeth seemed to have conked out already.

I knelt on top of the sheets. They were soft and silky. I yawned, and then, *You'll be under these sheets with Elizabeth*, a terrified voice in the back of my head said.

You're running for your life from the Ladies who control the magic books and the dude who believes in free knowledge because they all want to kill you. Where you sleep really shouldn't be a priority, the other voice sighed.

It doesn't matter. She held your hand. She thinks you're brave, the first voice crowed.

I lay down, staring at the back of Elizabeth's head.

Brave doesn't mean she would date you. You don't even know if wizards date, the second voice said.

She thinks you're brave. She doesn't want you dead. She even held your hand.

I slipped into sleep before my brain could finish duking it out.

———

"Where's Elizabeth?" Devon's question yanked me into the waking world.

"Wha d'ya mean?" I sat up, blinking at the colorful lights that still danced on the walls. Everything looked the same as when I had drifted to sleep. But Elizabeth was gone. The covers on her side of the bed had been thrown back.

I swore so badly Devon muttered, "Damn, dude."

"Let's go." I pushed myself to the bottom of the bed and slipped on my sneakers. Part of me wanted to pull the phone out of my pocket. But somehow I didn't think picking a spell at random would really help if Lola wanted to keep us separated and trapped here.

I held my breath as I stepped into the blue fabric, half-expecting to be stuck in its folds for the rest of my life. But I passed back out into the front room as easily as I had left it.

Elizabeth was sitting on the red fainting couch next to Lola with her back to me.

"I still don't see why this has anything to do with me," she said, unsteadily lowering her teacup onto its saucer.

"It's the seeing that got you tangled up in all this." Lola wrapped her arm around Elizabeth's shoulders. "And don't worry, it's not all living like a bridge troll with fabulous shoes. You're not magic, Sugar, you're simply not as easily deceived. Even my darling Eric can't see my beasties outside for what they are."

Elizabeth shuddered hard enough I could see it shake Lola's arm.

"Fate dragged you into this mess to see what that pack of helpless boys can't." Lola took Elizabeth's face in her hands and tucked her blond hair behind her ears. "It's funny how a girl like you can't see how very special you are." Lola glanced at me. "Good thing Bryant here knows."

My cheeks burned as Elizabeth looked over her shoulder at me.

"I'm only here because I suck at Calculus," Elizabeth said. Bright tears balanced in the corners of her eyes. "If I hadn't needed a tutor, I wouldn't have seen the fire start, or gone to Bryant's dad's, and Eric never would have seen me. I'm only here because I'm stupid."

"You aren't stupid." I crossed around to the front of the couch. My mom still lay there, like she was taking the best nap ever. "You're great at lots of things. You're really good in all your other subjects. You're great on stage. And you're beautiful, and nice, and incredibly brave. You figured out the phone was magic and you didn't try to run away. You wanted to help, that's what landed you here."

My heart soared up into my throat as Elizabeth smiled at me, blushing the gentlest pink. "You're brave too, Bryant. And really, pretty great."

My throat was too tight to form words like *thanks* or *I love you.*

Luckily, Devon took my terrible non-word sigh as a cue.

"And you could be good at math if you wanted. Your dad wants you to be a math genius and not an actor"—he took Elizabeth's hands in his—"and then suddenly you can't do math anymore. You aren't stupid. You're rebellious. That makes you cool in my book."

"I don't suck at math on purpose." Elizabeth shook her head.

"Don't argue with the boy." Lola shook a finger at Elizabeth. Her nails were a brilliant bright blue this morning. "He knows more than those good looks give him credit for. And besides, even if you were top of your class in every subject the world has ever seen, you would still be in my sitting room right now. 'Cause that's how fate works, sugar. The Devil's in details. But fate, she don't give a shit."

"Eloquent as always." Eric walked through a strip of scarlet fabric. "I thought I heard the dulcet tones of teenaged angst."

"I would be nice about the suffering of their tender young hearts if I were you, darling, since you barely managed to escape being a teenager yourself," Lola said.

"Surviving twenty years of this life has been a feat, hasn't it?" Eric smiled.

"You're twenty?" I asked, louder and maybe a little more disbelievingly than I should have since everyone but my unconscious mother spun to face me. "What?" I sputtered, flushing for the second time in two minutes. "You just seem older."

"Surviving below will steal years off your life, add years to your soul, and never let you die in peace," Lola said.

"And that is why you in your grandeur escaped." Eric poured himself a cup of tea from the pot on the table and took a biscuit from an overflowing tray.

It wasn't until I saw the steam rising from the biscuit that I noticed the wonderful smell, and my mouth started watering.

"Go on." Lola waved at the tray without looking at me. "I made them for you all. And you should be grateful my banishment, which you so lovingly call escape, left me alive and topside, or you would be huddled under a bridge with a dead mama. If you had even survived this long without my help. Which I highly doubt would have happened."

"Not in a million years." Eric smiled, lifting his cup to Lola. "My savior."

"As long as we agree on something." Lola stood up and walked over to the little desk in the corner. Her long, silk, embroidered bathrobe swished at her ankles.

"My mom." I froze with the hot biscuit in my hand. "Is it light out now? Can you fix her?"

"Fix her?" Lola laughed as she rummaged around in the drawers. "Isn't it cute how he says *fix her* like she's an engine with a bad spark plug?" Lola reached down, and her arm disappeared up to her elbow in a drawer that was at most six inches deep. "I can heal her. I can use my immense—" there was a clattering of things toppling over. "Damn those little things. Where was I?"

"Your immense..." Eric prompted.

"Thank you, darling. I can use my immense magical prowess, power, and knowledge to save your mama's life." Lola stood up, holding a handful of something. "But if you want to talk about the very woman who gave you life like she's an automobile, that's fine with me. I'll *fix* her for you."

"Thank you," I said sheepishly as Lola started pulling things out of her fist. It was like a magic show where the magician keeps drawing yards and yards of scarves out of her hand. But instead of scarves, there were glass vials filled with sparkling liquid, two silver trays, a violet and a pale blue candle, a wooden mortar and pestle, and a silver spoon.

"Darling, you come be my mixer." Lola poured some of the liquid into the wooden bowl.

Eric obediently popped the rest of the biscuit into his mouth and walked over, picking up the pestle and lazily stirring as Lola added a few drops of blue, then purple, then red.

I wanted to ask what she was doing, but something in the pale pink smoke rising into the air kept me silent.

After about a minute, she moved on to the first tray, dripping the ingredients right onto the surface. After a few different vials had added their contents, she picked up the spoon to stir what was on the tray. I thought I would hear the scrape of metal against metal, but instead the spoon sloshed like it had been dipped into a bathtub.

Another few minutes passed before Lola tapped the spoon on the edge of the tray, knocking off the few stray black drops that had clung to it. Eric stopped stirring in the wooden bowl, too.

"Did I tell you to stop?" she snarked as she picked up the violet candle and stuck it to the middle of the tray.

Eric rolled his eyes and kept stirring.

Lola started mumbling at the candle. I tried to listen to the words, but they were all strange. Lower and more guttural than the ones I had found on the phone.

When she finished, the tip of the candle burst into flame, making lights dance in my eyes as the glow settled down to normal. Well, normal except for burning pink. She took the wooden bowl from Eric and whispered something into it before dumping its powdery contents onto the second tray and picking up the pale blue candle. A puff on the tip, and a gentle teal flame shimmered to life. Lola smiled and settled the candle onto the middle of the second tray.

"*Erbracina*," she said loudly, and with a popping *hiss*, both the candles puffed out and their smoke drifted down, flowing onto the trays.

"Nicely done." Eric cocked an impressed eye at the trays.

"You know how I love praise for my excellent work." Lola lifted the candles, laying them on the desk before picking up a tray in each hand and carrying them to the table in the center of the room. "Now comes the hard part."

"Hard part? What else do you have to do?" I asked.

"Oh not me, love. You." Lola pointed at the trays. "You have to pick which one you want to give your mama."

I looked down at the trays. One had a pill on it, a capsule filled with pale blue powder. The other—a tiny stone so purple, it looked almost black.

"What's the difference?" My heart raced in my chest as I imagined all too vividly having to solve some terrible riddle or do something magical when I didn't know anything but how to whip up a tornado.

"One wakes your mama up"—Lola indicated the stone—"and the other keeps her sleeping." She pointed to the blue pill.

"Then give her the stone."

"If that's what you want, love." Lola nodded. "But what happens when she wakes up? You have enough folks out to kill you that getting dead shouldn't be too tough. Do you think your mama's gonna let you just waltz out there on your feet or in a box and not do anything to try and stop it? Do you think if she's with you, she won't end up getting hurt again?"

My throat was so tight I couldn't make words. I looked at my mom. Sleeping on the couch. Halfway to dead because she had tried to save me.

I shook my head.

"The pill," Lola said, "it'll cure what the Ladies did to her, but it won't let her wake yet. She'll stay asleep and safe here till you come back and get her up and running."

"What if I don't make it back?" I croaked. The reality of the words shattered me inside.

I had to follow Eric to survive. Following Eric might get me killed. I would never get to see Mom again.

"Then I'll wait to give her the stone. Even if it takes a hundred years for the Ladies to lose her scent. I've got the time and the house room. I'll make sure she stays safe."

"And wakes up in a hundred years to find out her son's dead?" Devon shook his head. "You can't do that to her. It would kill her just as much as the Ladies would."

"This isn't your choice." Lola held up a hand to stop Devon from talking. "It can only be Bryant's. Even I can't see who makes it out of the shadows that crawl around under our feet. But I know mamas, and I know what it's like to watch yours die."

The room fell silent. Everyone stared at me as I looked at my mom. I wanted her eyes to open. I wanted to talk to her and ask her what I should do. But I knew what she would say. She would tell me I couldn't go underground, especially not without her.

"You'll keep her safe?" I asked, not bothering to hide the tear snaking from my eye.

Lola nodded. "I won't let anyone get to her, love."

"Blue pill."

Lola lifted it off the tray and slipped it into my mom's mouth. Blue haze poured out from between Mom's lips, wrapping itself around her. The haze got denser and heavier, so thick I couldn't see her face anymore, so thick I wanted, *needed* to rip it away. To hug her and tell her I loved her and I was sorry for every mean thing I had ever said and for every time I had been a pain in her ass. But the haze would keep her alive. So I sat and watched my mother's face disappear behind its veil.

Tears ran down my cheeks as the haze turned into a cocoon, shimmering as it solidified.

"Take her to the low room, darling," Lola said.

Eric stepped forward and lifted the cocoon with one hand, pushing it in front of him like it weighed nothing. He walked out through an orange patch of curtain.

"The low room is the safest place I have," Lola said.

Elizabeth slipped her hand into mine. Three days ago I would have given anything to have her hold my hand. But right then I would have given anything to go back to how things were before, when the worst problem I had was figuring out how to get the most beautiful girl in New York City to give me the time of day.

"You two aren't coming either." I glanced at Devon. "I'll go with Eric, but you can't—"

Elizabeth and Devon lit into me at once, but it was Lola that cut over both of them. "Sugar and sweetie are going with you." Her voice rang oddly in the room, like the walls were made of marble instead of fabric. "I know you want to save your friends, and that makes you a good kid. But fate brought all three of you into this, and the only way it's going to let any of you walk away before this thing has played out is by dying. Your mama was never meant to get involved. But those golden threads of fate have you three tied up in a little bow."

"But neither of them can use magic." I paced in front of the table.

"Stop moving and eat a damn biscuit." Lola threw one to me.

Its warmth was comforting in my hands. I took a bite and felt the panic raging in my chest back away just a little.

"Have you ever heard the saying fight fire with fire?" Lola asked.

I nodded.

"Well, sometimes that works, but sometimes you need a bucket of water or a fire extinguisher, you get me, love?"

I lifted my chin to nod, then shook my head.

"There are more ways to fight magic than by tossing spells at it." Lola walked over and took the biscuit from my hand, pressing the rest of it into my mouth. "You only have to see the path and take the leap. None of you will survive if you don't go together. I don't even need to look into the shadows to see that, love."

"You're my best friend, Bryant." Devon rose. "Your fight is our fight. I'm not walking away from this."

"Neither am I," Elizabeth said.

"Ah, the nobility of youth," Eric drawled as he walked back through the orange curtain. "Have I ever been that noble?"

"I can tell you you haven't." Lola smirked. "Now darlings," she said, suddenly serious, "the only thing I've got is a strong feeling that this is trouble like you've never seen before." She took Eric's chin in her hand. "I hate wearing black. It depresses me to no end. So, do Lola and favor and come back alive. I don't want to wreak havoc on my wardrobe."

"We'll do our best." Eric kissed Lola on the cheek and squeezed her hand for a moment before striding toward the black curtain. "Let's get this motley army on the march. We have an evil to destroy and a regime to topple. It's going to be a long day."

"You kids take the rest of the biscuits." Lola's voice was thick as she pressed biscuits into each of our hands. "I'll take care of her. You take care of him."

"Yes ma'am." I looked back at the orange curtain. "And thank you."

"Anytime, love," Lola called after us as we walked out into darkness.

21

I didn't mind the walk through the dark on the way back out of Lola's. It didn't feel like I was being trapped forever this time. Instead, I didn't want the blackness to end. Once we got through, I would be leaving my mom behind and leading my best friend and Elizabeth to do something dangerous that could get us all killed. Well, really Eric was doing the leading. But that didn't make me feel any better. Not even a little bit.

The blackness ended, and we were standing at the top of the wall. The sun was high in the sky, and the chaos of the midday bustle echoed under the overpass.

Eric started walking down the wall, keeping his chin tipped up and away. I did the same, trying not to panic as I stepped out onto what should have been a drop but felt like level floor. I looked at the steel trusses high above me, which got farther away as my feet carried me out.

Right when I was getting used to the sensation and my heart had figured out what a normal rhythm should be, I took another step, and the flat smooth ground wasn't there. I waved my arms in the air like an idiot for a second and fell forward, hitting the gravel hard with both knees.

"Watch out," Eric said, completely unfazed, as the rest of the crew marched down the wall, Elizabeth walking normally, Devon looking up like I had been, "the last step is a doozy."

"Thanks," I grunted as I pushed myself to my feet.

"Well, it was already too late for you." Eric shrugged.

"But we appreciate your consideration." Elizabeth all but floated off the wall.

Devon teetered at the edge for a second, feeling the air with his toe, before jumping down to solid ground, muttering, "Weird. This is way too weird."

I agreed.

There was a faint rustle of tarps and cardboard as the homeless emerged from their homes.

"Good morning," Eric said. "We're going to be on our way now."

The big guy stepped forward, lifting his chin and tipping his head to the side.

Elizabeth gasped behind me.

"Take care of Lola for me," Eric said, "and if there are any others sleeping for the warm months, wake them. There could be visitors coming who wish to do Lola harm."

The man glared at Eric through the lower edge of his eyes for a second before he nodded, and all of them retreated into their tents.

Eric started to walk away and Devon followed, but Elizabeth stayed frozen on the spot, staring.

"You all right?" I asked softly.

"Lingering is unwise after we've said our goodbyes," Eric called back, not slowing.

I took Elizabeth's hand and pulled her around the corner and out of sight of the tents, to where Eric was examining the shabby street. The nearest store had windows covered in plywood with the words *Still Open!* spray-painted on in bright blue. Flickering neon signs that had no hope of competing with daylight advertised *lowest price cigarettes* and *best bananas in downtown.*

"This way should be fine." He set off farther into the city, but Elizabeth grabbed his arm with her free hand, still not letting go of me.

"What *were* those things?" she demanded. "They...they looked different last night."

"Sunlight casts away disguises," Eric explained. "It's what it is meant to do. But they are still Lola's loyal guards who now protect Ms. Miller as well. So, perhaps you shouldn't be so concerned with what they are and think more about the good they are doing." He pulled his arm free and strode away.

Devon shrugged and followed Eric. Elizabeth and I took the rear.

"What did you see?" I asked quietly when I had finally gotten her to walk at the same pace as the others.

"Shadows," Elizabeth whispered, her eyes wide like she was still staring at something. "Last night, they looked like dogs. Like dark wolves with big teeth.

But this morning"—she took a shuddering breath—"this morning, they were rotting. The big one's hair was torn away so I could see bone. They're all dead."

"It's not uncommon for the dead to serve," Eric said. I hadn't noticed he had fallen in step next to us. "Especially when they owe the living."

I shuddered, trying not to think of what kind of debt could follow a person into the grave.

We walked in silence after that. The street sounds were so normal, which made it doubly weird that I couldn't shake the coldness on the back of my neck as the dead wolf people guarded my mom and we passed dilapidated basketball courts and increasingly upscale bodegas.

In good ole New York fashion, in three blocks, we had left the scary streets behind and were surrounded by Starbucks.

"Where are we going?" Devon asked as he narrowly dodged a Chihuahua hell-bent on peeing on his ankle. "Thanks, lady," Devon grumbled at the owner. "There should be a law about who gets to own a dog in the city."

"We're going to Beville." Eric hadn't slowed his pace during the dog incident, so we all had to run a few steps to catch up.

"Beville, check" Devon said, "but if you haven't noticed, none of us know where or what Beville is."

"Which is why I'm leading the way." Eric pointed forward and kept walking.

"Not good enough." Devon ran two steps and planted himself in front of Eric. "You don't get to lead us blind. Tell us where we're going." He crossed his arms and gave Eric the scowl he usually saved for jerks who catcalled the girls he was busy hitting on.

"To Beville." Eric raised his hands to stop Devon from talking. "The simplest way possible. Well, not simplest, but most expeditious and surreptitious, considering our circumstances."

He moved to step around Devon, but Devon blocked his way again.

"You know, either you are very brave or have very little self-preservation instinct," Eric said. "In either case, get out of my way."

"Not until you tell us where Beville is," Devon growled.

"I thought that would have been obvious." Eric raised a black eyebrow. "Beville—Below the Village."

"You mean SoHo?" Devon asked as Eric sidestepped him and started down the street again.

"I said *below*," Eric corrected. "Not *south of*."

"I hate that guy," Devon whispered. "I really hate that pretentious asshole."

"Most people do," Eric called back. "I consider it to be one of my charms."

"People hating you is not usually considered an attribute," Devon said.

I punched him hard in the arm. "Don't piss off the guy who knows magic!"

Devon rolled his eyes. "I guess if it's the best you've got."

"The best I've got is my patience in not turning you into a sewer rat. But as you don't seem to be appreciative of my kindness..." Eric turned a corner and clapped his hands. "I thought I remembered there being a stop here."

He started down the steps to the subway station. The familiar bouquet of dank, rats, and pee crept into my nose as we jogged after him. There weren't too many people in the station, just some homeless making themselves, well... at home. I glanced back at Elizabeth, but she was looking around the platform like nothing was weird. Maybe the homeless guy eating a sandwich in the corner really was just a homeless guy this time. Part of me wished I could have seen Lola's guards the way Elizabeth had. Part of me was really grateful I couldn't.

Eric walked over and stood behind the yellow line, leaning forward to stare down the tunnel.

"What are we doing down here?" I followed his gaze. "Are we going to wait for no one to be looking and run down the tunnel?"

"You can get to Beville that way if you know the right path," Eric murmured softly as the three of us crowded around him. "But every wizard knows those walking paths. There are a few fake walls in subway stations that hide shortcuts, but those are easily watched. It takes a fine mix of daring, magic, and wisdom to find the...other ways."

"And let me guess." Devon's voice dripped with sarcasm. "You have just the right mixture?"

"Precisely." Eric smiled. "So, I do know of a way in where our arrival will go unnoticed."

Lights appeared in the distance, and a chain of cars roared their approach.

"Whether any of you are brave enough to follow me is another question entirely."

The doors *dinged* open, and we followed Eric onto the train.

"Stand clear of the closing doors," the voice warned.

It should have said *Stand clear of the megalomaniac wizard.* Or *Stand clear of evil mist and shadow dogs.* Or better yet *Stand clear of imminent death and destruction.* But the subway voice only cared about the damn sliding doors. So, I stood clear, and the train lurched forward.

I waited to see if Eric would take a seat or grab the handrail, but he did neither. Instead, he walked to the back of the car, to the door that led out. You know, the one only used by drunk dudes who need to pee or people with a strong death wish.

The train rocked back on forth, twisting around corners as we hurtled through the dark. Eric grabbed the handle and wrenched the door open. And I mean wrenched. They don't make those things easy to open. Mostly because they should never ever be opened.

"Out we go." Eric bowed and held the door open for us.

Devon made a sound halfway between a *tsch* and a growl, which I could barely hear over the noise of the tracks, and went out. Elizabeth followed. But I stayed frozen. Partly because I was terrified of going out onto the forbidden platform while the train raced around in the dark, but mostly because I could feel terribly judgmental eyes on the back on my neck. I turned around.

There was a lone old black lady sitting there, staring at me disapprovingly. Like she was angry I was tossing away all the work she and my other guardian angels had done trying to keep me alive over the years by doing something this stupid.

"We're running short on time," Eric said, snapping me out of it, and I placed one reluctant foot in front of the other. Freakin' peer pressure.

The light reflecting from inside the car cast shadows on the tracks racing below my feet. But around the train was mostly darkness. Every once in a while, a wall flashed right up next to us, but that only made it feel like the tunnel was trying to reach out and grab me from the tenuous safety of the platform.

Eric stood at the right side of the tiny bit of metal we were all crammed onto. "We only have a window of a few seconds," he shouted, his voice immediately swallowed by the rush of wind. "If you don't jump at the right time, there's nothing I can do for you. Get ready. Keep to the very edge. It makes it easier."

Elizabeth stepped to stand next to him.

"We're nearly there."

Devon joined Elizabeth.

"Jump hard, and aim away from the tracks."

"You want us to jump off of the train?" I puffed, when the horror finally registered.

"Yes!" Eric shouted. "In three, two, one!"

He jumped, and Elizabeth and Devon followed. Not thinking, or at least trying really hard not to, I took two giant running steps and leapt out into the blackness.

22

I thought I would meet a wall, but I fell through the air past where a wall would be, then hit the ground with a thud that shook my teeth and sent pain searing through my shoulder.

"Bryant!" Elizabeth screamed.

Coughing, I rolled onto my back, and found a dim streetlight hanging right over my head.

"Are you okay?" Elizabeth helped me sit up. Her face was pale and terrified as I reached up to touch my own with the arm that I could move to make sure everything was in the right place.

Devon appeared in front of me. "That was crazy, dude."

"I said we had a very brief window." Eric stepped next to him.

"Well, maybe you should have been a little clearer on why it was so brief!" Devon spun around, clenching his fists. "We're not some puppets you get to play with. We *break*, asshole!"

"I know how easily humans die, actually," Eric said calmly, rubbing his fingers together.

"Then why the hell did you try to get all of us killed?" Devon shouted.

"If I had wanted you dead, you would be dead," Eric shot back.

"Really, because it's not like you haven't tried to kill us bef—"

"Stop!" Elizabeth shouted. "I think the priority shouldn't be a pissing match of who has the better bad ideas. Can we focus on the fact that Bryant's arm looks dislocated."

I finally thought to glance down at my own shoulder as my shock ebbed. My arm did look funny. It was drooping down from where it should have been sitting in the socket.

"At least he didn't hit the wall," Eric sighed.

"What wall?" The words weren't even out of my mouth all the way before I turned and looked over my deformed shoulder. A concrete wall rose not three inches from the skid mark where I had landed. A little farther right and having my head dislocated would have been the problem. "Found the wall."

"I can fix the shoulder." Eric knelt next to me.

"Do you need the phone?" I pulled it out of my pocket. It was still shiny, black, and completely unharmed from me nearly getting myself killed.

"No." Eric took the phone and held it in his hand for a few seconds before passing it back to me. "The phone is an accumulation of knowledge, free of the rules of impartment, available at your fingertips. I already have a significant amount of knowledge stored in my brain. *Crantanolous.*" He slipped the word in like it was nothing.

With a terrible *pop* and shooting pain that made me want to vomit, my shoulder went back into its socket.

"*Keeiieeahhwhaaadiidowwww,*" I whined, but Eric was still talking.

"Since you have no magical knowledge except for what's in that phone and it would be easier to stop the Ladies and Thaden"—cold breeze tickled the back of my neck—"if I have an assistant, it is in my best interest to keep you alive and fighting, and the phone will help with that. Do try and keep it safe, though. As far as I know, it is one of a kind."

"And what about Elizabeth and me?" Devon clearly couldn't stop himself from Eric-baiting. "Are we just cannon fodder?"

"Guys!" I raised my now-working arm. "Remember, ya know, threads of fate, Lola, sticking together?"

Devon took a deep breath and tipped his head up, muttering a string of curses the sailors of Fleet Week would have been proud of. "Fine, we follow the twerp and hope he doesn't get us killed." He reached down and helped me to my feet.

My arm felt better, but the rest of me still felt like I had jumped off a speeding train.

"But the next time you ask us to do something that might get us killed," Devon said, stopping Eric mid-stride, "you tell us what the hell it is first. No more jumping blind."

"Fine." Eric nodded and began walking again. "Then it would probably serve you best to know we're taking an illegal entrance into the backside of

Beville, which is full of the most desperate kinds of wizards who really don't appreciate uninvited guests and will be perfectly willing to rob and murder us just as quickly as say hello."

"And we chose this way in because?" Elizabeth asked, slipping her hand back into mine like it was routine. I liked it.

"Because it's the only entrance I've ever found that isn't watched by the Ladies or Thaden. And I would rather try to reason with thieves than let either of them know we're here."

Soon, we were out of reach of the one streetlight. Eric muttered something and a light flickered on in his palm, reflecting off the dirty walls. The farther we walked, the weirder it seemed that there had been a random streetlight in the middle of a dark tunnel.

"Why was there a light where we jumped off?" I asked after another minute, more to make a noise that wasn't our footfalls and the distant rattle of the trains than because I needed an answer.

"I put it there," Eric said. "Stole it from a nasty abandoned corner and hauled it on the train. I did receive some very strange looks when I boarded the subway."

I pictured him carrying a full-size lamppost onto a train. My brain said it was impossible, but then, you know, magic...

"I jumped off and planted it there," Eric kept talking, "did a spell to keep the thing lit. It keeps the shadows away. And the last thing you want to jump into is shadows."

"Shadows?" I asked, feeling suddenly like I was back at the summer camp my mom had made me go to where the counselor told us scary stories that made me too afraid of trees to go near Central Park for a year.

"Not literal shadows," Eric said. "I mean things that hide in the shadows. Dark servants created by the magic of wizards who died long ago. Creatures that have crawled up from their own realms and taken refuge in the blackest places of Beville. Not that foul things can't exist in the light—they merely prefer the darkness. And I prefer not to be surprised by things lurking out of sight."

As he spoke, the way his voice echoed in the tunnels slowly changed. The walls weren't eating the sound anymore. And there were noises coming from up ahead.

I listened hard, trying to figure out what I was hearing, but a sickening *crunch* underfoot stopped me. I jumped back, afraid I had broken something. Where my shoe had been was now a small pile of broken white bones. Bile shot up into my throat. I had stepped on a skeleton.

"You okay?" Elizabeth asked.

I nodded, not altogether sure I could open my mouth without spewing.

"Why are there dead things down here?" Devon asked, poking at the shattered bones with his toe.

"Most dead things end up underground," Eric answered, his fast, controlled gait eating up the tunnel.

"Yes, but I thought people lived down here. Wouldn't they want to keep their place corpse-free?"

"In the nice parts of Beville where people build houses and take pride in their surroundings," Eric said as we came to a fork, and he turned left without hesitation, "you would be hard pressed to find anything as unappealing as a dead rodent. But out here where people are outcasts, there's more concern with survival and less worrying about keeping up with the Joneses."

"But why are they outcasts?" I asked. "Did they do something wrong?"

"Not wrong, no." Eric led us down another tunnel, this one barely taller than Devon. "It's more that the people on the outskirts aren't really magical enough to be considered wizards and accepted into our society. But they aren't normal enough to live aboveground with the rest of you. They have enough magic to be noticed, but not enough to be special. It's unfortunate, really."

Eric's voice dropped, and it really did sound like he was sympathetic. "It's not their fault they were born between worlds, yet they're made to suffer for being different. Most resort to crime eventually, but then I suppose if everyone blames you for being born wrong, there must be some relief in doing something wrong. Then at least you have a concrete memory of what you're being condemned for."

"And there's no way to teach them?" Elizabeth asked. "You can't tutor them in magic? Or help them fit in with us in the city?"

"It might be possible if wizards cared to try." Eric's voice darkened as we turned another corner. "But in Beville, being *other* makes you unworthy of help. No matter how desperately you need it."

Suddenly, we stopped short. I had been so busy wondering if I even had enough magic to be considered an outcast to notice the tunnel in front of me until I bumped into Eric.

The tunnel wasn't wide, no bigger than the space between two platforms in a subway tunnel. But both sides had been lined with tents. Made of old Disney bedsheets, filthy canvas, and patchwork t-shirts stitched together, some stretched twenty feet. Others were barely wider than my shoulders. Lights glowed in a few of them, and the noises of life came through the fabric. The tinny *clunk* of a person stirring a pot with a metal spoon, the dull rumbles of people talking and snoring.

Eric headed down the row, and I held my breath, waiting for everyone to emerge from their fabric homes like Lola's guards had. But no one looked out at us. Even the old man lying on the ground barely lifted his head to glance at us. Finally, I let myself breathe, and instantly regretted it.

The air smelled worse than a porter potty at a World Series game. Elizabeth clung to my hand, and if it hadn't been for the fact that I still thought that somewhere in this hell I might actually have a chance with her, I would have thrown up right where I stood.

It took longer for us to march through the row of tents than it did to walk three long city blocks. In front of us was a stretch of dim light, and then nothing but dark. I itched to run into it and away from the stench, but Eric kept a slow, steady pace.

"Funny how you strutted through like that," a voice called from behind as we passed the last tent. "No saying hello to friends, no partaking of the fine commerce Spells End has to offer. It's like you think you're walking down a highway."

I stared at the back of Eric's head, waiting for him to say something. It was a few seconds before he turned.

"Spells End is a lovely place, but we are in a bit of a hurry." Eric's voice was light and friendly, like he knew whoever had stopped us.

I turned to see who he was speaking to. Ten people flanked us. All filthy. All glaring.

"If you're going to use Spells End as a highway," the man at the front said, "you're going to have to pay the toll." The man smiled, baring his blackened, rotting teeth.

23

W e all stood in silence for a moment, waiting to see what Eric would do. "A toll?" he asked calmly.

Part of me expected lightning bolts to shoot out of his hands, blasting our way to freedom.

"That's right." The man stepped forward, flashing the rot in his teeth.

"And that's a new rule? I mean, I've never been asked to pay a toll before," Eric said, "and I've come and gone from Beville many times."

"New rule." The man gave a gigantic grin. I wanted to look away, but there was something hypnotizing about the way he slowly drew forward. "Times change. Now you pay to cross."

"Right then," Eric said to the man before tossing over his shoulder, "Bryant, call our friend and let him know we'll be a little late as we have to sort out this matter of a toll."

"Phones don't work down here." The leader snorted. "Didn't you say you've crossed our way? Out at Spells End, we don't get to call for help, sorry."

"Well, as you said, times change," Eric said. "As does technology. Call our friend, Bryant."

I reached for my normal phone, realized there was no way a non-magic phone would do anything so far underground, then pulled the black phone out of my pocket instead.

Who am I supposed to call?

My mind raced. I could call Lola, but I didn't know her number. I definitely shouldn't call Thaden. And this phone didn't have a call button anyway.

"And how much am I to pay?" Eric asked.

"Two-Hundred," the man said. "Each."

"You expect me to have eight hundred dollars in my pocket?" Eric laughed.

I opened the *At a Glance* tab.

"Only if you expect us to let you pass," the man said.

Offensive spells. Definitely offensive.

"That's funny, because we've already passed through your little settlement."

My eyes flew down the screen. Why did the words all have to look like nonsense?

"And it's strange to me," Eric said, "that you would wait to demand a toll until we were past your homes. That says quite clearly to me that you have no legal right to do so."

"We're in Spells End." The man edged closer. "Legal don't hold water here. We make our own laws."

Kuraxo. I tapped the spell and scanned the description.

"Well, even if you make your own laws," Eric said, stepping forward so he was close enough to reach out and touch Mr. Tooth Decay, "that means you do, in fact, have laws. Do you understand the concept of a contradiction?"

"Do you understand we'll tear you apart and no one'll find your bodies?" the man smirked.

"Ready for that call, Bryant?" Eric asked.

"Y-yes," I stammered.

"You really want to die on your phone?" the man growled.

"Put in the call to *Erunca!*" Eric shouted. A bright ball of lightning appeared by the ceiling.

Before I realized Eric was doing a spell, the ball had split itself into ten lightning bolts that streaked toward the ten from Spells End.

"*Kuraxo!*" I shouted over the screams. The ground beneath our feet shook.

"Run!" Eric turned and tore down the corridor.

I darted after him, glancing behind my shoulder to make sure Devon and Elizabeth followed. A dull *crack* echoed through the tunnel as the floor gave a fierce jerk.

"Run faster!" Eric shouted as we all sprinted full tilt through the darkness.

The ground was soft dirt, filth made of forgotten rot. The only light was the beam that radiated from Eric's hand. My lungs burned. My legs ached. The tunnel slopped down, but it seemed like whatever depth we were running toward, we would never arrive.

The screams and the ground cracking seemed miles away when Eric finally led us to a dead end. He swept the light from his hand through all the shadows before leaning against the wall.

"Next time"—Eric patted the one hair that had gotten windswept back into place—"when I ask you to do a spell, please choose something that might not get all of us killed. I have very strong preferences on how I die, and a cave-in has never made that particular list."

"You told me," I panted, clutching the stitch in my side, "to make a call. I did."

If it hadn't been for Elizabeth and Devon leaning against the wall next to me just as out of breath, I might have felt bad for feeling like I was going to die. But instead, I glared at Eric.

"Perhaps I should give you credit for not actually collapsing the tunnel on our heads, and, theoretically, you might not have caused severe damage to the subway system or to the street above, so that is something," he said, apparently unfazed by my death glare. "But we should work on unspoken communication for the future. If we survive long enough to have a future. And the odds of that are dwindling every moment."

"Really?" Devon pushed himself away from the wall. "We jumped off a speeding train and made it through the den of thieves you decided was the best path to lead us through. I'd say the plan is going about as well as we could have hoped for."

"While I am willing to admit," Eric said, "the fact that we're alive to have this argument is a feat, the point in my leading us through the *den of thieves* was to be sure we could enter Beville without anyone who wants to exterminate us being the wiser so I could lay our trap. But now everyone in Manhattan will know the ground shook below the Village, and Thaden"—the wind licked my neck—"and the Ladies will both know it was magic that did it, which means not only will they be looking for whatever caused the ground to split between Spells End and Beville, but soon they will be hunting us."

"Look, Bryant didn't mean to——" Elizabeth began, but I cut her off.

"Bryant didn't *mean* to?" I croaked, my throat paper-dry from running. "Of course I didn't mean to! I was told by a sociopath to do magic. I don't know how to do magic. I don't know how to fight! So, don't blame me—"

"I wasn't——" Elizabeth tried to say, but I was on a roll, and the words kept flooding out.

"All I wanted was to return a guy's cellphone. It should have been Devon who picked it up. Then he would be the one trying to figure out what the hell a spell is supposed to do while mole people are threatening to kill him! Devon would be good at it."

"What do you mean *what a spell is supposed to do*?" Eric crossed his arms. "Didn't you tap on the word and check the effect?"

"I tapped on the word, and it said *Causes a split in the ground*," I shouted. "Causes a split in the ground, not an earthquake!"

"How else did you expect the ground to split?" Eric asked, his voice so calm, it made me want to spit.

"I don't know!" I shouted. "A subtle widening of the Earth would have been nice."

"Subtle widening of the earth?" Eric chuckled. "Nothing about magic has ever been subtle."

"How would I know that? I found a phone, you told me I'm a wizard, and my mother is trapped in a cocoon! I don't know how magic works. Because someone"—I pointed a shaking finger at Eric—"only ever tells me things like *I'll kill you*, or *run*, or *make a phone call!*"

"Let me ask you something." Eric pressed his fingers together and planted them under his chin as though he were praying. The light stayed between his palms, making strange shadows dance across his face with every word. "When you were little, did your ice cream ever fall off the cone?"

"What?" I dragged my hands through my hair to keep myself from punching Eric.

"Did your ice cream ever fall from the cone?" he said slowly.

"Yes!" I started pacing. I wanted to run or kick through the walls. Anything that would get me out of the tunnels.

"Well, when your ice cream fell on the ground, what did your mother say?"

"Not to listen to crazy men who never figured out life could be lived in Technicolor," I growled.

"Very funny," Eric said. "I think perhaps a more accurate representation would be that she told you not to tip the cone or the ice cream would fall down. On this, your first encounter with the terror that is gravity, I believe it's safe to assume she didn't bother with Newton's law of universal gravitation. You were young, and the loss of the ice cream mattered more than what made it fall." Eric grabbed me by the shoulders, keeping me still. His fingers dug into my skin. "This is your first foray into magic, and knowing how the rules work is not nearly as important as staying alive.

"So, I am sorry about your ice cream, but from now on, take the phone literally, do everything I say, and try not to have any more temper tantrums. I already have Sir Moody Pretty Pants pouting because he isn't in charge and there is no one here for him to use his incomparable charm on. I can't try and win this thing if you get angry because you're being asked to play without knowing the rules of the game. I can fill you in this far: win or die." Eric held my gaze with his dark blue eyes. "Are you ready to follow me and do as I say? We don't have time for lessons."

I wanted to scream at him to go to Hell. But without Eric, I couldn't find my way back up to the street, let alone avoid the Ladies.

I nodded.

"Thank God for you, Elizabeth." Eric let go of me. "Leave it to a seer to be the one who can keep her head on straight."

Elizabeth let out a high, strained laugh. "I don't know what being a seer is. I've been creeped out by dark corners and weird things my whole life, and now I'm supposed to believe it's fate that I imagine monsters? I don't understand any of this anymore than Bryant does."

"And yet you're taking it so well." Eric patted her on the shoulder. "And that's the way to do it. Roll with the punches until you get your footing."

"Unless one of those punches kills you," Devon said dryly.

"Well, you have heard of rolling over in your grave, haven't you?" Eric said with a smile that, for a split-second, made me believe he thought he had made a joke. A very bad joke. "Now that we've finished with all this unpleasant worrying about our place in the magical world, we need a plan. A new plan." Eric paced the dead end, his hands still clasped below his chin. "We need to plant the seed. Let Thaden and the Ladies know where we're hiding without letting them actually know we're waiting for them."

"Then, what?" Devon asked.

"Then we watch as they fight each other and take on whoever is left standing when the dust settles," Eric said.

"Doesn't that seem a little shady?" I asked, remembering all the stories of knights and chivalrous armies my mother had read to me. "Isn't it wrong to set our enemies up and wait it out while they do the work for us?"

"You can call it shady." Eric shrugged. "I prefer the term survival savvy. Besides, it's not as though either party is innocent. My conscience is clear."

"Mine, too," Devon said. "How do we leak the information?"

"That's the thorny part." Eric tilted his chin up to stare at the ceiling. "We could send each a message that we want to meet them to discuss turning over the phone and just let them arrive for the same meeting."

"A monkey would see that coming." Devon shook his head. "If you're playing two people, you can't let the play come from you."

"What do you mean?" Elizabeth asked.

"We ask them to meet us, they'll send scouts or set traps," Devon said. "They have to think it's their idea to come and fight us. Then they'll be searching for us, and not our plan."

"I agree with your reasoning." Eric nodded politely. "But how do you propose to get the message of where we are lurking to two parties without actually telling them? Implanting thoughts into someone's mind is magic only the Ladies can accomplish."

I shuddered at the thought of the Ladies playing around inside my head.

"We don't have to plant it in their heads." Devon smiled. "We just have to make sure they hear it from someone who isn't us."

Eric's damn eyebrow shot up again. "And how do we do that? There are very few people in this world I trust, and all of them have been banished from Beville."

"We don't need your shady banished friends," Devon said. "All I need is a cafeteria."

"Cafeteria?" Eric asked.

"Point me to where you people eat." Devon grinned. "And I'll make sure we're surrounded by the big bad wizards in no time."

24

I felt numb as Eric led us back into the tunnels and to the now-familiar crunch of bones under my feet. I didn't ask questions I wouldn't want the answers to. I just walked through the dark, not marking the endless twists or turns. Just walked.

Elizabeth was next to me, not looking at me.

"Hey," I whispered. Devon and Eric both looked at me, but Elizabeth kept her head firmly forward. "Look, I'm sorry I was an asshat who snapped at you."

Eric rolled his eyes, but Devon grinned and gave a tiny thumbs up Elizabeth probably saw.

"I know you were trying to be on my side and I—"

"Bit my head off," Elizabeth said.

"I mean, that really covers a lot of it," I muttered.

"I get that you may not remember," Elizabeth said, "but we've been in class together for a really long time. I've probably sat next to you for a thousand hours of my life, even though you've never noticed."

My heart stopped beating. It seemed impossible that I would still be walking while my heart was stopped.

"And you were special way before you found a cellphone," Elizabeth kept talking, apparently unaware of my impeding death from heart stoppage. "You're smart. Really smart. And sweet. If you weren't a wizard, you would probably cure cancer or end hunger or something. So don't act all shocked that our lives are depending on you. You were always the type to have lives depending on you. But you were too nice and shy and humble to figure it out. Don't blame me for seeing it or for speaking up. Apparently that's like my thing."

We all walked quietly for a moment. "You're wrong," I said, glad for the darkness as my face burned.

"Wrong that you shouldn't hate me for seeing the truth?" Elizabeth's melodic voice verged on snapping. "Or wrong that you're going to be important whether you like it or not?"

"Wrong that I didn't notice you." My throat was so tight I could hardly breathe. The back of Devon's neck tensed as he pretended not to listen. "I noticed every time I sat near you and every time you walked by. I always notice you."

I always notice you. I wanted to curl up on the floor and die. Forget evil mist Ladies and cellphone programmers. I told the girl of my dreams that I always *notice* her.

Please let the tunnel collapse and put me out of everyone's misery.

"If you've always noticed me," she said finally, "then it should be clear I really am right."

"Is this what high school does aboveground?" Eric asked as a light came into view down the tunnel. "Turn all its victims into blubbering, blushing, hormonal messes who can do math but don't understand love or fate?"

"Pretty much," Devon said.

"Hmm," Eric sighed. "And I thought life in Beville was trying."

"It's nice to see you boys agreeing on something," Elizabeth said as the first house came into sight right behind a sign that read *Center Street*.

I had expected more tents leaning up against the tunnel walls, but the residents of Center Street had built houses. Real, two story houses.

Sort of.

The tunnel had been carved out high above so the ceiling sat at least thirty feet overhead. Lights had been set into the stone, casting the already weird buildings in a warm, eerie glow. Half of them looked like the old brick town-houses from up in the city, complete with wide stoops and fancy front windows. But the other half had given up on the Upper West Side vibe and decided to go rogue in a way no HOA would ever approve.

A giant log cabin had been wedged in next to a house that didn't seem to know quite what shape it was supposed to be. At first glance, it looked like a fancy country home with bright blue shutters. Then I blinked, and the friendly shutters had turned into gaping black windows. Rain pounded and lighting split the air right in front of the house. I glanced at Elizabeth. She was looking at it too, but she didn't seem afraid. So, I checked the house again. This time it looked like a lighthouse with an invisible sun beaming right down on it.

"Are you sure the mist ladies can't see us out their front window?" Devon asked, yanking my attention away from the stone tower the changing house had morphed into.

Devon pointed to a bright white construction made out of some sort of matte metal. The front steps were paper-thin strips of white that floated lazily in the air. The whole thing looked like something out of a sci-fi movie.

"The Ladies don't live down here." Eric waved to a person with shockingly red hair who appeared in the shimmering square that was one of the white house's windows. "They would never live with the masses."

"And the masses all live underground?" Devon murmured. "Fun."

"It allows us the freedom to live a life of magic while having the convenience of a central location like Manhattan." Eric led us down the street.

The curved cobblestones turned to bricks, which turned to sand as the sidewalk changed with each house. "Ideally, I think we would all prefer to live aboveground and have a city of our own," Eric continued, his voice barely loud enough for us to hear, "but with the way the human race has expanded, there is very little habitable room to hide. Modern fiction isn't wrong about the chaos that would ensue if regulars knew magic existed. People seem so determined to hate anything they can define as *other*. Wizards would be no exception. So, down we went, where the people of the city think myths and monsters live."

"Couldn't you go to the rainforest or Antarctica?" Elizabeth whispered as a face stared at us through a stained glass window.

"If you don't mind spiders, snakes, or the constant prospect of freezing to death. Of course, there are wizards who choose to live in such places," Eric said.

"But you're stuck underground?" What I didn't ask was, if *I* would have to pack up a suitcase and move down here. If we lived through the day. Not that I had anything to pack anyway, since I had successfully destroyed both my parents' homes.

"The Consortium came to Manhattan long before it was a buzzing metropolis. We are too ensconced here," Eric said. "This is where our community was built, and this is where it will stay."

"But—" I began.

"I never question why normal people toil endless hours to pay astronomical Manhattan rent they truly can't afford." Eric's dark eyebrows drew together. "The Big Apple is an addictive place. Beville may require sacrifices, but excitement is not one of them."

We had reached the last house on the street, which was a giant glass edifice Frank Lloyd Wright might have had a hand in. The sounds in front of us changed. Besides the waterfall rumbling through the glass house, there were voices echoing down the tunnel. Lots of very boisterous voices.

We rounded the corner and walked onto Commerce Street. The street name seemed to fit. The tunnel was lined with shops. A normal looking storefront sold electronics, and a low, gross stone building had a rotting sign out front that read *Cheap Herbs*.

In front of the largest, pale stone place was a group with steins in their hands. It looked like something out of a pirate movie. They were all swaggering and talking loudly while slopping their drinks. A lady in the center of the crowd stood on a table, acting out some story that had everyone around her roaring with laughter.

"Damn." Eric spread his arms and pressed us back into the shadows between two buildings.

"Why damn?" I peeked around the corner as the mob cheered and the woman's laugh boomed over the whooping.

"Technically I've been banned from the Witches Brew," Eric said. "Most people have at some point, but Mildred really does seem to dislike me."

"And you didn't think to mention his before?" I whispered.

"It's the middle of the day." Eric huffed. "I figured she would be sleeping."

"So, now what?" Elizabeth asked. "We can't walk into a place that's banned you and casually drop the fact that we're here trying to hide from some murderous maniacs."

"He can't walk in." Devon smiled. "But I can."

"Devon—"

"You know I've charmed my way into far worse places than a magic Ren Faire pub, Bry." Devon checked his hair in the window. "Besides, they'll never suspect a lowly city dweller of planting information."

"He does have a point." Eric looked Devon up and down. "They'll know he's not from Beville right off. We don't get many strangers walking our streets."

"Then he can't go in," I said. "It's too dangerous."

"I'll be fine." Devon waved a hand a little too casually through the air.

"We should find a way for us all to stay together." Elizabeth caught Devon's hand, not to hold it, just to stop its flippant motion. "You don't need to be the hero, Devon."

"But I do it so well." Devon looked away from Elizabeth and toward the pub. "Besides, I'd rather die working on a plan than hiding. Anyone have any cash?"

"I'd rather none of us die," I said, but Devon wasn't listening as he took a handful of bills from Eric.

"We'll meet you in the gray stone house down the next street. Lark Lane." Eric patted Devon on the shoulder. "Stay safe. And just knock on the door."

"See you in a bit, then." And with that, Devon was gone.

I wanted to scream at him to come back. Or to go instead of him. But Eric was right. If anyone was going to charm their way into us not getting killed, it would be Devon. So, I watched my best friend walk helpless into a pack of witches.

"We need to go." Eric slunk into the far side of the shadows. "It will take us a while to cut around out of sight."

"We can't leave him," I said.

Devon had arrived at the edge of the pub crowd.

"I didn't think I would ever find myself saying something nice about that one, but his combination of debonair bravery, charm, and inability to understand that death is lurking around the corner might be what keeps him alive." Eric took both my shoulders and spun me to face him so I couldn't see Devon anymore. "Don't feel like you're throwing him to the wolves. What we've got ahead of us is worse than walking into a pack of angry wizards. For all we know, Devon might outlive us."

I nodded. I didn't know what else to do.

"Then let's go," Eric said, "or we won't beat Devon to the gray house, and then he'll be stranded on the street."

"I should have gone with him," Elizabeth murmured as we cut around the side of the building. "He shouldn't have gone in alone."

"Where we're going we need the best eyes we've got." Eric led us down another alley and out onto the strangest street I'd seen yet.

The buildings here were so black, they looked like shadows leaning out of the tunnel walls. As we rounded the corner, the noise disappeared as quickly as though someone had slammed a door behind us. I looked around for a street sign as whispers from unseen mouths floated through the air. But there were no signs, and the light from above was only bright enough to cast shadows.

"Where are we?" I breathed.

The soup of whispers in the air seemed to hiss in response.

"It doesn't technically have a name," Eric whispered back like he was in a library, "but I've always called it Shady Lane."

"Cute," I said as something brushed past the back of my neck at the same moment that Elizabeth screamed.

"Bryant!"

I spun around, expecting to see someone attacking her, trying to pull her away. But she was swiping her hands around me like she was trying to push away something that wasn't there. Only...there was. Her hands made contact with something I couldn't see. But I heard the *thud* as her punch landed.

"Elizabeth, no!" Eric raced over to pull her from whatever she was pummeling. "Stop! Stop, Elizabeth! They won't hurt him!"

"Then why was that monster touching him?" Elizabeth shrieked.

I spun around, trying to see the monster. But, nada.

Elizabeth's eyes darted around, her fear only growing. "Did you bring us here so they could kill us?" she spat at Eric. "You cowardly piece of shit!"

"I brought you here to ask these fine people for help," Eric said.

Elizabeth tore a hand free and slapped him across the face.

"And they might be a little more willing to help stop the Ladies from killing us if you stopped trying to hit them."

"Unless"—I heard a voice distinctly coming from thin air—"the Ladies are trying to destroy you for a worthy reason." As the voice spoke, a shadow formed next to me. It grew thicker and darker, gaining dimension with each word.

"Charles." Eric smiled and reached out to shake the shadow's hand.

"I didn't think I would see you again," Charles said, "after the last time you set Commerce Street on fire."

"That." Eric waved a hand dismissively. "There were a few underworldlings roaming around, and the pub was the simplest place to corral them."

"You burned Mildred's pub." Charles laughed. The sound came out like a rattling wheeze.

"No one ever remembers you saved their life," Eric sighed. "All they remember is the structural damage."

"You never change, Eric," Charles said. "I'm afraid the only thing that will kill you is death."

"Then let us hope I don't change today." Eric smiled.

He was talking about dying and smiling. I had followed a psychopath onto a street full of shadow people. And the street *was* full of shadow people now. Filling every doorway, more stepping toward us every moment. I reached back and took Elizabeth's hand. Somehow, the fact that I could feel her warmth as her heart raced made the whole thing a little better. We weren't in a mausoleum. Yet.

"And why is it that you would die today?" Charles asked. "If it's the Ladies you're afraid of, surely they have not been so precise. The last time I heard of them deciding upon an execution, it took them three years to carry out the order. The poor man died of fright before they ever bothered coming for him."

"I'm afraid the Ladies have been tracking us since last night." Eric bowed to Charles. "My friends and I have come to beg for your help in escaping their wrath."

Charles gave a crackling laugh, which sounded like it was shaking the ribs I couldn't see. The rest of the shadows cackled, too, filling the darkness. It took a minute for Charles to calm himself down enough to talk.

"You want our help in making sure the Ladies don't kill you?" Charles finally choked out. "You know our solution to avoiding the Ladies, and I doubt you will find it appealing since you have never accepted our path before."

"Nor could I today," Eric said. "The shadow path isn't mine to tread."

"What shadow path?" If these people knew a way to survive, it would be worth it.

"He's fresh, isn't he?" Charles asked Eric.

"You've no idea." Eric smirked, gesturing for Charles to explain.

"The Ladies control all the magic aboveground," Charles said. "Every spell, every potion, every incantation that has ever been written down is in their Library. They dole out pieces of knowledge like every wizard is standing in a bread line. And with their rules of impartment, the magic can't be shared. They may give me *estuna*." A light shone behind Charles, casting his shadow into deeper relief. "You can say the spell, but unless the Ladies themselves have given you the knowledge, it would only be a word to you."

Like a dog doing tricks under the dark eyes of the crowd, I sounded out, "*Estuna*." The moment I said the word, I knew nothing would happen. It felt soggy and heavy in my mouth, the texture of it on my tongue making me gag.

The shadows around us laughed.

"Doesn't feel nice, does it? Helluva copyright protection." Charles said when the laughter died down. "They keep us starving for knowledge to maintain their power."

"That's terrible," Elizabeth said.

Charles and the other shadows nodded as one.

"More than you might realize. Having magic pulse through your veins without a way out is painful." Charles' voice lowered as he spoke. "To live to half your potential, not allowed to reach what you were born to become, illiterate to the language that flows through your blood."

"But I never felt any pain," I said. "Does that mean I'm not really meant to be all magical?"

Eric answered this time. "Your magic is undeniable. You wouldn't have felt the pain. You didn't know you were meant for magic."

"It's the atrophy that's painful. Imagine never knowing your fingers should flex," Charles said. "It wouldn't hurt you, wouldn't trouble you at all. But you've lived your life with hands that move. Imagine losing that now."

"That's...I'm sorry," I said lamely.

The Ladies had crippled the wizards they ruled. Suddenly Thaden didn't seem like such a bad guy. Then I remembered that if all went well, he would be trying to murder us in the next few hours.

"But magic didn't begin with the Ladies or The Consortium's Library." The light behind Charles faded as he stepped closer. "Magic began deep in the bowels of the earth. Below the rocks where the dead lay. We dig into the darkness, finding the magic piece by piece. Filling ourselves with the power the Ladies have stolen from us."

"And the magic turns you into shadows?" Elizabeth's voice shook as she spoke.

"Traveling through the darkness leaves its marks." Charles reached out to her. "Eventually the darkness stops washing off, and we become shadows."

Elizabeth took Charles' hand in her own.

"But with the coating of the darkness, we find the light of knowledge." Charles smiled. "And isn't the spark of illumination worth living in the shadows?"

"No." Eric stepped between Charles and Elizabeth. "Not when the same knowledge can be gained without losing the ability to go aboveground."

"Thaden has granted you so much power?"

"Thaden is a monster, and I was too full of myself to see it." Lines creased Eric's brow, and for a second, he looked lost. Not snarky or brazen, but truly remorseful. It kind of scared me. "I thought Thaden would give us a path to freedom, but his way would only leave magic chained to a different master."

"If the Ladies want you dead and Thaden won't take you, your only choice may be to join us in the shadows."

"The choices we have may look very different come morning." Eric smiled. "Order will soon crumble from above and below."

Charles took a step back.

"The dark one and the light are going to battle today," Eric said as the shadows closed in. "Neither party wants us to survive. The darkened death will draw us all into the blackness forever. The Ladies will never let us walk freely in the light. Would you be content to let wizards live forever in the middle? Buried in a living tomb?"

Whispers flew around the street. Words I couldn't hear or didn't understand. But one syllable rang out clear. *No.*

"Then help us!" Eric's voice pounded through the darkness. "We have an opportunity today that won't come again for a century. And if you help me, my friends, if you stand by my side when the spells shatter our walls, we *will* break free!"

The shadows cheered. And that was the moment I realized Eric was the hero. In a world I didn't understand, following plans I didn't know about, and doing magic I didn't think could be done. Somehow on the way from the Meatpacking District to the Village, I had become the sidekick in my own story.

25

I t took a few minutes for the crowd to stop cheering long enough for anyone to speak. Charles told us to follow him. Eric said something about claiming the day, and the shadows cheered some more. It was like a magical shadow pep rally. Finally, when I was afraid someone would break into a valedictorian speech, the crowd surged down the street.

"It seems you've won the majority, brother." Charles clapped Eric on the shoulder as he led us away. "But be mindful," he added so quietly I could barely hear, "if you lead us to our end, the shadows will follow you forever."

I shuddered even though I didn't know what Charles meant.

"Is he really your brother?" I whispered as we wound deeper down Shady Lane. I know it might seem like a weird thing to be worrying about when you're being escorted by a swarm of silhouettes planning a major battle, but it was the only thing in the conversation that made enough sense for me to try and hold onto.

"Brothers in arms," Eric said.

"Right." I nodded even though Eric wasn't looking at me.

I kept waiting to turn off the street or go into a house, or maybe for the whole parade to turn into a scene from Les Miserables, where we would all stand on tables and sing about freedom.

We reached the end of the tunnel where a solid wall blocked our path, but our companions kept going, melting into the pitch black.

Eric kept walking in front of us like everything was normal. But the closer we got to the shimmering black stone, the more crushing the atmosphere became. My heart picked up speed. The shadow wizards might be able to survive walking through the wall, but not me. I would be smothered into oblivion.

"We can't go in there," I whispered.

"Of course we can," Eric said, all blasé as he stepped into darkness.

I panicked. "Elizabeth." I grabbed her hand, pulling her back the moment before she would have disappeared into the solid stone. "Don't go in there. You'll die."

"You can't see it, can you?" Elizabeth tipped her head to the side like she was studying me.

"There's nothing to see."

A shadow pushed past, jostling me into the crowd.

"Trust me." Elizabeth laced her fingers through mine. "There is a way through." She smiled. And she wasn't afraid or worried. She was perfect, her hair shining against the shadows.

I nodded and closed my eyes, letting her lead me onward. I waited to walk into a wall or for the darkness to crush my lungs till there wasn't enough left of me to breathe. The air got thick for a minute, like I was walking through a storm made solid, but then it became cool and damp. And I took a deep breath. It smelled like a forest after the rain. Not such a bad smell, not the scent of a place where you were going to die any second. I opened my eyes.

I wished I hadn't.

Things moved all around me, but it was like I was catching the movement out of the corner of my eye. Flickers that told me I was surrounded by a hundred things just out of sight.

Charles had faded among the rest of the shadows, his voice just discernible as he shouted orders, but the only people I could see were Elizabeth and Eric.

"What's happening?" I whispered.

"Charles is talking to people," Elizabeth said. "They're putting on armor, but not like any I've ever seen. It's like they're covering themselves in smoke."

"For protection against the Ladies," Eric said.

"Why can both of you see this and I can't?" I grumbled as the largest flicker yet moved past me.

Elizabeth gasped. Whatever had walked in front of us was huge.

"Because I've trained for years to be able to see the things that roam in the darkness." Which, incidentally, grew denser as Eric spoke. "And Elizabeth has a born ability to see what lurks beneath the surface of the world."

"Didn't you mention you've been seeing things creeping around for years?" I asked, trying desperately to keep from squeaking.

"I..." Elizabeth struggled for words as I tightened my hold on her hand, clinging to the one tangible thing in this world of nightmares. "I mean, I've always been afraid of the dark. Like I could see something there, hiding. But I couldn't see it like this. Living people with faces. I chalked it up to being a wimp with an overactive imagination."

"But then why today?" I asked, my voice growing louder as my fear turned into anger. "Why can she suddenly see all this crazy stuff now? What did you do to her?"

"I didn't do anything to her," Eric said. "Elizabeth has always had a special sight. Fate simply chose this time for her to become a true seer."

"Fate?" I half-shouted. "Fate decided I should find a phone and become all magical? Fate decided Elizabeth should be a seer? And what has fate decided for you? That you should go talk to shadow Charles and start a magical war under Manhattan?"

"Fate builds on what is already there." A shadow moved out of the corner of my eye, and there was Charles. "We have wanted the same things Eric has been working for for years. When Thaden appeared"—a *whoosh* like a terrified whisper shot around the room—"we thought he would be the answer. A way to knowledge without a life in the darkness. We are not shadows, but students of the oldest magic. Thaden promised us a way out, but his way is filled with more death and despair than we are willing to bring into the world. Thaden wants control. Not freedom. Living under his rule would be no better than living under the Ladies."

"Right, okay." I clenched my head in my hands. "None of this makes any sense. Am I just supposed to go along with the fight between the black pieces and the white pieces like this is a game of chess? I'm getting dragged through this crazy shit, and I'm only seeing the surface. I don't even know which side I should be on."

"On this side." Elizabeth took my face in her hands. I stared hard into her sparkly eyes, and for a moment, the world stopped spinning.

But I couldn't stay still. Things were still out of control, still uncertain.

"How can you even trust Eric," I directed my words at a shadow I thought might be Charles, "if Thaden is your enemy and you know Eric worked with him? He's only fighting Thaden because he messed up and now Thaden wants to kill him."

"Don't question why allies are allies," Eric cautioned.

"None of us are innocent," Charles's voice came from a different shadow than the one I had been speaking to. "When you're trapped between two different evils, one can begin to look like a savior. We've been fighting for a freedom away from the shadows and the Ladies for a long time. Eric isn't the first to have seen false promise in darkness."

"Thank you, brother," Eric said.

"And I'm just supposed to trust that this is a great idea?"

The shadow of Charles's head bobbled like he was nodding.

"You have to, Bryant," Elizabeth said.

"Because Lola has my mom, and if I don't do what Eric says, I may never get past the decaying dogs to stage a rescue?" My voice sounded dry to my ears, like I had just aged ten years.

"Because the Ladies are out for blood. *Our* blood," Elizabeth said. "They didn't speak to us or try to make things right. They went right for the kill."

"Eric tried to kill us at my dad's."

"And he failed," Elizabeth said. "Which means if he doesn't turn out to be the one we want to support, we'll kill him."

"I suppose that's as good a vote of confidence any leader of a rebellion can hope for." Eric laughed.

"If you're going to call yourself the leader, you should probably get to the leading." Charles' voice came from right behind my left shoulder. "Coat the girl first."

"Do what?" Elizabeth said.

I spun to face the voice, pushing Elizabeth behind me.

"You need to be able to see," Eric said, his voice so calm I wanted to deck him.

"She can see," I growled. "She can see all your friends surrounding us."

"If she were coated, she would be able to see without being seen," Charles said.

"But then I would never be able to go home." Elizabeth's voice shook. "You said the shadows can't go aboveground."

"If they coat you in shadow, it will wear off in time," Eric said. "The effects outside the tunnel would be minimal and temporary. If we want to be able to see the battle as it happens, we need you to be able to get close."

"It won't hurt," Charles said. He was close now. He had crept around my back between me and Elizabeth.

"Don't!" I shouted, but I couldn't move my arms. They were pinned to my sides by hands I couldn't see.

"It will feel like a cold fall rain," the shadow said.

Elizabeth looked terrified as the shadows closed in.

"Stop!" I screamed as drops of black appeared on the top of Elizabeth's head. It was like someone was pouring a bucket of ink over her, the black dripping down her head, covering her face, her arms, hands. "No!" I roared, but the blackness didn't stop. It was swallowing Elizabeth, changing her into something I couldn't see. "*Aarantha!*"

I reached for the tips of Elizabeth's fingers and pulled her close to my chest as the wind whipped around us, howling into a twister.

Screaming cut through the wind. It sounded like the people on the outside were as scared as I was. But I couldn't see them. Only shadows dancing in and out of the wind.

"Bryant, stop!" Elizabeth screamed. "Stop it!" Her warm cheek pressed into mine. "I'm okay. He didn't hurt me."

Slowly, I let go of the spell. And when I say I let go, I really mean I stopped wanting to destroy everything in sight for killing Elizabeth, and the funnel cloud sort of went away. But *letting go of the spell* sounds way cooler and much more like I was in control, so we're going with that.

Part of me expected the shadows to attack as soon as the wind died. I think Elizabeth thought the same thing since she kept close, her back pressed to me. Her arms reached back and she grabbed my hands. Her breathing resonated through my chest. But all I could see was a wisp of smoke where Elizabeth's bright blond hair should have been.

"*Aarantha*," a voice whispered from somewhere deep in the darkness.

"How did he find *Aarantha*?" another voice hissed.

"The Ladies have that magic!" a third voice cried. "He has come from the Ladies."

"No!" I shouted as the rumble of anger surged through the crowd. "I found the spell on Thaden's phone. It's on a list of defensive spells. That's why I've used it."

But the rumbling didn't stop. It worsened, the voices encircling us. Eric backed up so he was only a foot from me. There was barely enough room to fit Elizabeth.

"There is no way the boy should have that magic!"

"He's in concert with The Consortium!"

"The phone is Thaden's!" I shouted, but no one was listening.

"The spell did not come from the Ladies." Eric's voice rang out clear over the crowd. "Look at him. Does the boy look like he's seen the magic of Beville? He's a city dweller. Thaden himself found a way into the great Library and stole the magic from the Ladies." The crowd quieted. They were listening to Eric like he was giving a speech in the state house. "Thaden made a device that could carry all the knowledge of our books out into the world. A device that is untouched by the Ladies' rules of impartment and allows magic to move freely into the learner. The boy found it. The magic opened itself to him. He used magic, massive magic without any knowledge of how it works, and he survived. He continues to use it and survive."

A hiss of *impossible* floated through the crowd.

"It is not impossible if fate has chosen him to be a part of this great day," Eric said. "The golden threads have drawn him here as they have drawn each of us. Do not fear this boy because his strand of fate has pulled him to this battle in days instead of the years it has taken the rest of us. He is here for a purpose. We are all here for a purpose. Our purpose is to clear a path to a better tomorrow. To a future where the choice is not between prison or darkness. This is a battle a century in the making. And the strings of fate pulled this boy here to stand at the point of it all! Who will stand with him?"

I was shouting, cheering with the crowd. We were going to change the magical world I didn't know anything about but had already ruined my life. And then I realized Eric was talking about me. That *I* was special. That I was somehow destined to be a part of a battle that would unfold in the next few hours. A battle that might get me killed.

But the cheering didn't stop, and hands I couldn't see patted me on the back and dragged me forward. I felt a hand close around mine and knew it was Elizabeth without whispering her name. Eric led us to the end of the shadowy tomb room.

I barely heard Eric shout *"Portunda!"* before the black wall shook, and a door appeared. The door wasn't bright or shining, but after the blinding darkness, even that little bit of color overwhelmed my eyes and I had to blink before I could clearly make it out. It was wood painted gray, but even through the thick coat, the wood looked heavy and old.

"Charles, will you come through with us?" Eric said.

"As you wish," Charles said.

My brain registered Charles giving commands, but the words floated right by me.

Then Eric opened the gray door, and I tightened my grip on Elizabeth's hand and followed him into the house.

But forward isn't always safer than back, even if back wasn't all that nice to begin with.

26

I spun around as the door shut behind me. There was a shadow next to the door. It didn't look frightening or thick. It looked more like the person making the shadow had forgotten to show up. Like Peter Pan's shadow had finally won his bid for freedom.

I took a breath and looked down to where I still held Elizabeth's hand. She didn't look like someone had dumped ink over her head anymore. It was more like she'd become a charcoal sketch of herself, drawn in gray scale with soft edges all around. The only white left was her eyes.

Elizabeth sighed. "Well, choices were made. Some choices were bad."

My laugh caught in my throat.

"I find the choice with the best chance of leading to my survival is usually the right choice," Eric said from across the room.

"And I don't have to be"—my voice faltered on the word—"*coated* to survive?"

"You won't need it for your work in the battle," Eric said, "and I have no intention of hiding my whereabouts. Alas, Elizabeth is the only one in need."

I wanted to say something witty or brave about work in the battle or even make fun of Eric for saying *alas*, but nothing came to mind, so I studied the room instead. I wish I could tell you that looking around this room didn't surprise me because I had already been in a vault of shadows and in a sub-overpass lair of a seer. But I don't know if I could ever achieve the level of cool required to not be shocked when I walked from a place of blackness into a

Victorian Row House, complete with lace curtains and plush window seats with fancy-looking green fabric covering the cushions.

There was a sofa near the table and a settee, at least I think it was a settee, near the fireplace where flames crackled merrily away. A fancy lace cloth covered the table in the middle of the room. And a silver tea tray with five china teacups rested on top. Like someone had been expecting the four of us to arrive. With a cup saved for Devon.

The walls were covered in bookshelves. Old books, new books, titles I recognized, some with titles in languages I had never heard of before.

"You know, if the Ladies came to tea, they would banish you from Beville for hoarding magical knowledge from The Consortium." Charles poured himself a cup of tea. Watching a shadow pour tea into a cup is freaky. It didn't seem like his hands should be substantial enough to lift the cup, let alone his intestines to process the tea.

I tried not to think about shadow digestion as Eric chortled, "Well, most of the forbidden books were given to me by you." He poured himself a cup and sat down. "Besides, I have the house well trained to hide all the less innocuous items should I have guests who might not appreciate my collection."

Without him saying a spell or clapping his hands or anything, the book-shelves trembled for a second before the bottom half disappeared. Now from the ground to my waist was normal wall with pale blue and white wallpaper.

"Handy." Charles took another sip of his tea.

"This old place has been in the family so long," Eric sighed, "I hate to bring the fight to her, but she's a tough old broad. I've taught her to mend herself, so she has as good a chance of making it through the night as the rest of us."

Elizabeth's hand started to shake in mine.

"Do you want some tea?" I asked lamely.

I think there was a whole conversation about tea being comforting in a play my mom had directed. Devon had been obsessed with it ever since. I'm hardly a fan myself, but in the moment, it seemed like the best thing to do.

Elizabeth nodded, and the movement of her head left smudges of black in the air that lingered briefly, before fading away.

I poured us two cups, adding cream and sugar carefully before stirring. It felt so bizarre. To be sipping our tea out of fancy, gold-decorated china while we waited to find out if Devon had managed to set us up to be at the eye of a battle.

Armed with cups, Elizabeth and I took the sofa. It was large enough that there could have been space for another person between us, but Elizabeth sat right next to me, her hip pressing into mine. My stomach jumped up and down like I had swallowed a hyperactive poodle.

"Devon should be arriving soon." Eric pulled the curtain back an inch and peeked outside.

"And he's told them to come to your house?" Charles said. "I suppose I should give you points for bravery."

"It would be terribly rude of me if I arranged for a battle on someone else's front steps." Eric's lips quirked. "Besides, all things being equal, I prefer to fight on ground that will fight with me."

"Fight with you?" I asked.

"I did say my house is very well trained."

"How do you train—" But I never finished my question as Elizabeth asked her own, and well, her topic took precedence.

"Won't they still be able to see me?" Her voice never wavered as she looked down at our hands that had somehow found their way back together. "I mean, I can see me."

"Thaden, yes," Charles said. The house groaned at his words. "But not the Ladies, and they're the ones whose tricks we may not be able to see until it's too late."

"Thaden," Eric said, "draws his magic from the same place as Charles and the other shadows. Think of it as being able to read the same language. If—"

"When," Charles interrupted.

"When," Eric conceded, "Thaden brings a few of his shadow beasties with him, Charles and his friends will be able to hold them back while Thaden is distracted by the Ladies."

"But whatever the Ladies bring along"—Charles' outline shifted like he might have been shrugging—"maybe we'll be able to catch a glimmer of them."

"And where I might be able to get a healthy gist of what's going on," Eric said, pointing to Elizabeth, "she can see the Ladies' magic for what it is."

"And now that we've coated her," Charles finished, "she'll also be able to see what Thaden is doing without being seen."

"So you're going to put me someplace high up where I can be safe while I watch my friends risk their lives?" Elizabeth's voice was hollow.

"They're going to put you someplace high up where you can try and help us win," I said. "We can't do this without you."

I don't know if I can do this at all. I wanted to shout at Eric that I was done. That I was in way over my head.

When this whole thing started, it was like I was snorkeling in shallow water. Maybe I couldn't touch everything at the bottom, but I could see the fish and the sand swirling. That was plenty, but now I had swum too far. Out over the deep where all I could see was dark water.

Before I could try and put all of that into words that didn't sound like they belonged in a creative writing competition, there was a knock at the door.

Eric's neck tensed, but as I moved to stand, he held up a hand to keep me in place.

"That could be Devon," I whispered. I don't know why I whispered, it just seemed like the thing to do.

"The house knows who it should let in," Eric said.

The distant *creak* of a door opening carried up the hall. A few footsteps, and then a door slammed. I held my breath, waiting for Devon to call out, but instead there was another *slam*. Then another and another. Footsteps pounded toward us along with a string of curses.

"Devon!" I shouted, and a second later, he sprinted into the parlor. His shirt torn, his face panicked, but it was Devon, very much alive. Something inside me unclenched.

"Is this place trying to kill me?" Devon panted, glaring at Eric. "The house *chased* me."

"Don't think of it as chasing. Think of it as escorting without words," Eric said.

I think Devon would have seriously blown up, but then his eyes found Elizabeth. "What did they do to you?" he breathed.

"My own personal camouflage and night vision," Elizabeth said. "I'm told it's temporary."

"Right." Devon nodded and looked to me. "Bryant?"

"I'm good," I said. "What happened to you?"

"*Pft.*" Devon shrugged. "It all went according to plan. Well, at least the important life or death bits. Everyone at the bar knows Eric is hiding in the gray stone house, the Ladies are after him, and he has something Thaden wants."

"And then they attacked you to stop you from warning us they're going to tip off Thaden and the Ladies?" Eric asked, pointing to Devon's ripped shirt. A trickle of blood marked his skin where it looked like he'd been scratched.

"What?" Devon looked down at his chest. "Ah. I mean, maybe a few of the guys who looked really tough wanted a piece of me for saying a few nasty things about our two sets of baddies. But Mildred wasn't having any of it. She pulled me into her backroom. And well, the scratches are from *her* when she got a little too intense about protecting me. It's okay though. I told her I had to defend my friends, and I think she swooned a little as I split."

"Only you"—Elizabeth shook her head, leaving smudges in the air again. Devon was smart enough not to say anything if he noticed—"would be able to walk into a group that wanted you dead and walk out with a woman swooning over you."

"And that's what makes him useful," Eric said. "How long ago did the minions scatter to their masters?"

"I would say about forty-five minutes since Mildred pulled me into a closet." Devon walked over and poured himself a cup of tea, chugging it before pouring himself another.

"Then they should be here at any moment." Eric stood, clapping his hands together. "Devon, you go with Elizabeth up to the lookout."

"I should stay down here to fight!" Devon's perfectly shaped brows pinched together.

"Fists and good looks won't be of use when the spells start to fly. Go with Elizabeth. Your job is to tell us everything she sees." Eric tossed Devon a mirror. "Stay low and out of sight, speak into this, and we'll hear you. Go through that door, and the house will lead you up the stairs." As good as Eric's word, a door appeared in the bookcase on the back wall.

"What about Bryant?" Elizabeth asked. "Where is he going?"

"He'll be far from the fighting," Eric said.

"Far from the fighting," I repeated. "What does that mean?"

"It means you'll be with the phone. I don't need you collapsing the tunnel on us while we fight," Eric said.

"So, I'm going to stand there with a deadly object and hope no one notices?"

"More or less," Eric said.

"It's a good plan," added Charles.

Devon's eyes whipped to the shadow at the same second he spat out his tea. "What the—"

But before he could ask why a shadow was talking, the house rumbled. It felt like we were in the belly of a growling beast.

"Showtime." Eric fixed his hair in the mirror. "Lady and gentleman, if you will." He took Devon and Elizabeth by their arms and led them to the new door.

"But Bryant—" Devon said.

"I'll be fine," I said, not feeling at all confident in that fact. "Take care of Elizabeth."

"Yes, that's all very sweet." Eric gave them a shove as the house rumbled again.

"Be careful, Bryant!" Elizabeth shouted as Eric slammed the door behind her, and it disappeared.

"You, too," I whispered to the books.

"Now you come with me." Eric walked me over to the fireplace. "Step through the flames and stay put." He pressed a mirror into my hand. "This will allow me to let you know if the plan changes."

"But I should be out there fighting with you," I tried, but Charles spoke gently over me.

"My apologies, but we don't have time for this." His shadowy hand pulled back the lace curtain.

"Listen to me, Bryant." Eric stared at me fiercely. "For some reason, fate has chosen you to survive. You played with fire and didn't get burned. You escaped me twice, and the Ladies. I was half-sure the shadow wizards would kill you for being a city dweller with the audacity to go to them asking for help."

"That wasn't my—"

"But you've survived," Eric said, his eyes dazzling. "Elizabeth is right. Fate has great plans for your life, and I won't risk those plans on my very own lawn. Part of living an extraordinary life is knowing when the game is up. A hero doesn't live forever." Eric gave me a shove, and I tumbled backward into the fire.

"Make your adventure great." Eric's words echoed as I fell through the dancing orange flames and into the darkness.

27

I was flat on a cold floor. The fire was gone, and I hadn't been burned.

I pushed myself to my feet and felt around. As far as I could tell, I was in a stone room the size of a walk-in closet.

Fumbling in my pocket, I pulled out the black phone. I pressed my thumb to the button, and the screen flicked on.

"All this for a phone," I muttered.

But then I heard Eric's voice in my head. *This isn't about a phone. It's about freedom of knowledge. It's about living outside the darkness.*

I scrolled across the screen to a button that looked like a ball of light. I tapped it with my thumb and instantly found the glowing sphere in my free hand, 3-D and working.

I had guessed right, the room was top to bottom stone. The same stone as the fireplace. There was a meeting of two—make that three—deadly forces a hundred yards away, and I was locked in a fireplace. I wasn't even a sidekick anymore. I'd been demoted to helpless bystander.

I sat down on the ground and leaned back against the wall. My blood pumped hard through my veins, my body telling me to run or fight. But I couldn't do either. I was trapped. And it didn't sound like Eric was planning on coming back for me.

A hero doesn't live forever.

I gripped my head with my hands, feeling my hair singe where I pressed the light to it. I couldn't even hold a magical flashlight without messing it up.

I screamed in rage and frustration. I roared and cursed. But when I stopped, the screaming didn't. The shouts came from my pocket, from the mirror Eric had given me before shoving me into this damn safe room.

I pulled out the mirror. Devon's face appeared.

"I don't know if this is working right." His voice cut clearly through the distant screams. It sounded like banshees wailing in anger.

"Just keep talking to it," Elizabeth said. "There's nothing else we can do."

"Fine, what do you see?" Devon asked.

"Flying at the end of the tunnel," Elizabeth's voice carried to the mirror like Devon was holding a phone on speaker near her face. "It looks like women. Shadowy women with big bat wings. Charles' people, too. They're running toward the flying women. I think they can see them. At the low entrance in the middle. Shit...."

Her pause made my heart leap to my throat.

"Devon, stay down, don't let them see you. It's the Ladies, but there's more of them. Thirteen I can see," Elizabeth said. "Eric, watch out! Behind the ladies. There are things."

"What things?" Devon asked.

"I don't know. I don't know what they are. They look like clouds, but clearer, cats maybe. Oh God, they're fast. Eric, in front of you!" Elizabeth shrieked, and I jumped to my feet.

Why was Eric out there fighting already? He was going to let them destroy each other, and then we would take on the losers.

Unless that hadn't really been the plan. Only what he had told me to keep me from trying to break out of the chimney.

"Sorry for the scare, Elizabeth," Eric said. "I think I've got them following me now."

"You thought right!" Elizabeth shouted. "Run faster. Eric, the flying shadows, there're more. They're penning you in."

I pounded my fist on the wall. Pain shot through my hand, and no, it didn't really help matters, as bangs, howls, and screeches came through the mirror.

"Keep going, keep going, you're almost clear," Elizabeth chanted. "The Ladies are still by the low entrance. They're watching the fight. Wait, there's something at the far end. I can't make it out. It looks like a shadow."

Everything went silent. I stared at the mirror, terrified the connection had been broken. Or, a hundred times worse, Elizabeth and Devon weren't there to talk anymore.

"He's here." Eric's voice broke the silence.

"Eric, get out of there," Elizabeth whispered, as though terrified to be overheard. But an instant later, screams of hatred like I had never heard before burst forth so viscerally, they shook the walls of my prison. It was like Hell had just let all its demons pour out onto the street.

"Elizabeth!" I shouted. "Devon! Get off the roof."

"Thaden." Elizabeth's voice was strong and clear. "He's got crawling things with him. And more women flying above. Eric, climb up on something, now. Spiders, I think they're spiders. Eric, the Ladies. They're aiming for Thaden. Eric, they aren't looking at you, run. The cats are leaving the shadows behind. They're coming toward you. Eric, run left, now!"

I listened as she gave him directions. It was like she was choreographing him as he fought.

"Good!" she shouted triumphantly.

A thunder blast echoed through the mirror. "Eric, one of the Ladies. She's turned away from Thaden. She's coming for you. The shadows are heading your way. Another Lady is leaving Thaden. Oh God! She sees me. Eric, she's coming toward me. Eric, what do we do? Eric!"

But I could hear Eric shouting spells, caught up in his own battle. Besides, he was on the street far below Elizabeth and Devon. They were trapped on the roof, helpless.

"Let me out!" I screamed at the chimney. "I said let me out!"

I waited stupidly for a moment like the walls would listen to me and realize that I had to get out. Of course, the dark stone stayed in place.

"Fine!" I shouted. "*Portunda!*" The word felt heavy in my mouth and the wall didn't move. Muttering curses under my breath that would have made Devon proud, I whipped the phone out of my pocket and started searching as soon as the screen flickered on.

"Eric, they're coming!" Elizabeth's voice echoed through the mirror.

I tried to scroll through the spells, but my fingers shook too badly.

"Get down!" Devon shouted a second before Elizabeth screamed.

"They're dying!" I bellowed. "My friends are dying. *Please* let me out."

Yes, screaming at a solid wall never did anything for anyone, but Elizabeth was in danger, and I didn't know what else to do. "Please, I have to save them."

With a *crack*, the stone in front of me split, leaving a gap barely large enough for me to fit through.

"Thank you." I squeezed through the opening. I wasn't back in the parlor. I was at the bottom of a wooden staircase lined with doors. They were spaced along the walls every few feet, not high enough up to be on the second floor, some at odd angles, and none where doors should have been.

The crack behind me shuddered closed, and I started running up the stairs. Except, if none of the doors made sense, how was I supposed to know which one led to the roof? As I raced up, the doors in front of me opened, slamming as I passed as though I was being chased—or maybe led to where I was supposed to go. I ran up and up, screams still coming from the mirror. It wasn't only Elizabeth and Devon I was hearing now, but also inhuman, high-pitched wails.

I ran as fast as I could, but the stairs still wound up. Maybe this was the house's way of keeping me safe, making me run and run while the others fought, never getting close enough to help them.

Just when I thought I would never reach the top, a door opened to my left. It was slanted toward me, like an attic hatch. All the doors in front of me and behind me slammed at once with a *bang* that pounded in my ears, but the hatch stayed open. As I neared it, I heard Elizabeth again. Screaming and terrified, but alive. I jumped from the steps to the trap door, pulling myself up and through without breaking my stride.

And then I was on a roof like any normal roof in Manhattan, covered in tar paper with a foot-high brick edge. For a horrible second, I thought I had run too far. That I was aboveground in the Manhattan skyline. But the sounds in the air weren't from traffic, and the lights above didn't come from the skyscrapers.

White things swooped over my head. Birds with raptor beaks, bat wings, and reptilian tails.

"Leave him *alone*," Elizabeth growled.

I spun to face her.

Devon was on the ground. He was unconscious, bleeding hard from his head, and Elizabeth stood over him, swinging her bloody fists at the birds as they dove at her, clawing and pecking.

"Elizabeth!" I screamed. Everything froze.

Then she looked at me. As her lips curved around my name, her voice was drowned out by the wailing screeches of the birds streaking straight at me.

And then it was like everything slowed down. I saw the birds, their feathers and their scales. Their red hateful eyes. Instinct told me to raise my arms and protect my face. But there was another, calmer voice, and somehow I spoke, "*Aarantha!*" The vortex formed around me, and I ran toward Elizabeth, ducking low as the birds tried to hit me.

"Bryant!" she screamed as I held her close, shielding her head with my arms as the winds fought to pull the birds away. But these birds weren't like the fire, mist, or shadows. They had wings to fight the wind. Their wings pummeled the air as they struggled to break free, screeching and howling. And something in their cawing made sense.

You will die, usurper of magic. You will die below the earth.

It was like I was understanding words I didn't know existed. And as the first bird broke free from the vortex, I wished I hadn't understood.

"*Abalata!*" I screamed, and the thick black unspooled from my palm, pummeling the bird and knocking it through the twister and far out of sight.

But there were still more birds calling for my blood. I gripped the phone in my hand and flipped to the fire tab, hoping I knew what I was doing. Tapping the fire button, I tilted the scale all the way to the burning edge.

Instantly, the flames filled the vortex, and the birds screamed. Terrible screams, almost human. Their feathers twisted and blackened, their scales charred, and one by one, they dropped out of the air. I clutched Elizabeth to me, waiting for the smoke to smother us or for something larger to catapult down to kill us.

But the last bird vanished into the flames. Still, I waited for a moment, the heat from the fire roasting my face, before I dropped the scale to the other end, extinguishing the inferno. I let the spell go, and the vortex faded away.

I took a breath. And then another. But nothing flew at us or crept over the edge of the roof. Elizabeth clung to me, not talking, just staring around. The only sounds were our shaky panting and the echoes of the fight far below.

"Devon," I said after a minute, kneeling next to him. Bruises peppered his face, and a gash on top of his head sluggishly bled, painting his skin and hair a bright, kitschy shade of crimson.

Elizabeth tore off her sleeve and pressed it to his scalp. "He was trying to protect me." Her voice was thick with tears as she bound his head. I think she had learned that in last year's spring play. "I was watching the battle, and then those things came."

The screams and bangs bellowing up were nightmarish. Noises that weren't even human. But I suppose the things I had killed weren't human either.

I laid a hand on Devon's chest. Once I made sure it still rose and fell, I crept toward the edge of the roof, keeping my head low until I was close enough to peer over the bricks.

I had never thought I would need to describe something like that. The roof was higher than it should have been. Six stories up at least, but even from here, the blood that coated the ground by the left tunnel shone red in the dim light, where wisps of shadow still battled shimmers of brightness.

By the low cavern, only two Ladies had been left standing. One of them was familiar from our run-in back at my mom's apartment. The other looked twice as old, bent over at the waist, hair hanging limp and spider-web-thin around bony features.

In front of the house was another Lady—the other one who had tried to off me at my mom's. She hovered between Eric and Thaden, her head twitching back and forth like a snake's as they all fought each other in a horrible three-way battle, trading spells and trying to shield themselves as the dark winged women flew overhead, casting spells on the Lady and Eric, and the shimmering things and spiders indiscriminately attacked everything that wasn't their master.

I wanted to watch, maybe find Charles. But even if I had been able to tell the shadows apart, I couldn't have pulled my eyes from Thaden. Tall and broad, like some hero from a storybook, with jet black hair that curled up at the ends.

He looked for all the world like my dad. My breath caught in my throat, and the cacophony of the battle disappeared.

My dad was Thaden.

He was going to turn around and make eye contact with me. Then we would have the big moment—*Bryant, it's true. I am your father.*—and the whole battle would stop. Every time he had missed my birthday, he was digging under the city tunnels, creating evil minions. Every overseas trip had been a sham. My father wasn't a workaholic businessman. He was a homicidal wizard.

But there was something much bigger than Thaden/Dad pushing out of the tunnel. Something dark and as large as a house that made me forget about shadowy family reunions. Eric was the first to see the monster. He froze, immediately forgetting the Lady and Thaden, and sprinted away, casting a green, shimmering spell in his wake.

The Lady aimed another spell at him, and waves of shaking red shot toward Eric, but before they even met their mark, the Lady turned and saw the ink-black monster. I didn't think it was possible for a Lady to turn any paler, but as the monster bore down on her, she turned white as a full moon. Her screams echoed up to the roof as the beast reached down and picked her up in its hands, squeezing her until the screaming stopped.

I wanted to throw up, but didn't have the time. Thaden was giving his creature orders, and the thing was turning toward Eric, who ran straight for the fighting shimmers and shadows.

"Stay with Devon," I said to Elizabeth, feeling like someone else was forming the words. "Get him back inside."

"Where are you going?" She grabbed my hand, looking terrified. "You can't go down there. There's a giant minotaur, in case you hadn't noticed!"

Part of me wanted to scream, *I have to stop my dad from murdering people*, but the other part knew it didn't matter if Thaden really was my absentee millionaire father. It was like fate was whispering in my ear that it was my turn to be a hero, no matter what waited for me on the bloody floor.

I looked down, trying to make out that mythic shape Elizabeth saw so clearly. But for me, it was just darkness on Eric's heels. "I have to help him," I said. "If he dies, we all die." And it was true. Even if Eric had meant to go out in a blaze of glory and leave me alive for whatever dumb thing he thought fate had planned after this, he was wrong.

"Bryant—"

"I have to," I said, trying to find the words to explain. But Elizabeth took my face in her hands and kissed me. My heart raced, and my head spun.

"Don't die," she whispered before stepping back to Devon.

I nodded and turned to the edge of the roof.

28

I stared dumbly for a few seconds, wanting to do something heroic like leap from the edge and to the battle below. But then I would be dead as soon as I hit the ground, and what good would I be to Eric then?

I took a deep breath and pulled out the phone, tapping my way to the *Quick Escape Spells at a Glance. Aarantha* was at the top of the list, but I wanted a way down, not a tornado to do even more damage to the top of Eric's poor, sentient house.

So, I scrolled down, hoping a spell would look right. *Escata.* The word jumped out at me like I had known I was looking for it. Like I knew the description was *a speedy decent with relative assurance of survival* before I read it.

I climbed up onto the brick parapet. The giant shadow was gaining on Eric. It was now or never. I wanted to look back at Elizabeth and Devon to make sure they were still safe. But I knew if I did, I wouldn't be able to step off of the roof and into thin air.

I took a deep breath and jumped, shouting, *"Escata!"* My speed didn't slow when I said the word. I was still falling, fast. I was going to hit the ground and break my legs. At best. And just as I closed my eyes so I wouldn't have to watch my own bones shatter, I hit something. Not something hard or bouncy. It was more like I had jumped off a high dive and into a pool of pudding.

I opened my eyes, and my feet were still a foot aboveground, and I was sinking slowly, too slowly. Charles' shadows at the far end of the tunnel were screaming as the monster closed in. I picked one foot up, and the air made a horrible sucking noise before my spell vanished and I fell forward onto the street, landing flat on my face.

Pushing myself off my stomach, I raced toward the monster. The black shadow looked taller and broader from down here. It was at least twenty feet high with shoulders as wide as I was tall, and giving off a terrible, angry roar as it waded into the shadows. A few charged him, a suicide run.

A high scream and a terrible crunch sounded from high in the air. I didn't need Elizabeth's breathless, "He ate that woman!" to come through the mirror to know the result.

And while the shouts of anger and fear carried through Charles' men, and the shrieks of the women flying above mixed with the growls of the shimmering white cats and the bellows of the minotaur, one sound carried above the rest. A low laugh that shook the walls and was more frightening than all the shadows and mist combined.

I spun toward the sound. Thaden walked slowly in the minotaur's wake, drinking in the panic. Veiled in inky black, his face was darker than the minotaur's shadow, but somehow, I could still make out the details. His mouth cocked in a triumphant grin. His eyes locked on mine.

I searched his features for something familiar. Something that would tell me my dad had a good reason for becoming the evil Thaden.

"Dad!" I shouted above the screams. "You have to stop this!"

For a moment the blackened face shimmered, transmuting into a mocking grin.

But the lips were wrong. The top one was so narrow, I could barely see it. And his eyes were set too far apart, and his chin too chiseled.

"You're not my dad." A laugh tumbled out of me, shaking my ribs, before another scream and crunch told me the shadow monster had eaten another one of Charles' people.

"I am the father of a whole new world, a world where magic will reign." Thaden's voice shook the air.

"Still way better than I thought." I ran a hand over my face. "Not that this isn't awful but—"

"I am glad death amuses you."

"Amused isn't really what I'm feeling."

"You might have a place in the world yet." Thaden smiled. "You have something that belongs to me." He was still a hundred feet away, but it might as well have been inches. My skin prickled.

For a second, I thought about lying, or running. But the phone was in my hand, and there was nowhere to go.

"Yep!" I finally answered, as loudly as I could muster.

"If you give me what is mine," Thaden said, "I may let you leave with your life."

"Really?" The tone of mock belief that came out of my mouth shocked me. I sounded badass. And knowing I sounded like I wasn't afraid kind of made me feel a little less like I had jumped helpless into a battle I couldn't even see properly, thinking my dad might be a mass murderer and finding out, no, a stranger was going to kill me instead. "Because I was under the impression you were the kind of guy who kills everyone who gets in his way."

"I am not unreasonable." Thaden stepped closer, his voice shifting to what in some version of reality might have been considered kind. "You did not know what you were doing. You were led astray by Eric Deldridge. But it was Deldridge that failed me. Deldridge that betrayed me. He was to sit at my right hand, and now he must die. But you could escape his fate. You could take the destiny he so carelessly threw away."

The minotaur roared behind me, but Thaden didn't even look up.

"Being able to use the spells on the phone without any proper training is remarkable." Thaden's voice was so low, it was just above a whisper, but I could still hear every word.

I hated it. That whole *whispering deathly things into your ear* thing is seriously creepy.

"Such natural ability is rare these days," Thaden continued. "Imagine how powerful you could become if you let me teach you."

"Teach me what?" I asked. The ground shook beneath my feet, and only my years of riding the New York subway kept me standing.

"To be a real wizard. A powerful wizard who will see the darkness and the light that control our world." Thaden was close, only a few feet away now. "Fate has pulled you here, boy. Fate has drawn you to greatness. Don't let this chance slip through your grasp. Give me what is mine, and I will show you a new world you cannot even imagine."

"You don't even know his name." Eric's voice came from over my shoulder. "Nor care to, Thaden. He may be very new to magic, but he isn't stupid enough to think you'll let any of us live. I thought you were the sort to allow new magic to thrive, but I was wrong. The only magic you want to survive is what you can control. You are no better than the Ladies. Trapped between a prison and a tomb, and I was fool enough to follow you."

"You stole from me." Thaden rounded on Eric.

"Stealing is such a dark term for losing something you lent me," Eric said.

"But I suppose semantics aren't important now that we're trying to kill each other."

"Do you think you stand a chance against me?" Thaden tipped his head to the side, examining Eric. "How strange that I never realized the extent of your delusions of grandeur."

"I did learn from the best." Eric bowed, not taking his eyes off his opponent. "*Bryant,*" he emphasized my name like he was trying to rub in that Thaden didn't know it, "do me a favor and keep that minotaur from eating me while Thaden and I continue our little chat."

"O-Okay," I stammered, taking a few steps back.

As soon as I was behind Eric, he launched into a long stream of words. The air in front of him glowed a reddish-purple before morphing into a glistening wall.

Thaden screamed something, his words strange and muffled. The ground at his feet cracked and more of the horrible spiders scurried out as he shouted something else and green balls of light streaked out of his palms. I ducked, covering my head, but instead of being burned to death, there was sizzling *smack* after sizzling *smack* as they hit Eric's purple wall and petered out.

"Bryant, the minotaur, please," Eric said as Thaden drew a deep breath.

"Right." I turned away from Eric and toward the sea of shadows.

Everything was darkness now. The thin, white glimmers the Ladies had left were gone. I glanced over to the short entrance where the two Ladies had been before I jumped off the roof, but there was no sign of them now. I hurried toward the shadows, trying not to think of the Ladies rallying troops to come in and kill us all.

I stared up at the minotaur as I ran. For a moment, I thought I could see him properly. The head of a bull with great deadly horns as thick as my torso, on top of the body of a man. But the next step, he was just a shadow again. My foot slid under me, and I tripped over something I couldn't see. But I could feel it. The thing I landed on. It was a person. A person long past moving.

I swallowed the bile that had flown up into my throat and pushed myself to my feet.

The minotaur had reversed course and was rambling back toward Eric and Thaden. He was going to get Eric from behind. Kill him before he could stop Thaden.

"*Abalata!*" I shouted. The black taffy mist pulled from my hand and shot out. For a split second, I was afraid the spell would go right through the shadow. But then the beast roared in anger and turned toward me.

I couldn't make him out, but if you ever have the misfortune of having a giant, angry minotaur staring down at you, you'll know what I mean when I say I felt his eyes ripping me to shreds.

This is how I die. Not a mugging or a fire or old and in bed surrounded by grandchildren. I'm going to be eaten by a minotaur, and there is nothing I can do about it.

The ground shook as he bore down on me, and I wondered if it would take the minotaur long enough to eat me that Eric might be able to beat Thaden. My eyes shot over to their battle. Eric was crouched on the ground with his arms over his head as Thaden floated above, showering him with spells that sizzled the air as they streaked toward Eric.

I'm going to be eaten by a minotaur, and it won't even have helped anyone.

"Bryant!" Elizabeth's voice came out of my pocket. "Bryant, there's black blood coming out of the minotaur's left side!"

"What do I do?" I shouted into the mirror as I pulled it out of my pocket.

"I don't know, but aim for there!" There was something in the way Elizabeth said it—like she actually thought I could fight a giant shadow minotaur—that made my mind race and not because I wondered how much being eaten alive would hurt, but because I was searching for a plan.

"*Abalata!*" I shouted again, not aiming for the minotaur's knee this time but for his left side. There was a howl of pain and fury as my spell hit its mark.

"*Erunca!*" I screamed as the minotaur lurched forward. Lighting streaked down from the ceiling. It was like watching a cloud being lit up by lighting. I could see the minotaur's teeth as he howled and his long, broken fingernails as he tried to bat the lighting away. But he kept up his progress, one shuddering step at a time.

"*Kuraxo!*" I shouted, and the ground shook. I turned and ran from the spell, hoping Eric and Charles' shadows wouldn't be caught in it, and the ceiling wouldn't cave in and bring down half of Manhattan on our heads. A *boom* scrambled my brains, and the earth rolled so hard, I fell forward.

"Bryant, he's on the ground!" Elizabeth screamed.

"*Parapus!*" I roared at the shadow spread-eagled on the cracked street.

Lines flew from me and hung in the air, outlining the figure I couldn't see. The minotaur bellowed in rage, but the lines held.

"What now?" I asked Elizabeth.

"Kill it," she said, her voice filled with horrible certainty. "He's tearing the lines apart."

The binding spell wasn't permanent on wizards. How long could it last on a minotaur? Hell, all I knew about minotaurs was my mom made me paint a foam sword for one of her educational shows in school so the hero could slay one.

A sword. You kill minotaurs with swords.

I looked down at the phone. But there was no icon for a sword. I scrolled down the list of *Last Resort at a Glance spells*, but nothing screamed medieval cutting weapons.

"I need a damn sword!" I shouted at the phone as the minotaur howled and the ground shook.

"Make one," Elizabeth said.

"There isn't an app for that!"

"You can do magic, Bryant. Magic a sword."

"Swords don't grow on..."

My words faded away as the minotaur shook in his binding, cracking the ground under my feet into razor-sharp shrapnel.

I grabbed a pointy-looking piece and ran toward the minotaur. "*Milkawa.*"

I didn't watch to see if it would work, I didn't have time. The rock grew heavier in my hand as I started climbing the thin bands that bound the monster like a jungle gym. There was nothing solid below my feet, but I could feel the minotaur's squishy flesh as I clamored to his chest and raised the rock high over my head. But it wasn't a dinky rock anymore. It was three feet long now and growing, with a vicious point at the end.

"You're too far left," Elizabeth warned from my clenched fist where the mirror cut into my palm as it pressed into the end of the rock sword. "You're not over his heart."

I shuffled right a little. "Here?"

"Up a bit," Elizabeth said.

I took a step forward, and the minotaur's chest shook as he growled.

"There!"

I plunged my sword down with all my might. The tip met something hard, but I pushed down with all my weight, not stopping until the back end squelched out of sight.

A whimpering scream shook the tunnel before the monster under my feet went still.

"You did it!" Elizabeth shrieked. "You did it. You did it!"

"I did," I panted.

You would have thought that killing the minotaur would have made the fight go quiet. That everyone would have recognized I had done something epic. But the battle hadn't stopped. Eric was standing now, and a dozen bright white whips surrounded him, shooting out at Thaden in turn.

I had to get to him. I started pulling at the sword, trying to free it from the minotaur's chest. The sound of blood and who knows what else squelching as I yanked the sword free was quite possibly the worst thing I had ever heard.

"Elizabeth, say something," I said as I slid down the dead minotaur's side.

"Why?"

"Because if I die, I don't want dead minotaur gurgle to be the last thing I remember." I leapt the cracks in the ground toward Eric, ignoring the spiders that clicked at my feet.

"Bryant Jameson Adams, you had better not die. I decided yesterday that I really like you, and I don't want you to die before we get to have our first date."

My heart jumped so high in my chest, I swear I flew the last twenty feet to Eric's side.

Eric was bleeding from a gash across his cheek. It looked worse on his bright white skin than it would have on a normal person. Well, possibly. What did I know about bloody battles?

"Took care of him?" Eric smiled. "I knew fate had something wonderful planned for you."

"There is nothing more wonderful than a glorious death," Thaden growled. "Let the shadows sing songs of your passing. The songs will last far longer than your lives ever could."

"You know"—Eric pulled himself to stand up straight, wiping the blood from his face with his sleeve—"I thought perhaps this battle was going to be my last blaze of glory. A chance to pass the torch on to a new wizard. But Bryant killed your minotaur, and the last of the Ladies have fled. So perhaps Bryant and I can both live to fight another night, and he won't be a new wizard alone in the world with only a phone and a dream to see him through. What say you, Bryant?" Eric raised a dark eyebrow. "You and me wreaking havoc. Running amok in Manhattan."

"Sounds pretty good." I smiled.

"Then how about we finish this for good?" Eric said. "Whichever spell you fancy."

"I will destroy you!" Thaden cried, "*Talisma—*"

"*Milkawa!*" I shouted, without anger or fear, my eyes trained on the rock at Thaden's feet. It was like I had always known the spell was supposed to be important. Like fate had made sure the word felt familiar on my lips.

The street underneath Thaden's feet swelled, rising and pulsing like a living thing.

"*Ilmatiot!*" Thaden shot back, and a vice closed around my chest, squeezing out every last ounce of air.

The stone from the street began to grow, wrapping itself around Thaden's legs.

Blood pounded in my ears as my vision grayed.

Thaden was wound to his chest in stone, and the column rose.

Pain shot through my knees as they hit the ground.

This is how I die. Far below the streets, lost in the blood of shadows.

Thaden's arms were pinned by the stone.

Maybe Eric will win. Maybe my fate was to make sure he lived. Not such a bad way to go.

A spell made my bones buzz as it shot through the air. Thaden's face twisted in terror, then everything went black. And it was a relief.

29

"Bryant," a voice pleaded.

Maybe it's my mom. Maybe she's dead, too. Oh God. She's gonna be pissed I got us both killed.

But the voice was lighter than my mom's. Shakier, too. Scared instead of mad.

"Bryant!" another voice chimed in. This one did sound angry. "Come on, man, you can't be dead."

Devon. Devon was mad at me for being dead. Warm prickles filtered down into my chest.

Clearly I'm not dead if fire ants are eating my lungs. Then, the pain worsened.

Someone was crying next to me.

Elizabeth.

"Bryant, you promised."

The pain in my chest morphed into an uneven throbbing.

"What are you doing?" It was Eric. He sounded tired but alive. If he was alive, Thaden must be dead. I wanted to scream at Eric to take Devon and Elizabeth and run before more monsters could come after them, but I still had no air.

"Saving my best friend, you asshole," Devon growled and the pressure on my chest grew.

Lips clamped over mine. Someone tried to blow air into my lungs, but they were solid metal now. Unable to be moved by air.

"Get out of the way," Eric said.

"We aren't giving up on him." Elizabeth's hair fluttered around my face as she tried to push her breath into my chest.

I wanted to thank her for trying, but the pain had taken over, lighting my veins on fire.

Maybe if they let me die, it won't hurt quite so much.

"I don't believe I mentioned giving up," Eric said. "*Palmuntra!*"

Agony like nothing I had ever imagined shot into my lungs.

Eric's going to torture me before he lets me die. Probably because I didn't stay in the chimney.

"*Palmuntra!*" Eric shouted again, and again the pain struck.

And didn't stop. It flooded my leaden lungs with air. I hacked it out, but more took its place. Things in my head, in my chest, spun out of control, while the voices around me cried, "Bryant!"

But then the pain in my veins ebbed away as wonderful oxygen raced through my body. I took a normal, though shuddering, breath and opened my eyes.

Elizabeth knelt over me. Tears had left wide, pale tracks through the charcoal that covered her face. Devon crouched next to her, the blood-covered bandage still on his head. Eric stood behind them, all traces of the battle gone.

"And he lives." Eric grinned.

I pushed myself to sit up, and the cavern swayed. Elizabeth wrapped an arm around me, holding me steady.

"Careful," she whispered over the moans of pain and cries of grief lingering after the battle.

In front of me was a pillar of stone. It was like Big Blue in the park, growing like a sped up video on crack.

"Thaden?"

"Eric chopped his head off," Devon said.

"So, he's dead?" I asked as the pillar of stone pierced the ceiling, pushing up like a new flower bursting through the earth. With a shuddering crack, the ceiling split, sending a shower of dirt and debris tumbling down.

"*Primurgo,*" Eric cried, and a shimmering dome enclosed us.

The dirt fell around it like filthy, polluted snow, glancing off the surface as though we were trapped in a perverted snow globe.

I waited for the ceiling to split in two. But after the dust settled, the ceiling stayed up, and the stone column continued to grow.

"I think Thaden is very dead," Eric said as the shimmering bubble disappeared.

"What about the Ladies?" I tried to push myself to my feet. Nope. My legs shook too badly.

"The Ladies will remain a problem for another day," Eric said. "But with so many of them gone, I would say it's safe for you to collect your mother and go home. I think you can officially be declared a hero. For today at least. One battle does not a true fighter make."

"Some hero I am," I muttered as Devon half-dragged me up.

"You are." Elizabeth stepped in front of me. "You kept your promise. You didn't die." She wrapped her arms around me and kissed me. Not fast, like she had before. But slow and deep. Holding me close like she didn't want to let go.

"Not dying is a very good beginning," Eric said after a moment. Or a century. I was never good at keeping track of time when Elizabeth kissed me. "And we did destroy Thaden and his minotaur, so I don't think today can be considered a waste."

Elizabeth took a step back, and I looked into her sparkly eyes. They were smiling at me. I wiped the tears from her face and the black washed away.

"Not a waste," Elizabeth said.

She took Devon's place with her arm around me, helping me over the cracked ground.

"Do you think Charles is okay?" I asked as we crossed the blood-slicked ground.

"He is." Elizabeth pointed toward the far end of the tunnel. "I can see him with his people." Her voice caught in her throat. "They lost a lot."

"They did," Eric said. "And not just today. Thaden had been picking them off for years. They are finally free to explore the dark without fearing him and his monsters."

"Why did you get involved with Thaden again?" Devon asked as Eric led us over to the low tunnel where the two Ladies had disappeared.

"Choices were made." Eric shrugged. "When you've spent your life stranded between two types of evil, one of the evils can begin to look like hope. But perhaps all you need is a catalyst to shake the rocks apart."

"Look, Bryant," Devon said. "You're a catalyst." Devon swayed little, and Eric caught him.

"I've forgotten how badly non-wizards do after battles," Eric said. "*Concursornio.*"

Devon breathed in sharply through his teeth. "Please don't magic my insides without asking me first." He shook his head hard and then stood up straight.

"You're welcome."

"You know," I said, scrunching up my nose against the words, "for a second there, I thought Thaden was my dad. Like he had lived a creepy double life and was trying to kill us all."

"I think your issues with your father are more a matter for a therapist than magical in nature," Eric said.

Devon and Elizabeth both started laughing, and in a second, I was laughing with them. It was weird, laughing as we walked away from battle, but it felt right. Like it was somehow an affirmation that the four of us had survived.

"This way please," Eric said.

I didn't want to leave the scene with the street cracked and the dead shadows to be buried, but Eric led us through the tunnel. It started sweeping up toward the surface. I didn't even want to begin to imagine how long it would take us to climb to the streets.

But soon there were lights hanging from the ceiling, casting our shadows across the ground.

Elizabeth gasped and took a step back, knocking me off-balance as she pulled her arm from around me.

"What?" I spun around, trying to find what had scared her.

"Don't you see it?" she whispered, before looking up to me. "No, I suppose you can't."

"What do you see?" Eric asked.

"We're all there, like a picture in a storybook." Elizabeth pointed to our dark shapes on the ground that looked like nothing to me. "The hero, the adventurer, the apprentice, the seer. All tied together by golden thread." Elizabeth smiled. "It makes one whole picture. The four of us. And it was always going to be that way."

"Fate pulls the threads as it sees fit." Eric stepped through the shadow.

"Just for the record," Devon asked, "who was the hero?"

Elizabeth laughed and wrapped her arm around my waist, not to hold me up, just because.

We walked a little farther until tiles began popping up, scattered in with the stone. A roar sounded right over our heads, but I wasn't afraid. It was only a subway car carrying people home.

A solid wall rose in front of us. Without stopping, Eric said, "*Portunda*," and a metal door with peeling-off white paint appeared.

Eric opened it, bowing for us to walk through.

The bright, industrial light made me blink for a moment before I saw that we were in the Columbus Circle subway station.

"*Portundo*," Eric muttered, and the door disappeared.

"Columbus Circle has an entrance to the magical underworld?" Devon shook his head. "Really, this is the best you could come up with?"

"It's a nice central location." Eric headed toward the stairs that led aboveground.

I looked at Elizabeth, but she was staring at her reflection in a poster.

The shadows had worn off her skin, but her hair was still jet black. "My mom's gonna kill me."

"It'll wear off eventually." Eric waved a dismissive hand as he walked back to us. "You've only been coated once."

Elizabeth looked at me, her sparkly eyes shining with tears.

"You still look beautiful." Blood rushed to my face.

She leaned over and kissed me quickly. An old woman next to me scoffed her disapproval, and Elizabeth pulled away, smiling.

"Well, I suppose it's only fitting for you two to be kissing after he slew a monster." Eric shrugged, leading the way up the stairs and to the street. I was starting to get used to him shrugging at me. There was something in his exasperation that felt comforting. Like I was destined to frustrate him.

"*Wooh*," Devon whistled as soon as we reached the street, and I didn't need to ask what he was talking about. A giant stone spire had split the skyline. Big Blue's rocky twin was peeking out above Times Square.

"I wonder what the reporters will say about that," I said, trying not to think of Thaden's body sans head locked in the stone.

"I suspect they'll call it installation art." Eric wove south through the awed crowd.

"And if they try to follow it to its root?" Elizabeth asked.

"Charles and his people will take care of it." Eric stepped out onto Broadway, gazing up at the stone tower.

"If Charles will take care of that," I asked, "what do we do?"

"We go collect your mother," Eric said, "let Lola know we haven't died, and after that, it's up to you."

"What do you mean?" I watched a helicopter fly overhead, circling the new addition to Times Square.

"Well"—Eric turned his gaze toward me—"you can collect your mother and return to being a normal high schooler. Apply to colleges. Work in an office. Try to find a way to give life meaning…"

"Or?" I asked.

"Or you can join me in a world beyond your imagination and dare to face adventures most can never even dream of."

A guitar began playing in the night. Cabs rushed past. Sirens echoed in the distance. All the sounds of New York I had known my whole life. But I was in a different New York now. One deeper and greater than I had ever imagined.

"One question," I said as an elderly black lady knocked my toe with her cane. "When my parents get new apartments, are you going to destroy those, too?

"I never try to predict destruction. It ruins the surprise." Eric grinned. "Just think of it as a nice fall cleaning. And I'm sure Devon and your charming girl-friend will be pleased to help you sort through the rubble."

Elizabeth laughed but didn't argue. I held her hand tight as we began the long walk to Lola's, strolling peacefully through the chaos of Manhattan.

In less than four days I had become a wizard, stopped a bad guy, toppled a regime, and gotten a girlfriend.

"I wonder what we'll be up to next weekend," Devon said as we passed by a stand of reporters all babbling about Big Blue and the stone tower.

"In my experience, it's best not to ask," Eric said. "The path fate has chosen for you will find you. And we'll meet the next adventure when it comes."

We walked through Times Square past Thaden's tomb. I ignored the chill tickle of wind on my neck and shoved down the feeling that someone was watching me.

I'm glad I did. If I'd known what waited in the shadows, I might not have been brave enough to stay in Manhattan.

Eric was right. Fate would lead us to whatever journey came next, whether we were ready or not.

SEVEN THINGS NOT TO DO WHEN EVERYONE'S TRYING TO KILL YOU

BOOK TWO

1

The monster dodged around the people of New York, daring to run within inches of the unsuspecting humans before darting down another path. But the tourists of Central Park were oblivious to the imminent danger charging toward them. Unaware that at any moment a magical creature could attack. Only one wizard was brave enough to hunt the beast. Only one wizard had the heart to defend the good people of New York.

"There!" Devon shouted, yanking me out of my inner monologue. "He's over there."

I bent double, squinting between the legs of the horde of tourists who crowded the Central Park paths. A streak of brown fur skidded across the frozen ground and off through the trees.

"Dammit." I pushed my way through the crowd. "Why is it still running?"

"Just come on!" Devon sprinted ahead of me, chasing the beast.

My lungs ached as I dodged people and trees, barely keeping the thing's tail in view. Buildings cut through the grass, blocking the creature's path. Soon we would have it pinned.

"Where does it think it's going?" Devon puffed. It was nice to know the last hour of running through the park had actually winded him.

A guttural roar split the air, and my heart sank as I recognized the brick buildings in front of us.

Of course the thing was running straight for the Central Park Zoo.

"We can't let it get in there!" I ran as fast as my exhausted, scrawny legs could muster. If that thing got into the zoo, there would be too many places for it to hide. Too many cages for us to search. If a zookeeper found it, it would make their career and headline news. And really ruin my week.

The creature dashed through a clearing in the trees as he made his final sprint for the zoo buildings.

"*Stasio!*" I shouted, my eyes fixed on the blur of brown fur. The air surrounding the thing shimmered for a moment before the creature smacked into the brand new solid box my spell had formed around it.

"Nice one, Bry," Devon panted, his hands on his knees as he stopped next to the creature.

"Thanks." I don't mean to sound like a prick, but I really was pretty proud of myself. A perfect, crystal-clear square, like Snow White's glass casket, sealed in the angry critter. "For a little guy, he's freakin' fast."

The fur ball squeaked and clawed against the spell like he had heard my words and found the word *little* to be insulting.

"He really doesn't look so bad." I knelt, letting the chill of the frozen ground drain the heat of the run from me.

"Doesn't look so bad?" Devon rubbed his gloved hands over his face. "How often do you see a two-headed squirrel the size of a house cat with a bright green lizard tail running through Central Park?"

Devon's description was on the whole completely accurate. Though the squirrel was a little smaller than my mom's cat, it did have two heads, both of which swiveled to glare at me. One had black eyes, the other creepy red. I shuddered as they simultaneously started chirping at me. The forked lizard tail curled up over its head like a scorpion ready to strike.

"Okay, so it's a little creepy. *Conorvo.*" The squirrel's makeshift cage shrank, stopping just short of squishing the little guy.

"What I want to know is how no one noticed him," Devon said as I shrugged out of my bright red backpack. "A weird little nut-hunting baby dragon running around New York for two months and no one said anything? How is that even possible?"

Nutty McDragon, because the little dude deserved a name, squealed as I slid him into my backpack and closed the zipper.

"Really?" I hoisted myself to my feet, legs shaky after having run so far. "After everything that's happened, you think people pretending not to notice a weird squirrel in Central Park is strange?" I pointed to the sky west of us where a giant blue flower cut through the trees of Central Park, and then to the south where a stone tower loomed over Times Square.

"Okay, okay"—Devon raised his hands in surrender—"but still, people, man."

"People." I sighed and followed Devon back toward the path.

Nutty McDragon squealed like a mutant demon in my backpack, but other than a few people looking nervously at their phones, no one seemed to care as we made our way west.

Part of me wanted to be disappointed in humanity for not caring about weird squirrels, giant flowers, and stone towers of doom appearing in Manhattan, but since I was the one who had caused all three of them, I couldn't be too mad.

See, I'm a wizard. A super new wizard. Once upon a time, about two months ago, I had four really bad days. I found a phone that holds an illegal magical library, destroyed both my parents' homes, defeated an evil wizard, pissed off some other crazy powerful people, and almost died a couple of times. Not to mention the, you know, obvious magical damage to Manhattan. But I came out on the other side alive, a wizard, and with a girlfriend who embodies all things wonderful in the world, so really the hell days were worth it in the end.

We walked past the chain-link fence that surrounded the base of Big Blue, protecting the giant flower from protestors and wannabe flower killers. Scientists were researching the flower as a genetic anomaly. On the other side of the crisscrosses in the fence, they circled Big Blue's base like they did every day. Doing all sorts of sciencey things. I could make someone's career by giving them Nutty McDragon, but I didn't need another disaster on my head.

"Winter is here!" a protestor screamed as we passed. "It's time for the plant to die!"

"Wow," Devon muttered. "Do they have nothing else to do with their time?"

There were at least twenty people protesting around this side of Big Blue. And I had to give it to them—it was a little weird that, while the rest of the park had succumbed to the December freeze, Big Blue had stayed just as... blue. But the sign that read *The Aliens are breeding, destroy their nest now!* was way off. Aliens didn't make the giant bloom. I did. I blushed and ducked my head as we passed the alien protestor, like he might be able to read my mind or something.

I'd seen news stories about protestors surrounding the Times Square spire, too—some claiming demons from the underworld, others angry about sinking real estate prices with the new massive mineral neighbor. I had been upholding my New Yorker obligation and avoiding Times Square lately, so I didn't really know how weird those protestors were. Only that they were there every day and really pissed about my accidental architectural addition.

"Let Eric know we're on our way," Devon said when we reached the far west side of the park.

I pulled my phone from my pocket, checking to make sure I had the right, non-magical phone before pressing my finger to the scanner and dialing Eric.

"Did you finally manage it?" Eric drawled in a bored tone.

"Hello to you, too," I said. "And yes I—"

"We," Devon cut in.

"—*we* got it. I'm taking him to my mom's."

"Delightful." I could almost hear Eric's eye roll through the phone. "I'll meet you there."

I hung up and slid the phone back into my pocket.

"Is your mom going to be okay with Eric and Nutty being at the apartment?" Devon's eyebrows scrunched together. A pack of girls in chic winter coats passed, and his face immediately smoothed into racially ambiguous perfection. The girls giggled and waved as they passed. Nutty McDragon squealed his displeasure at the noise.

"Mom'll be fine with it." It wasn't true. I knew it wasn't true. Even Nutty, who was squirming around in my backpack more than any magically-contained creature should be able to, knew it wasn't true. But I didn't really have another choice, so we kept walking to my mom's, Devon winking at every remotely attractive woman, me trying to look inconspicuous with my shrieking backpack.

"You got a sewer rat in there?" An old black lady eyed my bag as we waited for a crosswalk.

"No ma'am, just trying to get his cat back from the vet," Devon said calmly as I opened my mouth to say...I don't know what. "The carrier broke, and it was the best we could do."

"It doesn't sound like any cat I've ever heard." The woman shook her head. "You better be careful playing with angry animals. Some bites don't heal too well."

"We'll be careful."

The woman *tshed* her disbelief at our promise and waddled down the street, shaking her head.

Devon grabbed my elbow and steered me away. My feet wanted to carry me south to my mom's old house, but seeing as that one had been mostly destroyed, we turned north instead.

The doorman didn't look up from the dinging video game in his hands as we walked to the elevator.

"What service," Devon whispered sarcastically.

We lived on the twelfth floor of this building, and the elevator protested the whole way up. It wasn't a great place, but it was what my mom could afford. My dad offered to buy us an apartment—he was already looking for a new place himself, so he had a real estate dude and everything—but my mom wanted nothing to do with it. The concept of taking help, let alone money, from my dad was enough to turn even Mom's best moods sour. So we ended up in a place with chipped linoleum floors that smelled vaguely of nursing home.

Voices carried through the door before we reached it.

"I don't even want to know what you're bringing in here," Mom growled as I slipped the key into the lock. "What are you bringing into my home?"

"Seeing as you've just contradicted yourself," Eric said, "I'm not really sure how to answer you, Ms. Miller."

"Hey, Mom," I said, cutting her off as I opened the door. "How are you?"

"It depends on why Mr. Deldridge"—Mom growled his name—"is here."

On cue, Nutty McDragon started squealing. The squirrel knew just how to get me in trouble.

"Oh good God." Mom sank into a chair as Mrs. Mops, our shaggy, gray, obese cat, leapt up onto the table by the door to bat at my bag.

"We found the squirrel," I said lamely, smiling to soften the blow.

"It only took you a week." Eric held out his hands for my backpack.

"But we found it." Devon flopped down onto the couch. "Had to run all over Central Park, mind you."

"One down, two to go." Eric pulled the shimmering cage that held Nutty McDragon from my bag. "At least we hope only two."

"Just try for optimism." Devon sighed and closed his eyes.

"I'm sorry," I said for the millionth time. You see, the same day I accidentally made Big Blue, I did another spell. One I thought hadn't worked at all. Only it had. Little bits of magic drifted off into Central Park and did a minuscule amount of damage to a few of the resident animals. And by damage, I mean an extra head and lizard tail. At least for Nutty. We hadn't actually seen the other two animals.

"What in the hell are you going to do with it?" Mom leaned in to examine Nutty, her eyes narrowing as he chittered at her. "I will not have an animal exterminated in my home."

My mom would never kill a mouse or rat or anything in our apartment. I never pointed out the irony of letting Mrs. Mops do the killing for her. I just wanted the rodents dead, and if Mrs. Mops wanted to be a vermin serial killer, so be it.

"Can you make him a normal squirrel again?" I sank onto the couch next to Devon.

"It might be possible." Eric held Nutty up to the light. "But it would be difficult to remove the right head. I'm not entirely sure which holds most of the poor thing's brain."

"So, what are you going to do?" I asked over Mrs. Mop's growling as her paws slid uselessly down Nutty's cage.

"Rehome it." Eric shrugged. "I can take it to Beville. The thing seems to have a reasonable temperament. There might be someone in need of a new pet."

"Would Lola want him?" I asked, thinking of her colorful home with lots of drapes to climb.

"Lola doesn't approve of rodents." Eric placed Nutty back into my backpack. "And I don't think Lola's guard would like him hanging around either. Don't worry, I'll find a home for him somewhere. You should concentrate on finding whatever other disasters you created."

"Any tips on how to start?" My feet throbbed at the very thought of tracking down the other two creatures I'd inadvertently created.

"The same I've given before. Track the magic in Central Park. If it's an animal that doesn't look right, catch it before we have any more magic making headline news." Eric strode to the door. "Call me when you've found something else."

And with that, Eric, Nutty, and my backpack were all gone.

"I really don't like that man." Mom got out the vacuum and started cleaning where Eric had stood. "I really, really don't like that man."

"I can meet him somewhere else." I spoke over the *whir* of the vacuum, hope rising a centimeter in my chest at the suggestion.

"You are not meeting him unsupervised," Mom half-shouted. "I may not be able to keep my son from being a wizard, but I will not have him fraternizing with criminals without supervision."

"Right." I didn't dare look at Devon. "You're totally right."

"Ms. Miller, is it okay if Bryant comes out with me tonight? I want to walk around, but it wouldn't be safe to go alone." Devon sounded disgustingly sincere, young, and hopeful.

"Of course, Devon." Mom nodded. "I think Bryant spending time with his *normal* friends is a great idea."

"Thanks, Ms. Miller." Devon and I both leapt to our feet.

My legs twinged in protest at being asked to move again. But sitting wasn't an option. We had places to be, and we still had our coats on and everything.

"Be back soon," I said as we walked into the corridor.

"You should invite Elizabeth," Mom called after us.

"Only your mother would worry more about you spending time with your mentor than your girlfriend," Eric said in a thoroughly bored and disdainful tone as he leaned next to our door, holding my red backpack.

My stomach did an Olympic gymnastics floor routine at the word *girlfriend*.

"Well, Elizabeth has never almost gotten all of us killed," Devon said as we headed down the hall.

Eric smiled. "Touché."

2

The steps down to the Columbus Circle subway station were crammed with people. New Yorkers looking harassed, tourists looking confused. A man with steel drums thumped out "O Christmas Tree" with a red-and-white top hat sitting in front of him for tips. The sun had started to set, and New York was ready for Christmas magic in a way only a city built on shining lights and commercialism could ever be.

"How long do you think we have?" Devon asked.

"Before my mom freaks out?" I asked, not wanting to voice the other options for answers to that question.

"If we make good time to Beville," Eric said, weaving through tourists with a vague look of disapproval on his face, "we should be able to get a full hour of training in and get you home before your mother begins to panic. It really would be much simpler if you could move to Beville, or at the very least were able to spend more than a few hours a week on your training."

"My mom can't know you're teaching me anything." I ducked under the flailing arms of a gaggle of girls trying to take a selfie. "If she knew, she'd want to be there, and then she'd know what we're doing, and then she could end up in a magical cocoon halfway to dead again."

"I totally agree we need to keep your mom as far away from magic as we can, Bry," Devon said as we made it inside the station. "But how long do you think she's going to buy you're only seeing Eric for critter capture reasons?"

"Listen to the boy, Bryant," Eric said. "I have a feeling Mr. Rhodes has spent a fair amount of time lying to ladies. He must be an expert by now."

"I resent that," Devon said as we passed the ticket machines.

A pack of tourists had lined up, trying to buy subway passes. The New Yorkers behind them looked like they might riot if the tourists couldn't figure out how to insert their credit cards stat.

"I may have worked my way through a fair number of women—"

"More like girls," I countered.

Devon ignored me "But I have never lied, cheated, or..."

They kept going, Devon prattling on about chivalry or something, Eric laughing snobbishly at him, both agreeing my mom would find out about my secret wizard training eventually. But their words got all muffled under the blissful humming in my ears as soon as I saw Elizabeth leaning against the subway platform wall.

She looked at me with her sparkly, perfect eyes, and her smile made my heart fly right out of my chest. Wind seemed to carry her gently toward me as her black and blonde-streaked hair floated around her shoulders.

Her fingers twined through mine, and she kissed me gently. As soon as our lips touched, my brain went even fuzzier, like I was living the happiest dream any human has ever had.

"We got one," Devon said, interrupting our moment and bringing me shattering back to Nutty McDragon-inhabited reality.

"Really?" Elizabeth turned to Devon but kept her hand firmly in mine.

"There are still two more to go." Eric led us down a side corridor. "And I doubt the next two will be as easy to catch."

"Thanks for that cheerful thought," I muttered.

Eric stopped in front of a blank stretch of wall, glanced around, then murmured. "*Portunda.*" With a tiny *crack* and a sprinkle of dust, a door appeared in the wall.

"Well, if you would help us, we could find them in a day and be done with it." Devon stepped through the newly created door.

"You and Bryant made the mistake—it is up to the two of you to fix it," Eric said.

My eyes swept the corridor. No one seemed to care that a door had appeared where it shouldn't have been. They were all too busy trying to avoid being pummeled by giant bags stuffed with Christmas gifts to spare us a glance.

Elizabeth pulled me gently through the door, and Eric shut it behind us.

"*Portundo.* It's good for you to work on your own, and I have other things to be getting on with."

A knot settled in my stomach as we started down the long, sloping tunnel. Tiles mixed with the rough stone of the floor, and dim lights hung overhead. I knew the walk down to Beville well. It had become a sort of tri-weekly pilgrimage.

I could meet with Eric aboveground to chat about catching the unfortunate critters, or for coffee and tales about the history and hierarchy of magic, but for actual spell practice, we had to go belowground to Beville. Where all the wizards in New York lived and no one would get too mad if I accidentally caught something on fire while trying to levitate. Unless I caught a person on fire. That guy had gotten really, really mad.

"Speaking of other things for you to be getting on with," Devon said after we had been walking in silence for a few minutes, "any word on our impending doom?"

"Mr. Rhodes, have you learned nothing about discretion?" Eric sighed.

"Elizabeth, are there any creepy crawlies listening to us?" Devon stopped and turned toward Elizabeth.

She squinted into the dark corners of the tunnel, watching shadowy details I couldn't hope to see. "We're alone."

"It is useful having a seer around." Eric nodded.

"A baby seer," Elizabeth corrected.

"Still more skilled than the rest of us." Eric bowed. "There have been rumors of the Ladies. Activity in the Consortium and rumblings in the Library. The Consortium hasn't reopened for business yet, but we can assume it will quite soon. The residents of Beville are growing restless without the Library's resources. And without the Ladies' rule, others have tried to step into their place."

"On a scale of one to ten, how screwed are we?" Devon asked casually.

"I'd give us a seven." Eric turned and continued down the sloping tunnel. "We didn't destroy the Ladies in the Battle of Beville. Thaden did that."

My neck tensed at the name. It's hard to shake the bone-chilling fear of the guy who tried to kill you, even after he's dead.

"Though they might be a little testy about my slight rebellion," Eric said.

"A bit of an understatement, but sure," Elizabeth said.

"And allowing signs of magic to be seen aboveground is strictly forbidden."

"Sorry," I mumbled.

"Which is why it is of the utmost importance you catch the animals you altered. It is a show of good faith that you are trying to fix your mistakes."

"And you think Bryant catching the freaky squirrel is going to make the Ladies forget all the things they've tried to kill us for? Or now that most of them got slaughtered while they were trying to kill us, you think they'll just give it up as a bad job and leave us alone?" Devon said, fear barely audible beneath his cavalier tone.

"Of course they won't," Eric said. "They will blame us for the loss of their comrades and the disruption of order. But when they decide to come for us, I would like to have as much reason and justice on our side as possible."

"And when exactly do you think they might come?" Worry wiggled in my stomach.

"In a few years," Eric said as we entered the cavern.

My stomach stopped doing the terrified tango. In a few years, I might be competent enough to defend myself.

"Or they might come tomorrow while you're all clustered together at your lunch table," Eric said, bringing the dancing belly right back. "That's the trouble with having enemies who are powerful and slow to age. They lack the sense of urgency one requires when planning an appropriate defense."

We cut sideways around the giant column of stone that jutted up from the center of the street. Cracked and crumbling bits of rock littered the ground, but the stone spire itself was perfectly smooth as it rose from Beville to Times Square. I shuddered, remembering casting the spell that trapped Thaden in the stone, but Elizabeth, Devon, and Eric didn't spare the thing a glance. I guess they were used to it after having walked around it every time we went to Eric's house. And I suppose when you're in an underground city of magic there are better things to consider strange than a column of stone.

Rows of houses pressed up to the wide stone walls, which soared to the ceiling thirty feet overhead. Some of the houses looked like normal brownstones from the city above. Others...not so much. One house had taken the shape of an enormous clock tower, and another tiny house perched high up in a tree. But we aimed for the gray stone house next to the white, clapboard Victorian.

The door to the house swung open as soon as Eric set foot on the stairs.

"Hello, old girl." Eric patted the doorjamb.

The floor of the house creaked as Eric stepped into the foyer, a low rumble that sounded almost like a cat purring filled the air.

"I'll see you in a bit." Elizabeth kissed my cheek and headed down the long hall toward the parlor where Eric kept his illegal collection of wizard-type books.

Devon and I followed Eric the other way, past the rows of shiny, locked, wooden doors, stopping at the very last door in the hall.

"You know, it really would be more useful if you went with Elizabeth and studied." Eric gave Devon a side-eyed glare as he opened the door to the training room. "You can observe Bryant learning magic as much as you like, but you will never be a wizard. Wizards are born, not created through observation."

"I like to think of myself as a chaperone." Devon grinned and pushed past Eric. "It's your job to train Bryant to survive the Ladies and whatever other shit your crazy magical mess can throw at him. It's my job to make sure *you* don't kill Bryant."

"Thanks, Devon." I punched him in the arm on my way to the center of the room.

I'd never say it out loud, but having Devon with me in training really did make our imminent death feel a little further away.

The training room had been a ballroom. Shining parquet floors sparkled under a giant crystal chandler. Wallpaper with gold inlay glistened above and below the intricately carved chair rail. Our footsteps echoed around the room that, by non-magic standards, was too large to fit in the house. A lot of the rooms in Eric's house were too large to fit in Eric's house. It always felt a little bit creepy, like I was standing in a place that wasn't meant to exist. But it was just another charming part of living with magic, accepting the impossible as a part of daily life.

"So what are we working on today?" I asked as I shrugged out of my coat and tossed it to Devon. "Lightning whips to bind attackers? Levitation to distract enemies? I made the cage work for Nutty."

"It is a pretty great cage," Devon said as Eric pulled Nutty out of my backpack.

"An excellent cage." Eric set Nutty on the ground. "*Vanexo.*" Nutty's shimmering cage disappeared. "But you need more of a challenge to be getting on with. *Libargo.*"

With a *screech*, Nutty grew, not stopping until he had reached the size of a Great Dane. Nutty thumped his arm-width tail happily on the ground, shaking the floor. The chandelier creaked in protest.

"Nutty," Eric said. Both of Nutty's heads swiveled to Eric. Light glinted off his black and red eyes. Eric smiled and pointed at me. "Attack."

"What the—" I didn't have time to finish swearing at Eric before Nutty launched himself at my face like he knew damn well I was responsible for his newfound two-headedness.

I opened my mouth to shout a spell, but couldn't think of a spell to shout that wouldn't hurt poor Nutty.

Nutty didn't care as much about hurting me. His claws dug into my shoulders, and his tail whacked me in the stomach, knocking the wind out of me. But his two mouths baring sharp teeth were the most terrifying.

"*Conorvo!*" I screamed the spell, but Nutty didn't shrink. I managed to get my bleeding arm under his stomach and toss him off me before he shredded my face. "*Primurgo!*" My shield shimmered into being around me.

Nutty threw himself at my shield, spitting and hissing.

"You cannot simply hide in a shield, Bryant." Eric rolled his eyes at me. "The point is for you to learn how to fight, not hide."

"Hiding sounds like a much better option!"

"You can do it, Bry," Devon cheered me on from his nice, safe, non-bleeding place by the door.

"You know what? Fine." I let go of the magic holding up my shield. "*Kunga.*" The spell whipped out and struck Nutty in the stomach like I'd sucker-punched him. He skidded across the glass-smooth floor, furry little butt over head. I didn't have time for the self-loathing at hitting an animal to set in before the demon had gotten back to his feet and charged, teeth gnashing.

"Oh, it's on."

3

"Ouch, ouch," I grunted with every step as I hobbled my way back out of the Columbus Circle subway station, wishing PETA would just come after me for battling an evil animal and put me out of my misery. "Ouch."

Elizabeth was kind enough not to laugh as she wrapped her arm around my waist to help me up the stairs. It was nearly ten, and the daytime crowds had cleared. It was nice not to be buffeted by people with every step, but it left more chances for people to notice me.

"You should just heal yourself, dude," Devon said in a stage whisper. "Eric told you to try it."

"Shh," Elizabeth warned as a man cut a wide arc on the stairs to avoid coming near me.

I didn't blame him. Dear sweet Nutty McDragon had left cuts on my cheek and arms with his claws and a nice bite on my right calf. My coat covered the blood on my arms, but not what leaked out of my face, and my pants were torn and gross.

"I was just saying he should." Devon shrugged.

"And risk healing my nose right off my face?" I whimpered as we made it to level ground, preparing myself for the rest of the torturous walk home.

"It could be a new fashion." Devon grinned.

"Really not helping, Dev." Elizabeth glared at him.

He shrunk a little under her sparkly glare. "I'm just gonna take the long way home." Devon stepped out of Elizabeth's reach, giving an Eric-like bow. "I'll see you at school tomorrow, oh wonderful squirrel tamer."

"Devon!" Before Elizabeth could shout anything else at him, he disappeared into a crowd of drunken tourists.

"It was a little funny," I said meekly.

"It's not funny at all." Elizabeth kept her arm around me even though we were walking on flat sidewalks. "Having your face scratched half off by a mutant rodent is not funny."

"A least it wasn't a mutant turtle," I muttered.

A tiny smile glimmered on her lips for a moment. "But what's your mom going to say? What are you going to tell her?"

"Bar fight?"

"It's not funny." Elizabeth stopped and stepped in front of me to look into my poop-brown eyes with her diamond ones. "Eric letting a monster maul you isn't funny. Hiding what we're doing isn't funny. I"—she ran her hands through her hair, mussing her multicolored curls in the most breathtaking way—"I know you need to train. I know you need to learn to fight. We all chose to be a part of Beville and magic and all of it. We all knew it wouldn't always be safe…"

"But?" I wrapped my arms around her waist. It still astounded me that she didn't tell me not to touch her. That she actually melted a little and drew herself closer to me.

"But," she began, tears glistening in the corners of her eyes, "if this is what a training session with a demonic squirrel—"

"A magically enhanced demonic squirrel."

"—leaves you looking like, what's going to happen when the Ladies decide to come after us again?" Elizabeth pressed on. "Or when some of Thaden's creatures decide to crawl up from the shadows? Or some evil asshole decides to take Thaden's place?"

"We'll figure it out."

She pressed her forehead to mine.

Even in frozen Manhattan, where the scent of gas and garbage were the usual aromas, Elizabeth smelled like fresh spring flowers.

"I almost lost you once." Elizabeth brushed her lips against mine. "I don't want to do that again."

I smiled. I mean a broad, soul-glowing smile.

It might seem weird since Elizabeth was talking about the time I had nearly died. But having the most wonderful girl in the world look truly terrified at the prospect of losing you can sort of make your heart grow three sizes.

"If something happens again—"

"*When* it happens," Elizabeth said. "This is Eric we're talking about. Disaster is a *when* with Eric Deldridge as our fearless leader."

"*When* some new scary thing comes our way, we'll be better prepared." I brushed the tears from her cold cheek with my equally icy thumb. "We've been training hard. I actually understand a teeny tiny bit about how to use magic. When another monster or Lady or whatever comes after us, we'll be ready. I promise."

A gust of freezing wind whipped down the street. Elizabeth huddled her face into my coat as the sudden cold tore past us.

"We should get home." Elizabeth took my hand and pulled me down the street as soon as the wind stopped. "There must be a storm coming."

But the prickle on my neck didn't stop when the night went back to its normal level of unpleasant cold. The feeling of dread followed me the rest of the way home and settled itself into my stomach as I wondered if it had been meteorology or fate that blasted us on the sidewalk.

I didn't say anything to Elizabeth as we walked hunched against the cold, gripping hands and moving as quickly as my hobbled leg could carry me. We didn't stop until we reached the florescent-lit lobby of my building.

"Do you want me to come up?" Elizabeth asked.

It wasn't like a *Do you want me to come up* in a Hollywood movie kind of way. It was a *Hey, do you want me to come and lie to your mom for you since you're incapable of lying in a convincing manner* sort of thing.

"I don't know." I touched the squirrel cuts on my face.

"Dude," the desk guy said, inexplicably choosing this moment to actually care what was happening in the lobby, "you should put some cream on that."

"Right, cream. Thanks." Elizabeth took me by the elbow and led me to the elevator. "We'll just tell your mom Nutty broke out of his cage."

"Eric was supposed to have left the building without us." I leaned against the wall by the elevator door, trying not to wonder why it was making such a low grinding sound. "Was I mugged?"

"She'd want to file a police report." Elizabeth frowned. Lines appeared on her forehead. They were the cutest little lines I had ever seen.

"We could say I fell?"

"And got perfectly lined up cuts and a bite mark?"

"Pissed off a dog walker with an angry dog?"

"Do you want your mom to make you get rabies shots?" Elizabeth asked. She bit her lips together and glanced up and down the abandoned hallway. "I think you should try a healing spell. Eric wouldn't have told you to do it if he didn't think you could."

I swallowed a laugh.

"You can't just walk around like this. Those cuts could get infected," Elizabeth whispered. "He may be a lizard squirrel, but you were still bitten by a wild animal."

I opened my mouth to argue, found I didn't have an argument to make, and sighed. "Fine, but if I end up with no nose—"

"I won't dump you." Elizabeth kissed the tip of my nose. "Just in case I never see it again."

"Thanks." I pulled the black cell phone from my pocket. Even after everything that phone had been through, it still looked perfect. Not a crack in the glass, not a ding in the case. I pressed my thumb to the scanner, and the screen instantly blinked on.

I swiped over to the healing app—a shimmering drop of blood against a white background. The image didn't make me feel any better.

"Should we go into the elevator?" Elizabeth asked as the door dinged open.

I shook my head, scanning the spells in the app. If something went wrong, I definitely didn't want to be sans nose and trapped in the world's jankiest elevator.

Flesh wounds. The straightforward description seemed promising. Like the phone was finally trying to make one damned thing easy. Like it had tried to idiot proof magical healing.

I clicked on the underlined words.

Healing a flesh wound is a rudimentary skill. The incantation to be used is Sinato. *If, however, there is venom present in the wound, the venom must be treated before the skin can be healed. If the venom is healed into the skin, the venom will become integrated with the new flesh and impossible to remove. Death will be inevitable.*

"Inevitable death," I murmured. "Sounds great."

"Does Nutty have venom?" Elizabeth asked.

"I don't think so. I don't feel sick or tingly or anything." I mouthed *Sinato*, rolling it around in my mouth until it felt natural. "Here goes nothing." I glanced up and down the hall one more time before speaking. "*Sinato.*"

The pain was instant. Like someone had poured boiling hydrogen peroxide into each of the cuts. I groaned and pounded the wall, trying not to shout as healing seared through my calf.

"Not in the hallway, dude," the desk guy called from around the corner, "or in the elevator. That thing is on its last leg."

Elizabeth rolled her eyes and pressed the button, making the doors open with a shudder. Wrapping her arm around me again, she half-dragged me into the elevator.

The subtle flickering of the lights sent bile flying into my throat as the elevator shook its way up, and the pain petered out.

"Do I look okay?" I asked as soon as I could open my mouth without fear of vomit.

Elizabeth took my chin in her hand and tipped my head around in the light.

"You look like you scratched your face too hard." She smiled and kissed my cheek, right where the cuts had been. "I think you just learned a new trick."

"I guess I did." I leaned in and kissed her. The world spun around me, or maybe the elevator was just super shaky, but time stopped, and I pulled Elizabeth in tighter. Her scent filled my lungs, and my heart galloped out of my chest.

The elevator *ding* yanked us out of eternity.

Elizabeth laced her fingers through mine, and we walked out of the elevator. With Elizabeth next to me, the dingy hall didn't seem so depressing. I couldn't smell old people and cheap cleaner, just fresh spring flowers.

"*Cliaxo*," I said, not wanting to let go of Elizabeth's hand to fish the keys out of my pocket. The keyhole turned, and the door swung open just in time for me to see my mom flop down onto the couch in an overly causal pose.

"Oh, Elizabeth!" Mom said brightly. "I didn't know the boys were meeting you."

"I caught up with them." Elizabeth smiled, bending to try and coax Mrs. Mops over to her.

"Did you have a nice walk with Devon?" Mom asked as Mrs. Mops growled at Elizabeth. The cat hadn't really trusted anyone but Mom since we abandoned her in the wreckage of our old apartment while we were running for our lives.

"I think he just needed some time to walk." Elizabeth pulled her hand out of Mrs. Mops' reach the second before she would have needed me to heal her with my new skills.

"I'm glad you all could spend some nice time together, doing normal things."

There was an awkward pause where my mom's disapproval of all things magical hung heavily in the air.

"Do your parents know you're out?" Mom looked at the clock in the corner. It was a big grandfather clock, which looked like it should be a family heirloom but in reality had been bought at a secondhand store when Mom was frantically scrambling to make this den of linoleum look homey.

"Sure," Elizabeth said a little too brightly. "I have another half hour till curfew."

It was a lie and I knew it, but I smiled along. The laundry list of things my mother didn't know grew by the second.

"Do you want Bryant to walk you home?" Mom offered. "I hate for you to be out alone at night."

"I'll take a cab."

I pulled out my wallet and grabbed a twenty. "Here." I passed the crisp bill to Elizabeth before Mom could come up with an argument against Elizabeth leaving alone.

"Thanks." Elizabeth rolled her eyes, playing the exasperated girlfriend of the rich kid perfectly.

"See you tomorrow, then." Mom headed to her bedroom, allowing Elizabeth and me a moment to say goodbye alone.

Elizabeth tried to pass the twenty back to me.

"Dad money." I shook my head. "Just keep it. And be careful."

"Always." Elizabeth brushed her lips gently against mine. "See you tomorrow."

My heart tightened in my chest as she shut the door. I leaned against the doorjamb, listening to her footsteps fading away.

I knew where she was going. To ride the subway. To sit on a dark corner. To watch the shadows and learn their secrets. She promised she was safe. So did Eric. They both said she was protected in a tone that meant I wasn't supposed to ask questions. But knowing the girl you're in love with is going to walk around Manhattan alone at night makes your heart panic, no matter who tells you she's safe.

When I couldn't hear her anymore, I went to the bathroom. The scratches on my face were barely visible. Little faint lines of pink cutting through the usual pastiness.

Elizabeth's parents thought she was interning backstage at a Broadway show. Another lie to another mom. Elizabeth wasn't practicing being a seer. Oh, no. She was living her theatrical dream. A horrible, unbelievable lie Devon and Eric had concocted.

Devon's parents thought I was going through a mid-teen crisis and Devon had become my personal handler. His parents hadn't bothered to ask if my having a nervous breakdown was going to be a bad influence on their son. They just let him stay out till all hours without question. Devon always seemed a little disappointed he hadn't been grounded for disappearing for hours at a time. He should have been the wizard. His parents wouldn't have minded him training with Eric. If they had even noticed.

Mom thought I was only meeting with Eric enough to fulfill my magical legal obligation of animal spell clean up and to learn enough magic to not accidentally blow myself up. She was super happy to let me wander around Manhattan with my girlfriend or best friend. Curfew didn't matter as long as there was no spell work involved.

And Dad...he thought his penthouse had been destroyed in a freak accident. He didn't know about the whole wizard thing at all.

It was so many lies to keep straight, thinking of it made my head pound and my half-frozen hands sweat.

All three of us had made the choice to be in the magical world. To learn and fight, to face danger and adventure. But the lying?

I don't think any of us had bargained for that.

4

"This isn't a proscenium stage," Mom's voice rang out over the actors who were being overly rambunctious for a 7:00 a.m. rehearsal. "You don't have the audience only on one side. The audience is surrounding you. You have to play to all sides."

"Excuse me, Ms. Miller," a tiny freshman piped in. "I thought you said we were supposed to cheat out so the audience could see us."

"You *were* supposed to cheat out when we had a stage." Mom's voice was a frightening mix of fatigue and frustration. "Our stage burned down, as I am sure you remember." All the theatre students nodded as one. "Since we don't have a stage, we are going to be performing in here." Mom swept her arms around, indicating the gym. She did it in an exciting and enthusiastic way that didn't show how depressing it really was to have moved from a giant theatre to a parquet-floored gym with acoustics only capable of making shoes squeal louder.

"Since we're going to be performing in here, we need to face all sides, we need to wear quiet shoes, and we need to project!" Mom had a manic look in her eyes, so I tuned out while she went on with the cleaning rehearsal for *A Christmas Carol.*

We should have been doing the show on the stage, but I accidentally burned down the whole theatre as my first act of magic. We should have been rehearsing after school when any of the poor actors had a shot at remembering their lines. I should have been sucking at helping my mom build a set, but there was no set to be built. Everything had turned into a pile of penniless theatrical poo after the fire, so I was painting signs for this afternoon's bake sale.

Wizard by night, cookie hawker by day. The oh-so-varied life of Bryant Jameson Adams.

They had gotten to the part where Elizabeth and Devon were both onstage. Devon was playing the young Ebenezer Scrooge and Elizabeth his love interest. For a minute, my stomach squirmed jealously as he knelt and proposed to Elizabeth, and I looked away as they kissed. It was weird—way, way weird—to have your best friend kiss your girlfriend. But better Devon than anyone else. Every other straight guy in school would kill to have Elizabeth Wick be their girlfriend. Devon was the only one I trusted to resist the lure of her sparkly eyes enough to not chase the girl of my dreams.

"Dammit," I cursed quietly as I looked at the sign I had been painting. The crooked letters now read *Cookis for sale.* I buried my face in my hands, half-tempted to search the phone for a way to erase paint, but it wasn't worth it. I chucked the sign and moved on to a new sheet of poster board.

I didn't get a chance to actually talk to Elizabeth or Devon until lunch. Devon and I had all our classes together, but they weren't really ideal places for conversation.

"You okay?" I asked Elizabeth as soon as she sat down at our table, her tray laden with something that looked like it could be spaghetti and meatballs if you weren't really sure what spaghetti and meatballs were supposed to be.

"I'm golden." Elizabeth smiled tiredly and snuck a bottle of coffee out of her bag, adding in a whisper. "The life juice of seers."

"Did you actually *see* anything?" Devon murmured after looking casually around. He did it well, like he was searching for a cute girl to hit on instead of prying ears.

"A few creepy crawlies." Elizabeth shrugged. "Nothing of any real interest."

"And you were safe?" I pulled my lunch out of its bag. I had been in the back of the faculty meeting where they discussed the health department almost shutting down the cafeteria a month before, and I hadn't been able to eat the food since.

"I was safe." Elizabeth nodded. "I was the safest girl in Manhattan."

"Except for the people who weren't out looking for things that go bump in the night and were tucked safely in their warm beds." Devon waved a French fry. "They were probably safer."

"Please don't mention beds." Elizabeth lifted her coffee, but before it could reach her mouth, a beefy hand caught it.

"What is this?" The evil lunch lady towered behind Elizabeth, her wide face twisted in a quasi-comical frown.

"My drink," Elizabeth growled, not releasing her grip on the glass bottle.

"The school board doesn't want coffee or soda in this school." The lunch lady's grating, low voice made the nerves in my neck twitch.

It was true though. A bunch of parents had banded together to get soda, coffee, and all things joyful banned from the school. They had ranted about negative health effects and concentration in class. Kids could pound a latte on the sidewalk, but pass through the school doors, and it was no coffee allowed.

"I'm so sorry," Elizabeth said, speaking in a cheerful tone through clenched teeth. "I totally forgot. But I mixed my medicine with it, so now I really need to drink it."

With a tug of her beefy hand the lunch lady yanked the coffee from Elizabeth's grasp, splashing the front of her shirt with brown. "I'm sure the nurse has your medicine in stock." The lunch lady grinned like a Cheshire cat, showing her yellowed teeth.

"You just splashed her." I leapt chivalrously to my girlfriend's defense. "You could at least say sorry."

The lunch lady's eyes flashed to me. She looked from my unruly hair to my clenched hands, and her smile grew. "How nice to find a hero in the lunchroom." With a laugh like she was hocking up phlegm, she turned and waddled away, holding her prize above her head for all to see.

"That woman truly is evil." Elizabeth's voice shook as she tried to sponge the coffee from her shirt with a flimsy paper napkin.

"If only you could tell her you needed the caffeine to stay awake after prowling the city by night to try and find the next big bad who wants to bring destruction and death down on all of us." Devon glared after the lunch lady.

"Move your hands," I whispered.

Elizabeth moved her hands and leaned toward me.

"*Nudla.*" I spoke the word below a whisper. With a *hiss*, the stain vanished.

"My boyfriend, the magical dry cleaner." Elizabeth kissed me on the cheek.

"Not in my cafeteria!" the lunch lady hollered.

Elizabeth sat back, grinding her teeth loud enough for me to hear.

"Are we all set for the bake sale?" Devon asked. I think he was more trying to distract Elizabeth from throwing her tray at the coffee thief than actually concerned about the cookies.

"We have everything in order." Elizabeth's jaw gradually loosened as she spoke so she wasn't talking through her teeth. "There are posters lining the halls. The cash box and merchandise are ready in Ms. Miller's office. And all of us will be released early from our last classes to sell at the final bell."

"Then move to the sidewalk to freeze while we sell the extras." Devon nodded. "I love live theatre."

My phone buzzed in my pocket. Not the magic one, the normal one.

I pulled it out under the table, careful not to let the lunch lady see in case she decided it was cafeteria contraband.

A text message showed on the screen.

You should be on lunch. Come outside now. Tell no one.

You would think the message had come from Eric or a mob boss. But there was a little tag underneath.

~Dad

My mind went blank for a second, then raced to think of what I possibly could have done to make my dad come see me at school. Or, more likely, send someone to come see me at school. Ever since Eric and I had fought an epic battle that destroyed my dad's penthouse that he still didn't know I was mostly responsible for, I had been on my best behavior.

Unless my dad had finally found out it was me who destroyed his home.

My stomach dropped past my butt and shattered. I stood up slowly, my legs shaking.

"Are you okay?" Devon asked. "You just got super pale, Bry."

"Oh God, is it venom?" Elizabeth turned white. "Does Nutty have venom?"

"What was on your phone?" Devon asked.

"A-a," I stammered dumbly. "A reminder I had a project. I set it for the wrong time. I forgot my paper. I'm gonna see if Mom can print it." I turned and ran out of the cafeteria before either of them could argue with my ridiculously lame and unbelievable excuse.

The weight of another set of lies twisted the shards of my shattered stomach.

I slowed my speed as I walked down the hall toward the front door of the school. I wasn't technically forbidden to go outside during lunch, but if I acted like something was wrong, I could get stopped.

It might seem weird that I was so freaked out about my dad asking me to meet him outside, and it wasn't just the cryptic message. Seeing my dad wasn't like a weekly or even monthly ritual. He was always away doing important business things. Most of my time with him over the last few years consisted of grabbing a coffee on one of his infrequent visits to the city. But since his penthouse got wrecked, he'd been in town more often than usual. Once to file the insurance claim, then to meet with a realtor, then to sign the papers on his new fancy brownstone. Unless he was here to purchase a priceless antique rug to go with the vibe of his new place, there was no reasonable explanation for him coming back so soon.

I made it out the front door without any more than a suspicious glare from the ancient biology teacher. For a second, I expected my dad to be standing outside, but he wasn't. And there wasn't a fancy black car waiting obtrusively in front of the school either. As I looked around, my phone buzzed in my hand.

Turn left.

I squinted down the street. At the far end of the block was a big black car.

"Great," I muttered, keeping my head down against the wind as it tore through my sweater.

I walked as fast as I could without looking like I was trying to escape from high school. As soon as I reached the car, the back door swung open, and a familiar voice said, "You should've stopped to get your coat, Bryant. You're going to freeze to death out here."

He didn't want me dead. That was a good sign.

"You said now." I slid into the backseat of the car and closed the door, keeping in the precious warmth.

Dad pulled me into an awkward side hug, ruffling my hair like I was still five. It only lasted for a moment, and then he leaned back in his seat looking cool and calm as ever. My dad was the opposite of me. Blue eyes, black curly hair just long enough to make him look like a Hollywood star, and a chiseled jaw to complete the Greek god look.

"How are you, Bryant?" Dad asked. "School going all right?"

"Yeah, fine." It wasn't his real question, and I knew it.

"Excellent." Dad smiled. "And how is your mother's new apartment?"

We were getting closer to it now.

"Not as homey as the old one, but it works." I shrugged, trying not to betray how much I hated the linoleum. "The neighborhood is good, and we have an elevator."

That might get all of us killed.

"It's amazing how much real estate is available in this area if you know where to look." Dad's tone was all contemplative, like he was just coming to a remarkable conclusion. "I bet there are some excellent places to be found—"

"If mom would only use your realtor?" I finished for him. "She's never going to go for it, Dad."

"Buying is a wise investment."

"She doesn't have money for a down payment." I felt like a traitor saying it out loud. That's the problem with having one super rich parent and one normal one—it's hard for them to understand each other. Mom was doing fine, but not fine enough to buy a two bedroom in Manhattan.

"She wouldn't need one," Dad said. "Not if she had someone willing to co-sign on the loan."

"No." I shook my head so hard the leather interior of the car went blurry. "No, no, no, no, no. Never in a billion years would Mom let you co-sign a loan for her. No."

"I want you to at least mention it." Dad passed me a shiny black folder. "There are ten properties in this area that would work well for you two. And the mortgage wouldn't be more than your mother is paying in rent with the right kind of loan."

"We're fine."

"This is as much for her as it is for you. You'll be off to college soon, but your mother will still be in the city. She'll probably retire a teacher in the Manhattan school system. Her life will be easier if she owns an apartment. At least try and convince her. It's for her own good."

"But..." I wanted to say no again and toss the folder on the floor of the car, but the *but* was he was right. If she could own a place of her own....

"And how is the theatre reconstruction going?" Dad pressed on, apparently unaware of the deep-seeded issues I was trying to sort through.

"Good, fine. The school had a ton of insurance." I tried not to let my mind wander to how much I had cost the insurance industry with my badly used magic. "It's going to take some time for all of it to come in and for reconstruction to start. We're doing some fundraisers to rent show stuff and a space for the performances until they can build a new theatre."

"I've heard as much."

"From who?"

Dad didn't answer. Instead, he reached down and pulled out a lunch bag. One of the kind that's tapered at the top like a folded over paper bag but is really made of fabric and insulation.

"Finding a space in Manhattan isn't easy or cheap." Dad set the lunch bag on top of the folder on my lap.

Hands shaking, I opened the bag. A mound of money sat inside. "How much?"

"A hundred thousand," Dad said like it was nothing. Like he really was just giving me lunch money.

"No, Dad, no." I tried to push the bag back. "She won't take it."

"She will if she doesn't know it's from me." Dad closed the top of the bag and shoved it back toward me. "You're working the bake sale. Slip it in with the rest of the money at the end of the day."

"'Cause that won't be suspicious."

"It doesn't matter if it's suspicious. If she can't prove it's from me, she'll have to take it." Dad grinned, and for a second I could almost picture him as the young idealist my mom had fallen in love with in Bryant Park.

"Why?" I begged. "Why do you, do *I*, have to do this? She'll be fine on her own. We'll figure it out somehow. We always have."

"Your mother and I may not always agree, and we definitely don't get along, but she is the mother of my son, and I want her to have a decent place to grow old in." He pressed the folder to my chest. "And she is an amazing teacher who has spent too much time building this program to let it crumble."

"Dad."

"I have more money than I could possibly use." He held a hand up so I wouldn't interrupt. "Don't argue with me because I want to do something good with it. Why should I be blamed if the good has to do with my family?"

"She won't go for the apartment." I felt my fight deflating like a shriveled-up balloon of dying hope.

"I'm only asking you to try."

"She'll know the money came from you."

"She won't be able to prove it."

"This is such a bad idea." I buried my face in my cold hands.

"It's a brilliant idea, Bryant. You'll see." He reached across me and opened to car door. "Now get back in there and try to learn something."

"Thanks, Dad." I stepped back into the cold. "I'll try."

"Good. I love you, Son." With a wave, my dad shut the door and the car pulled away, not pausing for me to call *I love you* back.

5

I stood on the sidewalk for a second, holding a folder of real estate printouts in one hand and a hundred thousand dollars in the other. It wasn't until I started shivering that I realized I really should go back inside.

Back inside and do what? Put the money in my locker and leave it until the end of the day?

"Dammit, Dad."

I turned to go back inside, but a wall of black blocked me.

"Do you really think it wise to be walking around outside without a coat?" Eric asked, one black eyebrow arched high on his alabaster forehead. "Have you decided to use a little trick from the phone to keep warm? It might draw unnecessary attention, but I applaud your embracing magic."

"I came out here to talk to my dad."

"The mystery father appeared?" Eric looked up and down the street as though hoping to catch a glimpse of him.

"Just because you've never met him doesn't mean he's a mystery." I started my trudge back to school.

"No, your lack of understanding of your patriarch makes him a mystery. And where do you think you're going?" Eric stepped in front of me.

"Back to school." I pointed over Eric's shoulder. "Back to slave away in my brick prison."

"I hate to ruin your plans for education, but I'm afraid there is other urgent business that needs tending to."

"What business?"

Eric took his phone from his pocket and pulled up a picture—a three-headed deer running across the GW Bridge.

"Oh sh—" I won't write out all the curses that flew from my mouth.

"This picture appeared on the Internet after one of your little casualties made a bid for freedom and caused quite a stir."

"Did it get hit?"

"Did it get hit? There are more important things to attend to than your bleeding heart, and no, we have no idea where the animal is." Eric's normally creepily blue eyes had gone dark. I had recently begun to recognize this as a sign he was going to get really serious about something I didn't understand. "We can only hope fate guided the beast as far from Manhattan as the thing can run. If the creature is going to stay in the wild, the farther from us it is, the better. They can call it a genetic anomaly or blame a plague or chemicals for the creature's existence."

"B-but that's g-good right?" I asked through chattering teeth. "I-I mean th-that leaves only one m-more left to find."

"Leaves one more left to find, but has, in all likelihood, alerted the Ladies to your misconduct."

For the second time that hour my stomach dropped clear out of my body. "What does that mean?"

"It means we can no longer allow you to learn while you search for the animals." Eric took my shoulders and steered me down the street. "It means the Ladies now have a legitimate reason to come after you. It means the terrible feeling that has been creeping into the corners of my life that something is waiting just out of sight to come after us is probably correct."

"Something else is coming after us? Like not Ladies or deer?" I pictured giant shadow monsters creeping out of the sewer and grabbing my ankles, dragging me farther underground than Beville, to swampy places of shadows and death. I dug in my heels, refusing to let Eric push me any farther.

"We have had two months of unnatural peace. Are you really surprised that placidity has come to an end?"

"Well, I was kind of hoping non-deadly fun had become our new thing." We stopped in front of the school steps. The few lunchtime stragglers braving the cold stared at me.

"Fate laughs at hope," Eric said. "We have things to attend to, Bryant. Now let's go."

I glanced from the folder in one hand to the lunch bag in the other. "Can I run in and get my coat? Just really quickly? I'm freezing." It wasn't a lie. I was frozen to the bone. I also didn't want to carry enough money to buy a small house in Upstate around the city with me while we searched Central Park for whatever animal I had accidentally altered.

"You want a coat? Fine." Eric muttered something under his breath I couldn't hear then reached into his pocket.

It was the most magician-like thing I had seen him do. It was like that trick where a dude in a top hat pulls a hundred scarves out of your mouth or ear. Only Eric was dragging something made of black wool out of his pocket. In a few seconds, he shook the fabric, showing a replica of his own black trench coat.

"Here." Eric strode down the street, leaving me gaping at the newly-fashioned coat.

I swore some more under my breath, yanked on the coat, and chased after him. It was a long coat that was perfectly tailored...for Eric. On me, the sleeves hung over my hands, and the shoulders sagged past my armpits. But it had a pocket deep enough for the black folder to lay rolled up in. As for the money bag, I did the safest thing I could think of and shoved it down the back of my pants. I'd had too much experience with pickpockets to leave something like that in an open pocket.

"Are you warm enough to preserve our magical lives now?" Eric asked when I caught up to him.

"It's very nice. Thank you." I tried to keep the sarcasm out of my tone.

"Just think of how well you could look if you visited a proper tailor. Then you could truly fit in on the streets of Beville."

"My life's dreams fulfilled," I said.

"I think the best place to start would be the castle." Eric dodged between cars in a way that would have given my mother a heart attack. I followed, trusting Eric to not let me die. "It may seem cliché, but that is a very likely place. Or perhaps by the water."

"What if the thing is already dead and mounted on someone's wall as a creepy trophy?" I asked as we weaved around a bunch of old ladies fighting over which bodega they should go to.

"While we can hope for that, we can't count on it," Eric said. "Fortunately, I have a friend meeting us who should be able to make quick work of finding the thing."

"A friend?" I wasn't sure if I should be excited or terrified.

"I hate to make him come out in the light, and favors will be owed, but such is the work to be done."

"You're going to owe someone a favor?" I had forgotten to walk for a few seconds, so I had to run to catch up. "Isn't owing a favor, like, a much bigger deal for magical types than for non-demented humans?"

"A debt left unpaid can chase a wizard into death itself."

"And you owe someone because of me?" My voice squeaked as I spoke. "You shouldn't have done...whatever it is you did."

We had reached the edge of the park, and Eric headed north.

"I am your mentor, and you are my apprentice. If the Ladies come after you for breaches of the magical code, then they will come after me as well. Your conduct reflects on me." Eric stopped and rounded on me so quickly I rammed right into him. "I am doing this for both of us, Bryant, and the source isn't such a terrible one to owe."

"Still, thanks."

Eric slapped me a little too hard on the shoulder and turned to study the street.

There wasn't all that much to see. The middle west side of Central Park isn't exactly a tourist hot spot on a freezing winter day. There were a few hardy folks trudging along, taking pictures of the leafless trees and snow-spotted grass. Natives hurried past, heads tucked down against the cold. And one sad bundle of filthy, mismatched clothes huddled against the wall.

"Here we are." Eric walked right up to the bundle of rags.

I hoped the mass of fabric wouldn't look up. I hoped there wasn't a person hiding under there. But the rags stirred, and a face appeared. A sad little fist clenched around my heart. It was a kid. He couldn't have been more than ten. His eyes looked vacant, like two glassy nothings above his sunken cheeks.

"I'm glad you were able to meet us." Eric gave a little bow as the boy stood.

The boy nodded and turned his eyes toward me. Recognition trickled through my brain.

"I've seen you before. At Lola's...you're one of Lola's guards."

The boy nodded, and a shiver swept up my spine. He looked like a child, a very hungry, dirty child. But I knew that wasn't true. Elizabeth could see Lola's guards as they truly were—rotting corpses of something not quite human.

The boy walked toward me. I clenched my fists to keep my hands from shaking. The boy leaned in toward me, looking for all the world like an animal sniffing, then he looked up to Eric.

"You're quite right." Eric smiled, though the expression didn't reach his eyes. "He does spend a considerable amount of time with Miss Wick."

"Elizabeth?"

Eric shot me a look that very clearly said *Don't ask questions right now*, so I bit my lips together and stayed silent.

"As we've finished introductions, perhaps we should get down to business." Eric moved toward the entrance to the park where a wide swath of asphalt created a walking path. "We're looking for a creature, hopefully small, though it is not necessarily so. It has been transformed in some way by this boy—"

I ruffled a little inside at being called *boy*.

"That is really the best information I have for you."

We were under the trees now. The winter sun fought its way through the bare branches, trying to liven up the mostly dead park.

"I have been assured you can make quick work in finding such a thing?" Eric paused to look at the kid as though waiting for some silent communication.

The boy/undead shadow monster tipped his head to the side for a second before rounding on me. He didn't even bother creeping closer this time. He walked right over and started sniffing me. He grabbed both my hands, so quickly I wasn't sure how to react, and took a good whiff of my palms. His hands were freezing, colder than the air or ice. Colder than any living thing should ever be. But then, the kid wasn't really living.

The boy turned and walked down the sidewalk before cutting north through the grass.

"Keep up, Bryant," Eric called over his shoulder as I ran to follow.

The lunch bag of money slipped down my pants, and I stumbled as I reached to hike it back up. The last thing I needed was a small fortune falling out the leg of my pants.

The kid sprinted in front of us. It was just like chasing a dog. He would sprint for stretches then stop and stand very still for a few seconds before taking off again. It didn't seem to matter what parts of the park we weren't supposed to enter either. The boy ducked under chains and leapt over fences in an unnatural way, leaving Eric and me scrambling behind him. Okay, Eric wasn't scrambling. He was running behind the undead kid like it was nothing. I was scrambling and trying not to fall on the ice while balancing money in the back of my boxer briefs.

"Why?" I panted when the sniffer dog stopped to stare at a bush after running us east for a few minutes. "Why are we just doing this now? Why didn't we kill the bad guy, win the battle, ask the favor, and catch the weird oopsie animals two months ago?"

"It was your place to clean it up on your own." Stupid Eric wasn't panting. "To rebalance the scales of magic as it were. You make the mess, you clean it up. Simple as that."

"Is this going to turn into some big fate thing now where I'm going to get my ass handed to me because you helped me?" Not gonna lie, it came out really whiny.

"Probably."

The boy snaked his way into the bush, squeezing between barren branches.

"But it's better to need to find a way to right the scales of magic than to give the Ladies a new reason to come after us."

Sniffer McDeadDog leapt back out of the bush and started running again.

"Can't I do, like, magical community service or something?" I panted between gasping breaths. "Help old ladies cross the dangerous streets of Beville?"

"Do you think *you* could survive the dangerous streets of Beville?" Eric turned to look at me, running backward with one black eyebrow perfectly arched.

"Isn't there anything?"

"We'll know when it comes." He started running forward again just as Sniffer stopped in his tracks, pointing high up in a tree.

6

A *bird.*

That was my first thought. I had made furry, many-headed bird. Then I noticed it didn't have wings. Then it hissed and moved farther forward on the branches.

Fear curdled my intestines as my mind floundered, failing to find a way to put the horror into reasonable terms.

"Rat king!" I screamed. "It's a rat king!"

The thing startled at the noise and swiveled its nine heads toward me.

That's right. Nine freakin' heads!

I stumbled backward, landing hard on my butt. I scooted back across the frozen ground as the thing undulated down the tree. It was worse than I had ever imagined, even after hearing the urban legends that give nightmares to every New York kid with a healthy self-preservation instinct. Nine rats joined together by a tangle of tails crept down the tree toward us. But the tails weren't joined by gunk or glue. They had melded together into one, veiny disk so it looked like a fleshy Frisbee had sprouted rats.

The nine weren't moving independently either. They were moving as one, inching down the tree, staring at me like they were being controlled by one brain. The rats were all the same size. Too big to be normal, too small to make moving as a unit impossible. But the most terrifying thing of all was the one pure white rat who seemed to be the host of the others' thoughts. Leading the path down the tree, swiveling his head toward the undead boy a split second before the others.

The boy rounded his shoulders, looking like he would have growled if he ever made noise.

The rat king looked to Eric who said in an overly calm voice. "The coloring does seem symbolic, doesn't it?"

"What?" I screeched. Big mistake—it made the thing look back at me.

"Well, Bryant." Eric stepped aside, leaving a wide path between the nine-headed monster and me. "We've helped you find the beast. Now catch him."

"Nope!" The scream tore from my throat as I leapt to my feet. "Nope. Not going near it."

The evil, disgusting monster chittered as it reached solid ground.

"Bryant, just trap the thing," Eric said tiredly.

But I couldn't remember a spell. I couldn't think of any words. So again I shouted, "Nope!"

I ran backward a few steps. I wanted to run all the way to Brooklyn, but I couldn't bring myself to look away from the monster's eighteen beady, black eyes.

"Bryant, you're being rather ridiculous."

Something heavy fell down the leg of my pants, slowing my progress as I stumbled over it. "No, no, no!"

The thing was only five feet from me.

"What the hell is that?" A voice spoke from somewhere behind me, and other voices answered.

"Wonderful." Eric sighed. "Bryant, we really need to be done here."

Done. I wanted to be done. I wanted the rat to be dead.

In a fit of theatre-bred frenzy, I remembered the Nutcracker and that little girl killing a giant mouse with her shoe. I reached down to pull off my sneaker, but there was something else on the ground. A nice, heavy, sturdy-looking bag.

I picked up the bag and threw it at the rat king. It hit him straight in the Frisbee of conjoined tails, making the thing scream as hundred dollar bills flew into the air.

"Money!" a voice screamed behind me. There were other words, too.

"Is it real?"

"Get it!"

"Watch out for the rat!"

"Stop!" I shouted at the top of my lungs. I didn't know what I was telling to stop, the rat king that was only a few feet from me, or the people trying to get to my dad's illicit bake sale money.

The monster hissed, baring its teeth.

"Oh dear." Eric tipped his head down, looking like I was the most disappointing thing in the history of the world as random people charged toward me, braving the rat for a chance at money. "*Dothranta.*"

Everything went black. If the people charging toward my dad's money hadn't started screaming, I might've.

There was a hissing sound, then screeching as something thumped to the ground. It might seem cowardly, but I didn't step toward the shrill *squeal*. I backed away, careful not to fall. With a *crack* and a *thump*, the screeching stopped, but the people were still screaming.

Someone banged into me, knocking me to the ground.

"Eric!" I shouted, hoping he would have a way to see in his darkness. "Eric!"

He didn't answer, but a hand grabbed the back of my jacket, hauling me to my feet.

"Eric?"

I could almost feel my legs again, but the hand dragged me back so quickly I couldn't keep my feet under me. As I fumbled toward the ground, the sun burst back into being. "What the hell?" I twisted around and fell to the ground. "Eric..." But it wasn't Eric who had hauled me out of the dark. It was the boy, gripping my coat in one hand and the bloody, dead rat king in the other. I screamed and rolled away, catching a glimpse of Eric walking toward me, holding my lunch bag in his hand.

But the people behind him weren't chasing the bag of money. They were still stumbling around in a panic like they couldn't see anything.

"You saved the money?" I panted.

"I wasn't about to let the masses take it." Eric tossed the bag, and it landed at my feet. "With any luck, it's all in there."

With a squishing *thunk*, the undead boy threw the very dead rat king at my feet.

"Why!" I leapt to my feet, clutching the lunch bag and trying not to vomit. Each of the rat's nine necks had been snapped. At least, their spines didn't look right anymore, so I assumed that was what had happened.

"Thank you for disposing of the creature." Eric bowed to the boy. "You went above and beyond our agreement. I won't forget it."

The boy stared at Eric.

"We are done," Eric said.

The boy turned and shambled down the park, any indication he could run completely gone.

"We should leave before the spell breaks," Eric said.

I glanced at the people groping around in the dark.

"What about that?" I pointed to the rat king corpse with a sinking feeling Eric would want me to pick it up.

"Can't you at least get rid of that much yourself?" Eric pressed a knuckle to the bridge of his nose.

I pulled the black phone out of my pocket and held my thumb to the scanner. The screen flashed on. I tapped on the icon that looked like fire. A level bar balanced beneath blackened logs blinked into being. Pointing the phone like I was going to take a picture of the pile of mangled rat, I pulled the bar all the way to the right.

With a smell that would make a sewer cleaner gag, a pillar of fire five feet high sprang to life. I covered my mouth and nose with the rich man's lunch bag and counted to ten before sliding the bar back to the left.

The fire poofed out, leaving nothing but a scorched circle of earth to mark the death of the rat king.

"Well done, Bryant." Eric didn't look proud. "Now let's go." He took off at a brisk trot, heading south the same way the boy had gone.

I ran after him, hoping the wind would blow the stink of burned rat off me.

It was over. We had dealt with the three animals. Nutty McDragon had found a home and a new career as a mangler extraordinaire, the deer was hopefully living it up peacefully in Upstate, and the rat from hell was dead.

I tripped over my feet as a guilty weight thumped into my stomach. I would be mad if someone hurt Nutty even though he had tried to take a chunk out of my face, but I was thrilled the rat was dead. I packed that moral quandary away for another time and bolted after Eric.

Once we were well out of sight of the rat king's funeral pyre, Eric changed his pace to a stroll. I skidded to a stop behind him.

"How long will those people think they're in the dark?" I puffed.

"They are in the dark," Eric said. "It's just a one-way darkness. It should be gone in the next few minutes."

"What are they going to say happened? Do you think they'll call the police?"

I didn't want to think of how giddy the Ladies would be if they found out I had messed up badly enough that a bunch of normal people got caught in a one-way darkness spell.

"They'll call for an ambulance before they call the police." Eric didn't seem too worried, so I let my fear go a bit. "There is no crime any of them will be able to think of that could take away the light. They'll come up with some fancy medical name for it and leave us well alone."

"Then it's done." I heaved a sigh of relief, letting the cold air of the park wash away my anxiety. "All I have to do is deliver this to the bake sale and I'll be good." I shoved the lunch bag back down the back of my pants.

"Indeed." Eric's voice sounded dark when he said it, like he didn't think we were done at all.

"Don't *indeed*," I begged. "Please, don't *indeed*. Haven't we done enough for one day?"

"We have by all measure. Now it's just a matter of if the day is done with us."

"What does that mean?" The question came out as a whimper.

"Have you ever had the feeling someone was watching you?" Eric turned onto a side path away from the rest of the people around us. "That there are eyes staring at the back of your neck?"

"Of course, everyone feels that sometimes."

"But have you ever felt the truth of it?" Eric turned down another path. "Known for certain there is someone waiting for a moment of weakness to strike?"

I wanted to say no, he was being paranoid, but I knew the exact feeling he was talking about. "When I had the phone, before I knew you weren't evil, it felt like a giant eye was watching me."

"Thaden was watching, and you were wise enough to know." Eric turned again, cutting back through the grass toward the edge of the park. "I've had the feeling of something creeping closer for days—"

"But we fixed it," I cut across him. "We got rid of the last bit of my mistake. It's all okay. The Ladies can't come after us for that now."

"We arranged a battle that killed most of their number. The Ladies coming for us is inevitable. Getting rid of the animals was only a means of postponement. They can't admit we caused the battle without admitting we still have the phone and acknowledging the triumph of Charles and his people."

I shuddered at the thought of Charles, a man made shadow, who risked everything to fight the Ladies and Thaden in the battle of Beville.

"They will find a reason to come for us."

"Maybe years and years from now, right?" I asked as we cut back out of the park and onto the sidewalk. "You said maybe years!"

"Or they might send someone else after us." Eric looked back over his shoulder and toward the park. "I've not heard of it happening, but I wouldn't be surprised if, weakened as they are, they turn to outsourcing."

"Outsourcing?" I screamed the word. "You think they want to outsource our murders?"

"There are three options I can think of, Bryant." He cut into the lobby of a fancy apartment building. Before the woman at the front desk could pop up to ask how she could help us, Eric led me through the marble-floored hall and out the side door into a courtyard. "Option number one: I have lost my touch. I no longer have a keen sense for impending danger, which leaves us open to a multitude of enemies yet unknown." Eric burst through the doors of a restaurant and strode straight through it and into the kitchen, scaring the poop out of the dishwashers as we cut back out to the street.

"Option two: The Ladies have decided that, rather than wait for a justified offense we have committed they want to admit to, they will hire someone to rid themselves of us without worrying about messy legalities, which leaves us open to attack from any scum who can do a spell and is looking to earn a few extra dollars in this sad world."

We ran down the steps to a subway station and back out the other side.

"Option three: There is another source that wants us dead. A person or entity yet unknown has decided Manhattan would be better off without us. And this, Bryant, is the most troubling possibility of all." Eric turned on me so suddenly I nearly tipped over trying to stop before I rammed into him. "This means someone we are unaware of is willing to use time and resources we cannot estimate to destroy us. Manhattan has just become a very dangerous place."

7

We spent the next half hour running in circles back to my school. I ran with my hand on the back of my pants, trying to make sure I didn't lose the money again. Eric wanted me to dash into school really quickly, grab Elizabeth and Devon, and run for the (relative) safety of Beville. But with the bake sale and, you know, school, there was no way to grab them without the faculty and my mom knowing we had all escaped.

"Try not to get into any life-threatening trouble," Eric ordered as he left me on the school steps.

I had missed all the time left before the bake sale, so all I had to do was walk nonchalantly through the halls with a ton of money in my underpants, hoping no one could smell the burnt rat carcass on my new magically-made coat.

Elizabeth was already at the table, laying out rows of cookies, brownies, and other sweet treats.

"Hi," I whispered as I reached her.

"Bryant." She threw her arms around my neck like she hadn't seen me in months. "Where the hell have you been? Your mom found out you were gone, and she's been flipping out." Elizabeth stepped back and slugged me in the arm. "She's been trying to call you. Devon and I have been trying to call you! Why the hell didn't you answer your phone?"

I reached into my pants pocket and pulled out my non-magic phone. Twelve missed calls from Mom, Devon, and Elizabeth.

"Damn. I didn't even feel it. I mean, there was sort of a lot going on."

"What's in your pants?" Elizabeth leaned to look behind me where I was still clutching the lunch bag.

"Don't freak out," I said.

Elizabeth tensed like I was about to pull the rat king out of my pants. Not that she knew I had almost been murdered by a rat king. I passed her the lunch bag and mouthed *open it.* Because mouthing is less suspicious, obviously.

"Jesus, Bryant." Her sparkly eyes got all wide. "Where the hell did you get this?"

"Dad. He wants me to dump it in with the bake sale money." I pulled Elizabeth around to the backside of the table as the bell rang and students appeared in the hall.

"What the hell is he thinking?" Elizabeth whisper-screamed.

"He really is trying to help." I ran a frozen hand over my face. "He wants to help the theatre program."

"And your mom isn't going to know exactly where this came from?"

"Bryant Jameson Adams." Mom's voice echoed down the hall.

Elizabeth shoved the lunch bag into my chest and I tossed it back to her.

"I'm not taking it!" Elizabeth yelped.

"Please!"

Mom was halfway down the hall, glaring at me with her laser eyes.

Please, I mouthed.

With a panicked glare, Elizabeth shoved the lunch bag under the table.

"Bryant, where on God's green earth did you disappear to?" Mom's voice was crazy calm and pleasant, but her eyes were furious.

"I-I." I had two choices: half truth or all lie.

"You were with him, weren't you?" Mom took my arm and dragged me out of the hallway and into an empty classroom. I caught one last glance of Elizabeth looking panicky before the door shut, locking me in with the mom monster.

"What makes you think leaving school to run around with him is in any way acceptable?"

The use of the word *him* was problematic. I could surmise she meant Eric, which was reasonable since I saw him a lot more than I saw my dad. But if someone said they had seen me get into a big black car she would know it was my dad. I needed more information.

"It was an emergency."

"What sort of emergency requires the attention of my sixteen-year-old son?" Mom's eyes glittered dangerously. "What task was so insurmountable that only you, and not responsible adults, could handle it?"

"It wasn't really an emergency per se." I back-peddled. "More like a time-sensitive thing that ended up taking longer than I thought it would."

"And what was this urgent matter that was more important than school?"

She had me again. I still didn't know which *him*. I took a risk and pulled the black folder out of my pocket. "Dad wanted me to give you this." The rolled up folder glinted in the light.

She pinched her lips together.

I had gotten it right.

She opened the folder and glared at the pages.

"The urgent situation was real estate?" Her voice was tight and strained. A bad sign, a very bad sign.

Time to Mom detonation: 10, 9, 8...

"He wanted me to show you the apartments his realtor found."

"And he thinks your lowly mother can afford any of these?"

6,5,4...

"He wants to help you buy it so you can have money to retire." I started backing toward the door. "He really does seem like he wants to help."

3,2...

I reached for the doorknob, hoping against hope I could slip out the door and run before she blew.

"Bryant Jameson Adams, why the hell is there blood on your shoes?"

Boom!

I froze with my hand on the doorknob and glanced down. Splashes of rat king blood dotted the orange and white of my shoes. I bent over and puked on the floor.

"Bryant!" Mom pulled me away from my own vomit. "What the hell is going on?"

"There was a rat king." My defenses were gone. "One of the animals I changed turned out to be a rat king and we had to chase it and I got blood on my shoes."

"And what about the folder?" Mom growled and waved the folder in the air.

"Dad gave it to me." I was going to pass out. All I could think of was the rat blood on my shoes. I needed to burn my shoes. That was clearly the only option. Amputating my feet might be necessary, too.

Mom went silent.

The smell of my puke made me gag again.

"Grounded." She pronounced it like a verdict. "You are grounded. No going out. No magic. I can't keep you from seeing your father, but I will be making sure he doesn't pull you out of school again."

"Yes, Mom." I knew I should say something about how I couldn't walk away from magic since there might be people trying to kill me, but when your mom is bearing down on you, you can't really fight back.

"Go home now. Get your books, and go home. No stops, no talking to anyone, straight home."

"Yes, Mom." I turned and headed for the door.

"Wait."

I turned back around.

Mom had her hand held out. "Phone."

I pulled my phone out of my pocket and handed it to her.

"The other one, too."

My heart skipped a beat. I needed that phone. I needed to protect myself and my friends.

"I need it." I shook my head. "I need to keep it with me."

"Why? What is going on that you need to keep the phone?"

Another battle raged in my exhausted brain. I needed the phone to fight whatever was following us. If I told my mom something was coming, she would either want us to flee the country or come up with some other crazy plan to protect me. Last time she had tried to save me from a magical problem, she almost ended up dead.

"There's nothing going on," I lied, and bile crept back up into my throat. "The animals are all gone so there's nothing going on."

"Then give it to me." Mom held her hand out again.

I pulled out the magical phone. It seemed heavier in my hand than it ever had before.

Mom stared at me, waiting for me to pass it over. My heart raced. I hadn't been without the phone in two months. I kept it with me always. A defense against the shadows, and Ladies, and death in general.

"Bryant."

Everything blurred as I placed the one-of-a-kind magical library contained in a portable device in my mom's hand.

"Now go."

Mom didn't know my head was spinning out of control. She just stood there, mom-glaring at me like she had taken away a video game controller.

"We'll discuss the length of your grounding when I get home."

I nodded. My mouth was too dry to say words. I opened the door to the hall, which had flooded with students. A mob surrounded the bake sale table. Elizabeth and Devon were barely visible behind the horde. I wanted to dive through the crowd and make sure Elizabeth hadn't been attacked for the giant bag of money. But I could feel Mom's eyes on the back of my neck. I would just have to trust Elizabeth and Devon to guard the money and my mom to keep the phone safe. She wouldn't get rid of it. She couldn't.

My hands felt fuzzy as I pulled my real coat and bag from my locker. Like maybe losing the phone had drained me of magic, and losing my magic had made my body numb.

But that wasn't how it worked. I was still magical. I was still Bryant Adams, boy wizard. I was just...helpless.

The streets were packed on the walk home. Hundreds of strangers surrounded me, and my one defense was gone. Every old lady felt like a terrible threat. Every businessman ditching work early had some evil, magical thing hidden in his briefcase. The kids running past me on their way home were goblins in disguise. I didn't even know if goblins existed, but I was absolutely sure those kids were evil.

I wanted to bolt for Columbus Circle and head straight for Beville. Tell Eric my mom had confiscated the dangerous magical device and make him fix it. But she would know I had gone to him. Then she would know something was wrong, and she would get hurt.

I took off at a run. Not heading for Beville, but back to the linoleum-floored apartment. Back to my bedroom, which I still felt like I was visiting. I dodged between tourists and locals, not letting the squeals of alarm or curses of frustration slow me down. I tore through the lobby and pounded the janky elevator button until the damn thing rattled to the first floor.

The doors dinged closed behind me, and I panted in the corner, sure the entire magical world knew I was defenseless. I'd trapped myself in a box where anything could come get me. Mist could pour in through the crack in the door. Winged monsters could rip open the ceiling and tear me to shreds. The doors dinged back open on my floor, and I squeezed through them before they shimmied apart all the way.

The keys fumbled around in my hands as I tried to find the right one and open the door. They slipped from my fingers and clattered to the floor so loudly it felt like I had just set off an alarm that wailed, *Helpless idiot alone in the hall!*

My heart thudded as I grabbed the keys and jammed the right one into the lock. I leapt into the apartment and flung the door shut behind me.

I leaned against the door, panting. I wanted to lock myself in my room and hide under my bed, but I had rat king blood on my shoes, and I smelled like burnt fur and flesh.

I ripped off my sneakers and risked death opening the apartment door long enough to throw my shoes as far down the hall as my non-athletic self could manage.

"*Nudla.*" I bolted for my bedroom. The spell hissed as it cleaned my clothes, and tingled my scalp as it scrubbed my hair.

I slammed my bedroom door and clicked the lock shut. I wanted to shower. A nice hot shower to wash away every trace the rat king had ever existed. But what if some unknown evil found me in the shower and I became the worst horror movie cliché?

"*Nudla.*" The spell tingled on my skin.

"*Nudla.*" I crawled up onto my bed, back to the corner, staring at the door.

"*Nudla, Nudla, Nudla.*"

8

I'm not proud of how long I hunched on the corner of my bed trying not to panic, fighting to remember that I wasn't completely helpless without the library in the phone.

After a while I started repeating all the spells I could remember in my head. I got to fifty and started feeling better. I was limited but not helpless. That's when feeling started to come back to my feet and I decided I needed to get to work before Mom got back from school and inevitably reamed me out about the bake sale money.

I pulled out my computer and went to a sketchy text-from-the-web site.

My mom took the phone. At home and grounded. If you need me, you'll have to come to me.

I sent that message to Eric, and the weight on my chest got a little lighter.

Mom took both my phones. Eric thinks there might be something bad coming. Contact him if you need help.

I sent the message to Elizabeth and Devon before sending a shorter message to Elizabeth.

Sorry I left you with the bag. I miss you.

I shut my computer and lay back on my bed. Things were happening too fast. We had spent months working on finding the deformed critters I had accidentally created, and in two days they were all gone. We had been on a long peaceful streak, but now Eric thought it was going to end. Truth be told, I felt it, too. Life was speeding up again, moving more quickly, like something dangerous was chasing us and time was trying to run away.

"I should be training!" I shouted at the ceiling.

Mrs. Mops howled from the living room in response.

I started going through the list of spells I knew again. If there was something coming, we had to be ready this time. I couldn't risk my friends' lives again.

———

"Bryant!" Mom's shout dragged me out of sleep. The sun had gone down, and the only lights left outside were artificial.

I instinctively felt my pockets for my phones. My stomach dropped as I remembered they weren't there. But Mom was home. If I could convince her….

"Bryant Jameson Adams!" Mom shouted. "Out here, now."

"Yes, Mom." Girding my loins, I went out into the living room.

Mom thumped across the room, pacing like a lioness.

"How was the rest of your day?" I tried to sound casual, but my voice got all wavery and gave me away.

"How was the rest of my day?" Mom repeated. "Well, after finding out my son ditched school for not one but two wholly irresponsible reasons, I went to the bake sale my students have been bending over backward to make work so we can try and keep the theatre department running. To try and preserve the thing I have spent the past twelve years building! We go to count the bank, and guess what I find?"

"You made a lot of money?" My voice cracked. That right there was why I could never ever be an actor.

"We made $102,421.54, Bryant." Mom stalked forward, more terrifying than any of the monsters I had ever faced. "How do you think that happened?"

"Really good cookies?"

"How much did your father put in?"

I swallowed hard and spoke as calmly as I could muster. "None."

"Don't you dare lie to me, Bryant. How much?"

"A hundred thousand."

Mom melted down onto the couch.

"He really wants to help with the program." I hurried to sit next to her, hoping to find a window in her moment of weakness. "He wanted to make sure you could rent a space for your performances."

"I used to be able to trust you, Bryant." Her voice sounded hollow, like I'd cracked something inside her. "You were such a good kid. I could trust you to tell the truth. I could count on you to be the responsible one."

"Dad wanted me to take the money. I told him you would know it was him. I said it wasn't a good idea."

"This isn't about the money, Bryant." She rested her head in her hands, looking more exhausted than I had ever seen her. "The last couple of months have been rough. Knowing you're out with Eric kills me. Knowing there are people who want to hurt you destroys me every day. But I thought I could count on you to be where you said you would be, doing what you said you'd be doing. And now I know I can't."

"That's not true, Mom." I shook my head. I could feel the conversation tilting, going in a direction I didn't know how to come back from. "I've been following the rules. It was just today." The lie burned in my mouth.

"It doesn't matter." Mom stood up. "I know you want to be a wizard, but this has gone too far. I'm sorry, but I can't let it continue."

"What?" I sprang to my feet. "I can't just stop being magical. I can't turn it off. That's not how it works."

"What do you want me to say? That I'll let you keep lying to me when I know damn well there are things out there I can't protect you from? The further you dive into magic, the more dangerous it gets. I won't lose my son to a pack of mole people!" Tears streamed down her face.

I hadn't seen my mom cry in forever. I forgot how to breathe.

"Even if I wanted to stop, I can't." I lowered my voice like I was talking to a spooked animal. "It's fate that pulled me into this, and it won't just let me walk away. If something dangerous wants to come for me, it'll come whether I'm working with Eric or not. He's helping me be ready. Eric is teaching me to be safe, to defend myself. Making me stop would make things worse, not better. Please, Mom. I promise I'll be totally honest from now on. But I have to do this."

She stood frozen, staring at me for a long moment. "Then I'll just have to take you far enough away that danger can't find you." She grabbed her purse and coat and headed for the door.

"That's not possible, Mom. You can't run from fate. It'll only make things worse." I sounded like Eric.

Mom rounded on me. "I don't give a damn about fate. All I care about is protecting my son."

"Mom—"

"I'm going to see your father."

"Dad doesn't know about any of this." I ran to the door, leaning against it with all my weight. "You can't tell him about magic. He won't understand."

"He'll have to." Mom glared at me so hard I dropped my hands. She meant it. She was really going to tell Dad, and there was nothing I could do to stop it. "We'll find a safe place for you far away from the city."

Before I could process what she'd said, she disappeared through the door.

I sank to the ground.

I was sixteen. Old enough to make my own choices. But if Dad really wanted me to leave the city, he would just hire men to come take me in the middle of the night.

I could fight them off. But I would have to use magic.

I could run away to Beville, but then I would be leaving my life and my parents behind. Elizabeth and Devon would know how to get to me, but that would be it. No Mom, no Dad.

I couldn't leave magic. It was in my blood. Getting rid of it would be worse than trying to rip out all my veins.

I didn't want to leave my family. They were my…my family.

It was an impossible choice.

In an unusual show of affection, Mrs. Mops banged her head against my thigh, purring effusively.

"You're so lucky you're a cat," I murmured.

I gave the cat a pat on the head, which earned me a deep scratch on the back of my hand.

"You've got nothing on Nutty." I got numbly to my feet and went to my bedroom, closing the door behind me. "*Portundo.*" With a faint rumble, my door disappeared, leaving a smooth patch of wall in its place. At least they wouldn't be able to come get me in my sleep. I'd wait until morning. Try and reason with Mom. If that didn't work, I'd find a way to take back the phone and make a run for it.

I curled up on my bed and stared at my new bit of wall, waiting for sleep to come back for me.

9

When the sun had started to rise, Mom woke me up. Not by shouting this time, but by pounding on the wall.

"I'm up!" I hollered. The words seemed so normal even though I was screaming them through my magical wall. I didn't bring my door back until I had dressed and packed my school bag. I even put on my coat in case I had to trap Dad and ten henchmen in a spell and make a run for it.

"*Pontunda,*" I said when I ran out of reasons to linger.

My door rumbled back into existence, and, taking a deep breath, I stepped out into the living room.

"Good God." Dad sat perched on the edge of the couch, eyes wide with terror as he watched me walk through the newly-formed door.

"Morning, Dad." I wasn't really sure which was weirder. My dad knowing I was a wizard, or my dad being in my mom's apartment. Dad hadn't been in Mom's place since she kicked him out when I was three.

"I told you, Leo," Mom said from her spot on the floor in front of the door to the hall.

"How the hell did this happen." Dad's face was sheet white. Like it wasn't his son Bryant standing in front of him, but just some freaky ghost who'd stolen my face.

"Fate mostly." I stepped into the living room, not letting go of my backpack.

"Fate?" Dad looked from Mom to me. "*Fate* made him able to do this. Fate turned my son all...all..." My dad mouthed like a fish. My dad, who made massive amounts of money talking to super important people, couldn't think of the words to say his son was a wizard.

I didn't know what to say to a man who looked at me like I was possessed, so I stuck to the fate thing. Like if I showed him the big picture first, maybe he would see I wasn't some weirdo. Magic was a huge thing, and the random pull of a golden thread meant I got to be a part of it. And it was awesome.

"Fate sort of has a different meaning with magic," I said. "And I've been—"

"Eric, the man who nearly got him killed, taught him about *fate*," Mom growled.

Mrs. Mops jumped into her lap, kneading Mom's panic sweatpants with her sharp claws. By *panic sweatpants* I mean the pants that meant she was on the edge of insanity and dressing for comfort on the way to the loony bin.

"And what sort of a"—Dad swallowed hard—"wizard are you, son?"

My heart flipped to my ears when Dad said *wizard*.

"A new one," I said. They were both staring at me so hard. "An apprentice, I guess."

"An apprentice." Dad nodded knowingly. I think he was happy it was a word he knew. His big fancy company had apprentices.

"I've learned a lot, but there's a ton more to go." I stepped toward Dad, hoping he would be the reasonable one and understand why what I was doing was so important. "There is a whole world of magic right here in New York, and I've only seen the very tip of it."

"And most of it's in New York?" Dad leaned forward in his seat, like he was leaning over a conference table.

"Well, the Library and The Consortium are here, so this is where magic has sort of congregated, but there's no rule about wizards having to stay here. It's just their home, and they want to stay in it. Magical roots, sort of literally with the shadows." I was rambling. Giving them too much.

"Then there shouldn't be a reason you have to stay in New York." Dad looked to Mom, who brushed Mrs. Mops off her lap but didn't stand.

"Your father and I are very concerned, Bryant. We know you love magic and want to be a part of it. But it scares us both terribly. I know how dangerous it is. I've seen it. It nearly killed me."

"Kate." Dad turned to Mom. Apparently she had left the being trapped in a lifesaving cocoon bit out.

Mom gave a tiny shake of her head.

"Your mother and I love you very much, and we are here because we're concerned for you."

"Is this an intervention?" I laughed harshly. "Are we having a magical intervention right now?"

We'd gone from not being able to say the *w* word to an intervention in a minute. My heart dropped back down to its normal spot and started thumping a panicky rhythm.

"We want you to be safe," Dad pressed on, "and the only way we can do that is to take you out of the city."

"Out of the city?"

Dad nodded. "There are some wonderful boarding schools only a few hours away."

It felt like he'd punched me in the gut. "Your big plan is to ship me off to boarding school?" I rounded on Mom. "You've been fighting to keep me with you in the city for years, and now you cave?"

"Bryant—"

"One afternoon!" I shouted. "I ditched one afternoon of school, which you started!" I pointed a shaking finger at my father. "So now you just want to pack me up and send me away?"

"It's not like that, Bryant." Dad's voice was firm and set, like he was negotiating with someone who didn't want to be bought out. "We're trying to keep you safe."

"I won't be safe! There is nowhere magic can't and won't follow me! The Ladies who almost killed Mom could come after me anytime they want. Shadow people could come after me. Monsters could come after me. And they won't care how far they have to commute to get to me! Running away and pretending I'm not a wizard isn't going to make me any safer. It's only going to make me less prepared!" My chest heaved, and I wanted nothing more than to fling open the door with magic and stomp away. But Mom was still sitting in front of the door.

"If you really think there are people after you, we can send you to school farther away. I have a friend on the board of an excellent school in England." Dad didn't even look sad. He was speaking perfectly calmly about shipping his only child to the other side of the ocean.

"How much did he say he'd give your program?" I spat at Mom. "A million? Two? Enough to rebuild the whole theatre? How much did he offer you to send your son away?"

She looked like I'd slapped her in the face, but I didn't care.

"Don't you dare speak to your mother that way." Dad stood up. He was taller than me, bigger than belonged in our living room.

"Don't pretend you get to make the rules in this house. You just found out about magic today, so don't think for a second you understand any of this." I turned and walked back into my bedroom.

"I understand you're my son." Dad followed me, but I'd already reached my bedroom window. "All I want is what's best for you!"

I rammed open the window. The ill-fitted glass shook in the frame.

"What the hell do you think you're doing?" Dad tried to step around me, but I ducked under his arm, planting my hands on the windowsill.

"I'm going to school." Without looking back I leapt out the window, muttering, "*Escata,*" under my parents' screams.

I freefell eleven stories before the air around my legs solidified, turning into invisible pudding that stopped me a few feet above the ground.

"Bryant!" Mom's terrified voice carried down from my window as I pulled one of my feet free and the spell disappeared. I didn't look up. I didn't want to see their faces and wonder if they were more afraid that I had jumped or that I had managed to stop my fall.

I walked out of the tiny courtyard and onto the sidewalks, not stopping until I was around the corner.

There was a lot to process. Too much to process.

My parents wanted to send me away, take me out of the only city I had ever called home.

No way I could let that happen.

I could stay in the city if I stayed away from magic.

I thought for a second about not using magic ever again. About slipping through life day to day without ever uttering another spell. My skin started tingling like every part of my body had fallen asleep at once. I couldn't stop doing magic. It would hurt. I had been warned before, but now I knew without a doubt it was true. And even if I wanted to dodge my magical fate, the Ladies, and whatever else might want to kill me, Eric, and quite possibly my best friend and girlfriend, would still hunt me down.

That left running away. Getting someplace where my parents couldn't find me and force me onto an airplane.

The look of pure hurt on my mother's face when I'd accused my dad of buying her off flashed in front of my eyes. I shouldn't have said that.

I took a step to go back to the apartment and apologize. But if I went back, we'd fight again.

I screamed, a horrible roar of fear and frustration. The sound echoed off the nearest building, and two women skittered across the street to get away from me.

I'd have to move to Beville. I'd move into the gray stone house with Eric and focus on my training. I might be a high school dropout tomorrow morning, but that was okay, right? Wizards didn't need diplomas, right?

My stomach gurgled as I realized I had a plan. I'd go to school, make it through to lunch. Then I could tell Elizabeth and Devon at the same time. I was going to be leaving the normal world to live with the magical mole people. Then I'd go.

Live belowground. All the time.

A weight pressed on my chest like Manhattan was practicing burying me alive.

Weird thoughts raced through my head as I walked toward school. Would I be allowed to come aboveground to take Elizabeth out on dates? Would I be allowed to get a job to earn money to pay for dates? Was there higher education for wizards? Would I be able to get into my college money to pay for it, or would Dad strip the account?

Every breath seemed like it would rip my chest apart. As I walked up the chipped steps and into school, a black car pulled up in front of the door. I dodged inside and hid behind the doorjamb, waiting for men in fancy suits to come in and grab me. Maybe they'd stick a needle in my neck.

But it was only a steady stream of students coming in through the door.

"Dude, what's your problem?" a senior asked snidely when he caught me peering around the corner.

"Nothing." Sweat pooled on my palms at the lie. I stepped into the oncoming crowd and craned my neck to look at the street.

The black car had parked, and two men stood outside it, their eyes sweeping the crowd.

I let muscle memory carry me to my first class. Devon was waiting, concern showing in his eyes with his first look at me.

"Not now," I said as he opened his mouth. "Wait for Elizabeth."

I couldn't go through explaining everything twice. It was a mark of how good a friend Devon was that he just nodded and didn't ask anything else.

He did keep giving me side-glances during that class and the next. The teachers' voices sounded like they were coming from underwater miles away. They were saying words, but I couldn't hear them. My ears were tuned to much softer sounds. My eyes darted toward the door at every *squeak* of a shoe on the hall floor or *rumble* of distant voices, waiting for Dad's cronies in suits to come drag me away or for Mom to come bursting in in tears.

But nothing happened.

I made it all the way to lunch with nothing at all happening.

10

The space of the cafeteria was overwhelming. Too many people, and too many doors. There was no way to spot where danger might come from.

Elizabeth sat at a table off to one side, an untouched tray in front of her, her eyes locked on me as I approached.

"Come on." Devon patting me on the shoulder nearly made me jump out of my skin.

I yipped like a scared Chihuahua. But no one gawked at me. They were all focused on the lunch line, where the evil lunch lady stood on top of a table, handing out snacks to the crowd.

Elizabeth stood and threw her arms around me as soon as I reached her. "Are you okay?" she whispered in my ear.

"No." That one simple word dissolved all the fight I had left in me. "Dad came to the apartment this morning."

"What?" Elizabeth grabbed my hand and pulled me down to the table.

"Your dad came over to your mom's place?" Devon said.

"Yeah. It was bad. They want to send me away."

"Away?" Elizabeth laced her fingers through mine, and a thrill ran up my arm.

"First, it was boarding school in Upstate, but when I said the Ladies could follow me there, it was England."

"England?" Devon whistled. "Your mom is okay with this?"

"I think it might have been her idea."

"But they can't." Elizabeth shook her head, and her curls swirled around her. "They can't just make you leave."

"They want to keep me safe."

"Are you"—Devon swallowed hard—"are you going to go?"

"He can't. He wouldn't be safe."

"I told them that. And then I jumped out my bedroom window and ran here."

Elizabeth clasped her free hand over her mouth, and Devon swore under his breath.

"You missed the line for treats." The voice made me jump. But it wasn't a giant dude trying to tackle me. It was the evil lunch lady holding out three bright pink cupcakes. "Everyone gets a free treat today."

"What?" It took me a minute to process Her Evilness doing something as nice as offering kids cupcakes. "I'm not hungry, thank you."

"A growing boy your age must be hungry all the time." She smiled, showing overly long teeth. "And a girl as skinny as you needs to put some meat on her bones."

"Meat on my what?" Elizabeth's cheeks got all sucked in like she was literally biting back the urge to scream at the lunch lady about body shaming.

"We aren't hungry," Devon said. "Thanks though."

"I even have gluten-free. I can bring some over."

"No, thanks," Devon snapped.

"Vegan?"

"No."

"Sugar-free?"

"These are great." Devon grabbed the three pink confections and set them on the table. "Thanks a ton."

"You have to try them. I made them special just for you kids."

"Fine." I picked up a cupcake and Devon and Elizabeth followed my lead. I took a giant bite of the surprisingly good treat and smiled. "It's amazing. Thank you for brightening our day."

"Thank you for eating my goodies." She shambled back to her table.

"What are you going to do?" Elizabeth asked as soon as she swallowed her bite and the lunch lady was out of earshot.

"Ask Eric if I can move in with him." I took another bite of cupcake to give myself something to do while they exchanged frightened glances. "I'll understand if you don't want to be a part of any of this anymore. I mean, if you don't want to see a wizard dropout—"

"Don't be a dumbass, Bry." Devon put down his partially consumed cupcake and punched me hard on the shoulder. "You're my best friend. Living in Beville won't change that."

"It'll be like having a boyfriend in Brooklyn." Elizabeth gave a faint smile. "I'll just have to commute to see you."

"I'll miss you." Tears burned in the corners of my eyes. I was so used to seeing them every day. To knowing when I woke up, they were in my near future. I would be giving that up along with everything else. Like sunshine and parents.

"It'll be okay, we'll—"

But I didn't get to hear the end of what Elizabeth was going to say. A *ping* rang through the air, and something like pink pixie dust whooshed up from all the tables.

"Elizabeth!" I shouted over the resounding *bang* as all the doors around me swung shut. "Devon!" They had both crumpled to the floor. Everyone in the lunchroom had crumpled to the floor. "Elizabeth!" I shook her shoulders, but she didn't move. "Help!" I scanned the room, searching for whatever had caused every student in the room to drop.

I expected to see a monster looming over the fallen crowd, or even a sheet of pearl white mist creeping in. But there was nothing but my classmates covered in pink shimmer powder.

"Elizabeth." I bent down to grab her under the arms. I could break open a door, drag her out to the hall, then come back for Devon. But a voice rang out over the cafeteria before I could lift her.

"You must be joking."

I looked up toward the growling voice. The evil lunch lady stood on top of the lunch counter, her steak-like hands on her hips.

"You?"

"Me what?" I stepped over Elizabeth and Devon, planting myself between them and the only other conscious person in the room. "What did you do to them?"

"You ate. I saw you eat." She tipped her head to the side a little too far. Like her neck didn't quite work the same way as mine.

"Did you poison them with glitter?" I took another step forward. "You sick f—"

"Poison is not my ends. Finding the one they're looking for. Collecting the magic one." She twisted her head the other way. "But it shouldn't be you."

"Shouldn't be me? Who the hell did you think it should be?"

Her gaze drifted past me to the floor. Straight to Elizabeth, who lay on the ground, hair shimmering around her like a halo.

Looking at Elizabeth was a mistake. In the second I had glanced away, the lunch lady had grown. Not all of her though. It was like her bones had decided to grow without telling her skin, filling out her wrinkles and sags, making her more frightening than any woman with a hairnet had ever been before.

"No matter." The lunch lady smiled. "They paid for one with magic, and I will deliver. My search led me close enough to find you."

"Who paid you to find me?" I took a slow step to the side, then another. My instinct to stay near Devon and Elizabeth warred with my need to draw the evil lunch lady's attention away from them.

"The ones who want you." She sneered, baring her nasty yellow teeth. "They pay well for fresh ones. How long I've had to look. Waiting and waiting for a fresh one for market. But market day has come, little piggy."

"People are going to eat me!" I halted my sideways progress, too stunned to move. "I don't know which is worse—the thought of being eaten or the irony of a lunch lady searching for human meat."

"Not human." She leapt off the counter, landing ten feet away without a sound. "They pay for magic flesh."

"To eat? I just want to be really clear on that." Her scent of bleach and meatballs reminded me of the importance of escape.

"Not my business what they do once they have you. I only deliver to my master." She smiled. But her lips didn't stop where normal lips should. They stretched back, showing her overly long teeth like an animal preparing to bite. "Best not to fight. They pay more for undamaged goods, and I've waited so long to make a sale. Years and years waiting for one precious item."

"An item for who?" I scooted back toward the front door. It was the largest and had a straight shot toward the main entrance of the school. All my years of plotting for a zombie invasion had finally come in handy. "I mean, if I'm going to be sold, I have a right to know who's doing the buying, don't I?"

"The buyer is not the business of the merchandise." The skeleton lunch lady weaved between tables, snaking her way toward me. Her protruding joints flowed too loosely in their sockets, her knees bending back too far, her fingers flexing like tentacles as they reached for me.

"I find *merchandise* to be an offensive term." I automatically reached into my pocket, my hand searching for the phone that wasn't there. Panic surged in my chest. I didn't have the phone. I didn't even have a way to text Eric and tell him that if I went missing, the six-and-a-half-foot-tall skeleton that used to serve bad pot roast had abducted me.

"You have much larger worries, little wizard." I barely saw her crouch before she sprang at me, flying through the air like a demented grasshopper.

"*Primurgo!*" I screamed the spell, and a shimmering shield appeared around me.

The lunch lady landed on it and smiled at me as she slid down the transparent surface like a kid surfing down a slide.

"Do you want to delay the inevitable, boy? Do you want to fight me?"

In truth, I wanted to scream *no!* and curl up on the floor until the she left, but I knew that wasn't an option. My mind raced, trying to think of something to say, and I spotted Devon's cool black shoes sticking out into the aisle.

Be Devon.

I pulled myself up to stand as straight as I could. "I mean, if you're trying to sell me, I don't think I have a choice but to fight. If you decide you just want to walk away though, I could be feeling generous."

"Cocky little wizard," she growled.

I took cocky as a compliment. It meant I sounded like I wasn't shit-face terrified.

"I don't know who you think you are, but I'm not going with you." I took a swaggering step toward my shield. "I'll give you ten seconds to walk out of this room and never come back. If you don't, there will be consequences." I drew out the word *consequences* like there was some deep, dark meaning I wanted her to understand.

"Consequences?"

"Yeah." I wished Devon and Elizabeth were awake to see me be such a total badass. "I'll have to teach you a lesson."

"If anyone needs a lesson, it's you, wizard boy." In one great leap she flew across the room and landed next to Elizabeth. Lifting her by one limp arm, the lunch lady dangled my girlfriend in the air like a rag doll.

"Don't touch her," I spat as panic squeezed my heart.

Skeletor sneered, and her teeth grew longer and sharper. "Drop the shield, or I kill your girlfriend."

"What?"

"I can rip out her throat. I can paint the floor with her blood. I'd like to see what's in those veins. Such a strong scent of magic on her I couldn't even find you. Magic and death, what has the pretty one been playing with?" She dipped her mouth toward Elizabeth's neck.

"Don't hurt her!"

"Drop the spell, and come with me. No more fighting, no damaged goods, no dead girl."

"Fine." I nodded so hard I thought I would snap my own neck. "Just don't hurt Elizabeth." I released the shield.

With a flick of the wrist the lunch lady threw Elizabeth across the room.

"Elizabeth!" I screamed as she hit the brick wall and crumpled to the ground.

"Oops." The lunch lady cackled, and the laugh shook her whole bony frame.

"If you hurt her, I will kill you." The words weren't even hard to say. They were too true.

"Come with me, or *I* start to kill. And I'm so good at it." The lunch lady took a step that carried her three feet closer to me. "Which should I start with? The actor?" She pointed to Devon's prone figure on the ground. "The jock?" She pointed to a boy in a football jersey I had never spoken to. A stab of guilt shot through me as I thought how much better it would be if she killed the boy without a name.

"You're not going to kill anyone." I moved backward as quickly as I could without looking down, feeling behind me with my foot for tables and limbs of fellow students. "I'm going to go with you, and I'll take my issues up with your bosses. You're just doing your job."

"And what a wonderful job it is." Her strides were so long she was catching up to me. Soon she would be close enough to grab me. "I could kill just one. To make the job more fun. Make them think the missing boy had lost his mind."

"Are you kidding? They would totally blame the lunch lady." I laughed, hoping I wasn't pushing too far and she would keep talking. "They would say I was a kidnap victim and the lunch lady tried to kill everyone. They'd call me a hero."

"A hero?" The lunch lady kicked one of the band geeks, sending him flying seven feet into the air. "There are no heroes in high school."

"You really need to work on your observation skills if you're going to stalk wizards. I'm starting to think you're not very good at your job." I was three feet from the door, out of reach of all the tables. "I mean, as if the meat loaf weren't enough to prove how incompetent you are."

With a howl, the lunch lady launched herself in the air, flying forward to pounce right on me.

"*Erunca!*" I screamed. A streak of lighting cut through the air striking her mid-leap. The bolt lit up her skin, showing her overgrown bones in sharp relief. I thought she would crumple to the ground, but instead she landed with a stumble and hitch in her breath as though I had punched her.

"I should have killed the girl. I suppose it's not too late," she hissed, twisting to leap back toward Elizabeth.

"*Parapus!*" Thin lines of black flew from my hands and toward the lunch lady like horizontal bars, but before they could *clang* tight around her she batted them aside with her overly long fingers.

"Do you really want to play with me, boy wizard?" She tipped her head too far to the side again. "I don't want to deliver damaged goods. But you give me no choice."

With the tiniest bend of her knees she pounced again, flying through the air so fast I barely had time to throw myself to the ground.

"*Hieata!*"

She gasped and gagged as my spell pummeled the air from her lungs, but she kept moving toward me, step by shuddering step.

I scooted sideways along the wall. She curled a finger in the air, beckoning me forward. I held my breath as she smiled.

One more step. I only needed her to move one more step.

I lunged forward and shouted, "*Abalata!*" A thick band of black sprang from my palm. I threw it as hard as I could, and it stretched like taffy, striking six inches away from the lunch lady's head.

She easily dodged sideways, her eyes dancing with glee, but that move was enough. She was away from the last of the students.

"*Calimarta!*" A great *crack* sounded overhead as a giant chunk of concrete fell from the ceiling.

Fear flashed through the lunch lady's eyes a split second before the chunk hit her with a sickening *squish*. I didn't even have time to want to vomit as blood and squishy body ooze spread across the floor.

"Elizabeth!" I raced to her.

All the people asleep on the cafeteria floor were still, well...still. The lunch lady's death hadn't released them from whatever magic she'd used.

"Elizabeth." I knelt next to her, too afraid to move her in case hitting the wall had done some horrible sort of damage. I wanted to call Eric and ask him what I should do, but there wasn't any time. Voices screamed in the hall, and thumping echoed through the room as someone tried to batter down the door to the main hallway.

I scrunched up my eyes, trying with everything I had inside me to focus. "*Concursornio.*" The air around Elizabeth shimmered for a moment, and I held my breath, wishing for her to wake up with every fiber of my being, hoping I hadn't made a terrible mistake and made everything worse.

Her perfect, glittery eyes fluttered open, and she gasped. The most beautiful gasp I had ever heard. She gave an exquisite cough and sat up. "What happened?" She looked around the room. "Oh, God." She was on her feet before I could stop her. "Bryant, what happened?"

With a crack, the hinges around the cafeteria door began to give way. "No time." I clasped her hand in mine and dragged her over to Devon who lay crumpled on the floor. "*Concursornio.*" The instant he stirred I leapt up onto the table. Closing my eyes, I tried to focus my magic out in every direction, which was really, really hard when the fire sirens started blaring. "*Concursornio.*" I felt the magic whoosh out of me harder than it ever had before. My head spun like I'd just inhaled some weird kind of fume. There was no time to let my head figure out how to be attached to my neck, so I climbed unsteadily off the table. Elizabeth wrapped an arm around my waist as I reached the ground.

"What the hell happened?" Devon asked.

"No time," I whispered as the door banged open.

The football coach and three other teachers tumbled into the room.

"Get out!" I shouted with as much authority as I could. "It's gas! I think there's gas!"

"Everybody out!" the football coach bellowed, lifting two barely-conscious students by the arms and dragging them away.

"We have to get out of here. Now." I grabbed Devon and Elizabeth by the hands and charged to the front of the stumbling crowd, which surged for the door. Everything was still covered in pink, sparkly dust. They wouldn't buy the gas story for long.

"We need help over here!" the English teacher shouted as she tried to shove the concrete chunk off the squished pile of former lunch lady.

Emergency lights flashed in the hall, and everyone charged toward the front door.

"Just keep moving," I spoke as loudly as I dared. "Don't stop for emergency workers or anything. We have to get out of here."

"Bryant!" Mom's panicked voice shot over the sirens as only a theatre person's could. "Bryant!" She raced down the hall toward me. I wanted to dodge out of the way, but there was nowhere to go.

"Are you okay?" Mom took my face in her hands, checking me over for damage.

"I'm fine, but we have to go."

"Let's get you to the ambulances." Mom tried to take my arm, but I shook her off.

"I can't."

People flooded around us, bumping into us as they fled in panic. But the four of us stayed, like a rock in the middle of a creek, immobile in the current.

"Bryant, there was a gas leak." Mom spoke between clenched teeth, hurt and fear showing in her eyes. "You need help. We can figure everything else out later."

"They can't help me, Mom. It wasn't gas, and it's not over yet. I have to go. We all do. Before something else happens to the school, before they find me again."

Mom's hands flew up to her mouth. "Your father has people outside. They can take you away." Tears streamed down her face.

"No they can't. If they found me here, they can find me anywhere."

"He's right, Ms. Miller," Devon said. "I don't even know what's happening, but I know hiding won't work."

Firemen charged down the hall.

"I'll come with you. We'll figure this out."

"You can't." Elizabeth said. "You have to stay here."

"No."

"We need you to make sure no one asks questions about Bryant, or any of us," Devon said. "He needs you to do that. We need you to stay."

"No, please." Tears coursed down Mom's face.

"We have to go. I'm sorry. I love you." The words hurt like a knife twisting in my gut. It didn't matter what had happened that morning. She was still my mom, and I loved her and I had to leave her in a panicked hallway.

Elizabeth squeezed my hand and started down the corridor, trailing Devon and me behind her like kindergarteners playing follow-the-leader. Men ran past, pushing a stretcher.

"Bryant, wait!" Mom lunged at me, throwing her arms around me. "I love you, baby boy."

Two of the men in dark suits my dad had sent came into the hall. I ducked, hiding my face in Mom's shoulder as they passed.

"I have to go," I murmured, pulling painfully away.

"Be safe." Mom pressed something into my hand and ran down the hall toward the cafeteria, shouting to the students, "Everyone get outside! Now!"

I glanced at my hand. The black phone sat in my palm, perfectly smooth and undamaged by its time away from me.

"This way." Elizabeth grabbed me by the arm, dragging Devon along with her other hand. We cut sideways out of the main hall and to the other side of the school.

Wide windows looked out over the sidewalk where students stood, gazing up at the school, some frightened, some disinterested.

Elizabeth hoisted one of the windows open. In one smooth movement she sat on the ledge, twisted to lower herself as far as her arms could reach, and dropped to the ground.

No one on the sidewalk seemed to care. It was sensible—a way to avoid the scrum at the front door. Devon jumped next. The black car had moved farther down the street, making way for the ambulances and fire trucks that had filed in in front of the school.

"Bryant, come on!" Devon hissed up at me, pulling my attention away from the unibrowed man pacing between the fire trucks.

I climbed up on the windowsill and tried to twist around like the others had. But my scrawny arms had had enough. My fingers couldn't hold me, and I crumpled to the frozen sidewalk in a heap.

Devon grabbed me under the arms and lifted me to my feet. Without a word, the three of us ran as fast as our tired and beaten limbs could carry us around the corner and out of sight.

11

The three of us sat scrunched together, panting in the back of the cab. My limbs tingled with fatigue, Devon looked like he was fighting a migraine, and Elizabeth was so pale she looked like Snow White.

"What the hell happened?" Devon whispered as the cabbie sped toward Columbus Circle. It wasn't far. Normally we would have walked. But I wanted to be hidden in the car, to disguise our scent, to run away and hide from more evil lunch ladies trying to kidnap me. Also, sitting felt really good.

"Not now," I whispered back after a long moment.

Devon scowled and shut his eyes.

"Elizabeth, can you text Eric and ask him to meet us at the entrance?" Mom had given me back the magical phone, but not the one that was actually capable of things like calling or texting.

Elizabeth pulled out her phone. A thin dust of pink glitter puffed into the air.

I held my breath, waiting for her to pass out again. But she just coughed and waved it away like it was normal dust.

"What is it?" she asked in a disgusted tone.

My head throbbed trying to make sense of the coma cupcakes. Eric would know. Eric knew everything.

The cab stopped, and I let him run the black credit card my dad had given me. The card went through without trouble. Apparently Dad hadn't cut me off...yet.

We went back down the familiar steps and squirmed through the expected crowd. My eyes scanned every person we passed, making sure they weren't growing into skeletal monsters.

"*Portunda*," I whispered as we reached the bit of wall that led to Beville. For a terrifying moment I thought the wall would stay solid, but the door appeared, and we slipped through, shutting it firmly behind us. "*Portundo.*"

We walked quickly down the corridor. It had begun to feel routine. A commute to magic. Now I wanted the walk to go faster, but I didn't know a way to magic the tunnel to be shorter.

"Now can you tell us what happened?" Devon asked as we left the tiled floor and moved into the roughly hewn portion of the tunnel. "I was eating a cupcake, and then I was on the ground covered in fairy dust with a really bad headache."

"The headache was probably me." I ran a hand over my face, trying to work what had happened into an easily explainable order.

"You're admitting to giving people headaches?" Eric spoke dully from the tunnel up ahead. "And here I thought you were only a pain in the—"

"Eric!" I cried, not even caring that he had been making fun of me. "I didn't know what spell to use to wake them up."

"Why did we need waking up?" Elizabeth asked as we reached Eric.

"My question as well." Eric gave us each a hard look before joining our group moving toward Beville.

"It was the lunch lady. The cupcakes she gave everyone had something in them to knock people out. She was looking for a magic one. She thought Elizabeth was the one, said she could smell magic on her."

"Smell it on me?" Elizabeth shuddered.

"But I was the one who didn't pass out, so she knew it was me. And then her bones got all long and gross, and her teeth grew. She, if you can even be a *she* when you're all demony, said she had waited a long time to find a young wizard and people were going to pay good money for me." I didn't even realize Eric had stopped walking until we were ten feet in front of him. "What?"

"She said people wanted to pay for you?" Eric asked, his face a stone mask.

"Said they would pay more if I was undamaged so I had to come with her nicely. She said"—the words caught in my throat—"she said she would kill Elizabeth if I didn't come with her."

Elizabeth laced her fingers through mine.

"And this lunch lady of yours didn't know you were the one she was looking for?" Eric asked. "She hadn't been sent specifically for you or tracked you by your scent?"

"She smelled magic but thought it was Elizabeth. I told you that." Frustration bubbled in my chest. What was the point in explaining everything if Eric wasn't going to pay attention?

With a muttered curse I didn't understand, Eric charged down the tunnel so quickly the rest of us had to run to catch up.

"What is it?" Devon asked, keeping pace with Eric.

"Worse than what I had hoped for is a descriptive beginning," Eric said, his words coming out evenly as we ran. "I'm afraid what you have just described is a Lancre."

"A what?" I puffed. The end of the tunnel came into view. It felt like we were running with a demon at our heels.

"A Lancre. In the simplest of terms, a witch hunter."

"Like a burning-at-the-stake kind of witch hunter?" Elizabeth asked. "I thought that sort of thing stopped a long time ago."

"It did." We turned onto the street and pelted toward the gray stone house. "But like all occupations, it evolved."

The door to Eric's home sprang open as we charged up the steps. Eric didn't speak again until we were all inside and the bolts had closed with a resounding *thunk*.

"Lancre started off as witch hunters, following one of the greatest haters of our kind that has ever been recorded." Eric led us down the hall toward the parlor. "But as time went on, magic immigrated to the New World, witches became more adept at hiding, and public execution of those accused of witchcraft became a less prevalent form of entertainment."

"Entertainment?" I asked, my legs getting wobbly at the sight of Eric's couch. I collapsed onto the finely upholstered sofa and buried my head in my hands. "Burning witches was entertainment?"

"The hunting, the trials, the executions, it was all for the appeasement of the masses. A way to pass the dark days of the past." With a *crack* the walls shook. I looked up in time to see the bottom half of the room change from wallpaper to packed bookshelves that matched the top half. Eric examined the bottom-most shelf as he continued. "When that delightful source of fun ended, the Lancre discovered they had to find real witches to fulfill their pleasures."

"Real witches?" Elizabeth squeaked. "They had been burning fake witches?"

"A person with actual magical ability would be incredibly difficult to restrain and kill. Of course, there were those who were too untrained to fight back or those who chose not to and became martyrs to magic.

"In most cases, however, it was only the unpopular or the too popular who were targeted and killed." Eric pulled an old leather volume from the shelf. The spine was a faded maroon with gold lettering that had flaked away in places. "Once the Lancre were forced to find real witches, they found themselves ill-equipped for the task. Using the magic they so despised, they altered their forms to become monsters like the one you met today."

Eric opened the book and set it on the table at the center of the room for us all to see. I pushed myself to my feet, my legs burning and stinging from even that small effort.

Elizabeth gasped beside me as she looked at the book. It was an illustration of a naked man with bones that had grown too long for his frame and teeth too long for his mouth.

"Dude," Devon whispered.

"Is this what you saw?" Eric asked.

"Yeah." My throat crackled like I'd swallowed sandpaper.

With a *snap* and a *rumble*, the surface of the table shook, and a silver tray with four steaming teacups, a teapot, and a plate of cookies appeared, growing from its surface. Eric snatched the book away just as the teapot would have knocked it from the table.

"So witch haters, who are witches, decided to change themselves with magic so they could trap people with magic more easily?" Devon added sugar to his tea, his hand shaking as he gripped the tiny spoon.

"Would that it were so simple," Eric sighed. "Fighting amongst witches is a time-honored tradition. Lancre are humans. Humans who have bargained with witches to have magical changes made to their bodies but still possess no magic themselves."

"But what about the cupcakes?" I asked, my mouth full of cookie. "They had poison and glitter in them."

"Potions require magical ingredients, not a magical creator," Eric corrected.

"But what witch would give a witch hunter potion ingredients and tracking and fighting skills?" Devon asked. "I mean, doesn't that seem like a terrible idea?"

"A terrible idea can seem brilliant to terrible people," Eric said. "In magically modifying Lancre, they become indebted to you, either constantly as hunting dogs, or let loose in the world with the knowledge that someday you will call upon them to do your bidding."

"That's sick." I hesitated with another cookie halfway to my mouth. Hunger won out over revulsion, and I bit into the gooey treat. Eric's house was a really good cook.

"It is sick." Eric sank back into one of the two winged armchairs, and Devon into the other. "It's even banned by the Ladies. One of their policies I wholeheartedly agree with."

"Okay." Elizabeth took my arm and guided me back to the sofa. "Let me get this straight. Someone broke the laws of the Ladies and created a Lancre?"

"Yes, they can only be created by witches and wizards." Eric sipped his tea, a look of skepticism on his face as though wondering where Elizabeth's thoughts might be heading.

"How illegal is making a Lancre?" Elizabeth asked. Her leg was pressed into mine even though the couch was wide enough for three people to sit. If we hadn't just almost been killed, it might have passed for a lunch date.

Me cozying up to Elizabeth, books all around us, white lace curtains covering the windows. We could make Eric and Devon leave us alone and spend some time kissing on the window seat, holding books in our hands, pretending we might actually read them.

"If you're thinking of asking Bryant or me to make a Lancre, I can assure you it won't happen." Eric ruined my lovely dream by speaking. "If we were to call Bryant's deformed animals a misdemeanor, creating a Lancre is a felony worthy of a life sentence. A Lancre is a thinking, plotting, magically altered being whose sole purpose is to track and destroy witches."

"So whoever made the lunch lady a Lancre must be a fugitive," Elizabeth said.

Eric nodded.

"So a fugitive sent a Lancre after Bryant."

"She thought it was you." I squeezed Elizabeth's hand.

"My best guess is she was told to find a wizard and given a general idea of where to go by her creator. From there she would lay in wait for new witches or wizards to show themselves. Since you and Elizabeth are so closely intertwined, it's not surprising she guessed wrong." Eric pinched the bridge of his nose. "What I want to know is who in New York would be foolhardy enough to set a Lancre loose in the city."

"She worked there for two years," Devon said. "She came halfway through our freshman year. She replaced the lady who gave me extra Jell-O if I winked at her."

"She was in the school before I was a wizard." I took a sip of tea, letting the hot liquid wash away the panic that had been building in my stomach.

"You were always a wizard, you simply hadn't shown any magic," Eric explained. "The scent of magic on you would have been too dull for her to track you specifically, but it would have been clear someone in the school possessed magic."

"Then why did it take her so long to come after me? I've been using magic for months."

"You burned down the theatre with magic." Eric leaned forward in his seat. "Everyone who was touched by those flames smelled like magic to the Lancre. It had to wear off enough for her to smell the continuing magic you three have been party to."

"But why—" Devon began, pointing to Elizabeth, but she cut him off.

"Wouldn't it have been easier to just wait around Beville and snatch someone than to stalk a school for two years?"

"The type that employ Lancre want fresh magic. Newly-formed wizards are what they trade in," Eric said.

My insides squirmed at the thought of being a thing for trade.

"But—" Devon began, huffing loudly when Elizabeth cut across him again.

"So a fugitive who specializes in kidnapping new wizards made a highly illegal magical modification to the lunch lady and laid in wait for years in New York, the heart of modern magic."

"Yes." Eric drew out the word.

"Then we should turn them in to the Ladies." Elizabeth smiled, her eyes dancing with some plan I didn't quite understand.

"The people who tried to kill us right out there on the street?" Devon pointed through the window. It was true. The Ladies had done their best to slaughter the lot of us a few hundred yards from where we sat. "We should just saunter up to The Consortium, knock on the door, and say, *Hey, I think I might have a couple of fugitives for you. But not us. Please don't murder us?*"

"The animals are gone," Elizabeth spoke excitedly. "They were the one thing the Ladies could legally punish us for. We didn't tell them to come to the battle. They can't pin that on us. The only thing they have on any of us is collusion with outside forces"—a really nice way to say Eric worked for a seriously evil dude, but whatever—"and possession of the phone. So we find whoever made the Lancre, turn them over to the Ladies, and ask them to call it even!" Elizabeth finished triumphantly, and the room fell silent.

Devon didn't even bother to slow clap.

"It would be a brilliant plan if the Ladies believed in law and punishment the way you are used to aboveground," Eric said slowly. "And I agree, stopping the maker of the Lancre is of vital importance, not only for Bryant's safety, but for the safety of all in New York. Turning the creator in to the Ladies might even be the wisest plan if we manage to catch them alive."

"But?" Elizabeth asked.

"Turning the creator in would hardly wipe our tarnished slate clean." Eric spread his hands and looked up to the ceiling. "I'm not sure there is a deed in Manhattan that would set our tally right with the Ladies. And if there were, it would be too dark to be done without losing one's soul."

I didn't ask if he meant literal soul or like *I did something that went against everything I believe in* soul.

"Okay, then." Elizabeth growled with frustration. "What do you suggest we do?"

"First, we find the creator and rid Manhattan of the evil of one who trades in new magic," Eric said, "then we go after the Ladies."

"Go after the what?" I yelped at the same moment Devon said much more calmly, "Go after as in *attack*?"

"The magic done at your school is the violation the Ladies have been waiting for. They can now come after Bryant without even needing to publicly mention their embarrassing defeat by Thaden, Charles, and of course, us." Eric bowed to the group. "The Ladies are weaker now than I have ever seen them, but removing an aboveground threat like Bryant would go far in proving their worth to those they rule. Whether by design or by accident, the creator of the Lancre just made Bryant a political target."

12

We talked about plans for a long time. Eric went on and on about how we needed to find the creator and bring them down, then go straight after the Ladies. Devon ranted about how we should go after the Ladies first. Eric said no. Elizabeth said everyone needed to calm down and eat, so we went to the dining room to sit around the shining wooden table, which was big enough to fit twenty people.

The table produced food, we ate, and they argued. I half-tried to keep up. My brain was too foggy to follow their fighting. We had to stop the creator before they made another Lancre to try and grab me or some other poor kid who was new to the magic crazy pot. I got that much.

We had to stop the Ladies who Eric seemed really, really sure were going to take my squishing the former lunch lady as the announcement that it was now open season on Bryant Jameson Adams hunting. I understood stopping the Ladies, too. I didn't want to end up murdered by mist or spending the rest of my life dodging them. And if the Ladies decided killing me was their best play to show they were still in power, it really was them or me.

It was the details that made the humming in my head buzz loudly over their words. We had to wait for daylight. There was a place to go and find answers. Go in the back way and take everything.

They argued around in circles until the three of them seemed to agree on something.

"Bryant, you've been awfully quiet," Eric said as the plates of whatever it was we had been eating dissolved back into the table. "Are you having second thoughts about joining the magical world? If so, I hate to be the one to tell you it's far too late to leave now."

"It's not that." I shook my head, shutting off the buzzing. "I just…" I took a breath and started again. "I get that we have to stop all the bad guys. I even get that fate likes to speed things up when stuff starts to go wrong. But last time we got into a big battle, the fight was coming after us and we really didn't have any choices. We were cornered and desperate and utterly screwed. Now we're picking who we want to go after and how? It just seems impossibly, I don't know…bizarre? Presumptuous with a hint of death wish? How are the four of us supposed to do all this? Are we going to bring Charles and his army of shadows with us?"

"As I've said, we're on our own." Eric didn't sound mad at me for not paying attention to his grand plan. In fact, he sounded more genuinely sympathetic than he had since the time we trapped my mom in a magical cocoon. "We are going to do this carefully, I promise you. With any luck, by this time tomorrow we'll have dealt with the unpleasant creator and be onto the Ladies."

"I really don't think you're helping." Devon rolled his eyes. "Look, Bryant. Like it or not we've become the people who have to stop the bad guys in order to survive. But we're better off this time. We're choosing to go after them. We're more prepared. It's going to make all the difference." Devon sounded so calm and sure I nodded despite the prickles of doubt and dread on the back of my neck.

"We should all get some rest." Eric stood. "There are plenty of rooms upstairs. The house will lead you where you need to go."

Elizabeth, Devon, and I headed to the shining wooden door that led to the hall. All the doors around us swung open like gleeful tormentors waiting for us to run the gauntlet. None of us had the energy to run as the doors slammed one after the other, *guiding* us up the stairs and into a hall none of us had ever entered before. The slamming of the doors kept chasing us down a corridor far too long to fit in the house, until we reached the end where three doors stayed open. I peeked into the first door. A large canopy bed with ruby-red hangings sat in the center of the room, looking warm and inviting.

"Ladies first." Devon bowed Elizabeth into the room. With a murmured goodnight, she closed the door and was gone.

I didn't like her being out of sight. It was too hard. The memory of her being flung at the wall by an evil, witch-hunting Lancre made me want to tear down the door just to see her safe and sound.

"Come on." Devon pulled me through the next open door. This room was different than Elizabeth's but just as Victorian and fancy. A white iron bedframe with flowery sheets took up the center of the room, and a scent like lavender filled the air. A painting of a castle hung on the wall next to a wide-set wardrobe that looked like it might lead to another world.

"Are you okay, Bryant?" Devon asked as soon as the door clicked shut behind us.

"Oh, yeah," I said a little too enthusiastically. "Just excited for all the dangerous adventuring we have coming up."

"I really want to punch Eric in his stupid wizard face." Devon slid down the wall by the door. "He talks like this is no big deal."

"I think the near-death thing is normal to him." I sank onto the bed. The metal frame creaked and groaned, protesting my weight.

"Normal for him isn't normal for us. We should be at home right now. I should be listening to my dad lecture me on how I need to find a nice girl like my friend Bryant did."

"Your dad says that?" I slid off the bed to sit eye level with Devon.

"All the time, dude." Devon nodded tiredly. "You're like his hero. You were even before Elizabeth."

"Wow." We sat in silence for a moment, like only best friends can. "You could go home, you know. You aren't the one the Lancre sniffed, so you probably don't smell any more magical than everyone else who got pixie-dusted today."

"I'm not going home. I'm not leaving you or Elizabeth. I may not like the idea of trying to take on two bad guys in the next few days, but if that's where you're going, it's where I'm going. I couldn't live with myself if I didn't. Better to fight than be the asshole who abandons his friends." Devon gave a tired grin. "Besides, I texted my parents while we were in the cab and told them I had things to do and wouldn't be home for a while. They've probably thrown all my stuff out the window and shunned me by now."

I returned Devon's smile like I thought it was a joke, even though we both knew he was mostly serious.

That was the problem with being Devon's best friend. I knew his parents weren't great, and I was duty-bound to never mention it. I wasn't allowed to ask why his parents always seemed to be relieved when he left the house or why once every third month they'd freak out if he was ten minutes late when they didn't want him around anyway, and he wasn't allowed to ask why I was terrified of anyone finding out my dad was super rich. It was how we survived.

"Remember when being a hero meant being the one to volunteer to climb the sketchy fire escape to rescue a ball? I miss that." Devon laughed. I think it was the saddest laugh I'd ever heard. "See you in the morning." Devon stood and walked out the door before I could think of something meaningful to say.

"Goodnight," I said to the woodgrain on the door.

I crawled back onto the bed and under the flowery quilt. I missed my bed. Not the one in the linoleum place. The one that had gotten blown up when I ruined my mom's old apartment.

I shut my eyes tight, trying to pretend I was back in the bedroom I had grown up in. Soon Mrs. Mops would come stick her butt in my face and dig her needle-like claws into my chest just to mess with me one more time before I fell asleep.

But a tap on the door came instead of vicious claws.

"Bryant?" Elizabeth's voice drifted through the door.

"Come in?" I said it with a question at the end. Like I was asking if it was all right for her to come in. Mostly because I wasn't sure if it was all right for her to come in.

But Elizabeth slipped through the door without any magical siren blaring, shouting to the world there was a girl in Bryant Jameson Adam's bedroom.

"How are you?" Elizabeth perched at the foot of the bed. Like it was normal for the two of us to be on a bed together.

"*Immummm.*" I'd lost my ability to say words. Two months of dating and now I had suddenly reverted to not being able to speak in front of Elizabeth.

"So about as well as me then."

I crawled over the squeaky mattress and wrapped my arm around her. She was shaking even though it wasn't cold.

"We'll make it through this, you know," I said with as much determination as I could muster. "It's going to be crazy, but we can do it."

"I know." Tears sparkled on Elizabeth's face.

"What's wrong?" The sight of her silently crying stabbed me right through the heart.

"I'm just"—Elizabeth took a shuddering breath—"I'm so tired. It's been months of this, and now we have to fight again. I just want to rest. Just for a while."

"It's been quiet for two months."

Elizabeth bit her bottom lip, the way she did in math class when she was trying to figure out calculus.

"Unless it hasn't been and you haven't been telling me." I paused for a moment, waiting for her to argue that of course I knew everything and she really just needed a nap.

But she just looked at me with tears in her eyes.

"What haven't you been telling me?"

"A lot," Elizabeth said. "I've been doing a lot."

I waited for her to keep talking, but she just stared at me, like she was stuck between scared and too exhausted to talk.

"Is that why Lola's homeless child guard sniffed me and Eric told him I knew you?" I said.

Shock flickered through Elizabeth's eyes before she nodded. "He's the one who keeps me safe at night. When I'm wandering around, studying the shadows. He's my guard dog."

"But you said he was terrifying. You said they looked like decaying man dogs." The thought of my girlfriend walking around Manhattan with nothing but a dead demon dog for company was horrifying.

"He does." Elizabeth shuddered. "But he keeps me safe. And he can find just about anything."

"You should have told me." I took both Elizabeth's hands in mine. "I could have gone with you. Given you someone alive to talk to."

"It wouldn't be allowed." Elizabeth shook her head, sending her hair cascading around her shoulders. "No non-seers allowed in training."

"Training? I thought you were just keeping an eye on things."

Elizabeth laughed. It started like a tiny giggle, but soon she was laughing so hard I was sure Devon would hear.

"Keeping an eye on things?" Elizabeth finally gasped. "How am I supposed to do that without training? I see creepy things in the shadows, but I can't always tell what they are. I know the shadows swirl by Pearl and Water Street, and not all the people are people in Bowling Green. But how would I know what I was looking at without training? Eric's library has given me some things to study, but it wasn't enough."

"Then how have you been learning?" I glanced stupidly at the door like Elizabeth's teacher would come charging in right on cue to introduce herself.

"Lola, mostly."

I breathed a sigh of relief. Eric's paramour had saved my mom. She was an amazing and powerful seer, even if she did live in exile under a bridge.

"She's been sending me out into the city with the boy, and he's been helping me track things. Different kinds of shadows so I could see them for myself, a few kinds of creatures normal people can't see, sometimes wizards who are trying to hide from the Ladies. Bad things don't always hide in nice places."

"Why didn't you tell me?" I tried to keep the hurt out of my voice. It wasn't like she was seeing another guy, but it still stung.

"I did, mostly." Elizabeth shrugged. "And I didn't want you to worry. You have your own training to think about, you can't waste time chasing after me."

"You aren't a waste of time." I took Elizabeth's face in my hands. "Nothing about you will ever be a waste of time."

"But it is." Elizabeth took a shaky breath. "I'm barely a seer. I'm not a wizard. I'm only talented enough to be able to tell evil things are coming. I can feel this darkness building and the patterns in the shadows are different, but I don't know what any of it means."

"What sort of evil things are coming?" I asked like a stupidly moronic idiot.

"I just told you, I don't know!" Elizabeth half-shouted, pulling away from me.

"I'm sorry, you did." I held out my hand to Elizabeth, waiting for her to take it. "You can see things I can't even imagine."

"It's like trying to read a language I don't understand. That uses an alphabet I don't know." Elizabeth wound her fingers through mine. "I can tell things are getting angrier and more frightened. Violent sometimes. But I don't know why. And knowing that I don't know makes it worse."

I scooted over to her, pulling her to my chest. She nestled her head on my collarbone. It was the most wonderful and terrifying feeling at the same time.

Elizabeth was there in my arms. The most perfect creation in the entire world wanted me to hold her. But that made it my job to protect her. To keep her safe from whatever might be lurking in the shadows I couldn't even see. The urge to take her hand and run back up to the city, find an airplane, and fly to the other side of the world surged through me. It didn't matter how far we had to run, or how long we had to hide, as long as I could keep Elizabeth safe.

Nothing mattered but keeping Elizabeth safe.

But the Lancre had found Elizabeth's scent, not mine. Even if I could convince Elizabeth to move to Thailand to live on an elephant sanctuary, she still wouldn't be safe.

"Is that why the Lancre scented you?" I asked, still holding Elizabeth tightly. "Because you've been spending so much time with the shadows?"

"No idea." Elizabeth gave a faint laugh. "I'm a seer, not a scenter."

"If you figure it out, will you tell me?" I pressed my lips to Elizabeth's hair, reveling in her scent of fresh flowers with no detectable magic mixed in. "Tell me everything. Because it is all important." I scooted back enough to be able to look into her eyes. "You are important."

"I just"—she gave a shaky sigh—"I didn't want to bother you. With everything you need to learn, and how hard you've been trying—"

I didn't let her finish. I leaned in and kissed her instead. And Lancre didn't matter, and shadows didn't matter, and leaving my parents didn't matter. There was only me and Elizabeth.

13

I would love to say I was super cool and when Elizabeth curled up with her head on my shoulder I totally slept super peacefully like I was finally complete and everything was right in the world. But I didn't sleep. Not really.

I'd drift off for a few minutes, then wake up suddenly, expecting my mom to come into the room screaming at me for falling asleep with a girl. Once I was awake enough to know my mom was definitely not going to come storming into Eric's house since she had no idea how to get to Beville, let alone which house Eric lived in, I'd fall back asleep. Then I'd wake up thinking Eric was going to come barging in with some coy remark about the follies of youth. Then I'd drift off again and think shadows were coming to steal Elizabeth away from me.

But Elizabeth slept, her breathing steady and her beautiful face calm. She slept through each of my mini freak-outs without so much as a murmur. Like she hadn't slept properly in months. Which might have been true. Which made me a terrible boyfriend for not noticing.

The cycle continued until the house decided it was time for us to wake up. The lights in the room all flicked on at the same moment the wardrobe doors gave a bang that would have shattered any normal glass.

With a scream, Elizabeth tumbled off the bed, hitting the floor with a shriek and a *thud*, while I leapt to my feet, standing on the bed and screaming, "*Primurgo!*"

The shield blossomed around the bed, but only the wardrobe moved. Its doors swung open to show a set of perfectly pressed clothes as the door to the hall flew open.

"Is that my cue to go?" Elizabeth whispered. The door opened wider in response. "Okay then." Elizabeth stood silently and crept out into the hall. As soon as she passed the threshold the door slammed shut behind her.

"Thanks." I rolled my eyes at the door.

The knob rattled in response.

"Though I don't see why you should care where Elizabeth sleeps." Heat flooded my face just talking to the house about Elizabeth sleeping in my room. I'm not sure how to explain it, but I swear I could feel the house judging me.

I headed for the door to the hall, but a barely visible narrow door behind the wardrobe swung open with a *creak*.

"What?"

The door opened a bit wider.

"Fine."

The door didn't lead anywhere dark or dangerous. Just to a bathroom with white and blue tiles. The scent of strong soap filled the air. The fancy carved showerhead hovering over the claw foot tub turned on as I stepped into the room.

"So now you're telling me I smell?"

Instant food delivery was great, and having a house that wanted to keep you alive during a battle also had some definite pluses. But when the house gets all judgey and tells you to bathe, it gets a little weird.

Not weird enough for me to refuse a hot shower, though. I mean, I had been covered in rat king blood and pixie dust, fought a Lancre, and run for my life since my last shower.

I didn't suspect anything until I climbed back out of the shower and reached for my pile of clothes on the floor. My fingers met nothing but smooth, cool tile. "Aww, come on!"

I ran into the bedroom, chasing the vain hope that maybe my clothes would be magically clean and folded on the bed. My hopes were smashed as soon as I got into the room. The bed was perfectly made, and my clothes were nowhere in sight.

"No, no, no," I groaned, turning to the wardrobe.

The doors gave a joyful little wiggle on their hinges, happily displaying the neatly hung clothes.

"I could just decide to go naked, you know!"

If a wardrobe could laugh I swear this one would have. Luckily, there were no enchanted roses to be had in this house, so the doors just wobbled a bit harder.

"Fine!" I yanked the clothes from the hanger. "You want me to wear a suit, fine!" Socks and underwear tumbled out of the dresser, landing at my feet. "Oh, how very kind of you."

I didn't look in the mirror as I pulled on the suit. The house was making me dress like Eric's mini-me. A black, three-piece suit with a white dress shirt, fancy black shoes that really didn't seem suited to running for my life, and even a black bowtie to cap off the turn-of-the-century horror. I snatched up the black bowtie. It wasn't even a clip-on. I had a horrible feeling that if I held the tie up to my throat it would tighten for me.

"Nope, that's too far." I threw the bowtie back onto the bed. "I draw the line at bowties."

Storming over to the door, I half-expected the knob not to turn until I completed the macabre ensemble. But the door opened easily, and I darted into the hall before the house had a chance to change its mind.

"Elizabeth? Devon?" I called, waiting dumbly in the hallway. It only took a moment for Devon to pop his head out his door.

His eyes traveled up and down my outfit before he bit his lips together to pinch back a laugh. "And here I thought I was the only one the house decided to mess with." Devon stepped out into the hall. He was dressed in an all-black suit that looked like it belonged on a billboard. He didn't have a white shirt with a dodgy collar. He had a fancy, black, collarless shirt with no place for a tie. I looked like an undertaker—he looked like an international spy. Sometimes having a super cool best friend sucks.

"You boys look nice." Elizabeth stood behind us smiling, looking like a time-traveling angel. She was wearing a 40s-style dress, like the ones my mom used for *Guys and Dolls* when the costumer couldn't find anything decade-appropriate for the show. It was all black with thin, white trim tracing a line around her neck and down the long rows of buttons in the front. Black stockings and lace-up heels completed the look of perfection.

"Wow," I breathed, blushing all the way down to my rebelliously unbuttoned collar. "You look...wow."

"You boys look pretty dapper yourselves." Elizabeth's heels clicked on the floor as she walked over and kissed me.

Time stood still. Angelic perfection, kissing me.

"Whoa." Devon coughed. "Get a room." He kept coughing. "But you already did."

Elizabeth pulled away from me and smacked Devon hard on the arm.

"Rude." Threading her fingers through mine, she led me back down the overly long hall toward the stairs. Devon followed behind, snickering at us.

"Breakfast in the parlor or dining room?" Elizabeth asked loudly as we reached the bottom of the stairs.

The doors on one side of the hall swung open and banged shut, ushering us toward the parlor.

"Thanks," I muttered to the house, not feeling really friendly toward the judgmental building who had made my friends look cool and me look like a stooge.

The smell of freshly baked bread wafted out of the parlor. Eric sat in one of the two large armchairs, balancing a teacup in one hand and a croissant in the other. Mouth watering, I headed straight toward the round table, grabbing a pastry and shoving it into my mouth.

"How very delicate of you, Bryant," Eric said dryly. "Though I suppose an elegant exterior can't immediately change the interior."

"Elegant?" I choked through my mouth full of food. "I look like a pallbearer."

"No one would have you as a pallbearer." Eric stood and batted my hand holding the rest of my croissant away from my mouth. "You've forgotten the tie. You look like a cretin with your top button undone."

"He looks dashing." Elizabeth smiled coyly as she poured herself a cup of tea.

"I'm not wearing the tie." I took a defiant bite. "And you can't make me." I finished with my mouth mostly full.

Eric gave a disgusted sneer. "After we've worked on your table manners, we can begin on the attributes of proper dress. You need to be taught bowties are cool."

"And why do we need cool new duds?" Devon asked as he settled into the other armchair. "Are we going for a trip to the country club?"

"Surprisingly correct." Eric nodded to Devon before pouring himself another cup of tea.

"Correct how?" I asked after the pause in explanation lasted long enough for Eric to pour the tea, add sugar and cream, and sit back down in his chair.

"While you lovely children—"

"Offensive, man," Devon inserted.

"While you younglings were sleeping blissfully, I was doing a bit of digging," Eric finished.

"What sort of digging?" Elizabeth leaned so far forward off the couch I thought she might fall.

"The sort of digging our lovely seer wouldn't be suited for. There are rumors in the city of a new dark wizard. One who fancies himself above the law. This prince of discord has been bold enough to set up his kingdom aboveground, and clever enough to keep his name out of the shadows."

"And he sent the Lancre?" I sank down onto the couch next to Elizabeth.

"Presumably." Eric took a slow sip of his tea. "I don't believe it was anyone who resides in Beville. I whispered to the shadows last night, and they've seen no trace of that kind of magic. It wouldn't be the Ladies. They can scent magic without the foulness of creating a Lancre."

"So this new guy is our only option?" I asked. "I mean, couldn't there be more than one rogue wizard who doesn't live in Beville?"

"Absolutely." Eric raised his cup to me. "I'm sure there might be dozens. But this wizard seems to have a taste for recruiting young talent. He's even lured a few children out of Beville with promises of magic aboveground."

"Does he deliver on those promises?" I asked. A shiver ran down my spine. I leapt up, way faster than the situation warranted, and began making myself a cup of tea, clanking the sugar spoon too hard against the cup.

"Please don't break the china, Bryant," Eric said.

"I mean, does he actually have some wonderful world waiting for the people he steals?" My hands shook as I took a sip of my overly sweet tea.

"I think *recruits* would be a more descriptive term than *steals*, at least for those he's convinced to leave Beville. But as for a wonderful world in the light, I truly don't know." A little wrinkle creased Eric's pale, white skin between his coal black eyebrows.

Eric saying *I don't know* was terrifying. He was always so annoyingly sure of everything. Him not knowing something was like a doctor telling you they didn't really know if you had cancer or not.

"But I doubt it," Eric said. "If he truly had something spectacular to offer, his discreet recruiting would have taken more from Beville, and the use of Lancre would be unnecessary."

"So he takes these kids and does what with them?" Devon asked.

"I have no idea, but that is what I intend to find out. We'll go to this prince aboveground, find out if he did, in fact, send the Lancre to lurk in your school, make sure none in his care are being harmed, and if he is guilty on either of those counts, we will ensure he can never hurt anyone again." Eric set his cup on the table and stood.

"Now?" I asked, my voice trembling enough to have all three of them look at me. "I mean, it's morning. Shouldn't we wait until afternoon?"

"Usually I would agree that a visit before noon is rude, but when seeking one's enemies, the rules of propriety can be set aside."

"So…now, then." Elizabeth grabbed my elbow and hauled me to my feet.

"Once you know where an enemy is, it's best to strike immediately before fate thinks you're lazy and decides to ruin your plans."

"Right." I grabbed an extra croissant and followed Eric out the door.

"You still haven't explained the suits," Devon said as he followed the funeral train down the hall.

"Where we're going, it would be best not to be seen as *other*." Eric stopped by the front door, pulling his long coat off a hook I'd never noticed before. Three other coats hung next to it. He swept a hand for us to take them. "While in your society blending in might be possible with loud and poorly made clothes, this is the camouflage of magic."

I grabbed a coat from the wall, hoping maybe I had gotten the cooler one this time. Nope. Devon looked like he was going to battle inside a computer, Elizabeth looked like a Kennedy, I looked like an asshat.

I slouched out of the house after Eric, doomed to be the dorky sidekick to the suave hero. Elizabeth slipped her hand into mine, and a warm glow started right in the center of my heart, burning away the icy cold jealousy. So I stopped pouting and puffed up my chest. If I was going to be a funeral director, at least I was a funeral director holding the hand of the most beautiful girl in the world.

"What?" Elizabeth asked, giving me a sideways smile as we entered the tunnel to Columbus Circle.

"Nothing." I grinned like the idiot I am. "You just look truly beautiful."

14

I really thought I would get a bunch of weird stares or at least some blatant avoidance on the subway for looking like a harbinger of death. But no one seemed to notice my undertaker-chic ensemble as we took the train to the lower east side.

"Where exactly are we going?" I whispered as another hundred tourists got off of the train, heading for Christmas merriment aboveground.

"You'll see when we get there." Eric smiled as he spoke.

I didn't trust that smile. "What do you mean, I'll see? Are we going to the Empire State Building? Please don't tell me magical forces have taken over the Empire State Building."

"Don't be foolish." Eric chuckled. "The Empire State Building hasn't been in magical hands for the last decade."

"Right. Who doesn't know that?" I leaned back in my subway seat.

"And here we go." Eric popped to his feet as the train rumbled to a stop.

"Allons-y!" Devon bowed, letting Elizabeth and me leave the train first.

A man in a bright red jacket leaned casually against the pole right outside our train door. I searched his face for signs of magic. Not that I knew what a sign of magic would be other than color impairment. But Eric walked past the red coat and headed toward the kiosk on the side. I searched the stand for a door to an enclave of magic, but Eric walked past that, too.

I kept searching everything we passed for a sign of something magical. The

stairs leading up to the street didn't turn into a slide to a forbidden underworld. The crosswalk sign wasn't blinking a secret message.

Maybe that dog trying to eat his own leash was the doorman for the secret
society of magical kidnappers. Or that old man gumming chestnuts was actually the wizard we were looking for.

"How do you do it?" I whispered to Elizabeth. "How do you see magical
things all the time? And spend nights looking for creepy shadows?"

"It's exhausting." Elizabeth sighed, not seeming to think there was
anything weird about the little girl having a tantrum and pounding her fists
against a frostbitten tree.

The crowds got thicker as we moved toward the more touristy streets.
Soon, we reached a scrum that blocked the whole sidewalk.

"Just great," Devon grumbled, cutting out onto the street.

Eric grabbed his arm. "If you want to be in on the fun, you'd best stay here.
We've arrived."

I looked up at the building all the tourists had jammed themselves in front
of. A giant black-and-white mock vintage sign hung out front.

The Game.

"You have got to be kidding me." A laugh bubbled out of me before I could
swallow it.

"Not in the least." Eric stared at me with one eyebrow arched high.

"This is it?" I asked through my torrent of laughter.

"Shhh," Elizabeth hushed as a harassed woman with three whining children turned to glare at me.

"The most popular tourist restaurant outside Times Square is where the
kidnapping prince of magic hangs out?" I whispered.

"It's an excellent cover when you consider it." Eric spoke so softly Devon,
Elizabeth, and I had to lean in to hear him. "A noisy place known for odd
goings-on. The expectation of strangers coming and going."

"A liquor license," Devon added.

"Crass but undeniably true," Eric conceded.

"So what do we do now?" I scanned the crowd. The throng pressed toward
a man holding a tablet at the door. All I could see of him over the crowd was a
wide top hat and lips pinched with impatience as people complained about
the long wait for a table.

"And why is everyone here to eat now?" Devon growled as a tourist stepped
on his toe. "Why are you pushing in line to eat now?" he snapped at the
offender.

"I don't want to get stuck in line waiting for dinner," the woman coughed in her gravelly, smoker voice.

"Lovely." Eric faced the door and muttered something under his breath.

The crowd parted gently in front of him, like an invisible wedge was plowing subtly through the mass of hangry people. Like Eric was Moses parting the red and green tourist sea.

I trailed in Eric's wake, keeping Elizabeth's hand clasped firmly in mine.

"We'd like a table for four," Eric said as we reached the man.

I forgot to be intimidated as the doorman surveyed us. I was too busy gawking at his outfit, which suddenly made mine feel subtle and chic.

Aside from the wide, black top hat, he wore a deep purple tailcoat to go with his ruffle-fronted shirt. His black leather boots came up to his knees, mostly covering his emerald green pants. He looked like a combination of a horseback rider and a court jester. The illusion was ruined as soon as he spoke.

"There's a wait." His tone was dry and low with a touch of menace. "It'll be about two hours before I have seating for you. You can wait on the street. We don't hold tables."

"A true pity that a magical place such as this is so lacking in customer service." Eric smiled calmly. "I suppose it's quite lucky for us we aren't here for one of the standard tables. We're here to dine with the proprietor."

With a fancy little flick of his wrist, Eric produced a black business card with shimmering gold letters that read *Eric Deldridge ~ Resident of Beville.*

The doorman looked down at the card for a moment, and then with another flick of Eric's wrist, it was gone.

"Just because you've found the place doesn't mean you're the type for entry to the private game," the doorman said.

"Oh, but we are." Eric took Devon by the shoulders and moved him to the front of our group. "I believe I can offer just the sort of merchandise that is of value in the private game."

The muscles on the back of Devon's neck tensed as the doorman looked him up and down as though examining a chunk of meat at a high-end butcher.

"Fourth floor. If you can't open the door, it isn't my problem." He stepped aside, bowing us in.

Eric reached for the handle, but before he could touch the knob, the doorman slammed his hand against it.

"One more thing." The doorman smiled, which was way scarier than his scowling had been. "Play The Game at your own risk."

"Of course." Eric grinned back.

If I didn't know Eric, I might have missed the *I might kill you later* glint in his eyes. Eric pulled open the door, and the crowd roared in protest.

The shouts of "We've been here for an hour!" "You said there were no reservations!" and "I slipped you a fifty!" fell silent as we entered The Game.

The hall in front of us was taken up by a wide, wooden staircase. To the right was a huge archway that opened into a bar, which, despite the early hour, was packed. Not that I'd had much experience in bars, but I knew right away why this one was in such high demand. Bartenders in pointy hats and long robes stirred smoking drinks with the tips of their wands.

Mounted animal heads hung over the roaring fire in the wide brick fireplace. And these weren't the average buck heads of normal creepy hunting cabins. They were mounted magical creatures. Or at least dead things that had been doctored to look like magical creatures. A face of something between a pig and a horse took the center space, flanked by an eight-legged ferret and a bright silver-and-purple bird with a florescent blue beak.

"This is what they think of us." Eric shook his head, sighing heavily. "Better that than the truth."

"The truth?" I asked as sparks flew out of the barback's wand, lighting the sconces around the room to thundering applause from the guests.

Eric rolled his eyes so hard I thought they might fall out. "This way."

We started up the wide, wooden staircase that wrapped around a fancy metal elevator.

"Better to think magic is something from a far removed world utterly beyond normal reach than a specter waiting for you to take one wrong turn," Eric said in a hushed tone.

"Hey," Devon said, "calling Bryant a specter is offensive. Almost as offensive as calling me merchandise. What the hell was that about anyway?"

"Having something to offer to the private game not only gained us entry into this vulgar place, it also gave us some very important information," Eric said as we made it to the second floor.

"Like what?" Devon asked.

"Like this is a place where a kidnapped teenager would be a hot commodity," Elizabeth said as we rounded the corner and the second floor dining room came into view.

Lights flashed in one corner as a man strapped to a wall writhed, screaming in pain. For a spilt second I thought the tortured guy was a teen stolen by a Lancre, living the horrible fate I had narrowly avoided. But then I saw the vaguely disinterested expression on his face as he screamed.

"He's an actor," I whispered to Elizabeth.

"A bad one," she murmured back as the man broke free of his bindings and stumbled forward into the dining room, lurching toward a group of high school girls who screamed like banshees.

As the man raised his hands toward a girl's throat, another actor burst through a curtain onto a balcony halfway up the wall bellowing, "Halt, my monstrous creation!"

The crowd cheered. I snickered.

"I did not intend to create a beast without a soul!" Balcony guy clutched his chest in mock heartbreak. "Now I must destroy my creation!"

Eric took my elbow, dragging me away from the floorshow and up the next flight of stairs.

A monstrous roar followed us up the steps. If I weren't so used to magic, I might not have noticed how the scream faded too quickly, like a spell had blocked sound from traveling between floors.

"What the hell is this place?" Devon said. "I mean, what kind of tourist lines up for this?"

"The ones who..." I lost the ability to speak as we made it to the third floor.

A man in a red uniform screamed as a light saber slashed through his stomach.

"What?" I shouted. "That's not right!"

"Bryant." Elizabeth tugged on my hand as, with a display of glitter and strobe lights, an android appeared in the wall.

"I cannot feel fear," the pale-faced android said. A gold droid toddled out to the center of the room, bowing to the pale android as Elizabeth yanked me out of sight.

"They can't do that!" I tried to get back to the door as the sounds of laser guns and *wooming* sword slices cut through the air. "That is cross-geek contamination!"

"I'm sorry if this place offends your nerd sensibilities," Eric said from the foot of the last staircase. "I promise as soon as we finish our business here, we can leave this place and its misplaced fandom forever."

"Misplaced fandom?" Devon spread his arms wide. "This place embodies a full range of awesomeness!"

Eric turned on the stairs so quickly Devon ran into him. "I didn't take you for one to indulge in things that weren't bound to attract women."

"I'm more than just a pretty face." Devon stepped around Eric to take the lead. "I have depths you know nothing about."

"Delightful," Eric said dryly as Devon stopped in front of a white-and-black checkered door.

15

The heavy metal door, without a window or doorknob to mar the chessboard design, blocked the top of the staircase.

"Well, Mister Depths-beyond-my-understanding, unless you've suddenly become learned in the magical arts, perhaps you could step aside," Eric said.

Devon growled as they switched places on the narrow stairs.

"Do you think it's a puzzle?" I asked in a stage whisper. The terrible feeling of being watched had goose bumps sprouting all over my neck.

"Perhaps." Eric ran a hand around the edge of the door. "Though I doubt it. This is a place of profit with a customer base of wizards who don't mind breaking the law. Making entry too difficult would be bad for business."

"But keep a better clientele." Elizabeth squeezed past Devon and me, squinting at the door.

"Anything of interest?" Eric moved his fingers between squares like they were doing some strange minuscule version of hopscotch.

"Not that I can see." Elizabeth tipped her head to the side.

"Well then, let us try for the obvious solution. *Cliaxo.*"

A deep *thunk* sounded within the door.

"And simple it is." Eric grinned and pressed on the metal. The chessboard surface swung slowly and silently. It wasn't until it was about halfway open that the thump of music carried out to the staircase. "Shall we?"

Eric didn't spare a glance to see if we were following. He was back in his element. Like the last two months of training had just been a hiatus from his real life of danger and sneaking up on people.

"In we go," Devon murmured, following Eric up the steps.

It was my turn to say something brave and/or cocky. My mind was suddenly blank as I turned to Elizabeth.

Say something cool, Bryant. Just one cool word!

"I've always liked chess." The words fell out of my mouth as involuntarily as vomit.

"Maybe we'll play sometime." Still holding my nonsensical and unworthy hand, Elizabeth climbed the last few steps with me.

For a moment, I thought there was some magical trick messing with my head. The black and white door had expanded into a room. Then I blinked a few times and realized the door was still swung open where it belonged—it was the checkerboard pattern that had eaten the room.

The floor was laid out in black and white squares. Unlike the rooms below that were crowded with tables, the center of this floor was almost entirely open. Edged along the walls were black and white booths made of fancy leather, which looked so soft I wanted to curl up and sleep on them.

The only real table in the room sat opposite the door we had just entered. A round, white marble table just big enough to seat four. Two white and two black chairs surrounded it. One of the chairs was filled. By the time my head managed to make enough sense of the room to notice the person staring at us, he'd already stood.

The man had bright white hair spiked into a Mohawk with black tips. His eyebrows and lips looked like he had painted them on with charcoal. But it was his cloak that made me cough a badly-hidden laugh. Black fuzzy fur piled high at his shoulders, like he thought winter was coming, and not in the Manhattan trench coat kind of way. Below the fluffy shoulder pads, a stitched insignia tied the checkerboard décor to the Ren Faire couture. Black and white chess kings crisscrossed right over the stranger's heart.

The man stared at me staring at him and smiled. "Fresh blood."

"Actually, Eric Deldridge." Eric strolled lazily into the room, seeming completely at ease chatting up the caped man. "While I am rather younger than most, I don't think the term *fresh blood* can rightfully be applied to me."

The cape man's smile broadened. "Eric Deldridge. I might have heard of you."

"Then it's even stranger that I have never had the pleasure of hearing of you." Eric reached the table and leaned in to shake hands with the cape man.

Some weird instinct made me move farther into the room. I don't know why. If cape man wanted to kill Eric, I don't know what I could have done about it. But I was Eric's apprentice, his second in the battle of life—at least, that's what I tried to tell myself.

"Kendrick McDonald." Cape man gave a little bow of his head. "And it should be a testament to this institution that you've never heard of The Game."

"What is The Game?" The words slipped from my mouth.

Kendrick glared at me as Eric shot me a warning look.

"The fresh blood speaks." Eric spread his arms wide, stepping aside for Kendrick McDonald.

"The Game is a place, and a thing. It's a way of life and death. It is meaning and power and you"—Kendrick leapt over the table, vaulting toward me —"you, fresh blood, might be an excellent new piece to play."

Kendrick stalked toward me, looking me up and down like I was a pretty girl and he was a gross construction worker.

"He's not a piece to play." Devon spoke so loudly his voice echoed around the room.

Kendrick leaned in, sniffing Devon. "You could play then. You won't survive, but it would be beautiful to watch you try."

"None of us want to play," Elizabeth said. "Whatever fancy game you think you've come up with, we're not interested."

"But you will be," Kendrick said. "Everyone loves The Game."

"If everyone wants to play, why did you need a Lancre to stalk my apprentice?" Eric's tone remained dry and conversational. Because, you know, I hadn't almost died or anything.

"Lancre," Kendrick said the word slowly. "Lancre?" he said again as though testing to be sure he really understood.

"You sent a Lancre to stalk a school." Eric paced the perimeter of the room, running his fingers along the backs of the leather booths and across the shining tabletops as though checking for dust. "The Lancre wasn't even very good, tried to take the girl instead of my apprentice. Your beast caused a fair bit of trouble as well. Made things unpleasant for us."

"*That* Lancre." Kendrick chuckled, nodding his understanding. "She's been out hunting for so long, I thought she'd been killed."

"You left a Lancre on the hunt with no supervision?" For the first time since entering The Game, anger sounded in Eric's voice.

"Don't be absurd!" Kendrick waved a hand in the air. "Could I supply The Game with fresh blood if I only had one, terribly unskilled Lancre hunting for me? We have some willing players, but they grow scarcer as the world begins to fear adventure. I have many Lancre."

"What?" Eric finally stopped pacing.

"I have Lancre in the city, across the country." Kendrick giggled. "I even have a few braving the far-flung reaches of Thailand, searching for something very special for me."

"You've set witch hunters free in the world!" Eric rounded on Kendrick. He seemed to grow in his rage as he walked slowly across the checkered floor. "You created monsters to kill our kind and told them to run along and have a good time?"

"Don't be absurd." A wide smile lit Kendrick's face. "If they killed their prey, who would there be to play The Game?"

Kendrick clapped his hands, and a *clang* shook the air. The door at the back of the room swung open, and a cage glided forward. The cage was partitioned into four quadrants, separated by thick metal bars, and each of the spaces held a thing in it.

"It's not too late for the fresh blood to join." Kendrick tilted his head, examining me once again. "He barely knows which end of a spell is pointy. Give me a month, and I'll have him fighting in The Game."

At the word *game* the things in the cage started to stir, coming to life like Kendrick had just set off their alarm clock.

"Bryant isn't going to play any game you have in mind." Devon stepped up to be shoulder to shoulder with me. He's voice was strong and sure, like he wasn't afraid of the cage that was still coming closer, or of the boy in the front of the cage who glared hatefully at me.

And it was a boy. A wild-looking boy near my age, dressed in black, furry leggings that were crusted in places, like he had forgotten to wash the blood of his enemies out of his clothes after a battle. In the front right corner there was a girl in a pure white, unstained dress. She didn't glare at me or even glance at Kendrick. She just stood with her back to us, moving her arms slowly through the air like she was doing some sort of demented warm-up.

There was a girl in black behind her, and a boy in white behind the other boy.

"These are the champions of the week," Kendrick cooed lovingly, like he was presenting his dog who had won best in show. "This one will earn out of the bars if he wins just once more this week." Kendrick trailed his fingers along the bars that trapped the boy in black.

"Is that what you do here?" Eric moved forward to examine the boy. "I had truly hoped it wouldn't be something so crude. I really must learn to lower my expectations."

"What are you talking about?" I asked. A prickle of understanding pressed on the back of my thoughts, but I couldn't get past the feral boy staring at me.

"Kendrick," Eric spat his name like it was a filthy word, "likes to kidnap young wizards and witches and train them to fight. Force them to fight. To the death would be my guess. It would have to be a very bloody sport to create enough income to support this expensive real estate."

"It is very lucrative." Kendrick rapped his knuckled against the cage. All four of the captives turned to stare at him. "And not just for me. It takes time to earn your way into the fights, time to earn your way out of indentures for the vast sums of money I put into my fighters' training, but if they can make it all the way through, they enter Manhattan free and stronger than anyone apprenticed to a coward who hides in the shadows of Beville could ever hope to be.

"So, what say you?" Kendrick pointed to me, and all the heads in the cage swiveled toward me. "It's not too late for you to join me. And since you walked so nicely in, I won't add recruitment costs to your account. You'll be out of your indentures in no time."

"Recruitment?" Elizabeth growled. "I think you mean attempted murder and kidnapping."

"Spoken like a true mundane human," Kendrick sneered. "What are you going to do, little girl, call the police? They can't get up the stairs."

"Don't talk to her!" I shouted, feeling my feet carry me a step forward.

"And what will you do, fresh blood? Call the Ladies? Tell The Consortium to come after me?" Kendrick tossed his head back and roared with laughter. "Have you been cowering so deep in the shadows you haven't heard? The Ladies are in hiding, buried in the fortress of their Library. They won't risk leaving safety to come after the likes of me."

"What did you say?" Eric stepped forward, his hands tented under his chin in his usual thinking habit.

"There is no one left to police us!" Kendrick shouted, over-enunciating each word as though Eric were hard of hearing. "They are too weak to leave their Library without being destroyed. Holding onto the books is the only thing that keeps them in power. They will hide between the stacks until the end of time. They won't leave the Library. They can't stop me. You can't stop me. Nothing in the world can stop me!"

"I really must thank you." There was a cheerful note in Eric's tone that was more terrifying than furry-bloody-leggings dude clinging to the bars of his cage and baring his teeth at me. "I've spent two months trying to work out a problem, and you've just handed me the solution!" Eric let out a triumphant laugh. "Fate can be a cruel beast, but I am so grateful to her for bringing me here today!"

"You've apprenticed to a madman." Kendrick laughed. "And not even one who knows how to turn a profit."

"Life isn't about profit." Eric stepped forward, planting himself between us and Kendrick. "But I'm afraid I don't have time to work through your moral values or lack thereof. At your advice, I'm afraid our day has suddenly become quite busy."

"You really are a—"

"Of course"—Eric cut Kendrick off—"I can't leave you here to plot the kidnapping of anymore innocent young wizards either, and as you so kindly pointed out, law enforcement is rather lacking these days."

"Then we are at an impasse." Kendrick bowed, and the locks on the four cage doors *clicked*.

"Not at all," Eric said, ignoring the four fighters moving toward their now-open cage doors. "There are two ways forward. You can come with me, and I will bring you to a nice comfortable place where you will never be able to harm anyone again. Your fighters will be freed and sent to appropriate homes to be re-acclimated to magical society."

Furry leggings boy leapt silently to the floor.

"The second option is you refuse to come with me and I have to destroy your establishment, free your captives the hard way, and send the types of shadows after you that you will not escape."

The other fighters climbed out of their cages and stalked forward on the checkered floor.

"The types of shadows that track for me are unwilling to let their quarry survive," Eric continued like there weren't four creepy people closing in on him, not even bothering to spare them a glance. "This is an opportunity I won't offer again. Call off your dogs, or I'll have to call upon mine."

"You think you can fight me?" Kendrick asked so softly I could barely hear him over the pounding of my pulse in my ears. "You think your little *dogs* can fight against my warriors."

"I find the term dog to be offensive," Devon said.

"I'd never call any of you a dog, Devon," Eric said. "And yes, we will fight you. And we will free the ones you have stolen from their homes."

A glimmer of joy shone in Kendrick's eyes. "Then let The Game begin!"

16

Bright lights flicked on, shining down on the center of the room. If the booths had been filled with spectators, we might have been doing theatre in the round. But this wasn't going to end with everyone smiling and bowing.

Eric and Kendrick locked eyes with each other. With one fluid flip of the arms, Kendrick tossed off his fur cape.

"Elizabeth, take care of the door, please," Eric said calmly. "Bryant, try not to die."

"What the hell am I, chopped liver?" Devon asked.

The heads of the caged four turned toward Devon.

"More like bait, but I thought it rude to say. *Kunga!*" Eric slipped the spell in at the end of his sentence. Kendrick doubled over and flew backward as though something very strong had kicked him hard in the stomach.

Then it started all at once.

The two dressed in white launched themselves at Devon.

"*Primurgo!*" I shouted. I didn't have time to make sure the shield was enough to protect Devon. The two in black had charged straight toward me.

The girl screamed something at such a manic pitch I couldn't hear the word, but white-hot pain cut deep into my shoulder.

"*Milkawa!*" I focused on the black square under the girl's feet. The floor writhed and squirmed, slithering silently around her ankles.

The boy with the fur pants didn't shout a spell at me. He just leapt into the air, arms outstretched like he wanted to give me a lethal bear hug.

"*Primurgo!*" I shouted an instant too late. With a horrible *smack*, the boy crashed into me, knocking me to the ground. Stars danced in front of my eyes so brightly I almost didn't see him pull his fist back. "*Abalata!*" A thick blackness sprouted from my hand, and I threw it at the boy's face, knocking him sideways off of me.

The girl in black screamed in rage. Blue light jetted from her palm, and I rolled away, yelping as the spell blazed past, burning my ear.

"*Erunca!*" I knew what the spell was going to do, but seeing the lightning shoot from the ceiling and strike the girl made me gag. But I didn't have time to consider the morality of unleashing lightning on someone who had been locked in a cage for who knows how long. Devon was screaming.

I turned toward him, sure I was going to see my best friend die. But Devon was still standing and very much alive, holding a chunk of table in his hands and swinging it at the girl in white, who had blood trickling down her cheek.

"Bryant, door!" Devon shouted.

I spun to Elizabeth, who ran her fingers along the crack of the closed metal door.

"Bryant, floor door!" A sharp, black something flew at Devon and landed in his table chunk with a *thud*. "Now, Bry!"

I don't know if it was a lifetime of friendship or sudden brilliance, but I knew exactly what Devon wanted me to do.

Focusing as hard as I could on the floor at the girl's feet, I shouted, "*Portunda!*" The floor split perfectly along the lines of the checkerboard, creating a two-square by four-square hole right beneath her feet. The girl fell with a shriek.

"*Portundo!*" The hole in the floor sealed back up with *crack*.

"Bryant, duck!" Devon shouted as a painful weight crashed into my back, sending me face first onto the floor.

I coughed, trying to pull enough air into my lungs to speak as something hard pushed into the back of my neck.

With a shout of pain, the weight disappeared. I rolled over in time to see fur pants hit the ceiling. Eric had turned away from his own fight with Kendrick to help me.

Kendrick had both hands in the air, rearing back as though preparing for a deathblow.

"*Stasio!*" I spat the word and leapt to my feet. The spell wouldn't hold

Kendrick for long, but Devon was under a table and the boy in white loomed over him, his fingers crackling with a spell.

"*Turso!*" A band of white lashed out at the boy's ankles, knocking him off his feet.

"Let's go!" Elizabeth shouted from the open door.

I didn't have time to wonder how Elizabeth had opened the door without magic. I darted to the table and hauled Devon to his feet.

"You can't run from The Game!" Kendrick shouted.

"Looks like we can!" Devon called back as we tore through the door and onto the stairs. Eric was out a moment behind us, muttering some long spell I didn't try to understand as we bolted for the next level.

The sounds coming from below were so blissfully normal. Awkwardly exciting music and the dull chatter of tourists. For a split second I thought we were just going to keep running. Down to the street and to someplace quiet where Eric could heal my shoulder and Devon's head. We rounded the corner and were nearly to the next flight of stairs when streaks of bright blue shot through the doorway. I tackled Elizabeth, pinning her out of reach of the spell.

My heart thudded out of control. I waited to hear screams of terror from the innocent diners, but all that came was a roar of tumultuous applause.

I jumped up, blocking Elizabeth from the doorway. At the far end of the room stood the girl dressed in white, purple flames crackling around her fingertips.

"The Game won't let you go." The girl's voice carried perfectly over the crowd.

It wasn't the pronouncement of doom that made my stomach drop to my toes. It was her voice. It was so...normal. Like any girl I would have talked to at school, if talking to girls were a thing I ever really did. She didn't sound demonically evil or even psychotic. She was just a girl who had been captured and brought here. Made to live in a cage and fight.

I was one magic cellphone and a crazy guy in a black suit away from being her.

"You don't have to do this!" I stepped forward, reaching my hands out toward her. "You don't have to fight for Kendrick. You can come with us."

The girl stared at me, tilting her head to the side. She didn't move as I cut through the tables, weaving my way toward her. "Just come with us, and you'll be safe."

"I've never seen them do this scene before," a woman's nasal voice cut over my words, breaking whatever truce the girl and I had.

"There is no life without winning The Game." Purple flames flew from the girl's hand, streaming toward me.

"*Aarantha!*" I caught the fire in the twister that formed around me. Clawing my hands through the air, I pulled the vortex into my palm, aiming it up toward the ceiling above, keeping the flames away from the bystanders.

People clapped and cheered as the vibrantly purple flames licked the ceiling.

Two men with glowing swords stepped forward.

"The Game will not be disturbed," one of the men said, raising his saber. It was sort of comical—him standing there in his pajama-like, white costume, glaring at me.

"I don't care about your game." Sweat dripped down my face from the sheer effort of keeping the flames away from the spectators.

"You haven't won your round yet." A woman in a red-and-black costume stepped forward, pointing her laser gun at my chest.

"I really think I'm starting to understand why you thought this fandom blending was so annoying, Bry. Ensigns and light sabers don't mesh well." Devon stepped up to stand next to me. "We're leaving, so back the hell off."

"You can't leave without winning." The girl in white let go of the fire spell, and the violet flames dissipated.

Like they had plotted it in the break room, the two space ninjas charged forward, light sabers raised.

A laugh rose in my throat before turning into a stone of fear as the glowing swords got closer to us. They weren't fake plastic glowing tubes or even the nicer Comic-Con variety. The blades of the swords crackled with very real, very dangerous magic as they slashed toward Devon and me.

"*Primurgo!*" I shouted. The blades of the sabers sparked as they struck my shield.

The woman dressed in red-and-black military attire started shooting at us with her laser gun. The globules of magic shook my shield, and the crowd roared.

"Drop the shield, Bry!" Devon shouted.

I let go of the shield as a chair flew over my shoulder, hitting one of the space ninjas in the stomach. Devon bull charged forward and, for a split second, I was absolutely positive I was going to see my best friend split right down the middle.

"*Abalata!*" I threw the black taffy from my hand, hitting the other sword bearer in the face.

Eric was on top of the tables, leaping from one to the next, dodging the blazing spells being shot by the space army chick. There was something building in his hands—a ball of crackling green light. He threw it at the woman, tossing her into a table, which crumpled to the ground. The crowd's cheering turned instantly to shouts of anger and fear.

"This way!" Elizabeth called from the far wall.

I glanced to Devon, who was on his feet, holding a sparking red sword. The man he had taken it from lay unconscious on the ground behind him.

"You can't leave The Game!" the girl in white roared as we ran for the far wall.

"*Parapus!*" Eric shouted.

Thin black lines flew through the air, binding the girl.

"*Kunga!*"

The girl doubled over as the air was knocked from her.

Elizabeth stood next to a plain, gray wall with shimmering panels on the floor. A console of buttons stood to one side.

"Hold on!" Elizabeth called as Eric leapt onto the glowing platform.

A shimmering swirl of glittery strobe lights clouded my vision as the floor disappeared from under my feet.

17

B efore I had time to scream we had passed through a chunk of black and were falling onto a squishy floor. Metal netting and thick bars obscured our view of the room outside. But the crowd in the steam punk dining room seemed to be totally calm as a monster walked through the rows of tables, holding a tray of display deserts.

"I almost fell on my sword," Devon panted, pushing himself to his feet, clasping a silver cylinder in his hand. "I almost killed myself with my light saber." With a flick of his wrist, the red blade sprouted from the silver tube, blossoming to magical life complete with a low hum. "Thank God they went for geek accuracy."

"We need to go. Now." I reached for the glow-taped knob on the elevator door.

The door was much lighter than it looked, like the metal netting was really only plastic in disguise. It swung open easily, and a spotlight flicked on, beaming right on the fake elevator. Every head in the dining room swiveled toward us.

My mouth went Sahara dry, and my hands started to shake in a way they hadn't when people were trying to kill me only a moment before.

"Come on." Elizabeth slid her hand into mine and dragged me out of the elevator and onto the little stage in front of it.

"They're not even supposed to be on this floor!" a prepubescent twerp shouted from his seat right in front of the stage. "They aren't monsters."

"You have no idea what monsters are, little boy," Eric said, taking his place at the front of our pack. "I assure you if you knew what really lurked in the shadows, you would never sleep again."

All the color drained from the boy's face and his lips trembled.

"The quality of service here is terrible," the boy's mother snapped.

"You have no idea, lady." Devon raised his sword as the door to the hall filled with mismatched employees.

The boy in furry black leggings stood at the center, flanked by space people, Frankenstein's monster, and a mad scientist.

"We are going to leave this building." Eric's voice echoed around the room like he was wearing a body mic. "You can either step aside and let us leave peacefully, or you can make us fight you."

The kitchen door swung open, and a line of bussers filed in, holding their trays up like shields.

"Not human, not human, not human," Elizabeth murmured in a panicked voice.

I tried to see what she was seeing beyond the uniforms and angry faces.

"Fine, we'll fight our way out." Eric raised both his hands. "But I absolutely refuse to apologize for any structural damage. *Elihi nustrum alief*"—Eric began walking toward the door, pushing with every step like he was trying to move a city bus by himself—"*manheil erbracina!*"

For one terrible moment, I thought the spell had gone horribly wrong and wasn't going to do anything but leave Eric closer to the flock of people who wanted to kill us.

But then a bright light flashed between Eric's hands, exploding out into a wall of light that shook the air and blasted the group off their feet. Frankenstein's monster's mask flew off his face as he smacked into the banister. Through the bright wall Eric had created I could tell something wasn't quite right. The monster's features were too animalistic, his nose too small, his mouth too large. For one moment of stupidity, I wanted to ask Elizabeth if she saw what I was seeing and if that was what the world looked like to her all the time. But Eric had started to sag under his spell.

"We have to get out of here." Devon charged forward, wrapping his left arm around Eric's waist while holding his sword in his right hand.

The line of busboys charged toward them, bellowing madly.

"*Erunca!*" I shouted, and lighting streaked from the chipped paint on the ceiling.

Only one of the busboys was quick enough to raise his shield and block my spell. The lightning bounced off the metal and hit the ceiling, leaving a black scorch mark where it struck.

The man lunged toward Eric and Devon, giving no sign he had noticed my attack at all.

"Devon, watch out!" As the words tore from my throat, Devon swung his sword, slicing through the busboy's wrist.

Everything in the world slowed as the busboy's gloved hand flew through the air, tumbling wrist over fingers until it landed with a *smack* right in the center of a table full of teenage girls.

"Move, move, move!" Elizabeth shouted over the shrieks of the girls.

Eric's spell faded from view as we ran toward the door. The ones who had been trying to block our path were sprawled on the floor. Large dents cracked the wall where bodies had struck plaster.

"Bryant, above us," Eric said, his voice weaker than I had ever heard, lacking its usual suave flare.

I glanced up as the *rumble* of footsteps pounded down the stairs.

"*Limbargo!*" I shouted at the banister, which grew into a cage-like barrier as we ran down the steps to the ground floor.

"*Expulso!*" a high voice shouted from the bottom of the stairs. A thick stream of red shot up the steps. I slammed myself into the wall just in time, pinning Elizabeth behind me.

"*Kunga,*" Eric rasped, knocking away the attacker.

But orders were being shouted in a horribly familiar voice. "Do not let them leave!"

At the bottom of the steps, the street came into view through the glass of the door. Masses still packed the street outside, desperate to come enjoy the kitsch, completely unaware people were trying to murder us.

Two men holding wands charged out of the bar, their long black robes billowing around them like they were filming a bad music video. One of the men flourished his wand.

"*Abalata!*" I screamed, terrified of what the wand might do. The black that flew from my palm knocked both the men's wands out of their hands.

"Good one, Bry!" Devon shouted, grabbing the handle to the outside door and moving to wrench it open. But the doorframe shifted and melted as Kendrick stepped calmly out of the bar, clapping his hands.

"You've done well." Kendrick smiled, like it was merely impressive that we had destroyed most of his restaurant and potentially killed a few of his people in the process of fighting for our lives. "Better than I thought. Making it all the way to the ground floor. Even the pretty, normal boy managed to find a way to make himself useful."

"Thanks," Devon growled.

Footfalls thumped on the steps as steampunk monsters, space soldiers, and intergalactic ninjas penned us in from above.

"I really think at this point you should be able to appreciate what we're accomplishing here." Kendrick spread his arms wide as a line of wand-bearing wizards formed behind him. "Look at the order I've created, the power. Isn't it worth a little bit of death and pain to be a part of something so wonderful?"

"There are very few things I believe are worth dying for." Eric pulled himself to stand up straight. "Forcing innocent children to fight will never be one of them."

"Well if they won't join you..." Kendrick shrugged. "Kill them."

A dozen wands raised toward us, glowing swords hummed to life above us, and for the tenth time since I met Eric Deldridge, I thought, *This is how I die.*

"The real pity is you didn't even get the wizards right," Eric said. "Real wizards don't need wands."

"*Dothranta!*" I shouted the spell as I leapt toward the door. Before I reached the solid wall, everything around me went black. I felt Devon moving next to me, raising his saber. "Don't kill me!" I yipped, before shouting. "*Portunda! Elizabeth!*" I called her name as the edge of the door reformed under my fingertips.

"*Tundina!*" Eric shouted the spell, and a horrible *whirr* sounded as I dragged Elizabeth and Devon out the door.

"Eric!" I bellowed as bright sunlight blinded me. "Eric!"

Elizabeth's hand slipped from mine as she dove for the door.

"Elizabeth, no!" I screamed, moving to charge after her, terrified the darkness I had created would swallow her forever.

Devon grabbed me around the middle, holding me back.

"Elizabeth!" Her name tore at my throat. "Elizabeth!"

Before I could break out of Devon's grasp, Elizabeth reappeared, her arm around Eric as he stumbled next to her.

"Block the door," Elizabeth ordered.

"*Portundo.*" The spell fell from my lips, making the door meld in with the rest of the restaurant front.

The crowd on the sidewalk clapped and shouted their approval of our show.

"Let's get out of here." Devon flicked off his sword and took Elizabeth's place, supporting Eric.

"We have to mark it," Eric mumbled, his face scary pale. Redness surrounded his eyes. "*Envasio.*"

A shimmering black X four stories tall appeared on the front of the building. It wasn't flat like paint. It shimmered and swirled like it had mass of its own. A hypnotizing mark with no non-magical explanation.

"The Ladies won't be able to ignore that." Eric smiled and sagged into Devon's arms.

Elizabeth led us through the gawking crowd and around the corner. My heart pounded like we were running for our lives. I mean, we had just left a horde of people/maybe-not-so-much-people that wanted to kill us. But Elizabeth walked calmly, and I don't think Eric could have run anyway.

It wasn't until we were two blocks away that any of us even spoke.

"Where do we want to go?" Elizabeth asked when we reached a set of steps leading down to the subway. There were a dozen entrances to Beville scattered around the city, all of them I knew of branching from the subway system.

"We should go to Beville, get Eric some help," I began, but Eric spoke over me.

"We need to get to the Statue of Liberty." Eric's voice rasped as he spoke. "We need to get to the ferry."

"Not until you've rested," Devon said. "You look like you're going to die any second. Let's go to Lola's, have her patch you up."

"We've just given the Ladies a reason to leave the Library." Eric wobbled toward the subway steps. "We might not have another opportunity like this for a very long time. Besides, a little rest and I'll be right as rain."

"I don't think—" I argued, but Elizabeth cut me off this time.

"He's right. We need to go now." She threaded her fingers through mine. "We have to keep going."

There was something in the definitive way she spoke that kept Devon and me from arguing as we hopped the train toward Battery Park.

We were too far south for the tourists to crush us on the subway. The rumble of the tracks under our feet soothed the adrenaline that made me want to kick through the door and run into the dark screaming for help. I guess if you spend your whole life in New York City, the swaying of the subway trains is practically like being rocked to sleep.

"Could you see in the dark?" Eric asked Elizabeth, his head leaning back against the subway window in a most un-Eric like way.

"What?" Elizabeth asked, sliding into the seat beside him. I hadn't even realized he was the only one to sit until she joined him.

"You came into the darkness of Bryant's spell to find me," Eric explained. "I need to know if you could see in the spell. If the spell is vulnerable to seers, we can't use it anymore."

"I couldn't see." Elizabeth sighed. "I just knew about where you were and like you enough to risk going back for you."

"Then I am both relieved and honored." Eric gave a tiny bow of the head that looked like he might have been falling asleep, but the train rumbled to a stop and it was time to walk again.

That's the weirdest thing about fighting. When you leave it seems like everything in the whole world should be in chaos. Like every person you pass should look terrified after the things you've seen.

But that's not how it works, at least not when you're fighting secretive magical battles. No one is supposed to know about things that can kill you with a spell, so they don't know to be afraid. They keep moving through their lives blissfully unaware, leaving you to stagger through their midst. Trying not to look like demons might be chasing you.

18

No one attacked us on our way to Battery Park. I held my breath as I passed over my black emergency credit card to pay for our tickets. I had destroyed part of my school (again) and run away from home. There was a very large possibility my dad had finally decided to cut me off and the card was now nothing more than a magnetized bookmark. But the card went through, and the lady handed us our tickets without even looking up from her computer. I magicked away the dirt and rubble from our clothes so the security guard didn't even give us a second glance as we climbed aboard the ferry.

The wind on the water was even more biting than it had been on land. Like it was determined to freeze off layers of our skin and rip them away forever. Part of me wanted it to.

"We should sit inside." Elizabeth glanced meaningfully at Eric.

He was just as pale as he'd been on the train, his eyes half closed as he gripped the rail to keep standing.

"Good idea." My voice came out all stupid and high like it always did when I was trying to sound calm and cool. "I'll grab us some cocoa."

"I prefer tea, personally," Eric said.

"Me, too." Devon took Eric's elbow, escorting him into the overheated interior of the boat.

There weren't many people inside. It was too late in the day for most people to be heading out for the Statue of Liberty and Ellis Island experience. Rows of upholstered, uncomfortable seats faced a giant TV playing a history film. In the back corner there were a few sticky looking tables. Devon led Eric that way.

"Do you think he'll be all right?" Elizabeth whispered to me as we waited at the snack counter.

"Aren't you the one who agreed we couldn't take him to be healed?" I muttered before turning to the girl at the counter. "Two cocoas, two hot teas, and four sandwiches." I hadn't realized how horribly hungry I was until I said the word *sandwiches*. We had spent the morning battling in a restaurant, but we hadn't actually gotten around to eating anything.

"What kind of sandwiches?" The girl pointed grumpily at the menu. "There are choices you have to make."

Choices. Like running for the Statue of Liberty instead of taking Eric somewhere to rest. Choices like attacking kids who had been locked in cages for who knows how long.

"Well?" the girl asked with an overly-dramatic eye roll.

"Four turkey sandwiches on wheat, and chips with all of them," Elizabeth answered for me.

I squeezed her hand, grateful she hadn't made me think about what we all should eat. I didn't even know how we had managed to stay alive.

I didn't really feel like I knew anything at all. We had gone to find out who was after me and had come out of the restaurant from Hell with way more questions than we'd woken up with that morning. I'd lightninged someone, Devon had chopped off a dude's hand, and Eric looked like he might die any minute. The only one who seemed to have it together was Elizabeth.

Elizabeth, who I was supposed to protect. Who I didn't know how to protect. And now we were on a ferry where our escape route would involve swimming in freezing cold, contaminated water.

Anger rumbled in my empty stomach. I didn't even know why we were on a boat, let alone why we were doing the New York tourist day planned by Satan.

"You okay?" Elizabeth asked in a hushed tone as the food girl collected our purchases at sloth speed.

"No." The word weighed heavily in my mouth. "I'm an idiot who felt like I was actually starting to get a handle on all this. But now I feel like I'm drowning again."

Elizabeth leaned in, brushing her lips gently against mine. All the anger and fear and panic melted away in her soft flowery scent. After an all too brief moment, she pulled away and looked into my poop-brown eyes with her perfect sparkly ones.

"You do have a handle on it. You used magic today like I've never seen you use it before. The four of us fought together, and we all walked out alive and really pretty unharmed." She took both my hands in hers. "There's a lot of things I don't understand either, but we'll make Eric explain. And what he doesn't know, we'll all figure out together. We're going to be okay, Bryant."

"Is that the gorgeous girlfriend or the beautiful seer talking?" I asked, quasi-hoping she would say she had seen a prophecy in sewer trash that meant this was all going to work out okay.

"Just your girlfriend." Elizabeth smiled, and my heart did a back hand-spring at the word *girlfriend.* "Who believes in her boyfriend and in her friends. We'll make it out of this."

A freezing gust of wind blew open the backdoor, sending flyers flying and the crewmembers sprinting to slam it shut. The wind stopped as soon as the door was rammed closed, but the cold feeling on my neck didn't go away.

"Do you want your food or not?" the counter girl said snidely.

We grabbed our overpriced meal and headed back to our table in the corner.

Eric sat slumped on one side with Devon across from him. Eric's eyes were closed, but he was speaking as Elizabeth slid into the booth next to him.

"There is no healing that I require," Eric murmured.

"Then what's wrong with you?" I asked, pulling my turkey sandwich from its cellophane wrapping.

"I used a spell too strong for my weak, mortal frame." Eric opened his eyes to stare right at me. "A thing which I highly suggest you never try. I barely survived the damnable thing. I doubt my charming apprentice would fare much better."

"If you knew the spell was too much for you, why did you use it?" Devon leaned across the table. "Or did you just try a spell without knowing what it would do?"

"Devon," Elizabeth whispered warningly.

"I think it's a legitimate question." Devon snatched a sandwich. "Is our fearless leader stupid or suicidal?"

"I would never try a spell without a relatively good idea of the conse-quences, unlike some people." Eric gave me serious side-eye as he took a long drink of tea, grimacing at the paper cup. "We were in a desperate situation that called for an unusual amount of magic to ensure our survival."

"And what if we hadn't been there to haul you out of the devil's meat shop?" Devon ripped the cellophane off his sandwich so violently you'd think it was the bread that had tried to kill us. "Would you just have asked for a time out so you could sit down for a little nap?"

"I wouldn't have used magic that strong if I didn't have people I trusted fighting by my side," Eric said. "If I thought for one moment any of you might leave me lying defenseless on the floor, I would have used normal amounts of magic to find an escape route for one. But as I trust you not to abandon me, it seemed prudent to find a way for all of us to escape."

Eric and Devon silently glared at each other while I took a few bites of my dry turkey sandwich.

"If we've established no one has a death wish and we all actually do like each other in some twisted way, would someone please explain to me why we're going to the Statue of Liberty? Not that I'm opposed to a historical field trip, but I thought we were going to try and stop the Ladies from killing all of us." Elizabeth took a sip of her cocoa.

"We're going to the Library," Eric answered.

"But the Library is up by Central Park. The entrance is at The Consortium, we've seen it," I said, wondering if Eric's use of too much magic had somehow affected his brain.

I knew I was right. We had seen at least the outside of The Consortium while we were hunting for Eric back in the days when he was still trying to kill us. The place looked like a normal, if unpopular, café on Central Park West from the outside, but the Ladies ran the place. It was the only outpost of magic aboveground in Manhattan. I guess the only *official* outpost would be more accurate. We had just blasted our way through a magical dining experience, after all.

"The primary entrance to the Library is, in fact, under The Consortium." Eric leaned his head against the wall. "But the Library isn't one basement of books. It's a vast system of tunnels holding the entire knowledge of magical civilization. It is a vast *living* space."

"I'm sorry, you emphasized the word *living*?" My throat was suddenly too dry to take another bite of gross sandwich. I tried to gulp my hot chocolate and burned my throat instead.

"Magic imbues the things it touches with magic," Eric said, slipping into his terse, teaching tone. "It changes places and things. My home isn't just a building—it has a spirit all its own. Beville isn't just a cave—it is a living, breathing place. You may not be astute enough to have noticed, but if you survive to return, taste the air in Beville. It's not the dank stench of a cave. The air is crisp and sweet with magic. Now take that magic, all that magic, and condense it into its truest form, into knowledge itself. Vast stores of knowledge.

The most potent and pure form of magic available. Lock it away for centuries and see how the walls change, how they breathe, how they move. I've heard tales of the Library rearranging the volumes all on its own. Organizing the world to its will. Presenting the magic it wants to be used."

"Wow," I breathed.

"Have you seen it?" Elizabeth asked, her eyes wide with wonder. "Do the books fly around? Or just transport instantly?"

"I have no idea." Eric sat up straight, his eyes looking more alert by the minute. "Other than the Ladies, no living person has been in the Library."

"Again with the *living*," I sighed.

"Thaden." Devon leaned across the table. "Thaden got in, didn't he?"

"Indeed he did," Eric began. "Thaden might have been evil—"

"Most definitely evil," I tossed in.

"But he was a genius, a very magically powerful genius. Many had tried to break into the Library before, but none had ever succeeded." Eric tore open five sugar packets and began dumping them out onto the table one by one. "Most died in the attempt. Years of theories and rumors led Thaden into the Library. Once I heard someone had managed to see the vast stores of our kind's most precious treasure, I knew I had to try it for myself."

"Of course you did." Devon shook his head.

Eric didn't seem to notice. He patted the pile of sugar on the table flat and picked up a stir stick. "I followed the same rumors that led Thaden on his successful quest. I found a way into the Library. And I was close, so wonderfully close, to breaking through. I failed." Eric traced lines in the sugar with the stick. "But I escaped with my life. A feat great enough to attract Thaden's attention. He had created the phone by then, using the magic he had taken from the Library. He told me of its glory, everything I sought deep underground handed to me in one convenient package. So I abandoned my dreams of entering the Library and joined Thaden's service."

"We all know how well that went," I said.

"Terribly well by all accounts." Eric didn't look up from his drawing. "We're all alive and stronger for having each other."

"It would almost sound sweet if I thought there weren't some near-death about to be added to that sentiment," Elizabeth said.

"And now we're going to have to succeed where I alone failed." Eric finally looked up, a hint of a smile twinkling in his eyes. "Kendrick was right. We don't need to search for each of the Ladies and fight them on the streets. That could take years. They would recruit new members to carry on their grudge against poor Bryant."

"And you, don't you dare leave out you," I interrupted, pointing an angry finger at him, which he ignored.

"The new members would hunt us as viciously as the Ladies we have already encountered. To gain our freedom we have to destroy the pillar on which they stand, the thing that gives them power over wizards. We have to take the Library. Without it, the Ladies cannot rule. They cannot attack us."

"You want to destroy the Library?" Devon said loudly enough that the few people trying to watch the Statue of Liberty film turned to glare at him.

"I would never dream of harming the Library in any way," Eric said. "I would rather die than risk damaging such a treasure. What I am suggesting is evicting the Ladies."

"You want to break into the Library and kick the Ladies out?" Devon whisper-shouted.

"Basically." Eric shrugged and set down the stir stick. "And lucky for you, I'm one of the few people who has attempted to break into the Library and survived."

"Now I feel great about it," Devon said.

"And I have a team with me this time." Eric leaned forward. "I know the where, and now I have the tools."

"Now we're tools," Devon growled.

"That still doesn't explain why we're on a boat heading toward the great metal lady." Elizabeth pointed out the window.

The statue had come into view through the glass, as green-tinted and surreal as ever, towering above the water. If this had been a normal school field trip, it would have been cool. I'd have taken a picture of the beacon of hope that greeted immigrants and felt grateful for living in a country where a lady with a torch could mean so much to so many.

Staring at her with overly sweet cocoa in my mouth, she looked like a sentry standing guard, blocking my hopes and dreams for survival with her giant green book of doom.

Eric tapped the table next to his flattened sugar pile. I had thought it was a nervous tick, his way of dealing with feeling like a steaming pile of poop, but he hadn't been doodling—he'd been drawing a map.

A long curve marked the west side of Manhattan with a *C* marking The Consortium's location on Central Park West. There was a long thin shape marked *BV* under the Village right over Beville. And crossing under the city, out into the water, and toward a crudely-drawn Statue of Liberty was a swatch marked with an *L*.

"The entrance to the Library that is officially listed is under The Consortium. But the Library expands well outside the city, down below the water where very special sorts of magic dwell. After all, if you're going to go through the trouble of digging, you may as well dig for something good."

"They mined for magic?" Elizabeth asked.

"Exactly." Eric nodded. "And it all might have come to nothing. I have no idea if the Ladies ever found anything under the earth they so diligently mined. But the work proved useful when the time came to build a second entrance to the Library. The world went to war, and it began to seem possible New York City could be attacked, even taken by foreign powers. That is when the Ladies built an escape route, lengthening the Library to give themselves a cozy place aboveground they could run to if foreign wizards stormed their gates."

"They would abandon the Library?" Devon asked. "That might make this easier."

"They would destroy it," Eric corrected. "Better to let the knowledge of the ages burn than have it in someone else's hands."

"But we're going to try and take it?" I squeaked. "What if they set the Library to self-destruct?"

"Then we burn with the books, but"—Eric held up a hand as I tried to speak again—"they won't do it while they're inside. And if the legends are as reliable as I am hoping, they would need to be at the statue exit to make it work at all."

"So if legends are right, and we can do something only an evil mastermind has managed, and if nothing goes wrong, *then* we'll drive the Ladies from the Library and take charge of magic in Manhattan?" Devon leaned back, crossing his arms over his chest.

"More than just Manhattan," I said. "The world. It's the Library for the whole world."

19

One thing I've learned about planning world domination or at least deadly attacks—it makes your stomach feel like it's made of cement. Like the weight of the world you're now trying to take charge of was in the awful turkey sandwich you bought on the ferry ride to your doom.

"It isn't the only library of magic in the whole world." Eric waved a breezy hand through the air like what he was talking about wasn't monumental and quite possibly disastrous. "Just the largest and most notable. Honestly, I have more books hidden in my home than the London Library has on its shelves."

"So best, most important library in the world, run by the murdering Ladies who are in charge of basically everything." I swallowed hard. It was good to know I could still swallow while panicking. "Just some sensible world domination for our afternoon enjoyment."

"We aren't plotting world domination, Bryant." Elizabeth reached across the table and took my hand. "We're going in to kick out some bad people."

Her soft, delicate hand in mine made the stomach cement melt away.

"And once we get rid of the bad people?" Devon asked, his brows knit together.

"We'll figure that part out if we survive," Eric said as a voice came over the speakers.

"*We are now arriving at the Statue of Liberty. Please check under your seats for your belongings, and keep your groups together. The last ferry leaves at 6 p.m. this evening. Please arrive at the docks no later than 5:50 for boarding.*"

The buzz of people moving toward the doors blocked out the rest of the words.

"Anything of interest, Elizabeth?" Eric asked as the herd moved us out the doors and into the freezing air on the deck.

"That kid stuck gum under the railing." Elizabeth pointed to a snot-nosed ginger in front of us.

"Splendid." Eric led the way onto the dock that ran up to the tiny island.

I had been to visit Lady Liberty for school field trips. Like six times. I had always taken the wide path straight to the front of the island where you could take a picture of the statue. Most of the people who got off the ferry shambled along that same route.

"Please don't tell me we have to climb to the top and jump off," I whispered, trying to sound like I was joking even though I was afraid that might be exactly what we needed to do.

"Don't be ridiculous." Eric shook his head, tipping his face up to the winter sun as we followed the flock of tourists. "We're going to find a quiet place to hide ourselves until the island has cleared and we can slip away."

"Until the island has cleared?" Devon said. "Why didn't we just bring your boat over here once the statue closed for the day?"

Devon had a point. Eric did have a little sailboat we'd ridden on while fleeing from the Ladies the first time we were all facing imminent death.

"Do you have any idea how much security there is around this island?" Eric asked, standing in the center of the path, casually scanning every person that passed. "Better to sneak out than in."

"And where do we wait?" Elizabeth asked. "And please tell me it'll be warm."

"Right…" Eric paused for a long moment, beckoning us all to the very edge of the path, before sweeping a hand through the air. "Here."

I noticed the change in noise first. It was like someone had clapped earmuffs onto my head.

"What?" Devon asked, his voice sounding perfectly normal, but as the nasty little gum boy passed, I could see his mouth moving as he shouted at his mother, but there was no real sound.

"Cool," I breathed.

"Now if we could all take a few more steps into the trees," Eric said in a tour guide voice.

"Don't tell me the spell moves with us." Giddiness bubbled inside me. "Okay, tell me the spell moves with us."

"It can shift slightly," Eric said in an exasperated tone. "Enough to get us off the path."

"And they can't see us?" Elizabeth traced her fingers through the air, which shimmered as flesh met spell.

"Or hear us. And just for you, Miss Wick." Eric gave a little bow. "*Relanto.*" The air around us warmed at once.

"You can wave your hand and make an impenetrable shield?" Devon growled. He alone didn't seem to be happy about the instant comfort.

"There is more to it than waving your hand. *Glasien.*" At Eric's word, the ground in the tent/shield glowed faintly for a moment. The chill disappeared from under my feet as the snow vanished, replaced by squishy, fresh grass.

"Nice," Elizabeth sighed and sank to the ground.

"Do you know how many times survival would have been significantly less painful if you had just waved your hand and made a shield?" Devon spat. "I can count two today."

Eric sighed, holding up both hands placatingly as Devon took a breath to keep railing.

"This sort of shield isn't useful in combat," Eric began. "It's too passive. A spell meant to harm could fly right through it. All it does is make a nice little silencing bubble with a touch of camouflage and a few dashes of something fancy that dissuades people from trying to walk through it. It does no good if someone is looking for you or if you are in an enclosed space. But for now it will give us all a chance to gain some much needed rest."

Devon stared at Eric, stone-faced. He looked like a racially ambiguous, clothed version of the David. Handsome, unflinching marble.

"Fine," Devon said after a very tense minute. "Just fine." He lay down on the newly formed grass, coat and all, his eyes fixed on the bare tree branches above us.

I wanted to talk to him, to ask him why he was so mad at Eric for being normal douche Eric, but we were trapped in an invisible tent with tourists unknowingly passing a few feet from Devon's head, so it didn't seem like the time.

"Do you see anything of interest, Elizabeth?" Eric asked again.

Elizabeth silently scanned the trees and people moving past. "Nothing magical."

"Good." Eric smiled tiredly and pulled off his jacket. With a perfect flick of the wrist, he laid it out on the ground and sat on the silk lining.

"Right." I pulled off my long coat. I didn't bother with the wrist flicking to lay it out flat. I just knelt and spread it out like a mere human. Then I held out my hand. Elizabeth took it and scooted over to sit on my coat. And suddenly I wasn't a stupid human lacking magical sophistication. I was a brave knight giving a beautiful lady a soft place to rest.

"What did you see in the restaurant?" Devon asked.

"Things." Elizabeth gave a little shudder. "People that weren't quite people. Their faces were wrong, or maybe darkness had taken bits of them."

"And Kendrick had them working in a restaurant?" I tried not to picture a server with a black void instead of an arm bringing me dinner.

"Kendrick is much cleverer than I had hoped, clever enough that I doubt we've seen the last of him. I expect he will be long gone by the time the Ladies reach The Game. "

"Great," I muttered.

"But if he's so smart, why did he put not quite people right in view of the tourists?" Elizabeth asked.

"He didn't. He dressed them up as characters or hid them in unnoticeable positions."

"The costume part I sort of understand. If I couldn't *see*, I probably wouldn't have noticed," Elizabeth said. "But it was super noticeable when the bussers attacked."

"When they were forced to defend The Game, then yes, it became notice-able," Eric explained. "But on any normal day, no one would notice anything strange because they refuse to look. You've asked before why Lola's associates appear to be homeless?"

"Yeah," I answered.

"The same reason bussers are an excellent disguise for the not quite humans or wizards in Kendrick's employ. Both are the type no one really wants to look at. No one wants to look the homeless man or the underpaid in the face. They don't want to acknowledge that part of the reality in which they so comfortably live. If you don't want to see something at all, imagine how hard it would be to see something awful in it."

"Unless, of course, you're a seer." Elizabeth sighed and curled up on my coat. "Then you get to see everything in every dark shadow and corner."

Eric gave a nod. "A terrible burden that is a great gift to our cause."

"Well, the gift is exhausting." Elizabeth yawned. "Wake me up if someone tries to kill us."

Her streaked hair splayed out around her like something in an art museum. Then she did the most amazing thing. Without even opening her eyes she reached up and took my hand, gently pulling me down to lie behind her. She wrapped my arm over her like a blanket and sighed, like because I had become her big spoon she felt safe.

Everything inside me melted, and I didn't care about the death-defying mission we were on. I was holding Elizabeth. My heart buzzed, and I held her tighter, letting my face touch the back of her hair, breathing in her delicious scent.

I closed my eyes, not caring if Devon and Eric thought I looked like an idiot. My arm rose and fell with each breath Elizabeth took. Soon her breathing was so slow and steady, I knew she was asleep. And I spun into blissful oblivion.

———

"You couldn't think I would forget it."

Eric's voice pulled me from sleep. The sun had sunk to the horizon, and the branches of the trees were silhouetted against the gray of the sky.

"I don't actually care what you remember to think about." Devon's voice was low and tense. "It's mine, and I'm keeping it."

I snapped my eyes shut, willing myself to fall back to sleep so I wouldn't be eavesdropping on my best friend.

"It's a magical object," Eric said.

"And I'm not magical so I don't deserve it?"

I slipped one eye open as a hum filled the air. Devon held the sword he had taken from The Game. Its red glow cut through the darkness, making the bare branches of the trees look like bloody fingers scratching the night in their fury to kill us. I squeezed my eyes shut again.

"It isn't about deserving," Eric said. "It's about safety."

"And you don't think I can handle a sword? I seem to remember chopping a guy's hand off while saving you a few hours ago."

"And I am eternally grateful for your assistance."

Devon made a noise somewhere between a *tsh* and a *growl*.

"I don't think a derring-do like yourself should be given an inconsistent magical object they can take into battle."

"I've fought with you twice now," Devon said coldly.

I wanted to smack Eric on the head and warn him that *when Devon uses that voice, either say he's right and apologize, or run for your life.* Those were the only two options available.

"I've stood in the middle of magical battles with nothing to defend myself. And it never once occurred to you that maybe you should mention magical light sabers exist? Or what about the tray shields the non-human bussers had? Do I not merit a way to fight? To defend myself and the people I care about? Am I just supposed to stand around being disposable?"

"I would never dream of calling you disposable—"

"But I am."

"What you are is one who has walked into dangerous magic and survived based purely on self-confidence and an inability to recognize danger," Eric spoke quickly as though trying to make sure Devon didn't interrupt. "What you are is someone who seems to place his own mortality at an extraordinarily low priority when protecting others."

"That's really rich coming from you."

"But I can defend myself," Eric said. "My magic is consistent. I can count on it. When I go into danger, I know exactly what my defenses are and how far they can be pushed. That sword is an enchanted object."

"An enchanted object that saved our lives," Devon jumped in.

"I'll give you that," Eric conceded. "But next time you need it, the sword could fail. Imbuing objects with magic is a tetchy thing. They can falter without cause. The spell can shift without warning. And it would leave you running into battle thinking you have a sword and ending up with a paper-weight. I never told you such things exist, because I prefer to keep those around me alive."

"And that's your prerogative?" Devon spat. "You get to keep us alive?"

"As the leader of this motley crew, it is my *duty.*"

"And it's my *duty* to keep the people I care about safe." Devon's voice shifted, and the *thud* of pacing footsteps echoed around me. "Has it ever occurred to you that I know I might get killed? The Battle of Beville, I was pretty sure I was gonna end up dead, but dying was better than abandoning my best friends. I'm scared shitless half the time. Everyone around me is doing magic and could kill me with a couple words, but I'm not going to leave the few people who actually matter to me in some underground world of weird-ness and just hope I get to see them again."

"You have a family," Eric said. "You have a whole life aboveground. That isn't a thing you should so freely sacrifice."

"Bryant is my family."

His words hit me hard in the chest. I squeezed my eyes shut to keep from crying.

"It's not like I have some great parents I'm ignoring to be here. Bryant and Elizabeth are the closest thing I have to a warm fuzzy family." Devon's voice dropped. "You've said it before—we're all in this together. I get that you all have these awesome powers that make you a part of magic. But I'm a part of it, too. Because I can't live with letting any of you get hurt. I can't survive standing on the sidelines while people I care about are in danger. That's a million times worse than getting hurt."

"Or killed?" Eric asked, his voice gentle.

"Or killed."

Tears leaked from my eyes.

"And here I thought you were simply incapable of fear."

"I spend half my life terrified." Devon gave a dry laugh. "I'm just scared of different things."

"Keep the sword." There was a shuffling on the ground like someone standing up. "And I'll find someone to fashion you a few more treats if we survive long enough to get back to Beville."

"Thank you."

"But please remember, Devon, fate can choose to twist magic in strange ways to fit her will. Twisting the magic in that sword would be an easy task for her."

"I know."

The urge to jump up, hug my best friend, steal the sword from him, and lock him in a safe room was overwhelming. But I knew Devon well enough to know he was right. Not being able to help was a worse fate for him than being hurt. And it was my job to make sure he didn't get so hurt we couldn't heal him.

20

"Time to begin." Eric's words were a relief since I had been lying there pretending to sleep for who knew how long.

Darkness had fallen in earnest now. Streetlamps lit the wide path even though there were no tourists to be seen, and bright beams of light shone on the Statue of Liberty.

"Was it some sort of feminist thing?" Devon asked lightly, all traces of his talk with Eric brushed away.

"I'm not sure I understand. *Nudla*," Eric said, and his coat was drycleaner-fresh with a tiny *hiss*.

"The Ladies chose their emergency exit from the Library to be at Lady Liberty." Devon brushed his coat off by hand.

I gave my coat a firm shake and used the same spell Eric had. The grass disappeared, but it didn't get the nice pressed lines on the sleeves Eric's had.

"More a matter of convenience, I think, though admittedly I've never asked." With a wave of Eric's hand, the shield around us disappeared. "This island is far enough away from the city to be safe in case of an attack, isolated enough to give some semblance of privacy, and nowhere that the exit could be stumbled upon accidentally."

"But how many tourists swarm over this island every day?" Elizabeth said.

I turned to ask if she wanted me to clean her coat, but she already looked perfect. I was so distracted by the swish of her skirt I didn't realize the others were cutting through the trees until Elizabeth almost slipped out of sight.

"The island is frequently invaded by tourists," Eric said once I jogged to catch up, like he had known I had fallen behind while marveling over the wonderment of my girlfriend. "But the entrance isn't on the island."

"Then please tell me there's a good reason we've been sitting here for hours," Devon said, his hand firmly in his pocket as we cut through the shadows. I had a strong gut feeling he was grasping his sword.

"Other than a nice rest in the fresh air?" Eric said. "Of course. The Library exit isn't on the island." He stopped at the edge of the water. "It's beneath it."

I scanned the beach, hoping for a hidden door to pop open or even for a chasm to appear. But Eric just stared at the mucky, nasty water.

"We have to get in the Hudson?" Elizabeth asked, revulsion sounding in her voice. It wasn't hard to see why.

The filth of the Hudson sloshed up against the shore of the perfectly manicured island. Plastic bottles floated next to rotting garbage. The whole thing was topped off with one distended, dead rat.

"You have got to be kidding me." I swallowed hard, trying not to hurl at the thought of swimming next to the dead rat and making a silent vow that if we lived through the night, I would really work on getting a stronger stomach for grossness. "There is no way anyone would swim next to that. Let alone the Ladies who fancy pure white fashion."

"Many wonderful things in this world are hidden right beneath the horrible. It's one of the safest places to be." Eric leaned toward the water, apparently unfazed by Devon, Elizabeth, and me glaring, horrorstruck, at his back. "It's quite simple, really. We dive in here and swim down. You'll see the entrance when you get close to it. Swim right in. There will be air waiting in the light."

"Swim toward the light." Elizabeth's voice trembled. "Great."

"I'll hop in first as a show of good faith. Best not to think about it too much." Eric stepped out to the ledge, and in one swift movement dove into the river, disappearing beneath the dark water.

"Lovely." Devon wiped his hands over his face. "I'd say ladies first but that would be cruel. See you on the other side."

Pulling himself up to his full height, he lifted his arms and dove into the water.

"Me next." Elizabeth stepped toward the ledge.

"I can go," I said. The thought of her having to swim through the muck was almost worse than doing it myself.

"If I go, you'll dive right in." Elizabeth smiled at me. "You wouldn't let me swim into the dark alone, would you?"

Then she was gone. She dove in like it was nothing. Like freezing water and dead rats were nothing to worry about. Like cancer-causing, flesh-eating diseases weren't in every drop of nasty river touching Elizabeth's perfect eyes and flooding into her dainty nose.

With a forceful kick, her heeled shoes sank out of sight.

It was my turn.

I took a deep breath, trying not to think of the bacteria I would soon be submerged in that was probably going to kill me before the Ladies ever got a chance. The current had pushed all the garbage right up next to the shore, so if I jumped far enough, I might be able to clear it and not actually touch the distended rat. I raised my arms like Devon had...and dove.

Well, tried to dive. It was more like falling a few feet from shore and belly-flopping into the water. The impact knocked the air out of my lungs, and river water flooded my mouth. I gagged and retched, but I couldn't even cough. It was too cold pull in any air. The rat had been stirred back into the current by my belly flop. He was missing one eye, and the horrible void glared at me as he drifted closer.

I gasped for air and dove, kicking and hoping it was only my imagination as something brushed against my ankle. I swam down into the cold. Certain I was going to die. The freezing water, the current, something was going to get me. I wasn't going to die in an epic battle. I was going to drown in the Hudson. A jogger would find my body. The police would come, and they would probably rule my death a suicide.

I swam down farther, and my lungs started to burn. Pressure surged in my ears. My whole head was bound to explode. The water was too dark to see any of the others.

Pain seared my lungs.

Would my lungs pop first or my head?

Maybe I had swum the wrong way and the others would all survive. They would be able to tell my mom what happened.

If they survived the Ladies.

The current of the river caught my coat, dragging me backward, or what seemed like backward. There was no light for me to fight toward. Nothing left but darkness.

My arms burned as the weight of my wet wool coat became too much. A new current grabbed me, dragging me farther down. Farther away from the air I so desperately needed.

Lights danced in front of my eyes.

Please let the others be okay.

More than anything I wanted to stop. To let the freezing water squeeze me into nothing so the pain would end. But I couldn't. I had to fight as long as I could to get to them. To help them survive. I owed all of them that.

The lights got brighter, burning my eyes.

No, not lights. One light. One impossibly bright light.

I was only seeing one bright white light.

I kicked as hard as I could, using my very last bit of strength and fell, heaving, onto a white marble floor.

21

"Bryant," a beautiful angel called my name. "Bryant!" The angel was mad. "Bryant, wake up!" The angel smacked me.

"Ow!" I coughed. Water tumbled from my mouth.

"Oh thank God!" The angel was Elizabeth, and she pulled me into her soaking wet, foul-smelling arms.

Devon sank to the ground next to me, his whole body shaking, his face a mixture of exhaustion and relief.

"You okay?" I asked him. My voice came out all raspy like I'd gotten overly enthusiastic at a football game.

"I'm good." Devon nodded, flopping his hair into his eyes.

"I told you we would all make it." Eric was not hovering worriedly over me. He stood away from us on the other side of the white room.

All four walls were made out of the same pure white marble as the floor. There were no lights in the room, just a warm, ambient glow that seemed to come from nowhere in particular. The only break in the stone was the ceiling, which was made of river. The surface of the water wasn't visible. But the river flowed over us as though we were sitting under a giant fish tank. But there was no glass. I should know—I'd just fallen through that ceiling.

"Where are we?" I struggled to my feet.

"At the exit of the Library." Eric turned an appraising eye toward me. "Did you hit your head?"

"I mean *how* are we here?" I pointed up to the water, pushing down the horrible feeling it was going to spill onto our heads at any moment and crush us all to death.

"Magic." Eric shrugged, turning back to the white wall in front of him.

"Thanks," I grumbled.

"I've told you before, breaking into the Library is dangerous." Eric ran his fingers along the marble like a pianist playing on invisible keys. "I need you all to do exactly what I say, exactly when I say it. There will be no room for argument. No time to second-guess my decisions. We're waltzing into the best security system known to magickind. If you move one hair out of my guidance, I cannot guarantee you will live to see the inside of the Library."

"And if we do everything you say?" I asked.

"Then I still can't promise your survival." Eric's fingers stopped, hovering a centimeter over the stone. "But I will feel terrible for a long time that you died a horrific death. Everyone ready?"

"Can't we get dry first?" Elizabeth asked through chattering teeth.

"No point." Eric pressed his fingers to the wall.

A *pop* sounded high above us followed by a *hiss* and a *slam*.

I looked up in time to see a thick panel of glass slide into place on the ceiling.

"We're trapped," I whimpered as water trickled into our cell from the edges of the glass.

"Not entirely." Eric's voice was calm enough to pull my horrified gaze from the falling water. He had stepped out of the room. Sort of.

A thin veil of mist separated him from the rest of us. And where he was standing wasn't flooding at the same alarming rate as the rest of the chamber. I slogged through the knee-high water toward him with Devon and Elizabeth close behind me. I dove toward the translucent wall and hit something hard with my face.

"Eric, let us in!" Elizabeth pounded on the mist, and a reverberating *thud* echoed around the room.

"Not yet, Elizabeth." Eric faced away from us, doing something I couldn't see. He swirled his hands through the air like a painter working top speed on a giant canvas.

"The water's getting high out here!" Devon shouted a few seconds later when the water reached our waists.

"I'm doing rather delicate work." The annoyance in Eric's voice wasn't as terrifying as the undertone of fear.

"We have to go back up." Devon turned away from Eric to the glass ceiling above us. "My sword might cut through it."

"It won't work," Eric said.

"Well, I'm not going to let us die out here!" Devon shouted.

"There is nothing you can do," Eric said.

I had followed a psychopath, and now we were going to be human sacrifices to buy his way into the Library.

Maybe that was how he got in the first time. Maybe it had been his plan from the beginning.

The water was up to our shoulders. Devon flicked his sword on and held it up toward the ceiling. The burning red blade was a few inches shy of reaching the glass.

"Elizabeth." I turned to her to say something deep and meaningful about how being with her was better than magic.

But Elizabeth didn't look at me. She was staring through the mist at Eric, watching him slice his hands through the air like she could actually see what he was doing.

"Elizabeth, what is it?" I asked as the water lifted me off my feet.

"Come on, come on," Elizabeth murmured, treading water.

"Elizabeth, what is he doing?" I shouted.

"Saving us."

The mist dissolved with a *whoosh*. The water surrounding us shot up toward the ceiling, like we were being attacked by a giant with a Shop-Vac. Each drop tore at my skin as it was sucked away. My hair hurt from being yanked toward the river. And then we fell. I hit the marble floor just as hard as I had a few minutes before and grunted as someone landed on top of me.

"Ouch," Elizabeth groaned as she rolled off of me.

"Are you serious!" Devon leapt to his feet. "Tell me you didn't know the room was going to flood."

"I'm perfectly happy to lie to you whenever you like," Eric said.

The mist separating him from us had disappeared, leaving an opening to a white tunnel in its place.

"We could have died!" Devon's shout echoed off the marble walls.

"Shh," Elizabeth hushed.

"We still might, and moving quickly is our best chance for making it to the Library alive," Eric said. "The hall won't remain open for long. If you'd like to come with me, I suggest we move quickly."

Elizabeth grabbed my hand and yanked me to my feet. Between the two near drowning experiences, my whole body shook. On the plus side, my clothes and hair were dry. And not like still sort of damp dry. Like creepy blow dryer dry.

"Come on." Elizabeth dragged me into the hall, pulling my attention from my super dry clothes. "Devon!" Elizabeth snapped.

Devon hadn't moved. He was still standing in the white box, glaring at Eric. "And what if we get in there and lightning strikes us? Or swords pop out of the walls and skewer us?"

"Stop being dramatic," Eric said. "We don't have time for it. You knew this was dangerous long before we dove into the water."

"But I didn't think we would be lied to!" Devon shouted. "After everything we've been through, you just walk through some mist and leave us to tread water. We are not pawns. We are the closest thing to friends you have. Friends don't abandon their friends."

"I wasn't abandoning you." Eric stepped out of the hall and reached toward Devon. "I promise I'll explain, but we have to go now. Or we will be abandoning Bryant and Elizabeth in the Library with no hope of survival."

"We have to go," Elizabeth warned, staring at where the wall had been.

Squinting, I could kind of make out a subtle solidifying of the air in the corners.

"Now, guys!"

"I really hate you sometimes," Devon growled and ran for the hall. A sound like breaking glass came at the same instant he faltered. A cut appeared on his cheek as he charged forward, Eric on his heels.

"What was that?" Devon wiped blood from his cheek.

"The wall regrowing," Elizabeth answered.

"It's a failsafe door to get into the library." Eric beckoned us farther down the hall while the white room with the square of Hudson hovering above disappeared behind a very solid, white wall. "You have to find the door, which is no mean feat, and everyone locked in the chamber has to perform the spell. A spell none of you are capable of."

"How does he know that?" I whispered to the solid white marble ceiling above. The ceiling didn't answer, which I was really happy about.

"Is that what all the hand flapping was?" Devon asked, his tone still angry.

"The use of arrow magic is arcane," Eric said.

The hall ate his voice, like the walls around us weren't solid and bare. The white corridor twisted off into the distance. The air lit with ambient light showed no marks or changes in the wall. It seemed too perfect, too harmless.

"It's an inconsistent branch of magic. One misplaced arch of the finger and you could very well die. Its use fell out of favor a few centuries ago. I only bothered to track down its few living purveyors when I discovered arrow magic was necessary to enter the Library. The only firsthand accounts of failed attempts to enter the Library I've heard are those of the people who stayed where the water floods in the first chamber.

"That portion is possible to break out of. I met more than one unfortunate soul who lost their compatriots to the mist in the arrow magic chamber. It's funny," Eric paused, "the Ladies who guard the books use magic that can't be written to guard them. It's almost as if they don't trust the books themselves."

A shiver prickled the back of my neck as Eric laughed like he had just told a wonderful joke.

"So you left us to drown because you needed to use out-of-date magic to pick a magical lock?" Devon asked. "That was you protecting us?"

"Exactly." Eric nodded and started back down the hall.

"And what near death are you tossing us into next?" Devon asked.

"It's not tossing, more of a sprinting wiggle," Eric said.

"What?" Devon growled between gritted teeth.

"Yeah, I concur with the *what*," I panted. We were only moving at a speedy walk, but the fear of whatever was coming next, combined with all the almost dying of the day, was confusing the hell out of my fight-or-flight reflexes.

"The Ladies were very smart," Eric said. "They didn't use one sort of barricade to block the exit. The arrow magic, the cogs, the chasm. All patterns the Ladies would easily know how to solve, which are exponentially easier going the opposite direction than we are currently traveling."

"Okay, so we swam the river, got past the arrow thing." My voice sounded annoyingly optimistic, even to me. "Now we just have to do the cogs and the chasm. That makes us, like, halfway there."

A faint grinding sound drifted from down the hall where the walls swerved to one side, hiding whatever the moving thing was from view.

"Theoretically," Eric said, pulling my focus from the sound.

"Whoa, whoa, what do you mean *theoretically*?" Devon asked.

"That's as far as I made it."

22

The grinding sound was overpowering even before the gateway came into view. The ceiling of the tunnel sloped upward to reach the top of a high arch. Sparkling silver bars covered the opening, obscuring my view of the moving things beyond.

"There really isn't much I can tell you about this." Eric squinted through the shining bars. "Keep up, don't touch anything, don't get crushed. If I ask you to do something, assume it's for your survival."

Devon rolled his eyes.

"Isn't that you wanted me to do?" Eric asked. "Give you an honest representation of what to expect?"

"Let's just go." Devon reached for the bars.

I expected Eric to stop him or for Devon to be electrocuted and die, but he grabbed the gate and swung it open.

My brain froze, trying to comprehend what was happening. It looked like the inside of a clock. If the clock were magical and massive.

Cogs with shifting shapes latched onto one another, moving sideways, pulling each other toward the unseeable ceiling or mashing themselves between other moving bits. Some of the cogs didn't appear to be totally solid. They would grow and shrink as they moved from one gap to another.

And the patterns on them—giant geometric shapes shimmered as they twisted around the surfaces, and smaller markings, like a language beyond my comprehension, floated in and out of view.

"There's no way through it," I said as the others stepped into the room.

"What's your problem?" Elizabeth whispered to Devon as Eric moved into the lead.

"Nothing," Devon murmured.

"Dev."

"I can't take partial trust," Devon answered barely loudly enough for me to hear over the cogs. "Either we're all in this together, or I'm not in it at all. I'm done being treated like a bystander or a child. I'm neither of those things."

Elizabeth opened her mouth to speak, but Devon had already walked away.

"The trick is to not get crushed to death while moving the cogs into the right position to free the path forward." Eric stood at center of the space, glowering at the cogs around him.

"It's like a puzzle." Elizabeth stepped in front of him. "Each of the patterns complements another, and if you put them together right…"

It was like she was in a trance. Two giant wheels wound around each other, their jagged, angular patterns not seeming to have any relation. Elizabeth reached forward, pressing her fingers through the air as though meshing the cogs together. But there was nothing there to mesh, only giant things that were going to suck her in and kill my girlfriend.

"Elizabeth, no!" I lunged forward a second too late. Her hands met stone.

The stone wheels shifted, and my heart stopped for a moment. But they didn't mash Elizabeth, because they weren't turning toward each other anymore. They were twisting and opening up, creating five little cogs that only took up half the space the two large ones had.

"I really did hope you were going to have a talent for this," Eric said with as close to a broad smile as I think he was capable of.

"The pattern made sense." Elizabeth blushed.

"I don't know of any seers who have tried to make it through the cogs, or at least not any who survived the attempt." Eric turned back to the wheels. "I had hoped your skills would translate to this particular task, but there was really no way to know. I could have done it myself." Eric approached a set of three cogs. One sat on the bottom and narrowed at the top, allowing the two great wheels to push it around and around. "I did it before, after all. But I was stuck in this room for three days before I managed to find the way forward."

"Three days!" I coughed.

"Yes." Eric leapt forward, grabbing a part of the pattern and twisting it sideways, creating a perfect set of parallel lines that spanned all three moving parts. The bottom cylinder dropped away, leaving a gap where it had been. "And we really don't have three days."

"So what should we be looking for?" Devon asked, his face betraying the same confusion I felt.

"I'm not sure either of you will be able to see it." Elizabeth didn't look away from the spire that swirled up and down from the floor. "It's like there's a missing piece to each of them. A place they belong they can't quite reach on their own. And you have to...." She threw herself forward, knocking the spire sideways where it kept turning, rotating a bit of the puzzle I hadn't even noticed before.

"Okay." Devon searched the cogs. "Okay."

"Please don't, Devon," Eric said, his tone kinder than usual. "The pattern is incredibly intricate and difficult to find. One wrong move, and things could go very badly."

Devon froze for a moment, his face somewhere between stone and demon killer. "Fine. The simple human will stay out of the way."

"I think this is one." Elizabeth pointed high above our heads to where five strands of the ceiling pulled in different directions, apparently oblivious to Devon looking like mutiny was in his near future.

Not leaving Devon's side, I stared up at the ceiling. Each of the strips had a different pattern on it, one like sweeping hills, another like binary code.

"There has to be a way it fits together," Elizabeth murmured. "How did you do it last time you were here?"

"Quite frankly, the entire room was different." Eric scowled. "I can't be sure, of course, but I feel like you could make it into this room a hundred times and never find the puzzle to be quite the same. You simply have to figure it out."

Eric jabbed a set of tiny cogs I hadn't even noticed. That portion of the wall came to a screeching halt.

Carefully, Eric pulled a gold cog from the pattern and carried it across the room. He glared at the wall for a moment, then inserted the cog into a crack barely large enough for it to slip through.

The floor shuddered as those bits of the puzzle shifted out of sight.

"Now we're getting somewhere," Eric said, his tone thick with concentration. "Elizabeth, keep an eye on the ceiling, if you will."

Eric stepped into the gap the last move had made as the wall he had stolen the cog from came back to life, moving in a completely different way than it had before.

"We're inside a lock," I whispered to Devon. "We're inside a giant lock, and they're twisting the tumblers by hand."

"You mean *you all* are." Devon's face was still stony.

"I don't see any of it." I shook my head in awe as Eric swiped a column forcing it to turn faster. The wall behind us twisted, and the floor shuddered again.

"I'm sure you will," Devon said. "Just look at it, and you'll see something great. A spell you have to do. Something amazing for you to accomplish."

"Devon." I took a deep breath. Devon was my best friend. Had been my best friend for years. But deep and meaningful conversations weren't things we did very often. "I know what it's like to feel useless."

"So I'm useless." Devon didn't even sound mad. "A useless kid to be led by the hand through the scary world of magic."

"No," I said quickly, "you aren't. You're a brave badass. What I'm saying is just because magic and seeing aren't your thing doesn't mean we don't need you. The number of times you've saved me proves it. We need you—I need you—just the way you are."

"Dammit, Bry. Are we in a chick flick now?" Devon smiled, not like a giddy smile, but it was something. "Good to know my utter normalness is handy."

"You have a sword, dude." I laughed. "My best friend has a magic sword. I think that's pretty—"

The floor gave another shudder, sharper and more violent than before.

"Oh no." Elizabeth stepped back from the far wall, which was much farther away than it had been when I'd stopped paying attention a few minutes before.

I scanned Elizabeth for signs of injury or impending death. She looked fine except for the horror on her face.

"Miss Wick." Eric leapt back into view.

"I thought I'd found one." Elizabeth's hands flew to her mouth, and the wall whirred. It was still turning like it was a part of the puzzle, but the whirring had changed. The tone of it was different. Dangerous.

"Everyone this way!" Eric dove toward the opening he'd made in the cogs.

I sprinted the few feet to follow him as Elizabeth dove into the gap.

A hand shoved me forward and I fell to the floor the second before a bright light flashed behind us and Eric bellowed, "*Primurgo!*"

Heat nipped at my back for a moment before the light dissipated.

"Devon!" I gasped, pushing myself off the ground.

"Human's alive," Devon panted from just inside the shield.

I slumped back onto my elbows.

"Everyone intact?" Eric asked, his pale face shining with sweat.

Elizabeth whimpered. "I thought I was helping. I'm so sorry."

"You are helping, Elizabeth." Eric let go of the shield and stepped over me.

"Helping doesn't mean perfection. But please don't make another mistake. The punishment will only be worse."

"Right." Elizabeth nodded, smoothing out her skirt. "No more mistakes."

Devon helped me to my feet as Elizabeth leaned in to examine a gear twice the size of my head.

The cog room was just the same as when we had fled from it a minute before. No signs of fire or exploding death.

"I think I found one," Elizabeth called.

"If you're sure, then do it." Eric stood staring up at the ceiling.

Elizabeth muttered a long string of curses and twisted a tiny hinge. From the shaking of the floor and the widening of the gap, she had been right.

"We should be nearly there." Eric pointed up to the ceiling. "Look how it's changed. The speed, the variation. Everything we do alters the pattern above. It's symbolic—it almost makes sense."

"Almost?" I asked.

"*Almost* can mean quite a bit when dealing with magic."

"Going to try another one," Elizabeth said. "Promise to miss me if I die?"

"Elizabeth, that's not funny." I spun to face her, and my heart leapt into my throat as she stuck her hand into a portion of the wall that looked like a giant jaw ready to chomp my girlfriend's arm off. "Elizabeth!"

She twisted her arm quickly, reaching up inside the jaw, and wrenched her arm back, yanking on something.

The jaw froze, and she pulled her hand away as the wall crumbled into nothing. The floor shook, but not in an evil *gonna kill you* kind of way, more like a *janky turntable on a stage* kind of way.

A *clang* shook the far wall as the gate we had passed through swung shut.

Devon ran forward and rattled the gate.

"Trapped is better than dead?" Elizabeth shrugged.

"We're nearly there," Eric whispered to the ceiling.

"And how do we get there?" I asked.

The room had gotten larger. None of the moving pieces I'd first seen were still there, and I still didn't have any idea what I was supposed to be looking for. If I tilted my head sideways and really focused, I could tell the movements were different. It wasn't a thousand pieces of a hundred puzzles. It had evolved into one giant puzzle with a few pieces just slightly out of place.

"I don't see anything else." Elizabeth stared frantically from one wall to the next. "I don't see anything else to change."

And then I did something stupid/brilliant. I closed my eyes.

It was a game I used to play when I was little and scared of the dark. If you can't see the monsters, try to hear them coming. All it had accomplished was instilling a healthy fear of Mrs. Mops, but that's beside the point.

Squeezing my eyes shut, I listened to the hum of the room. The grinding and whirring of the cogs had changed with every switch in the walls. The new tone was brighter, as though there were less density for the sound to fight through. But a lower buzz still rumbled from the left corner.

"Over there." I pointed like an auditory divining rod. "The change needs to be made over there."

"What?" Elizabeth said. "Where?"

"I don't know." I moved over to that side of the room, squinting at the squares that rotated like a Rubik's cube. "But it's something here."

Elizabeth squinted at the squares as they clinked together, switching between silver, gold, and shining white. "Here." Elizabeth reached her hand forward. "No here."

"You do know you really need to be right, right?" Devon whispered over my shoulder.

"Not helping." Elizabeth's hand shook as she reached forward. "Really not helping." With a quick swipe, she struck the square the instant five whites lined up. "Bingo," Elizabeth breathed.

The floor shook again as the squares smoothed out. The wall, still covered in cogs, gears, and moving parts, had pushed back so it was almost like we were standing in a square room.

"And here we have it," Eric said from the center of the room.

The pattern on the ceiling had changed yet again. The middle three strips moved one way at three different speeds while the outer two moved in the other direction at the same pace, like tracks made by the wheels of the car.

"Anyone have a stick to poke it?" I asked.

"Devon, lift Elizabeth," Eric said casually.

"Plié on three." Devon took Elizabeth's hips. "One, two, down, up."

In one smooth motion, she popped up to sit on his shoulder. My mom would be thrilled dance classes had yet another practical application.

"Slow the center," Eric said.

Elizabeth reached up and dragged her fingers along the center strip, slowing the speed. Without waiting for further instruction, she swiped her hand along the second strip like she was spinning a roulette wheel, doubling its speed.

"You're going the wrong way." Elizabeth dug her fingers into the third strip and flung it the other direction.

A picture appeared, shimmering and moving in a breathtaking way. And at last, the pattern made beautiful sense. Waves drifted along the top of the water, with bubbles and froth surrounding the giant creatures swimming beneath.

I could have stood there watching for hours.

But a *clink* sounded, and the gate we had entered through swung open.

"No." Elizabeth slid down from Devon's shoulder. "No, no, no. We came from that way!"

"Not so quickly." Eric walked slowly toward the gate as though he still thought the room might chew us up.

"But we did come through that way." I followed Eric.

"We came through the gate, but it led someplace very different," Eric said.

"But how is that—" My protest at the impossibility of this magic disappeared.

We weren't in a shining, white hall. We were standing on the edge of a ravine seventy feet wide and so deep the bottom was lost in blackness.

"So how do we get across?" Devon asked.

"I have no idea," Eric said. "I never made it past."

23

"You never made it past?" I tested each of the words on my tongue to see where I might have gotten confused or slipped into an alternate reality.

"No." Eric glowered at the chasm as though the depth blocking his path were a personal affront.

"So you've fought shadows, mist Ladies, and magical kidnappers, and a hole in the ground stopped you?" My words came out more like a cry for help than a question.

"If you think you can do better, then please, go ahead," Eric said.

"No, I..." I stared at the endless pit of black, my insides freezing at the thought of it. "It just makes the hole sound really awful."

Devon chuckled behind me. "Evil hole of death."

"Okay," Elizabeth said bracingly, stepping up to the edge of the cliff and sliding her hand into mine. "You couldn't get across by yourself, but we're all here together now. The four of us together can work it out."

"That is my hope." Eric tented his fingers under his chin as he stared across the gap.

There was a doorway straight ahead of us, a silver gate like the one we had passed through moments before, but this one had glass set between each of the bars. Warm blue light filtered through the panes, and shadows drifted in and out of view.

"Uh, Eric," I whispered. "Are there people watching us?"

We all froze for a moment, watching the shapes twist behind the glass. It could have been flickering torchlight, or people waltzing...or the Ladies spinning in joy as they plotted our deaths.

"No," Eric said finally. "They did that for two days the last time I was here."

"You spent two days trying to cross this and failed?" Devon asked.

"It's more like shadows than actual people." Elizabeth cocked her head to the side, watching the glass.

"Shadows like *big bad evil* shadows?" I crossed the fingers on my free hand, hoping if there were monster shadows there wouldn't be a giant minotaur included.

"No, like shadows of things that have happened." Elizabeth shivered. "Eric, what's it like in the Library?"

"No idea. I've never been in it." Eric knelt and began crawling along the side of the cliff, trailing his fingers through the open air.

"There's no spell to fly across?" Elizabeth asked.

I pulled the black phone out of my pocket. The trip through the river had done no damage and the screen blinked on as soon as I pressed my thumb to the scanner. I'd spent countless hours in the past two months pouring over every app in the phone. Reading all the spells, trying to find a spare bit of brain to store them in. Making the spells a part of my magical knowledge base so I could use them without running into the rules of impartment the Ladies had created to stunt magical learning.

But nowhere had I found a spell for flying. It had been a horrible disappointment. No enchanted brooms, no spell to sprout wings, not even a flying carpet.

"Flying isn't a thing wizards do," Eric said.

"Okay," Devon said. "What about throwing? You could throw each of us across. I mean you can move furniture, why not a person?"

"For many reasons," Eric said, not looking up as he scoured the ground, "but the short of it is no. That would still count as flying. I could hit you with a spell and hope it knocked you in the right direction, but that is a risk I'm not willing to take."

"But *escata* lets you kind of—"

Eric cut me off. "That is not flying, it's falling with style. I can assure you there is no possible way for you to fly over the gap and land undamaged on the other side."

"Great," Devon grumbled.

"Elizabeth, do you see anything of interest?" Eric asked.

Elizabeth took a long moment walking the edge of the chasm where Eric crawled, staring into the pit and over to the other side. "Nothing. As far as I can see it's just a deadly deep pit."

"Okay," I said, steeling myself to be brilliant. "These walls are made of rock, right?"

I was right. The walls that surrounded us weren't made of the glistening white marble of the halls. They were plain old rock like we had jumped into an Indiana Jones movie.

"So we use a spell to carve out a portion of the rock and magic it into a bridge." My words tumbled out. "Carve out a plank to lay across the crack."

"It won't work," Eric said, finally standing. "The rock can't be changed."

"But—"

"Feel free to try." Eric raised his hands placatingly.

I cringed, sure if he was so positive, this was obviously going to end badly for me, but we had to do something.

"*Caruson.*" I pointed at the wall like my finger was a knife ready to dig out stone. Pain shot through my finger, up my arm, and into my neck like I had just poked the third rail. "Gah!"

"You should have warned him." Elizabeth smacked Eric hard on the shoulder.

"I had to be sure it wouldn't work if someone else tried it." Eric shrugged.

"Maybe the way across is on the other side of the creepy glowing door." I rubbed the back of my neck, which stung like it had been attacked by bees. "Maybe there's a lever for a drawbridge on the other side."

"Thaden got through," Eric said. "If he managed it, there's a way."

"He might have summoned demons from Hell to ferry him across," I said.

"Please be realistic, Bryant." Eric sighed, like of all the things I'd seen, mentioning demons from Hell was one step too far.

"Or he jumped," Devon said.

I turned toward him. He had been quiet for long enough that, being the horrible friend I am, I had lost track of him. Now he stood at the edge of the chasm, his toes a centimeter from the abyss.

"Somehow I doubt Thaden was suicidal," Eric said. "A leap like that would kill you."

"Bryant jumped out his bedroom window and lived." Devon didn't move away from the edge.

"My window was high." I took a slow step forward. "This could lead to China."

"Can you shine a light down and see how far it goes?" Elizabeth asked.

"The light just disappears," Eric said. "The pit is too deep for magic to penetrate."

"It's the only way forward. We have to try." Devon didn't look at us. He just stared into the pit.

"Supposing we were to jump and by some miracle we survived the fall. How would we get back out of the dark?" Eric asked. "Here we can get back out to the river. Down there we could starve to death."

"Not my fault you didn't pack snacks." Devon inched forward.

"Dev, this is crazy," Elizabeth said. "Even if Bryant and Eric could cushion the fall, I can't see what's waiting down there."

"That's the problem with you special people." Devon smiled. "You only see the magical ways. But when all other choices are gone, you only have the obvious path left. Forward means down." He moved forward an inch, spreading his arms wide.

"Devon!" I screamed, lunging toward him a second too late.

He tipped forward out of my grasp.

"*Escata*!" I screamed the spell, but Devon was falling too fast. Before the word had left my lips, Devon had been swallowed by the black.

I should have listened for a *thump* or a cry for help, but I couldn't stop myself from screaming. "Devon! Devon!"

"Devon!" Elizabeth's shout joined mine.

My best friend was dead. Devon. The brave one. The one with unbeatable suave and daring was dead. Lost forever. We wouldn't even have a body to bury.

I clasped my hands over my mouth to stop the terrible screams from coming. I didn't know I was crying until tears fell onto my fingers. He'd been my best friend since forever. Always there. Always Devon. Sobs banged in my chest. I'd never thought of not having Devon around. In all the madness, I never really thought I could lose him.

"Dev." Elizabeth knelt next to me, because somehow I was kneeling. I wrapped my arms around her, holding her as tight as I could, desperate not to lose her to the pit as well.

"Devon!" Eric called, his voice thoroughly lacking the utter horror of Devon's death. "Devon?"

"We should have grabbed him." Elizabeth coughed through her tears. "We should have found a way to stop him."

"Devon?" Eric called again. "Devon, can you hear us?"

"How could he hear us?" I jumped to my feet. "He's dead. My best friend in the world is dead. The closest thing I'll ever have to a brother—" I choked on the words as a fresh wave of tears took hold. "He was a better man than you'll ever be, and now he's dead. Don't be such a dick."

"Devon, have you had quite enough?" Eric asked.

"Quite enough? You son—"

Devon's voice cut me off. "Aww, come on." The words drifted up from the ravine.

No, not up—out.

"Can't a guy enjoy people crying and saying how wonderful he is?"

"Devon, where are you?" I called at the same moment Elizabeth shouted, "I'll kill you, Devon Rhodes!"

Devon walked out of the chasm on the other side. And I don't mean climbed, I mean walked. Stepped out of the black in the middle and walked onto the stone on the other side.

"What?" I sputtered. "How?"

"You knew he didn't die?" Elizabeth shrieked, punching Eric in the arm so hard he actually made a pained noise.

"I suspected." Eric rubbed his arm and stepped toward the edge.

"How?" Devon asked from across the chasm. "Because I didn't make a splatting noise?"

"The way the black swallowed you," Eric said, like we all should have noticed the movement of the light while my best friend was jumping to his death. "It moved like you were jumping under something, not into something."

"Well, take the leap, folks." Devon spread his arms wide. "It's not too bad a fall."

"Devon Rhodes, I swear I am going to make you pay for this," Elizabeth growled as she stepped toward the edge.

"Me first." I stepped in front of her.

She raised one eyebrow at me in a shockingly Eric-like way.

"I don't think I can watch you fall," I said.

She brushed her fingers along my palm, and a tingle ran up my spine. Without taking a breath or thinking, I jumped.

I thought it would be a long fall. I thought air would *whoosh* past me, making my hair stand on end. But by the time I realized I had just jumped into a bottomless pit, I landed hard and fell forward in an awkward, gangly way. The landing didn't hurt much more than if I had jumped from the bleachers at school. It didn't feel nice, but I was on my feet in a second.

"Bryant?" Elizabeth shouted. "Are you okay?"

"I'm fine!" I looked up at where I had jumped from. The edge of the cliff was distorted, looking both too far away and too close at the same time. A few feet out from the edge a solid ceiling of black began, and on the other side was another gap, this one clearer with Devon waving me over.

It only took me a few seconds to walk across the invisible black floor beneath me. I took a breath preparing for a jump up, but when I stepped toward Devon I was just...on the other side.

"See? Not so bad." Devon beamed.

I took a page from Elizabeth's book and punched him in the shoulder.

"And you just thought it would be fun to not tell us you weren't jumping to your death?" I averted my eyes as Elizabeth jumped. "How the hell did you know you weren't going to splat?"

"I didn't." Devon shrugged. "I mean not *for sure* for sure. But it was what we had to try, so one of us was going to have to do it. We can't go back from this, Bry. We aren't here on a leisurely pleasure trip. We're here because the Ladies want all of us dead. Because creepy Kendrick McDonald wants us dead and you in a cage. We can't afford to fail. That would mean bad people and death."

"But that doesn't mean you get to jump!" I tore my hands through my hair. "I get that it's hard, and I get that we have to do this, but that doesn't mean you can charge into something stupid without the rest of us. We're a team. We need you. And not as a guinea pig for deadly things. No more risks, Devon."

The smile slid from Devon's face. "You know how you had to jump before Elizabeth? That's the way I feel about you. All of you. I can't watch people get hurt, Bry. Not when I can stop it. I just don't have it in me."

Elizabeth emerged from the chasm like she was just walking out of a shadow. She nailed Devon in the shoulder and pulled him into a hug. "I'm so mad at you right now."

"Good to see you, too." Devon's smile slid back into place.

Eric walked out of the dark. "That was surprisingly pleasant, all things considered." He dusted off his jacket, making sure a stray piece of filth hadn't marred his perfection. Because that sort of thing matters when you're breaking into a magical library.

"So now what?" I asked, staring at the gate. A silver handle melded seamlessly into the bars, like it was just an ordinary door that happened to glow all magical and blue.

"I believe we should open it." Eric reached toward the handle.

"And if all sorts of monsters jump out at us?" Elizabeth whispered.

"Then I suggest Mr. Rhodes get out his sword."

The blue glass of the door reflected the red light of Devon's sword as a faint hum sounded behind me.

I held my breath as Eric turned the handle and the gate swung open, bathing us all in bright blue light.

24

I don't know what I expected, but as I stood there blinking, I knew this wasn't it. Deep blue light flooded the air, just as the white light had done before, cutting shadows deep into the divots and niches of the roughly hewn stone walls. There were no people or even monsters waiting for us beyond the gate, but I couldn't shake the feeling there was something *there*. I don't even know if I can describe the feeling of knowing there are a hundred eyes staring at you and knowing those eyes don't exist at the same time.

"What is this place?" I whispered, following Eric into the blue light.

"Are you sure we should be here?" Elizabeth asked.

"Of course we shouldn't. That's the point." Even Eric kept his voice low.

A *creak* and a dull *thud* made me gasp and spin around as the blue door swung shut.

"Check the knob," I whispered, proud my voice didn't sound like I was about to poop my pants.

Thankfully, the knob turned easily.

"No point in locking the emergency exit." A laugh wobbled in my throat, completely blowing my cool act.

"We should keep moving." Elizabeth took my hand, not in a girlfriend way, but in a *for the love of all that is holy, don't leave me alone here* kind of way.

"I wholeheartedly agree." Eric stepped farther into the hall.

"I don't see any books," I whispered as we reached the first nook. Peering into the shadows in the niche, there were no book spines or even scrolls to be found.

But there was a shape floating in the shadows. Bone white with gaping black holes for eyes.

"Skull!" I scampered to the other side of the hall, dragging Elizabeth with me, but the opposite niche held another skull. This one missing teeth.

"This isn't a Library, Eric." Devon held up his sword, its red glow making the skull look even more terrifying.

"I didn't know where they put them." Eric reached out and caressed the skull. "They've all just been taken." He leaned down, speaking to the skull. "You must have been someone very important."

"Eric, explain right now," Elizabeth snapped.

"We've found the catacombs." Eric looked up, excitement and wonder lighting his eyes. "I've always wanted to see them, and here they are, hidden right along with the Library."

"So we are still aiming for the Library?" I asked.

"Of course. That is the mission," Eric answered.

"Just checking." I held my free hand up. Elizabeth clung to my other hand so tightly, I couldn't have let go even if I'd wanted to. Not that I'm complaining.

"Who are, I mean, *were* these people?" Devon leaned in close to one of the skulls. "Is it like Merlin or something?"

"Possibly. It could be any number of truly incredible people." Eric spoke reverently, something I wasn't used to from him. "It could be my grandmother for all I know."

"But what are they doing here?" Devon asked. "I mean, I was sort of kidding. If Merlin did exist, wouldn't he be buried in England somewhere?"

"At one point." Eric stepped slowly away from the niche. "We should keep moving. We're in the Library now. We've no way to be certain they went to tidy up the mess at The Game. And even if fate favored us with their departure, they could come back at any moment." He turned and walked down the hallway.

I hoped it would just be a few skulls of famous dead witches and wizards and then done, but no such luck. They just kept going on and on. Some of the niches were small, just large enough to fit a solitary skull. Others were massive with ornate pedestals holding up the bones. A wide alcove held a base of carved gold with an inscription on it in some language that didn't use our alphabet. I teetered on the edge of asking Eric if he knew what the words said, but I didn't want to linger with the skulls for a second more than necessary.

"I still don't understand why there are skulls in a library," Elizabeth said when we reached the first full skeleton. All the bones floated in midair with no visible supports. It was like a living person was standing in the coffin-sized hole in the wall, but all their tissue and squishy bits were invisible.

"When you spend your life in magic, the magic itself starts to seep into you," Eric said softly. I wasn't sure if he was afraid of disturbing the dead or of the Ladies coming after us. "A dead witch or wizard's bones hold power."

I audibly gagged.

"Not for any sort of magic you would be interested in, Bryant." Eric glanced back over his shoulder. "Try not to desecrate this sacred place with your vomit."

"Sorry," I muttered.

"Most bone magic is done by humans who are trying to find a way into the magical world," Eric continued. "Only the darkest of wizards would dare use another wizard's magic after his death."

"A dark wizard like Thaden?" Devon asked.

"Exactly like Thaden," Eric said. "Which might explain how he became so very strong toward the end. If he stole bones and words, he made himself nearly invincible."

"The nearly part is very lucky for us," I whispered.

We passed a hollowed out area larger than the ones we had seen before, but shorter too. Three skeletons barely as tall as my shoulder hovered an inch above the ground, all holding boney hands. My brain couldn't decide between thinking it was beautiful or demonic.

"Are they like, from Salem?" Devon whispered.

"Possibly." Eric leaned in to give the bones a closer look. "If I had time to examine them I might be able to learn more."

"And this is why we need placards and docents," I murmured.

An archway loomed in the distance. I said a silent prayer to whoever was willing to listen to wizards on a breaking and entering spree that nothing to do with death would be on the other side of that arch. Either lots of dead people or us getting killed. Both would have been terrible options.

"My God." Eric ran into the next room.

"Eric." I ran after him. It only took me a second to see the thing he had seen that I instantly wished I had never seen.

Piles and piles of bones. Not jumbled up, but laid out in patterns. Long leg bones arranged in sturdy stacks to support a sea of skulls.

"How many in this room have I met?" Eric's hand shook as he reached out to touch a skull.

The weight of it all suddenly settled in my chest. All these people were the ones who had come before me. I may not have a blood relation to any wizards, but these were the ones who mined for the spells that were the language that gave me power. These people had created Beville and built the Library. These were my people.

It felt like the whole Hudson had poured down on my body. I couldn't breathe, I couldn't think. The weight of centuries of magic smothered me. I only knew I needed to get out.

"We need to go," I panted, not caring if I looked like a coward. "We have to get out of here."

Taking the lead, I stumbled down the row of skulls and shinbones. I ran the length of a city block before the tunnel twisted. A brief moment of relief lifted the weight from my lungs, but around the corner was just another long line of bones.

Trapped. I'm going to be trapped forever. Literally forever. My bones will just join the pile.

I broke into a full out run. Vaguely, I heard voices behind me telling me to come back, but I didn't want to be trapped in the deep blue light forever. The tunnel swerved into another corridor. A section of this bone wall had collapsed, leaving skulls scattered on the floor. I leapt over jawbones—which had detached from their craniums and were strewn on the ground—like I was playing hopscotch with death.

The crumbled section of broken skulls showed what was behind. A jumble of ribs, vertebrae, and other bones I never knew the names of. I leapt over the bones, desperate to get away. My foot skidded on a shinbone, and I hit the floor, smacking my head on the stone.

Not bothering to check if I was bleeding, I scrambled to my feet and kept running. Around another corner to a small room, where the bones were laid out in a fancy pattern, long bones crisscrossing around skulls. Words had been engraved high on the wall. *Honor those who bled.*

I was incapable of thinking about who might have bled, because there was no blood left. No pulses or hearts. Just bones. An impossible sea of bones.

All I could do was run.

Around the next corner the light changed. The blue filtered out, and a warm, normal looking glow called from the end of the hall.

A carved archway, thicker and fancier than any I had seen before, surrounded the exit. Words I didn't understand were inscribed in the stone. For a spilt second, I thought the archway would collapse, trapping me with the bones forever. Leaving me to starve to death.

I dove through the arch, like it was a closing hatch in an action movie, and skidded to a halt on my stomach on the floor beyond. I lay panting on the ground, panic subsiding as I chanced a glance at the walls and didn't see a single bone.

Pounding footsteps came from behind me.

I cursed under my breath as I suddenly remembered I was an asshat who had abandoned his friends.

"Elizabeth," I panted as I shakily pushed myself to my feet. "Elizabeth, I'm sorry."

Two figures moved out of the faint shadows by the arch.

"Elizabeth, run!" I shouted a second too late. The others had all sprinted through the archway, their faces a mix of anger, fear, and, in Devon's case, vague amusement.

"Behind you!" I pointed to the shadows as the arch crumbled, leaving a solid wall in its place.

"How exciting," Eric said, stepping in front of Elizabeth and Devon as the shadows began to take shape.

Longs fingers formed and disappeared. Dark fog swirled around their legs, like skirts blowing in the breeze.

It was...beautiful. Calm. I'd seen monsters come out of the shadows before, and there had always been a sense of evil oozing out of them. But these shadows seemed peaceful and kind. Which of course made me panic again.

"Eric, what's happening?" Elizabeth asked as proper hands and feet formed out of the shadows.

"I'm afraid to say I really haven't a clue."

A face formed. Wrinkled, worn, and smiling. Dark hair streaked with gray swirled into being.

Then two black women stood, smiling judgmentally at us.

"After all that work he just finds his way down here anyway." The first woman shook her finger at me.

"On the plus side, he made it here without getting himself killed," the second said.

"I don't know if I would call that a plus or a sign of being extra stupid," the first retorted.

"What?" I sputtered. I had been prepared to be attacked but not verbally.

"If you'll allow me to introduce myself." Eric stepped forward and gave a little bow, head to toe the pretentious douche I had met two months before. Not that I thought he had ever really changed, just maybe loosened up around us.

"Eric Deldridge." The first woman gave a bow. "Wizard, adventurer, fighter, who has escaped coming into our walls more times than I can count."

Eric bowed again, giving no sign he was flustered at someone keeping tabs on his near death experiences. "Quite right. Though I am afraid you have me at a disadvantage as I have no idea who you are."

"We are the ones they don't speak of," the second lady said. Now that my initial shock was over it was easy to tell she was younger than the first. Her hair only had tiny traces of gray.

"That would explain us not knowing who you are," Devon said.

Both of the women looked toward him.

"And this one doesn't belong to us," the older woman said. She dipped her head and studied Devon from the ground up. The warm glow of the light that seemed to come from nowhere, because why not, reflected off the white streaks in her hair.

"Strange we should know the name of one whose bones we shall never carry," the younger woman said. "But as I live and breathe, Devon Rhodes has broken into the Library and taken a stroll through the Vault of the Dead."

"I think I like *catacombs* better," I muttered.

"And dear, sweet Elizabeth Wick." The older lady stepped forward, arms outstretched toward Elizabeth. "Such a dear, sweet, brave girl."

"Don't touch her!" I yelped as the woman took Elizabeth's hand.

"You run through the dark looking for shadows, trying to find a way to help." The woman touched Elizabeth's cheek. "I'm sorry if my shadow added to your fear."

"I'm sorry," I said loudly enough that everyone turned to look at me, "but you know all of us, and apparently you've been scaring my girlfriend. So, I really need to know exactly who you are."

"Oh young love." The older woman laughed. "It's been such a long time, I hardly remember what it feels like."

"Something between sunshine and stupid as I recall." The younger woman laughed.

"I have seen you before," Elizabeth said. I couldn't tell if she was afraid or in awe. "I've seen you all over the city."

"We had to keep an eye on you, child." The older woman smiled. "When we find one like you, it becomes our happy obligation."

"And who are you that keeping an eye on young seers and hiding in dark corners is a part of your duties?" Eric asked like he was asking what borough they were from.

"We are the guardians of the dead." The younger woman spread her arms wide. "You have passed through our gates, and we welcome you to eternity."

My heart clenched in my chest, and both women burst out laughing.

"Don't scare the boy so." The older woman chuckled. "We have spent too much time trying to protect this one to scare him to death on our doorstep."

She looked into my eyes as she spoke, and they weren't filled with the terrifying void of a dark eternity. Their brown depths were caring and warm. Deep wrinkles formed around her eyes as she smiled at me, like centuries of laughter had carved themselves on her face.

"We are the ones who guard the dead. We are the seekers and buriers of the bones. We are two of the sisters who have been ordained to search the world for our deceased charges and given the honor of protecting them in death."

"But we're not dead," I said in a tone I hoped wasn't insulting. "So, why do you know us?"

"You follow a sweet boy for years making sure he doesn't get himself killed, and he doesn't even notice you," the older woman said.

"Typical," the younger added.

25

"You've been following me?" I squeaked.

"Not all the time. We have too much to do," the older woman said. "And it hasn't been just the two of us either. The Vault of the Dead can't be left unattended. We rotate *keep the child alive* duty."

"Why have you been following him?" Elizabeth stepped away from the women, taking my hand in hers.

Devon moved back too, blocking the women's path to me.

"Merlin's shiny bones, there's no need to protect the boy from us." The older woman tipped her head back and laughed.

I flinched as the sound ricocheted off the stone walls.

"You know about fate?" the older woman asked.

I nodded.

"The golden strands that bind all things together. That twist and pull and alter the way the world works based on her sorry whim?"

"Yeah," I said, hating myself for sounding like a kindergartener on the first day of school. "Yes, Eric's told me about fate."

"And Lola, too, no doubt." The younger woman nodded.

Eric's neck stiffened. "You know so much about us, might we at least know your names?"

"We gave up our names a long time ago. I won't insult the girl I used to be by dragging her into this dark place." The older woman didn't even bother looking at Eric. Her gaze stayed fixed on me. "If you know about fate, you know some people are wound up tight in the web, caught in so many different strings that to pull them away would leave a hole right in the middle of the pattern."

"Some holes are meant to be torn," the younger woman said. "Like a fire burning through the forest, you've got to clear out the old lives to make room for the new."

"But there are some folks"—the older woman raised a finger, pointing at my nose—"who are right in the middle of things. Who are needed for fate to push the world forward."

"And some of those people don't have the sense God gave peanuts and can't seem to keep themselves alive," the younger said.

"It has been a monumental amount of work trying to keep the web of fate intact when you keep trying to yank yourself out of it by dying. We have spent the last fourteen years keeping you alive." The older woman spoke the last word like a threat.

"Only fourteen?" Devon asked, a hint of humor in his tone.

"That was the first time he tried to wander out into traffic." The older woman gave a pinched smile and shook her head at Devon. "Tore his hand away from his mother and chased a puppy down the street."

"Good lord, that puppy wasn't even cute," the younger *tsked*. "Some stringy-looking nasty thing."

"I'm not even a dog person," I murmured. My brain couldn't move past the dog to people following me around trying to keep me alive. "I like cats."

"*I like cats*." The older laughed. "That's why we've had so many problems with him."

"I've guessed it before," I said. Devon, Elizabeth, and Eric all looked at me. "I mean, not really like *Hey, there's crypt keepers saving my life.*"

"Crypt keepers?" the younger scoffed.

"But I sort of thought there might be a league of older black women trying to keep me alive..." I felt stupid and horrible for saying it.

But it was true. I couldn't count the number of times some old black lady had grabbed me by the hoodie and yanked me back before I could daydream my way into traffic. Or stared at me judgmentally enough that I stopped whatever stupid thing I was doing. Or asked why my backpack was screeching like I had a demonic mutant squirrel in it.

"You really have been following me." Somehow the revelation didn't feel creepy.

"I think there might be hope yet," the older said.

"But why?" Elizabeth asked. The women turned cold eyes on her, and she added hastily, "Not that I'm ungrateful for you keeping my boyfriend alive."

A thrill ran up my spine as she called me her boyfriend. Even while facing my judgmental, crypt keeper fairy godmothers, she still wanted to claim me.

"But why would you? Out of all the people in New York, or all the wizards even, why would you help Bryant?" Elizabeth finished.

"A very good question," Eric said.

"Thanks, guys," I grumbled.

"It is not our place to riddle out fate. We are only given glimpses of her plan," the older said, her voice more serious than it had been. "We see darkness, and we see light. The future can go either way. One push, and it could all tumble down."

"So Bryant's the guy standing on the middle of the magical good-and-evil teeter-totter?" Devon asked.

"How poetic," the younger said. "And yes, the fate of this one gangly boy reaches further into the golden strands than even we can see."

"You're seers?" Elizabeth asked.

I couldn't really blame her for skipping over my straddling good and evil. As far as I knew, Elizabeth had only ever met one other seer before.

"And witches," the older answered. "You have only one gift."

"One feels like a lot," Elizabeth said.

"How did you end up down here?" Devon asked. "This isn't like a seer retirement home, is it?"

"He thinks we're retired!" the older cackled.

"Another very good question, though," Eric said, stepping toward the women, his spine totally straight, looking regal in his suspicion. "I didn't think the Ladies would want other women running around their Library."

"We haven't seen the books in ages," the younger said, a hint of something nasty in her voice.

"Don't blame the child," the older said. "We've known for a long time how short the memories of those topside can be."

"Topside? Like not dead?" I gulped.

The women ignored me and pushed on.

"More than a century before your time, magic was dangerous for women," the older began. "Even more dangerous for women of color. The Ladies took control of the Library. They seized a way for women to shape the future of magic in Manhattan. It was a beautiful thing to behold."

"When they decided to bring all magical kin to a safe resting place, they knew they needed guards. Keepers of the dead who could travel out into the world to collect the bones of those who needed protection," the younger said. "They didn't want men. Men would want to steal their power. Men would want to make their place under the Library greater than the Library itself. And that could never be allowed."

The older stepped forward. "We were a ready workforce. Trained to follow orders, happy to have a safe place to call our own. The Ladies named us the keepers of the dead."

"Wait," I said, accidentally cutting the younger off as she opened her mouth to speak. "Are you the originals? Have you been living underground for a century?"

"Let's just say we don't begrudge our trips topside to keep you from dying." The older woman smiled. "It gives us a nice chance for fresh air."

"But if you work for the Ladies, haven't you been going against them in keeping Bryant alive?" Elizabeth asked. "Again, not that I'm not grateful," she added sheepishly.

"The Ladies do not own us, nor do we work for them." The older woman spoke sternly. "We work for the dead. We assist fate to protect the future and keep the vault from filling before its time. But if the Ladies wanted to kill Bryant, we would not interfere."

"Death in battle wouldn't be an accident or even a misstep on the part of a foolish boy."

My face flushed hot.

"It would be the will of fate," the younger woman continued. "And we do not try and cheat fate."

"We hold too many within our walls who have been foolish enough to try just that." The older shook her head solemnly.

"Well then," Eric said, a little more brightly than the situation seemed to call for. "Let us hope fate holds favor with us today. Though it is good to know our bones will someday rest in such capable hands."

"You're welcome." The older bowed.

"We should be going." Eric turned to all of us. "There is much to be done."

"But I'm standing on a teeter-totter of doom! I want to know more about the teeter-totter and the knot of threads that…"

The older woman shook her head at me. "There are some things best not to know. Has it ever occurred to you that knowing too much of the future would only make it harder to keep walking toward it?"

"So it's bad?" My stomach seized up like all the strings fate had to offer had tangled themselves around my intestines.

Now the younger woman shook her head. "You just worry about keeping yourself alive. Fate's planned picture is bigger than you need to be worrying about."

"And don't trip over a book and die in the Library," the older said. "We can't follow you in there. Now go on. A whole lot of tomorrows are waiting on today."

"Tomorrows for me?" I asked.

"Go on." The older flapped her hands at me, shooing me down the hall.

"Okay, okay." Leaving my seer godmothers behind felt awkward. I wanted to hug them or ask for their address to send them a thank-you pie. I settled for "Thanks for keeping me alive."

"Try not to waste our hard work," the younger said, raising an eyebrow at Eric's back.

"Any advice?" Devon asked. "On, you know, surviving?"

"Turn back the way you came and find a nice quiet place to live out your years far away from here," the older said without a hint of sarcasm in her voice.

"I'll keep that in mind." Devon nodded.

"Till we meet again." Eric turned and gave one final bow.

"May it be years from now," the older woman said.

"See you around?" I asked.

The younger laughed dryly. "Try not to make us work too hard."

Elizabeth took my hand and led me down the hall. The back of my neck prickled familiarly. I could feel them watching. It wasn't quite as weird a feeling as it had been before.

"You okay, Bry?" Devon whispered.

"Just found out the keepers of the dead have been keeping me alive because I'm at the center of a knot in the web of fate that could tip the balance between good and evil." I shrugged. "It could be worse. At least there are no skulls here."

The corridor we traveled down was definitely nicer than the ones packed with bones. The warm glow hanging in the air made the stone walls seem pretty if not friendly.

"I still can't get used to it," Devon said after we'd been walking in silence for a few minutes.

I knew him well enough not to ask what *it* was.

He chewed his lip for a while before talking again. "The whole magical fate thing. That there's an invisible web that pulls us all around. And has you hogtied. It feels...prickly. Like I can feel it on my skin."

"You've spent enough time around magic, I wouldn't be surprised if you are actually starting to feel it." Eric stopped and looked at Devon appraisingly. "Perhaps magic will become your second language."

"Thanks?" Devon said to Eric's back as he kept walking, then mouthed to me, "What does that mean?"

The walls around us were hypnotizing. Not smooth and not covered with sharp ridges, but instead carved in gentle curves, like someone had lovingly scooped away the rock one minuscule spoonful at a time. Ahead, a branch in the tunnel came into view, one side sloping up, the other down.

"What's the plan?" I reverted back to whispering. The divergence of the hall suddenly made it real again. We were here to fight the Ladies.

"The upper path would be my best guess for getting into the main Library." Eric didn't stop walking forward. He didn't even slow down.

"Okay, so we take the upper path and then what?" I whispered. "How do we drive the Ladies out? Are we going to pen them in? Are we going to surprise them by charging the wrong way into The Consortium?"

"Perhaps" was Eric's only answer.

"Eric." I grabbed his arm, making him stop freakin' walking. "What are we going to do? What is the plan?"

"There is no plan," Eric said. "Quite frankly, I didn't think we'd make it this far."

"What?" Devon said.

"And I've never been in the Library," Eric pressed on. "I've never even seen a map of the Library. Obviously if I had, I would have known the Vault of the Dead was here. I can't formulate a plan without knowing what is ahead. I don't know why you would expect me to."

"Because you're the leader! You're the one who's supposed to know what to do!" I whisper-shouted at him.

"Well, I'm sorry to disappoint." Eric extricated his arm from my grasp. "But I'm nothing more than a wizard trying to leave this world a little bit less of a wreck than I found it." He straightened his bow tie. "And if I can have an adventure or two along the way, so much the better."

"Okay." Elizabeth stepped between Eric and me. "So we don't have a grand plan. Let's start small. What are we doing right now?"

"We're going up that hall and looking around," Devon answered. "We're going to see what's up there. We're going to keep quiet, scout the area, and find out if the Ladies are here. Then we come up with a plan."

He sounded so brave, so confident, I had to fight the urge to cheer.

"And what if the Ladies find us before we find them?" Elizabeth narrowed her sparkly eyes at Devon.

"We fight like hell and hope no one dies."

26

Stalking through secret tunnels on your way to a forbidden Library can be kind of fun and exciting. But a few minutes into the upper tunnel and the deadliness of it all crept back into the adventure, and my palms slicked with sweat. After the third time I wiped my sweaty hands on my pants, a set of wide, polished double doors came into view.

"We shouldn't knock, right?" I whispered as we reached the doors. Shining brass handles stood out against the deep chocolate color of the wood. They towered over us, at least twelve feet high, looking more like they belonged in a mansion than in an underground stone tunnel.

"After me, I think." Eric stepped forward and took the handle.

I held my breath, waiting for the door to grow teeth and bite Eric in half, or to shock him and send him flying down the hall. But the handle just turned. Smoothly and quietly, as though the door saw regular use.

Giving us a nod, Eric swung the door slowly open. Standing on my tiptoes, I peered over his shoulder, waiting for spells to start flying.

Eric gasped, and *abalata* balanced on my lips as I waited to begin the fight. But Eric stepped forward, and I gasped, too.

We were at the bottom of a long spiral, which towered high above us. The space was wide enough for a few school buses to do donuts in. The walls around us bore carved white marble busts of women's faces. I recognized the one nearest us. She had been killed at the battle of Beville. I wanted to search the stone faces for the Ladies who were still alive and out for our blood, but I couldn't pull my gaze away from the ceiling high above.

Each tier of the spiral was more than twenty feet high, and at the top of the fifth level a beautiful mural of the night sky covered the ceiling. The stars weren't painted with normal gold paint. They were glittering as though someone had ripped stardust from the sky and trapped it in the picture.

A shining wooden banister wound its way down the five stories, and right beyond the rail, shelves peeked into view.

"It's massive," Devon whispered.

"It's beautiful," Elizabeth murmured.

"It's...it's..." I couldn't think of anything to add.

Eric said it for me. "It's magic."

I wanted to whoop, charge up the stairs, grab a book, and start finding out what I, Bryant Jameson Adams teen wizard, was really capable of. If it hadn't been for Devon taking my shoulder as I took the first step toward the tightly spiraled stairs that led to the next level up, I might have.

"They could be right up there," Devon whispered.

The edges of the shelves were visible, but, magic or not, it would be easy for a person to stay low and peer at us through the rails. The utter joy of it all drifted away, replaced by the horrible feeling of being watched.

Eric took the lead once again, keeping near the stone busts that lined the walls. Even the statues seemed to be glaring at me. A horrible fleeting vision of cameras implanted in their eyeballs sent a shiver through my spine.

The steps in the spiral staircase were made of metal set in an intricate swirling design. The swooping curls had been worn away in places. How many times had the Ladies climbed these steps for their feet to wear away that much metal? How many thousands of books had the Ladies carried with them?

I crept up the stairs, trying not to let the metal *thunk* with my weight. My fingers buzzed with anticipation, itching to hold just one of the books. I'd read through most of Eric's volumes on magic, but these were new, forbidden.

At the top of the stairs I closed my eyes for a moment, preparing for the breathtaking beauty of knowledge I was about to behold.

"No." Eric's horrified whisper tore me away from my beatific anticipation.

My eyes sprang open, ready for death to rain on us from above. But Eric was just standing there, staring at the floor-to-ceiling shelves, his face pale and vaguely ill looking.

"What's..." My voice faded away as I looked at the shelves, made of beautiful shining wood that gleamed in the light, with delicate scrollwork carved around the edges. They were utterly empty.

"No," Eric murmured again, as if refusing to accept reality could somehow change it. "No!" He took off running the circle of the layer. I charged after him, my heart pounding in my chest. I glanced over my shoulder just long enough to be sure Devon and Elizabeth were following before looking back to the shelves.

They were *all* empty. Perfectly dusted, wood unscratched, and totally empty.

Eric charged up the steps to the next level before I could catch him. I tore up the stairs, praying the next level would be filled with books, but the shelves were bare.

"Eric!" I hissed as he sprinted the circumference of the next level. "Eric, come back!"

He didn't listen, so we all just kept running after him, passing shelf after empty shelf. I tried not to do the math. How many books missing from how many shelves?

Thousands. Just on one level. Thousands and thousands of one-of-a-kind books. Centuries of irreplaceable knowledge.

"Eric, stop!"

He ran up to the next level, his footfalls clanging on the metal steps.

The Ladies were going to hear him. Any second they would come charging out to kill us. But there was no way to stop Eric without making even more noise as he circled the third floor and up the steps to the forth.

I was in way better shape than I had been the first time I had run with Eric, but he was still faster than the rest of us. I was barely up the steps to the fourth floor when he clambered up the stairs to the fifth.

"Eric!" I panted completely in vain. Tears burned in the corners of my eyes. I don't know if it was because we had done so much to get to the books and they weren't here, or if I was terrified of what the Ladies might have done to them.

At the top of the last flight of stairs, the view was different. The ceiling reflected a shimmering pattern of stars on everything around us. It should have been breathtaking. Half the circle was covered with shelves, but the other half was taken up by three large doorways. Eric knelt in front of one, his head in his hands.

I ran over to him, searching the other doors for signs of evil, killer-mist Ladies.

The door Eric had collapsed in front of was covered in bars like an old-fashioned bank vault or jail cell. I held my breath, hoping there wouldn't be more skeletons hidden in there.

There were no white bones in the locked room. Nothing that even resembled people. The space was as big as my mom's linoleum-floored apartment, and the walls had been scorched black by fire. Scattered around the room, under chunks of burned shelves and the blackened remains of a single chair, were the singed remnants of books.

"Why?" Eric whispered. "How?"

"We have to keep moving." Devon reached down to Eric.

"Everything." Eric sounded like his best friend had been burned in the room with the books. "Everything for centuries, gone."

"We don't know that." Devon seized Eric's arm and dragged him to his feet. "All we know is the shelves are empty. That doesn't change what we came here to do. We have to drive the Ladies out, and if we get a chance to question them along the way, all the better."

Eric swayed. "Records from around the world. Scrolls and papyrus."

"Eric." Devon took Eric's face in his hands. "We will find out what happened to the books. I promise we will do whatever it takes to find them. But we have to keep moving before the Ladies find us."

"Too late," Elizabeth said, her words shockingly loud as they resonated off the ceiling.

I spun to face her, expecting to see a knife at her throat, but she stood alone, pointing at the farthest door where three Ladies waited, mist lapping at their feet.

27

Tendrils of cold tore at my skin. Elizabeth, Devon, and I froze, staring. The childish idea that if you don't move they can't see you seemed to have taken over all our instincts.

"Where are they?" Eric growled.

His perfect hair spiked out of place. His eyes gleamed wildly. He was a man filled with grief and rage and was more terrifying than I had ever seen him.

"Where are the books?" Eric spat, stepping in front of the three of us. "What have you done with them?"

"The intruders came to steal our books," the oldest of the Ladies said. Even from a distance, her overly wrinkled skin seemed paper thin and crackly. "And now they can't find them."

"They'll just have to die without seeing the precious books," the second Lady said, a savage joy filling her voice as it bounced off the ceiling and echoed around the landing. "Our books cannot be stolen."

"We haven't come to steal anything." I felt my lips form the words, so I knew it had to be me speaking.

"Then why would they come?" the last Lady said, her voice higher than the other two. Like she was barely a teenager trapped in the pure white form of the Ladies. "Why would they come to die if they have nothing to gain?"

"We seek to gain nothing," Eric said, his voice so low it was more frightening than if he had been screaming. "We've come to take everything from you. *Erunca!*"

Three bolts of lightning streaked down from the star mural like Zeus himself had thrown them. With a *hiss*, the Ladies scattered, dodging Eric's spell.

"I will cast you out of your power." Eric stalked toward the Ladies, magic crackling around him. "*Enestoliot.*" Lightning formed in Eric's hands, surrounding his fists before he threw it at the nearest Lady.

Mist formed in front of her, eating the power of Eric's spell, lighting the cloud from within.

"Kill them all," the wrinkled Lady said the moment before she charged Eric.

The high-voiced Lady launched herself over the railing, and for a moment I thought she would fall, but a wind rose around her, carrying her straight toward Devon.

"Oh, of course the young one is attracted to me," Devon laughed, pulling his sword from his pocket.

"*Primurgo!*" I shouted, blocking the Lady from Devon, but I couldn't wait to see if the spell had done any good because the last Lady had come for me, sweeping along the railing like a misty-white bat.

"*Abalata!*" I screamed, throwing the black from my hand as soon as it formed. It found its mark, hitting the Lady square in the stomach. She doubled over for a second, just long enough for me to watch Elizabeth scream, "This way, you old hag!" from the doorway where the Ladies had appeared. She took off down the hall, the wrinkled Lady swooping after her in a rage, Eric chasing them, bellowing a spell that streaked red through the air.

That moment of worrying about why my girlfriend was trying to get herself killed was too much. The Lady I was facing had pulled herself upright and hovered six inches above the ground, glaring at me.

"*Telinto*," the woman said casually.

A white-hot something slashed my face, spraying my blood across the marble floor.

"*Kunga!*" I shouted.

The woman flew back, hitting the rail.

I waited for her to take a step forward. "*Turso!*" The spell knocked her feet out from under her but not in the direction I had intended. Instead of falling face first on the floor she tipped backward over the railing.

"No!" I screamed as she fell out of sight. But there was nothing I could do. I spun to Devon, who looked like he was dancing with the Lady he fought.

She giggled wildly like they were playing a game. Grasping a sword of mist made solid, she beamed with joy while she dueled Devon. I ran toward the fight. If the Lady got tired of playing games with him, she could slaughter him with a whisper.

Devon parried her blow just like he'd done to Tybalt in *Romeo and Juliet* two years ago and shouted, "Go after yours, Bry. Finish it!"

The Lady lunged forward, and Devon arched his torso to the side, barely missing being sliced by her blade. "Is that the best you've got?" Devon laughed.

I didn't know what the right thing to do was, but my feet carried me to the bannister in two long strides, and I vaulted over the wooden rail. "*Escata.*" I kept my eyes on the floor far below as I fell, spotting the Lady as the feeling of landing in pudding began.

Bright red blood dripped from her head, staining her otherwise perfect whiteness. She opened her mouth, but I was a split second faster.

"*Aarantha!*" A whirlwind formed around me, pressing the Lady back into the wall. Mist pulled from her like yarn unraveling from a blanket.

Through the roar of the wind I heard a muffled shout. Pain shot through my arm as a deep gash appeared.

"*Erunca!*" Streaks of lightning swirled though the vortex in jarring strips.

The Lady screamed in agony the instant before a cut appeared right over my heart.

I coughed at the pain, wanting nothing more than to press my hands to wound, but I couldn't let go of my spell.

The Lady's eyes peered through the wind, glowing with hate and brimming with joy. She wouldn't stop until she killed me.

"*Caruson!*" I bellowed, hoping my half-formed plan would work. A round of crashes circled the room as each of the marble busts broke free from their bases. The stone heads caught in the twister, flying toward the living Lady.

With a cackle she batted one out of my storm, sending it flying toward my head.

Throwing myself to the ground, I dodged the marble missile. A second head exploded two inches from my own. The voice inside me that believes things work out in the end for good people told me to duck again. To try a spell to pin the Lady to the wall until Eric could find a way to lock her in the burned vault.

Then I pushed myself back to my feet, and my eyes landed on the bright red streak of my own blood smeared across on the floor. The Lady was going to kill me. And then she would move on to my friends.

"*Ilmatiot.*" Dread filled me as I said the spell. I had never used it before. I didn't know the surge that would fly through me as magic blasted from my body. I didn't expect the moment of hollowness once the spell reached the

Lady. I didn't know how strong my panic would be as she gasped, fighting for the breath I squeezed from her body.

She clawed at her throat like she was trying to free the thing that was choking her, but that wasn't how the spell worked.

Thaden himself had used it on me. I knew all too well the horrible searing pain as her lungs fought to expand, the dizzying crash as she fell to the floor, the panic as she realized there was nothing she could do.

I didn't let go of the spell. I could've stopped it, could've let her breathe. But I didn't. I stood there in the center of the tornado I had created and watched her die.

She gave me one last hateful glare before her eyes went blank.

28

One more for the Vault of the Dead.

That was the sick thought in my head as I let go of the twister. My knees buckled, and I hit the marble floor.

I wanted to curl up and never move again. I probably would have, but Devon screamed high above, and I knew I had to keep going. Devon, Elizabeth, Eric—they were why I had to fight. They needed me, and I couldn't abandon them to wallow in fear.

"*Sinato*," I said as I stumbled to the stairs. The sting of the spell healing my skin hurt almost as badly as the cutting itself.

Devon screamed again.

"Devon, hold on!" I shouted, running faster than I had in my entire life.

I caught a glimpse of him rolling away from a shattered piece of banister.

"Hold on, Devon," I whispered as I reached the fourth floor. "Just hold on."

A shriek of laughter from the Lady made my heart vault to my throat. But there were still sounds of fighting. Fighting meant alive.

"I'm here!" I shouted as I leapt the last few feet to the fifth floor.

"Good timing," Devon growled through clenched teeth. The Lady had him pinned to the wall, her mist sword pressing on his light saber in an attempt to force him to decapitate himself.

I stared at them for a moment. Devon poured sweat, his muscles shaking from the fight. Blood seeped from a cut on his neck, dripped from his hand,

and covered his thigh. The Lady beamed like she was gleefully awaiting a ride on a Ferris wheel of death, her white untainted.

"Anytime, Bry," Devon grunted.

My mind raced, trying to find a spell that would stop her from decapitating my best friend without me accidentally decapitating my best friend. I had nothing.

Schoolyard instinct took over. I grabbed a piece of the broken banister and charged, screaming at the top of my lungs. My wordless battle cry shook the ceiling.

The Lady wasn't dumb enough to let go of Devon just because I was howling at her, so I raised the hunk of wood high and bashed her on the head with it, knocking her away from Devon.

I opened my mouth to start a trapping spell, but Devon got there first, plunging his sword into the Lady's chest. She didn't even scream before she went limp.

Gasping for breath, Devon pulled his sword free. There wasn't any blood. The heat of the blade had cauterized the wound. It was like she was meant to have an awkward burned hole in the middle of her chest.

"You okay?" Devon panted, tearing his eyes from the dead Lady. His eyes didn't have the crippling fear of having just killed someone that sloshed painfully around in my chest. He looked hollow.

"Fine." I swallowed. There wasn't time to worry about emotional trauma or anything more than if either of us was about to bleed to death. "Let me help." I raised my hands to do a healing spell.

"There isn't time."

Ignoring him I muttered the spell and watched his skin shimmer as it healed the cut on his neck—which was too close to his jugular for comfort—the swiftly bleeding wound on his palm, and the gash across his thigh.

"We have to go." Devon ran to the door where Eric and Elizabeth had disappeared before his skin had finished knitting back together.

We ran quietly. I wanted to ask Devon what the plan was, but I knew what he would say. *Find Eric and Elizabeth, make sure they don't get killed, try to make sure we don't get killed either.*

The doorway they had taken led to a hall that looked...normal. Well, normal for my dad's super rich friends.

Evenly spaced chandeliers dripped from the ceiling, marble tables held vases of flowers, and paintings hung in gold leaf frames. The first painting was the size of a car and showed a man standing on top of a rock, summoning lightning from above. I wanted to stop and study it, to find out who the magical man was. But singe marks marred the fancy red wallpaper, and swatches of the patterned rug had been torn away. We ran on, the thickness of the tattered ground muffling our footfalls.

I kept listening, waiting for Elizabeth to scream. It's weird to hope someone will scream, but screaming means alive.

Devon grabbed my arm as we reached the double door at the end of the hall, yanking me back before I could wrench them open.

"Shhh." Devon leaned close to the doorjamb, pausing for a moment before opening the door a crack and listening again.

"Let's go," I whispered.

"Who's in a hurry now?" Devon pulled the door open far enough to peek into the next room. "Empty."

The square room was empty at least as far as people. Matching desks were laid out in a grid on the shining wooden floor. All of the desks had been cleared but three.

Only one now.

The thought shook me to my spine as we ran across the parquet floor, our shoes clacking. A door led out of each side of the room. All the doors were closed. Panic surged, gripping my lungs. There was no way to know which way they went, and no time to search.

"There." Devon pointed to a scorch mark above the left-hand door.

I charged toward the door, not even caring if it wasn't Eric being brilliant at all but a trap from the wrinkled Lady. I reached the door first and wrenched the knob, not giving Devon the time to listen. The girl of my dreams and the man who brought me into this world were fighting somewhere, and I had to reach them.

"How dare you!" The Lady's shriek of rage flew down the narrow corridor we'd just entered, echoing off the concrete walls.

My heart leapt. If she had someone to scream at, someone was still alive and fighting her.

The hall ended in a sharp corner, and lights flashed around the bend. I sprinted down the corridor, my feet barely touching the floor.

A crash of a spell striking something solid rattled toward us.

"*Ellisium!*" the Lady screamed.

"You are finished here!" Eric bellowed. "You are done. I will not allow you destroy one more ounce of magic."

As I rounded the corner, bright red light nearly blinded me and I skidded to a stop. Shielding my eyes, I tried to understand the scene in front of me.

Elizabeth was on her feet, four limbs attached and breathing like a champ, next to Eric who had streams of red light pouring out of his palms. The Lady screamed, trapped inside a glowing scarlet cocoon, which had tipped her onto her back and pressed her toward the floor as though the spell held the force of gravity itself. Only the strength of her own magic kept her hovering a foot above the ground.

"Tell me where the books are," Eric growled.

"The books are not meant for men like you," the Lady spat. Even in the red light her skin shone white, making her look more like a corpse than a person capable of speech.

"Tell me where you've hidden them." The magic in Eric's hands redoubled, squeezing in around the Lady.

Her face twisted in rage and pain as she screamed. "You will never see those books, you foolish child."

"If I am a child to you, then know a child has taken your Library, a child has overthrown the Ladies, and a child will find where you've hidden the books." Eric's eyes danced in the light of his own magic, giving him the look of a madman rather than a wizard.

"The books have not been in these walls since you walked on this earth." Each word the Lady spoke seemed to cost her energy she didn't have. "The best of us have sought them and failed." A laugh like a scream flew from the Lady, echoing off the walls. "Die in the attempt, fool."

A *whoosh* of magic tore through the hall, knocking me over as it dove into Eric's spell.

And the last Lady went limp, falling to the floor in an undignified heap.

"No!" Eric bolted forward and grabbed the Lady, taking her by the shoulders and shaking her so hard she looked like a shriveled rag doll. "You don't get to be dead!" He began murmuring under his breath.

"Eric," Elizabeth said, her voice shaking.

Eric didn't look up. He held the Lady in his arms. She didn't look terrifying anymore. Just old and sad.

"Eric!" Elizabeth said loudly enough Eric couldn't ignore her. "Eric, she's dead."

The world froze for a moment. The enormity of the truth settled around us, falling heavily on my skin.

I know it sounds crazy, but for the first time, and only for a split second, it was like I could feel the strings of fate. Feel the golden strands that had surrounded the Ladies snap. The long line of women who had ruled magic for so long was gone, the last of them lay dead before me. My skin prickled like the threads were searching, finding a new life to latch on to, adding more weight to the web that already wrapped so tightly around my life.

And then the feeling was gone.

Eric let go of the Lady, and she fell back to the floor. "She had no right to die."

"That wasn't you?" Devon asked, sounding as tired as I felt.

"She did it to herself, to keep the books from me. From the people who deserve them." Eric cursed and banged his fists on the concrete wall. Shock-waves of magic flew from his hands, denting the surface.

"Where are the other two?" Elizabeth asked.

"Dead."

Elizabeth looked into my eyes as I said the word, and I knew she knew. She saw the horrible fear that had settled just above my spleen. She saw the panic in my eyes. I had killed a witch. A human. Not fought for my life and vaguely wondered later if my opponent had survived. Not incapacitated and let someone else make the final blow. Not killed a monster before it could squash my friends. I had watched the life leave the Lady's body, and I wasn't sure if I regretted it. Elizabeth didn't need to be a seer to see the burden death had laid on me.

"We did it." There was no triumph in Devon's voice. "We took the Library from the Ladies."

"It wasn't supposed to happen like this," Elizabeth said.

"No one was supposed to die." The word *die* tasted like bleach in my mouth.

"There were supposed to be books!" Eric buried his face in his hands.

"Eric." Devon laid his hand on Eric's shoulder. "We came here to take the Library from the Ladies. To make sure they weren't in power so they couldn't come after us for what happened in Beville. The Ladies are gone. They can't hurt us or anyone else ever again."

"But the books." Eric dragged his hands across his face so hard it looked like he'd tear his own skin off. "What good is the Library without the books? How can we tell the magical world the Ladies are gone and so are the centuries of magical learning we've been begging for all our lives?"

"The books haven't been here during your life," Elizabeth said. "The whole time you've been wanting them, the shelves have been empty."

"Can we not be here right now?" I asked. Having a conversation over a dead body was too much for me.

No one said anything, but Elizabeth took my hand and led me away. I didn't look back to make sure Devon and Eric were following us. I didn't want to see the body again.

"Why weren't there any mist monsters?" Devon asked when we reached the room with the desks and shut the hall door firmly behind us. "I'm not complaining, but why didn't we meet any of their nasty little friends?"

"Only the Ladies could be allowed in the presence of the books." Eric sounded numb as he spoke.

"And little killer mist pets didn't make it through the ban?" A laugh rose in my throat and died before it made a sound.

"They kept their secret from their minions though it cost them their lives," Eric said.

"Which way?" Elizabeth asked.

The temptation to curl up and sleep under one of the desks overwhelmed me. I didn't want to find a way out. I didn't want to go into the crisp winter air and see the world was still turning like I hadn't just killed someone.

But the world doesn't wait for you to be ready.

Numbly, I walked to one of the doors we hadn't been through. It led to a short hall lined with doors, sort of like the wing we slept in in Eric's house. Not bothering to close that door, I moved on to the last one and was greeted by a long staircase.

The steps weren't made of fancy metal. They were worn wood like we had accidentally stumbled into the basement of a brownstone.

"This way?" I asked. Not waiting for a response, I climbed the steps.

The first stair creaked and I started to shout a spell before realizing the step wasn't trying to attack me.

"What did Thaden take?" Eric asked as we trudged up the stairs. "He broke into the Library. He found the spells he put on the phone. If the books weren't here—"

"The burned room," Devon said. "My Lady said Thaden torched the last of the books in the vault. Said she'd burn me in there, too."

"He just burned them?" I hate to say that I hated Thaden, but I did. He tried to kill me, and it all sort of spiraled from there. Knowing he'd burned precious magical records tripled my loathing. I finally understood what it must have been like to find out the Great Library of Alexandria had been burned, and the feeling was nothing less than utterly sick.

"He recorded the knowledge in the phone for his own use and destroyed the rest," Eric said as the stairs finally came to an end. "I have never conceived of such depths of evil."

A door waited for us at the top of the stairs. Nothing strange or beautiful, just a door with a faint scent of food wafting through.

The door moved with one quick shove, and I knew where we were before Devon said, "The Consortium."

We had made it all the way back. Under the river, through Hell, and back to midtown. I didn't know whether to laugh or cry.

"I'll get food." Devon headed toward the swinging door in the back. Suddenly it seemed like a hundred years since we'd eaten the overpriced turkey sandwiches from the ferry.

"Is there anyone back there?" Elizabeth called after him.

Because that's how wonderful she was. Thinking of things like if there's henchmen making eggs.

"All clear," Devon called back.

Eric sagged into a chair, looking utterly defeated even though we'd just won.

"Thaden knew." Elizabeth slipped into the chair opposite Eric. "He must have seen the empty shelves. He knew there were no more books. Why didn't he tell everyone? Why did he bother fighting the Ladies at all? He could have just told everyone the books were missing, and the Ladies would have lost all their power over Beville. Over everyone."

"Missing?" Eric said. "Thousands of books don't just go missing. If the Ladies couldn't find them, they were stolen by someone very brave and extremely magically talented."

"How do you know they looked for them?" I asked. My brain had gotten to the muddy phase where you can't quite understand the flow of your own thoughts, let alone anyone else's.

"*The best of us have sought them,*" Eric recited the Lady's words. "They would only call themselves the best of anything. If the Ladies were looking for the books, someone else took them."

"Who?" Elizabeth asked, wiping blood from the cuts on her forearms. It looked like the Lady had clawed her.

Feeling like the worst boyfriend in the world, I murmured, "*Sinato*" and held her hands as the spell knitted the skin back together.

"Eric?" I asked after a long moment. "Who could have taken the books?"

"A hundred unlikely people," Eric sighed. "And I haven't the faintest clue as to where to find them."

"But I still don't understand why Thaden didn't tell everyone the books were gone," Elizabeth said. "It would have wreaked more havoc than anything else he could have done."

"If you found out a priceless treasure was missing, would you tell everyone, or would you search while no one else knew there was anything to even be searching for?" Devon said, laying a chocolate cake and four forks on the table. "That kitchen is shockingly bare." Devon shrugged when Eric raised a questioning eyebrow at him.

I grabbed a fork and tore free a bit of cake. "Do you think Thaden found the books?"

"No," Eric said, sounding more himself after a bite of cake. "If he had them, he would have told everyone. Thaden never found the books."

"So now we have to find a way to do something Thaden never managed?" Devon stabbed his fork into the cake a little harder than necessary. "I might need coffee to go with this cake."

Eric froze looking at Devon. "You'll help me find the books?"

"We'll all help you find the books," Devon said. "And figure out a way to stop Kendrick McDonald from hunting Bryant and whatever other new blood he's after."

"That's a really big to-do list for only being two items long." I shoved a huge bite of cake into my mouth. I don't know if the Ladies had been excellent bakers, outsourced, or just magicked the cake into being, but it was moist perfection. The rush of sugar flowed through my veins, and suddenly trying to take down a wizard-trafficking ring and find a few thousand lost books seemed not entirely suicidal.

"Do we tell people the Ladies are dead?" Elizabeth asked with the most tantalizing crumb of cake on her lip.

"No," Eric said. "Having the Ladies be gone without having a new government in place would be chaos."

"Are we going to turn Elizabeth pasty and make her a fake Lady?" Devon asked.

"Are we going to bleach Devon and dress him in drag?" Elizabeth countered.

"Neither." Eric stood, ignoring Devon and Elizabeth staring each other down. "I happen to know a seer who has spent far too long living in exile. I think a change in address is just what she needs."

"So we grab Lola from under the bridge and make her the head of the magical world?" I asked.

"Yes." Eric's face lightened as he walked toward the window that looked out over the park and Big Blue in all its early morning glory.

"Then we stalk Kendrick McDonald and make sure he can't hurt anyone again?" Elizabeth led me to the window, wrapping her arm around my waist so she could lean into my shoulder.

"Precisely."

"Then we find the books and create free knowledge for magickind?" Devon joined the group.

"Exactly."

"And hope all of our parents will take us back and we're not expelled from school?" Devon added.

"I have plenty of spare room in Beville." Eric smiled. "And I hear The Consortium might need a new busboy besides."

Devon glared at Eric.

"All the best magical restaurants have busboys with swords." Eric bowed.

"I want a magical shield," Devon said. "Maybe a suit of armor, too."

Devon started to laugh, and then we were all laughing, because there was nothing else to do.

We stood together in the window of The Consortium, watching the Christmas tourists pass. None of them knew there was no line for a table at The Consortium. None of them knew we had all almost died. And none of them knew we had all just agreed to take on most of the magical world to save magickind. Whether they liked it or not.

THREE SIMPLE STEPS TO WIZARDING DOMINATION

BOOK THREE

1

Don't panic.

Elizabeth's voice echoed through my head.

Don't panic.

But there was no way out. After everything I'd survived, after fighting my way through blood and monsters and tombs, I was trapped.

There would be no plaque marking the place of my demise. People might vaguely wonder what had happened to Bryant Jameson Adams, boy wizard, but they'd never know the real truth—there are some things even magic can't save you from.

Just don't panic.

"Bryant." Mom shattered the dulcet tones of Elizabeth's imaginary voice. "Are you listening?"

"Yes?" My voice wiggled at the lie.

"Bryant, your mother and I are trying to talk to you." My dad set down his glass of wine and leaned across the dining room table.

"Right." I nodded. "Sorry, just thinking about...homework." My voice wiggled again.

Mom and Dad looked at each other like some weird silent communication was flickering between them.

I'd been trapped in the Twilight Zone. Stuck in a world where fate had somehow twisted my broken-home life so my parents had decided they were okay with speaking to each other. So okay with not communicating solely through lawyers that we should have a family dinner. The three of us. At a table. Together. For a whole meal. If that wasn't a sign of impending doom, I don't know what could be.

"We're worried about you, Bryant," Mom said. "Ever since the incident before Christmas, you've seemed a little strained."

"Strained?" My voice cracked.

Mom pointed to my plate. "I made pancakes for dinner, and you've barely eaten."

Of the four pancakes she'd piled onto my plate, I'd only managed to get through one.

"They taste different cooked on rich people pans," I said.

Mom bit the corners of her mouth to keep from smiling.

A crease formed between Dad's perfectly sculpted eyebrows.

"I'm not saying there's anything wrong with...this." I waved a hand around the fancy dining room with its ultra-modern light fixtures, giant marble tabletop, and weird abstract painting that could very well have been done by an elephant. "It just doesn't feel like a breakfast-for-dinner kind of place."

Dad took a bite of his pancakes, washing it down with a sip of wine. The bottle probably cost more than most people spend on groceries in a week, but whatever.

"Pancakes aside," Mom said. "We're worried about you."

"Your mother and I have been talking," Dad said.

I gripped the edge of the marble table. "Don't even mention boarding school or becoming a sheepherder in Ireland. I'm not leaving Manhattan."

"We know." Mom reached across the table and took my hand. "You can't leave being a wizard behind. We've come to accept that."

Dad made a weird noise in his throat that sounded like he had not at all come to accept that his seventeen-year-old son was a wizard locked in a web of fate that had yanked him near death a few times.

Mom shot Dad a glare.

"You need help, Bryant," Dad said, waiting for a nod from Mom before pressing on. "Professional help."

"I'm learning about magic from Eric," I said. "That's about as great a magical education as I'm going to get."

"Professional psychological help," Mom said.

It took a second for my brain to click the words into place. "You want me to go to therapy?"

"Whatever is going on with you," Dad said, "it's too big for a kid your age to be dealing with on their own. It's been two months now, and you're still stressed and antsy."

I wanted to flip the marble table and scream that of course I was stressed and antsy! I'd squished a monster, killed a Lady, and helped secretly topple the magical government. A nervous breakdown seemed really natural, all things considered.

But knocking over furniture didn't seem like a great way to get out of therapy.

"Stressed is my natural state," I said. "You've just never been around long enough to figure out your son is a permanent ball of anxiety."

Everyone went quiet.

Guilt joined the anxiety weighing in my stomach.

"Sorry," I muttered.

"Don't apologize," Dad said. "I can't fault you for telling the truth."

"Well, you're around now," I said. "That's nice."

I didn't launch into the details of how weird it was to have my dad trying to see me for more than a quick cup of coffee as he floated through town on business, how inconvenient it was that he had chosen now to take his father gig super seriously, or how I had totally noticed him standing way too close to my mom while she made pancakes in his super fancy kitchen and that it gave me more anxiety than the time I'd almost gotten skewered by a magically made light saber.

My dad's a good guy, and I love him. So better awkward than absent...I guess.

"You need help, Bryant," Mom said. "I may not know anything about magic, but I know my son. You aren't sleeping. You don't laugh like you used to. You need to talk to someone."

"And say what?" I dug my fork into my now mushy pancakes. "Hi, I'm Bryant, and I'm a wizard. Some bad people were after me, but now they're not and I still feel like they're looking over my shoulder? What's the point in going to therapy if being honest with the doctor would get me locked in a mental ward?"

"You've at least got to try." Dad laid his hand on Mom's shoulder, like they were the picture of bliss. Like we were somehow going to morph into the kind of family that didn't need therapy or custody lawyers. "I've gotten in touch with one of the best psychologists in New York. There's no harm in talking to her."

Both my parents stared expectantly at me, Mom still clutching my non-pancake spearing hand.

"I'll give it a try," I said. "But if they lock me up and Eric has to come rescue me, I take no responsibility for the structural damage."

"Good." Dad leaned back in his seat. "You have an appointment at 4pm tomorrow."

"Great." I spent the rest of dinner half-listening as Dad asked Mom about the architect the school had hired to rebuild the theatre. Then Mom asked Dad about how things were going at work now that he'd restructured his job to spend more time in New York with me. Then they made plans for us to do something that involved a bunch of family bonding over the weekend.

I tried to pay attention, but I couldn't quite manage it. My brain was too busy trying to figure out how to talk to a therapist without mentioning magic, or that I'd killed somebody.

After dinner, Dad had his driver take Mom and me home in his fancy, leather-interior car.

Two months ago, Mom would rather have trudged through a blizzard than take a ride from Dad, but things were different now. They'd united in their two-person club. The *My Son the Teenage Wizard is Having an Emotional Crisis and Someone's Probably Still Trying to Kill Him Support Group.*

Okay, so they didn't know about the last bit. As far as my parents were concerned, we had "scared" the evil mist Ladies who wanted me dead out of Manhattan, and now everything was hunky-dory and I was moving up in my magical studies like a pro.

They didn't know Eric, Devon, Elizabeth, and I had taken over the Library. They didn't know when we broke into the Library, all the one-of-a-kind books on magic were missing. They didn't know all the Ladies were dead, and that I'd killed one of them myself. And they definitely didn't know we'd sworn to find the missing books no matter what.

Dad's driver let us out at the building where Mom and I lived.

Mom waved to the doorman even though she knew full well he wouldn't look up from his video game to see who had strolled into the lobby.

I took a deep breath, inhaling the scent of old people and cheap cleaner. I hated that smell, but at least it was familiar.

Mom didn't say anything until we'd climbed into the janky elevator and were rattling our way to the twelfth floor.

"I'm proud of you." Mom brushed my hair away from my face in that semi-endearing *I'm judging you because you need a haircut* way.

"For what?" I ran a hand through my hair and let it flop back into my face. It really did need cutting.

"For being willing to accept help," Mom said. "That's a very grown up thing to do."

"Thanks." I made myself smile.

"Things are going to get better. You'll see."

The elevator rumbled to a stop, and a hum filled my chest, a thudding buzz that didn't stop even as we walked into our apartment with the chipped linoleum floor. The rumble kept going while I brushed my teeth and climbed into bed. I tried to tell myself my stomach was mad from eating pancakes at night, but I'm just as bad at lying to myself as I am at lying to other people.

As I lay in bed, trying to ignore the pain of Mrs. Mops' claws digging into my thigh, I knew things weren't going to get better. We'd had two months of magical peace. Two months of trying to figure out our lives in a post-Ladies ruled world. But fate had more it wanted us to get done, and we weren't going to be able to move on with living our actual lives until we had finished saving the magical world.

2

———

"I just don't know how much longer I can take it." Elizabeth leaned her head against my shoulder. Her scent of summer flowers cut through the smell of coffee and fresh-baked pastries that filled the dining room of the Consortium.

I took a sip of my cappuccino, blocking the wonderfulness of Elizabeth's fragrance enough that I could focus on her words instead of drifting into the lovesick, blissful state where concentrating got really hard.

"I understand they're mad," Elizabeth pressed on. "I did technically run away from home for two days."

"And break into the Library and secretly take over Manhattan's magical government," Devon added from behind the counter.

"They don't know that," Elizabeth said. "My parents think I went on a post-traumatic tear through the city after seeing my lunch lady squashed in a tragic accident. And they still think being grounded indefinitely is fair."

"I'm sorry." I kissed her forehead. Bubbles of joy tickled my lungs as my lips touched the softness of her skin.

"I don't think the problem was you panicking from the squashing and running away," Devon said. "I think the problem was their daughter disappearing with her boyfriend for two days."

"Don't side with my oppressors," Elizabeth said.

"If living with your parents is so rough, there's always room at the Consortium Orphanage." Devon tossed Elizabeth a deep purple apron with silver letters across the front, which read *The Consortium*.

Her face paled. "I'm so sorry, Dev."

"No worries." Devon sat on the counter that separated the kitchen area of the Consortium from the main body of the empty restaurant.

"I should have thought." Elizabeth stepped away from me and took his hands. "I could have it way worse. I'm sorry."

"It's really fine." Devon kissed the back of Elizabeth's hand in a way that would have made my stomach curdle with jealousy if anyone besides my best friend had tried it. "Life post-parents really isn't so bad. I've got sweet digs, a job that pays pretty good, and my teachers feel so sorry for me I've been snatching A's on everything I turn in. And I don't have to hide that I'm running around with magical people."

"Not lying about magic anymore would be great, but," Elizabeth sighed, "perspective is important."

"Not as important as keeping off my counter." Lola swept in from the kitchen. Her sapphire blue turban matched the flowing, full-length romper she wore. Her nails glittered a deep violet, which lay somewhere between sapphire and the Consortium's standard purple. Her only concession to the fact that she had taken over running the restaurant that had been the front for the magical Ladies who ruled New York were the sequined flats Lola had donned in place of her usual high heels.

"We don't have customers," Devon said.

"Of course not, sweetie," Lola said. "I have no interest in havin' strangers off the street comin' in here to bother me. But if a health inspector were to saunter past, see you perched on my clean counter, and decide to inspect this place, how do you think he would feel about the people I've got helpin' me in the kitchen?"

"Fair enough." Devon slid off the counter, tossing Lola a crooked grin.

"Now, go earn your keep and eat everything I baked." Lola shooed us toward the kitchen.

Elizabeth slipped her hand into mine.

I could feel the tension radiating from her shoulders all the way down to her fingertips.

"Don't be scared, sugar," Lola said. "You know full well they don't bite. Usually."

Elizabeth shook out her shoulders as Devon swung open the door.

The kitchen looked like any other restaurant kitchen, not that I'd been in a ton, but everything seemed standard. Giant walk-in fridge in the corner, massive oven, pots hanging all over. It wasn't until you got to the quasi-dead staff that things got a little weird.

Sniffer McDeadDog, Lola's resident homeless-looking kid, shuffled toward us, holding a tray of fresh croissants and muffins.

"Thanks, little man." Devon took a croissant, shoving half of it into his mouth.

"Thanks." I opted for a muffin.

"Thank you." Elizabeth's words were barely audible as she reached for a muffin. She kept her hand steady, as though reaching toward a wild animal. Which, I guess, is sort of what she saw.

I squinted at the kid, trying to see the dead, decaying, half-dog, sort-of person thing that was what Elizabeth saw when she looked at Lola's guards/kitchen staff. All I could see was a kid who looked sad and hungry enough to eat all the food in Manhattan.

As much as being a wizard could be rough at times, I never envied Elizabeth being a seer. Looking into the shadows and finding darkness staring back is not something I could be brave enough to do and ever sleep again. But Elizabeth could. My brave, beautiful, amazing girlfriend.

"Bryant." Devon waved a muffin at me with laughter in his eyes like he'd been waving the baked good for a while.

"Sorry, what?" I took a giant bite of my muffin. Gooey blueberry heaven greeted me.

"Do you want to bring anything to your mom?" Devon asked.

"No," I said. "She can be on her own for breakfast."

"Then let's go." Devon grabbed his backpack from the place where I'm pretty sure some chef would be chopping up meat in a normal restaurant.

"Is that all you're taking?" Lola asked as we walked back out into the empty restaurant.

"The pack will give out the rest on their rounds," Devon said.

"Try not to find too much excitement before you get back here." Lola wiped her pristine counter.

"I can't promise anything." Devon winked.

I grabbed my backpack from where I'd dumped it by the front door and passed Elizabeth hers. Devon held the door open, and together, we stepped out to greet another morning in Manhattan.

Big Blue in all her glory loomed over Central Park. The giant bloom still hadn't seemed to notice that every other leafy plant in New York had given up on life for the winter, but I guess that's standard for magical botanicals.

"Spill it, Bry," Devon said before we'd made it to the end of the block.

"Spill what?" I checked the edges of my cappuccino cup.

"Whatever's got you only taking one bite out of Lola's fresh-baked muffin," Devon said.

I stared down at the muffin in my hand. For a fleeting moment, I considered shoving the whole thing in my mouth so I would have a really good excuse not to talk for a few blocks.

"Does it have something to do with why you didn't want to bring your mom breakfast?" Elizabeth peeked sideways at me from behind her curls. Most of the black had worn away, leaving only thin dark streaks weaving through the golden tendrils.

"My parents want to send me to therapy," I said.

"Therapy?" Elizabeth choked on her coffee.

"Like *sit on a couch and spill your deepest thoughts to a professional so they can help you work through your innermost demons* therapy?" Devon said.

"Yeah." I took a long drink of my coffee, waiting for them to tell me how screwed up I'd been lately and how seeking professional help was a great idea because clearly the trauma of killing someone was eating my brain.

"Are they insane?" Elizabeth said.

"Is this like a regular therapist, or did Eric help them find someone in Beville?" Devon asked.

"Human and highly recommended," I said.

"They've lost their damned minds." Elizabeth's cheeks flushed to a pale rose color. "You mention you're a wizard, and you're going to be locked up. If you tell them you have the weight of the magical world on your shoulders, I'm not going to get to see my boyfriend anymore because he'll be in a closed ward."

"I tried to explain the institutionalized problem." Having Elizabeth tell me I wasn't insane for thinking my parents were crazy made my stomach feel a lot less like I'd swallowed concrete. I took a giant bite of muffin.

"You're going to have to lie," Elizabeth said. "Tell the shrink you need to work on building coping mechanisms to handle the trauma of the school fire and seeing our lunch lady squished. If they ask anything else, say you feel abandoned by your father."

"Bryant's not a good enough liar to get away with that," Devon said.

"I know, right!" I shoved the rest of my breakfast into my mouth.

"We could try coaching him?" Elizabeth said.

"Before my 4pm appointment?" I asked.

Devon pinched the bridge of his nose. "Is there a spell you could use on the doctor?"

"Not unless you want me to trap my shrink in a magical cage to prove to her that I really am a wizard."

"I'll talk to your mom," Elizabeth said, "try to convince her this is a terrible idea."

"Thanks, Elizabeth." I wrapped my arm around her shoulders. Having a normal human problem to worry about with my friends almost qualified as a fun morning activity. I tipped my face up to the sky, enjoying the sunlight peeking down between the buildings.

"I don't think you should talk to Ms. Miller," Devon said as we reached the bottom of the school steps.

"Why not?" Elizabeth asked.

"Because Bryant's parents are fussing about sending him to therapy and not some boarding school in another country. Let them feel like they've won a big victory over the scary magical world. It'll keep them off Bryant's back."

Elizabeth bit her lip, her nose wrinkling in thought. "Do you think if I volunteered to go to therapy, I might convince my parents to unground me?"

"No," Devon laughed. "I think the only way you're going to snag a *get out of jail free* card is by dumping Bryant."

An iron coil tightened around my gut. "That's an even crazier idea than me going to human therapy."

Elizabeth looked to me, her sparkly eyes narrowed. "Is it?"

"Yes. Because we're happy, and I"—I balanced on the edge of saying *I love you and you're the thing that makes getting up in the morning really worth it*—"I think we should stay together."

"We'd get more time together." Elizabeth threaded her fingers through mine and led me up the stairs and into school. "Right now, I can only see you for an hour before and two hours after school because my parents think I have extra rehearsals for the school play. And, while coffee at the Consortium is great—"

"I am a pretty bangin' barista," Devon said.

"—if I were allowed evening and weekend hours away from home, I would have more time to help Eric and learn from Lola," Elizabeth pressed on.

"But don't you care about us?" I said.

"What do you mean?" Elizabeth detached her hand from mine.

"And this is my cue to find my locker." Devon bowed and disappeared into the shambling crowd of tired teenagers.

"Bryant?" Elizabeth furrowed her perfect brow at me.

"I mean…" I stared into the horde of students, half-hoping for something to lunge out and try to kill us so I wouldn't have to have this conversation.

"You'd be free from grounding, but we wouldn't be together. If you don't want to be my girlfriend anymore, I understand." Saying the words tore at my chest like someone had just violently removed one of the puzzle pieces of my heart. "It was bound to happen eventually. You've always been too good for me."

Elizabeth blinked at me. "You think I'm too good for you?"

"Yeah." Heat raced to my face, not because I was embarrassed to tell Elizabeth I would never be worthy of her, but because panic threatened to burst through my now fractured heart. "The whole danger attraction thing wasn't going to drag you along forever. I just, I thought I had more time."

"More time." Elizabeth's voice sounded hollow, like I'd broken something in her, too.

"I'm not saying I want us to break up. I'm not ready for us to be over yet." The words tumbled out of my mouth as involuntarily as vomit.

"Yet?"

"I want to stay with you." I reached for her hand.

"But you think I'd walk away from us?" She didn't reach for me. "I'm only your girlfriend because of all the crazy we got dumped into?" A faint shimmer of silver pooled at the bottom of her eyes.

"Elizabeth."

The bell rang, sending the sleepy throng scurrying.

"I have to get to class." Elizabeth turned away.

"Elizabeth, wait." I reached for her arm.

"I can't be late." She stepped into the flow of bodies and let them sweep her away.

I stood frozen as the corridor emptied, trying to figure out how I had messed everything up so royally.

It wasn't until the second bell rang that I finally sprinted for class, ducking in just in time to avoid a tardy.

Devon looked at me as I sank into my seat. Years of friendship let me read the question in his eyes.

How much trouble are you in?

I think I might have just ruined everything.

I dragged my hands over my face.

I'd hurt Elizabeth. I'd said something awful, but I wasn't quite sure what.

She *was* too good for me. Anyone with two eyes and half a soul would know that. And I'd just proven it by being a horrible idiot.

She'd never known me when I wasn't a wizard, not really. Not in a boyfriend way. But the lure of dating a wizard wasn't going to last forever.

I spent the whole morning circling through our conversation in my head, trying to figure out which bit of truth had been the one that hurt.

I will never know how economics are affected by wars, or what the meaning of Frankenstein's monster might be, because all I could think of in class was how to make sure Elizabeth didn't cry anymore.

I'd finally worked out where everything had gone so terribly wrong when the bell rang for lunch. I grabbed my books and started for the cafeteria as quickly as I dared with teachers on the prowl for any dangerous-looking activity.

I closed my eyes as I passed the technicolor memorial mural for the squished lunch lady who had tried to kidnap me and threatened to kill Elizabeth. Still, just knowing the two-dimensional, angelic version of the Lancre was staring at me from the wall made sour stir in my stomach.

I made myself swallow as I weaved through the horde of hungry students.

Elizabeth wasn't at our usual table on the side of the room. I scanned the masses for her blonde and black hair.

"She's not here." Devon laid a hand on my shoulder, guiding me to sit.

"What do you mean?" I didn't stop searching until Devon held his phone up in front of my face.

A message from Elizabeth showed on the screen.

Feeling sick. Got the nurse to send me home. Let Ms. Miller know I'll be missing rehearsal after school.

3

A way to turn back time, that was what I really needed. Even as I searched through my spell-filled phone in the back of the fancy car my dad had sent to haul me to therapy, I knew I wasn't going to find a spell that could undo my fight with Elizabeth.

I scrolled past the app for healing spells, the fire app that had started it all, even poked around in defensive spells before putting the black phone into my pocket and pulling out my regular phone. The one with the cracked screen that could actually do important things like make phone calls.

I'm really sorry.

I typed to Elizabeth. I wasn't sure what else to say.

I hope I didn't just destroy everything seemed too dramatic. *I love you and would do anything not to lose you* would probably make everything worse.

Can I call you tonight? I sent the message.

I stared at my phone, waiting for her to reply, until the car stopped in front of a gleaming office building.

"I'll be back to pick you up after your appointment," the driver said.

I looked to the front of the car, acknowledging the driver for the first time—because sometimes I'm a self-absorbed, trust fund prick who treats everyone horribly.

The driver was older than my dad. He had kind eyes and a wedding ring on his finger. He'd probably been married for thirty years and knew exactly what to say to the girl of his dreams when he'd royally screwed up.

As I opened my mouth to ask the driver to save me from my doom, the cabbies behind us started blaring their horns for the poor guy to move.

"Thanks for the ride." I climbed out of the car, letting the depressing scent of New York City sink into my soul.

The security guards inside had my name on file. They snapped my picture and checked my ID before sending me up the elevator to the fifteenth floor.

I followed the signs for Dr. Spinnek's office, making my way past a tax attorney, a divorce attorney, and an acting agent.

I don't know if Dr. Spinnek was a marketing genius or had just accidentally ended up on a floor full of businesses that could funnel stressed out clients directly onto her couch.

I reached the fancy glass door with Dr. Spinnek's name painted on it. The gold and black lettering sent a shiver down my spine. My gut reaction was to grab for the black, magic-filled phone and storm through the door, spells blazing.

Dr. Spinnek could be a Lancre sent to kidnap me and deliver me to her master. Or a lost Lady who had come out of hiding to seek revenge.

Or a super expensive therapist Dad was paying to make me less jumpy and neurotic.

My heart skipped a beat as I pushed open the door and stepped into a waiting room, complete with potted plants, soothing music, and a glass-fronted fridge filled with fancy bottled water.

A guy in a purple suit sat at a desk blocking the door to Dr. Spinnek's office.

"Mr. Adams?" Purple suit guy stood, extending a hand.

I glanced at his palm, searching for signs of a spell that might kill me, before realizing the poor guy just wanted to shake hands like a normal human.

"Hi." I shook his hand and tried to give a sane-looking smile. "It's Bryant."

"Of course." Purple suit smiled. "We're happy to call you whatever makes you feel most comfortable. Please have a seat, Bryant."

"Thanks." I sat in one of the four, high-back chairs that had been artfully placed around the room.

I should be with Elizabeth. Or at the Consortium. Or training. Or doing homework.

I pulled my normal phone back out of my pocket. Elizabeth hadn't texted back. Not that she should have texted back within five minutes of me messaging her. She just usually did. Unless she wasn't planning on speaking to me ever again.

Hot panic burned in my throat.

"Mr. Adams." A woman with a salt-and-pepper bob stood by the office door.

"He prefers Bryant, Dr. Spinnek," purple suit said.

"Bryant, it's nice to meet you." Dr. Spinnek held her arm to the side, gesturing me into her den of despair.

"Right." My backpack felt like a lead weight as I lugged it into her office, which had too much furniture to be practical.

A desk with two chairs sitting in front had been placed near a wide window. To the other side of the room were a sofa and an extra chair.

"Where do you want me to go?" I asked, like I was a kid trying to figure out where to sit on the first day of kindergarten.

"Wherever you feel most comfortable."

Part of me wanted to be a real smart ass and sit at the chair behind her desk. But what if that made her think I had serious and deep-seeded issues? The more issues she thought I had, the more likely she'd be to ask important questions that could wind up making me spill my guts about the whole wizard thing, which would get me landed in a mental hospital where I wouldn't be able to see the girlfriend who probably hated me anyway.

I gripped my backpack to keep my hands from shaking and plopped down onto the couch.

"Shall we jump straight in?" Dr. Spinnek sat on the chair facing me, notepad in hand.

I tried not to think of poor purple suit guy transcribing the notes of my insanity. If he was even allowed to read the notes. I'm not an expert on doctor-patient confidentiality laws.

"Are you okay, Bryant?" Dr. Spinnek stared at me, her pen hovering over the paper.

"Yeah. I'm fine. I don't even really know why my parents wanted me to come here. I'm well-adjusted and make good grades."

"To be completely frank, whatever reasons your father had for scheduling you to see me don't matter as much as how you and I can use this time productively for you." She set her pen down on the seat next to her like it was some kind of symbolic declaration that she wouldn't be passing notes on my innermost secrets. "We're going to be chatting for the next hour, so what do you want to talk about?"

"Nothing."

"Are you sure? You seem stressed. Is everything okay at school?"

No, everything is not okay at school. There's a memorial in the lunchroom to the Lancre/lunch lady I squished because she was trying to kidnap me to bring me to a guy who wanted to make me fight to the death. And there's a bunch of witch-hunting Lancre left in the world stalking other people, and we toppled the Ladies' rule, and they were the best chance we had of getting rid of the Lancre.

"School is fine." I swallowed hard. "A lot of work, but high school is supposed to be tough."

"That's it? Are you finding enough free time to spend with your friends? Connection to a support system of peers is important."

I spend every spare moment trying to find a way to save the magical world with my friends, and sometimes we have cake and pizza.

"I mean, I'm not the most popular kid, but I have a few good friends," I said. "I mean, that's all you really need, right? The rest of it is just white noise."

"That's a very healthy way to look at it, but does your closed circle make you feel isolated?"

Until you've lived with a deadly, world-altering secret you're keeping from the magical mole people lurking below the village, not to mention everyone else in the world, you don't know what isolation is.

"No. Between my best friend and girlfriend"—I waited for the happy buzz to surround my stomach that I had grown so accustomed to whenever I said the word *girlfriend*. A tiny panic monster gnawed at my gut instead—"I…I don't have time for hanging out with other people anyway."

"Girlfriend, huh?" Dr. Spinnek smiled. "Tell me about her."

"She's perfect." I shrugged. "She's brave, and smart, and strong, and the most beautiful girl in the world. But even if she looked like a toe, I wouldn't care, because she'd still be her, and nothing could be better than Elizabeth."

"Wow. Sounds like she's pretty great." Dr. Spinnek picked up her pen, ditching her symbolic neutrality.

I watched it wiggle across the paper, trying to guess what she was writing about me.

"How did the two of you get together?"

I burned down part of my school and then we fought in an epic magical battle, and the rest is history.

"Fate sort of pushed us together?" I said.

"Fate?" Dr. Spinnek looked up at me. "How did fate do that?"

By pulling the golden strings that wrap around all our lives.

"There was a fire at our school," I said. "I was with Elizabeth when we had to evacuate. I guess we sort of bonded through trauma."

"Hmm." Dr. Spinnek's pen picked up speed.

"*Hmm* what?"

"Do you still think about the fire?" Dr. Spinnek looked up at me.

"Not really." I leaned back on the couch, trying to look casual. My leg started twitching like an out of control jackhammer. "I mean, it sucks, because it was my mom's theatre at the school that burned down, and it's going to be a while until they can build a new one, but I'm not, like, scared of fire or anything."

"How about Elizabeth? Does the fire still affect her?"

Well, she's now a seer who's been sucked into the magical crazy pot. So, I would say the fire ate her life and spat her out on the other side of sanity!

Heat crept up my neck. I clutched my backpack to my stomach.

"Yeah. I think it's a little different for her."

"How do you mean?"

"I don't know. I mean, I've had a weird few months. Part of my school got burned down, my dad's apartment got demolished, my mom's place collapsed." I ran my hand through my overly long hair, leaving palm sweat in the strands. "But I didn't lose anything. I live in a new apartment, but other than that, my life got better. Elizabeth...all she got was a whole bunch of crazy stuff and me."

"Oh?"

"And I said something really stupid to her, and now she's mad at me." The word vomit began. "She has every right to be mad at me. I mean, she's grounded for the rest of her life because of me. All the crazy horrible stuff that's happened is my fault. If she'd been sick the day the theatre burned down, she might have gotten missed by fate. She'd still just be perfect Elizabeth, living her safe, happy life.

"But she was there, and I dragged her into this mess, and soon she's going to realize she'd be better off far away from me. Because no relationship is worth this much stress and trauma."

"Bryant"—Dr. Spinnek leaned forward—"the fire wasn't your fault. You can't feel guilty because of a freak accident. Whatever effect it's had on Elizabeth—"

"This isn't going to work." I jumped to my feet. "I'm sorry for wasting your time, but I'm sure my dad will pay you for whatever."

"Bryant"—Dr. Spinnek stood—"beginning the process of talking through your problems can be difficult, but walking out my door won't make things any better."

"Staying in here could make things a whole lot worse."

She didn't block me from the door.

Purple suit jumped to his feet but just gaped at me as I bolted from the office and into the hall.

I didn't stop running until I reached the elevator. I jabbed at the down button until the doors popped open, then leapt inside.

I'd made everyone's lives worse. Devon was living below a fake restaurant and hadn't spoken to his parents in months. Elizabeth had nearly been killed more than once. My mom had almost died. My dad had lost his apartment and given up traveling.

The doors swished open on the ground floor. Normal people who hadn't ruined anyone's lives bustled about their business, leaving slush all over the polished marble floor. Like I left magical poop slush all over my friends' and parents' lives. Leaving them, like the poor lady with the red vest and mop, desperately trying to clean up my ever-growing mess.

The red vest lady looked up, giving me a bland smile that shattered my panic and left me with nothing but desolation.

I wandered back out onto the street without a real plan of where to go. I'd have to call my dad and tell him about the appointment. Tell him not to have the driver come collect me.

Then...I didn't have a then.

"Out of your session already?" Eric stepped in front of me, one pure black eyebrow arched high on his pale forehead. "And here I thought you'd run overtime with all the fixing they need to do on you."

"It's not funny."

"Not at all," Eric said. "But your premature dismissal is odd."

"I wasn't dismissed. I bolted. I can't talk about my issues without mentioning things I'm not allowed to talk about!" I shouted so loud, a woman spilled her coffee down her pink peacoat in her rush to get away from me. "Great. Now I'm the crazy guy shouting on the street."

"I'm sorry you've lost your reason, but we really must be going." Eric started down the sidewalk, not bothering to ask if I had something better to do with my time than follow him through the cold, mucky streets.

"I can't."

Eric stopped and slowly turned to face me. "Can't?"

"Whatever it is you're trying to drag me into, I just can't deal with it right now." I walked toward Eric, stepping in a puddle on my way. Icy, biohazard-filled sludge flooded my sneaker. "I'm sure that whatever reason you had for stalking me to my shrink is super important. Fate dragged you here today so we could stop some major catastrophe. But I just can't."

Eric stared at me for a long moment.

And I just stood there in the middle of the sidewalk, waiting for him to scream at me.

"I'd been wondering when this would happen," he said very calmly.

"When what would happen?"

"When you would hit your breaking point. After everything you've done, you were bound to snap. To realize how monumental the past few months have been. To feel the weight of the magical world that fate has so unceremoniously thrust upon your shoulders. I understand the crushing impossibility of living up to the destiny you've been handed.

"But the mere fact that you are an underprepared wizard does not change the task at hand." Eric looked up toward Dr. Spinnek's office. "So, I give you two options. You can stop. Take a breath. Find a way to cope with the wonders and horrors magic has brought to you. Heal, reflect, then deal with the consequences of walking away from the path fate has prepared for you."

"The path fate should have handed to someone else." My voice cracked. "Elizabeth, Devon, my parents...all of them would be better off if I wasn't a wizard."

"Would they? If you're sure." Eric walked down the street, leaving me behind.

"You're just going to leave?" I chased after him.

"You seem intent on believing your innate magical ability has been a curse on those you care for. I don't believe there is anything I can do to convince you otherwise." Eric didn't slow his pace. "And, as much as I care for your emotional wellbeing, I'm afraid I don't currently have the time to argue the finer points of the responsibility that has been placed upon you."

"You can't argue it, because it's true." I followed Eric as he rounded the corner and headed uptown.

"In a way, your argument that Elizabeth, Devon, and your parents would be better off, had you been a regular teenager with nothing more pressing in his life than grades and socializing, is completely valid."

Eric might as well have stabbed me in the heart.

Pain shot through my chest. I wanted to sit down in the slush and freeze to death, but he was still moving, so I clutched my backpack even harder and jogged to keep up.

"Their lives might also have remained untainted by magic," Eric said. "Your parents would still despise each other, Devon would be living miserably with his parents, and Elizabeth would still believe she was worth nothing more than her pleasing personality and pretty face."

"She's so much more than that," I puffed.

"Ask Elizabeth and Devon if they would prefer to go back to their lives before they knew about magic, and I guarantee you both would choose to remain a part of the magical world."

"But—"

"And if you could, for one moment, look past your immediate circle to the larger consequences of your joining magical society." Eric didn't even acknowledge I had tried to speak. "If you hadn't found the phone Thaden entrusted to me, it would undoubtedly have fallen into the hands of a normal human. I would have found the phone and taken it back without Thaden or the Ladies being any the wiser. Neither would have had reason to come after me. The battle of Beville would never have happened. Thaden would still be lurking in the shadows, slaughtering any who came too close to his dark realm.

"The Ladies would still control the Library. They would still be punishing any who dared speak against them and slaughtering those who actively rebelled. Most importantly, we still wouldn't know the books in the Library were missing. We would still be suffering in the darkness of ignorance while hundreds of years' worth of magical learning could be turning to dust.

"Discovering your wizardhood may have made your life more complicated—becoming a part of the magical community has undoubtedly given you more responsibility than a seventeen-year-old should bear—but you have changed the magical world for the better. You've saved people, Bryant. There are wizards who are only alive today because fate chose to bring you into this mess."

"But I killed that Lady." My feet stopped moving. I swayed on the spot, not seeing the street around me. Not seeing anything besides the hateful look in the Lady's eyes as I crushed the air from her lungs. My balance steadied as Eric laid a hand on my shoulder.

"With lives such as ours, the slate will never be clean. We can only hope when the tally is counted, the good we have done will far outweigh the bad. You killed someone in battle. An evil person who ended many lives before she set her sights on murdering you. Her mark on your slate will show the monster she was. But your life is far from over. There is so much work to do. Imagine the marks that will be left if you abandon the path fate has laid out for you. You might not see their deaths with your own eyes, but if we don't finish what we started, more will suffer."

"What's option two?" My words came out thick through the tears freezing their way down my cheeks. "You said you could think of two options for me, but you only gave me the first one."

Eric smiled as my eyes focused on his face. "You follow me to do something incredibly unwise and potentially catastrophic."

"Yeah." I wiped the tears from my cheeks with the back of my hand. "Let's go do some damage."

4

When Eric said we were going to do something unwise and potentially catastrophic, a trip to Times Square wasn't what I'd had in mind.

Despite the weight of my backpack, my shoulders crept toward my ears as we walked downtown.

I tried to be smart, tried to focus on not bumping into the people around me and not walking out into traffic, but every few steps, my gaze would flick up to the giant, stone spire that peered over the buildings.

I gripped my backpack straps, letting the fabric absorb the sweat that beaded on my palms even though it was freezing outside.

"Who here loves comedy?" A man with a fistful of flyers dodged in front of a pack of tourists. "If you want the true New York experience, you've got to check this out."

The dude's comedy-hawking partner eyed me.

"I'm not a tourist." I looked away from comedy dude, and my gaze slipped right back up to the stone spire.

I hadn't been near Times Square in months. Honestly, I'd been doing everything humanly possible to avoid going anywhere near Manhattan's biggest tourist trap.

A lot of it was because I am a New Yorker and avoiding Times Square is a matter of pride. More of it was because I didn't want to think about what was trapped in the stone spire. Namely Thaden's headless body.

Someone had mounted a red, flashing light on the tip of the spire, like they wanted to make sure no air traffic rammed into my accidental architecture.

I tried not to wonder how deep they'd had to drill into the stone to mount the light and if they'd struck evil wizard bones.

But, if they had struck evil wizard bones, had they noticed? Did the cops know there was a corpse hovering over Times Square?

An off-brand mouse mascot toddled up to me, miming that I should pay to take a picture with him.

"No thanks. I have enough nightmares already." I dodged to Eric's other side.

A weird robot with cracked plastic armor came at me from the corner.

"I don't want a picture!" I shouted.

The robot flicked me off and marched up to a family of five all toting shopping bags like they were prepping for the retail apocalypse.

"I thought you wanted to avoid screaming on the street?" Eric asked.

"Easy for you to say." I leapt out of reach as a superhero tried to pull me in for a photo-op. "The tourist baiters always leave you alone."

"If you would allow me to alter your wardrobe, as I have often offered, they would leave you alone as well." Eric crossed over to the portion of Times Square they'd blocked off so tourists could wander without risking getting hit by cabs.

I studied Eric from his long black coat to his black leather shoes, trying to decide if looking like a high school undertaker would be worth establishing a more Manhattan vibe.

I thought of asking Devon to give me a chic makeover instead of resorting to Eric's help. But then I started thinking about what Elizabeth would say if I showed up at school with a whole new look, and then I remembered she probably wouldn't care what I looked like since I had screwed up so royally I might not even have a girlfriend anymore, and then I almost puked on the sidewalk.

I turned my attention back to the oddly less distressing subject of the spire.

The stone giant poked up right through the center of the concrete island in the middle of Times Square. Someone had put a plexiglass wall around the base to block the flocks of tourists from reaching the spire. I peered through the hordes getting their pictures taken with the monstrosity and caught a glimpse of the people on the inside of the wall. Official-looking people with computer tablets and glasses, all of whom seemed like they were studying my magical creation.

Those poor scientists would spend years looking for a reason for why the spire had shattered the earth. I wasn't worried they'd find Beville, figure out what had happened, and sue me. Eric swore there were enough spells protecting the underground wizarding settlement that no regular person would ever find their way through the tunnels to reach it. Also, my dad has amazing lawyers.

I did, however, feel really awful that these people, who could have been studying things like predicting earthquakes, were going to be wasting years of their careers on my creation.

My feet started pulling me toward the plexiglass wall as a thousand insane explanations bounced around in my head, fighting to be the thing I would shout to make the poor geologists stop wasting their time.

"No, no, no." Eric took my arm, swiveling me to face the line of people waiting to buy discount tickets to Broadway shows. "I admire your desire to tell the truth, but under no circumstances can it be allowed."

"They're wasting their lives," I whispered as Eric led me to the back of the line of ticket seekers.

"Most people are. The majority of humans toil toward goals they will never reach while barely scraping by from one paycheck to the next. Those scientists are being paid to work in their chosen field and gaining excellent publicity in the process."

"But—"

Eric pointed to a man in a white lab coat who stood just outside the plexiglass wall, posing for pictures with tourists.

"Have you ever seen a geologist treated like a celebrity by the masses?" Eric raised one black eyebrow.

"No."

"Then let them enjoy their moment and let us move on with our work."

"Fine." I made myself let go of my backpack straps and shoved my hands into my pockets. "What work?" I looked from the people around me to the concrete beneath my feet, searching for something remotely magical. "If the work involves seeing a show, we should bring Devon and Elizabeth."

There was no happy tingle in my chest.

I pulled out my non-magical phone. No new messages.

"Do you know what show you'd like tickets for?" A girl with a braid reaching most of the way down her back stepped up to Eric and me. A big button on her red vest read *Let me help you choose!*

"Umm," I began.

"We're looking for a very particular production," Eric said.

"Which show?" the girl asked.

"It's Fosse meets Sondheim with a Miranda twist," Eric said.

"What?" I didn't bother trying to swallow my laugh.

"Right." The girl pursed her lips. "I think I have some good options available for you. Have you seen Chicago?"

"No, thank you." Eric waved her away. "You can't help me."

"Good luck." The girl shook her head and went to help someone farther down the line.

"What was that all about?" I asked.

"You should clear your schedule for this weekend." Eric tented his fingers under his chin. "I have an odd feeling we're going to be quite busy for a while."

"No. Please don't have any feelings. Or if you have to have feelings, make an appointment with Dr. Spinnek. She can help you work through the mound of issues brewing in your messed-up mind. Because if you're trying to find a magical place where Fosse meets Sondheim—"

"Do you folks know what show you're looking for?" A girl with jet-black hair stopped next to us.

Eric tipped his head, studying the girl from her black leather boots to the brochures in her hand, and finally landing on her creepy blue eyes.

"I'm looking for a very particular show," Eric said.

"Which one?" the black-haired girl asked.

"It's Fosse meets Sondheim with a Miranda twist." I stepped closer to Eric's side.

"Ah." The girl's smile faltered before growing broader. "I know the one you're talking about, but they don't sell those tickets here."

"Pity," Eric said. "I've heard it's an experience unlike any other."

"I can give you the address of the box office." The girl reached forward, like she was going to hand Eric one of her flyers.

"How kind." Eric seized the girl's wrist. A tiny light glowed beneath his palm, and the girl gasped. "But I do think it would be better if you walked me there yourself."

"Let go of me." The girl's smile vanished as she bared her teeth like she wanted to bite through Eric's jugular.

"Do not cause a scene," Eric said. "If you do, I'll have to tell the Ladies about the special experiences you've been offering."

A hint of fear flickered through the girl's eyes. She opened her mouth to speak.

"Do not try any magic. It will cause you a significant amount of pain. All I want is a moment of your time and a few answers," Eric said. "Behave, and I won't tell the Ladies how many of their laws you're breaking in the middle of Times Square."

"I'm not that attached to New York," the girl whispered. "I'll kill you and find a new city to sell in."

"The line's moving." The lady behind us overenunciated in our direction. "If you don't want tickets, get out of line."

"We're still deciding." I shot her a nearly apologetic smile.

A tiny *zap* sounded behind me. I spun back toward Eric and the girl as she swallowed a whimper and a faint burning smell filled the air.

"My name is Eric Deldridge." He stepped closer to the girl. "This is my apprentice. If you'd like to fight us, you can try. But I encourage you to consider your odds of winning, as well as the price the Ladies will demand for using magic in such a populated place."

They stared into each other's creepily blue eyes for a long moment.

I kept waiting for the girl to spit in Eric's face, scream that the Ladies were all dead, and stab him in the gut.

But instead, she gave an *I'll kill you later* smile and said, "The customer's always right."

"Perfect." Eric nodded and, keeping his grip on her wrist, led her away from the line.

"Finally." The lady behind us glared at me as I passed. "I can't stand rude people."

"You know what?" I rounded on her. On this middle-aged, fanny pack wearing, bad dye jobbed woman who stared at me like she wanted to speak to the manager of Times Square. "You are the reason New Yorkers don't like tourists. I bet you send your food back at every restaurant. I bet you never tip your server. You set your bag on a seat on the subway, you stop in the middle of the sidewalk for a selfie, and you don't turn off your cellphone before you see a Broadway show. Well, your vacation destination is my home, so if you don't like the way I act, get out of my city!"

A pack of teenagers began to clap.

"Come along, Bryant." Eric grabbed my arm, leading me away.

"Delinquent," line lady spat.

"I'm on the honor roll, you tourist hag!" I shouted back at her as Eric hauled me out of Times Square.

"If you could draw a little less attention," Eric said.

"I've heard of Eric Deldridge," the black-haired girl said. "But no one mentioned his apprentice was one spell away from the deep end."

I glared at the girl, and the faint glow coming from where Eric gripped her wrist caught my eye.

Then I remembered we were doing something important that didn't include ranting at nasty tourists, and my rage bubble popped, leaving me tired, deflated, and super wary of why Eric had bothered to drag the girl away from Times Square.

Eric didn't slow as he led us farther from the tourist hordes and didn't stop until we'd reached an outdoor parking lot—the kind where they use machines to lift the cars so they can stack more vehicles in the tiny space Manhattan allows.

He whispered something at the lot attendant, and the dude's eyes sort of glazed over for a second as we walked past.

"Maybe I should tell the Ladies about you messing with regulars," the girl said as Eric weaved between cars to reach the back corner of the parking lot.

"You wouldn't be so foolish," Eric said. "You can't possibly be delusional enough to think the Ladies would let you go about your business. You've been selling potions to humans."

"What?" I squeaked.

"The price for your experience just doubled."

"Experience?" I repeated the word, waiting for a shiver to rattle my spine. But there was no magical warning of impending doom. Just a faint odor of rotting food and my fingers going more numb from the cold by the minute.

"That's what you want from me." The black-haired girl wrenched free from Eric's grip.

Eric let go, but the light from under his hand didn't fade. It solidified like a rope leading from his palm to the girl's wrist.

"I have no interest in the experience you offer," Eric said.

"What sort of *experience* are we talking about?" The dread I'd been waiting for finally shook my shoulders. "Like a show? Like the death matches at The Game?"

The girl tensed as I said the words *The Game*.

"Nothing so perverse," Eric said. "Or, perhaps much worse, depending on her skill."

"Four hundred dollars and you can try it for yourself." The girl pulled her arm farther away from Eric, then hissed in pain when sparks flew up the rope that connected them and zapped into her flesh.

"I don't think I've been fully clear on your situation." A weird little smile lifted Eric's lips, and he got this glint in his eyes. I hadn't seen him with that look since the time he was trying to kill me.

"I don't think you understand how fast I could kill you." The girl flicked her foot, and a knife shot out of her boot, flipping end over end up to her palm.

"*Stasio!*" I shouted.

The magic flew out of me, rushing to surround the girl as she gripped her knife and slashed for Eric. Her blade met the see-through wall of my spell with an ear-splitting screech.

"Thank you, Bryant." Eric still calmly held on to his end of her glowing tether.

"I'll kill you," the girl spat.

"Yes," Eric said, "I suppose that would be your aim. I don't think Kendrick left you fit for much else."

5

"You don't know anything about him." The girl slashed her knife against my shield again.

The screech of metal on spell stabbed into my ears.

"Kendrick, like the man who owned The Game *Kendrick*?" I looked from Eric to the girl.

"Bryant and I have a reasonable familiarity with Kendrick. We defeated him in his own establishment." Eric ignored me completely.

"No one defeats Kendrick," the girl growled.

"Kendrick McDonald who tried to have me kidnapped *Kendrick*?" I gripped the magical phone in my pocket as I searched the growing shadows between the cars for any hint of attack. "What does he have to do with a ticket hawker from Times Square?"

"My apologies for not bringing you up to speed earlier, Bryant." Eric didn't actually sound sorry. "I had hoped I was wrong."

"That doesn't actually give me any more information," I said. "You know that, right?"

"I've spent the last two months looking for Kendrick," Eric said.

"You'll never find him." The girl smiled as she dragged her knife across my spell.

The screeching cut so deep into my ears, the pain radiated down my throat.

"I've come to the unfortunate realization that you might be right." Eric gave the girl a nod. "But I can't simply turn my back and pretend Kendrick isn't kidnapping, abusing, and murdering young wizards."

"It's not him who kills." The girl pulled against the tether that bound her to Eric.

The glowing rope had stayed intact even as it reached through my spell. More sparks crackled along its length, racing into the girl's wrist.

She smiled at the pain that time.

"No, Kendrick does not wield the knife himself," Eric said, "but forcing teenagers to fight and kill for his profit is an even greater offense."

"You have no idea what you're—"

"How many did you kill to earn your way out of The Game?" Eric asked.

The hatred around the girl's eyes faltered for a split second.

"You fought in The Game?" I asked.

"I won. I earned out, and now I'm free."

"I'm so sorry." My words sounded frail and meaningless even to my own ears.

"I'm strong enough to survive aboveground." The hate jumped right back up onto the girl's face. "The weaklings in Beville could never live like I do."

"My thoughts exactly," Eric said. "Kendrick bragged that his champions lived aboveground. Secure in their magic. That was all I needed to begin searching for you. I'm sad to say you weren't even that hard to find."

"I can't hide from my clients."

"Clients for what?" I felt a buzz in my pocket. Dread and hope mingled in my stomach.

"Kendrick's former champion has been brewing potions and selling them to humans," Eric said.

"What?" I froze with my hand halfway out of my pocket. "You've been hurting humans? After everything Kendrick did to you—"

"None of my clients complain." The girl smiled at me. I think she was trying to be alluring, but really it just looked like she wanted to eat me alive. "Let me out of here, and I'll give you a free taste. The experience is even stronger for wizards."

"Bryant wants none of your street magic," Eric said.

My pocket buzzed again.

"Are you sure?" the girl asked. "He's pretty twitchy."

"It's his natural state," Eric said.

"I know, right?" I switched my grip to my non-magic phone.

"Fine then." The girl tossed her knife into the air, flipping the blade end over end before catching the hilt. "You're not going to kill me. You would've gone for blood before now. From what I hear, you're not too popular with the Ladies—"

"You have no idea." The words popped out of my mouth along with a weirdly desperate laugh.

Eric raised one eyebrow at me.

My pocket started buzzing like someone was calling me.

"Sorry, can I just—" I pulled my phone out of my pocket.

"Is he serious?" the girl asked.

My screen shone with one terrifying word. *Dad.*

"Shit."

"Bryant, if we could focus for a few more moments?" Eric said.

"Right." I ignored the call and flipped over to my messages. Two from Dad. Zero from Elizabeth. "Sorry." I shoved my phone back into my pocket.

"Kendrick was right," the girl said, "kids who apprentice to normal wizards come out soft. Weak."

A little crack formed in the eggshell-thin layer that had been holding back the tide of my utter self-loathing and panic.

"On the contrary," Eric said. "While I would never shove my apprentice into a death match, he went up against Kendrick's protégés and won. Don't let an odd exterior distract you from the power of the wizard within."

"Thanks, Eric." Sadly, I may have blushed a little.

"Fine. What do you and wonder wizard want from me?" the girl asked.

My pocket buzzed again. I gripped my hands together behind my back to keep from reaching for it.

"Are you going to steal my stash?" The girl flipped her knife again. "Are you going to try and make me cut you in on the cash flow?"

"On the contrary," Eric said, "I want nothing to do with your tawdry business. I might drop a hint in the right ear that the Ladies should stop you, but I have no desire to sell your hallucinogens, nor to partake of them."

"Then what do you want?" She froze, studying Eric like she might somehow make sense of him.

"I want information," Eric said. "You're going to tell me where Kendrick moved his operation. In exchange, I'll forget I ever heard about your little enterprise."

"Even if I knew where Kendrick had gone to ground, I wouldn't tell you. Let the Ladies come after me. I'd rather deal with them than whatever Kendrick would cook up to punish me for betraying him."

"Does it really count as betrayal if he kidnapped you?" I asked.

"Well then," Eric said, both of them completely ignoring my excellent point, "I'm afraid things are going to have to become much more unpleasant than I was hoping."

"Let me out of here, and we'll see how unpleasant I can make things." She screeched her knife along my spell again.

That time the awful-feeling sound dug all the way down my spine.

"I'm afraid that's not possible," Eric said. "I went to the trouble of capturing you, so I can't let you go unless I gain something for my time. I have a reputation to uphold."

"Then what do we do with her?" My thoughts flew to the Library and the extra bedrooms below where Lola could take care of her and rehabilitate her into a productive member of wizarding society. But then Kendrick's graduate would know the Ladies were gone.

Eric's house had plenty of room, but then we'd have to guard her ourselves.

"The river seems the safest bet." Eric shrugged. "I hadn't meant to kill anyone today, but we can't always choose how our plans turn out."

"You're going to dump me in the river?" The girl laughed.

"We may have to," Eric said. "It's a horrible way to go, but—"

"I'll kill you," the girl spat.

"Funny. Thaden told us basically the same thing before we killed him," I said, like I was cool and not having a nervous breakdown. "If we managed to get rid of him, we can do the same to you."

"It's dark enough now." Eric looked out toward the street. "We should be able to move her without causing too much of a stir."

"I don't know where Kendrick is." For the first time, the girl looked a little afraid.

"Which is what has led us to this unfortunate impasse." Eric yanked on the rope that bound them together, pulling the girl closer to my spell and away from the brick wall behind her. "Close in the back, Bryant."

"*Stasio.*" I made the invisible wall wrap all the way around her. "*Conorvo.*" Her cage shrank.

"I can give you someone else," the girl shouted as my spell pinned her arms to her sides.

Eric held up a hand, and I stopped my shrinking spell.

"Who?" Eric said.

"If you don't like Kendrick, I bet you hate the Lancre," the girl said.

Dread crept up my neck and wrapped around my brain.

"More than you will ever know," Eric said.

"I know where there's one in New York," the girl said. "Her location should be enough to excuse capturing me."

"Having a witch hunter to defeat would fill out the tale of this evening quite nicely." Eric nodded. "But we've already dealt with a Lancre in Manhattan."

The girl looked from Eric to me.

"I squashed her." The normal sour didn't rise in my throat.

"Which one?" the girl asked.

"There's more than one?" Eric stepped closer to her cage.

"There were two that I knew of in New York," the girl said. "Kendrick mentioned one that he'd left at a school."

"That's the squashed one," I said.

"The other works in a store," the girl pressed on. "She scents the shoppers for magic."

"Interesting. Where?" Eric tented his fingers under his chin.

"Let me go first."

"No way," I said.

"I agree with Bryant." Eric clapped his hands together. "You will tell us where the Lancre is. Bryant will release you. I will seize whatever illicit potions you have on your person as insurance. If your information is good, I dispose of them. If you're wrong, I place your wares in the Ladies' path and let them follow the scent right to you."

"Fine." The girl let out a long breath.

She told us where the Lancre was stationed, and I started to wonder if I'd somehow taken a hallucinogenic potion and just didn't remember doing it. Maybe the whole day had just been some messed up trip.

"Let her go, Bryant." Eric spoke in a tone that suggested he was repeating himself.

"Sorry." I let the spell go.

The girl glared at me like she might attack.

"*Frico.*" I yanked the knife from her grip and, in a feat of athleticism I wish Devon had been there to see, actually caught it by the hilt.

"Your stash?" Eric held out his hand.

"You're going to step into the wrong fight." The girl reached into her pocket and pulled out a little orange prescription bottle. "You're going to bait someone you shouldn't mess with, and your guts will end up all over the floor."

"Potentially." Eric took the bottle and tucked it into his own pocket.

"I hope I'm there to see you bleed out." The girl held up her wrist that was still bound to Eric's hand.

"We all must dream of something." The rope disappeared from Eric's grip.

"I do hope you were right about your *experience* being non-lethal. If I find out otherwise, we may meet again."

The girl spat a string of curses that Devon could have learned from, dodged between cars, and bolted out of sight.

"Now we're getting somewhere," Eric said.

"No." I shook my head. "No. Just no. We can't." I leaned against a car. The alarm blared to life as the lights stared blinking.

"I always appreciate your subtly." Eric turned, walking away from the screaming car and back toward the front of the parking lot.

"I never appreciate your sarcasm." I chased after him.

"What are you doing back there?" The lot attendant ran toward us, holding a baseball bat in one hand and a cellphone in the other.

"*Dothranta*." As soon as Eric spoke the spell, the man stumbled to a stop.

"What's happening? My eyes!" The man swung his bat, taking out the window of a shiny red sports car.

"Just hold still for a while," I called loudly enough for the man to hear over the now two, blaring car alarms. "It'll be okay."

The man ignored me and swung the bat again, leaving a giant dent in the side of a Tesla.

I flinched and turned away, blending in with the crowd that had gathered around to watch the man destroy a fleet of mid-life crises in auto form.

"Call Devon," Eric said. "We'll need him to meet us."

"Now?" I'm ashamed to say that came out super whiny. "Can we please go after the monster tomorrow? Elizabeth is pissed at me and may never speak to me again no matter how much I grovel. I ran away from therapy and am probably grounded forever—"

"Which is exactly why we should act now," Eric said. "Before the grounding is in place and before your heart is broken."

"You think my heart is going to get broken? You think Elizabeth is going to dump me?" I stopped in my tracks, unable to force my feet to move. "She is, isn't she? And I deserve it." My breath started coming in shallow gasps as the frozen, filth-covered sidewalk began to bend and shift under my feet.

Eric pinched the bridge of his nose for a moment before taking two steps back to stand next to me. He sighed before wrapping an arm around my shoulders in what he seemed to think was a comforting way.

"Breathe," he said. "Whenever things get bad, you've got to remember to breathe."

It felt like the outside of my lungs had been soaked in cement, but I made them expand and accept air.

"Good." Eric guided me north. "Elizabeth may end your relationship."

Pain shot through my chest.

"Such is young love," Eric said. "If she chooses to end things, you'll try and win her back. If that doesn't work, you'll respectfully walk away."

"Do you think I could win her back?"

"I think every day that Lancre is hunting in this city is another chance for a young wizard to be handed over to torment and probable death at Kendrick's hands. I also think you've been through enough to know that, while heartache is terrible, we are not lucky enough to be able to dwell on such possibilities. We are the type that dives into danger. We haven't the time to wallow in dread or despair."

"Okay." I nodded a little too much, making the world spin around me. "We can take out a bad guy. We can help people."

"There we are," Eric said. "Now, call Devon, and ask him to meet us."

"Right." I pulled out my normal phone. "I can do this."

"That's the spirit."

I wanted to punch Eric for talking in such an oddly comforting voice, but I punched in Devon's number instead.

"Bry." Devon answered on the second ring. "Where have you been?"

"Long story." I brushed my shaggy hair out of my eyes and made myself stand up straighter. "But you're never going to believe where I need you to meet me."

6

We stood outside the massive glass cube that rose above the street, watching as New Yorkers and tourists alike streamed down the stairs, anxious to get their technology fix.

"The girl was playing you." Devon shook his head as he stared down through the glass to the subterranean store. "There's no way there's a Lancre in there."

"And what makes you believe that?" Eric asked.

"Background checks for hiring employees." Even as Devon spoke, his hand drifted into his coat pocket.

"They background checked the lunch lady," I said. "They must have. She worked at a school."

"I see I have once again failed you." Eric frowned. "While *we who dwell below*"—he said the phrase with a weird emphasis that was no less obvious than just saying *wizards*—"are not known for our love of technology, there are those among us who are more than capable of doing enough hacking to create a false background, and there are some fine forgers who are quite willing to help those with the funds to pay."

"I don't know if that's cool or creepy," I said.

"Shall we?" Eric bowed us toward the door.

"It feels wrong, doing this without Elizabeth," Devon said.

"While Miss Wick's aid would be helpful, the last thing we need is to get her into even more trouble with her parents," Eric said. "She needs to keep training with Lola. Any further restrictions on her time would prevent that."

"Okay," Devon said, "but I'm not going to be the one to tell her we left her out."

"Right." A weird hollow formed in my chest as I followed Eric toward the door.

"You okay?" Devon said, quietly enough Eric could pretend not to hear.

"She still hasn't messaged me back." I pressed my hand to my chest. My ribs seemed solid, like all my inside bits hadn't leaked out. But the hollow where my lungs were supposed to be made it hard to breathe.

We stepped inside the glass cube and onto the glass platform that led to the glass spiral stairs.

"Have you heard from her?" I asked.

Devon stopped on the top step, earning a glare from a lady who held a shiny smart phone in her hand like it was a newborn baby.

"Devon?" I asked.

"I called her." Devon headed down the stairs. "I texted after lunch, but when I didn't hear from her, I gave her a call on my walk to the Consortium."

"What did she say?" I almost tripped over myself as I raced to the bottom of the steps to block Devon's path.

"Look, Bryant, you're my best friend," Devon said.

"She asked you to dump me for her?"

Devon took me by both shoulders, steering me out of the path of the rest of the customers. "I know you worship Elizabeth. I know you think she's the best thing that has ever been on this earth."

"Because she is."

"But you don't trust her not to break up with you over being grounded?" Devon said. "You think she's going to ditch you because of one stupid, relatively small fight?"

"But—"

"Stop worshiping your girlfriend and start understanding she's a badass who's marched into battle by your side."

"Yeah, but—"

"She didn't dump you after the Library." Devon clapped me on the shoulder. "She won't dump you now. As long as you stop freaking out and have an actual conversation with her. Listen to her. And when she says she's crazy about you, too, try believing her."

"That was shockingly wise," Eric said.

"Thanks." Devon smacked me on the shoulder again. "I've been spending a lot of time with Lola."

"She is the wisest of us all," Eric said. "But, as much as I appreciate any improvement to Bryant's understanding of women, we do have a purpose here."

"Oh, right." I actually looked around the store for the first time.

Don't judge me too harshly. I was having a day.

The glass spiral staircase had led us down into the center of a white marble space that looked too much like parts of the Library for my comfort.

High tables laid out with tablets, watches, computers, and phones were spread around the store. To one side, people had crowded together as a young dude with platinum hair taught them how to download music onto their phones. By the wall, guests stood in front of a counter, waiting for the genius employees to fix their devices.

None of the guests or employees looked remotely magical.

"Try to be careful," Eric murmured before walking away from Devon and me, heading toward the table of people learning how to use their phones.

I wondered what the people would think if I showed them everything my magical phone could do.

"Can I help you?"

I jumped at the question.

Abalata was already halfway out of my mouth when Devon much more reasonably said, "Actually, we're just looking around for now," to the girl who had spoken.

"Is there anything in particular I can direct you to?" The girl's voice was a little too chipper. Like she had eaten the employee handbook on how to greet guests and the corporate jargon had somehow taken over her soul.

"Not really." Devon punched me a little too hard in the arm.

"My dad said I could buy myself something," I said. "He said I could get whatever. So, I'll just browse for a while, I guess."

"Right." The girl blinked at me for a second. "Well, just ask a team member if you need any help."

"Thanks." I took Devon's elbow, leading him toward the row of smart watches.

"I think that's the first rich kid thing I've ever heard you say," Devon laughed under his breath.

"Yeah, well it sounded better than the truth."

"Touché."

We hovered over the table of watches for a minute. I tried to picture myself wearing one. Then I tried to picture all the information on my magical phone available on a magical watch.

"You're clear," Devon whispered.

"*Nudla*." The fingerprints and few flecks of dust that had been on the watch table disappeared with a *hiss*.

I looked up and scanned the workers nearby, searching for anyone who seemed to be sniffing the air like a nightmare-inducing child catcher.

Everyone appeared to be completely absorbed in the wonders of technology.

"Maybe that spell doesn't make a smell," Devon whispered. "Maybe it cleans the scent out of the air as it works."

"Okay." I took a deep breath and wandered my way over to the table with the phone lesson.

"Can I help you find anything today?" A man about my dad's age stepped into my path.

"We're just looking," I said.

"Let us know if you need anything." The Dad-age man smiled as he glanced between Devon and me for a moment longer before walking away.

"It's him." I gripped Devon's arm and whispered in his ear. "It's totally him."

"Or he thinks we're going to try and steal something," Devon said.

"Right. That's another possibility." I headed over to the spot where they displayed the computer monitors that were both too large for anyone to actually need and too bulky for Devon and me to be accused of trying to steal.

"Try another spell," Devon said.

"I don't know a lot of spells people won't notice." I spoke out of the corner of my mouth. "And as much as we want to be found, I really don't want to be noticed."

"Is there anything in the phone?" Devon turned to look at rest of the store, like he was girl trawling.

"That won't cause structural damage?" I reached into my pocket to pull out my magical phone and froze when movement caught the corner of my eye.

A girl walked by. She was young, like barely out of high school, and she had a bandage wrapped around her palm like she'd sliced it on something.

"*Sinato*." I said the spell without really thinking. It just sort of slipped out like a natural response to someone who looked like they needed to be healed.

The girl gasped, gripping her hand to her chest. "Ow, ow, ow."

"Are you okay, miss?" Dad-age employee came over to check on the girl.

"My hand just"—the girl sucked in air through her teeth—"it stings so bad."

Devon grabbed my elbow and led me away. "Did you—"

"I could probably get arrested for that, couldn't I?" I gripped my phone even harder. "Oh, that was a bad thing to do."

"Maybe not the best idea you've had." Devon looped us to the other side of the glass staircase.

I peeked around toward the girl, wanting to make sure I hadn't somehow sent her into the magical equivalent of anaphylactic shock.

She'd pulled the bandage off her hand and was gaping at her palm.

"Looks like you didn't do any damage," Devon said. "Maybe try something that doesn't mess with strangers' flesh next?"

I pulled out my phone and pressed my thumb to the scanner.

"If you're looking for a new phone," another employee said as he stopped in front of us, "I think you'll love facial recognition technology."

"I'm not looking for a phone today," I said.

"He's really attached to his," Devon said as I flipped through the icons on the phone.

Nothing from healing. Definitely not the fire app. A solid no from the pretty tree icon—that one had caused enough damage.

"We can upload a phone's memory into a new device as long as it's been transferred to the cloud," the employee said.

"I'm sorry, what?" I looked up.

"If you don't want to lose the information on your phone," the employee said, giving me a much friendlier smile now that it looked like I might buy something, "just upload all your data to the cloud, and we can transfer everything to a brand-new device."

"And how hard is that—"

"Bryant," Devon cut across me.

"Right," I said. "Not in the market for a phone upgrade."

"Let me know if you change your mind." The smile dude walked away.

"Come on, Bryant," Devon said. "Just turn out the lights or something."

"I don't know how to do that without creating total darkness." Panic welled in my chest.

I should have gone over the plan with Eric more thoroughly. I should have kept an eye on Eric, who was I didn't know where as I stood there staring at my phone, freaking out.

"Just do something little," Devon said.

I took a deep breath and focused on a leg of a nearby table. "I really hope they have insurance. *Kunga.*"

The table leg buckled, and the whole thing tipped with a tech-cracking *crash*, sending tablets smashing to the floor.

"Subtle," Devon murmured as a flock of employees ran toward the table, and the people around the relatively minor destruction scattered like they knew damn well I'd just done magic.

Still, no one came charging at me.

"I don't think I can try anything bigger without being super obvious," I said.

"Everything is fine, ladies and gentleman." The Dad-age dude calmed the crowd. "Please pardon our mess. We'll have this cleaned up in just a moment."

I bit back my urge to say that I would pay for the damage.

"I think the girl lied to Eric," Devon said. "Let's get out of here."

We took two steps toward the glass spiral staircase, and the whole thing shattered.

7

I didn't even scream as the stairs crumbled, sending shards of glass flying through the air.

Acting on pure instinct, I grabbed Devon and pulled him close to me. "*Primurgo.*"

My shield blossomed around us, blocking the glass from reaching our skin.

"Tell me you didn't do that." Devon spoke under the frightened cries of the other customers.

"It wasn't me." I let go of my shield, hoping no one had noticed it in the chaos of the stairs collapsing.

"We need the police!" a woman ten feet away from me shouted into her cellphone. "I think we're being attacked."

I didn't really see how it happened, but the phone woman was suddenly flying across the room as though she'd been tossed by a spell I most definitely hadn't created.

And then the greeter with the super perky, corporate-trained voice was standing where the woman had been, a smile curving her lips as her limbs started to grow.

"Lancre. Lancre. Lancre." I tugged on Devon's arm, shoving him behind me and backing him up all at the same time.

"Sorry, folks," the girl spoke in her super cheery voice, even as her bones stretched and her teeth elongated, "no one is leaving here tonight. We apologize for the inconvenience."

People screamed. Lots of people screamed. And there was scattering and hiding under tables to go with the excessive screaming. One man, who looked like he belonged on Wall Street, just stood in the middle of it all and started bawling.

In all the shouting and chaos, I still couldn't see a hint of Eric.

"Okay." I took off my backpack and shook my shoulders out. "I can do this."

"You?" The cheery girl/Lancre tipped her head too far to the side. "You don't look the type."

"I really think Kendrick needs to update your training," I said. "You're the second one who's overlooked me."

"But your friend is hot." The Lancre pouted.

"Thank you," Devon said. "You're very...not hot."

"No flirting with the evil creature." I glanced over my shoulder toward Devon.

In the split second I looked away, the Lancre leapt over two tables and landed right in front of me.

I looked up into her creepy face. The skin on her cheeks had stretched so taut, I could see the ridges where her teeth met her gums.

"Let everyone else go. There's no need for people to watch this."

"Watch what?" She bared her teeth at me. "I'll just tuck you in my pocket and carry you home."

"Gross," I said.

Sirens blared outside, and lights started flashing through the glass cube high above me.

"We're out of time," I said. "The cops are here. There are humans here. Let everybody go, and then I'll kick your ass."

I actually said all that in a cool voice, too.

"Let them watch!" The Lancre leapt away from me and tossed aside a table four guys were cowering under. "There is magic in this world." She grabbed one of the men by his collar and chucked him against the wall.

The people in the store screamed as the man crumpled to the ground.

"There are witches and demons." She picked up another man and threw him against the display of massive monitors.

The other two men scattered like cockroaches.

"And do you know what we do with witches?" the Lancre asked.

"Sell them to Kendrick?" I said.

"You're spoken for," the girl said, "but these people, all of them, they've seen magic. They'll hunt the witches down and watch them burn."

"A purist." Eric strode through the broken glass. "That's not what I expected to find in such a place."

"The stairs are gone," a voice shouted from above. "We need a ladder in here!"

"We will not suffer the witches to live." Great globules of spit flew from the Lancre's mouth.

A dark figure appeared in the glass cube as a fireman started rappelling toward us.

"Oh dear. *Balatha*." A sheet of glowing gray shot from Eric's hand and rose toward the gap in the ceiling.

The rappelling fireman landed on the spell with a *thunk*.

"I cannot allow you to escape," Eric said. "I desire information, but stopping your hunt is a duty that must come above all else."

With a scream, the Lancre launched herself at Eric.

Eric spoke a spell as he dove to the side.

"Is there anything I can help you with today?" The Dad-age man stepped up beside me.

"Umm," I began, but the man launched himself at me, tackling me. I hit the ground hard.

"*Abalata*." The black of my spell pooled in my palm, and I threw it at the man's stomach, knocking him off me.

Devon stepped in front of me as I scrambled to my feet. With a flick of his wrist, his glowing red sword *voomed* to life.

"I didn't think we were coming to find two Lancre," Devon said.

Dad-man bared his oddly pointy teeth, but he didn't grow. His bones didn't get longer. His skin didn't get stretched out in a creepy, vomit-inducing way.

"Not a Lancre!" I shouted as the man launched himself at Devon.

I raised my hand to do another spell, but something hit me hard in the side, knocking me to the ground again. My head smacked against the floor, and spots danced in front of my eyes as something landed on my chest.

The nice dude who'd wanted to help me upload my data to the cloud had pinned me down.

"Is it all of you?" I tried to punch the dude in the face, but with a move so fast it looked like the matrix had glitched, he turned his head and sank his teeth into my knuckles.

I screamed as his teeth met my bones.

"We will find all of you abominations." My blood dripped down his chin as he closed his hands around my neck. "You're bound for auction. The rest will burn."

"*Exci*," I coughed out the spell.

Blood spurted from the guy's nose, but he didn't loosen his grip.

I swung my bloody hand and punched for his face again. This time, my fist made contact.

His grip on my neck loosened, but before I could think to pull in more air, Dad-age man leapt over me with Devon following right behind, light saber blazing.

Upload dude gripped my neck harder.

I tried to raise my hand to punch again, but my whole arm felt heavy and a little numb.

I grabbed the dude's chin with my other hand, pushing him up and away from me, then kicked as high as I could, catching the dude in the back with a grand battement and finally finding a bit of gratitude for all the dance classes Mom had made me suffer through.

The dude sagged toward me, and I opened my mouth to start another spell, but with a sickening *crack*, a laptop smacked the guy in the side of the head, and he rolled away.

"We don't choke people!" A Mom-type lady stepped over me toward the upload dude and smacked him in the head with the laptop again.

Blood flowed from the cloud dude's head, but the computer didn't look harmed at all.

And that is how you win brand loyalty.

I tried to leap to my feet, but the room sort of swayed around me.

The red glow of Devon's sword shone in one corner. Customers had packed in behind him, trapping the Dad-age man and Devon together like they were in a cage match.

Eric and the Lancre battled in the middle of the store.

I don't mean to sound like a jerk who doubts his friends, but I was more concerned for Devon than for Eric, so I started toward him.

But the room began to sway even worse as I tried to walk across the giant chunks of broken glass.

The Lancre dodged Eric's spell and leapt up, twisting while she was in the air, changing course like a creepy squirrel as she veered toward Eric.

Eric dove out of the way, rolling across the broken glass and leaping to his feet.

But something had fallen out of his pocket. An orange bottle.

I recognized that orange bottle.

I reached down like I thought I could snatch it up on my way to help

Devon, but the room tilted again, and the glass in front of me glittered as I tipped toward the ground.

I fell to my hands and knees. Pain shot through my left hand and both my legs, but I couldn't feel anything in my right hand. It was like it didn't exist.

I looked at my right hand, and the world did a flippy swirl.

Weird gray lines led away from the blood that dripped from my knuckles.

"That's really bad." I fell to my side, and my doomed hand knocked the pill bottle farther away from me. "Get back here you."

It felt like I was talking in slow motion as I dragged myself through the glass toward the bottle.

"Are you okay?" the Mom lady/head basher/laptop durability tester crouched in front of me.

"Bottle. I need the bottle." I tried to reach for it, but my whole right arm had gone numb and just sort of laid uselessly on the ground.

"Okay, hun." The lady grabbed the bottle and popped it open. "You're going to be okay."

I tried to speak, but the lady shoved something into my mouth before I could make myself form words.

The thing tasted like cherry lip balm and fizzed on my tongue.

"Should you take one or two?" The lady's words slowed down and her face brightened like I had added an angelic photo filter to her image.

"You're pretty." I collapsed onto my back, right beneath the glowing gray of Eric's spell.

There were four firemen on the barricade now. And people in helmets standing around the sides.

One of the firemen had a pick. I watched as he swung it for the shield. It struck Eric's spell with a tinny *thunk*.

"No, that's a bad key." My words slurred together. "If you're going for the cliché, do it right." I hummed a decent starting pitch. "Do you hear the people sing..."

And...I could.

Like I had just wished it into being.

The lady parted her lips, and the most lovely, inhuman sound drifted from her mouth. Like angels had come down from heaven or New Haven to fix my arm.

I reached up to touch her perfect face, but the angel screamed as a head rolled right up next to me.

I looked over to find the blank eyes of the Lancre staring back at me.

"Gross."

I turned back to the lady, because she was nicer to look at than the severed Lancre head, but she had run away.

"Damn." I looked up in time to see the sky open.

Beams of light poured down from above, surrounding me with warmth and security.

"So, this is how I die." It didn't seem like such an awfully bad way to go.

Everything was warm and light and peaceful.

The sky above turned even brighter, like a beautiful beam beckoning me home. And then the light shifted, and it wasn't a shapeless glow anymore.

Two sharp eyes peered at me as a mass of shaggy, gray fur filled the sky.

"Mrs. Mops?" I tried to lift my head, but I couldn't even move my neck anymore.

"It's all right," Mrs. Mops said. "I've come to help you."

"You never help me," I said. "You just scratch me and put your stinky ass on my face."

"Just take nice, slow breaths," Mrs. Mops said.

"Why do you always try to make me sniff your cat ass?" The world shifted again, wobbling beneath me. "That's not so good."

Mrs. Mops smiled in a way cats should never smile.

"No," Eric's voice cut through the rumble of Mrs. Mops purring as she led me into the great unknown. "That boy is in my care. I will take him."

"Are you his guardian?"

A giant hand joined Mrs. Mops in the sky, scratching behind her ears.

"Then you have no right to refuse medical aid for this boy."

Mrs. Mops' weird cat arms reached toward me, drawing me up into the Heaviside Layer where good felines are reborn.

There were so many cats waiting for me in the sky. So many excited voices and bright lights.

"I never knew kittens liked to party." My words slurred as a chill drifted into my chest.

I guessed I should have known cats would like lots of flashing lights in their afterlife. Maybe that's why they spend so much time chasing laser pointers. They're searching for their own glimpse of heaven.

A herd of cats joined Mrs. Mops.

Dozens of them dancing and purring, skittering around the lights as joyful yowls filled the air.

Cats surrounded me, like pallbearers, carrying me into a place where the light wasn't as bright.

"I never said goodbye. Elizabeth is going to be so pissed."

A something banged by my feet, and the ground began to rumble as I burst into song.

"Up, up, up to the dead cat heaven."

8

I'd felt pain before. From falling down the stairs at my old apartment, to falling up the stairs at school, to having all the air crushed from my lungs by Thaden.

None of that prepared me for the pain that burned through my right hand as the singing cats disappeared.

"I understand," a voice said, "but I've been sent in as a specialist to take care of this little love, so why don't you just let me scoot on in and see how he's doin'?"

Something soft grazed my skin. The pain in my hand doubled, and everything faded to black.

"What do you mean you don't know what did this to him?" The low angry voice sounded familiar.

"What's more important right now is gettin' this boy healed," another voice said. "We can figure out the *what* behind this mess after I save your son's life."

"Trust her, Leo. She saved me before."

Mom? I tried to say the word, but somehow puke came out of my throat instead.

Hands lifted me, rolling me onto my side.

"Let it out, love. I know it feels awful, but you gotta let the badness come out."

Searing hot sour flew from my mouth, and everything went black again.

Sound came before pain the next time I woke up.

"If this is what he's up against…" I recognized my dad's voice. "He's just a kid. This is too much for him."

"Your son isn't a child," Eric said. "He's a wizard and one who has faced far greater danger than we met tonight."

"Is that supposed to make me feel better?" Dad said.

"No," Devon said, "but it should make you trust him. And trust us to have his back."

"Did…" Mom paused like she'd shuddered. "Did anyone at the store pick up his scent? Are they going to be hunting him again?"

"Only the same man who already tried to kidnap Bryant once." If I didn't know Eric so well, I might've missed the hint of a lie in his voice. "And he is now three servants poorer after our fight."

"We should let him sleep," Lola said. "He can hear us."

"I will not—"

"Come on, Leo," Mom said. "He'll be okay."

I wanted to tell them not to leave, but I couldn't manage to move.

A door clicked shut and everything went quiet.

———

I f you've ever had sand ground into your eyes, you'll know what mine felt like when I finally woke up for real. It took me a while to actually wrench my eyes open more than a slit and a dozen painful blinks to get them to focus on anything.

The ceiling above had been painted pure white, so I knew I wasn't at home. There were no weird ceiling tiles, so if I was in a hospital, it had to be a fancy one.

I took a deep breath, testing the probability of my puking, before turning my head to the side.

I was in a bedroom I'd never been in before. It was small, and there weren't any windows.

I would have worried that I'd been institutionalized, but Mom and Dad were sleeping in armchairs in one corner, while Devon and Elizabeth slept in another corner, wrapped in blankets as they leaned against the wall.

I lay still for a minute, letting the glow of gratitude for all of them sitting by my bedside soothe the ache in my stomach from the night before.

I wanted to say something cool or brave to wake them all up. Like *I knew fighting the battle would be worth it to come home to all of you.* Or, *I never doubted you would stick by my side.*

But all I could think of was *Do any of you know if Mrs. Mops is still in my apartment or has she become the high ruler of the afterlife?*

So, I settled on sitting up instead.

I moved my right hand to push myself up and screamed in pain.

"Bryant!" Mom was on her feet in a second like she hadn't even been sleeping. "Honey, are you okay?"

"Fine." I swallowed hard and tried to look like I wasn't about to pass out. "I'm fine."

"I'll go get Lola." Devon ducked out of the room.

"Do you need to go to a hospital, Son?" Dad asked.

"No. I'm okay." I tried to sit again.

Mom perched behind me, looping an arm around my back to help me up.

I swallowed more bile. "My hand hurts like hell, but other than that, it's not bad." I finally looked at my hand.

Gauze covered everything from my wrist to my fingertips, but it wasn't like normal, drug store gauze. The material was green and had a thick scent that smelled distinctly of magic.

"It's to draw the venom out," Mom said. "Lola made it up special last night. She promised your hand will be functional soon enough."

"That's good," I said. "I don't think I'm coordinated enough to survive with one hand."

I glanced over to Elizabeth.

She stood with her back pressed into the corner. She didn't smile at my self-deprecation or tell me I'd be fine one-handed.

"Where are we?" I looked back to my parents.

"We're in the Library." Lola breezed into the room, holding a silver tray. "Devon called after the ambulance took you away—"

"I got to ride in an ambulance, and I don't even remember it?"

"You were high out of your mind." Lola pulled up a chair and sat by my bed. "Which might have been a blessin' considering how badly you were bit. Whatever was in those tabs Eric confiscated kept you from feeling the full brunt of the venom."

"It still felt awful," I said.

"You were very brave." Mom's eyes were all watery.

"Let me look at you." Lola leaned close to me.

I let her look into my eyes and my throat and feel up and down my arms. She dripped something out of a vial onto my bandages, and steam rose from the gauze while an icy chill sank into my hand, dulling the throbbing pain.

Part of me hated being poked at in front of Elizabeth, but I was too weirded out by everything else to argue.

There were just too many levels of weird for my post-venom-and-drug-induced-hallucination-of-my-cat-being-God brain to process.

Dad had his hand on Mom's shoulder like they were some kind of unit, which was super weird thing number one.

Mom, Dad, and Lola were all in the same room. Weird thing number two that, for all I knew, signaled the beginning of the apocalypse.

Weird thing number three—Mom and Dad were in the Library, which, until we killed them, the Ladies hadn't allowed any outsiders in for longer than I'd been alive.

Fourth and scariest weirdness of all, Elizabeth was still in the corner and hadn't said a single word.

"A few more hours, and you should be able to move your hand just fine," Lola said. "There's nothing I can do about the scarring. At least, nothing I'm willing to risk for cosmetic damage. But a wizard like you can do with a few scars. It proves to fate that you're strong enough to fight."

Dad's shoulders stiffened at the word *fate.*

"Now that we are well into the morning," Lola said, "why don't you fine folks come on up to my restaurant? From what I hear, Miss Miller already likes my muffins."

"We should—"

"We would be happy to come with you." Mom cut across Dad as she helped me to lie back down on the bed. "I could use some breakfast, and I'm sure Bryant needs more rest."

"But—"

Mom took Dad's hand in hers. "Come on."

Lola held the door open for my parents.

Dad didn't even look back at me as Mom led him out. He just stared down at her hand holding his.

"I should've tried harder in therapy," I said.

I waited for Elizabeth to laugh, or say I was right to have run away. Or yell at me for agreeing to go after the Lancre without her.

I looked her way.

She was still just standing silently in the corner.

"Thank you," I said like a lame idiot, "for being here."

She nodded.

"Did your—" I tried to put my words into an order that wouldn't make things worse. "I hope you don't end up getting in trouble for being here."

Three Simple Steps to Wizarding Domination

"You almost died, Bryant." Elizabeth's voice came out all low and rough, like she'd been sick since I'd last seen her. "I really don't give a shit what my parents think."

"I'm glad you're here." I wiggled my elbows under me, trying to sit up without using my hand.

"You should have called me." Elizabeth didn't leave the corner. "You shouldn't have gone into that store without me."

"We didn't know—"

"The first time I heard about a new Lancre shouldn't have been when Devon called me crying to tell me my boyfriend was on his way to the emergency room."

"You're right," I said. "We should have waited until morning. Found a time when you could come with us."

"You should have called me when you found out about the store and let me make the decision for myself." Elizabeth finally took a step toward the bed. Anger radiated off her in thick waves. "How I handle my parents is my problem."

"But if you get in more trouble, I won't be able to see you at all."

"Do you even want to see me?" Her voice shook, and my heart shattered. "Do you even want me to be here right now?"

"More than anything."

"Then why would you push me away when you need me?"

"I'm sorry, Elizabeth. I'm so sorry. I never should have gone with Eric. I freaked out after I bolted from therapy, and it all just spiraled."

"Don't apologize for following Eric on some stupid *nearly get yourself killed* mission. I get it. He's Eric. One minute, it's a normal day, and the next, everyone's trying to kill you. It's just how life works when he's around."

"We still should have called you. I mean"—I took a deep breath—"I should have called you."

Elizabeth nodded. One of her curls broke free from the others to rest on her cheek. I wanted to tuck that curl behind her ear so badly, my fingers tingled and my broken heart hummed.

"I'm sorry for what I said at school, too." I held out my non-bandaged hand to her. "The last thing I would ever want to do is hurt you."

She stared at my hand for a minute before stepping close enough for her fingers to graze mine.

"I know," Elizabeth said. "And I shouldn't have gotten so mad. I just never thought about us having an expiration date."

"What?"

"Which is completely stupid." The words tumbled out of her mouth in a very me-like way. "I mean, we're seventeen. We're not even really adults yet. We still have to worry about college and careers. And that's if some big evil thing doesn't kill us before we hit our six-month anniversary. I just never considered the possibility of us breaking up." Tears glistened in the corners of her eyes. "How ridiculous am I?"

"You're not."

"Yes, I am." Elizabeth dragged her fingers through her hair. "What do I want us to become? Romeo and Juliet? Dead in some tragic story? All the couples like us I've ever read about either end up dead or with the story fading to black before their real lives start.

"We run around trying to save the magical world from every horrible thing fate throws our way, and if we both live to the end, then what? We go back to being normal teenagers whose biggest worry is if they'll be bored over spring break? What if we can't do normal? What if saving the world ends up breaking us up?" A tear raced down her cheek. "I've come to grips with dying in a magical battle, but you walking away...it hadn't even occurred to me."

"Elizabeth." I took her hand and drew her down to sit on the bed beside me. I wrapped my arms around her, holding her tight and pressing my lips to her hair.

She laid her head on my shoulder. Right on the little groove that seemed like it had been made as a place for her to feel safe.

"I'm not walking away," I said. "I will never walk away from you. I guess I just haven't ever been able to think of a reason you'd want me to stay."

Elizabeth tipped her chin up, brushing her lips against mine. She tasted like rose-flavored sunshine. Every thought of danger and breakups and hand venom disappeared as I pulled her closer, feeling the curve of her body fit perfectly with mine.

Her lips parted as she gave a happy little sigh.

I wanted to stay in that moment forever.

Elizabeth kissed me again, harder than before, sending tingles zooming all over me. My head spun as I tasted more of her. I fell back in the bed, and she came with me, digging her fingers through my overly long hair.

I gasped, and she pulled her lips away from mine, shifting so her nose barely grazed my cheek.

Her heart pounded against the side of my chest like we were meant to be one person.

"I couldn't walk away from you any more than I could walk away from magic," I whispered. "I love you."

I hadn't meant to say it. Hadn't had a plan. But the words slipped out, and my heart stopped beating.

Elizabeth's eyes were extra sparkly when she leaned up to look at me. "I love you, too. For a million reasons you'd never believe."

My heart shattered again, but this time with absolute joy, bursting through its cocooned layers of self-doubt, and sending a brand-new heart worthy of being loved to live in my chest.

I leaned up, letting myself taste her lips again.

"Just promise me whatever hell we're about to jump into, we're going together?" Elizabeth said.

"Do you know something I don't?"

"Only that Eric's been prowling around the Library since I got here, and that can't mean anything good."

I shut my eyes, refusing to let the daunting exhaustion of jumping back into another disaster smother the blissful joy that filled me. "Through shadows, battles, and magic, we stay together."

9

The rest of the morning passed with Lola sprinkling more stuff on my hand and Mom and Dad spending more time looking concerned while standing awkwardly close together. Dad didn't look happy about a witch/seer taking care of me, but he didn't leave or complain that his phone wouldn't work all the way down in the Library so I guess that counted for something.

Eric never showed up, and Devon didn't come back. I tried to feel hurt that they weren't huddled beside my sickbed, but Elizabeth stayed with me so I didn't really mind them ignoring my plight.

Also, I was sort of over the whole sickbed thing after the first hour.

"I really think I'm fine." I kicked my feet out of the bed when Mom brought in my dinner tray, with Dad close on her heels, of course, because why wouldn't my divorced parents be attached at the hip? "I can come up to the restaurant and eat with everybody else."

"Absolutely not," Dad said. "You were almost killed less than a day ago. You need rest."

"But I've had medicine." I held up my bandaged hand, which was still vaguely steaming from Lola's last treatment.

"How does your head feel?" Mom laid the back of her hand on my forehead.

"It doesn't matter how his head feels," Dad said. "We should take him back to the hospital. Or bring him to my house. I have a private physician on retainer."

Mom turned to Dad and wrinkled her nose. "We should go see Lola, Leo."
Dad furrowed his brow. "Why?"

"There are some things you should learn about magical healing." Mom rubbed his shoulder. "Bryant's probably fine to get up, and a blood screen might give a lab tech a heart attack."

Dad swayed a bit.

"When Lola put me in a cocoon, I felt great when I woke up," Mom said.

"What?" Dad's eyes got super wide.

"Come on. We'll find wine." Mom led Dad out of the room.

As soon as the door closed, I tossed away the blankets.

"What are you doing?" Elizabeth asked.

"Finding my shoes." I tried to crawl under the bed, realized my hand was not as healed as I had thought it was, and did an awkward belly flop instead.

"I haven't seen your shoes." Elizabeth took my arm, helping me to my feet. "But we can ask next time Lola comes in."

"It can't wait." I kept Elizabeth's hand in mine as I went to the door, willing to brave the Library in sock feet if it meant escaping from the sick room.

"Why can't it wait?" Elizabeth asked.

"Because I think something in my brain clicked back into place and, well, depending on when the hallucinations started—"

"Hallucinations?"

"Mrs. Mops was God, and there was singing." I opened the door and peeked out into the hall. There were doors leading up and down the corridor, but not a single parental unit in sight. "But before I took the weird drug potion thing, the one who bit me said something, and I need to tell Eric."

I felt sort of like a stooge creeping down the hall in my socks, though it did make being quiet a lot easier.

At the end of the hall, we entered a room filled with empty desks. Three of the desks had had things on them when we took over the Library, but after hunting through everything for anything important, we burned the Ladies' stuff.

I won't lie. It was super cathartic.

I led Elizabeth toward the part of the Library where all the books had been stored before they were stolen.

If I hadn't known there'd been a big fight in the long corridor, it might have been a pretty place to walk. Lola had fixed the singe marks on the red carpet that led down the fancy hall, and Eric had mended the chandeliers that lit the space. But just knowing there had been so much damage done ruined the ambience for me.

I didn't take the time to look at all the oversized portraits that hung on the walls, even though they did represent the people who were my magical lineage.

I held my breath as we went through the door at the end of the corridor and out into the Library proper.

I had never gotten used to the Library. The way footsteps echoed across the vast, round space. The sparkling stars that beamed their light down from the mural of a night sky on the ceiling. The intricate railing that blocked the five-story fall to the bottom of the stacked floors of bookshelves. The horrible sinking feeling in my gut at seeing all those shelves empty.

"Eric?" I didn't even have to shout to be sure my voice would echo all the way down to the bottom level.

"Eric?" Elizabeth called.

We both waited for a moment, but Eric didn't answer.

"Did he go back to Beville?" I almost kept the hurt at being abandoned by my mentor out of my voice.

Elizabeth tugged on my hand, leading me back the way we'd come. "Maybe he's aboveground."

My legs started to burn a bit as we cut back through the room with the desks and up the worn, wooden stairs that led to the Consortium, but Elizabeth's fingers were laced through mine and I would have run a marathon if she'd asked me to.

The familiar scent of baked goods and coffee greeted us at the top of the steps.

I don't know why, but a shiver shook my shoulders as Elizabeth pushed the door open and we stepped out into the restaurant.

Lola, Mom, and Dad sat at a table near the window, each with a glass of wine in front of them.

Lola was the only one facing me. She gave me a little smile but didn't say anything as Elizabeth and I slipped through the door to the kitchen.

"It's still not right." I heard Devon's voice before I managed to catch a glimpse of him through the heavy haze that filled the room.

"You're new," Eric said. "And non-magical at that."

"But I got an A in Chemistry," Devon said.

We wound past the counters where ready plates would have waited in a commercial kitchen and to the massive stove in the corner.

Devon stood over a pot that billowed steam. Even with sweat pouring down his brow, he still looked like a model.

Eric stood beside him. He'd actually taken off his normal black suit jacket, though he still looked strangely posh in his white shirt and black bowtie.

"Hey guys." I gagged on the sour air. "I didn't die."

"We're aware," Eric said at the same moment Devon said, "I didn't think you'd be up so soon."

"And clearly you've been waiting with bated breath for me to arrive." I pulled my shirt up to cover my nose, realized I wasn't wearing the shirt I'd been in when I'd been bitten, and shoved the horror of wondering who'd changed my clothes down into the deepest parts of my brain where I'd hopefully never think of it again.

"What are you cooking?" My eyes started to leak as I leaned closer to the stove.

"Nothing good," Devon said.

"But what—"

"What did you want to tell Eric?" Elizabeth stepped between me and the now sparking pot on the stove.

"Right!" I dropped my shirt from my face and tried not to breathe through my nose. "After I got bitten, but before Mrs. Mops was God—"

"What?" Devon dropped his stirring spoon into the pot and cursed.

"The dude who bit me said I would be sold, the rest would be killed."

"Who's the rest?" Devon asked.

"The purchase of young wizards is a vile act we already knew Kendrick to be guilty of," Eric said.

"I don't know if he meant Kendrick specifically." A weird shudder ran up my spine. "Venom dude said the word *auction*. Like there was more than one person who might be willing to pay money for me."

A chill swept through the impossibly steamy kitchen.

"That's some really screwed up shit, Bry." Devon dragged his hands over his sweat-soaked hair.

"Auctioning off young wizards." Eric tented his fingers under his chin.

"Is this some kind of dark net, human trafficking thing?" Elizabeth gripped my good hand even tighter.

"No idea." I wrapped our hands behind her back, drawing the girl I was in love with closer to my side.

"It does leave us with some interesting questions and rather horrifying possibilities," Eric said.

"We can't let your parents know," Devon said. "I think your dad might need therapy after today. I don't know if he can take much more without locking you in a boarding school in England."

"I'll whisper to the shadows and see what evil I can find," Eric said.

"But what if it is an online thing?" I asked. "I mean, normal humans use the internet to do horrible things to each other."

"There was a time I would have believed well enough of wizards to think such a thing impossible." Eric sighed. "Unfortunately, I can no longer excuse that sort of naiveté."

"You said there were magic types who could make fake identities for things like Lancre to pass background checks," Devon said. "Can you ask one of them to search for a wizard trafficking ring on the internet?"

"I'll see what favors I might be able to call in. Whatever any of us can do to stop this ring, we need to do it quickly." Eric picked up his fancy black jacket from the counter. "The stir we caused with the Lancre—"

"You mean destroying a store and being almost killed?" I cut in.

"—will not go unnoticed by Kendrick or whomever else the Lancre and her minions were planning on selling Bryant to," Eric finished.

"Not to mention we destroyed a major retail location," Devon said. "People saw us fighting the Lancre and her minions. Word of something that big is going to trickle down to Beville. And then all the magical mole people will want to know why the Ladies aren't coming to take us away."

"I wish you weren't right." Eric headed toward the door to the front of the restaurant.

"Where are we going?" I chased after him. "I have to find shoes and my coat."

"We are going nowhere." Eric stopped right in front of the door and spun to face me. "I am going to whisper into the shadows. Devon is going to stay here and work on his stirring skills."

"Rude, man," Devon said.

"Elizabeth is going to help Lola sort through whatever might be seen," Eric pressed on. "And you are going to go home with your parents and finish recovering."

"What? No." I let go of Elizabeth and chased after Eric. "I can help. I feel better!"

"Honey, you're up." Mom stood from her seat at the table with Lola.

"I was just telling Bryant I thought it would be best if you took him home to recover," Eric said. "No use in all of you puttering about here. A good night's sleep, and Bryant will be right as rain in the morning."

"But—"

"Rest well, Bryant." Eric waved and strode out the door.

"But I don't have any...shoes."

———

D ad didn't care about my lack of shoes or coat. He only cared about getting as far away from the Consortium as possible. He kept me pinned in the restaurant while he called his private car and then walked me across the sidewalk in my sock feet, which was definitely in the top fifteen most questionable choices I'd ever made.

Elizabeth had stayed beside me the whole time we were waiting for the car, and this amazing, warm glow had filled my whole body. But by the time I'd gotten back to my linoleum apartment, I was cold, my feet were damp, and I'd realized I hadn't asked Elizabeth what she was going to say to her parents when she finally went home.

As soon as I'd managed to shake my parents off and get into my room, I sent Elizabeth a message.

Thank you for being amazing. If there's anything I can do to help with your parents, let me know.

My fingers hovered over the screen for a long moment before I typed in the rest.

I love you.

I held my breath while the little dots danced as Elizabeth typed back.

I'm already home. Everything's fine. You're supposed to be resting. I love you, too.

A thrill of absolute, untaintable joy ricocheted through my chest, and I suddenly realized how tired I was.

I had already passed out on my bed before Elizabeth's second message came through.

There are people here. I think they came for me.

10

Prickles in my chest and a nasty smell wafting up my nose woke me the next morning. I opened my eyes to find Mrs. Mops' butt half-an-inch from my face as she dug her claws straight into my ribs.

"You smelled better when you were God." Without even appreciating the wonderful normality of it all, I pushed Mrs. Mops off my chest.

The dim light of my room caught on the back of my right hand. Somehow, I'd pulled my bandage loose while I slept, and my skin peeked out through the gauze. Charcoal-black lines cut across my pale hand like some weird tattoo.

Both my hands shook as I pulled the rest of the bandage free.

A set of dots marked where teeth had pierced my skin. Dark lines traced along my veins, where the venom had mixed with my blood, then faded away on my forearm.

I took a few deep breaths, shoving down the nausea and vanity that made me want to scream.

"I'm alive." I threw my covers back and climbed out of bed. "I'm alive, and the thing that bit me isn't. I'm alive, and my friends are alive." I dug into my dresser for clean clothes. "I wasn't going to have a career as a hand model anyway."

I alternated between staring at my hand and avoiding looking at it entirely as I got dressed, tried to find my backpack, realized I hadn't seen my backpack since the store, and had a momentary freak out about not having school books or my homework.

I shoved my phones into my pockets without even looking at them and went to find my mom to ask if she could write a note explaining how I had lost all my school stuff without mentioning magic.

I opened my bedroom door, stepped into the living room, and the world stopped like my brain had decided to do that weird record scratch noise.

My dad was lying on the couch, curled up under a worn *Doctor Who* blanket. His bare feet hung off one end, and his normally perfect hair was matted against his face.

"What the hell?" I whimpered.

"Shh." Mom took my scarred hand, leading me toward the nook of the apartment that was supposed to be a kitchen. "Don't wake your father."

"What is he doing here?" My face had gone cold. I think my heart had forgotten that its job was to pump blood.

"He was worried about you and didn't want to leave." Mom smiled at Dad over the rim of her coffee cup. "I can't imagine he's comfortable on the couch, but we should let him sleep as long as we can."

I squinted at my dad, trying to see if he was a shadow monster in disguise.

"Do you want some breakfast?" Mom stepped in front of me, blocking my view of Dad.

I squinted at her too, but I couldn't see any hint of a monster. "I'll eat at the Consortium. I lost all my school stuff. Can you write me a note?"

"Sure, honey." Mom ruffled my hair. "Your dad had a new coat brought over for you last night. I'll see if he can have a new backpack sent to school for you, too."

"Right." I nodded. "I gotta go."

I stepped around my mom and to the door where a brand-new coat just like my old one waited for me. I tried not to wonder which of Dad's interns had been sent to scour Manhattan for it as I squinted at Dad one last time to make sure I didn't see any hint of a monster.

When I got into the janky elevator, I started to reach for my phone. I wanted to text Elizabeth to see if she could come squint at my parents for me. But then I saw my own hand again and decided leaving it firmly hidden in my pocket was better for everyone.

The street held the normal, weird winter haze of gas rising from the grates in the sidewalk. The air carried the usual scent of car exhaust, pee, and trash. Everything seemed to be totally normal.

Except my dad sleeping on my mom's couch.

I had decided to ask Lola and Eric if they knew any magic-friendly therapists before I reached the Consortium. Not because I didn't want my parents not to scream at each other—that part was great. I just didn't have the emotional fortitude to deal with them being nice to each other *and* the inevitable fallout when they went back to the good ole' screaming routine.

I pushed open the door to the Consortium without actually looking inside.

"I just need one, simple spell."

The unfamiliar voice froze me halfway into the restaurant.

Lola stood behind the counter, a tray of croissants in hand. She'd traded her usual Norma Desmond-style turban for shoulder-length black curls. Her romper of the day was a deep purple to match the awning outside, and she'd already painted on her usual red lips and fancy eye makeup.

But there was still something terrifying about her as she loomed over the man on the other side of the counter.

"You've come here lookin' for a spell?" Lola said.

"Yes." The man's shoulders crept closer to his ears as he nodded. "I want to do some work on my house in Beville. I need a binding spell to secure the wood."

I let the door close behind me.

"Come get some breakfast, love." Lola didn't look at me as she spoke.

The man from Beville didn't glance my way either as I crept across the dining room toward the counter.

"You want a spell for somethin' a hammer could do?" Lola pursed her lips at the man.

"If I could just speak to the Ladies," the man said. "I've money to offer and—"

"The Ladies don't see lowlifes like you anymore," Lola said. "You are beneath their bother. You want a spell, it's me you've got to convince. If I decide to help you, I will bring your request to the Ladies."

"But I—"

"If I give you the spell," Lola cut across the man, "how will you use it to help the common good?"

I slipped a croissant from her tray. "Thanks," I whispered before ducking behind the counter and into the kitchen.

Sour-scented steam filled the air.

Devon stood by the stove, glowering at a pan whose ingredients seemed to have caught fire.

"Devon." I coughed when the steam hit my lungs. "I think you should stick to being a barista."

He looked up from the pan, then shut off the flames on the stove. "Didn't realize it was getting so late."

"Late?"

"What do you want today?" Devon headed over to the coffee machine. "Cappuccino?"

"Sure." I took a step toward the stove.

Sniffer McDeadDog shambled out of the back corner and grabbed Devon's cooking disaster before I could peek into the pan.

"What were you trying to make?" I asked. "Lola already has—"

"Do you know what Elizabeth wants?" Devon turned on the coffee grinder, blocking my attempt to re-ask my question.

Trying not to look at my messed up hand, I pulled my phone from my pocket to message Elizabeth.

There were three messages on my screen.

One from Mom - *Come to my office. I'll have a new bag waiting for you.*

One from Dad - *Did you want another red backpack or would you prefer black?*

And one from Elizabeth - *There are people here. I think they came for me.*

I had thought my heart had stopped before, but this time I actually felt it. The whole world froze in a bubble of horrified terror.

There was no sound. No blood flow. No movement.

Just all-encompassing fear.

The message was more than eight hours old.

Eight hours since she'd messaged me.

I forced air into my lungs and willed my heart to restart as I unlocked my phone and pressed the button to call her.

My hand shook as I held my phone to my ear.

Her phone didn't even ring.

This is Elizabeth Wick, please leave a message. Or, if you need something in a hurry, just send a text.

"Shit."

"Are you okay?" Devon looked up from the coffee machine.

I bolted back out of the kitchen and through the dining room, punching a simple message into my phone. *Call me now.*

I sent the message. She'd be pissed at me for making it sound like I was dying.

If she's not already dead.

I sprinted west toward Elizabeth's apartment, running with a speed I couldn't have managed before becoming Eric's apprentice.

"Bryant!" Devon shouted behind me, but I didn't slow down. "Bryant!"

Traffic blocked my path.

I turned the corner and sprinted north.

"What the hell is going on?" Devon caught up to me. I don't know if it was a mark of friendship or experience that he didn't try to stop me. He just ran beside me as I plowed through the mass of humans on the sidewalk.

"Something's wrong with Elizabeth." I forced the words out past the knot of panic in my throat. "Someone went after her."

Devon pulled his phone from his pocket as I dove through a pack of preteens on their way to school.

"Eric," Devon panted, "get to Elizabeth's. Something's wrong."

We reached the corner where I had to turn west again. Cars honked as they zoomed south.

"*Lubula.*" I started running across the street before the spell was completely out of my mouth.

Shouting and the squeal of brakes filled the air as the force of my magic shoved the cars back.

"Bryant, that's a bad idea." Devon stayed beside me.

I didn't need to turn and look at him to know he was afraid. Not just for Elizabeth, but of me using my magic in broad daylight.

"She messaged last night and I didn't see it." Heat burned in the corners of my eyes. "If a Lancre got to her—"

"Then we'll find her. No matter what's happened. We're going to get Elizabeth back."

I didn't slow my steps as I burst through the door of Elizabeth's building.

"You boys can't—"

I didn't wait for the doorman to finish yelling at us. "*Dothranta.*"

I didn't even feel guilty when the doorman screamed as the one-sided darkness surrounded him.

Sprinting up the corridor, I raced past the elevator and to the stairs. There were no cracks in the walls, no blood spattering the floor. There was no hint at all that anything horrible had happened in Elizabeth's building.

I shoved open the door to the third floor and skidded to a stop in front of apartment 334, pulling my magic-filled phone from my pocket before banging on the door.

"Elizabeth!" My voice echoed down the empty hall. "Elizabeth!"

My heart skittered as I heard footsteps inside Elizabeth's apartment.

"Elizabeth." I moved to step forward as the door opened, but it wasn't my girlfriend waiting on the other side.

"You." Elizabeth's mom glared at me. If you took away the angry expression, caked-on makeup, and thirty years, Mrs. Wick would have looked just like her daughter. "I don't know what you think you're doing, but shouting in the hallway is unacceptable."

"Where's Elizabeth?" I peered over Mrs. Wick's head. Everything inside the apartment was pristine without a hint of a struggle.

"My daughter's whereabouts are of no concern to you." Mrs. Wick began to shut the door.

Devon stepped forward, planting his shoe in the gap. "Actually, they really are."

"She messaged me last night." I tried not to let my voice waver. "I didn't see it until now. She said someone had come after her. Elizabeth is in danger. I need to help her."

"The only danger my daughter faces comes from worthless teenage trash like you." Mrs. Wick's face shifted into a pinched, smug smile. "I let my daughter run wild with you for too long. I should have recognized the danger you posed sooner. I should have put my foot down the moment she mentioned dating a theatre teacher's son. I have made mistakes, but I am putting them right."

"How?" Devon asked.

"That is none of your concern," Mrs. Wick said. "Now get out of my building."

"Where is she?" I gripped my magical library of a phone, trying to think of any spell that might help me without making things worse for Elizabeth.

"Get out," Mrs. Wick spat.

Devon pushed himself farther into the doorway so he loomed over Mrs. Wick in a very Lola-like way. "Where is Elizabeth?"

"I'll call the police." Mrs. Wick didn't shrink under Devon's glare.

"Tell me where she is," I said. "I just need to know she's safe, and we'll go. You won't have to see us ever again."

"You're right, I won't." Mrs. Wick stepped away from Devon and farther into her apartment. "When they bring Elizabeth back, she'll be my sweet daughter again. Not some little whore who runs away with boys. They'll remind her what it means to be a good girl. How important it is to respect her parents. Too bad your families can't afford Soaring Horizons. I'd suggest both of you be sent into the program."

11

I didn't even notice the cold as I sat on the steps outside Elizabeth's building. I'd sunk to the level of numb where things like freezing to death don't seem to matter anymore.

Devon paced in front of me on the sidewalk, but he seemed to know better than to try and offer words of encouragement.

Elizabeth had been sent to Soaring Horizons, a place I'd only ever seen mentioned on the brochures in our guidance counselor's office. I could picture the cover of the brochure. Somber-looking kids in dark uniforms standing at attention while angry-looking wardens lorded over them.

Elizabeth didn't belong in a place like that, but she'd been sent away.

Because of me.

All my fault. It's all my fault.

All my fault.

The vicious chorus repeated in my head over and over.

"What's happened?" Eric didn't even sound out of breath when he sprinted around the corner. His gaze flicked between me and Devon. "Where's Elizabeth?"

I opened my mouth, but I couldn't make words come out.

A furious sadness shone in Eric's eyes.

"Her parents sent her to a scared straight program," Devon said.

"A what?" Eric stepped closer to us.

"They paid people to take her away." Devon dragged his hands over his face. "I think her mom's words were something like to teach Elizabeth how not to be a little runaway whore."

I barely scrambled to my feet in time to puke over the side of the steps instead of onto my shoes.

"If it's legal for parents to send their children to such places, surely it can't be that bad," Eric said. "She's safe. She'll be fed and—"

"And who knows when she'll come back?" My voice cracked in my raw throat. "They could keep her locked up there for months. They could not let her leave until college." Every breath throbbed in my chest as I tried to fight back my angry tears.

"Ah," Eric said. "That is unacceptable."

"So what do we do?" Devon said.

"A rescue may be in order." Eric tented his fingers under his chin.

"We can't do anything!" I stormed off the steps and onto the sidewalk. "We can't rescue her. This isn't like the Library or Kendrick or the Ladies. Anything we do could make things even worse for her than I've already managed."

"Bryant." Devon took my arm, but I shook him off.

"I can try talking to Mrs. Wick again. Maybe I can convince her Elizabeth disappearing was all my fault and vow never to see her again." I swallowed the sour that soared back up into my throat. "Or I can see if my dad can pay off the Wicks. Or maybe he can buy Soaring Horizons. My dad's got plenty of money. Money can fix anything."

"Bryant"—Devon stepped into my path—"money can't fix the things we've faced."

"This isn't a magic thing. This is real life. Elizabeth's real life," I said.

"Magic is real life." Devon gripped both my shoulders. "All the things we've done are very real. Elizabeth is a seer. The place her parents shipped her to is filled with pissed off kids and very angry adults. How many shadows is that kind of hell going to attract? How long can we leave Elizabeth stuck in there with things only she can see before someone notices she's different?"

"We have to get her out," I said.

"That's more like it." Devon turned to Eric. "Do we wait for nightfall, or should we find the place now?"

Eric raised one dark eyebrow. "I'm afraid it might be a little more complicated than that."

"Complicated?" Devon repeated.

"I assume this place is run solely by humans?" Eric said.

"I hope so." A thousand new terrible possibilities ran through my head.

"Then my usual tactics of suave and daring may be less than useful," Eric said.

"But if there aren't wizards at Soaring Horizons, we can just slip in and out," Devon said.

"Of course." Eric nodded. "The actual act of extracting Elizabeth from confinement should be simple enough, but what are we to do with her once she's free?"

"We keep her from getting taken again," I said.

"She's a minor," Eric said. "And while I have no fear of the police, their searching for a kidnapped girl might draw an unfortunate amount of attention to the Consortium. Not to mention the trouble it could bring to you and Bryant."

"I don't care about trouble." I balled my hands into numb fists. "I don't care about the police or the Consortium. We have to help Elizabeth."

"And when her parents refuse to see her again?" Eric said. "When she can't return to school because the same people we've saved her from will come to collect her again? What then?"

"We wouldn't leave you," Devon spat.

"And I'm not suggesting we abandon Elizabeth," Eric said. "I'm merely pointing out that running after her, spells flying, might be the worst decision we can make. We need information and a plan. We are not only dealing with Elizabeth's immediate safety and comfort, but her future as well."

I made a noise somewhere between an *ehh* and a growl as I dug my knuckles into my eyes.

"Are you going to be ill again?" Eric's voice radiated disappointment.

"I have an idea." I let the spots dance in front of my eyes as I tried to think of a more reasonable plan. "It's such a bad idea."

"Sounds great," Devon said. "Let's go."

I tried to talk myself out of it as we headed east. I almost managed to convince myself I had better options as I texted both my parents that I'd puked on my way to school, gone to Lola to get checked out, and she thought I should rest for the day.

I had just begun to grasp a better plan, but as I walked into the fancy lobby, whatever brilliant thought I'd had faded away. So I handed the security guard my ID and headed up to Dr. Spinnek's office alone.

I didn't pause outside the frosted glass door. I just walked in like I had an appointment with the therapist I'd run away from.

Purple suit guy had changed into a cerulean suit. And I only know the name of that color because of a fight my mom had with a costume designer when I was in ninth grade.

Purple/cerulean suit guy barely blinked at me before jumping to his feet. "Bryant, I didn't have you on Dr. Spinnek's schedule today."

"I'm not on her schedule," I said. "But this is an emergency."

Cerulean suit's mouth shifted to be one flat line as he reached for the phone on his desk. "If you're having a psychiatric emergency—"

"Don't call anybody." I stepped forward and shut the door to the hall behind me. "I just need to talk to Dr. Spinnek. Whatever her hourly rate is, my dad will pay triple. He'll give you triple her hourly rate too if you get me into her office."

I hated tossing my dad's money at people, but Cerulean's eyes got wide for a second before he nodded and moved toward the doctor's door.

He knocked lightly before calling in, "Dr. Spinnek, we have a surprise guest."

It sounded like I'd just walked onto a game show. Either that or *a surprise guest* was code for *call the ambulance and make sure they bring a straitjacket and sedative.*

But Dr. Spinnek's door opened a moment later. "What sort of surprise guest?" Her gaze landed on me. "Oh."

"I need to talk to you right now, and I'm willing to pay."

Dr. Spinnek stepped back into her office and closed the door.

"I just need a minute!" I shouted.

A rumble of voices carried through the door.

"Was she with a patient?" I pressed down the flicker of guilt in my stomach.

"The doctor always has a patient," Cerulean said.

"I'm very sorry, but we can start again next week." Dr. Spinnek opened the door to her office.

"Start again next week?" A woman stormed into the waiting room. "I'm not starting this again. Therapy isn't working. I want a divorce."

A teary-eyed man followed in the woman's wake. "But we're making progress, real progress."

"And we can continue that progress next week," Dr. Spinnek said. "David will help you make an appointment."

The wife stormed out as Cerulean David sat behind his desk and Dr. Spinnek ushered me into her office.

"Bryant"—Dr. Spinnek gave me a calm smile like I hadn't just bought my way into her office and potentially caused a divorce—"why don't you take a seat? I wasn't sure you'd want to see me again after you left our last session."

"I'm not here to talk about me." I paced the middle of the office, ignoring Dr. Spinnek as she looked pointedly at the couch where I'd sat before.

"Well, if you aren't here to talk about you," Dr. Spinnek said, "I don't know what help I can—"

"It's about my girlfriend."

"The perfect one you'd adore even if she looked like a toe?"

I paused my pacing for a moment. "You're a really good listener."

"That's why they pay me the big bucks." The doctor smiled.

"Right." I started pacing again. "My girlfriend, Elizabeth, she got into trouble."

"What sort of trouble?" Dr. Spinnek drifted over to her desk. For a second, I thought she was going to reach for her phone, but her fingers landed on her notepad instead.

"Her parents think she's a bad kid. Which could not be further from the truth. I mean, she did stay away from home for a few days when our lunch lady got squished, and yeah, she snuck out when I almost died this week."

"You almost died?" Dr. Spinnek froze with her pen halfway to her notepad.

"Yeah." I hid my black-marked hand in my pocket. "But it wasn't that bad. And your boyfriend almost dying has got to be on the list of top reasons why it's maybe okay to bend the rules. But Elizabeth's parents don't care. They're convinced she's awful. Her mom even called her a whore."

Dr. Spinnek pursed her lips. "There are some harsh biases young girls run into when it comes to sexuality that it can be hard for a young man to understand."

"Which is sexist bullshit, and we should overthrow the patriarchy." I dug my fingers into my hair, remembered the marks on my right hand, and shoved the magically scarred appendage back into my pocket. "But the more immediate problem is Elizabeth being sent to Soaring Horizons."

Dr. Spinnek's lips got even pursier.

"I can't leave Elizabeth in a place like that," I said. "She hasn't done anything wrong."

"Only a legal guardian can sign a student out of a residential program like Soaring Horizons." Dr. Spinnek went to sit behind her desk. "As much as it seems like Elizabeth may not fit in with the usual clientele at Soaring Horizons, there is nothing you or I can do to get her out."

"But my dad has money," I said. "Lots of money. If I can get a lawyer and you tell them she doesn't deserve to be in some program—"

"It's more complicated than that." Dr. Spinnek held up a hand to keep me silent. "I don't know Elizabeth. I haven't even completed a full session with you."

"But—"

"Soaring Horizons does have an excellent success rate and a passable reputation." Dr. Spinnek opened her desk drawer. "I never recommend my patients to such programs, but I do have some literature on Soaring Horizons."

"But I don't—"

"If you were to want to help Elizabeth leave Soaring Horizons before her parents formally withdraw her from the program, I would suggest you help her find legal counsel. Perhaps emancipating herself from her parents would be the best option." Dr. Spinnek set a shiny brochure exactly like the one from my guidance counselor's office onto her desk. "While becoming legally and financially independent at a young age can be stressful, it would give Elizabeth the freedom to reject her parents' desire to enroll her in such a facility."

I reached forward to grab the brochure.

"However"—Dr. Spinnek slid the brochure out of my reach—"considering I'm not entirely sure of your mental state, I'm not convinced Elizabeth wouldn't be better off where she is."

"I promise she's not." I didn't bother trying to keep the desperation out of my voice. "I'm the mess. I'm the one with nightmares and freakouts. I'm the one who can't walk into the cafeteria without feeling like the ceiling is going to collapse and crush me. I'm the one who's having oddly large issues with his dad flirting with his mom while also trying to deal with major problems that should never fall into a teenager's hands. Well, okay, Elizabeth is a big part of that, too. But other than responsibilities above our age bracket, some sleep deprivation, and parents that are way worse than I thought they were, Elizabeth is perfectly fine."

"Then it sounds like you need some sessions with me," Dr. Spinnek said. "I'd say once a week. With a commitment to sit through every session and make a genuine effort to work through your issues."

"I would walk through shadow monsters and deadly mists and fire and whatever other hell this world can come up with to protect Elizabeth." I snatched the brochure out from under her hand. "I'll sit on your couch for an hour a week. But first, I've got to get my girlfriend back."

12

I didn't call my dad until I was firmly in the cab between Devon and Eric. It seemed super weird for the three of us to be piled into the back of a car that smelled faintly of rotting fabric softener. It was usually Devon, me, and Elizabeth huddled in the back of a cab.

Soon. I'll get her back soon.

My dad answered on the second ring. "Bryant, are you feeling better?"

"I lied about being sick." I rushed through the words, not giving Dad time to ask questions. "Elizabeth's parents sent to her this awful residential program, and I have to get her out."

"That's interesting." Dad's voice was super calm, like he was surrounded by people and didn't want to give them a hint of how messed up his son's life was.

"I went to Dr. Spinnek for help."

"That's an excellent resource," Dad said. "I'm proud of you, Son."

"Maybe hold off on the pride," I said. "I sort of promised you'd pay Dr. Spinnek a lot for seeing me without an appointment."

"I'm not concerned with the cost."

"Good, because I have to see her once a week for a while." I shut my eyes tight as the cabbie turned toward the George Washington Bridge. "And I might need help from a lawyer, too."

"And why's that?" Dad's calm façade started to slip.

"Dr. Spinnek suggested we help Elizabeth become an emancipated minor and she said other legal things, too, but there could be shadows where Elizabeth is. We can't wait for courts. So I might need to be bailed out if this plan goes wrong and I get arrested for trespassing."

"I think maybe you should head home and rest," Dad began. "I'll send a car—"

"Also, maybe bail money for Devon and Eric if it comes to it," I said. "We're going to try and be subtle, but I wanted to say I'm sorry in advance and you can take it out of my college fund."

"Bryant—"

"I love you, Dad."

I pressed the button to end the call and turned my normal cell phone to silent.

I hated ditching my dad with that kind of information, but I did think getting bail money might be easier if he had a little backstory.

"This ride isn't going to be cheap," the cabbie said as we hit bridge traffic.

"Don't worry," Devon said. "We can pay."

I pressed my hand against my wallet that held the black emergency credit card my dad had given me.

"I'll pay when we get there," I said. "But turn the meter back on and wait for us to come out. If you stay, I'll tip the whole fare back to Manhattan."

I was throwing my dad's money around like it was sludgy snowballs, and I didn't even care.

I studied the brochure as we drove toward New Jersey, and despair threatened to overwhelm my soul.

There was the familiar picture of the guy lording over the kids in dark uniforms. There was another picture of teens helping each other climb a really high wall. And then there were testimonial quotes like:

After years of worrying about my son's future, I now know I won't be visiting him in prison.

Soaring Horizons turned my daughter from a pothead who was flunking out of school into a respectable young woman with a promising future.

I don't worry about where my child is at night anymore. This is freedom like I've never known.

My hands trembled as I fought the urge to tear up the brochure.

There were more quotes on the inside and an email address to contact for pricing on the back, but there wasn't any useful information.

I suppose it made sense for the brochure not to include details like floor plans, security weak points, and if there was anyone with magical affiliation onsite, but those were the bits of information I actually needed.

"You gotta breathe, Bry," Devon murmured.

I took a deep breath, letting the nasty cab air fill my lungs.

I'd gone into battle fairly certain I was going to die and come out all right. I could get Elizabeth out of lock down.

I didn't have any other choice.

We all sat quietly as the cabbie honked his way across the G.W. Bridge and into Jersey.

Devon chewed the inside of his cheek and stared out the window as we rode. It looked like he wanted to say something but couldn't in front of our driver.

Eric sat normally for a few minutes, then tented his fingers under his chin.

"What?" I muttered.

"Hmm?" Eric looked straight through me.

"Why are you doing your weird *tent my fingers under my chin* thinking thing?" I asked.

"I think I may have just realized something." Eric lowered his gaze to the brochure still clutched in my hand. "You can sell just about anything if you find the right market."

"How did we get to marketing?" Devon leaned around me.

"Take Soaring Horizons, for example." Eric tapped the glossy image. "Parents pay an exorbitant amount of money to have someone else discipline, and by that I mean *raise*, their children. It's a matter of connecting the product with the buyer. That's the link all salesmen must find. Don't you see the brilliance of it?"

"Maybe you should make an appointment with Dr. Spinnek." Devon leaned back in his seat.

"Perhaps." Eric tented his fingers under his chin again.

"Dr. Spinnek said she'd never recommend anyone get sent to Soaring Horizons." I dug my fist into my stomach, trying to fill the panicky hollow that had taken the place of my organs.

"Here we are." The cabbie turned down a side street that cut past a line of normal houses and onto a wooded drive that didn't seem to belong in the suburbs.

I gripped the magical black phone in my pocket and squinted out the window, searching for a hint of shadows, witches, or any other kind of trouble.

I couldn't see anything but trees until we reached a high metal fence with a guard minding the gate.

The guard stepped up next to the car, clipboard in hand, taser on his belt.

"Whoa." Devon leaned back in his seat as the cabbie unrolled his window.

"Name please?" The guard said.

"Ah"—Eric leaned forward—"I believe it's actually me you'd like to speak to."

The guard gave a heavy sigh before walking around to Eric's side of the car.

Eric rolled down his window and pulled something out of his pocket with a quick flick of his wrist.

"I've been sent by this young man's father to check the boy in for immediate care." Eric passed a black card with purple writing to the guard. "The finances should be being taken care of as we speak."

The guard glared at Eric's card for a minute before passing it back.

I caught a glimpse of the purple words.

Eric Deldridge. Estate manager for Leo Adams.

Manhattan, New York

"What's the other kid here for?" The guard leaned closer to the window and fixed his glare on Devon.

"That one?" Eric frowned. "I hate to say it, but he's rather the spare that no one can ever seem to get rid of."

Devon tensed beside me.

"I have instructions to check him in as well," Eric said. "It's not my place to say too much about Mr. Adams' business or his son's indiscretions, but placing both young men into Soaring Horizons' care seems to be the best way to avoid a rather nasty lawsuit."

"Admissions office is right inside the main building." The guard stepped back and swiped his card against the panel on the gate. "I'll let them know you're on your way."

"When can I get a magic business card like yours?" I whispered to Eric as the cabby pulled through the gate.

"When you have the mental fortitude to maintain the writing you want to appear on it while speaking to someone," Eric said.

"So never?" Devon said.

"Don't be rude because you're the spare." I leaned forward to peer through the windshield.

I don't know if it was some weird *my dad's super rich* bias, or if it was just because the brochure was so fancy and shiny, but when I'd pictured the place Elizabeth's parents had sent her, I hadn't pictured gray cement buildings that looked like they belonged on a military base.

The middle building was four stories high and flanked by two, long, single-story structures. Peeking through between the cement buildings was a track where teens in dark uniforms were running laps accompanied by angry-looking adults.

The car stopped, and I passed my black credit card to the driver. Out of habit, I held my breath as he ran the card, waiting to see if my dad had cut me off the second I'd mentioned the possibility of needing bail money.

"Are you sure you want me to wait?" Mr. Cabbie asked.

"Yep," Devon said. "There's no way I'm spending more time here than I have to."

Eric got out of the car and stepped aside, waiting for me to follow.

"As loathe as I am to admit it," Eric said, "I think it best if we part ways. Devon and I will get into admissions and ferret out what information we can. I suggest you try and find Elizabeth. If you need a distraction, give me a call, and I'll be glad to oblige. As much as I happily maintain my distance from normal human society and try and do as little damage as possible, I find this place to be foul and have no qualms with causing a bit chaos."

"What kind of chaos?" I asked.

"Best to hurry now." Eric shoved me down behind the cab as the front door of the building opened.

"Has Mr. Adams' financial officer contacted you yet?" Eric said, not giving whoever had come out of the building a moment to speak. "I have meetings in the city I'm going to be late for if we can't wrap this up soon."

"I'm glad my fate is less important to you than meetings," Devon said.

I hid behind the cab, lying on my stomach like a fool, as Devon and Eric walked away.

"Great. Just freakin' great."

I scrunched my eyes shut and tried to think.

My mind was a void where only panic could exist.

I don't want to make myself sound too incompetent. Compared to where I'd been less than six months before, I was super skilled and ready to take on the magical world.

Magical being the key part of that statement.

"I really hope my dad is ready with bail money." I pushed off the frozen ground, leapt to my feet, and bolted for the side of the main building. Pressing myself against the cold concrete, I sidled down the alley toward the track.

Peering around the corner, I watched the students run circles on the track. I needed a spell to hide myself, but I'd never seen anything like that on the phone. I looked toward the trees on the far side of the track. There was a high, wooden wall like the one in the brochure between me and the woods. If I could make it that far—

"What are you doing back here?" An angry-looking man strode toward me. "Out of uniform is ten points."

"What?" My voice squeaked a little as the warden bared down on me.

"Speaking out of turn is another ten," the man said.

"But you asked what I was—"

"Are you aiming for running laps all night?"

"*Turso.*" The spell just sort of popped out of my mouth, and then a white light hit the man in the ankles.

He tipped forward and fell to the ground.

"Oh shit. Oh shit. *Parapus.*" Thin lines flew out of me and wrapped around the man on the ground, trapping him.

"What in the hell is going on here?" The man fought against his bonds.

"*Laruga.*" I said the silencing spell before the man had a chance to scream. Panic buzzed through my chest like I'd eaten a beehive for breakfast. I took a deep breath, trying to keep my speaking voice steady enough to say a spell while the voice in my head kept shouting *This is bad, this is bad* on repeat. "*Geminesta protura.*" A tiny tingle of magic rushed through my fingers as I reached into the man's pocket and grabbed the lump of material I'd just created.

You know that completely unrealistic magic trick where the magician keeps pulling scarves out of someone's ear? That's nothing compared to dragging a full uniform to match the warden's right out of his pocket.

The warden stared at me with wide and slightly afraid eyes.

"Listen, sir." I pulled the uniform coat on over my own jacket. "I know you're thinking that as soon as you stand up, you're going to run and tell everyone that some freaky kid trapped you and invaded the school. I could stop you from doing that, but I honestly don't want to hurt you, even though you seem like a real jerk. So, since I don't want to be the evil dude in this situation, I'm going to give you some advice instead of squishing the air from your lungs or shooting lightning through you.

"No one is going to believe what I just did. Telling anyone about it is only going to make things worse for you and won't make a difference to me." I pulled the too-big uniform pants on over my own jeans. "So when you get set free, instead of ruining your career by telling everyone you've been hallucinating, tell them you fell and you think you're getting the flu. Go home, eat a nice dinner, and tomorrow when you wake up and wonder what the hell happened to you and how some kid managed to take a scary guy such as yourself down without breaking a sweat, just remember you had the flu. And fevers can do weird things to your memory."

I reached down to snatch the guy's hat. He twisted his head and tried to bite me.

"No biting." I grabbed his hat and shoved it over my floppy hair. "I'm really over biting."

Squaring my shoulders and tipping my chin up in a way that would have made Eric proud, I strode out toward the track.

13

I started off by walking along the track. I hadn't seen teens anywhere else, and searching the open area seemed like a better idea than going into one of the cement buildings and hoping I might stumble upon Elizabeth at exactly the right moment.

I kept my pace to a steady half-march, half-strut. I held my chin high and glared at every student I passed like I was Hell's hall monitor.

I studied each of the groups running by, searching for Elizabeth's blonde hair with tiny black streaks. I knew she wasn't outside before I'd made it halfway around the track.

Still, I watched the groups running past, searching for...I don't know what. Seeing things was supposed to be Elizabeth's part of the whole magic gig. I wanted to tell myself there were no shadows or monsters to be found at Soaring Horizons, but the truth was I might not be able to see them even if they were crawling around my ankles.

Letting out a long string of mental profanity, I took a deep breath and waited for the next group to come running by.

I stepped forward before the last one in the pack could pass.

"You. Stop," I said with all the authority I could muster.

The slowest boy stumbled to a stop in front of me. Panting, he drew himself up to a creepy attention before actually looking at me.

His face shifted from robotic stiffness to veiled curiosity as he looked from my slightly oversized clothes to my *way too young to be an authority figure* face.

"Yes, sir," the boy said.

"I'm looking for a student," I said.

His curiosity stopped being veiled as he wrinkled his forehead at me. "Shouldn't you collect a roster from the office, sir?" He kept his tone formal.

"She's a new student." I stepped closer to the boy, ready to magically silence him if he tried to call for help. "She just got here last night."

"I should keep running, sir." The boy moved to rejoin his group.

I blocked his path. "Please."

"That right there means you don't have the authority to ask."

"But I need to. I—" I fought to shove my desperation into words. "I just need to find her and make sure she's okay. They took the girl I love away in the middle of the night and brought her here. If I don't find her now, I don't know when I'll see her again."

I held the boy's gaze for a long moment. I was just about to open my mouth to ask how much money I had to pay him to get an answer and if he happened to know his bank routing number, but he spoke first.

"I wouldn't know who this girl of yours is." The boy looked over his shoulder to where his group was coming back around the track. "They keep all the new victims in C Building for the first 48 hours or so. Let them cry it out before sending them to join the rest of us."

"Thank you." I gave him a nod and kept moving around the track, keeping my face turned away from the wardens running their charges past as I headed straight for the building labeled *C*.

I don't know why my heart was racing like I was about to jump off a cliff. But there was something about walking toward C Building that made it feel like the world was starting to tip.

A digital lock tried to block my path, but a simple muttered *cliaxo* popped the lock open.

The inside of the building smelled like bleach and despair.

Voices carried from down the hall, their bored tones sounding more like a meeting than anything that should be happening where Elizabeth was being held captive.

Part of me hated myself for thinking of her that way. Trapped, conquered.

Elizabeth was the strongest, bravest person I knew. She'd faced evil with nothing more than her ability to see the faces of her enemies for what they really were.

But as I walked down the corridor, everything in me screamed that she'd become a prisoner.

There were doors lining the hall. All made of metal, each with a window at the top.

I moved from one side of the corridor to the other, peering into each of the windows, looking for a room that might hold Elizabeth.

The first room looked more like a nurse's office than anything else, though there didn't seem to be a nurse on duty. The next had a set of four desks facing a blank chalkboard.

The next had a bed in it. A cot shoved in the corner. Like a cell.

Sharp pain sliced through my chest. Elizabeth's parents had sent her to teen prison because of me. Whatever Elizabeth had been through, whatever path fate had decided to drag her down, I'd been the one to start it.

The next room had a person sitting on the cot. A boy who might've been a few years younger than me.

He looked up, saw my face in the window and charged the door, screaming at the top of his lungs. His shoulder hit the metal with a *thud*.

I bolted to the other side of the hall, ready to magic open a door to hide from whoever would come and check on the screaming kid.

But no one came.

The tone of the voices coming from down the corridor didn't even change.

Willing my pulse to steady, I kept searching.

The next bedroom was empty.

The one after that held a girl with short black hair.

I held my breath as I moved to the next door down. A pull centered right over my heart dragged me forward, like fate or love or my soul was drawing me toward the window.

I peered through the glass.

Elizabeth lay curled up on the bed, facing away from the window.

"*Cliaxo.*" My hand shook as I opened the door and stepped into Elizabeth's room.

"I'm still not hungry." Her voice sounded like she'd been crying for hours.

"Elizabeth." Her name fell from my lips with more gratitude than I knew a word could hold.

Her head snapped toward me. She was on her feet and in my arms before I could make it halfway across the room.

"You're okay." I held her tight. The stench of the place hadn't stolen Elizabeth's delicious scent, but she trembled in my arms with fear I didn't recognize. "Everything is going to be okay. Eric and Devon are here, too. We're going to get you out."

I felt her freeze, stiffen in my arms, like terror had zapped through her.

"No, Bryant." She let go of me and stepped away.

"What do you mean *no*? I have a cab waiting out front. Eric can create a distraction if we need him to—"

"I can't leave." Elizabeth brushed away her tears before they could properly fall from her eyes.

"Yes, you can. That's why I'm here."

She let out a shuddering breath. "My parents said if I don't make it through the program, I shouldn't bother coming home."

The air whooshed out of my body.

"I don't want to be here, Bryant. I belong at home, at school with you and Devon. But if I don't stay here, I won't have parents anymore."

"No, that's not true." I took a step toward her. She didn't back away, but she didn't reach for me either. "Parents say they won't forgive you, but they don't mean it."

"Devon's parents did. My parents do. It's different for you. Your mom and dad both know about magic. They might not like what you're doing, but at least they know you aren't a psychotic delinquent." She didn't bother brushing away the fresh batch of tears that spilled down her cheeks.

"So, we tell them." I reached forward, daring to brush her tears away. She leaned into my touch. "You're a seer, Elizabeth. That's never going to go away. I'll show them some magic."

"It's not worth the risk. Even with the Ladies gone, exposing magic—"

"You are worth every risk!" My voice bounced around the tiny room.

Elizabeth looked to the door, waiting for one of her jailers to come.

They'd all ignored the screaming boy. I didn't think they'd come to make sure Elizabeth was safe either.

"Look, you can't stay here," I said. "What if a Lancre catches your scent like the one at school did? What if there are shadows hiding in the corners of this hellhole?"

Elizabeth shivered and glanced toward the corner.

I looked behind me, but I couldn't see anything there.

"You are a seer. Locking you in with things only you can see won't help anyone. You wouldn't be safe, and—"

"We can't tell my parents." She shook her head, sending her curls fluttering around her shoulders. "They'd never understand."

"I'll work magic strong enough to make them understand."

"Magic is bigger than me, Bryant," Elizabeth whispered. "Whatever the Lancre and Kendrick are doing is bigger than me. Finding the books is bigger than me."

"Then come help us." I took her hand, lacing my fingers through hers. "If you want to stay in here to keep your parents happy, I'll go. I'll wait for them to let you out. I'll write you a letter every day and save them all in a box so when you get back to New York you'll have a whole book of how much I missed you. But saying that you staying in here is better for magic or wizards is just plain wrong. We need you. Devon, Eric, and I need you."

Elizabeth swallowed. "I won't have a family anymore."

"Yes, you will. Even if it's not your parents. You have me and Devon and Eric. Lola loves you. My mom loves you. My dad will love you. I'll split my college fund with you. There's a ton of money in there."

Elizabeth attempted a laugh.

"If you want to stay here, that's your choice." I took her face in my hands and pressed my lips to her forehead. "But if you come with me, I swear to you, you will never be alone."

"Okay." Elizabeth leaned closer to me. "Okay, let's get out of here."

I held her tight. "I love you. You're going to be okay."

"What the hell are you doing in there?" A voice shouted from the other side of Elizabeth's door.

14

An angry woman with a pointy face and sallow skin peered through the window.

"Is she human?" I whispered.

"I can only see her face," Elizabeth said. "So, probably?"

The woman looked down toward the lock on the door.

"What do we do?" Elizabeth gripped my hand.

"Something stupid." I turned toward the back wall. "*Portunda*."

The wall trembled as a door formed where one never should have been.

The lock beeped behind us as Elizabeth shoved the concrete door open.

"What have you done?" the pointy lady shouted, like Elizabeth and I were vandals.

The part of me that was emotionally exhausted and had forgotten how logic works wanted to ask the lady what non-magical explanation she could come up with for a random door forming. But Elizabeth and I had already darted through the new door and out into the open.

"*Portundo*." I sealed the exit before the pointy-faced lady could chase us through.

A full pack of students had stopped following their warden around the track and just stood, staring at us.

"Not good," Elizabeth whimpered.

I pulled out my normal phone and dialed Eric as I led Elizabeth toward the path between buildings.

I could see the cab waiting out front.

I picked up speed, heading straight for the yellow-painted safe haven.

But the warden I'd bound up earlier charged toward me with three other really angry-looking despots right behind him.

"A distraction would be great!" I screamed in the general direction of my phone while Elizabeth dragged me away from the warden's posse.

By then, all the teens had stopped sprinting around the track. They watched, their reactions ranging from glee to fright, as Elizabeth and I tore around the backside of the main building with the formerly bound warden and his buddies running right behind us.

I tried my best to focus on the people who were chasing us and not the innocent kids behind them. "*Dothranta.*"

The warden and his flunkies screamed as my spell trapped them in a one-way darkness.

"The cab is for us," I said. "We just have to—"

An alarm cut through the air, wailing like I'd just tried to invade a secret military base.

"What the hell is this place?"

A line of older, angrier-looking students/inmates appeared on the other side of the building, trapping Elizabeth and me between them and my one-way darkness.

"Got any bright ideas?" I asked.

"Try something not dangerous." Elizabeth dragged me back toward the darkness, cutting a wide path around the spell.

I didn't have time to stop and look at the spell list on my phone for ideas, and the blaring alarm made thinking through the spells I'd memorized impossible.

We should have come to save Elizabeth at night.

I should've hidden under her cot.

I should've gone with Devon to the front desk to check myself in and let Eric go after Elizabeth.

"Call the police!" the formerly bound warden kept screaming over and over as we ran past. "Call the police!"

I took a deep breath and summoned all the focus the alarm and screaming would allow. I fixed my gaze on the patch of ground where the formerly bound warden had dropped to his stomach and was trying to crawl to safety. "*Stilgarna.*"

I expected a stream of water to come up from the ground, confusing the wardens and making mud so it would be harder for them to chase us.

Nope.

I didn't know until that moment that *Stilgarna* uses whatever water is available. So using it over, say, a main water line for a place that houses two hundred kids, would cause a spontaneous fifty-foot geyser.

With a *clang* and a sputtering *hiss*, a tower of water knocked the warden aside as it soared into the air.

"Oops."

We sprinted between the buildings toward the cab.

The cabbie had gotten out of the car and moved to stare down the alley to watch my impromptu fountain show.

"We're ready to go." I opened the back door of the cab and pushed Elizabeth inside, then turned to face the main building and whatever else the horrible place had to throw at me.

Devon and Eric trotted down the steps toward the cab.

"Did you find her?" Devon said.

"Yes, I found her." I sprinted around to the far side of the car and dove into the seat beside Elizabeth. "What happened to you causing a distraction?"

"We did cause a distraction." Devon hopped in on Elizabeth's other side.

"The alarm was the distraction." Eric got into the front seat. "I thought it best to be subtle."

"Real subtle, buddy." The cabbie climbed back into the car and started driving up the long driveway. "I don't want to be the kind of guy everybody hates, but you'd better make good on tipping well."

"I will," I said. "I promise I will."

Elizabeth slipped her hand into mine.

A warm tingle ran up my arm, and all thoughts of property damage faded from my mind.

"Where do you want me to take you?" the cabbie asked.

I opened my mouth to give the Consortium's address, then realized it wasn't really my decision to make. I looked to Elizabeth.

Tears brimmed in her sparkly eyes.

"I just want a shower," she said. "I don't where the best place for me to do that is anymore."

"Some choices will have to be made," Eric said. "But you will be the one making them. Don't forget how much value that freedom holds."

Elizabeth nodded and squeezed my hand tighter. "The Consortium then."

The closed gate loomed ahead of us. The guard stood right in the middle of the road, blocking our path.

"One of you take care of him," the cabbie said. "I don't run people over, even for good tips."

"Just pull up beside him," Eric said.

The cabbie shook his head and swerved to stop with Eric's window right beside the gate guard.

"Excuse me, sir," Eric said. "I believe they need your help at the school. There were alarms going off and I heard someone say to call the police. Have you called the police?"

"What are you—"

I don't know what Eric muttered while the guard was talking, but the gate slammed open.

"Thank you for your assistance," Eric called as the cabbie sped away, racing through the gate and onto the wooded drive. We passed the suburban houses that didn't seem to belong so close to a hellhole like Soaring Horizons and whipped out onto the main street just before a cop car tore into sight and bolted down Soaring Horizons' driveway.

"That was good timing," the cabbie said.

"Are you always this chill?" Devon asked.

"Yep," the cabbie said. "You drive enough people in Manhattan, you see everything."

"Do you have, like, a card or something?" Devon asked.

"You always tip well?" the cabbie asked.

"Yes." I looked down at Elizabeth's hand clasped in mine.

The cabbie pulled a yellow-and-black business card from a holder on his sun visor. "Give me a call when you need me."

I got out my normal phone so I could put the information in under *SOS Car.*

My dad had texted. My mom had texted.

Elizabeth leaned closer to me and brushed her lips against my cheek. "Thank you for coming for me."

"Always." I wrapped my arm around her, letting her lean on my shoulder.

I stared at my phone for a long time as we drove back to the city.

I just couldn't think of what to say to my mom and dad.

I'm sorry I make you worry all the time. Thanks for not kicking me out like my friends' parents, seemed a little dramatic and presumptuous at the same time.

I'm sorry you're mad, but I'd risk anything to protect Elizabeth didn't seem like it would really help anything.

When pre-bridge traffic slowed, I finally typed a message to my parents.

We got Elizabeth back. The place her parents sent her was awful. Her parents aren't going to let her go home, but I don't know if they'll just ignore her like Devon's parents either.

We're going to the Consortium. I need to protect her, but I'm in over my head. I think I need your help.

A horrible mix of shame and fatigue boiled in my stomach as I re-read the words.

We'd gotten Elizabeth out of Soaring Horizons, but what if her parents tried to send her back? What if they tried to report her as missing? What if our school wouldn't let her come back? There were too many *what ifs* magic couldn't fix.

I sent the message and closed my eyes.

My phone buzzed before I'd managed to take a deep breath.

I'm on my way. I'll have my lawyer with me. Make sure there's nothing at Lola's Nikki shouldn't see.

I kissed the top of Elizabeth's head and let her scent fill my lungs.

Everything would be okay. My dad would make it okay.

I think that cab ride was the first time I realized that the difference between Batman and a creepy dude stalking people and whispering at shadows was a lot of money and a friend who really believed in him.

15

Devon and I had been banished to the kitchen.

Lola and Eric had disappeared to somewhere without telling me where they were going, which was super not cool considering how insane the last few days had been.

Mom and Dad were sitting in the dining room of the Consortium with the lawyer and Elizabeth.

I'd wanted to stay and hold Elizabeth's hand, but Dad had said no and his lawyer Nikki had agreed and Elizabeth hadn't argued with my banishment.

If I peeked through the crack beside the kitchen door, I could see Mom and Elizabeth sitting opposite Dad and Nikki.

Mom kept rubbing Elizabeth's back in that super comforting mom way.

Elizabeth looked exhausted and sad, but she was holding it together.

"I wish Lola had left behind some food." Devon hopped up onto a counter a health inspector would definitely have told him not to sit on.

"You've been practicing cooking," I said. "Make something."

"I don't think you'd want to eat anything I make."

I pressed my eye against the crack beside the door.

Elizabeth was nodding, and Mom was smiling encouragingly.

Nikki looked to my Dad, and he said something I couldn't hear.

"She's going to be okay," Devon said. "I mean, it'll be hard, but Elizabeth is tough. She'll come out just fine."

Elizabeth brushed tears away from her cheeks.

I leaned against the wall and sank down to the ground. "Do you ever hate me?"

"Hate you?" Devon asked. "Hate's a strong word, but you are my best friend so it is my prerogative to want to punch you in the face every once in a while."

"Thanks, but I meant for dragging you into the whole magical mess. If I wasn't a wizard, or if you weren't my friend, you'd never have gotten mixed up in all—"

"And I'd still be living with my parents who'd decide once a month they actually wanted to be parents and who spent the rest of their time making it really clear they'd rather I not be around." Devon hopped off the counter and came to sit on the floor by me. "No thanks. I'm better off at the Consortium Home for Wayward Youths."

"But is Elizabeth?" I dug my knuckles into my eyes. "Is she going to hate me forever when she figures out this is—"

"If you say *my fault*, I'm going to punch you." Devon clasped my shoulder. "Remember that time fate drew all of us into this thing? If I've learned one thing from being your magical wingman, it's that the guy with the magic needs people standing behind him. You may get the fancy wizard title, but Elizabeth and I both need to be here. And not just for you. To protect all of magickind, which, though I love you man, is way bigger than you.

"So, stop throwing a pity party and trying to make your wizardom bigger than Elizabeth's fate and the choices she and I have both made. She's not just here to be your girlfriend. Elizabeth Wick is here to help save the world from the forces of evil."

"Right." I let out a long breath and opened my eyes. "You're right."

"I know."

"So what am I supposed to do now, oh wise one?"

"We'll figure out what Elizabeth needs us to do for her, then we stop Kendrick, then we find the books and offer free knowledge to the magical world." Devon shrugged.

"Think we can get all that in before dinner?"

"Nope, but we can probably order some pizza."

"That sounds amazing." I reached into my pocket to get my phone to order a pizza, but the door opened before I could think through the logic of having food delivered to a fake restaurant.

Elizabeth stepped into the kitchen. Her eyes were puffy, and her cheeks were pink from crying.

I leapt to my feet and held my hands out to her in an awkward *I'd really like to hug you right now but only if you feel okay with being touched* kind of way.

Elizabeth stepped toward me and let me wrap my arms around her. She leaned her forehead against my shoulder for a moment before speaking. "Your dad wants to talk to you before he leaves."

I tensed.

"He's being really great." She nestled deeper into my arms. "He's paying for the lawyer, and she's going to file all sorts of papers so my parents can't try to send me back to Soaring Horizons. She said something about needing documents for when I apply to college next year, but I got stressed and I could only hear buzzing for a while."

"We'll sort it out." I tipped Elizabeth's chin up and brushed my lips against hers. "We've got time, and we'll figure out the paperwork as it comes. You're here, and you're safe. We can sort everything else out later."

She kissed me again. Her taste lingered on my lips.

"Go talk to your dad," she said. "Then your mom's going to help me find clothes to get through the weekend, and then I have to figure out schoolbooks, and homework. Then I'll probably curl up and cry for a while."

"I'll be there when you cry." I kissed her forehead. "I'll even make sure I have tissues for you."

"What a gentleman." Elizabeth gave a weak but real-sounding laugh.

"Bryant, honey"—Mom peeked into the kitchen—"your dad has to run back to the office."

"Right." I let go of Elizabeth and squared my shoulders. "How mad is he, and am I getting sent to boarding school?"

Mom raised one eyebrow in a way I think she'd picked up from Eric and held the door wider.

When I went into the dining room, Dad and Nikki were by the front door, Nikki hovering close to my dad. Like, inches from my dad. Like *let me smell your cologne, you sexy beast* close to my dad.

"Hey, Dad," I said way louder than was necessary.

Nikki looked my way, gave me a bright smile, and stepped, like, three inches farther away from my dad.

"Bryant." Dad didn't move away from smiley Nikki at all. "I think we should have a talk before I go back to the office."

I inserted myself into the thin space between my dad and Nikki, almost knocking over smiley McLawyer face in the process. "I'm really sorry about the money for the cab ride, and for calling you and mentioning maybe needing bail money."

"What?" Mom said.

I grabbed her arm and pulled her to stand awkwardly close to Dad with me.

"I just panicked," I said. "Elizabeth means everything to me, and I couldn't think straight not knowing if she was all right. And I know it's different because you're my parents, but I think I finally understand how worried you guys are when you think I'm in trouble. I thought I was going to suffocate, and it was awful."

"It is a terrible feeling." Mom gripped my hand as tears pooled in her eyes.

"I'm really grateful to you guys for helping Elizabeth." I pulled Mom and Dad into a big hug with me. "I love you guys so much. I'm glad the three of us are together."

I gripped them both tightly for a second before sidling away, leaving Mom in Dad's arms.

I turned to Nikki, planting myself firmly between her and my parents. "Thanks so much for helping Elizabeth. My family really appreciates it."

"I'm happy to help." Nikki gave me an extra big smile. "Elizabeth seems like a really bright and special girl."

A tiny tremble of guilt rattled in my stomach.

Nikki was helping Elizabeth. Yay.

Nikki was eyeing my dad over my shoulder. Boo.

I opened my mouth to say...I don't know, something along the lines of *it creeps me out that my dad keeps hitting on my mom, but you're sure as hell not joining the family, though please do take my dad's money to help my girlfriend.*

Thankfully, Lola and Eric breezed in through the front door and saved me from myself.

"Where is she?" Lola asked.

"She's in the kitchen," Mom said. "She's hanging on."

Lola reached for my mom, and they walked arm in arm to the kitchen.

Eric eyed Nikki. "If Bryant's not needed for anything further, we have some business to attend to."

"Business?" Dad stepped up to stand beside me.

Eric shot a sideways glance at Nikki. "After all the excitement of the day, taking the time to refocus Bryant's energy in a *constructive* way seems to be a worthwhile endeavor."

"Right." Dad sounded skeptical.

I wanted to give Dad the full Eric translation of *your son had a meltdown and caused property damage, so I'm going to make him do really hard spell work until I'm sure he's not going to accidentally catch the Consortium on fire,* but I couldn't really say that in front of Nikki.

"Probably a good idea," I said. "I could use some extra tutoring."

"Perfect." Eric bowed me toward the door.

"Don't you want to work here?" I asked.

"There are some specific books I'll need to find for this lesson."

My heart soared up into my throat, did a joyful pirouette, and skittered its way back down to my chest. "I'll grab Devon and Elizabeth."

"Elizabeth has—"

"No need to bother them," Eric cut across my dad. "I'm sure Devon will want to help Elizabeth get settled in. Lola can bring them along later."

"Right..." My mind raced as I tried to figure out what exactly Eric was trying to tell me.

"Shouldn't you wait and ask your mother?" Dad said.

Sometimes, I forgot he'd only bothered trying to be an involved parent for the past two months.

"Just tell her I'll check in with her before dinner, but I'll probably eat here with Elizabeth." I started to follow Eric, but Nikki stepped closer to my dad. "Maybe you and Mom should have dinner together. After the stress of having me for a son, neither of you should eat alone."

Dad's face brightened up. "I'll ask your mother what she wants for dinner."

"Great!" I hurried after Eric. He was already a block away from the Consortium by the time I managed to catch up to him. "So, what's going on?"

"We're going to go to my house in Beville," Eric said. "You ruptured a water pipe today and reminded me how much training you have yet to complete. While I appreciate how far you've come in your spell work, you undeniably lack finesse."

"But you said *books*." I whispered the last word.

"Yes, Bryant," Eric said. "I do have several of those in my home, and there are presently none in the Library."

"Well, if we're just doing spells, why couldn't we wait for Devon and Elizabeth?"

"I want to do a bit of poking around in Beville on our way," Eric said. "After the incident with the Lancre and today's blatant magic so close to the city, I want to be sure there are no whispers of the Ladies losing control. Considering all Elizabeth has been through today, I don't want to subject her to the shadows, and it would be rude to take Devon with us and leave her without her new situational sibling."

"It's going to be weird being the only one not staying at the Consortium." I pulled my normal phone from my pocket.

"I don't live at the Consortium," Eric said.

"I'll believe you aren't sleeping over with Lola as soon as I believe my dad isn't hitting on my mom."

"What happens between Lola and me is beyond the purview of your apprenticeship," Eric said, "though, admittedly, I should have clarified the difference between staying somewhere and living somewhere. I live in Beville."

I sent a quick message to Devon and one to my mom.

I slowed my pace as we reached the Columbus Circle station, trying to think of something to message Elizabeth.

Eric's hauling me away to make sure I don't make any Big Blue-style mistakes. I'll see you tonight. You're the strongest person I know. I love you.

Little dots danced across the bottom of my screen as I walked down the steps.

I love you, too. Be careful. If you do grow another giant flower, try for purple this time.

My heart did a massive swoop in my chest as I chased Eric into the station.

He didn't go through the weird door that normal people never seemed to notice popping in and out of existence. He headed straight for the train platform.

I should have known that was a bad sign. Should have bolted for the surface and back to the Consortium so I could be with Elizabeth, but I was too busy being happy to realize I was rushing toward my impending doom as I stepped onto the train and was whisked away into the darkness.

16

"No hesitation," Eric warned.

"I know." I bounced on my toes, trying to convince my body not to freeze in fear, as the narrow platform between the subway cars rattled under my feet.

"One, two, three." Eric leapt off the platform and into the dark.

I dove after him without letting myself consider the deadly stupidity of jumping off a moving train.

Pain shot through my shoulder and sizzled in my face as I hit the ground, skidding across the dirt before rolling to a stop in front of a lit lamppost.

Eric was already standing and brushing imaginary dirt off his black coat by the time I struggled to my knees.

"Why couldn't we come in through the entrance at Columbus Circle and then go creeping through the back alleys of Beville?" I touched my cheek, hissing in pain as blood coated my fingers.

Eric leaned against the lamppost. "The information we are seeking today is best gathered discreetly. I thought it wise not to stroll into Beville through the front door."

"*Sinato.*" I grimaced as the sting of my healing spell swept through my cheek and shoulder. "If you were going to steal a lamppost to light up your death-defying back door to Beville, couldn't you have stolen a crash pad, too? Or a few hundred feather beds to soften the landing?"

"I've never had trouble with the jump."

"Well, good for you." I wobbled to my feet, gripping the wall to keep the ground from swaying.

"Come along." Eric turned away from the train tracks and headed down the tunnel.

"Where exactly are we going?"

"To see what the shadows whisper."

I opened my mouth to ask what sort of shadows we were going to be looking for, then closed it, and gave a shrug to Eric's back. He'd helped rescue Elizabeth. The least I could do was go eavesdrop on some shadows in return.

Unless they were the sort of shadows that tried to kill you. Then we should have waited for Elizabeth so she could at least tell me what lurked in the dark before the monsters went for my jugular.

An awful squirming in my gut made me miss the stinging in my face.

I glared into the growing shadows as the glow from the lamppost faded behind us.

"*Heliono.*" A sphere of light appeared in my palm.

Shadows danced along the walls. Even if I hadn't known things lived in the tunnels below Manhattan, the wavering darkness still would have been terrifying.

Eric walked in front of me, strutting along like being in a roughly hewn tunnel was as normal as strolling through Central Park.

He cut to the side down a narrower passage, then into another corridor where the walls looked ready to collapse. How he knew where we were going, I don't really know. It's just an Eric thing. Storming through the world like he owns it and somehow making it out on the other side with an epic triumph worthy of gallery paintings.

For one fleeting moment, I thought of asking him if he really did know where we were going or if he was just that good at pretending to know every-thing. Then I crushed a rodent skull under my foot and snapped back into the grim reality of what other things could be lurking in the shadows that pressed in around the edges of my light.

The farther we got from the subway lines, the staler the air became. The streets of Manhattan had nothing on the stink of the tunnels belowground. I pulled the neck of my shirt up and pressed it firmly over my nose with one hand while holding my sphere of light out with the other.

I had only taken Eric's back entrance to Beville once before, and though I had been terrified and confused at the time, I didn't remember the stink being so bad.

Something squished beneath my foot. I didn't look down to see what it was.

You will not puke. You will not puke.

Eric stopped and turned to look at me like he'd somehow heard my thoughts.

He waited to speak until I stood right beside him. "Do you remember the naïve and terrified child you were the first time you visited this tunnel?"

Eric had spoken so softly, I opted to nod instead of saying out loud *Yes, I remember because it wasn't that long ago, and I'm not sure how much better off I am now than I was then.*

Eric glanced down the tunnel. "I need you to be that boy now. Do not let them see how competent you are. Do not let them see the phone."

I nodded again.

"You are, however, allowed to speak," Eric said.

I rolled my eyes.

Eric started forward and spoke again, this time loudly enough to carry down the passageway. "I'm not your tour guide through the world of magic, nor am I your babysitter. If you are determined to place yourself in unnecessary danger, then on your head be it. I'm finished helping you."

"What?" I said.

"I can no longer bear the burden of your incompetence."

"Thanks?"

Eric wound a finger through the air like he wanted me to keep talking.

"I'm just trying to learn." I'm a terrible actor. I sounded like an infomercial. "I haven't been a wizard for very long and I'm doing my best, okay? What I need is a teacher, and if you're not willing to help me, then...then..."

Eric shot me a glare.

"Then I'm going to have to find another teacher?" I squinted into the shadows, trying to find whoever I was supposed to be performing for.

"And where do you suppose you're going to find a fool willing to spend their time attempting to help someone as horribly inept as you? If the Ladies were willing to take in wayward teen wizards, I would deposit you at the Consortium this evening and make you their problem."

"Well..." I swallowed hard, trying to think of something to say and hating myself for refusing to participate in the improv camps my mom ran in the summer. "At least the Consortium has decent coffee."

Eric looked back at me with one eyebrow raised.

"And if I'm doomed to be a second-rate wizard, why do you bother trying to teach me at all?" That line came out more convincingly, because it was true. I had never really understood why someone as epically awesome as the occasionally egotistical jerk that is Eric would want to teach a dork like me.

"Because I am more afraid of the damage you could cause uneducated than I am horrified at the amount of time I am wasting in this pursuit."

A rustling sounded in the tunnel up ahead. Like the scraping of things being dragged across the dirt.

It took all my will power not to imagine a serial killer dragging bodies through the dark in front of us.

"I'm seriously considering charging your father per-hour for my work," Eric said. "How much is that man worth? I want to be sure to charge him a fair rate."

"I don't know." That part was true, too. I'd never thought to ask my dad his net worth. "Somewhere between obscenely rich and grotesquely wealthy? Many moochin' dollars? Lots of millions worth? Flies in private jets rich? Has a lawyer that shows up to last-minute meetings rich?"

"Then three-thousand dollars an hour to tolerate his idiot son seems like a fair rate. Is there a number I should call to arrange a contract, or can you deliver cash?"

"I'm not bringing you cash."

"Then I'll contact your father and arrange payment by more official means. Though I will have to bill him for the time it takes to get everything set up."

"You're a jerk." I made the mistake of pulling my shirt away from my face to scowl at Eric's back.

The stink had only gotten worse the farther into the tunnel we'd traveled. It wasn't quite the smell of death. More like burned rubber, sewage, and onions had had an unfortunate stench baby.

"What the hell is down here?" I scrunched my shirt back over my nose. "If you're leading me toward some slop monster, I'm going to make sure my dad cuts your pay to $2,000 an hour."

"My rate isn't up for negotiation."

"You're such a—"

A flash of light exploded in the tunnel. For a split second, I could see piles of trash pushed up against the walls, strips of fabric hanging down from the ceiling, and a grate blocking the path in front of us, then blackness swallowed me again, blocking out even the light from my spell.

Pain crashed into the backs of my legs, buckling my knees and knocking me to the ground. The thump and groan in front of me were the only indications I had that Eric had fallen as well.

"Eric," I coughed his name.

Something hard slammed into the back of my neck.

"*Hie—*"

———

My mouth had gone fuzzy. Like I'd eaten too many sour candies and gone to sleep without brushing my teeth. I tried to move my tongue to my lips, but something blocked my tongue from moving. A thing that was actually fuzzy.

I opened my eyes but couldn't see much through the thick bag over my head. My shoulders ached from my arms being pinned behind my back. My wrists stung from their bindings, which seemed to buzz with a faint something that felt almost like electricity.

Huh, I've been kidnapped.

That was my first stupid and unhelpful thought. But as far as I could figure, what with the bag over my head and all, I had definitely been kidnapped.

From standing in a dark tunnel to tied to a chair in less than a minute.

Or maybe way more than a minute. I had no clue how long I had been out.

"Ehm." I tried to say Eric's name through my gag. "Eram!"

A sound to my right, like a toe tapping, was my only answer.

I'd never tried a spell without being able to speak before. Eric had never really mentioned how horribly things might go if I tried to mutter my way through magic.

Telinto. I silently rolled the spell around in my mouth, trying to sort out how best to form the word through my gag.

I took a deep breath to try the spell, and a decisive "Uh-uh," came from my right.

Eric. Can you hear my thoughts? If you can, tap three times.

Though I had often gotten the impression Eric could somehow read my mind, no tapping came.

Wiggling my wrists, I tested my bonds. I squeaked a grunt as a sharp shock jolted my skin, numbing my hands.

I took a few deep breaths, making sure I wasn't going to puke on my gag, before trying to move my feet around. They weren't bound. A bubble of hope floated into my chest before I remembered I had been in the tunnels of Beville when I was kidnapped, so a wizard who could trap me with a spell was the best case scenario for my captor, and there were options way worse than shadow monsters I couldn't bring myself to consider. Standing up and trying to run blindly to freedom would most likely have just ended up with me being dead.

The air didn't smell too bad through the bag over my head. That was nice. Elizabeth and Devon weren't being held with me. Also a huge plus. My parents knew I was with Eric. Not super helpful, but at least they wouldn't think I'd just vanished for fun and decide my punishment should be spending more than an hour a week with Dr. Spinnek.

A laugh jostled my ribs before I realized how funny that really was. I would rather be kidnapped with a bag over my head than be on a comfy couch feeding a professional psychologist a massive pack of lies. My laughter grew until I started choking on the gag, but I still couldn't stop myself. Tears streamed down my covered face.

A sigh came from my right.

"Shut up," a voice growled in my left ear.

"Ae-e." I tried to apologize through my gag, but the feel of the fuzzy fabric on my tongue, like I had tried to eat a teddy bear, made me laugh again.

Something hard hit my ear. "Be quiet. Now," the voice said.

I swallowed my shout at the pain radiating from my ear down my neck.

"Keep bothering me, and you'll be sorry."

I don't know if this makes me sexist, but I was kind of surprised when I realized the voice belonged to a woman.

I sat back in my chair and waited for Eric to break out of his bonds and save us. Before I had fallen from my laughter-in-the-face-of-danger mood and drifted into a more reasonable state of worrying about surviving, sounds of fidgeting and rustling came from my right.

"What?" the woman spat.

"Thank you for taking off the hood," Eric said, unimpeded by a gag.

"I'll shove it back on if you don't have something useful to say."

"I have a great many useful things to say. But I would prefer a glass of water before we begin our discussion," Eric said.

"No."

"Very well," Eric said. "Put the hood back on. But do be careful not to let either of us die. If it's money you're looking for, you'd be losing out on a fortune by allowing anything to happen to either of us. If you're after something more interesting and worthy than monetary gain, my apprentice might be a bit useless, but I've heard of some who enjoy eating the flesh of young wizards."

"Eyy!" I shouted through my gag.

"What the hell kind of monster do you think I am?"

"It's difficult to gain an accurate assessment of someone who's kidnapped you," Eric said.

I pictured him giving a sanctimonious bow of his head.

"I do apologize if I caused any offense," Eric said.

I couldn't hold back my groan at that one.

"I also apologize for my apprentice."

Something hit my chair, jostling me.

"Ehh!" Another shock flew through my wrists.

"What were you doing this far down in my tunnels?" the woman asked.

"Water," Eric said, "then I'll be happy to answer your questions."

That time the pain came from something hard hitting my shin.

That's when I decided being kidnapped really sucks.

I wasn't super afraid. I had been through too much for being tied to a chair to scare me. I was just annoyed. I needed to get back to Elizabeth. She was counting on me to be there to comfort her, and my being kidnapped was interfering with my sacred boyfriend duties. I tipped my head back and tried to stare at the ceiling. Through the fabric of my headbag, I could make out the shape of the light coming from above. A chandelier with about fifty flickering candles hung just behind me.

"I should have killed you in the tunnels," the woman said.

There was a sound like pouring water.

"I can't drink that with my hands tied," Eric said.

A sound of splashy choking came from my right.

I gave a low chuckle.

"You're very kind," Eric said. "Now what did you wish to discuss?"

"Why did you come into my tunnels?"

"I must have taken a wrong turn," Eric said. "To be honest, I was trying to lead my apprentice through the more unsavory parts of Beville. I would hate to give the impression that I'm attempting to shirk my duties, but the boy's parents seem eager to give him to me on a more permanent basis and taking him into my home is a prospect I do not treasure."

I wanted to say I didn't fancy the idea of living with him either, but...gag.

"I don't believe you," the woman said. "You're too well put together to be stupid enough to wander this way without a better reason. Did you come here to dig for spells? To mine in the shadows with the others?"

"I have no interest in being coated in darkness for the rest of my days. I've spent enough time around Charles and his people to know such a life is not for me."

"Charles?"

"We're good friends. Fought in the battle of Beville together."

"Eric Deldridge," the woman growled. I don't mean that poetically. She growled like an angry beast as she said his name, and the first trickle of worry that being kidnapped might be more than an inconvenience seeped into my angsty, teenaged brain.

"At your service," Eric said.

"You're an idiot for coming down here, and I am one very lucky woman."

"If it's ransom you're looking for, then I can't argue with that. The boy's father has enough money you could renovate this rat-infested tunnel into a very nice home."

"I'll slice you to pieces."

"I don't believe you."

A hacking laugh came from the woman.

"I don't doubt you'd enjoy eviscerating me," Eric said. "I simply have more faith in your business savvy."

"I can kill you and still profit from the boy."

"If you ask for ransom for the boy, you'll have to let me go as well. What if he were to go to the Ladies and tell them you'd murdered me? They might thank you for getting rid of me, but they'd kill you with their next breath for ending the life of a wizard."

"I'll sell the boy. I know people who'll keep him far away from the Ladies. You can rot down here. Your flesh will feed the rats and no one will ever know what happened to Eric Deldridge."

"I'm not sure exactly what reputation I have this far down in the tunnels, though I can't help but be flattered at how well you know my name."

"Names fade in time."

"Fair enough," Eric said. "Since you seem intent on keeping my loathsome apprentice alive long enough to make a profit off him, might I give a suggestion in hopes of preserving my own life?"

A long moment of silence dragged past.

"You do whatever you please with the boy. Ransom him, sell him, it has little to do with me. As for my own predicament, I can offer you something far more valuable than money in exchange for my life."

"What?" the woman asked. "You happen to have bones waiting around to be used? You really don't seem the type. Of course, I can just kill you and wait for the rats to finish eating."

I gagged on my gag.

"Books," Eric said. "I have access to books on magic. I can offer you three books in exchange for my freedom."

"Three books?" the woman said. "Is that all you have?"

"No, but it is all I am willing to part with."

"Ten books," the woman said.

"Eight, and I will stay with my apprentice until he is taken by someone who will keep him far from the Ladies. Now that he knows I have illegal books, I can't risk him going to the Ladies with the information."

"Eleven books, and I'll let you attend the auction," the woman said.

"Auction?" Eric said. "This is a more worthwhile evening than I had hoped for. Eleven it is."

17

The weight of both phones in my pockets kept me sane as my limp body drifted through the tunnels. I don't know if it was Eric steering my floating form through the darkness and he was being extra nice for getting me sent to auction, or if the woman's magic kept me hovering and she was trying to prove she was a humane kidnapper by making my journey smooth. Whichever it was, they kept my head from ramming into the walls as we wound our way through the tunnels.

I couldn't see. I couldn't move.

I wished I couldn't smell.

Unfortunately for me, my nose was working like a champ. From the musty room where I'd woken up, we went back through the stink from Hell and then into someplace that smelled like a burning woodstove.

For a while, I tried to rally my body to fight against the spell the woman had placed on me. But I couldn't do anything. No wiggling, no spell speaking, no nose plugging.

The slight hint of fear swimming around in my gut at the thought that I might actually end up being sold to someone who wanted to buy a teenaged wizard for who knows what terrible purpose was the only thing that kept me from being really bored.

After what seemed like an exorbitantly long time, sounds of life came from up ahead. The echo of people shouting, the clanking of metal against metal, and the howling of dogs all pounded through the corridor. A few seconds later, the onion-flavored stink of sweat slammed into my nose.

I sighed and accepted the fact that I'd probably never be able to get the horrible stank of the underground out of my nasal passage.

"What have you got there?" a man asked.

Something thumped hard against the floor.

"I've got a boy for auction," the woman said.

"No auction scheduled today," the man said.

"I'm not going to wait for Wiltzer to decide he wants to make money," the woman said. "Put out the word that I've got a boy up for sale and tell Wiltzer to call a bidding session for tonight or I'll auction the boy on the street myself."

"That's not how things work around here," the man said.

"Do I need to take my business elsewhere?"

"On your head be it," the man said. "You won't get as good a price."

"Bah."

"What's he here for?" the man asked.

"I'm only here as a witness," Eric said. "I want to be sure the thing is done properly."

"Try not to bleed on anything," the man said. "And if you die, do it in a corner."

I started drifting forward again. The space we had entered was big. From the sound of it, really big. I could sense people passing close to me, feel the wind of their movement whispering against my skin, hear their footsteps as they passed by.

Being frozen suddenly became a lot less okay.

Eric was outnumbered down here, and not in the normal Eric *damn the odds* kind of way. Whatever his plan had been when he started shouting about the size of my dad's bank account, something had gone very wrong. And from the sound of it, he'd been injured in the process.

He was going to need my help. We were going to have to fight our way out.

"Are there books available for purchase here?" Eric asked.

"You're giving eleven books to me," the woman said. "I don't think you should concern yourself with any more illegal merchandise."

"Quite the opposite," Eric said. "I've been going through second and third-degree purchasing channels, spending a fortune on whatever texts my sources see fit to bring me. Imagine what I could gain by purchasing a book directly from the dealer. I'd be willing to pay you a fee for introducing me to the right people."

"I don't understand you," the woman said.

My floating stopped suddenly, giving my stomach an unpleasant slosh.

"One minute you're willing to trade me books, the next you're looking to buy more."

The woman's weight pressed on my ribs as she leaned across my torso toward Eric.

"I should just charge you more, leave you without a dime left to buy shit."

You're drowning, Eric. Find a way to set me free so I can help you!

"We've agreed on eleven books," Eric said. "I will gladly give you the eleven. If you don't want to help me locate a new book source, so be it. But I will pay you no more than the promised amount for my freedom. A deal is a deal. If you choose not to abide by your promises, then I hope you are willing to live with whatever burden that debt may place upon your shoulders."

"I don't know the book man." The woman's weight lifted from my ribs. "He doesn't deal with my type, but I know someone who might be able to introduce you."

"I'll pay $2,000 for the introduction," Eric said. "I would offer you another book, but I'm afraid I won't have access to any more unless your connection pans out."

"You've got yourself a deal," the woman said.

A sudden waft of wet half-dead dog drifted past me.

"If you would be so kind as to allow the boy to stand on his own," Eric said.

"So you can let him run away? I don't think so."

"You'll get a better price if people see him moving around," Eric said. "Leave him tied and gagged, by all means. I am enjoying his silence to no end. But rumor of tonight's auction is bound to circulate eventually.

"If there is even the slightest chance the people of Beville might find out I lost my apprentice and had to stand helplessly by while he was sold, I must at least make sure he sells for a reasonable sum. I don't know if I could show my face at the pub if anyone knew the boy I'd spent the last several months struggling to shape into a competent wizard sold for a few hundred dollars."

"You're evil," the woman said. "You should have found your way down here a long time ago."

Fingers fumbled across my forehead and yanked the bag free, taking several of my hairs along with it.

A beautiful woman glared down at me. Not like *normal person on the street* gorgeous, but *otherworldly, might as well be an elf in a movie* kind of beauty. Her skin glistened with a dewy glow. Her eyes were the light blue of a perfect summer sky. Her mouth had a rich cherry hue that made her look like a badly dressed, slightly filthy princess.

"You try to get away," the beautiful woman said, "I'll gut you and auction your corpse off piece by piece."

The weirdness of the gritty voice coming out of the beautiful face distracted me so much, I didn't even hear her speak the spell that ended the invisible gurney that had been supporting me.

I hit the ground with a grunt.

"*Eshan.*" A crackling light zapped from the woman's fingers and wound around my neck, like a more sinister version of the tether Eric had used on the hallucinogen-hawking girl from Times Square.

The heat of the spell pressed uncomfortably against my skin.

"Stand," the woman said.

I lay on the ground, staring at her.

She held the other end of the spell in her hand like some kind of magical leash.

"Stand," she ordered again.

The end of the leash she clasped in her hand shone bright. The light zipped toward me along the cord, bringing a wave of heat that burned my neck.

I whimpered through my gag and struggled to my feet as fast as I could with my legs asleep from floating for so long and my hands still bound behind my back.

"This way." The woman tugged on the leash in her other hand.

My gaze followed the string of light that wound around Eric's neck. Dried blood stained Eric's forehead, and a cut on his cheek looked like it might crack back open with one errant grimace. But other than the glowing collar around his neck and the bit of blood, he looked okay.

Eric glanced at me for a split second before looking to the woman. "Lead on."

She stepped forward, but I forgot to move.

My leash tightened, and another flare of heat burned my neck. Neither the woman nor Eric bothered to glance back as I gasped at the throbbing sting.

I stumbled along behind them, tears of pain trailing down my cheeks and being absorbed by my gag.

"I never believed there was anything besides shadows beneath Beville." Eric's hands were tied behind his back like mine, but his shoulders were relaxed and his face calm, like being tied up was a mutually agreed upon adult activity.

"People like you aren't allowed to know," the woman said. "This place isn't for you."

The tears in my eyes stopped enough that I could actually see some of the space around me. I'd expected a high-ceilinged cavern with buildings along the wideset walls the way Beville-proper had been built. I'd expected wrong.

The cave ended only a few feet above my head, and the lights set into the stone did little to ease the claustrophobic effect. There were no real buildings in sight, either. Stalls and tents filled the place, like I'd ended up in Hell's flea market.

The people moving from stall to stall were young, old, super icky, almost normal, but they all had that same vibe of having been underground for way too long.

When I first heard about Beville, I thought that was where the legend of mole people living in the subway tunnels had come from. But as the woman led me—literally since I was on a freakin' leash—through the stalls, I realized this place was where the stories of creepy sub-subway societies must have started. Either that or there was a worse place even farther belowground, but I didn't have the mental capacity to think about that.

Some of the stalls we passed sold normal-looking stuff like toothbrushes and food. A few sold old things like tarnished knives, and weird, lumpy sacks of leather. I stared as hard as I could at Eric's back, hoping he might feel my gaze and say something comforting like *Don't worry, there isn't a human heart wrapped in that stained bit of leather,* but he kept walking.

A pack of dogs tore down the aisle, howling and sniffing at everything within reach.

One got really friendly with my butt as a man who looked too old to be alive shouted, "You'll be soup if you don't shut up!"

The dog seemed to take the man seriously and abandoned his invasion of my nethers.

"Did Thaden know of this place?" Eric asked as we turned down a wider path of roofless wooden shacks.

"Maybe," the woman said. "Never saw him here. We're not the type he ever cared to deal with."

"Hmm." Eric paused for a moment, leaning over what seemed to be a pewter cauldron.

"*Hmm* what?" The woman yanked on his leash, sending a flash of light toward Eric's neck.

If the spell burned Eric, he didn't show his pain.

"It's a rather strange place to be," Eric said.

"The underground wasn't built to live up to your expectations."

"You misunderstand," Eric said. "I meant your place in the magical world.

The Ladies have long considered people like yourself to be below their notice. Not powerful enough to be a threat to the order of our world. Not useful enough to be cultivated as a part of wizarding society. And with their horrible underestimation of your capabilities, you've built a system of illegal trade and commerce that never could have existed had you been what the Ladies think of as worthy."

"Don't insult the woman who can kill you." The woman snatched at the air, and a knife appeared in her palm.

"I meant no insult at all. I am genuinely impressed with the amazing amount someone in your position has accomplished."

"Eh a ea," I muttered through my gag, sick of not having a clue what they were talking about.

"I mean she is not like you and me, Bryant," Eric said. "I hope this won't embarrass you too much for your young heart to ever recover, but you were captured and are about to be auctioned off by a woman who was born with no magic of her own."

The woman growled at him.

I glanced down to the leash around my neck.

"There are some things about magic you are too naïve for me to have risked teaching," Eric said. "Now that my duties as your mentor are nearing their completion, you'll have to ask your new master to explain the finer aspects of bone magic."

18

B one magic.

My stomach shriveled to the size of a walnut, leaving me with a well of terror where my insides should have been.

I didn't know much about bone magic. Eric had only ever mentioned it once while I was having a nervous breakdown in the catacombs hidden within the Library. You know, the Vault of the Dead where the Keepers of the Dead protect the bones of the dead from people who want to steal bones and use the power left behind by dead wizards to do spells? That awful place.

When Eric had mentioned bone magic, I hadn't really been in a place to ask a ton of questions about how a person could use the power left in a wizard's bones to create magic for themselves.

But now that the woman who had kidnapped us was using bone magic to make up for the fact that she hadn't been born with any power of her own, I had a few super urgent questions.

Did she kill a wizard, actually have rats eat their flesh, and then use the freshly chewed bones for spells?

Did she dig up a corpse and steal their bones?

Did she have the bones of her magically inclined grandma hidden down her shirt, and had said grandma left them to her in her will?

Did she plan on selling me off bone by bone to the highest bidder, and was I supposed to be alive while they cut me up?

Of course, I couldn't ask any of those very important questions as the woman led us to the only fully walled building I'd seen in Hell's flea market, because I was still freakin' gagged.

The woman looked sideways at Eric. "If he decides to gut you for being a prick, I get full rights to your books."

"Whatever my house offers is yours." Eric gave a little bow.

I studied the walls of the building in front of us rather than focus on the manic gleam in the woman's eyes. The whole thing was built from old-looking lumber, but the wood hadn't aged like wood would aboveground. There were no weather marks on the planks or signs of rot, only a feel of age. Like the building had seen one too many nasty things and given up on the world.

Voices, music, and the clinking of glasses came from inside.

"Seems like a lively place," Eric said. "Pity I've never made my way here before."

The woman tugged on both our leashes, pulling us through the door.

If anyone in the bar thought two people being led around by their necks was weird, they were smart enough not to show it. A few heads turned our way, but everyone went back to their drinks and sketchy meat-on-a-stick meals like my being kidnapped was a normal Friday night thing.

The bone witch dragged us to a booth and shoved us both into one seat. Smiling at Eric, she wrapped the ends of our leashes around the table.

"You must know I have no intention of running." Eric leaned back against his still-bound hands.

"You must know I'm not stupid," the woman said. "Be good, boys."

With a last check of our leashes, she strode off across the bar.

"We don't have much time." Eric's lips barely moved as he spoke. "Do not attempt to use any magic while in the witch's bonds. You'll do harm to yourself and won't help either of us. When your opportunity comes, run. The tunnels here are all sloped. Head uphill, and you may find your way out in time."

The *may* part was super comforting.

"If you should escape without me, go to Lola immediately. Her guards will be able to follow your scent back to this place. They'll understand what must be done."

I glared at him with all my might.

"Try not to anger the bone witch," Eric said. "I really do think she might be willing to gut you."

I leapt six inches out of my seat as the woman pounded on the table. "Been having a nice chat?"

"Imparting a few final words of wisdom," Eric said. "The boy has been a poor apprentice to me. I would hate for him to make the same mistakes with his new master."

"Well, apprentice"—the woman leaned close to my face—"try and look moderately intelligent. One of your potential buyers is on his way."

"Ehaw?" I muttered.

Neither Eric nor the woman bothered to answer me as a man squeezed himself into the bench on the other side of the booth. For a split second, I expected him to say *Ah un mah he nay* and pull on the end of a leash of his own so a lady in a gold bikini could lie beside the table glaring up at him. But the blob of a man spoke real words.

"Someone from the top level was stupid enough to come down here asking for books?"

"Not at all," Eric said. "I was foolish enough to be captured by your compatriot. The desire to find a book source came as a convenience as I was already bound for a trip to the underground."

"What sort of wizard is he?" The slug-like man leaned across the table, squinting at me.

"Passable," Eric said. "Of moderate talent and intelligent enough to retain information. He does, however, lack commonsense and has a wavering self-preservation instinct."

"Ey," I grunted.

The slug's greasy forehead wrinkled as he tried to raise one of his too-thin eyebrows.

"Convincing the boy to do something even moderately dangerous is nigh on impossible," Eric said. "He will, however, walk into traffic while daydreaming if you don't keep an eye on him."

The first part was mildly true. The second, completely true.

I shrugged my apology for sucking at keeping myself alive.

"How much are you looking to get for him?" Slug turned to the bone witch.

I don't mean to be rude by referring to the guy as slug. I would have asked his name, but...gag.

"I'm looking to get whatever the auction will give me," the woman said.

"I'll give you $1,500 for him right now," Slug said.

$1,500 for me. It was impossible not to be insulted.

"I'm not parting with him for less than $10,000," the bone witch said.

"I suppose it depends on what you're selling him for," Eric said. "If one was willing to deal with the people aboveground to make money off him—"

"None of us would take our business up there." The bone witch spat on the floor.

Eric pursed his lips. I knew him well enough to understand that look. All the cogs in his twisted little brain were turning at once.

If the woman took me aboveground, she could easily get millions of dollars from my dad. Eric had even shouted about my dad being rich in the tunnels, so the lady had to know I was valuable. But she didn't want my dad's money.

"I'm glad to see you're a woman of your word," Eric said. "If you're looking for the highest bids on this boy, sell him to the fighting circles. I'm not sure how long he'd make it, but a stringy little thing who has a modicum of fighting ability would be a crowd pleaser. And when he should eventually fall, his bones would still be available for other purposes."

"The boy can fight?" Slug leaned across the table.

"Not with any sort of finesse," Eric said. "But he did help me kill Thaden at the battle of Beville."

Slug and the woman exchanged a glance.

"You've an interest in books?" Slug asked.

"A ara ree?" I growled.

Eric dug his heel into my toes.

"I am about to find myself bereft of volumes," Eric said. "I'm hoping to find a source who might have the ability to help me rebuild my collection in a timely manner."

"Books are about the hardest thing to find," Slug said. "If you'd rather some shadows who will swear their devotion to you, I can have you a healthy fleet of bondsman before morning."

If I didn't know Eric so well, I might have missed the flicker of danger in his eyes.

"I can get you bones," Slug pressed on, not seeming to notice Eric plotting his death. "I can even find you some artifacts, but books..."

"If you've nothing to offer, then I'll have to take my business elsewhere," Eric said.

"Funny, coming from a prisoner," the woman said.

"I have a source in France," Eric said. "It takes a very long time for her to come through, but at least she can deliver. And $5,000 a volume isn't too great a price to pay."

"Let me have his tether," Slug said. "I'll take him to Dupont."

"He's my prisoner," the woman said.

"Do you want me to tell Dupont you lost him a client willing to pay $10,000 a book?" Slug said.

"Five is the price to which I've become accustomed," Eric said.

"Ten is what you'll pay," Slug said, "and you'll be grateful for the opportunity."

"I suppose one must adjust one's price with the market." Eric smiled. "I'm sure what Dupont has to offer will be more than worth the expense."

"The tether?" Slug held out his hand.

The bone witch lifted Eric's leash away from mine and yanked on it, pulling him halfway across the table. A crack of light burst from the line around Eric's neck.

Eric's eyes barely twitched at the burn.

"You will deliver what you owe," the bone witch whispered. "Or I'll take my payment in bones."

"I am a man of my word," Eric said. "You needn't fear I will forget you."

"I don't have time for this." Slug flapped his hand in front of the bone witch's face. "Tether. Now."

The bone witch plucked the glowing strand out of her palm and handed it to Slug. She shuddered as the magic lost contact with her skin. More than shuddered. Flickered. Like the projector that created her being had somehow been bumped.

"Come, topsider, let's go and make me a very rich man." Slug struggled to free himself from the bench, then dragged Eric to his feet. The crowd parted, letting Slug weave through their midst and to the back of the bar.

And then Eric was gone, leaving me alone at a booth with the kidnapper who held the other end of my leash. I stared into her creepy bright eyes for a long time, trying to convince her without words that letting me go would be a really great idea.

"Sometimes, I forget how dumb Beville makes people," she finally said. "If you end up surviving whatever your new master purchases you for, try and pick a better mentor next time. One who won't sell you out to save their own skin."

I kept staring at her.

"Does he have more books in his house?" She leaned across the table, pressing her lips to my ear.

The truth was, yes, Eric had a few hundred books hidden in his house, but whatever Eric's plan was, however it had gone wrong enough for Eric to warn me to run uphill and hope I didn't starve to death in the dark, I wasn't going to tell the bone witch about Eric's secret treasure.

I leaned back as far as I could with my bound hands mashing into the seat behind me and shook my head.

B.W.—because if I couldn't ask the bone witch what her name was, then I had to make up something to call her what with the strong possibility she'd be the last human I'd have a conversation with before I was sold, murdered, and had my bones ripped out of my corpse for spell work—glared at me for a solid minute before speaking again. "Did you actually fight in Beville?"

I nodded.

"You must be worth something if you survived." B.W.'s eyes glinted as their color shifted to a dazzling, deep midnight-blue. "Let's go get you sold before someone decides to cut your throat."

"Aur?" I mumbled.

She slid out of the booth without answering my question and jerked on my leash.

Heat flared like someone had just lit a fuse wound around my flesh. Tears stung my eyes again, not because I was crying, just from the pain so close to my head.

I stumbled after her toward the door of the bar, blinking at the shadows, trying to catch a glimpse of Eric. But he and Slug were nowhere in sight.

There was no hero charging in to rescue me. Only sad, rundown people nursing their dirty-glassed drinks.

A pack of dogs raced across our path as we stepped back "outside." None of them stopped to sniff my butt or paid me any attention. The people we passed didn't seem inclined to look at me either, like if they didn't notice me, then they wouldn't have to feel guilty about my being sold.

B.W. weaved between stalls, cutting toward the sidewall away from where we'd entered Hell's flea market.

Soon, the wooden booths were replaced by tents that had their flaps tied shut, like the people who lived there had turned in for the night.

I shivered as we walked down the long row of tent homes, trying not to wonder if there were any kids stuck living down here.

If I could have spoken, I would have asked what we were doing in the residential section if I was supposed to be getting sold off. Before I could think through a way to communicate my question without the use of my hands or mouth, a wide opening in the wall came into view.

A pack of people milled around the entrance, under a sign that had been painted on the cracked stone.

Wiltzer's Underground Auction.

Cash Only.

No spitting. No children.

The people parted as B.W. led me past. This time, everyone did pay attention to me. A man leaned in, peering at me through his thick glasses. A boy barely older than me snapped a picture of me on his phone. A woman swung her cane, trying to hit me in the shins.

I leapt over the cane.

Cane lady gave a satisfied nod.

More than thirty people waited inside the auction hall. Most of them had already taken seats on the wooden benches facing the low stage, and those that had been at the entrance filed in behind me like I was the pied piper of human traffickers.

"I'm going to take out your gag," B.W. said. "Don't think it puts you any closer to getting away from me. You'll do what you're told, or I'll hurt you. Do you understand?"

I nodded.

"*Frico.*"

The gag shot out of my mouth, taking the top layer of skin from my tongue with it.

I coughed and gasped, trying to breathe through the horrible dryness the fuzzy material had left behind.

"Can I please have some water?" My voice crackled like I hadn't spoken in a year.

"No." B.W. yanked on my leash, sending a zap of heat to my neck as she dragged me up to the stage.

The platform was nearly as high as my waist.

I stumbled, trying to figure out how to climb up without using my hands.

B.W. pulled so hard, I landed face first on the stage, screaming at the pain searing around my neck.

"Shut up," B.W. growled. "You look weak. They won't pay as much for a weak one."

"Good." I struggled to my knees. "I hope you don't make enough off me to buy a cup of corporate coffee."

She slapped me across the face. The blow vibrated my eyeballs, sending the room spinning.

"Don't make me damage the merchandise." She grabbed me under the arm and hauled me to my feet.

"You don't want to know how things turned out for the last person who said that to me." I planted my feet and turned toward the audience, keeping my chin up and my gaze steady.

If I was going to be sold and murdered, if Devon and Elizabeth were going to have to search through the shadows to find out what had happened to me, I didn't want them to be told I had cowered and cried.

I stood onstage, surrounded by monsters in wizard form, and for once, I, Bryant Jameson Adams, was truly brave.

19

"Shall we begin?" A booming voice carried from the back of the auction hall.

All the chatter in the room faded away. I watched from my place onstage as the man who'd spoken prowled his way to the front of the audience.

I had expected someone in a suit and tie. Or at least a top hat and vest. But the man was wearing faded jeans and a polo shirt. He had jet-black hair and super pasty skin, a mark of one who had dived deeply into magic, but the dingy clothes and potbelly sort of ruined the wizarding vibe.

"Ladies and Gentlemen, welcome to Wiltzer's Underground Auction." The man leapt onto the stage without seeming to try. "It is always a pleasure to have you come to my auction house, and for so many of you to show up for such a last minute affair"—he shot a scathing glare at B.W.—"well, I guess that just goes to show how dedicated my patrons are. I suppose that's what comes from cornering the market."

A rumble of laughter rolled through the audience.

"For this evening's event, we have only one item up for sale," Wiltzer said.

"I'm not an item," I said.

Only a few people looked at me.

I took a deep breath and used my diaphragm to project so well my mother would have cried with pride. "I am not an item. I'm a person."

"It speaks." Wiltzer clapped me on the shoulder so hard my knees buckled, and I had to lurch forward to stay standing.

"Why would anyone want to buy a scrawny topside kid?" the old lady who'd tried to whack my shins asked.

"He's a wizard," B.W. said. "Fought in the battle of Beville."

The crowd seemed to consider me more carefully.

"And..." B.W. gave a dramatic pause, "until a few hours ago, he was Eric Deldridge's apprentice."

A hush rippled over the horde, and then like a director had given a cue, they all leaned forward in their seats, hunger filling their eyes.

"Tonight might be an interesting evening after all," Wiltzer said.

Sweat beaded on my palms. I wanted to wipe them on my pants, but I couldn't move my hands enough.

"This whole thing is pointless," I said. "I'm not worth as much to any of you as I am to my family topside. Mr. Wiltzer, if you contact my father, I guarantee you'll make more than any of these people can afford to pay."

"There's more to be gained in this world than dollars. We can't let a treasure like Eric Deldridge's apprentice leave our community, can we?" Wiltzer raised his hands toward the crowd, who roared their agreement. "When a treasure filters down to the underground, do we let it leave?"

"No!" The shout echoed around the room.

The thumping rhythm of stomping feet pounded from the audience. The stage shook, and the sound vibrated in my chest, sending my heart racing.

There's a way out. There's got to be a way out.

But Eric had said not to use magic, and there were more than fifty people between me and the door. And a shanty town between me and the labyrinth of tunnels I'd have to run through to escape.

Wiltzer waved a hand through the air, silencing the crowd.

"The bidding starts at $10,000." Wiltzer shoved me down to kneel.

The pain of my knees hitting the stage didn't pierce the numb terror racing through my veins.

"Do I hear 10,000?" Wiltzer spoke so fast, I could barely understand the patter. "Ten in the back, do I have ten-five? I have ten-five from the lady down front. Do I have eleven?"

I didn't know how much I had in my college savings account, but as the bidding went on, I knew if I had access to that money, I could outbid all of them. A phone call to Dad's accountant, that was all I would need to save my life.

"15,000, can I get a fifteen?" Wiltzer asked.

A hand shot up from the back of the crowd.

I glanced to B.W. I didn't know what her cut of my sale would be, but she looked like Christmas had come again.

"Do I hear sixteen for Eric Deldridge's apprentice, do I hear sixteen?" Wiltzer said.

"45,000 for the boy." The voice came from the very back of the crowd.

Murmurs fluttered through the audience.

I couldn't see the person bidding, but the voice itself made the hairs on the back of my neck stand up. My gut twisted as I tried to ignore my fight or flight reflexes.

"Well, then," Wiltzer said, "do I have 46,000?"

The murmurs stopped, like no one wanted to be mistaken for offering $46,000 for my sorry ass.

The person from the back moved forward in the crowd. People parted ways to let him pass. A bright white Mohawk tipped with black sliced through the horde like a shark swimming forward to eat me.

Then I caught sight of the face, and my whole body froze.

Kendrick McDonald stood at the lip of the stage, grinning like he'd just won a Tony award.

"No." My throat burned from the effort of forcing out the one word. "I will pay you one million dollars not to sell me to this man."

"Do you have it in cash?" Wiltzer asked Kendrick, ignoring me completely.

"I do." Kendrick waved a hand, and the teenaged boy who'd taken a picture of me before stepped forward, holding out a large bag. "Unless anyone here wants to outbid me, I suggest you take my offer and go home a much richer man."

"Why do you even want me?" I asked. "The Game is shut down. Your fighting ring is done."

"Not at all." Kendrick took the bag from the boy and tossed it up onto the stage. "Your interference at The Game was a setback, of course, but really, I should thank you. I'd grown complacent. I'd been thinking on too small a scale. But"—he turned to face the crowd—"Ladies and Gentlemen, I am thrilled to announce that after a brief hiatus, The Game is back and more alluring than ever."

He leapt up onto the stage, grabbing my hair and yanking my head so I had to face the crowd.

"There will be blood, there will be death, and there will be more glory for the winners than any of you could have imagined." Kendrick leaned down, meeting my gaze. "And Eric Deldridge's apprentice will be featured on opening night."

"I'm not going to fight anyone," I said. "You kidnap kids and brainwash them. I'm not going to battle one of your victims."

"You won't fight to save yourself?" Kendrick asked.

The cold eyes of the Lady I'd killed flickered through my mind. Her anger, her pain, clawed at my soul. But I couldn't bring myself to regret what I'd done. I wasn't sorry for killing her, even if it had broken a piece of me and I'd never be totally whole again.

"I'll fight you," I said. "You're a monster. If I beat you, I save innocent lives. But I'm not going to kill kids you've abused just to save my own sorry skin."

"Well, if you won't fight," Kendrick said. "Then I guess I'll just sell tickets to your execution."

He grabbed my leash from B.W.

She hissed as the spell left her flesh, and I yelped as Kendrick yanked me to my feet.

"Give me your weak, your frightened, your youths who are wasting away belowground. The wretched refuse of our magical world." Kendrick looked out over his audience.

Every person on the auction floor watched him, their eyes lit with admiration and something like hope.

"I will make champions of them." Kendrick grinned. "A generation strong enough to lead us into the light. No more hiding and begging for scraps. No more waiting for the human world to collapse on us. We are a great people. And my champions will lead us to a glorious new day!"

The slow clapping of a single person carried from the back of the room.

The crowd parted as though pushed by some invisible force, leaving an open space between Kendrick and Eric freakin' Deldridge.

"You know," Eric said, "if your new world weren't going to be built upon a foundation of kidnapping, human trafficking, and murder, I might be tempted to join your cause."

Eric's hands were unbound, and there was no sign of Slug. The only thing that made me sure I hadn't imagined Eric being hauled away with a leash around his neck was the bright red welt peeking up above his white shirt collar.

"I was hoping you'd join us." Kendrick bowed. "It seems only right you should watch me take your apprentice from you, as you stole my protégés from me."

"Some of them escaped?" I asked.

"I have no use for weaklings who run from danger." Kendrick sneered.

A bubble of hope floated up through my terror. Even if Eric and I never made it out of the underground, some of Kendrick's kidnapped teenagers had gotten away. In my sorry little life, I had actually helped someone.

"I warned you, Kendrick," Eric said. "I told you if you didn't stop, I would be forced to send shadows after you that you would not survive."

"And yet here we are." Kendrick yanked my leash down, sending me crashing to the floor.

My forehead bounced against the wooden planks, blurring my vision as I twisted toward the silent crowd.

"Your apprentice is mine," Kendrick said, "and you will soon be dead."

B.W. stepped forward. "Eric Deldridge owes me—"

"*Erunca*," Kendrick said.

The lightning of the spell flew from the ceiling, striking B.W. in the chest. As the light shot through her body, her face morphed. Her eyes darkened, splotches marred her cheeks, patches of her hair disappeared. She fell to the floor, screaming and clawing at her changed face.

"Hush, woman," Kendrick said. "I'm trying to enjoy myself."

"Normally, I hate having to waste time dealing with someone like you twice. But in this case, I can't express how grateful I am. If you'd hobbled farther away to lick your wounds, I might never have found the underground and this despicable auction house." Eric smiled as his gaze slid over the crowd. "But you all kindly showed up to purchase Bryant's life. Each of you is a purveyor of wizard flesh, and you've saved me the trouble of having to track you down individually. It's really more convenient than I could have hoped for."

"Am I the only one who's tired of listening to this arrogant prick speak?" Kendrick clapped his hands.

The teenaged boy who'd taken the picture of me stalked toward Eric. Five other teens emerged from the crowd to follow.

"Kill him," Kendrick said.

"I would encourage all of you to consider your next decision." Eric looked to each of the teens in turn. "You've been treated in an unforgivable manner, forced to grow accustomed to violence in order to survive. You are victims. But even the most abused of victims becomes the villain when they choose to inflict the damage done to them on an innocent. Walk away now, and I will consider you a friend. Fight on Kendrick's behalf, and you stand on the wrong side of a line that should never be crossed."

"Attack!" Kendrick ordered.

Light began crackling around the teens.

I opened my mouth to tell Eric to run and leave me behind. But I froze, my mouth gaping, as a line of people stepped up behind Eric.

Well, sort of people.

Lola's guards stared at the approaching teenage posse, their filthy faces completely calm. Behind them, a line of shadows with blurred edges blocked the exit into the cavern proper.

"My friends don't take kindly to those who buy and sell wizard flesh," Eric said. "You have committed terrible crimes, and your time of payment has arrived."

"*Calimarta!*" Phone boy shouted.

"*Primurgo,*" Eric said. The shield blossomed over him as a chunk of rock cracked free from the ceiling and fell toward his head.

Lola's guards raced into the crowd, blocking Eric from view.

I wriggled my way to my knees as the shadows joined the fight.

"Take the brawling outside!" Wiltzer shouted.

One of the shadows leapt up onto the stage. The shape held something dark in his hand.

"I said ou—"

The shadow's dark blade ran through Wiltzer's gut before he'd finished his sentence.

I clenched my eyes shut as blood spattered the stage.

"Let me out," I called to the shadow.

Kendrick tightened his grip on my leash, pushing his fist into the side of my neck.

"Eric," I coughed out his name, but the white-hot pressure of the collar on the front of my throat was too much to let me properly shout for help. I opened my eyes a crack. "Please."

The shadow faced me. He lifted his blade toward Kendrick, but the cane lady jumped up onstage, cracking her stick across the shadow's back.

"Filthy, do-good scum." Cane lady whacked the shadow in the back over and over until the darkness didn't move.

A small figure leapt up onstage, kicking cane lady's feet out from under her and sending her tumbling to the ground below.

Sniffer McDeadDog stared at me. His sad, wide eyes nothing like the decaying dog I knew lay beneath the illusion.

"*Kunga.*" Kendrick's spell hit Sniffer in the stomach.

He contracted as though punched, but the blow didn't stop him from leaping forward, baring his dog-like teeth.

The kid sank his teeth into Kendrick's wrist.

Kendrick howled and let go of my leash.

I collapsed to the ground, gasping for air as the spell around my neck faded.

With a bang, the kid fell to the ground.

"Don't hurt him." I rolled toward the kid, who lay unmoving on the stage.

Sniffer's sad eyes found my face.

"You sick bastard!" I forgot about not using magic and not being able to move my hands.

With coordination the likes of which I had never possessed in my life, I leapt to my feet and launched myself at Kendrick's stomach, knocking us both off the side of the stage and into the fighting masses below.

We landed hard, and I managed to ram my shoulder into Kendrick's neck.

He coughed and gagged.

I kicked as I kept him pinned to the ground, doing my best to fight without my hands.

Someone grabbed me, hauling me off Kendrick.

"Let me go." I fought against my captor.

"Thought you'd want your hands loose," a voice whispered in my ear.

I moved my hands in front of my face, staring at my palms in utter amazement of my newfound freedom.

"Thanks," I said, but there was no one standing behind me. I had no idea who'd freed me.

I lowered my hands just in time for a sizzling spell to hit me square in the chest. I stumbled back, crashing into the lip of the stage as Kendrick got to his feet and dove toward the fight.

As soon as I could gasp a breath, I shouted, "*Abalata!*" and shot the black of my spell toward the back of Kendrick's head.

He stumbled forward as my magic struck its mark.

Pain shot through my arm as something sliced into my skin.

I spun to see B.W., her silver knife in hand. Her face was half back to the overly beautiful way I'd first seen it, but patches of whatever spell she'd used on herself were still missing. "You don't get to run away."

B.W. lunged forward, aiming her knife for my chest.

"*Stasio.*" The clear walls of my spell pressed in around her.

I turned away from her shrieking, terrified face and looked back at the fight. Blood and bodies dotted the ground, but Kendrick stood in the center of the room, four of his cronies surrounding him.

Eric flung a middle-aged man at the far wall and rounded on Kendrick. Magic crackled from Eric's fingers as he raised his palms.

"Give up." Eric stepped toward Kendrick.

The four cronies tightened their pack around Kendrick.

"You call me a monster and then bring your swarm of beasts to spill the blood of wizards," Kendrick said. "You are more like me than—"

One of Lola's guards leapt toward Kendrick, soaring over the cronies' heads.

"No!"

I heard the scream but didn't have time to figure out who had shouted.

A blast of light knocked me back. My head cracked against the edge of the stage. Spots danced in front of my eyes as a *bang* shook the ground.

20

"Eric." I forced myself to my feet, swaying as I tried to get the room to hold still.

There were bodies on the ground. So many bodies. But Eric was still standing, glaring down at the sole remaining survivor from Kendrick's side of the fight.

"Surrender, and you will be allowed to live," Eric said.

The girl didn't look up at Eric. She knelt where Kendrick had been right before the flash of light. But there was no Kendrick, not even in corpse form. He and two of his cronies had disappeared, leaving the lone, living girl kneeling beside a boy who couldn't have been more than seventeen.

The boy didn't move. Not even to breathe.

"I am not without mercy," Eric said. "You were forced into Kendrick's employ, but you do not have to share his fate."

A shadowy hand took my arm, guiding me away from the front of the stage and toward the outer wall of the room.

"Kendrick is going to give us a better world," the girl said. "He is going to lead us into the future."

"Kendrick is attempting to become a very rich man by making the next generation of wizards slaughter each other," Eric said. "A new day for magic is dawning, but it will not be one built on greed and the murder of innocents. You will live to see that beautiful new world if you come with us peacefully."

"The world you live in deserves to burn!" the girl screamed.

Everything slowed for a moment. I saw the girl raise her hands, saw the flames burst from her palms, shooting toward Eric.

But he was on the other side of the room, beyond dozens of dead bodies, too far away for me to reach in time.

"*Aarantha!*" I funneled the twister of my spell toward the flames, trying to shoot the deadly fire up, away from Eric and toward the ceiling. But another force crashed into mine, a spell stronger than I could hope to produce. The two spells smashed together, trapping the flames in the center of the room.

Screams of pain crashed through the panic in my mind. I let go of my spell, but the flames and screams disappeared before the wind I'd created died.

A circle of scorched ground marked the place where the girl had knelt beside her fallen friend. There weren't even any bones left for the world to remember their magic.

Everything stayed silent for a breath that somehow seemed to take forever. '

"Check them all," Eric said.

The shadows and Lola's guards moved between the fallen bodies, making sure our enemies stayed down, helping the ones on our side who had been wounded.

B.W. lay sprawled on the ground. Her stomach covered in blood. The façade that had made her beautiful gone.

I was glad she was dead.

"Bryant." Eric walked toward me.

I couldn't stand still, waiting for Eric to reach me, waiting for him say something wise about protecting innocent lives and the burden that defense laid upon us. I stumbled to the stage, crawling up onto the platform with shaking arms.

Sniffer still lay on the ground. His gaze tracked me as I crawled toward him.

"Are you okay?" I asked, even though I knew he couldn't speak.

I'd hoped he would nod or something, but he just stared at me.

"Eric, I need help!" I took the boy's hand in mine. "You're going to be fine."

Eric knelt beside Sniffer.

"We need to take him to Lola," I said. "Can I move him?"

Eric hovered a hand over the kid, doing I have no idea what. "This won't be the end of him, but he needs to rest in a safe place."

"I'll be gentle, okay?" I lifted the kid. I'd expected some kind of weight in my arms, but he was as light as an oversized teddy bear. Sniffer had saved my life, and he weighed less than Mrs. Mops. "Thank you."

He blinked up at my face but said nothing.

"They're gathering outside," a shadow spoke from near the entrance to the larger cavern.

I squinted at the blur of darkness but couldn't make out any features to know who had spoken.

"Thank you, Charles." Eric leapt off the stage and strode to the door.

By the time I'd climbed awkwardly off the stage with the kid in my arms and picked my way through the bodies left on the ground, Eric had already stepped beyond the boundary created by the shadows and guards to face the crowd.

"My fellow witches and wizards," Eric began, "I've come here today with a warning. The magical world is changing. Gone are the days of doing terrible things and hiding beneath the notice of the Ladies. Know you are watched. If you kidnap, enslave, or murder, you will be brought to justice."

I slipped between the shadows, stepping out to stand behind Eric's shoulder.

Hundreds of people stood in the cavern, staring at him. Even the ones who held bats, knives, or chains just stood, staring at Eric.

"I am watching you. The shadows themselves are watching you," Eric said. "And they will not spend years waiting for fate to punish you for your crimes. If you are found harming your magical fellows, you will be brought to *our* justice. Bury or burn the monsters we killed today. They are your people, not mine. But remember them the next time you decide to abuse an innocent, for you will share their end."

Eric walked forward like he was daring the people to block his path.

I stayed right behind him, keeping the kid tight in my arms. Four of Lola's guards flanked us, shambling along, the blood on their clothes and faces the only indication of the vicious fighters they'd been minutes before.

The crowd parted, letting us pass. I glanced back to see if the shadows were following as well, but Charles and his people were already fading, blending into the dark edges of the cavern. Whether they were staying to stand guard or taking some other path home, I didn't know.

The crowd didn't seem to either. By the time we'd reached the back of the pack, most of the horde had filtered away down the other alleys winding through the warren of tents and stalls.

Eric kept a calm pace as we walked to the opening where B.W. had finally taken the bag off my head. A pack of dogs sat by the entrance, their ears perked up.

The kid shifted in my arms. I watched him make eye contact with each of the dogs we passed. I wished I knew what Sniffer was trying to tell them.

The dogs gave a single round of barks before scattering.

Eric turned to the guard closest to him. "If you would be so kind as to lead our way out."

The guard stepped in front of Eric and started up the sloping tunnel.

My whole body ached. The skin on my neck burned like the leash still wound around it. My legs trembled as we started uphill, but I didn't want to sit down or sleep. I didn't care how much I hurt. I had to climb up to the surface. Fresh air for me, a safe place for the kid to rest.

I needed to see Elizabeth and Devon. I needed to know they were all right and that there was something in the world beyond blood and fighting.

I stayed as close to Eric as I could as we trudged through the dark passages. We'd just left a bunch of people dead on the floor, and I didn't feel guilty. I couldn't.

Maybe I've already broken that part of my soul. Have I just gone numb to horrible things?

I pressed down the question. I wasn't ready to deal with that answer.

"How did they find you?" I asked.

Eric followed the guard around a corner and up another passage before speaking.

"I would like to take a moment to encourage you not to be angry," Eric said. "When fighting a great evil, there are times sacrifices must be made."

"Sacrifices?"

"They've been following us since we left the lamppost. I explained my aim to our allies, and they rallied to the cause."

"What cause?" I stepped up to walk beside Eric.

"Ending the trafficking of wizarding youths," Eric said. "Once I knew there was a genuine auction where kidnapped young wizards were sold, our necessary and immediate course of action became clear."

I stopped, swaying enough that Sniffer grabbed on to the front of my shirt. "You set us up to be kidnapped so I would get auctioned off?"

"The fastest way I could devise to find where the auction was taking place was to be led there by someone from the underground. I needed to connect the merchandise with the buyer. Trying to convince them I wanted to be a part of their horrible activities as a buyer could have taken months. Innocent lives would have been lost in our delay."

"Why didn't you tell me?" My voice echoed through the darkness. "I thought I was going to die!"

"That was rather the point. You needed to believe your life was at risk. If you'd known you were going to be rescued, no one would have believed you were in danger. I hate to offend, but you truly are a terrible liar."

"Fair." The anger rolling in my gut shrank a little. "But that was still a real asshole thing to do."

"If there had been another way to stop those vermin in a timely manner, I would have taken a different path." Eric placed a hand on my shoulder. "I'm sorry for the distress you've experienced, but I had no doubt if I'd asked you to accompany me on this mission, you would have agreed."

"I..." I looked into Eric's eyes.

He thought I was brave enough to walk into an underground lair as bait in order to save total strangers from a terrible fate. I took a deep breath, ready to tell him that the fact that I'd run off to help Elizabeth without thinking about my own safety didn't change the horrible truth that I really was a coward who lacked social conscience and didn't deserve that kind of confidence.

But the thing is, I really wasn't that mad about the whole *bait* situation. And, if he'd asked me beforehand, I'd like to think in some weird version of reality I'd have been brave enough to say yes. And I know this might sound like I'd lost my mind from the trauma of being led around on a leash, but maybe it was more important that he thought I was brave enough to risk dying to save strangers than it was if I thought I was brave enough to go through with such an insane plan.

"I guess I really should work on my acting skills." Yep, that was the super meaningful thing I finally settled on saying.

"Perhaps." Eric waved on the guard who'd stopped two feet ahead of us without being asked not to leave us behind. "Though I do rather enjoy how terrible you are at lying."

"Glad someone does." My chest shook with a weak laugh.

The kid stared up at me.

"Eric likes to make fun of me," I explained.

"I've never made fun of you. I can't be blamed for your quirks any more than you can be credited with my brilliance."

"Like I said," I whispered to Sniffer.

The guard led us through a tunnel so narrow I had to turn sideways to not hit the kid's head on the wall.

"What do we do about Kendrick?" I asked. "I don't think we're lucky enough for him to have just turned to dust."

"We'll hunt him down," Eric said. "It will take time, perhaps years. But I will witness Kendrick McDonald's death."

"What about the kids he already has? We've got to get them out."

"Indeed."

"Just indeed?" My lungs had started to complain about the exertion of walking continuously uphill, but I still didn't recognize where in the tunnels we were.

"We've driven the snake from his den. Now all we need to do is find where in the darkness the reptile is lurking. Charles will search the underground for more information on Kendrick and others who enjoy his abominable sport. Now that the shadows have scented his blood, it will be easy to trace his steps back to whatever dark corner he'd been calling home. I'm sure Kendrick will have fled once again, but we can hope Charles will find more information there."

"Shouldn't we be going with him?" I looked to the kid. "After I get you to Lola."

"Now that we've found the underground, Charles will be able to search its warrens more thoroughly than either of us could manage," Eric said. "Besides, you and I are going to be quite busy."

"With what?" My incredulous whimper is not something I'm proud of.

"Things that are best spoken of outside the darkness," Eric said.

Books.

My fingers tingled in excitement. I wanted to ask if I had guessed right, but there really were some things best not to discuss when you couldn't tell what lurked in the shadows.

If we'd had Elizabeth with us, she would have been able to tell if there were any weird creepy crawlies listening in.

Elizabeth.

"Did Elizabeth and Devon know about the plot to get me sold to Kendrick?" My voice wavered. "Were they in on the wizard trafficking sting operation?"

"No. Lola knew of my plan, but I thought it best not to tell Devon and Elizabeth. I didn't want to add more worry and trauma to the weight Miss Wick is carrying. And, while I would trust Devon with my life, trusting him not to tell you of the danger I was dragging you into is a very different matter."

"They are going to be so pissed at you."

"I've battled monsters. I'm sure I can withstand the wrath of two teenagers."

A rumbling sounded overhead, and dust floated down from the corridor ceiling.

"Did you fill my parents in on your plan?" Panic zinged through my chest. "I was supposed to message my mom before dinner. Is it even still Friday night? Oh, they're gonna kill me. Between Soaring Horizons and disappearing, I might as well start planning my funeral. Save Devon the trouble of making a playlist."

The kid twisted in my arms.

I looked down at his face.

He didn't show any real expression, but a sense of calm washed over me. Like he'd said something really reassuring even though I hadn't heard him speak any words.

"Thanks for that," I said.

"I placed Lola in charge of dealing with your parents," Eric said. "I've no idea what she told them, but she has a way of smoothing out the cracks in even the roughest of surfaces."

The guard slipped into a slit in the wall I wouldn't have noticed if I hadn't seen a person/dead dog thing disappear through it. Eric slid through the gap without pausing. A moment later, his hands reached back through the darkness.

I shifted the kid, carefully moving his weight so I wouldn't hurt any injuries hidden by his human façade.

Eric lifted him through the darkness so I had no choice but to follow.

Maybe that was the trick for me. I wasn't a pathetic, useless coward who'd spent months freaking out about killing someone in self-defense and almost lost the girl he loved in the process. I was a hero who lacked self-motivation skills. I could be brave and daring as long as I didn't have to actively choose to run at the battle.

I stepped into the stone crack. Cobwebs touched my face. But after one sideways-shuffled step, I was in a wide tunnel complete with subway tracks.

I took a deep breath, enjoying the faint stench of rotting garbage and urine.

"If I do end up grounded for life, do you think Lola could find room for me at the Consortium?" I lifted the boy from Eric's arms.

"There is plenty of room at the Consortium," Eric said. "Though I assume your parents would rather keep you in their homes than let you live down the hall from the lovely Miss Wick."

Heat shot into my cheeks.

Sniffer blinked up at me.

21

No one in the cluster of commuters said anything to us as we walked up the subway tunnel and climbed onto the platform. A wide half-circle formed around us, like everyone wanted to be able to keep us in their peripheral vision, but with at least ten feet between our pack and them. If anybody thought it was weird that I was carrying a silent child while surrounded by bloody homeless people, no one cared enough to try and save the boy from the potential serial killer that was me.

We got on the train, and I sat with the boy on my lap. I watched the patches of darkness and light race past as we moved uptown.

A nagging thought tickled the back of my brain, refusing to leave me alone as the doors dinged open at each new stop and a fresh set of people saw us and said nothing.

The commuters on the subway were willing to sit silently by while people just ambled past covered in blood. No one asked if someone was hurt or called the cops to report the possibility of a murder in the subway tunnels. No one tried to save the boy from being kidnapped.

They were bystanders. Complacent in the drama of life.

Sometime between when I'd found a phone in the back of a cab and when I'd been auctioned off, I had stopped being like the platform people. I couldn't stand by and watch things happen anymore. Like it or not, I had become an active participant, not just in the chaos of my life, but in the everyday drama of the world.

I sat up a little straighter, making eye contact with the people who glanced my way. I sent a silent dare out to each of them, willing them to care. Willing someone to ask if any of us needed help and who the kid's parents were and how he'd been hurt.

The train reached our station, and our pack left the subway car, a wave of whispers trailing behind us.

As soon as I hit the steps climbing out of the station, my phone started vibrating like crazy.

"Are you sure Lola said she'd handle my parents?" I didn't even try to fish my phone out of my pocket. My parents probably already thought I was dead. A few more minutes wouldn't make a difference in how bad the fallout was.

It had gotten late/early enough that a steady trickle of cars raced up Central Park West.

The lights inside the Consortium blazed bright, like Lola had been worried about her guards finding their way and had lit a beacon for them to follow home.

"I have seldom been so excited for a cup of tea," Eric said.

Before Eric could reach for the handle, the front door of the Consortium burst open and Devon raced outside.

"Bryant." Devon stopped in front of me, his eyes wide and face pale. "What happened to you?"

"Oh, my sweet little baby." Lola stepped up behind Devon, her gaze fixed on Sniffer. "Did somebody hurt you?"

"He saved my life," I said.

"Oh baby, we need to get you someplace to rest." Lola lifted the kid from my arms and carried him inside. The rest of her guards followed her.

"Where have you been?" Devon asked. "Lola's been pacing since midnight."

"Why did your life need saving?" Elizabeth stood in the shadows by the door, her face pale, her arms wrapped around her middle. She was wearing a brand-new, baggy sweater.

My heart broke a little. I should have been there when she got back from finding new clothes with my mom. But being with her would have meant Wiltzer's auction staying open. But Elizabeth needed me.

"It's a long story." I shivered as my body finally noticed the cold. "Are you okay?"

Elizabeth winced.

"Our harrowing tale is one best told away from prying ears," Eric said.

"Right." Elizabeth opened the door, holding it wide for us to enter.

"You look like hell, Bry," Devon said. "You're going to have to get cleaned up before you go home."

"And heal the mark around your neck." Elizabeth took my arm, gripping it tight as she laced her fingers through mine.

"That may be a bit more difficult," Eric said. "Devon, if you could be so kind as to bring us some tea and food."

I think if Eric hadn't sounded so horribly tired, Devon might have refused, but he just said, "Don't get to the good stuff without me," and headed to the kitchen.

"Why exactly will healing the things on both your necks be difficult?" Elizabeth asked. "You couldn't fix the scars on his hand either. If Bryant can't be healed anymore—"

Eric held up a hand to quiet her. "It has nothing to do with Bryant's ability to heal. Only the sort of enemies we've been facing. The witch who gave us these marks"—Eric pulled his collar aside, displaying the red welt that circled his neck—"used bone magic. Magic that evil leaves marks even Lola might not be able to heal."

"Great," I said. "I've always wanted to live my life stuck in gloves and turtlenecks."

"Order up." Devon shoved his way out of the kitchen, bearing a tray filled with tea and fresh-baked muffins.

I must have started drooling because Devon gave a half-hearted laugh and tossed me a muffin. "I think stress baking might be a new thing for me."

"I think that's a great idea." I took a giant bite, which shockingly didn't taste like sour butt.

"You have food. Now what happened?" Elizabeth asked.

"All Lola would say was that you had business in Beville." Devon set the tray on the table. "I think she was worried about us chasing you down there."

"We should have been with them from the beginning." Elizabeth stared stone-faced at Eric.

"It wasn't necessary," Eric said, and I swear there was a hint of guilt in his eyes. "We destroyed a haven for the ones who have been stealing wizarding youths and gained some very useful information along the way."

"And why didn't you want to bring us in on the fun?" Devon poured a cup of tea and pressed the warm mug into Eric's hands.

"You're both too human to have been able to attend the festivities," Eric said.

"And you didn't bother telling us you were going to do something dangerous?" Elizabeth asked. "Didn't mention to anyone you'd be disappearing until 4:30 in the morning?"

"It's that late?" I pulled out my phone.

Ten messages from my parents. Not too bad considering I'd been kidnapped.

"I didn't think anyone would be waiting up for us," Eric said. "I'm sorry if we worried you."

"Terrified." Elizabeth tightened her grip on my arm. "The right word isn't *worried*, it's *terrified*."

"I'm sorry, Elizabeth," Eric said. "All your fear is my fault, and I deeply apologize. But there are more important things to discuss than my lack of consideration. I have a lead on the books."

"You do?" Devon leaned forward.

"While Bryant was brilliantly working his way into the heart of the wizard trafficking circle," Eric said, not really how I remembered it, but I didn't fight him on making my part in the night's events sound more heroic, "I found a man who deals in magical books."

"But we're not looking to buy books," Devon said. "Even if we had the kind of money it would take to purchase a library's worth of books one at a time, there's no way we'd be able to get back the whole collection the Ladies lost."

"I'm afraid you're right on that particular count," Eric said. "I don't believe the books have all been left in one, unharmed unit."

"What do you mean?" Elizabeth leaned closer to the table, loosening her death grip on my arm.

"I believe whoever stole the books either lost some of them, or has sold off a portion of the collection," Eric said.

"How big a portion?" The bubble of certainty in my chest that had screamed I was a productive member of wizarding society started to deflate. "Are we going to go through all the work of tracking down the books to find out there're only a hundred left?"

"It would be impossible to sell the majority of the volumes," Eric said. "Most are of the type that could only be found in the Library. Think of it as selling a rare stolen artifact. Even if sold in the darkest of corners, people would hear of the Mona Lisa changing hands."

"Then why do you think any of the books were sold?" Elizabeth asked.

"I'd been suspicious since we found out the books had been taken." Eric took a sip of his tea. "There have always been illegal printings of books. The practice began the day owning books on magic was banned by the Ladies. I've acquired many volumes that were printed after the ban came into effect. In the early days, before the rules of impartment, there were many who, like Charles, dedicated their lives to searching the shadows for hidden magic. Some who allowed themselves to be coated in shadow took the risk of recording the information they discovered to pass along to others. But I have found a few books of such quality that I often wondered how they escaped the Ladies' purge."

"Purge?" I grabbed a second muffin from Devon's tray and shoved half of it into my mouth.

"When the Ladies took control and decided to limit the dissemination of knowledge." Eric chose a muffin and took a much more delicate bite than I had.

"And..." Devon said.

"They rounded up all the books," Eric said.

"Like, burned them?" Elizabeth furrowed her brow.

"Nothing of the kind," Eric said. "It would have been impossible to convince people to turn in their books if they knew the knowledge was doomed. The Ladies were far cleverer than that. They told the magical masses the books had been tainted. Evil plots were in the works to slaughter wizards through misinformation."

"How would that work?" I asked.

"Somehow, spells in certain books were altered," Eric said. "A twist to the language that would cause the spells to have deadly results. The Ladies sent out news of the altered spells, then asked everyone to turn in their books so the language could be secured."

"And people went along with it?" I asked.

"Not at first." Eric sipped his tea. "But after a rash of spell-related deaths, people turned over their volumes en masse."

"It was the Ladies wasn't it?" Elizabeth said. "They changed the spells themselves."

"A likely guess," Eric said. "Unfortunately, so much time has passed, I doubt we will ever know if the Ladies themselves committed the heinous crime of tampering with the foundations of magic."

"Can we get back to the books being sold?" Devon poured himself a cup of tea.

It didn't take a seer to read the tension on his face. His clenched jaw made his chin look more chiseled than ever, and his eyes were wide like he'd pounded six cups of coffee while waiting for Eric and me to turn up.

"I've sometimes found books and wondered how they survived the purge." Eric pushed away from the table. "I think it might be best if we go downstairs."

"Fine, but I'm taking the food with me." I snatched up the plate of muffins.

"I wouldn't dream of depriving you after the evening you've endured." Eric took his own teacup and headed for the door to the stairs at the back of the room.

"I've got the tea tray." Devon hurried after Eric, moving faster than the pot of boiling water should have allowed.

The door closed behind them, leaving Elizabeth and me in the restaurant.

"I'm sorry." I took her hand. "I didn't know I was going to be gone for so long, and I didn't want you to worry. It all just sort of happened."

"It always *just sort of happens*." Elizabeth laced her fingers through mine. "What did Eric do? He said he stopped the people at the auction, but how?"

"Well…" I swallowed hard, trying to buy time to find a better way to say it. "Basically, everyone who was bidding on me but Kendrick is dead, and Eric told the other people he'd be watching them and to be good or more death would happen."

Elizabeth's face went super pale.

"It was a big fight." I wrapped my arm around Elizabeth's waist, holding her steady. "Charles was there, and Lola's guards. It was over pretty quick."

"I should have been with you."

"With how Eric got us in, I don't know if bringing you and Devon would have worked. And we could see all the people we were fighting."

"We can't keep doing this."

My heart froze in my chest.

"The answer can't just be fight our enemies and hope it's them who ends up dead and not us." She leaned her forehead against my shoulder.

I know this makes me an asshat, but I was way more okay with her worrying about the death thing than her worrying about being my girlfriend, which is super screwed up but that's just the honest truth.

"Eric means well." She nestled closer to me, and my insides melted into gooey bliss. "And I'm not saying we were better off with the Ladies in charge, but we can't keep fighting and killing. It's not right, and eventually one of us won't make it back."

I leaned away enough that I could tip her chin up. Her sparkly eyes met mine, and I would have stood up to a dragon if it meant wiping her worry away.

"We'll figure it out." I brushed my lips against hers. "We'll find a way to—"

"Peacefully rule the magical world?"

"Yeah." I kissed her again. "We'll write laws and everything. We'll make things better."

"Sounds simple." A hint of a smile curved Elizabeth's lips.

22

Even though I could hear Devon and Eric talking, and I was holding the hand of the most incredible girl the world has ever known and had a plate of really good muffins to boot, I had a horrible, creepy feeling in my stomach as we went down into the Library.

The sound of my shoes bouncing off the walls seemed like it might somehow summon the ghosts of the Ladies to come slaughter us. Not that I knew if ghosts were a real thing, but my gut clenched in a way that seemed to scream danger lurked just out of sight.

"Elizabeth," I whispered quietly enough that Devon and Eric wouldn't be able to hear, "are there any creepy crawlies in the corners?"

Elizabeth's gaze swept around the circular space as we joined Eric and Devon.

She gave a tiny shake of her head just before Eric started to speak.

"I first noticed the phenomenon a month ago." Eric led us past the caged room that still had singe marks on the floor from when Thaden had burned the remainder of the Ladies' books. He stopped at the railing, staring down at the levels below us. "At first, I thought the Library was simply trying to refill itself."

"You are aware we have no idea what you're talking about." Devon set down the tea tray and leaned against the railing next to Eric.

I let my plate of muffins join the floor buffet.

"Don't ruin his big moment." Elizabeth nestled against my shoulder.

My stomach gave a joyful squirm.

"I acquired this book in the underground." Eric pulled a thin, red volume from his pocket. The worn cover had been marred with dark splotches.

I didn't want to know what Eric meant by *acquired*.

"A volume of summoning spells the likes of which I'd never seen. I don't think the book's former owner understood the treasure he possessed. This text wasn't created by someone digging through the shadows, hunting for knowledge. It's too old, too precious. This book came from the Library." With a flick of his wrist, Eric tossed the book out into the open air.

"No!" Devon lunged for the book.

Eric grabbed his shoulder, keeping him from tipping over the railing.

I opened my mouth to try and shout a spell to stop the book from falling to its doom, but the book wasn't plummeting down the five stories of empty shelves. It had started floating across the open space, gliding through the air like a feather blown by an invisible giant. The book drifted past the third-floor railing and out of sight.

I sprinted for the spiral stairs, dragging Elizabeth along with me. I ran down the first flight and straight to the next, stopping at the third-floor landing and scanning the polished wood of the empty shelves for the red spine of the book.

"There!" Elizabeth started running first this time, dragging me around the loop to where the book perched alone on the shelf.

The volume sat upright, like there were books on either side to keep it in place. We skidded to a stop in front of the book. I expected it to topple over from the vibrations of our footfalls, but the spine stayed perfectly still.

"How did that happen?" Elizabeth tipped her head to the side, studying the book.

"Lift it off the shelf if you like." Eric strode up behind us.

Fingers trembling, I reached out and touched the book. If there was an invisible force holding the book up, my fingers couldn't feel it. I lifted it from the shelf, reveling in the feel of the worn fabric cover.

"Let it go," Eric said.

I didn't want to let the book go. I wanted to sit down on the floor and devour every page, but I tipped my hand, holding my breath as the book slipped toward the floor and drifted back up to the exact same place on the shelf.

"That's one hell of a Dewey Decimal System." Devon took the book from the shelf, dropped it, and watched it glide right back into place.

"The Library's books have been sold on the black market," Eric said. "I've spent the last month sorting through my personal collection. I had inadvertently purchased two of the Ladies' volumes."

"No wonder they were so determined to stop people from owning books," Elizabeth said. "I mean, apart from having the knowledge and spell market cornered. All it would take was one wizard figuring out Library books were in circulation on the black market, and people would start wondering how the books had gotten out of the Library."

"And the Ladies would have been screwed," I said.

"Elegantly put." Eric raised an eyebrow at me.

"You said you'd found a lead?" Devon dragged his hands over his hair.

"The man who sold me this book," Eric said. "He had one specific point of contact for the procurement of his finer texts."

"And who is this contact?" Devon's face sank into a skeptical scowl.

"It's not a *who* so much as a *where*," Eric said. "The books have been coming from right here in the city, from the library to be exact."

"We're in the Library," Devon said. "Unless there's some secret passageway hiding a stash of books we haven't found—"

"Not this library." Eric walked over to the railing and stared up to the star-coated ceiling high above.

"If you say there's another magical library hidden underground, I swear—" I began.

"No." Eric held up a hand to stop my panic. "The New York Public Library. It seems our precious volumes have fallen into the hands of a human."

I squinted at Eric with my mouth a little bit open as I tried to reason through a scenario where a normal human managed to rob the Ladies' Library and survive.

"If a normal human has magical books," Devon said, "and the wizards he's been selling them to haven't, I don't know, murdered him—"

"Then to what lengths has this librarian gone to survive?" Eric tented his hands beneath his chin. "That is the problem we face."

Devon gripped the railing with both hands. "What time does the library open?"

"Do we have to go when it opens?" I tried to sound daring. It came out whiny. Saving the world has a learning curve. "I'm just saying, we could sleep and go in the afternoon."

"When fate leads you to information, you don't turn your back on the gift," Eric said.

"In case fate decides we're lazy and yanks the rug of golden strands out from under us." I sighed. "I know, you've explained it before."

"So what time?" Devon said.

"I need to think through our strategy," Eric said. "Facing a wizard is one thing. Facing a human who's survived magic is quite another."

"Devon and I are coming with you." Elizabeth stepped between Eric and me. "There will be no more running off without us. No more plans made behind my back."

"You've had a trying time, and—"

"And I'm still here," Elizabeth cut across Eric. "So don't delude yourself into thinking I can't handle whatever shadows are lurking around the book dealer. I'm not going to be shoved onto a shelf like a vase that might break. I gave up my family to be here. I have to make it mean something."

Devon took Elizabeth's hand and held it tight.

Jealousy curled through my stomach. Not because Devon was holding my girlfriend's hand, but because she needed someone who really understood what she'd sacrificed to be a part of the impossible world of magic. And I couldn't be that person for her, no matter how badly I wanted to be.

"We'll all go together," Eric said. "Though, under the circumstances, I think a reconnaissance trip would be an excellent first step. If we spook the dealer and he flees with the books, it could take us months or years to find another valuable lead."

"Sounds great," I said. "Go case the place and see if we can spot anything weird. But maybe we could sleep first?"

"The library doesn't open for a few hours," Eric said.

"Where do my parents think I am?" I cringed as soon as the words were out of my mouth, but Devon and Elizabeth didn't seem to notice my horrific faux pas.

"You and Devon went on a video game binge and both passed out after too much pizza," Elizabeth said. "Lola didn't have the heart to wake you, but she promised to keep you out of my new bedroom."

Heat flashed into my face so quickly I thought I might die. "Right."

"I need to think." Eric turned back to the red book balancing on the shelf. "I'll see you in the Consortium in a few hours."

"You're not going anywhere, right?" Devon crossed his arms and glowered at Eric's back.

"No," Eric said. "Though I do wonder what the right direction might be."

"Great." Devon headed toward the stairs. "You keep working on that."

Elizabeth took my hand and led me along in Devon's wake. The metal stairs clanged dully under our feet. The swirls of the design had been worn down by years of footsteps.

I could almost picture it in my head—the Ladies running up and down the stairs as they devoured all the information the Library contained. It was hard to mesh the images of the eager scholars with the evil despots, but maybe they hadn't been evil when they'd started. Or at least, they'd thought they were doing what was right.

Devon didn't say anything until we'd started up the fancy carpeted hallway.

"Do we really think there's a human book dealer hidden in the New York Public Library system?"

I ran my non-Elizabeth claimed hand over my face. "Sure. Why not? Sounds like fun."

"It would make sense," Elizabeth said. "You'd need to know about books to actually understand the market value of the stolen volumes."

"But do we really think he's human?" Devon asked. "Like really, truly, plain old human?"

"Probably not," Elizabeth said. "But we'll find out."

We cut through the sad, empty desk room and into the hallway of bedrooms.

I stared down the row, trying to remember which door I'd slept behind when I'd been bitten.

"Don't make mistakes you have to feed." Devon went into the first door on the right.

Elizabeth held my hand and led me farther down the hall.

"I don't remember which one I slept in." My head swayed a little, like my body had realized a bed was nearby and decided to shut down.

"Stay with me." She didn't look at me. She didn't even say it like a question.

She just opened the door to a room toward the end of the hall and led me inside.

Pale blue drapes covered the institutional-style walls, a deep purple comforter had been laid out on the bed, and shopping bags sat in front of the little dresser.

"Your mom and Lola work fast." Elizabeth gave a brave smile.

"Are you sure I can stay in here?"

"I really don't care." Elizabeth kicked off her shoes and pulled me down to lie on the bed beside her.

23

I'm not proud of the amount of drool that coated my hand when I woke up a few hours later. I am, however, super grateful that by some miracle my drool hadn't made it into Elizabeth's hair.

I lay in bed for a minute, curled up as Elizabeth's big spoon, trying to figure out a way to get the drool off my hand without waking her up, before I started wondering what had woken me up.

Blinking my gritty eyes, I looked toward the door, saw a shadow hovering over me, and freaked the hell out.

"Shit!" I tried to spring to my feet to defend myself, but I was caught in the blankets, so I tumbled face first to the ground as Elizabeth shouted, "What?"

"Shadow!" I yelped, trying to wriggle free from the sheets.

The shadow shifted in the darkness, and a face hovered just above mine. Sniffer McDeadDog blinked down at me.

"Oh," I panted as I managed to get one leg out of the covers. "You're okay then?"

The kid blinked some more.

"Elizabeth, does he look okay?" I asked. "Did Lola fix him?"

Elizabeth tipped her head to the side and squinted at the kid, not even shuddering at the decaying dog-like creature I knew Sniffer to be beneath the human illusion.

"He's got some bandages." Elizabeth stood and stepped over me. "But I think he's okay."

"Good," I said. "I'm glad you're okay, buddy."

The kid blinked at me some more.

"Did you need help? Is someone looking for us?" I felt like I was asking if anybody had fallen down the well, but communicating with someone who doesn't really answer is way harder than most people realize. "Is there something you need us to do?"

The kid went to the door and opened it, then looked back, waiting for me to follow him.

"Cool." I yanked my shoes on and grabbed my coat for good measure. "Let's go for a walk. I mean stroll. Not like a *walking a dog* walk."

"Quit while you're ahead," Elizabeth whispered as we followed the kid into the corridor.

Devon was already leaning against the wall outside his door. A smile snuck onto his sleep-creased face as he spotted me and Elizabeth coming out of the same room.

"Naughty, naughty." Devon shook his head. "Lola's going to have something to say about this one."

"Okay, Casanova." Elizabeth took my hand.

"Did the kid wake you up, too?" I asked, trying to pretend my face wasn't burning with a horrible blush.

"Yep," Devon said. "He usually only comes to wake me up on school days."

"The Consortium alarm clock system?" Elizabeth said. "I do have a clock on my phone."

Devon shrugged.

The kid looked back to make sure the three of us were following before trotting down the hall.

"Maybe Lola's making a special breakfast," Devon said. "Or she's going to go *in loco parentis* on the two of you."

"Or we're supposed to be at library downtown soon," Elizabeth said.

"True," Devon said, "but I bet we get breakfast first."

We followed the kid up the worn steps and into the restaurant. I could hear Lola in the kitchen, talking to someone as she made breakfast, but Sniffer didn't lead us toward the kitchen or to a table. He headed straight for the front door and booked it outside.

I paused in the doorway, pulling up the collar of my coat. "Do you want us to follow you?"

Sniffer looked back and blinked at me.

"That's a yes." Elizabeth led me out into the cold morning.

The sidewalks were quieter than they would have been on a weekday. The

Saturday strollers had taken the weekday bustlers' place, moving at a pace that was slow for Manhattan, but would still be considered speed walking in most other cities.

Sniffer kept glancing back as we followed him down the street, like the kid was afraid we'd get lost without him. He cut around a corner and headed east, only pausing to stare at a dog walker and her six charges who all sniffed in the kid's direction.

As soon as the dogs passed, he started hurrying along again, not slowing until he reached a newsstand.

"Elizabeth?" I whispered as the kid just stared at the booth on the sidewalk.

"Looks normal to me."

"What is it, bud?" I stopped beside the kid. "Are you okay? Do you need more rest?"

"I don't like homeless hanging out by my stacks," the newspaperman growled.

The kid bared his teeth at the man, then went right back to looking down at a pile of newspapers.

"Get outta here kid," the newspaperman said.

"It's nice to know you've got a heart of gold," Devon said. "This kid looks like he hasn't eaten in a week and you just yell at him?"

"I will chase you off this block."

I wanted to tell the newspaperman good luck with trying to make the four of us do anything, but my brain had gotten completely stuck on the paper Sniffer was staring at.

The headline was simple, startling, and utterly terrifying.

Teenage Shenanigans Cause Serious Problems

And right beneath, in grainy black and white, was a picture from the Lancre-infested store, complete with Devon's glowing sword.

My hands trembled as I picked up the paper.

A photo from Soaring Horizons with a tower of water erupting from the ground took up the bottom part of the page.

I started scanning the article from the beginning.

Mysterious property damage has been plaguing the Manhattan area since the appearance of Big Blue in the fall. The giant flower that dominates the once peaceful section of Central Park has been called everything from a miracle to a science project gone wrong. With the addition of the spire in Times Square not long afterward, and the unauthorized street art that caused the closure of the popular tourist destination The Game during the holiday rush, we here in Manhattan have started growing accustomed to unexplainable intrusions in the order that holds our borough together.

But those odd occurrences have taken a sinister turn with two major incidents of mysterious vandalism having caused injury in the past week. And eyewitness accounts seem to place the same people at both scenes.

The police have begun investigating...

I couldn't actually feel my hand as I reached into my pocket and pulled out the coins I needed to buy the paper. I just tossed them onto the counter and turned back toward the Consortium.

"Bry?" Devon took my shoulder.

"We have to get back to Eric," I said. "And I think we might need to talk to my dad."

I let Devon lift the newspaper from my hand.

"Damn," Devon murmured, "my sword looks really good in security pictures."

"And this is why superheroes wear disguises." Elizabeth took hold of my arm.

To normal people passing by, it might have looked like she was clinging to me for warmth, but really Elizabeth was steering me and making sure I didn't flip out and run away.

"Hey, buddy." I looked down at the kid. "Thanks for the heads up."

Sniffer blinked at me before disappearing between two buildings, moving quickly enough I knew he didn't expect me to follow.

"How many times has that kid saved my butt now?" I tried to laugh, but it came out like a weird gurgle. "I owe him a lot. That's a big magical debt I have to pay."

"It'll be okay," Elizabeth said. "Magic and fate might demand you pay up, but at least you owe one of the good guys."

"Right." I nodded. "That's nice."

"Uh oh." Devon stopped for a second before hurrying down the sidewalk.

"What *uh oh*?" I jogged after him. "You don't get to *uh oh*."

"*While the police have yet to release any more information on the suspects involved in the incidents, we have been informed that the ongoing investigation into these occurrences has become a top priority of the NYPD*," Devon read. "They even want people to call a special tip line if they know anything."

"Well that's not great news." Elizabeth let out a long breath as we reached the door to the Consortium. "I'm really glad I've already met Nikki."

"I'm really glad my dad can pay Nikki." I pulled open the door, bracing myself for the tirade I was sure Eric was about to launch into.

But the dining room was still empty.

"Lola?" Devon called as we headed toward the kitchen.

"Back here, sweetie," Lola called. "I made quiche."

The scent of coffee and food wafting from the kitchen made my mouth water, but I walked slowly, letting Devon lead the way. Because I'm a coward, and if Eric was going to start freaking out about the NYPD, I was totally okay with Devon being first in line for the firing squad.

Devon tucked the newspaper under his arm as we entered the kitchen. Not that he'd needed to hide it since Lola and Eric didn't even look up.

"Food's on the counter." Lola waved us toward the waiting pot of coffee and tray of cheesy quiche, then went right back to fussing with the bandage wrapped around Eric's neck.

"It doesn't seem to be doing anything," Eric said.

"First of all, how would you know if it's doin' anything?" Lola said. "You can't see your own neck. Second of all, I warned you that fixing damage done by bone magic is tetchy at the best of times. Third and most importantly, you are tryin' to rush my work. I don't like it when you rush my work."

"So, Lola"—Devon poured himself a cup of coffee—"I don't want to interrupt your being mad at Eric's obvious lack of appreciation for your amazing skills."

"I appreciate her talent," Eric said.

"Sure you do," Devon said. "But if I could bother you for a moment."

"You already are." Eric twisted to glare at Devon.

"Hold still." Lola took Eric's shoulders, making him face front in his chair.

"We've run into a bit of a problem." Devon slid a slice of quiche onto his plate. "This breakfast looks amazing, by the way."

"Sweetie, why are you laying it on so thick?" Lola pinched some bright blue powder out of a bowl and sprinkled it over Eric's head.

"It seems as though we may have attracted the attention of the newspapers this week," Devon said. "Also, maybe the cops, too."

"What?" Eric stood and strode over to snatch Devon's newspaper.

"If you don't mind, I'm having a conversation with the lovely woman who took this poor child in," Devon said.

"I'm not letting any cops or reporters near any of my charges whether or not they deserve it," Lola said. "So you can stop with the sweet talking and bring me a cup of coffee."

"The world would be such a simpler place without security cameras." Eric frowned at the pictures in the paper. "The images aren't clear enough to really look like us."

"I'm just the student who broke out of Soaring Horizons," Elizabeth said. "Are we taking bets on if the cops talk to my parents?"

My stomach shriveled into a tiny, terrified raisin.

"Do I call Nikki?" I asked.

Eric pursed his lips. "I don't think so. Getting that lawyer involved would only make her even more suspicious than she's already bound to be. And all they can see in this picture is you running away from a catastrophic pipe leak, which really doesn't imply magic as much as delayed maintenance."

"I mean, I may have made a door where one shouldn't be—"

"We have no evidence of there being footage of that," Eric said. "Nor can they try and blame the collapse of the stairs in the electronics store on us. We are completely innocent of that particular destruction. All we did was defend ourselves."

"Not quite how I remember it, but that's what we'll tell the cops when they come banging on the door of the magical library we happen to be sitting on top of." Devon sipped his coffee.

"What do we need to do?" I snagged a wedge of quiche, not even bothering with a plate, just shoving it into my mouth.

"We're going to the library to search for the book dealer," Eric said.

"Wa han." I tried to speak through my mouthful of heaven.

"We must," Eric said. "It could take weeks before the police even begin to associate us with these incidents. If the book dealer finds out about our overturning the terrible status quo belowground, they could run. We cannot risk losing the best lead we've found in the last two months."

"Might I make a suggestion?" Devon asked.

Eric gave him a little bow.

"Maybe we don't all walk through the city wearing the exact same coats we wore in the footage from the store?" Devon held up the newspaper.

I looked down at my coat. It was a fairly generic water-resistant winter coat, but you could match it plain as day to the identical old one I'd been wearing in the picture.

"Hmm." Eric tented his hands beneath his chin.

"Don't *hmm* like you're considerin' wearing the same coat out of pride, darlin'," Lola said. "You're the one who decided he wanted to make a better world. You don't get to fuss about an outfit. Don't worry, I'll make sure you're still a handsome devil. Come on, let's get you all incognito and ready to track down the heritage of our great people."

24

I was born with poop-brown hair, poop-brown eyes, and pasty skin. It's the lot I was dealt in life.

But I ended up a wizard that fate likes to wrap herself around with an amazing girlfriend who didn't seem to mind the poop-colored hair, so I'd sort of stopped worrying about it.

Maybe that's why I hadn't noticed my hair and eyes darkening to a shade closer to a shot of espresso that somehow made my pallor seem a little less pathetic. Or, maybe Lola was just skilled enough at whipping magic out of the drawers and cabinets in her room that she could manage to make anyone look good. Whatever it was, as I stared at myself in the mirror, for the first time ever, I wasn't pathetically ashamed of what I saw.

She'd combed my floppy hair to have a tidy part, which somehow made the ends have a little curl like my dad's. She didn't try to dress me as an under-taker/mini-me version of Eric, either.

I have no idea what special kind of magic Lola used to whip up a peacoat in an emerald-ish green that cut around my shoulders in a way that made me look like an actual man instead of a gangly kid. The dress shoes and slacks seemed like a bit much, but I liked that the turtleneck mostly covered the new red scar around my neck, so I was willing to give up my sneakers.

Devon looked like his normal, awesome self with a fancy new charcoal coat.

Eric glowered in the corner because Lola had refused to dress him in black and had given him a camel color coat that somehow made his jet-black hair seem even blacker. She'd given him a turtleneck, too.

Elizabeth sat in the corner while Lola worked. She was actually enjoying herself enough she had to bite her lips together to keep from laughing at Eric's snobby pouting.

By the time Lola smacked Eric on the butt with a spun-up sweater, Elizabeth had given up on pretending not to laugh. The sound of her joy mixed in with the rest of us laughing, and a tiny bit of the guilt that had lived lodged behind my lungs for months filtered away. Not all of it, or even most of it. Just enough to make me think that we were all meant to be together like this, and fate really would have found a way to make it happen even without all my screw-ups.

When Lola finally walked us to the front door of the Consortium, the whole *the cops may or may not be looking for us* thing seemed a little silly.

We strolled out into the chilly morning, and I was just happy to be walking through Manhattan with my friends.

"Do we have any sort of a plan?" Devon had to bring my joy crashing back down.

"Do we ever?" Elizabeth asked.

"Of course we do," Eric said. "We are going to go into the library, discreetly look for anything that might lead us to the dealer—with Elizabeth's assistance, of course—and hope we find something."

"And if we don't?" Devon asked.

"We reassess." Eric led us down the steps to the subway.

"That sounds easy." I wrinkled my forehead as worry crept into my post-makeover euphoria.

"Yep," Elizabeth said.

"This is going to get messy, isn't it?" I asked.

"Yep," Elizabeth said.

I watched the people in the subway car as we sped downtown. No one seemed to be staring at us like they knew we were on the front page of the paper, but people were looking at me differently. Like I'd become something more than just another blob for their eyes to glide past.

And the guys who ran their skanky gaze over Elizabeth looked at me differently, too. More like they wanted to congratulate me on having an awesome girl holding my hand and less like they were wondering how I was blackmailing Elizabeth into sitting beside me.

I sat up taller and wrapped my arm around Elizabeth's shoulders, owning the fact that the most gorgeous girl in the world had chosen me.

We got off the train at Bryant Park and headed east toward the front of the library.

I kept my gaze on the massive building, letting Elizabeth guide me through the tourists and locals battling for sidewalk space.

In a way, it sort of made sense that magic would hide in the massive library. It was two blocks long and way fancier than any normal library needed to be. Grandeur like that could easily attract the kind of people who stole magical books and sold them on the black market.

The weirdest, darkest things like to hide in the shadows or mix in with the refined. I have no idea why, that's just how it works.

Elizabeth paused at the bottom of the steps that led to the front doors, staring at each of the massive stone lions for a moment.

"Please tell me those are just sculptures," Devon said.

"I think so." Elizabeth took a step closer to the right-hand lion, squinting at the curves of his mane. "Everything's just a little blurry. I didn't get a lot of sleep last night. My eyes are tired."

"Great." Devon led us up the stairs. "This is starting off really great."

"Thanks." Elizabeth swatted Devon's shoulder. "Let's go stare at stuff."

It was my turn to steer Elizabeth through the passersby as we climbed up to the terrace that surrounded the library. With three arched doorways surrounded by fancy columns, it felt sort of like we were entering a government building. The way the Library we'd taken from the Ladies should have been if it were aboveground and had any people left in it to actually govern the magical world.

Elizabeth walked in through the center door with the rest of us trailing behind her, like she'd become our tour guide through the paranormal. She took a moment looking around the vast entryway before heading to the stairs that led farther up.

I had visited the library before—for research for school, for an author program, to hide in the air conditioning when it got too hot in the summer—but I'd never really taken the time to actually prowl through all the rooms the public was allowed to visit.

Elizabeth paused near an old writing desk in one room and laughed at a map that had California marked as an island, but she didn't warn us about any magic lurking in the corners.

A John Milton quote had been etched in gold above one of the doors. *A good book is the precious lifeblood of a master spirit, embalmed and treasured up on purpose to a life beyond life.*

And yes, I did modernize the spelling on all of that. You're welcome.

"Sorry," Elizabeth said as we circled the massive reading room that's way bigger than a football field, "as far as I can tell, there's nothing odd going on except that guy pretending not to have a massive crush on his friend."

I looked toward the crushing dude. He sat next to his friend, blushing to the roots of his blonde hair, as though watching his friend take notes was the most breathtaking thing that had ever happened in Manhattan.

"Romance is wonderful, but not what we came here to find," Eric said.

"That guy is slicing pages out of a book." Elizabeth pointed to a guy in the back corner.

"Despicable," Eric spat.

"I could ask at the desk," Devon said.

"What?" I coughed out a laugh and shrank into the neck of my fancy new coat as a passing librarian glared at me.

"This place is packed with rare books," Devon said. "I can just go ask if they have any old books on magic or spells."

"Or we could look it up." Elizabeth pointed to the computers.

"I can't charm a computer," Devon said.

I headed toward the computers, trying to think through keywords other than *stolen books* to search.

"I'd rather not rely on your charm at the moment," Elizabeth said. "I don't want a librarian doting on you. Quite frankly, I think I may have a librarian phobia."

I claimed a computer and stared blankly at the search screen.

"I don't think you have any reason to fear the librarians," Eric said.

"Because Devon is so charming they'll all crumple at his feet?" Elizabeth gave a soft laugh.

"No," Eric said, "because your aversion to librarians most likely stems from your interactions with the Ladies, and as we've learned they lost their books long before any of us were born, they really didn't do much work as librarians, now did they?"

"Okay," Elizabeth said. "That still doesn't mean I have to like librarians."

"You should talk to my therapist." I started typing in random words. "Maybe she can do a group discount."

"Or couples therapy," Devon said.

"Dev."

I didn't turn around as the two of them launched into a whispered argument.

Magic Books gave back way too many results.

Ladies Rule Manhattan got a little weird.

Books Stolen From Library was shockingly unhelpful.

"Honestly, I think you should both visit your guidance counselor," Eric said.

"Because I really need a motivational poster in my life right now," Elizabeth said.

Beville.

I typed in the word, assuming I'd get something about Bournonville Ballet, but *The Building of Beville* came up.

My hands froze over the keyboard, every one of my nerves vibrating like I'd just found the Lost Ark.

"Guys." I managed to get the one word out.

"She's pretty great, and you're going to need her help with college applications," Devon said.

"I think I found something." I didn't even turn around to look at them. I was too afraid that if I so much as glanced away from the computer screen, my discovery would disappear.

"That is very interesting," Eric said.

"Where's the book?" Devon peered over my shoulder.

"We have to request it at the desk," I said.

"Do it." Devon nudged me in the ribs.

"Perhaps we should consider our options." Eric tented his hands under his damn chin. "We are only here for reconnaissance."

"Really?" Devon said. "Of all the times to err on the side of caution, you choose now?"

"This is a lovely room," Eric said. "Damaging this architecture would be a true tragedy."

"I'm requesting the book." I grabbed a little pencil and scrap of paper and scribbled down the information from the screen before striding over to the massive librarians' station, which sat like a blockade of desks and fancy wooden dividers at one end of the reading room.

The lady at the desk smiled and beckoned me forward.

"I'd like to see this book, please." I held out my form.

She squinted as she tried to decipher my atrocious handwriting. "I'll send downstairs for it."

"Downstairs?" Elizabeth stepped up beside me.

"Yes." The librarian nodded. "We only keep the oldest, newest, and most requested texts on hand. Everything else is stored in our underground facility. It'll only be about ten minutes if you'd like to take a seat."

"Thanks." I gave the librarian a smile that probably came out a little creepy before heading toward one of the long reading tables.

"I didn't know there was underground storage here," Elizabeth said.

"Underground is where creepy things like to hide." Devon leaned backward, peering behind the librarians' desks toward the narrow elevator door tucked between shelves.

"We could wait here for the book and see if it's actually about the magical Beville. Or see if anyone tries to kill us for requesting it?" I offered.

"Or we get into that elevator and go see where the books are stored for ourselves," Eric said.

"I thought we were only here for reconnaissance." Devon grinned.

"The knowledge of generations could be below our feet right now. I will not let hesitation rob us of those irreplaceable riches," Eric said.

"Yeah, screw architecture," I said. "When fate gives you information, you use it."

"So, do I cause a distraction while you all run for the elevator?" Devon looked around the reading room as though searching for which item could cause the most damage.

"I'm pretty sure there are security cameras here." Elizabeth gripped his wrist.

"There aren't too many people behind the desk." Eric pursed his lips. "I should be able to sneak us past."

"I love a good *should*." Devon stood, brushing off the front of his coat in a very Eric-like way.

"After me, then." Eric led us toward the side of the wall of shelves, dividers, and desks the librarians had barricaded themselves behind.

Elizabeth laced her fingers through mine, and a warm tingle shot up my arm, erasing the very reasonable fear that had been brewing in my gut.

Eric stopped at the desk nearest the elevator. "Pardon me." He spoke to the librarian in a low and urgent tone. "I don't mean to shock you, but there's a gentlemen in the back tearing pages from a book. I heard him mutter something about selling them on the—"

Eric didn't even get to finish his half-lie before the librarian scrambled around the bookkeeper-holding pen, gathering his fellows for battle against the defacer.

Five librarians darted out of their shelter and toward the back of the room, heading straight for the book butcher.

"If it's Maury again, I'm punching him before I call security," the last librarian in the line grumbled as she passed.

"Near me, if you would." Eric stepped to the very edge of the desk and murmured a spell. I felt the tickle of magic against my skin, but I couldn't see any effect of the spell. "Moving slowly would be best. The spell is a simple, penetrable camouflage."

"Ah. Invisible, yet useless," Devon whispered.

"You're in a good mood, today," Elizabeth whispered back.

"The spell is also not thoroughly soundproof." Eric opened the gate to the librarians' stronghold.

I stayed close on his heels as we slipped behind the desks.

"Maury, you aren't supposed to be in here!" one of the librarians shouted.

Two more librarians abandoned their posts in the fortress of desks, racing to join the rest of the bookkeeper pack.

"Oh dear." Eric leaned away from the charging librarians while I yanked Elizabeth out of their path.

But Devon was still stuck in the opening on the wrong side of the gate.

"*Turso*," I whispered.

The spell should have knocked the librarians' feet out from under them, but they both just sort of wobbled for a second before collapsing toward each other and falling to the ground.

Devon leapt over them and to Eric's side.

"What are you doing back here?" One of the librarians twisted to glare at us.

"Umm."

Elizabeth grabbed my arm, dragging me away from the man who'd been gaping up at me.

"Where'd they go?" The guy sat up, staring wildly around.

"What are you talking about?" The other librarian asked in a muffled voice as she tried to stop the blood flowing from her nose.

"Sorry," I whispered.

"Maury, put the book down!" A low voice bounced around the room.

"Points for subtlety," Devon said.

"We've avoided structural damage." Eric pressed the elevator button.

"Go team." I huddled close to the others as the elevator doors dinged open.

We all slipped inside, and Devon pressed the button. "Going down."

25

E levators are terrifying places.
Not because I have little faith in the mechanics who maintain them, but because when you step into an elevator, you are voluntarily locking yourself in a moving cage. Which, for someone who had spent the last five months knowing various people wanted him dead, is a real problem.

As the elevator started to go down, I took a shuddering breath and made a mental note to talk to Dr. Spinnek about how to deal with my elevator fear.

Then I realized I should probably talk to her about my tendency to vomit when under pressure or stressed.

But then I should also talk to her about my newfound determination to be an active participant in the world.

Then I realized I really did need massive amounts of therapy right before the doors slid open, letting us out into the book-filled basement I had never known existed.

"For the glory of magic." Eric stepped out of the elevator and into a concrete hallway that looked more like something out of an action movie where we were going to have to run from mutants and desperately try to close the elevator doors before they ate us than a space that had anything to do with magic.

I pulled the spell-filled phone from my pocket as I stepped out into the corridor.

Something moved in the corner of my vision. For a split second, I thought we'd run into a mutant rodent guard who would chew off our faces to keep us from finding the magical books, before realizing it was a little trolley with a book in a basket trekking along on a tiny train track.

"Whoa." I stepped closer to the tracks as the basket tipped, keeping its book safe as the trolley started climbing the wall.

"Bryant." Elizabeth tugged on my hand.

I hadn't even realized Devon and Eric had gone down the ramp without us.

"Okay," I whispered, "but you have to admit that's super cool."

"Very cool and not the magic books we're looking for." Elizabeth tightened her grip on my hand, keeping me close beside her as another little book trolley went by.

"So cool," I whispered.

We didn't see any librarians or magical people as we crept down the concrete hallway. Voices came from up ahead, but not the scary kind of voices you'd expect in the tunnels below Beville. More like the teachers at school prowling the staff room for a cup of coffee.

The talkers came into view, behind windows that spanned one whole side of the hall.

I tipped my chin up and walked like I was not only supposed to be there, but was also considering buying the whole library as my own personal weekend retreat.

A man in a guard uniform stepped out from behind the glass and into our path. "May I please see your IDs?"

He said it in such a nice, friendly way, like he really did believe we had IDs and we'd just forgotten to clip them to our shirts.

"Of course." Eric pulled his card out of his pocket. "I actually have several questions for you regarding the safety of your collection. We've come to inspect how the manuscripts are handled. If my client is going to donate his father's collection of volumes, we need to be sure they'll be secure."

"I won't waste my father's collection," I said.

"I can assure you our books are handled with the utmost care, Mr. Deldridge," the guard said. "But I think you're probably supposed to have a meeting with—"

"The people who are currently handling a book defacer by the name of Maury?" Eric said. "They sent us down ahead of them. I think they didn't want us to see the disaster one rogue patron can cause."

"Maury's upstairs?" The guard's neck tensed.

"Shouldn't you already know that since you're supposed to be security?" Devon said.

"I should take the books to another library system," I sighed. "How disappointing."

"No, not at all." Sweat beaded on the guard's brow. "Every library has its book loon."

"*Book loon.*" Eric smiled. "I like that. Do you have security cameras that can show us how your people are dealing with the loon? I've recently discovered I have a fascination with security cameras."

"Of course, Mr. Deldridge." The security guard bowed Eric toward the glass-enclosed rooms. "I'd be happy to show you our camera system while I contact the curator."

"Perfect." Eric glanced at Devon. "My assistant can pull up a list of the titles Mr. Adams wishes to donate."

Devon and Eric flanked the security guard as they walked away.

Eric gave a flick of his hand behind his back, pointing Elizabeth and me down a twist in the corridor.

"Come on." I studied the concrete walls with disdain as I walked down the narrow hall, doing my best impression of the time my dad had lowered his standards enough to step inside my public high school.

"See anything?" My question came out like I was portraying a snooty duke in a school play.

"Not really." Elizabeth ran a hand across her eyes. "Everything looks fuzzy."

"Fuzzy like how?" I glanced toward Elizabeth.

"Like I got eyelash glue in my eyes."

I stepped in front of Elizabeth, blocking her path. "Can you see me?"

"Yeah, up close is fine. Everything else is a little blurry."

I licked my lips to try and stop my mouth from going so dry I'd choke on my own tongue and wrapped my arm around Elizabeth's waist, keeping her tucked close to my side as we continued down the corridor.

"I don't want to freak you out," I said, "but you went three months without sleeping and never complained about your eyes going fuzzy. What are the chances of someone being able to make it so your super seer vision is wonky?"

"Lola never mentioned anyone being able to do that."

We reached the end of the corridor. A room filled with metal shelves stretched out in front of us.

"But if someone were to have lost knowledge from stolen books?" I whispered.

Elizabeth leaned closer to me. "I don't know."

"Okay." We started down the row of shelves. "We're going to be okay. I won't let anything happen to you."

The shelves in this space weren't the kind you'd find in a normal human library. They were the fancy kind that you could move back and forth with the press of a button, so you could get to books when you wanted to and then mash the shelves right up next to each other when you didn't need to walk down those rows.

"There's got to be some sort of summoning spell," I said.

"Or we look up *The Building of Beville*." Elizabeth dragged me to a little computer in the corner.

My skin started to prickle as Elizabeth clicked away on the computer. I should have saved the paper I'd written the information on upstairs, or insisted we stay with Devon and Eric.

"Got it." Elizabeth stopped typing and took my hand, leading me between the rows of moving shelves.

"What if we find the books but the dealer isn't here?" My heart thundered in my chest.

"We take whatever books there are and make a run for it." Elizabeth shrugged.

We kept walking and walking down the rows, going farther than it seemed like the underground space should have been able to stretch.

"I think it should be..." Elizabeth squinted at the label on the shelves then cut down a row walled with books.

I didn't like the books being packed in on either side of me, but before real panic could set in, we'd reached the other end of the row and were out onto another wide pathway.

"It should be right here." Elizabeth stopped next to a shelf that had already been moved aside like someone had just come to retrieve *The Building of Beville*.

I let out a long breath as I stepped into the row. Books towered on either side of me. I wanted to stop and read all their titles. See how many of them might have something to do with magic. But Elizabeth walked down the row without pausing.

"*The Building of Beville* should be right here." She reached toward the shelf.

The skin on my arms and neck started to tingle, like fate had drawn me into magic just so I could arrive at that exact moment. So that I, Bryant Jameson Adams, teenage wizard, could reunite magickind with the knowledge of ages.

But then too many things happened at once.

I realized the book we were searching for was already gone, the tingle on my skin changed from a buzz to a horrible stinging, and Elizabeth screamed as the shelves started sliding in toward us.

Gritting my teeth against the ache that burrowed down into my bones, I grabbed Elizabeth's arm and dragged her back down the row.

A green light flashed as I hit some invisible barrier that knocked me back onto Elizabeth. We both hit the cold concrete.

"Bryant!" She managed to get up first and yanked me to my feet.

We raced toward the other end of the row, but the shelves were creeping too close, squeezing in on either side like we'd taken a chute into the trash compactor of a spaceship.

"*Primurgo!*" I shouted the spell, but nothing happened.

Elizabeth pulled away from my grip.

I didn't want her to step away from me. If we were going to be crushed, I wanted to die holding her in my arms.

She grabbed an armful of books on the shelf at waist height and tossed them onto the floor.

A gasp came from the end of the row.

A man with bright red hair stared in horror at the books on the ground.

But Elizabeth didn't pause. She dove into the gap she'd just created, knocking away the books on the other side of the shelf.

"No, no, no!" the man at the end of the row shouted as I chucked a few extra books to the floor. He slammed his fist against the wall, and the shelves stopped sliding toward each other.

I didn't trust the danger was over. I dove after Elizabeth, knocking my head on the metal of the shelf above me, and squirmed out into the next row in a horribly awkward way.

"Come on." Elizabeth grabbed me under my arms, hoisting me to my feet.

Sprinting to the end of the row, I caught a glimpse of the red-haired man running away between another pair of shelves. Elizabeth and I tore after him, catching up to him before he made it to the end of the row.

"*Abalata!*" I shouted the spell, the spell I knew well, the spell I'd used to save my life more than once, and nothing happened. We kept chasing the redhead. "Stop!" Shouting at him didn't do me any more good than the spell had.

He dodged out into the next aisle, heading toward an emergency exit.

"Stop, or I'll burn the books!" I shouted.

The redhead's footsteps faltered.

"I'll burn them all." I made my voice sound confident and strong, like I was actually a person who not only had a lighter on him, but would also consider burning a few million books.

The man took a few more slogging steps.

"We just want to talk," Elizabeth said. "Tell us what we want to know, and you and the books don't have to get hurt."

The redhead started to turn around.

"We're looking for the books that were stolen." I took a step forward. "You're too young to have taken them yourself, but I think you know who did."

"I don't know what you're talking about," the redhead said. "Security will be here any second. We can't have lunatics coming into our storage area."

"Is he a monster," I whispered to Elizabeth.

"Everything's still blurry," Elizabeth said, "but he seems normal."

"Look"—I took another step toward the redhead—"I know you know about the books. *The Building of Beville.* Whatever shield kept us from leaving that row when you tried to smush us to death."

"I never—"

"Lying will get you nowhere," I said. "I'm giving you a chance to give me the information I want before my friends catch up. I promise this is as peaceful and polite as things are going to get."

The redhead's face twisted into a sneer. "You're not the first to try and steal the books." He pulled the ring off his finger and chucked it at me.

I grabbed Elizabeth and yanked her between two shelves, shielding her with my body as the ring exploded in a haze of steaming purple and green.

I pulled my turtleneck over my nose and ran back out into the aisle. I don't know what the smoke was made of. It stung my eyes, making everything blurry.

But I could still hear.

Footsteps pounded, not toward the emergency exit, but back the way we'd already come.

I grabbed Elizabeth's arm and dragged her down the aisle, keeping one hand in front of me, trying to save myself from going face first into a bookshelf.

Through my murky vision, I caught a glimpse of the freakin' ginger the second before the smoke alarm started blaring.

"Just great." I kept running after the redhead, not just because I wanted the books. I was also hoping he was smart enough to have had an escape plan before setting off a smoke bomb inside.

We rounded a corner, and the redhead was there, waiting for us with one fist raised high.

I let go of Elizabeth and ducked low, barreling toward the redhead's stomach.

He twisted out of my path, and the thing he'd been holding fell from his hand.

I watched the tiny chunk of carved white fall to the ground.

"Bone magic!" I swerved to change course, grabbing the collar of the redhead's coat and punching him hard in the back of the head.

He reached into his pocket as he stumbled forward.

"Bryant!"

I turned toward the shout.

A bright red light blossomed to life as Devon pulled out his glowing sword.

26

"What the hell!" the redhead screamed as he tried to run away from us. Devon charged into the redhead's path, grasping his sword in one hand while slipping his other hand into his pocket.

"Devon, watch out!" I shouted as the redhead reached into his own pocket. I leapt forward, ready to tackle the redhead rather than let him use bone magic on my best friend.

Devon was faster. He whipped a purple, sparkly water gun from his pocket and sprayed the redhead's feet.

"Ahh!" The redhead screamed as he toppled forward, his shoes suddenly stuck to the ground with grayish-green goo.

"What?" I stumbled to a stop, staring down at the redhead.

"Stay away from me!" The redhead lifted his hand.

Devon squirted the redhead's fist, covering it with goo.

"What is this stuff?" The redhead tried to unclench his hand, but Devon's goo wouldn't let his fingers move. "Who the hell are you people?" He tried to kick out of his shoes and crawl away.

"I can keep spraying you." Devon planted himself in the redhead's path, sparkly water gun aimed straight at the redhead's head. "Trouble is, I'm pretty new to this potion game, and I've only figured out how to brew the trapping potion. I don't actually know how to make the untrapping part yet."

"Potions?" I asked. "When did you start messing with potions?

Elizabeth elbowed me in the gut.

"You can't do this to me," the redhead said.

"I'm afraid you'll find we can." Eric stepped up to stand beside Devon. "You, sir, have clearly been meddling with some things that ought not to be meddled in."

"Running a legitimate business is not meddling," the redhead said.

"No," Eric said, "but selling books stolen from the Ladies is bound to bring disastrous consequences."

The redhead tried to reach for his pocket with his other hand.

"Don't make me," Devon said. "I sincerely don't know how to unstick you."

The redhead lay on the floor, glaring up at all of us with hate and fear. "Security will come."

"And you'll explain to them that wizards have invaded the library?" Elizabeth laughed. "I think not."

"Where are the books?" Eric asked.

"*The Building of Beville* is on its way upstairs," the redhead said. "I'm sure a librarian at the desk would be happy to help you."

"Not the volume you placed in the system that anyone could request." Eric knelt beside the redhead. "The books you are selling. Where in this building are they? Tell us, or my friend will stick your hands together in a quite possibly irreparable way."

The redhead spat on Eric's shoe.

"All right then." Eric grabbed the redhead's hands pinning them together behind his back.

"They aren't here!" the redhead shouted. "I'm not dumb enough to keep them here."

"A hand, Bryant." Eric and I grabbed the redhead under his arms, dragging him out of his glued-to-the-floor shoes and onto his feet.

"Devon, if our new friend tries to run—" Eric began.

"Goop him, or slice him?" Devon grinned.

"Your choice." Eric nodded and led us toward a glowing exit sign. "Since you are the one who came prepared, I feel it's only fair."

"I was prepared," I muttered, choosing feeling miffed at Devon getting the praise over being terrified of why my magic had suddenly abandoned me.

"You're not going to get away with this," the redhead growled as Eric kicked open the emergency exit door.

"Of course we are," Devon said. "Your bigger worry right now should be how much damage are you going to take before you realize I'm right."

The redhead didn't argue as we marched him up the concrete steps.

It didn't take long for us to reach a metal door.

Devon flicked off his sword. "I'll pull it back out if you make me." He shoved open the door, which led us out into Bryant Park. "Allons-y." Devon pushed the redhead forward.

The redhead shuddered as he stepped in a puddle.

I gave a sympathy grimace as city goo soaked through his paisley socks.

"Start talking," Eric said, "now."

"If you think—"

"Don't be belligerent," Eric said.

I followed the others, stepping fully free of the library, and it was like a weighted blanket had been lifted off me. Or like I was shedding some giant cocoon.

Elizabeth gasped and blinked.

I took her arm.

"Oh, I can see better now and he's definitely human, but there is some weird glow of death around him that I do not like." She took a few deep breaths like she was trying not to puke. "Why couldn't I see before? What made my eyes go blurry?"

"Keep moving." Eric tightened his grip on the redhead's arm, half-dragging him out onto the lawn.

I locked my gaze on a water bottle someone had tossed on the ground. "*Conorvo*." The bottle shrank to a doll-sized, dinky thing. I took a breath. The city air flooded my lungs, and I suddenly realized that not being able to access my own magic was nearly as terrifying as being kidnapped.

"Start from the beginning." Eric sat the redhead down on the side of a stone boundary/railing.

"I'm not going to—"

Devon pointed his sparkly water gun at the redhead's face.

The redhead shuddered. "What do you want to know?"

"How did you get the books?" Eric said.

I kept ahold of Elizabeth's arm, keeping her steady as she sat on the stones four feet away from the redhead. She still had a look of horror mingled with disgust on her face.

"I work in a library." The redhead sat up straight and tipped his chin toward the massive building. "I have access to millions of books."

"This would be easier if you didn't play dumb." Devon aimed his sparkly water gun at the redhead's crotch.

"I will put you on the *do not sell* list," the redhead said. "I don't care how much you offer, you aren't buying shit from me."

"You're right." Eric snapped his fingers, and a little bolt of lightning appeared in his palm. "We're not buying anything. We're going to take all the books you have, and we're not giving you a cent for them. Now, if you cooperate, you'll minimize your suffering. If you fight us, we'll have to take a little trip across town, and your day will become infinitely worse than it already is."

Eric had a gleam in his eye that the redhead somehow wasn't smart enough to interpret as *I'm really just looking for a good reason to kill you, so please keep defying me so I won't have to feel guilty about your death.*

"It's not worth it," the redhead said. "Whatever you think you're after, I promise, it's not worth it."

"I assure you," Eric said, "even one of those precious books is worth more to me than your life. Do no test my determination."

"It doesn't matter what I tell you," the redhead said. "I'm doomed anyway."

"Doomed." I laughed. Not like a little laugh. Like a loud, carrying guffaw that made the lady pushing her dog past in a stroller turn to glare at me. "That is such a defeatist attitude." I took a breath to make myself calm down. "I mean, you're a human who tried to squeeze a wizard and a seer to death between two bookshelves. Sure, we got out of it, and yes, we had backup, but you don't plant a trap like that unless you think someone is coming for you. And you'd have to be a real idiot to think that a smushing spell and throwing a few enchanted bones would be enough to save you when people like us finally came knocking on your library's door."

"People like you weren't supposed to come after me," the redhead said, "just pay me and walk away."

"Well, things didn't turn out that way," Devon said. "So are you going to pout about it, or are you going to answer our questions?"

"Where are the books?" Eric held the lightning bolt toward the redhead's face like he was offering him a cookie.

"I have all eight in another location." The redhead leaned away from Eric.

"Eight?" I said.

"Another location?" Devon shifted his wrist and squirted the weird goo onto the railing next to the dude.

"My apartment." The redhead flinched and shifted toward me. "I have them in my apartment."

"And the rest?" Eric drummed his fingers against the bolt, making it crackle, giving off a scent like a lightning storm had just busted through midtown.

"That's it," the redhead said. "I don't have any more."

"Do not test me." Eric tossed the lightning shard at the redhead's sock-clad feet.

The redhead yelped as the bolt left a singe mark in his sock. "That's literally all I have."

"Liar." A fresh bolt appeared in Eric's hand.

"I'm not lying," the redhead shouted loud enough for the passing Mahattanites to glance our way.

"Should we take this somewhere else?" I whispered.

"I will not be taken to a secondary location." The redhead tried to stand, but Eric shot a tiny bolt right into his chest. The redhead coughed.

"Don't think you can make me feel sorry for you," Devon said. "You tried to kill my best friends."

"Look"—I let go of Elizabeth and stood beside Eric—"I know that from your perspective this is going to be really hard to grasp, but we're not actually the bad guys. The books you've been selling were stolen from some very, very, excruciatingly bad people, so you're really lucky we're the ones who are trying to get some information."

"Maybe I'd believe you if my hand was free." The redhead held up his goo-covered fist.

"Maybe I'd try to free you if you hadn't tried to kill my friends." Devon shrugged.

"Can we just start with an easy question?" I said.

"Not here we can't." Elizabeth nodded toward the street corner where the dog stroller lady was talking to a policeman.

"Let us walk." Eric looped his arm through the redhead's. "Where is your apartment?"

"I'm not going—"

"*Frico*." The redhead's wallet flew out of his pocket and into my waiting hand. "Our friend William lives all the way up in Hell's Kitchen."

"Why up there?" Devon looked redhead William over. "Why does magic like to cluster together like that?"

"Are you actually asking me?" Redhead William asked.

"Yes." Devon poked William's elbow with his water gun.

"It's a rent-controlled apartment and the super answers his phone," William said.

"Bryant, call our driver friend," Eric said.

I was about to argue that calling my dad's driver would be a terrible idea, but then I remembered my *SOS Car* entry for the world's best cabbie.

He answered on the second ring. "Hello?"

"Hi, this is the guy from the New Jersey fare yesterday." I kept my tone all calm and chill. "Is there any chance you could swing by the northwest corner of Bryant Park to pick me up?"

"Triple the fare and a good tip?" Cabbie asked.

"Absolutely." A bubble of super mature pride grew in my chest even though I knew full well I was just offering up my rich father's money.

"Be there in a few."

"You're not going to get away with this," William said.

"Is it because of the bone magic you've still got waiting in your pockets?" Elizabeth asked.

Eric slid his hand into William's pocket, biting back a tiny gasp as he closed his hand around something.

"What did you do to the library to make it so I couldn't see right?" Elizabeth asked.

Eric pulled the thing from William's pocket and slipped it into his own coat.

"The other one, too," Elizabeth said.

Devon reached into William's other pocket but didn't react as he grabbed whatever the librarian had stashed in there.

"That it?" Devon asked.

"Yes," Elizabeth said. "Now it looks like death is surrounding you two instead of him. But it doesn't answer why I couldn't see inside the library. I should have known there was something awful lurking in the basement the moment I stepped into that place."

"Maybe you're just not that talented," William said.

"Nonsense," Eric said. "I myself had trouble with my magic once we reached the basement level. Even maintaining a simple illusion in the reading room took an extraordinary amount of concentration."

"Maybe you're not that talented either." William shrugged.

Devon dug his heel into William's toe.

"Were I less experienced or lacked confidence—" Eric began.

"That's never gonna happen," Devon said.

"—I might be inclined to believe such a lie." Eric ignored Devon. "However, I have faced darkness far beyond what humans with bone magic create as they plunge the murky depths of evil. Whatever barrier, or perhaps the better term would be dampening, you cast around the library was not simply bone magic created by one desperate and repulsive human. There was knowledge behind the act. Knowledge I suspect you gained from the books you have hoarded away from their rightful owners."

"Rightful owners?" William coughed a laugh and strained against Eric's grip. "You don't even know what you're talking about."

"I believe it might be you who has less information than he knows," Eric said.

A cab pulled up and stopped right in front of us.

The world's best cabbie looked out his window. "I only have room for four."

"And if your tip goes from great to obscene?" I asked.

"Hop on in." The cabbie didn't say anything else as Devon, Elizabeth, and I all crammed into the back with William while Eric climbed into the front seat.

Once we'd packed ourselves in like sardines and actually managed to close the door, Elizabeth shifted to sit on my lap and heat raced into my cheeks. Suddenly kidnapping/capturing a bone-magic-using librarian was a great weekend treat.

Eric read William's address off his license, and the cabbie nosed out into traffic.

"You're all a bunch of idiots," William said.

"Why do you say that?" Devon tossed his sparkly water gun from one hand to the other.

"Excuse me, sir." William leaned toward the cabbie. "These people are holding me against my will. I'm a victim, and I need your assistance."

"What are you doing?" I peeked around Elizabeth to ask.

"You want one prisoner, try dealing with two." William gave a self-satisfied smile. "You'll have to hold both of us now."

"You folks really are into role playing." The world's best cabbie laughed. "Runaways, prisoners, you should start one of those murder mystery party groups. I bet you'd make great money."

"Thanks." Devon smiled at William. "Always good to know we've got a driver on our side."

"You people are insane." William shuddered.

"That's debatable," I said. "But I am working with an excellent therapist."

We all sank into silence as we made our way uptown. I had questions I wanted to ask, but I didn't want to push our cabbie-luck. I also didn't want to be the one doing the asking if it was going to mean me having to throw tiny shards of lightning at a guy I'd only met, like, an hour before.

But the guy had tried to squish Elizabeth and me to death, so he really did deserve a bit of zappy pain.

But we were the good guys, so we should be trying not to hurt anyone.

But if we didn't hurt him and we let him keep the books hidden from us, how much pain would we be causing the magical community by failing to find the lost knowledge of generations?

But was it really our job to find the knowledge since we weren't the ones who'd lost it in the first place?

But the ones who had let the books get stolen were now dead because we'd killed them, and there was no one but us to try and right this wrong that had happened before any of us were born.

So...yeah maybe we were going to have to zap him, and maybe it was our *duty* to zap him.

But then I thought about what we'd have to do if the zapping didn't work. And then I started wondering what we were going to do with him once we had our answers since we obviously couldn't just let him go. And we couldn't ask Lola to watch him forever. Sticking her with a bone-magic-using asshole who'd tried to kill Elizabeth was not okay.

But what other choices did we have?

None. We had no choices. We were the ones who were supposed to make good choices that steered all magickind toward a brighter future, but all available choices led to badness.

Elizabeth wrapped my arms around her middle and leaned back so her face was next to mine.

"Breathe," she whispered too quietly for any of the others to hear. "Just keep breathing. We'll get through this together."

I held her close and buried my nose in the scent of her hair.

I'd finally been starting to get a handle on magic. The morality of ruling the magical world was another story entirely.

———

27

William's building looked a lot like the one I'd lived in with my mom before I accidentally destroyed it the first time the Ladies tried to kill me.

The cabbie stopped out front and swiped my black credit card while Eric swiped William's keys.

"Thanks again," I said as I slid out onto the sidewalk.

"No problem." The cabbie smiled. "Call if you need anything."

"In we go." Eric held William's keys in his hand but muttered a spell to open the door rather than actually use them.

The lock turned without a noise.

My heart rocketed up to my throat as I wondered if William had used whatever spell-dampening weirdness he'd created at the library on this building, too. I looked down at his socks. "*Nudla.*" With a tiny *hiss*, all the nasty sidewalk gunk vanished from the paisley-patterned material.

"Don't magic me," William said.

"Way too late for that, dude." Devon shoved William into the vestibule.

"Do you see anything?" I whispered to Elizabeth.

"Just the weird shroud of death coming from Devon's and Eric's pockets." Elizabeth took my hand. "But at least I can see something, so that's better than in the library, right?"

"Right." My voice was so strong I almost convinced myself.

"We don't have an elevator here," William said as Eric opened the door on the other side of the tiny vestibule.

"You don't?" Devon raised an eyebrow at William.

"Not a working one," William said. "It's a rent-controlled building with a good super. Having a working elevator would be way too much to ask."

I didn't argue as we climbed the five flights of stairs, not only because exercise saves lives, but also because I didn't want to be in a tiny moving cage with the guy who had tried to use bone magic on me.

We stopped at apartment 6B.

Eric stared at the door for a long moment before turning toward William. "If there is any danger lurking within, any protection spell, any hidden bone magic, tell me now. If I have to defend my people to escape your home, I will feel no guilt when your tricks cost you your life."

I gripped Elizabeth's hand as panic tightened my chest.

"You've already said I'm only human." William's cheek twitched. "What could I possibly be trying to hide?"

"*Cliaxo.*" Eric looked to the lock on William's door. The lock turned, and he pushed the door open, holding William by the scruff of the neck as he forced him into the apartment first.

Elizabeth let go of my hand to step in front of Devon and me. "No offense, boys." She peered through the door, checking the corners of the tiny studio apartment before stepping inside.

"Anything?" Eric asked.

"A haze." Elizabeth's gaze slid across the floor as she stepped inside. "It's like a low-lying fog, but there's no breeze stirring it."

I took a giant step into the apartment and the fog I couldn't see, choosing the possibility of being attacked by an unknown spell over the chance of being separated from Elizabeth.

"What is it?" Eric asked.

"I have no idea." William sank down onto his narrow couch. "There's been enough weird magic books in this apartment, it wouldn't surprise me if I'd opened a Hellmouth."

"Don't be foolish," Eric scoffed. "We are here seeking magical texts, not scary legends to frighten high schoolers."

"Don't diss the high schoolers." Devon walked over to the bookcase that took up the wall in the bit of the apartment that bridged the space that was meant to be a kitchen and the twin-sized bed that made up the whole bedroom.

The top shelf of books were normal ones that you'd find on any wizard-obsessed reader's shelf. Fantasy novels where wizards always know what to do when their enemies are surrounding them, and the actual consequences of changing the world never involve therapy.

The next shelf down was taken up by more novels, all of which had super worn spines.

The lowest shelf was filled with backpacking travel guides. Most of those looked like the pages would fall out if I touched them.

"So, where are the eight magical books?" Devon asked.

"Will you kill me as soon as I tell you?" William asked.

"Not at all," Eric said. "There are too many other questions I'd like answered."

"Like who stole the books in the first place." I leaned against the apartment door.

"I thought you'd already decided I was the thief," William said.

"You are the dealer," Eric said, "which, while a horror in itself, is not the same as being the one who actually took the books from their rightful place."

"Rightful is in the eye of the beholder," William said.

"You're way too young to be the one who broke into the Library," I said. "You say you have eight books somewhere in this apartment. Eric is going to make you tell him where they are."

A bolt of lightning appeared in Eric's palm.

"But," I said, "I'm a lot more interested in where you got those eight books, and all the others you've sold off."

"Let us first see if the books are truly the ones we've been seeking." Eric twirled the lightning bolt between his fingers. "If you could please just tell me. I'd hate to indulge in the vulgarities of forcing the information out of you in such weak-stomached company."

"I can take it." Elizabeth hopped up to sit on the kitchen counter.

"I was speaking of Bryant," Eric said.

"Rude," I muttered.

"I want to make a deal," William said. "I'll give you one of the books for free, and you leave me alone."

"Absolutely not," Eric said. "I'm taking all of them. And not just the few volumes you have in this tiny apartment."

Sweat beaded on the back of William's neck. "Then just kill me."

"Do not try my patience," Eric said. "It's been a very long week."

"I don't think threatening him is going to work." I stepped away from the door and to the front of the crappy couch.

"Why do you say that?" Eric frowned.

"He's got lip sweat." I pointed to William's face. "He was just outside with no coat, and he's sweating through the back of his shirt. His eyes are darty. I don't think he's taken a deep breath since we came in here, but he was calm and sassy in the park. The dude's panicking hardcore. And I don't think it's us he's afraid of. He's more worried about whoever might find out we found him."

The sweat on William's face doubled.

"Look, I get it." I crouched down to be eyelevel with William. "More than you could ever know, I understand the fear that comes with diving into the shit show that is magic and not realizing you're in over your head until you're drowning. But making Eric hurt you to get the books won't make it better for you. It'll just put you in pain while you wait for whoever it is you're so scared of to show up.

"But like I said, we're not the bad guys, so tell us what happened. Give us a reason to help you. We fought against literally the worst evil magic Manhattan can offer, and we won. So be on our side, and maybe we can keep you safe."

William just stared at me.

"Eric?" I prodded.

Eric sighed. "If you assist us and you truly have a right to fear whomever is making you sweat so copiously, then I would consider aiding in your survival as a show of good faith."

William let out a shaky breath. "The books are under the bed."

Devon moved to reach down.

"Hold it." Elizabeth hopped off the counter and knelt beside the bed. She reached forward and trailed her fingers through the air. "Move the bed and grab them from the other side."

She and Devon went to the head of the bed and shoved it away from the wall, letting the metal legs scrape across the wooden floor until a cardboard box came into view.

"What would have happened if he'd reached under there?" Eric asked.

"No idea." William leaned back. "The book I read just said how to cast the spell, not what it would do if anyone besides me reached through it."

"And you were going to let Devon—"

"Of course he was," Eric cut across me. "He doesn't trust us, and disabling or even killing Devon would leave one less of us standing between him and freedom."

"Can't blame a guy for trying," William said.

"Yeah, I really can." I gripped the magic-filled phone in my pocket to give myself something to do besides punching stupid William in the face.

"You had a book that taught you how to make a barrier spell with bone magic?" Devon set the box right in front of the couch. "I didn't think those nastier bits of magic would be recorded in books."

"Many human horrors are recorded in books," Eric said. "Why should evils of magical making be any different?"

Elizabeth reached toward the box.

"If something happens to her"—I leaned down to glare into William's eyes—"I will kill you. Do you understand?"

William nodded.

"Verbal confirmation," I growled.

"Yes," William said.

Elizabeth opened the box, flipping back the flaps that had a shipping label printed in some language I couldn't read.

I held my breath as she reached inside and pulled out a stack of eight books.

"That's my entire stash," William said.

Part of me wanted to sit right down on the floor and start reading through the books, but I didn't want to turn my back on redhead *I'm panicking, but I might still try to kill your best friend* William long enough to dive into the wonders of knowledge.

"These all seem like the kind we're looking for." Elizabeth read the spine of each book before passing them to Devon, who passed them to Eric.

"Are they from the Library?" Devon asked.

"I can't know for sure without testing them." Eric ran his fingers across the covers as he gathered the books in his arms. "But they do seem to be genuine."

"Great," Devon said. "Now where are the rest?"

"Those are all I have," William said.

"The important part of that statement being all *you* have." Eric handed the books to Elizabeth as though passing over his firstborn before turning back to William. "You'll have to forgive my bluntness, but quite frankly there is not any sort of a chance that a man like you has been selling books to a man like Dupont, who resells them for an exorbitant rate belowground by the way, without any wizard aiding you."

"Dupont is reselling?" William leaned forward. "That filthy, little—"

"He also gave me your location with very little coercion required. You should make better friends if you're going to be in such a risky business," Eric said. "And, as you clearly are the merchandise source for a man with prolific sales aspirations like Dupont, that means you've funneled far more than eight books through your tiny apartment. So, we must ask again, where are the rest?"

"I have no idea where the stock is stored," William said. "And that's the complete truth."

"Stock?" My stomach twisted. Just using a word like *stock* to describe the magical knowledge of all wizards seemed like an insulting commercial term that could only mean all the books we'd been chasing for months had been portioned off to be sold.

"If you don't have the stock," Devon said, "who does?"

"I..." William looked up to the patchy white paint on his ceiling. "If I tell you about that, there's no way I can get out of this alive."

"Why's that?" Elizabeth asked. "If you're more afraid of the person who has the books than you are of us, you're making a really bad judgment call. Not because we'll make sure you die a more painful death, but because we might actually be able to help you get away from whoever convinced you using bone magic was a good idea. Where did you even get the bones? You're clearly a topsider. I don't think you're even related to any wizards."

"How do you know?" William studied Elizabeth as though finally realizing she might be more dangerous than the rest of us, even though she was the most glorious girl to have ever walked the earth.

"You didn't complete your boundary spell in the library or here. You left open sides both times," Elizabeth said. "If you had a great uncle who had ever dealt with someone like Eric Deldridge, you would have done a better job of protecting your merchandise."

"Thank you, Elizabeth." Eric gave her a little bow.

"She didn't say it was a compliment," Devon said.

"Who dragged you into this?" Elizabeth spoke softly, like she felt genuine compassion for William.

"It was never supposed to happen." William's shoulders sank. "I was just trying to have a good time in Greece."

"Greece?" I asked, which earned me an elbow in the stomach from Devon, but William didn't seem to have noticed me talking.

"I was just trying to find dinner, and then this woman offered me shots of Raki, and I said I loved Raki. Then we were drinking, and I ate duck, and then we were talking about books. It seemed like such a nice night, just talking and drinking, lots of drinking, and then she was saying I should sell imported books. And then she was saying the books were magic.

"I started laughing, thinking it was a joke, but she made the whole square where we were eating go silent." William's eyes got wide with remembered fear. "Then she made the stars blink out, and everything went dark. She gave me all these instructions for what she wanted me to do, and then she got up and left. Sound came back, and the lights blinked back on. I woke up in the morning and thought I'd just gotten too drunk and imagined the whole thing."

"How long did it take for you to realize you'd met a genuine witch?" Eric tented his hands under his chin.

"Two weeks after I got home from my trip," William said. "I got a package of three books and a note with specifics on how to sell them and what prices she wanted me to get. If I didn't have the money from the sales deposited in an account in two weeks, she'd come after me."

"So, you just went along with it?" Devon asked.

"Of course not," William said. "I tried to send the books back. But the box ended up back outside my door the next day. When I got in the shower that night, blood came out of the taps instead of water."

"Damn," Devon whispered.

"So I tried to sell the books," William said. "I followed all the instructions, but I didn't get any bites. The day I was supposed to deposit the money came, and I didn't have anything to put in the account. I got home that night, and my entire apartment had been filled with hornets. I had to go to the hospital for the stings. When I finally got to come back home, there was another box of books to sell, and a promise that if I didn't get it right, no amount of Emergency Room bills would save me."

"So you figured out the method of selling," Eric said.

"I had to," William said. "That lady knows where I live. I even tried to move once. I put in an application on a new apartment, and three hours later a letter slid under my door telling me not to bother packing, I wouldn't be going anywhere."

I scrubbed my hands over my face, weighing my sympathy for William against his almost killing Elizabeth and me and not caring about potentially murdering Devon.

"What about the bone magic?" Devon asked. "Was that in your instructions from the witch? Is that the kind of magic she uses?"

"I have no idea how that lady stole the stars," William said. "I found a couple of things in a book she sent me to sell and bought some bones off Dupont during one of our deals. I had to do something to protect myself."

"Do you even know which wizard's bones you're using?" A shudder shook my shoulders as an odd tingle tickled the back of my neck.

"Dupont never said." William swallowed so hard, I wondered if puke had soared into his mouth. "But whoever those bones used to belong to, they're dead now. They don't need the bones or the residual magic those tools contain."

"Did you just call bones tools?" It was my turn to swallow mouth puke.

"I'm trying to keep myself alive," William said. "Whatever term you prefer for the things I use to keep breathing makes no difference to me."

"Those bones belong to our ancestors." Eric spoke in a dangerously quiet tone. "The only term I have for you is *grave robber*."

Devon laid a hand on Eric's shoulder. "Where's the bone magic book?"

"You already have—"

"Don't lie." Devon reached into his pocket and pulled out the hilt of his glowing sword. The bright beam burst to life with a flick of his wrist. "You're a human trying to survive in a world of wizards and you found something that could help you defend yourself. Even a spineless tool like you isn't dumb enough to sell that book."

A weird, cornered animal kind of rage took over William's face. "The book is mine. I'm dead without it, and I'll kill you to keep it."

"I've already sliced off a dude's hand with this sword," Devon said. "Let's see how it chops off a foot."

"Die trying, asshole!" William slammed his feet against the floor, and the air flashed a bright white.

28

"Elizabeth!" I screamed her name as I dove to protect her from the bright flash of light.

"Get down!"

Something crashed into my side, knocking me to the ground.

Bright fire crackled through the apartment, whooshing through the air and rising up to the ceiling to devour the patchy paint.

"Block the door," Elizabeth shouted in my ear.

"*Portundo!*" I gagged on the sharp scent that filled the air as I spoke the spell.

Asshat William crawled toward the place where the door had been, staying on his knees, keeping his head out of reach of the flames.

"There's no way out!" I choked on the air that stung my lungs. I coughed out the bad air, but the next breath was even worse.

"No!" William pounded on the wall where the door had been.

"You're not getting out of here." Devon scrambled toward William in full beast mode, while Eric grabbed me by the front of the shirt and wrenched my turtleneck up over my nose and mouth.

Eric didn't say anything, he just stared at me with something that looked frighteningly like fear in his eyes.

"Stay low." Elizabeth shoved the box of books to Eric before crawling toward Devon and William.

Devon pointed his sword at William's throat. "Where is the book on bone magic?"

"Open the door, or we'll all burn," William said.

"Where's the book?" Devon lunged toward William, aiming for his right shin.

I started to close my eyes against the coming foot amputation but gasped as the light of Devon's sword flickered and died before reaching the book dealer's flesh.

The noxious air flew in through the fabric of my turtleneck and blasted down into my lungs. The room swayed as my body begged for pure air. Logic screamed to crawl toward the door, but Devon blocked my path, staring down at the now useless tube of metal in his hand.

William didn't waste the moment. He lunged forward, knocking Devon to the floor and wrapping his non-gooey hand around my best friend's throat.

With a shout, Elizabeth kicked out, catching William in the face with a battement worthy of a Rockette.

William grunted and rolled to the side, leaving Devon gasping for air.

I tried to crawl toward Devon. I needed to cover his face, to keep the bad air from hurting his lungs. But my arms shook too badly for me to manage moving on all fours. Desperate yet vague thoughts about holding a wet cloth over my face floated through my mind as I dragged myself across the floor toward Devon.

Elizabeth had gotten to her knees and hissed in pain as she fumbled along the kitchen counter, reaching close to the flames for I didn't know what.

Devon gulped down the foul air as he reached into one of his coat pockets, but William had already slipped his hand into Devon's other pocket.

I tried to pull in enough air to speak a spell but started retching on nothing before I could form words.

William ripped his hand out of Devon's pocket, holding what I can really only describe as a graduation tassel made of bones. He pulled back his hand like he was going to slap Devon in the face with the morbid regalia, but Elizabeth swung first.

She cracked William across the head with a plate, which shattered as he fell backward, away from Devon.

I reached forward as far as I could, grabbing for the tassel William still clutched in his hand.

He flicked his wrist, smacking my hand with the bones. Pain shot through the back of my hand, up my arm, into my neck, and down to my spleen.

My scream used up the last of the air I had in my lungs.

A muffled shout right beside me pulled my attention back to the fact that William wanted me dead.

I looked toward him, trying to think of a way to defend myself without using a spell.

Elizabeth swung a saucepan at William's head at the same moment Devon squirted him in the face with his sparkly purple water gun.

The grayish-green goo spread over William's face as Elizabeth's blow knocked him to the ground.

"The window." Eric's voice rasped from the far side of the room. "Come to the window."

Devon and Elizabeth each grabbed one of my arms and dragged me across the miraculously tiny apartment to where Eric knelt by the window, gulping down air.

"The door," Devon said, "can you open the door?" He didn't sound like he was dying of the awful smoke as he grabbed the back of my coat and propped me halfway out the window.

"This way is better." Eric passed the box to Elizabeth and grabbed her around the waist. "Pardon the intrusion."

He rolled, flipping both of them out the window.

Elizabeth squeaked a scream as they fell toward the sidewalk far below.

"Come on." Devon gripped my waist, hoisting me so our bodies were mostly out the window.

"William," I coughed.

Devon glanced back.

The tiny movement shifted his weight just enough to press on my stomach.

With a weird gurgle, green spewed from my mouth.

"Bryant!" Elizabeth called from far below.

I wrapped an arm around Devon and launched us out the window. I couldn't stay to help the guy who'd tried to kill us. I couldn't risk not making it back to Elizabeth.

"*Escata.*" I choked out the spell and gripped Devon as hard as I could. But we hadn't fallen straight down. We were tipped at an angle.

The air around us seemed to solidify as we neared the ground, but I didn't have the strength to fight gravity to get upright. We sank facedown until we were three feet off the ground, the invisible pudding-ish barrier surrounding us like a nice soft place to sleep.

"Bryant." Devon shifted, and my comfort vanished.

We fell the last three feet and hit the mucky sidewalk.

Groaning from the impact took more air than my body had to give.

"We have to go." Elizabeth grabbed me under my arm, trying to help me up.

But my legs didn't seem to want to work. "Why does falling always have to hurt so much?"

Devon added his grip, yanking me to stand.

"Stay close," Eric said.

I looked to Eric, trying to think of something snarky to say about how I wasn't going to be able to stay close to anything that intended to move, because the only thing I was capable of doing was sitting on the sidewalk and waiting for my favorite cabbie to come back for me.

But then I noticed the cluster of people surrounding us. With their phones out like they were filming us.

A guy stepped closer to Eric, tipping his phone like he was trying to get a better angle of the unfortunately white flames now leaping out of William's window.

"Do the darkness thing." Elizabeth looked to Eric.

Eric raised an eyebrow.

"Just do it," Elizabeth whispered as a lady crept toward me, pointing her phone right at my face.

"*Dothranta.*"

At Eric's whispered word, everything around us went black.

Just in time for sirens to start wailing down the street.

As the people caught in the spell started to scream, Elizabeth let go of me.

"Elizabeth?" I coughed out her name.

I heard a thump and someone shouting as they fell over.

I gripped Devon's shoulder, trying to stay on my feet as we groped our way forward, away from the sirens.

Something hit me hard in the face. "Watch out!" I rasped at the person I couldn't see.

"What happened? What did those freaks do?" The terrified shriek dug down into my spine.

"Not so tight," Devon muttered as I clutched his shoulder so hard my fingers hurt.

"A bit to your left," Eric called through the darkness.

Devon and I shifted left.

"No, not you," Eric said. "Devon, drag him right."

"I'm walking pretty well here." I tried to straighten up, but my lungs seized at the movement.

"Hey, who did that?" a man shouted behind me. "Give that back!"

We took another step forward, and without any sort of warning, light flashed back into being.

"I really hate that spell." Devon lugged me over to Eric's side.

Eric had a suspicious amount of color in his face, but not the good kind. A weird yellow tinged his skin, and blue rings had blossomed under his eyes.

"Where's Elizabeth?" I asked, daring to let go of Devon in my hurry to find her.

I spun around and tipped toward the pavement. Devon barely grabbed me in time to keep me on my feet, but I caught sight of Elizabeth inside the one-way darkness spell, picking her way through the people, fumbling in the darkness to steal the phones in their hands.

"On your right," Eric directed. "Up a hair."

"God I love that girl," Devon said as Elizabeth slipped a phone from a lady's grip and ducked away before the woman had time to lunge for her.

"Me too." I sagged against Devon's side.

"We need to leave," Eric said.

"I don't think I'm done." Elizabeth started creeping toward a teenage girl who'd sat down on the pavement and started to cry.

"Now, Elizabeth," Eric ordered as the fire trucks stopped beside the hysterical crowd beneath the white flames that still poured out of William's window.

With a hint of fear on her face, Elizabeth turned toward Eric's voice, holding her cellphone-filled hands in front of her as she walked toward us.

"A bit to your left, if you would," Eric said.

The moment Elizabeth shifted her path, Eric tossed a tiny little shard of lightning right at the phone in the crying girl's hand.

The girl screamed and threw her phone aside.

"It had to be done." Eric reached forward and grabbed Elizabeth's arm.

She blinked as she staggered toward him, then shoved all the phones into her coat pockets. "I don't know if I got them all."

"We have more pressing worries." Eric gripped the box of books to his chest.

"Everyone out of the way." A firefighter called as she climbed out of her truck. "Clear the sidewalk!"

"Help!" a giant man screamed. "Do you have a flashlight? We need help!"

"Come on." Devon shifted his grip on me to better help me stumble away as cop cars joined the fire trucks.

"A little grace, Bryant," Eric said. "We can't look suspicious."

"He just looks drunk," Devon said. "I've seen kids tipping way worse than him on a Saturday afternoon."

"Hmm." Eric pursed his lips.

"I have been behaving very well as a ward of the Consortium." Devon raised his free hand in defense.

"How are you mobile and making jokes?" I looked to Elizabeth. "How do you still look gorgeous?"

"I don't think the poison in the air was meant for humans," Eric said.

"Poison?" Elizabeth slipped her hand into mine.

"But not like *poison* poison, right?" I asked.

"It most definitely was," Eric said. "At the moment, we are both, in fact, dying."

I turned toward Devon's shoes as green vomit flew from my mouth.

"Aww man." Devon quickened his pace, hauling me forward at a half-jog. "This is something Lola can fix, right?"

"We can hope," Eric said.

"I'm sorry about your shoes, Devon," I said. "I didn't want to, but I can't puke on my girlfriend."

"Don't die, and I'll forgive the shoes."

"Deal." I puked on him again.

I don't know if fate was trying to be helpful or if Manhattan geography just worked in our favor, but the stumbling jog from Hell's Kitchen to the Consortium only took enough time for me to vomit on my best friend two more times.

Before the black/really sort of purple awning came into view, Elizabeth had let go of my hand to wrap her arm around Eric's waist since he'd started to sway like a rum-drunk pirate.

Sniffer came tearing out the front door of the Consortium before we could open it. The kid tipped his head, glancing between Eric and me before running back inside.

"He's a good kid." Even saying those few words felt like my throat was being torn out.

"Do we need to go downstairs?" Elizabeth held open the door as we all stumbled into the restaurant.

"Here," Eric panted, "we can stay here."

"What the hell is happening?" Lola burst out of the kitchen with the kid on her heels. "I thought you were going to poke around and find a hint of information."

"We found books." Eric set the box on the table as he sank into a seat.

"Well, I hope you live long enough to read them." Lola turned around and strode back into the kitchen.

"Down you go." Devon lowered me into the seat across from Eric.

"I can clean your—"

"Save your strength," Devon said.

"I..." I tried to wave a hand flippantly through the air, but I caught sight of my hand and realized my skin had gone the same icky yellow as Eric's except for the black lines left behind by the venom and the new bone tassel-shaped burn that cut through it all. "This week sucks."

"As long we as all survive, that'll be enough." Elizabeth pushed my sweaty hair off my forehead.

I looked up toward her.

Somehow, in all the chaos and poison smoke, I hadn't realized her hair had been burned. She brushed some of the singed strands away from her face, the hair crumpled and fell to the floor, but it was the shiny redness of her hands I couldn't look away from.

"You're hurt." I tried to reach for her, but a sharp pain in my side made lifting my arm that far impossible.

"We'll worry about me after you two are patched up." Elizabeth laid her wonderfully cool hand on my cheek. "Just sit back and breathe."

Lola burst back out of the kitchen with a metal box in one hand and a half-full blender in the other.

"Sweetie, plug this in." Lola handed Devon the cord for the blender.

He ducked behind the table as she set down her metal box.

"Now, what sort of mess did you get yourselves into?" Lola asked.

"I think it was bone magic," Elizabeth said. "I'd been able to see a haze on the floor, but then William stomped his feet and this weird fire started and the smoke seemed normal to me, but Bryant and Eric got sick."

"I'm gonna have a lot more questions that are gonna need answering later." Lola reached into the box and pulled out something like a berry-shaped bit of onyx. She threw it into the blender along with a few leaves, something that looked like a dried, small creature's leg, and...I don't know. Other things. I stopped watching after the leg bit.

"Sweetie, fetch the finishing powder," Lola said.

Devon tore through the restaurant and into the kitchen.

"I'm going to have to make a run to Beville the way we're burning through my supplies these days," Lola said.

"Once you've saved me, I'd be happy to run the errand for you." Eric spoke with his eyes half-closed.

Devon raced back out of the kitchen with a mason jar of what looked like shimmer powder, or at the very least something shiny that had nothing to do with desiccated legs.

Lola unscrewed the top of the jar, tossed a pinch into the blender, and turned it on. "Two cups," she shouted over the noise.

Devon ducked behind the counter and came back with two coffee mugs.

"Thanks, sweetie." Lola stopped the blender. The odd concoction had somehow turned a dazzling blue as it was ground up. She poured some into the two cups and passed one to me and one to Eric. "Drink up. Whatever storm you just started isn't going to be weathered by anybody with one foot already in the grave."

29

It took an hour for Lola's magic smoothie to make me feel more like I'd had the flu and less like I was literally going to die.

Lola wrapped the burns on Elizabeth's hands and put some stinging goop on the burn the bone tassel had left on me. Then she put some cream on the hand-shaped bruise around Devon's neck.

By the time she was done patching our sorry asses up, the whole restaurant smelled like a weird combination of juice bar and antiseptic.

Devon watched everything Lola did carefully, like he was taking mental notes. A weird worry sank into my gut as I wondered how I had become such a bad friend that I hadn't noticed how much he was doing to try and protect the rest of us.

"Well"—Lola picked up her metal box and blender—"you should all survive the day. Unless you find some other snake's den to hop into."

"I never hop," Eric said.

"Uh huh." Lola kissed his cheek. "You keep tellin' yourself that, darling."

"I don't hop," Eric muttered in a very un-Eric like way.

"It's more of a daring dive." Devon mimicked Eric's voice and raised one dark eyebrow in a very Eric-like way.

"When did you start dabbling in potions?" I sniffed the goo on the back of my hand.

"When you were dying and there wasn't shit I could do to help." Devon pulled the sparkly water gun from his pocket. "This is the only potion I've actually gotten to work. It's just a sticking solution, but—"

"But it saved our lives." Elizabeth reached out to squeeze Devon's hand, wincing from even that little movement.

"I don't like bone magic." Devon furrowed his brow. "I don't like that my sword couldn't touch it, I hate that it tried to poison you guys, but the fact that we lost the book he used to cast those spells—"

"Makes everything worse," I said. "We don't even know what else he could do."

A silence fell over us as we all avoided mentioning that whatever William might have been able to do to us, chances were he was dead, and his human bones couldn't be used to hurt anybody.

"How many books on bone magic do you think the Library had?" Elizabeth asked.

"Since the Ladies chose to hoard all the bones of the dead in the vaults below," Eric sighed, "I would hazard to say quite a few."

"Which means a lot of terrible stuff you've never even heard of could be waiting for us in Greece," Devon said. "If that's even where the book thief really is."

"If those books are even really from the Library." I looked at the cardboard box on the table.

It had been singed on one corner, and a bit of street sludge had spattered across the shipping label on top.

"Shall we see if our venture was worth it?" Eric pushed himself to his feet, his jaw tightening as he tried to mask his pain.

I didn't bother hiding my groan as I stood up.

Elizabeth wrapped her arm around my waist as we made our way to the stairs that led down to the Library.

The world wasn't swaying anymore, and I could definitely breathe better. But I still liked having her close to me. Not just so I could feel that she was safe and breathing. I needed her beside me to remind me why it was worth it. Why I wasn't supposed to feel guilty that I had jumped out a window and left William behind.

None of us spoke as we entered the Library and headed toward the railing at the center. We just all stood side by side as Eric opened the box.

He stared down at the books for a moment, and something between grief and reverence crossed his face before he tipped the box upside down and let the books fall.

My breath caught in my throat as the books all twisted in the air, soaring toward shelves on the levels below us.

"He really was selling books from the Library." Devon gripped the railing with both hands.

"I thought…" I dug the knuckles of my non-maimed fist into my forehead, trying to mash the words into the right order. "Somehow, I really thought that whoever had stolen the books might have done it to protect them from the Ladies. Like they were trying to free the books and give knowledge back to the people. Like maybe they were like us. And really it was just somebody pulling off a huge magical heist. It's just—"

"Disappointing," Devon said.

I dragged my hand over my face, trying to get rid of the twisting in my gut like someone had just told me dodos were extinct all over again.

"They stole the books and moved them far from the Ladies' reach," Eric said. "I can appreciate their dedication if not their cause."

"Someone shipped all the books out of the country." I tried to keep myself from panicking over the logistics of sneaking thousands of books through customs.

"So we're going on a summer trip to Greece?" Devon shrugged. "Could be worse."

"I'm afraid we can't afford to wait that long," Eric said. "We've been lucky thus far. The Ladies were unpopular and reclusive. Wizards spend so much of their time trying to avoid the Ladies' notice, no one's started to suspect they're gone. If the people of Beville should discover we've taken control of the Library and the Consortium—"

"Which they're more likely to do now that we busted some human trafficking heads," I cut in.

"And made the front page of the newspaper," Devon added.

"And I'm really not sure I got all the cellphones people used to film us jumping out a window in Hell's Kitchen." Elizabeth gnawed on her perfectly pink bottom lip.

"—whoever has the books could sell them all off without having to worry about the Ladies coming to kill them. They could auction the books as quickly as they wanted without needing to go through the precaution of using a patsy like William to make the sales," Eric said.

"Great. Just great." Devon stared up at the ceiling for a long moment. "How soon are we leaving?"

"Spring break?" Elizabeth said. "It's not too far off."

"Within a few days," Eric said. "That should give us time to get things in order."

"But what about school?" Elizabeth said. "And my appointment with Nikki, and the spring play..."

Her voice drifted away as Eric raised one black eyebrow.

"Sorry," Elizabeth said. "Reflex."

"I don't have a passport." Devon crossed his arms like he was daring Eric to say he'd be left behind.

"I have a resource," Eric said. "We'll get you a fake."

"My parents have my passport," Elizabeth said.

I wrapped my arm around her waist, holding her close.

She relaxed a little, like I might actually be enough to make her feel not so alone.

"We'll get two fake passports." Eric gave Elizabeth a nod.

"No magic carpets to get out of the country?" I asked.

"Bryant, I have told you on more than one occasion, there is no magical way to fly."

"But maybe there is." Elizabeth took my non-gooey hand in her bandaged one and leaned over the railing, looking down at the levels of empty book-shelves below us. "Somewhere, in one of the books hidden in some dark corner, maybe there is a way to fly."

"What a wonderful world that would be." Eric smiled. A genuine, full-of-hope kind of smile I'd rarely seen on him before.

I've never been sure of Eric's proper age, but as he gazed out over the barren Library, he looked like a twenty-year-old ready to take on the world. And for some stupid reason, it made following him to a foreign country in search of a criminal mastermind, who quite possibly possessed magic we knew basically nothing about, a little less scary.

"We're going to need plane tickets," Devon said. "Luggage, passports, hotels in Greece."

"Any way you could convince your dad to pay?" Elizabeth asked.

All three of them turned to look at me.

"Isn't there some magical fund you could draw from?" I whimpered.

"The Ladies left behind no treasure I've been able to discover," Eric said. "I do have my own personal funds. I don't mind dipping into my savings."

Eric having savings was simultaneously comical and sobering.

"I'll ask my dad," I said. "I'm not sure how well it's going to go. Any chance your passport dude is a hacker who could help me bust into my college fund early?"

"Let us aim for the legal route first," Eric said.

"Because legality matters all of a sudden." Devon rolled his eyes at Eric.

"It's best to stay on the light side of the law." Eric headed back toward the restaurant, and the rest of us followed. "When possible."

Fatigue mingled with my newfound sense of purpose.

Elizabeth kept her hand in mine as we climbed the spiral stairs.

"Anyone have any suggestions on what to tell my parents about us needing money to disappear to another country?" I asked.

"You could tell them you and Elizabeth are eloping." Devon laughed.

Heat rushed to my face.

"I think we need an option that won't make his parents panic." Elizabeth jabbed a finger into Devon's back. "I need Nikki's help, remember? I don't even know if I'm allowed to leave the country. I don't want Bryant's dad telling her I'm running off to Greece to become Mrs. Bryant Adams."

Electricity zinged through my entire body. The heat in my face sank to my stomach in a delicious ball that radiated pure bliss.

"Maybe we can get to Greece and back without Nikki, or Child Protective Services, or my parents knowing I'm gone." Elizabeth kept talking like I hadn't been struck by the lightning of love.

"I don't fancy the idea of undertaking this journey without a seer," Eric said, "but if you can't come with us, I understand."

"I'm coming." Elizabeth tightened her grip on my hand.

"Bryant could tell his dad he has a sudden interest in columns and statues?" Devon said.

"We're in Manhattan," Elizabeth said. "He could go to a museum here."

"It's a school trip he forgot to tell them about?" Devon said.

"My mom works at our school," I said.

We all headed through the room with the desks where the Ladies used to sit. I glanced toward the door that led to the hall where Lola and her guards, and Devon and Elizabeth, lived.

Just the people who slept in that one hallway were worth facing whatever international criminal, evil mastermind waited for us across the ocean. It didn't matter that fighting turned me into an emotional wreck. It didn't matter that balancing the morality of governing was way beyond my skill set. It didn't even matter that I'd almost died three times in the last week. I'd take on the whole world if it meant keeping the people I loved safe. And if I happened to save the magical world along the way, I could live with that, too.

"If I may give one small piece of advice, Bryant?" Eric said. "Perhaps you should pack your bag before you tell your parents you're leaving."

"Don't worry, Bryant," Devon said. "You can just agree to more therapy if they get pissed at you."

"Careful," I laughed. "They might try and send Dr. Spinnek along as a chaperone."

In hindsight, a chaperone might have been a great idea.

FIVE SPELLBINDING LAWS OF INTERNATIONAL LARCENY

BOOK FOUR

1

They can smell panic.

I knew the truth of it down in my very soul, but I couldn't get my heart to stop racing. Hiding my sweaty hands in my pockets, I kept my pace steady and my chin tucked enough that none of my adversaries would think I was looking for a fight.

One of the pack swerved too near me, but the surrounding horde didn't leave me any room to dodge. A letterman-clad monster rammed into my shoulder.

I stumbled, pulling my hands out of my pockets to save my balance.

"Dude, what the hell happened?" The letterman's beta grabbed my wrist, pulling my hand closer so he could get a better look at the charcoal-colored lines that traced my veins and the angry burn that splatted over the black web.

"Cooking accident." I wrenched my wrist free and shoved my hands back into my pockets. I could feel the pack's eyes following me, tracking my steps to see if I would be easy prey.

The glistening gate to my sanctuary shone just out of reach.

Abandoning caution, I dodged through the throng and dove into the safety of homeroom.

I closed my eyes for a moment, willing my heart to slow.

"Are you going to move?" a tired voice asked from behind me.

"Sorry." I shoved my hands deeper into my pockets and slunk to my seat.

Logic screamed that no one in my high school could possibly know that two magical near-death experiences had created the new scars on my hand. There was also no way my homeroom teacher could have discovered I was a teenage wizard who'd, through a series of super unfortunate and very unlikely events, become entangled with the fate of magic.

And, since I hadn't even told my parents yet, the tired girl who glared at me as I sweat through my turtleneck definitely didn't know I was supposed to be flying to Greece in forty-eight hours so I could track down/steal from the thief who'd gutted all wizarding knowledge.

No, the people around me definitely didn't know any of that. All they saw was the seventeen-year-old geek who somehow had the coolest best friend and most perfect girlfriend and totally didn't deserve either.

I sank into my chair and kept my gaze fixed on my teacher's desk.

'Cause, here's the thing—and I don't want to sound like I'm a douche—if I wanted to, if the kids in my class were to actually gang up on me, I could defend myself.

Five months ago, when I found out I was a wizard and went from being plain geek Bryant Jameson Adams to wizard geek Bryant Jameson Adams, I stopped being defenseless.

I could trap my classmates in darkness. I could pin them all to the wall. I could...accidentally light part of the school on fire...again.

But my magic and battle savvy weren't meant to be seen by the regular humans aboveground. Here, trapped in the corridors of teenage angst and swaddled in the unending drama of dating, grades, and cliques, I wasn't a wizard who fate had drawn into the very center of the battle for what the magical community should be. I was just Bryant, the nerd whose mom ran the school drama department.

I'd always been able to almost cope with the strange difference between school Bryant and wizard Bryant, but having visible scars even magic couldn't mend made pretending to be normal during school hours a lot harder to manage.

The bell rang, and I glanced over to Devon's usual seat, ready to see his face and know I wasn't just a freak who had somehow hallucinated the fact that a settlement of wizards lived below the subway tunnels. But Devon's seat stayed empty as the teacher started class.

I gripped my non-magical phone, trying to decide if sneaking it out of my pocket to text Devon was worth the risk of

A) Being caught with a phone in class and

B) My teacher noticing all the damage that had been done to my right hand in the last week and freaking out, therefore sending me to

1. The guidance counselor
2. The school nurse, or
3. Skipping all the in-school steps and just notifying Child Protective Services, thereby forcing my poor overstressed mother into coming up with a logical reason for the two types of brand-new scars.

I dug my hands deeper into my pockets and tried to ignore the aching in my gut that whispered my best friend could need me to save his life.

Before I'd started hyperventilating, but after I'd managed to get a good start on a brand-new ulcer, Devon breezed into the classroom, beaming like he'd just won a Tony Award and been crowned Prom King on national television.

Devon sauntered right up to the teacher and handed him a slip of paper.

Mr. Ruler of Homeroom read the note before giving Devon a smile. "Congratulations, Mr. Rhodes."

"Thanks, sir," Devon beamed. "I'm really stoked."

"Please don't use words like *stoked* and throw away your shot." Mr. Ruler of Homeroom waggled a wrinkled finger.

"Of course, sir." Devon gave a little bow and slid into his seat, throwing me a thumbs up.

My gut stopped eating itself, but I still couldn't muster the courage to pull my hands out of my pockets as we drifted from class to class.

With random teachers stopping Devon in the hall to wish him luck, it was easier to believe no one knew about any of my weird secrets. Being in the presence of the great Devon Rhodes meant getting seen as wallpaper on a regular basis. Sometimes being ignored sucked. Sometimes it felt like Devon was the best friend equivalent of me wearing an invisibility cloak, which was super awesome.

"You ever going to ask?" Devon set his lunch tray down on the table with a satisfying *thunk*.

"Ask what award you won that's mysteriously taking you away from school starting Wednesday?" I pulled my sandwich from my lunch bag using only my left hand.

"Not an award." Devon took pity on me, opened the baggie, and pulled out my sandwich. "I've been invited to interview for early admission to college. Not bad for a guy who's been disowned."

"And the school is just going with it?"

"Well, after the official-looking letter I turned in this morning and the confirmation call Eric made to the principal, why would anyone doubt me?" Devon winked.

"If you say we're stealing a convertible and dancing in a parade, I'm sending you to Dr. Spinnek." I peered over the heads of the crowd, searching for Elizabeth.

"I haven't seen her," Devon said.

I finagled my normal phone out of my pocket.

No messages.

"What did your parents say?" Devon asked.

"Nothing."

"Because they've suddenly decided letting you leave the country to track down stolen books is a good idea or because you haven't told them yet?"

"Do I really need to answer that?" I shoved my sandwich into my mouth.

"You have to tell them, Bry. We need to book tickets."

I nodded as I chewed, still scanning the cafeteria for Elizabeth. I even dared to glance toward the mural honoring the Lancre lunch lady I'd squished. Elizabeth was nowhere in sight.

"She was fine this morning." Devon joined me in searching the cafeteria. "We walked to school together."

A moment of jealousy pinged in my stomach. I wanted to walk to school with Elizabeth, but as the only one of us who didn't live at the Consortium, and given the fact that my mom had been super freaked out about the tassel-shaped burn on my hand, I hadn't had time to get to the Consortium for my normal *coffee and make sure the world hasn't ended* time with Devon and Elizabeth.

I swallowed the half of my sandwich I'd shoved into my mouth. "What if she's been snatched? What if her parents came after her? What if there are shadows in the girls' bathroom and she's been trapped just out of reach?"

"First of all, take a breath," Devon said, "I'm sure Elizabeth is fine. Second, if she's in an epic battle against evil shadows in the girls' bathroom, we'll just invade the girls' bathroom. Third, we have enough real problems to stress about. Don't start freakin' out about things that aren't actually a problem."

"When do I get to start freaking out?"

"I'll let you know." Devon shrugged. "For now, just eat your sandwich."

"Sure."

I slipped my right hand out of my pocket, keeping it hidden as I typed two messages.

The first one, I sent to Elizabeth—*Are you okay? I love you.*

The second, I sent to my mom—*I haven't seen Elizabeth today. I don't know where she is. Can you check with the school office? I'm freaking out.*

I tucked my phone and hand back into my pocket and shoved the other half of my sandwich into my mouth.

"You didn't even ask what school I was going to visit about early admissions," Devon said.

"Okay, what—"

My phone buzzed.

I'm fine. Been stuck in the guidance counselor's office all day. I don't need rescuing, but I would kill for a cup of coffee.

"She's in the guidance counselor's office." I grabbed my lunch box.

"So, then she's fine." Devon stayed seated.

"I mean sure, like *monsters and evil people aren't trying to kill me* fine," I whispered. "But she might need emotional support. I'm the boyfriend. It's part of my job."

"Good for you, Bry." Devon winked at me. "You go earn your place as boyfriend."

"I will." I puffed up my chest and strode away with as much confidence and gusto as someone clutching a lunchbox can achieve.

There wasn't a rule about having to stay in the cafeteria during your assigned lunch time, but I still had a gnawing worry itching the back of my neck that someone was going to come barreling down the hall, shouting that I should be anywhere but near my girlfriend.

The door to the guidance counselor's office came into view, as shiny and surrounded by cheerful posters as ever.

I slowed my steps as I passed the cartoon characters standing under skywriting that read *One small change can make a huge difference* and was walking creepily slowly by the time I got to the poster of a kid wearing lab gear with the words *Building a brighter future starts with you!* badly photoshopped around her.

I lingered near the crack in the guidance counselor's door, listening for sounds of emotional distress.

An oddly familiar voice that wasn't Elizabeth's rumbled through the door.

I was just about to go full creeper and press my ear to the crack so I could figure out why I knew that voice, when the ancient biology teacher came toddling down the hall.

Giving him a nod, I picked up my pace, hustling halfway to the end of the corridor before making a U-turn to go back for another eavesdropping pass.

I tried to look cool and calm as I scanned the hall, timing my arrival at the guidance counselor's door so I could press my ear to the crack without any authority figures noticing.

I was so busy making sure the janitor wasn't going to turn down the corridor toward me, I didn't notice the guidance counselor's door swinging open as I leaned in to listen.

"Bryant!"

At the usually non-terrifying sound of Elizabeth saying my name that close to my ear, I screamed and dove away from her, landing on the grubby linoleum with less dignity than a balloon handler during a windy Thanksgiving Day Parade.

"Are you okay?" Elizabeth grabbed my arm to help me up.

"Yeah, I was just pass—"

"Mr. Adams, what happened?" The guidance counselor stepped toward me, her gaze fixed on my screwed-up hand.

"Project for stage makeup class," Elizabeth said. "I think Bryant's found a new talent."

"I didn't know you had a real interest in the performing arts." The guidance counselor furrowed her brow.

"He likes working backstage, just not being near the spotlight." Elizabeth widened her eyes. "Aren't you supposed to be meeting Devon?"

"Yes. Yes, I should go to do that now." Because saying things like that is exactly how you avoid suspicion.

"If you have a moment, we could talk about some very interesting arts opportunities," the guidance counselor said. "Even with the theatre having burned down—"

"I am so sorry to interrupt," the super familiar voice said, "but I'd like to cover just a few more questions before I go on my merry little way."

Lola stepped out into the corridor.

My brain did that weird thing where the entire world seems to blip for a second. Like your mind can't put two things together that should never, ever be together, so it just goes *Nope, I'm out!*

Lola's hair was all curly, and she'd switched out the sparkly romper she usually wore at the Consortium for a deep-blue power suit.

I blinked at Lola, trying to figure out if the last five months of my life had been some sort of weird hallucination.

"We're very excited to be workin' with Miss Wick," Lola said. "But to best serve each of our charges, going over their complete academic record is essential."

"Of course." The guidance counselor bowed Lola back toward her office. "I'm just so thrilled Elizabeth has been given this opportunity."

I kept staring at the door after it shut behind Lola.

"Come on." Elizabeth threaded her arm through mine, leading me away.

"Is that really Lola?" My question sort of came out as a whimper.

"Yep."

"Why?"

"After all the drama with my parents, I've been offered a place with a special teen mentorship program," Elizabeth whispered. "I'll be starting off my time with Steps to Independence with a two-week retreat to make sure I'm prepared to live on my own. Had to get it cleared with the guidance counselor, of course."

"When did this plan happen?" I asked.

"When I was up late last night, researching reasons I could disappear for a bit without your dad's lawyer freaking out." Elizabeth shook her head, sending her blond-with-tiny-black-streaks curls fluttering around her like a shampoo commercial. "Nikki is great, but I have a feeling telling her I'm running away to Greece might make her reconsider whether or not she wants to help me."

"I have a feeling Nikki would help whoever my dad told her to."

"What did your parents say about Greece?" Elizabeth stopped in front of her locker.

"I'm a coward who hasn't told them yet. But I love you." I tried to give a winning smile that probably looked more like a grimace.

"Do you need Devon and me to be there when you talk to them?" Elizabeth reached into her locker, pulling out a green hoodie.

"I..." For a moment, I considered being a selfish prick and making my friends, who'd given up any relationship with their parents, help me with my parents. "I'll be fine. I think I've got a game plan worked out."

By *game plan* I meant *decent lie*, but whatever.

"Let me know if you change your mind." Elizabeth handed me her sweatshirt. "Try it on."

"Isn't this supposed to work the other way around?" I glanced down the hall, waiting for one of the lettermen to come shoulder-check me again.

"We're a modern couple who won't be controlled by the outdated rules of the patriarchy," Elizabeth said.

"Okay." I pulled on the sweatshirt, which was so new it hadn't even pilled up on the inside.

Elizabeth took my hands and pushed my thumbs through the sneaky little holes in the cuffs, leaving enough of the dark green fabric hanging over my hands to hide my scars.

"You're brilliant." I used my weird hand to tuck her hair behind her ear and didn't catch a glimpse of the damage.

"You're welcome."

2

"I'm glad you were both able to join me." I pressed my palms to the kitchen table to keep my hands from shaking.

My parents sat opposite me, filling Mom's tiny linoleum kitchen to bursting. Mom cradled her coffee and looked ready to fall back asleep in her comfy sweater. Dad had arrived in his work suit like he'd been up for hours.

They both stared at me for a long moment until I remembered I was the one who was supposed to be talking.

"I know last week was really rough," I said, "and I want to thank you for being so supportive."

"We love you, Bryant," Mom said.

"I'm finding it hard to be supportive of your coming home with new scars every two days." Dad laced his fingers together with his hands planted on the table like we were in some sort of business negotiation.

"I did start off by saying last week was rough. And"—I pressed on before Dad could pull out some sort of contract obligating me not to get any more scarred up than I already was—"I really think things are looking up."

Mostly true, though not exactly detailed.

"Go on." Dad leaned back in his chair.

"Eric and I found something," I said. "The break we've been looking for."

"Break in what?" Dad asked.

"A way for me to have a higher education," I said.

"A break in you going to college?" A crease formed on Dad's forehead.

"Not exactly college," I said. "Wizards don't have a university accreditation system. But there's a spot in Greece that has more books and knowledge than any other place in the world, and Eric and I have discovered an opportunity that makes this the perfect time to visit."

"Greece?" Mom clutched her coffee even tighter.

"It's the chance of a lifetime," I said. "I mean, I'm learning a ton from Eric, but there's so much in Greece even he doesn't know. And it's the same for Devon and Elizabeth."

"What would Devon and Elizabeth have to learn from a Greek wizard?" Dad asked.

Sometimes having smart parents really sucks.

"So, so much. About the history of magic and how the magical Manhattan we live in came to be," I said. "And there will be no Ladies in Greece. No Beville. No shadows who have our scent. Just a chance for all of us to learn about magic."

"If Greece is so safe, why didn't you go sooner?" Mom said.

"Because the opportunity to go to the place with the books wasn't a thing then." I dug my nails into the table. "And the chance won't last for long. We have an invitation to arrive in Greece the day after tomorrow. If we miss it, we might never be offered entry again."

My parents stared at each other. I could see the silent communication flying between them, but it was in some sort of parent language I couldn't understand.

"It's like getting an invitation to a workshop run by Fosse and Sondheim, Mom," I begged. "This is a once in a lifetime opportunity. This could be my only chance to be really, truly good at something."

Mom took a deep breath and looked at Dad one last time.

"I think it's a good idea for you to go," Mom said. "But there are some conditions. You need to check in at least twice a day."

"I'll have your phone set up to work overseas," Dad said. "And you'll be traveling with a chaperone."

"I can't have a chaperone," I said. "We're doing wizardy things."

"You are not going to a foreign country with only Eric Deldridge as supervision," Dad said. "Your chaperone can drop you off where you're going to study and pick you up at night."

"Okay," I said, "but I need money for plane tickets and hotels."

"You have the credit card. Feel free to use it wherever you like." A devious twinkle filled Dad's eyes.

"Is this some *you'll be watching me* thing?" I shrank down in my seat.

"It's only responsible to keep an eye on credit card transactions." Dad shrugged.

Mom looked at Dad, and she had a little glimmer in her eyes, too. Like she was proud of his stalking parenting skills, or maybe she was just super shocked that when I'd woken up at 6:30 a.m. filled with self-loathing for not having been brave enough to talk to my parents about leaving the country and decided to text Dad to ask if he'd come for breakfast, he'd knocked on our door at 7:15. Either way, she patted his hand when she said, "Well, if that's all settled, we've got to get to school."

Her fingers lingered on his for a moment.

If I had known any therapists in Beville, I would have called to schedule myself an appointment before I'd even left the breakfast table.

But I didn't. So I fled to my room and tried not to imagine my parents sitting creepily close to each other as I pulled on Elizabeth's sweatshirt. I walked to school with Mom, not bothering to say how pointless it was for me to go to class since I would be leaving the country for I didn't know how long the next day.

By the time I sat down in first period, I'd already texted Devon, Elizabeth, and Eric that my dad had agreed to pay. By the time I reached lunch, all I had to do was type my credit card number into a bunch of different pages on Elizabeth's phone to book the trip.

"How did you even find all this so fast?" I asked, trying not to think of how much money I was casting into the internet to buy four tickets to Greece. It was enough to pay my mom's rent for a month. My dad wouldn't even notice the money had been spent.

Except that he was going to be stalking my credit card.

"I've been poking around." Elizabeth took her phone back after I had pressed the purchase button. "I wanted to be prepared. Last one."

She pulled up a payment screen for a hotel.

"I figured I'd only book us two nights in Athens right now." Elizabeth handed the phone back to me.

"And from there, we can try to figure out where a master criminal hid a few thousand books," Devon said. "I'm starting to think we'll be back by the weekend."

"We can hope." I pressed the purchase button and watched more of my dad's money drift away into the ether. "All we have to do is find the books and then figure out how to smuggle them back into the country." I took a long drink of my juice, trying not to panic. "Shipping a few thousand books shouldn't be a big deal."

"We can worry about transport after we find the books." Elizabeth held my hand, and my panic shifted into gleeful *I'm going to Europe with my girlfriend* excitement.

"Now we're just two forged passports away from saving generations of magical knowledge." Devon dampened my glee.

"Eric told me he's got it covered," Elizabeth said.

"Which probably means someone's going to try to kill us before we actually get our hands on the papers." I chugged the rest of my juice. "When are we meeting him?"

"Elizabeth and I are supposed to go right after school," Devon said. "You don't have to—"

"I'm coming with you," I cut across Devon. "I usually really like Eric, but that doesn't mean I trust his sketchy contacts."

"I won't mind the company." Elizabeth leaned over and brushed her lips against my cheek.

"Not in my cafeteria," a grating voice shouted over the chaos of the hungry teens.

I froze, instinct telling me to reach for the phone in my pocket, reason telling me the Lancre lunch lady had been dead for months. Instinct won out, and I slipped my hand into my pocket as I turned around.

A middle-aged woman with a hairnet and scowl weaved through the now-staring students, heading right for our table. "There will be no PDA in my cafeteria."

"Who are you?" Devon looked from her hairnet to the lunch line where the other, nicer hairnet-wearing lunch ladies were still doing their jobs of, I don't know, feeding the students.

"I'm the one in charge," the middle-aged hairnet snapped. "And I won't allow any of this teenage, hormone-fueled lust in my lunchroom."

"Lust?" Heat shot into my face.

"It's fine." Elizabeth packed up the remainder of her lunch. "I needed to drop by the guidance counselor's office anyway. Maybe she can give me some tips on not showing any emotion or *lusting* after my boyfriend in public. God forbid teenagers form actual attachments. I can kiss my grandma on the cheek, but the school should have something to say about me doing the same thing to a guy."

"I won't take any lip from students." Hairnet sneered as she lumbered closer.

Elizabeth took my chin, tipped my face up, and kissed me. Like full-on *I forgot how to breathe because she tasted like roses and all things good* kissed me. My insides turned to goo, and the whole world disappeared.

And then Elizabeth stopped kissing me, and the world reappeared just in time for the entire cafeteria to start applauding.

"See you after school." Elizabeth brushed her lips against mine, curtsied for the still-applauding crowd, and strode out of the lunchroom.

The lunch lady stood there, sputtering. She said things about write-ups and inappropriate behavior, but people were still clapping and oohing, and the world was still wobbly because the most beautiful girl to have ever existed had kissed me in front of everyone. And the burn of embarrassment from all those people staring at me joined with the fire dancing around in my chest that made it quite impossible to hear whatever the lunch lady was yammering as Devon put my food back into my lunchbox, pressed it into my hands, and yanked me to my feet.

"If you want to write us up, tell the principal." Devon's words drifted through the haze in my brain. "If you just want to take your misery out on someone, find another victim. Or better yet, a therapist."

Devon dragged me to the front of the cafeteria as a renewed round of applause began.

"Where are we going?" I asked as we strode down the corridor and the sounds of the cheering crowd faded.

"Anywhere but in there." Devon's voice had a dark tinge to it, an angry kind of determination I wasn't used to hearing from him.

"Look"—I slowed my steps as we neared our next classroom—"I appreciate you standing up for Elizabeth and me, but as long as Elizabeth doesn't get into trouble, I really don't care."

"I know. I'm just over being treated like a kid when I've literally fought battles to save lives." Devon let go of my arm and ran his hands over his hair in a way that somehow made it look even chicer than when he'd styled it. "I'm not sure if it's because I'm out of my parents' apartment and living at the Consortium, and we're dealing with things the teachers here couldn't even begin to understand. Or maybe it's just that I'm not totally convinced the lunch lady isn't another Lancre come to kidnap my best friend."

The thought of another Lancre hiding in the school brought me crashing back into reality.

"I just couldn't stand her looming over us." Devon ran his hands over his hair again, upping its style...again. "I know I'm not the magical one, but it's starting to feel like existing in this school is tearing away pieces of the person I'm supposed to be. Beville is more real to me than this concrete cage."

"Devon—"

"I think Greece is going to be good for everybody. Get away from New York. Get stuff done. Find the books and restore the Library once and for all. We've just got to get on the plane and everything will get better."

I sat in our next class, not bothering to actually pay attention. I was too busy trying not to stare at Devon while I wondered what would happen once we did find the books. There'd be shipping and customs to deal with. We'd have to restock the shelves, and then find a way to tell the magical population of Manhattan the Ladies were gone. The evil women who had ruled over them for so long were no more. And then...I didn't know what the *and then* was. I didn't know how to tell a bunch of angry wizards there was no longer anyone in charge.

3

I held Elizabeth's hand as we walked from school to the subway stop at Columbus Circle. The crisp winter air stung my cheeks as the wind whipped between the buildings. I took a deep breath and allowed myself a moment to appreciate that, sure, my face would probably be red for the rest of the day, but at least the wind toned down the natural stink of the sludge-filled city.

"How cold is it supposed to be in Greece?" I asked as we weaved through the crowds and down into the subway station.

"Shouldn't you have looked that up before you started packing?" Devon asked.

"Do you actually believe he already started packing?" Elizabeth poked him in the back.

"I didn't want to look suspicious." I took the lead, heading toward the blank bit of wall off to the side where no one ever seemed to want to look. "If my mom found a packed suitcase under my bed and didn't know why I'd squirreled away a week's worth of underwear, I'd be doomed to even more therapy. *Portunda.*" I muttered the spell at the wall. An instant later, a door appeared.

Playing it as cool as I am capable of, I opened my newly formed door and let Elizabeth and Devon through before following and closing the door behind us. "*Portundo.*" My door disappeared, leaving us with a solid wall behind and the path to Beville ahead.

Elizabeth peered into the shadows along the edges of the tunnel.

I held my breath for a second, waiting for her to say there was something lurking that was going to jump out and try to kill us. But she slipped her hand into mine and started walking toward Beville.

We didn't speak as we headed deeper and deeper underground. The steady sounds of our footsteps dug into my skull in a way that wouldn't have bothered me before the whole wizard thing. Before people wanted me dead, silence meant better opportunities for daydreaming. Post-discovering my wizardishness, silence meant a better chance to hear evil things sneaking up on you. Things like Lancre, shadows, monsters, wizards who want to sell you, wizards who want to kill you...

I shook my head, trying to stop my brain from creating a complete list of all the things in Beville that might want me dead.

It didn't work.

Somewhere between evil spiders crawling up from depths even deeper than Beville and the children of the Minotaur I'd killed months ago, footsteps carried from farther down the tunnel.

I held my free hand forward, ready to attack whatever beast had come for our blood, but it was only Eric, striding up the tunnel like he literally had no concept of fear.

"I thought we were meeting you at your house," Devon said.

"That was the plan." Eric waited until we reached him then matched our pace, continuing down the tunnel.

"But?" I slipped my hand into my pocket, gripping my magical phone as I waited for whatever horror Eric was about to spring on us.

"The forger refuses to leave her lair," Eric said. "I had hoped, with a large enough financial incentive, we might be able to avoid going to her. But she made it clear she will not be coming into my home."

"Wait," Devon said, "which is it? She refuses to leave her lair, or she refuses to go into your home?"

"Does it matter?" Eric asked.

"Of course it does." Elizabeth spoke slowly as she squinted into the shadows. "Not wanting to go into your house is smart. You've trained your house to defend you. The doors chase people. Rooms appear and trap people."

"But not wanting to leave her lair is different," Devon said. "Then we've got to wonder if she's agoraphobic—"

"Or knows something we don't," Elizabeth continued. "And if the forger who deals with all the dark deeds of Beville has a good reason not to want to leave home—"

"Should we be walking the streets belowground?" I let go of my phone and held my non-Elizabeth claimed hand in front of me as subtly as I could manage, ready to shout *Abalata* at the first hint of anyone trying to murder us.

"Would you like the comforting response or the absolute truth?" Eric asked.

"The truth." My voice wavered a little.

"I'm not sure," Eric said. "I can smell something in the air. Change. Dissatisfaction. Revolution."

"But we already did the revolution part," I whispered as we reached the end of the tunnel.

"We did. The rest of Beville did not," Eric said. "The people have always been displeased with the Ladies but too terrified to fight against them. Now that the Ladies haven't tormented or killed anyone in more than two months, the whispers of malcontent have become murmured conversations of dissent."

I let myself look at the base of the giant spire I'd grown during the Battle of Beville. I knew the massive stone reached all the way to Times Square where it rose up with the skyscrapers in a way that defied geologic reason. I knew Thaden's headless body was trapped inside. I knew that battle had weakened the Ladies enough we'd managed to break into the Library, defeat them, and take over.

I couldn't imagine what it was like for the people of Beville who didn't know those things.

"How long does it take to go from the murmur stage to the revolution stage?" I asked as we headed down the street where Eric lived.

"I'm afraid I'm not sure of that either," Eric said. "Throughout the Ladies' rule, there was never a rebellion that survived long enough to truly begin."

"That's not completely true." Devon raised one perfectly sculpted eyebrow.

"As far as we are concerned"—Eric raised a perfectly sculpted eyebrow right back—"it is."

A weird feeling, like I was being watched from the windows of the surrounding houses, nibbled at the back of my neck.

I looked up to the arched ceiling thirty feet overhead. The lights set into the stone gave off an eerily warm glow that did nothing to stop the neck tingle. The weird difference in architecture from one street to the next didn't help either.

The houses changed as we entered what looked more like a suburb than the townhouse-ish vibe of Lark Lane where Eric lived. We passed by some sketchy shops and a few houses that looked like they wouldn't pass inspection aboveground.

I kept waiting for Eric to stop in front of one of the shops—I mean, they definitely looked like illegal dealings would be up their alley—but his pace never faltered.

We weaved down streets I'd never seen before and somehow turned onto a row I definitely remembered.

There were a couple of normal-looking brownstone houses and a log cabin crammed onto the street, just because. But it was the house that couldn't seem to decide what shape it wanted to be that made me forget I was supposed to be walking.

First, it looked like a theme park castle. Then, it flipped to a tropical hut. Then it went all haunted house, complete with wind rustling through the half-dead trees that appeared out front. Then it became a medieval castle, complete with a moat where the sidewalk should have been.

"Come on." Elizabeth tugged on my hand, and we jogged a few steps to catch up to Eric just as he stopped in front of the whitest house I'd ever seen.

The whole thing was built out of some weird, matte metal that looked like it belonged in a sci-fi movie. The front steps were paper-thin strips of white that floated lazily in the air. The windows shimmered in a way that made me not quite sure if they were glass or if I was actually looking at some sort of hologram.

"Here?" Devon whispered. "Really?"

"What were you expecting?" Eric paused for a moment, like he was girding his loins, before climbing the steps.

I held my breath, waiting for the thin strips of white to give under his weight, but the stairs stayed steady as he knocked on the front door.

Maybe I had just gotten too used to Eric's sentient house and the way its front door would just swing open and let people in when it wanted to. Or maybe I was used to how people aboveground peeked through the peepholes in their doors and then decided if they wanted to answer or pretend they weren't home so they could go back to binge watching streaming television. Whatever the reason, I definitely didn't expect the top half of the door to give a weird shimmer and fade away to be mostly transparent.

I also didn't expect to see a girl my age standing on the other side of the door, her arms crossed and face set in an epic scowl as she glared at Eric.

"I do believe we're right on time," Eric said.

The girl tipped her head to the side. Her super red curls bounced with the movement.

"I have brought cash as requested," Eric said.

The girl's lips narrowed into a frown.

"I give you my word as a wizard we were not followed by the Ladies," Eric said. "You will not be risking your security by letting us in."

The girl raised her hand toward the transparent part of the door. For a moment, I thought that would be that. The door would become solid, and we would just have to find a human forger who could make us passports overnight.

But then, with a *hum* so faint I barely noticed it, the whole door shimmered before disappearing.

"We made a deal for two passports, Deldridge," the girl said. "Why the hell do you have three people with you?"

"Raven." Eric gave a little bow. "It is as lovely to see you as ever. My apprentice does not need a passport. He has a legitimate document. However, he is intimately connected with the two in need of papers. Also, finding a way to leave him out of this little errand would have been more trying than I have time for at the moment."

"That's not my problem," Raven said.

"I'm the one paying for the trip." I took a little step forward. "And since I'm funding it, I have a right to make sure the passports we're buying will work. I don't want to have wasted thousands of dollars on plane tickets if these two can't even get through airport security."

"I didn't know you needed a backer." Raven gave an unfriendly grin. "How the mighty have fallen."

"Not fallen," Eric said. "My resources remain steady. However, my humble wealth cannot compete with the accounts to which Bryant has access. Really, you should be thanking me for the introduction."

Raven examined me, from my worn sneakers to my generic, water-resistant winter coat. "I appreciate the unlikely ones." She turned and walked away, going farther into her house.

"Keep close." Eric stepped inside.

For one horrible moment, I thought the door would reappear and trap Eric in the house. We'd be on our own trying to find the books. I'd have to be the one to break it to the people of Beville that they'd really been free of the Ladies for a few months, but we'd been too busy searching for the stolen books to tell them.

But then Devon stepped inside, and Elizabeth dragged me through the door with her.

I gripped Elizabeth's hand as the handle-less door shimmered back into being behind us.

4

The matte-white walls inside the house didn't make me feel better about being locked in with Raven. I glanced back at the door, ready to whisper a quick *Portunda* just to be sure I could make the door reappear. But Elizabeth gave a tiny shake of her head, so I silently followed her farther down the pure white hall.

I'd been in Eric's house often enough that the fact that the hallway was way too long to fit in Raven's house didn't really freak me out. So, as I kept walking down the plain white corridor, it took me a minute to figure out why there was a bubble of panic rising in my chest.

The whole house seemed to be giving off a faint *hum*. It came from the walls, the ceiling, and if I really concentrated, I could even feel it buzzing in my feet as I walked.

"I hate to be rude," Eric said.

"Then don't be." Raven didn't change her pace.

"You give me no choice," Eric said. "Our time is precious these days, and, though I appreciate the theatrics of leading us down an unending corridor, I'm afraid we need to keep our business brief."

"I'm not wasting your time, Deldridge," Raven said.

"So you've moved your work room since my last visit?" Eric asked.

"Nope. Just letting the house do its work," Raven said.

"I'm sorry, what?" I took a few quick steps, dragging Elizabeth forward so we were right on Devon's heels.

"The walls are gathering images," Raven said.

"Wouldn't it be easier to just take a normal passport picture?" Devon asked.

"Sure." Raven stopped and turned around to face us. "But the walls aren't analyzing your faces for the passports. I'm more interested in finding out if your faces match the people I've been looking for."

"What?" My voice cracked enough to make heat shoot up into my cheeks. "Why would you be looking for us?"

Elizabeth squeezed my hand super hard with a grip that quite clearly said *Please don't speak. You're a terrible actor. You will make things worse.*

"I'm not sure if Eric told you," Elizabeth said in a voice that wasn't suspicious, "but Devon and I aren't wizards. So whoever you're looking for, it can't be us."

"Actually, I think it makes you better candidates." Raven tapped the wall, and a portion shimmered and vanished, leaving a doorway in its wake.

She walked into the room, and Eric followed her without any hint of trepidation.

Devon glanced behind to give Elizabeth and me a shrug before stepping up to the door. "Whoa." His eyes lit up like it was Christmas morning as he walked out of sight.

"I hate the going through the doorway into the unknown thing," I whispered as Elizabeth and I took our turn stepping up to the door.

The room beyond was...not what I expected.

"Whoa." I copied Devon's astonished joy as I took in the full wall of monitors, massive bank of computers, and workshop table filled with shiny machine bits like we'd just walked into a superhero's secret lab. "This is the best place ever."

"Yeah." Devon drifted to the corner of the room where a silver coat, which looked almost like a fencing jacket, hung next to a silver shield.

"You're still pursuing your side projects?" Eric leaned over the table with his hands tucked behind his back, peering at the bits of metal and wire that were probably going to be used to build something awesome.

"You're still causing chaos." Raven sat at a keyboard and typed, her fingers moving faster than I could ever hope to achieve. "Well, I guess that's not really true. Even you've never been brazen enough to cause so much trouble topside."

Videos popped up on all the screens. White walls, tall tables covered with electronics, people milling around trying to decide what to spend their money on.

My stomach sank as I recognized the subterranean store.

"There is no need for this display, Raven." Eric clenched his hands behind his back like he was stopping himself from stopping her.

"We're just about the get to the good part." Raven pointed to the top right monitor just as the glass spiral staircase at the center of the white store shattered.

On the next screen over, my shield spell shimmered to life.

Right below it, Devon's sword grew with a red glow.

"The cops have all this footage, of course," Raven said. "They've been careful to keep the decapitated woman off the news. I mean, they have to be. How could they explain to the regulars that a Lancre had been in the store? Long bones, long teeth. The cops aren't stupid enough to call that monster *human*."

"What have they been calling it?" I asked.

"I'm more interested in what the Ladies have been calling it." Raven spun in her chair to look at Eric. "The pipe breaking at that creepy boarding school—"

"It wasn't a boarding school." Elizabeth shivered.

"—I can understand the Ladies ignoring that," Raven pressed on. "Water pipes break. Vandalism happens. The school was filled with juvenile delinquents, so a little destruction makes sense. But that—"

Raven pointed over her shoulder at the largest of the screens.

There was no sound, but from the way screen-Eric's mouth moved, I could tell he was shouting a spell as the Lancre leapt toward him. The tape slowed down for a second, like Raven wanted to be sure we could all see the shift in the air as Eric's spell flew toward the Lancre.

I knew what was coming but somehow couldn't make myself look away as the spell sliced through the Lancre's neck.

The video went back to normal speed as the Lancre's body fell to the ground and her head rolled out of the frame.

"The police are losing their shit trying to figure out how a monster's head just fell off her body." Raven reached behind her and pressed a button. The videos started over from the beginning. "It's not like they can prosecute you, of course. They couldn't explain to a jury how you killed the monster that shouldn't exist. But they have footage, Deldridge."

"And how did you find the tapes?" Eric tented his fingers under his chin.

"Because I'm not like the rest of Beville. I'm not just biding my time underground, fiddling around with magic. I'm a tech girl." Raven spread her arms wide. "Tech starts with topsiders. Monitoring what happens aboveground is in my best interest. That and"—she pointed to a monitor just as one of the Lancre's minions bit into my hand—"it's perfect for my viewing pleasure."

"What do you want?" Devon stepped forward.

"The human asks first?" Raven smiled.

"What do you want?" Devon said again.

"I want to know why the Ladies haven't come after you yet. I want to know where it is you're fleeing to with the very expensive passports you want me to make. And I want to know what kind of awful mess you're trying to drag all of wizard kind into by exposing us to the topsiders, Eric Deldridge."

We stayed silent for a long moment.

I rocked back on my heels as my body begged me to flee from Raven's simmering glare.

Eric took a deep breath. "The Ladies have never been known for their swiftness in carrying out punishments."

"The cops have you on video. Even the Ladies wouldn't take their time reacting to something like that," Raven said. "Lie to me one more time, and you won't get any passports out of me."

I watched Eric thinking. His face was completely still, but somehow I could see all the cogs turning in his head.

"The Ladies are dead," Eric said.

I made a sound somewhere between a whimper and a gurgle.

"I said no more lies." Raven stood, kicking her chair back toward her computers.

"It's no lie," Eric said. "They've been dead for two months. We've taken over the Consortium and the Library."

"Bullshit."

"What you see on that video are the consequences of our trying to stop a Lancre placed in the store in hopes of searching out new wizards to be sold at auction in the horrible settlement far below Beville." Eric stepped closer to Raven.

"There is nothing below Beville," Raven said.

"I assure you there is." Eric pulled aside his collar. "A bone witch gave me this scar when she kidnapped Bryant and me and then tried to sell him. We disposed of most who were indulging in the foul trade of purchasing wizard flesh, but we have yet to deal with Kendrick McDonald. Surely you've heard of him. He ran The Game until we drove him out of business."

"Do you actually think I'm dumb enough to believe this?" Raven stepped so close to Eric she had to tip her chin up to look him in the eyes.

"I haven't even come to the great tragedy of our tale," Eric whispered. "The

Library is empty. It has been since long before we were born. The books were stolen, and the Ladies hid the truth of their shame from all of us. We need the passports to try and find the books."

"Bullshit." Tears sparkled in the corners of Raven's eyes.

"We're running out of time, Raven. The knowledge of our ancestors is being sold off on the black market. It drifts further away from our grasp with every lost day. I am asking you to help save the legacy of our people. Anything the police find, any anger from the people of Beville when the truth comes out, it's all meaningless compared to saving the books. Nothing can matter as much as the books."

"You're wrong." Raven spoke so softly I could barely hear her words. "There are books in the Library. The rules of impartment still stand. I won't believe in the fairy tale of the Ladies' death, or any other heroic daydream where you rescue us all."

"Your phone, Bryant," Eric said.

"What?" I gripped my pocket. "No."

"Your phone." Eric held out his hand. "You'll get it back unharmed."

My hand shook as I reached into my pocket and pulled out my one-of-a-kind magical mobile. The black case didn't have a ding on it. After all we'd been through together, the screen hadn't even been scratched. The distance from my pocket to Eric's hand felt like a million miles as I reached forward and laid the phone on his palm.

Eric pressed his thumb to the scanner and started scrolling through spells.

"What are you doing?" Raven shifted to stand beside Eric, peering at the phone.

"Here." Eric stopped scrolling. "Go on. Speak the spell."

"I'm not a kid on the playground anymore," Raven said. "I'm not going to fall for your tricks."

"Try it," Devon said. "What have you got to lose?"

Raven moved her mouth for a moment as though she were soundlessly practicing the word.

I shifted to the side, placing myself between Elizabeth and Raven before she could speak the spell.

"*Viodula.*" A little *whoosh* filled the air as Raven spoke, and then...nothing.

I glanced around the room, searching for whatever it was the spell had done, but everything in the room looked the same.

Except...for the laughter in Elizabeth's eyes. And Devon's eyes. And the slight twitch of Eric's lips, like he was determined not to smile. And the awe on Raven's face as she stared at me.

"What?" I looked between the four of them. "What?"

"Well, I couldn't let her read a spell that might prove dangerous to us." Eric handed me back the phone.

"But what spell did you give her?" I looked at the screen.

For violet pigmentation.

That was the whole damn description.

"What did you do to me?" I shoved the magical phone into my pocket and pulled out my normal phone.

"I think it actually looks pretty nice." Elizabeth giggled.

"What is it?" I turned on the front camera of my normal phone and spent a solid ten seconds blinking at the image.

I looked normal. Pasty skin, brown eyes, casual purple hair.

"Put it back." I rounded on Eric.

"We'll see if there's a counter spell later," Eric said.

"If?" I said.

"How did you do that?" Raven asked. "The Ladies never gave me that spell. I shouldn't have been able to use it."

"The phone is free of the rules of impartment," Eric said. "Thaden created it when he broke into the Library and burned the few volumes the Ladies had left. We took the same path into the Library and found the shelves empty."

"If?" I said again.

"It really looks pretty decent, Bry," Devon said.

"I've told you," Eric said, "the Ladies are dead. The rules of impartment hold no sway over the passing of new knowledge. Their reign of ignorance has ended."

"If!" I shouted.

"After all you have sacrificed to protect magic, are you really making this much of a fuss about hair?" Eric sighed.

"Why didn't you have her magic your hair?" I asked.

"The spell could have chosen to affect any of us," Eric said. "It was purely the luck of the draw."

Elizabeth wrapped her arm around my waist and laid her head on my shoulder. "I like the punk look. It's rebellious."

A happy little squirm wriggled up my spine as I pictured myself becoming an epic revolutionary worthy of posters being hung on bedroom walls in Beville.

"The books really aren't in the Library?" Raven sank down in her chair.

"They aren't," Elizabeth said. "We're going to bring them back. But we have to go tomorrow, and we have to have those passports."

"It shouldn't be up to the four of you," Raven said. "There shouldn't be any humans involved. We should let the people of Beville know what's happened. Send an army after the books."

"And when the information falls into the wrong hands?" Eric asked. "Free knowledge is a beautiful dream, the pursuit of which has nearly cost me my life more times than I can count. But how many people in Beville would take the knowledge of the Ladies' demise and use it for their own gain? To extort, to hurt without fear of punishment, to try and hoard the books for themselves."

"You really are on your own then." Raven buried her face in her hands.

"No, we're not," Devon said. "You just joined the team."

"I'm not on anybody's team." Raven stood and went to a machine in the far corner. "The only person whose side I'm on is me."

"So you're building magical armor for yourself?" Devon pointed to the shield and jacket on the far wall.

"I'm building armor to sell to the highest bidder." Raven pressed a few buttons, and the machine started whirring like a printer. "And trust me, even purple-hair can't afford my creations."

"What's your starting price?" I asked.

5

- *Socks*
- *Underwear*
- *Pants*
- *Sweaters*
- *Shirts*
- *Raincoat*
- *Phone 2x*
- *Phone charger 1x*
- *Wallet*
- *Passport*
- *Sunglasses*
- *Hat to cover my purple freakin' hair*
- *Hipster scarf to cover my neck scar*
- *Toothbrush*
- *Toothpaste*
- *Deodorant*
- *Sunscreen 'cause I'm pasty*
- *And...*

I was up most of the night thinking about the *and*.

I'd traveled before. I'd even been out of the country before. But for some reason, I couldn't stop feeling like I was completely unprepared.

It was after midnight by the time Mom and I realized there was no way boxed dye was going to cover my new purple do. Two in the morning before she'd finished adding thumbholes to my shirts and I finally zipped my suitcase and climbed into bed.

I'm really not sure I actually fell asleep before my dad came with his car to take me to the Consortium.

Mom rode with us. And, even though I could have walked and definitely didn't need two parents to accompany me on the two-second ride, it was nice to have them with me. Almost like they were escorting me to my first day of larceny kindergarten.

When the three of us got out of the car, the lights in the Consortium were already burning bright.

"Right. Well, I guess this is it." I turned to my parents, giving them each as good a hug as I could manage through my winter coat. "You guys go and get some coffee before work." I held the car door open for them to both climb into the back.

"You need the car, honey," Mom said. "Your dad and I can walk."

"No, it's fine," I said. "I know a really great cabbie, and—"

"A cab can only fit four people," Mom said.

"But we only have four people." I pointed to the Consortium window where Devon, Elizabeth, and Eric were all saying goodbye to Lola.

"Five people," Dad said. "You plus four others. That makes five."

"But I bought four tickets." I blinked at my dad, trying to get my early morning brain to figure out if I had somehow forgotten how to count or if Dad thought he was coming with me.

"Don't worry," Dad said. "I added a ticket for her."

"Her?" I looked to Mom.

"Your chaperone." Mom smiled just as a cab pulled up and a woman stepped out onto the sidewalk.

She wasn't the big burly security type, or even the prim protective Mary Poppins type. She looked more like a *just out of Grad school and super happy to intern for next to no pay* type.

"Dad, if we could just…" I pointed to the shadows on the far corner of the Consortium's awning.

"Sure." Dad smiled as I left my rolling suitcase in my mom's care, grabbed his arm, and dragged him away from Miss Chipper Intern.

"What's going on?" I whispered.

"I told you you'd have a chaperone," Dad said.

"I didn't think you were serious. We're going to do magical things. If this lady sees magic, what am I supposed to do? What if she hears the word *wizard* coming out of my mouth and decides to turn me in to Interpol?"

"That's not how Interpol works."

"People can't find out about magic, and the"—I stopped myself before saying *mission*—"studying"—I continued in a not at all super suspicious way—"I'll be doing is all about magic and spells and things regular people aren't supposed to know about."

"You were a wizard for months before I knew," Dad said. "If you kept it from me, you can certainly keep it from Cindy."

"That's entirely different, and you know it," I whispered. "I wasn't riding in cars with you. I wasn't stuck on an international flight with you."

"If you're really concerned about Cindy finding out anything she shouldn't, just be sure Devon and Elizabeth do all the talking." Dad clapped me on the shoulder like he knew damn well he was putting me in a corner with no wiggle room. "Better get going. Don't want to be late for your flight."

I turned back toward the car to find Mom and Cindy talking like they were old friends. No, not friends, coconspirators in my international oppression.

"Are we ready?" Eric led Devon and Elizabeth out of the Consortium. He eyed Cindy. "Did you call a cab, Bryant?"

"Nope." I took my suitcase from Mom and dragged it back to the trunk of Dad's car. "With my chaperone Cindy here, we make five, so we're all going to be riding in Dad's car."

Eric stayed still as stone for a moment. "Perfect. The last thing I would want is to be your babysitter. Being your tutor is work enough for anyone."

I waved through the Consortium window to Lola, who stayed firmly inside in her feather-trimmed dressing gown, and crawled back into the car.

Cindy climbed into the seat opposite mine. "Hi Bryant, it's really nice to meet you." She reached for my hand.

I considered being super petty and refusing to acknowledge her existence, then realized that might only make her watch me even more carefully.

"Nice to meet you." I shook her hand. "Sorry my dad is shipping you overseas to nanny me."

Cindy laughed. "I'm not coming to be your nanny." Cindy paused to greet Elizabeth and Devon as they climbed into the other two backseats.

"Then why are you coming?" A touch of hope flared in my chest as I actually deluded myself into believing maybe we were just giving Cindy a ride to the airport and then she would be heading off on some other errand for my dad.

"Your father hired me as your translator and driver." Cindy waved out the window to my parents as the car pulled away. "From what Mr. Adams tells me, no one in your group speaks Greek or has a driver's license."

"Your dad has a good point." Devon closed his eyes and leaned back like he was actually calm enough to sleep.

My normal phone buzzed in my pocket.

Why did I receive no warning, and how are you getting rid of her? Eric messaged me from the front seat.

I thought my dad wasn't serious, and I have no idea, I messaged back.

I could feel Eric's disappointment radiating toward me from the front of the car.

Sorry, I added.

Elizabeth reached over from her seat beside me and laced her fingers through mine.

I looked to Cindy, waiting for her to say that really her job was translation, driving, *and* making sure I didn't touch my girlfriend. But the chaperone was looking out the window, watching pre-dawn Manhattan speed by and not giving a hoot about my mild PDA.

"By the end of the day, we'll be in Greece." Elizabeth gave me a dazzling smile, and I couldn't tell if she was actually excited to be flying to another country or just putting on a show for Cindy.

I focused my gaze on Elizabeth, trying to pretend there wasn't a stranger sitting opposite me and the fate of magical knowledge didn't rest on my incompetent shoulders. "It's gonna be great." I was so wrapped up in how sparkly Elizabeth's eyes were, it actually came out in an almost convincing manner.

We didn't hit much traffic as we made our way out of the city and to the airport. It was too early for most people, and we were heading against the commuters anyway.

Before the fact that the next time I slept in a bed I'd be in a different country than my parents really sank in, the driver pulled up at the departures terminal and got out to unload our bags.

Five rolly bags, three backpacks, one purse, and one douche wizard who probably had so much hidden in his pockets he didn't need a bag.

Everything was going fine as we checked in, handed over our rolling suit-cases, and headed to airport security. It was easy, like we were just regular people going on a nice international trip.

Until we got in line to get our IDs checked to go through security. That's when my sleep-deprived brain freaked out.

"Ma'am, you need a passport to get on your flight." The ID checker had about as much compassion/enthusiasm as a hired princess at her third preschool party of the day.

"This is a special kind of license," no-passport lady said. "I can get through. I promise."

"Your promise doesn't have any sway over the law."

The law.

What an abstract yet firm construct.

Because people had drawn lines on a map, the law said we needed fancy printed papers to leave our part of the game board. The absurdity of it brought a laugh to my throat, just before the reality of having two illegal passports in our party shot panic through my veins.

The line moved forward, inching us closer to the ID checker.

But was having faux passports really that bad? They had all the right information on them...I hoped. I hadn't checked.

But Raven had seemed like she wanted to help. So she wouldn't have done anything weird to the passports...probably.

But did she actually care about obeying the human-style laws? Did she care about any laws?

I mean, now that the Ladies were gone, technically there weren't any laws governing the wizards in Manhattan.

Which on the one hand was very cool. Wizards didn't need the Ladies doling out spells like a miser who has yet to be visited by the spirits of Christmas past, present, and future. We didn't need arbitrary lines on a subterranean map telling us where magic could be used and where it was banned.

Except, maybe we did.

What if, without the Ladies, all the wizards of Beville just decided to hop right on up into Manhattan. Whether they meant to or not, they'd cause chaos. There would be too much magic flying around for anyone, even the normally oblivious Manhattanites, not to notice.

First, the reporters would panic.

Then, the police would panic.

Then, everyone would panic and start calling wizards freaks and we'd end up locked in weird magic-proof cages where they would do experiments on us to find out if they could make us into mutant super soldiers.

But some wizards would stay free.

And they'd have to fight back.

They'd be declared evil for standing against the human government, but all reasonable wizards would know they were vigilantes, fighting for the freedom of magickind.

My daydreams of epic magical battles waged in Times Square wouldn't be daydreams anymore. The whole city, maybe even the whole world, would be dragged into an existence where wizards were creatures to be used or feared.

The only thing protecting us from that awful fate was the laws put in place by the evil Ladies we had overthrown. And as soon as the people of Beville found out the Ladies were no more, the laws would dissolve like cotton candy dipped in a puddle by a sad raccoon.

And it was our fault. We had started the beginning of the end. We'd been trying to help, but leaving a void where laws should be would make things worse in an unforgivable way.

"It's wrong." My words came out as a strangled whisper. "It's all wrong."

"Is he okay?" The ID checker stared at me. She held Devon's fake passport in her hand, and Elizabeth already had hers out and ready.

They were both breaking the law. They were going to be dragged away and locked up and I was going to be put in a research facility by some secret branch of the human government and I wouldn't be able save my friends.

"No." I shook my head so hard the airport went blurry. "No, no we can't do this. It's too dangerous. We can't trust Raven." I reached for Elizabeth's passport.

"Sure we can." Elizabeth moved her passport out of my reach as the ID checker grabbed her walkie-talkie.

"He's terrified of flying," Devon said with a hint of humor in his voice I in no way appreciated.

"I am not—"

"I don't think *terrified* quite covers it." Elizabeth looped her arm through mine, squeezing tight. "We've been through this—planes and birds are both built to fly."

"He had a raven attack him when he was little." Devon took his passport and ticket back. "He's been afraid of flying things and Edgar Allan Poe ever since."

"He's been seeing a really great therapist." Elizabeth passed her papers over. "And as soon as we get him to the gate, he'll be taking a nice dose of Dramamine. The drowsy kind."

"Yep," Devon said. "Just enough to calm him down."

"We don't want a fuss in the airport." The ID checker set her walkie-talkie down and returned Elizabeth's passport like it wasn't fake at all.

"No fuss." Elizabeth lifted my hand, making me give the checker my papers. "Just a phobia and some early morning brain fatigue."

"Right." The lady scanned my passport, made a few marks on my paper ticket, and passed everything back. "Have a nice flight. And remember to stay calm or they can and will remove you from the airport."

I answered with a weird sort of guttural whimper.

"Breathe, Bryant," Elizabeth whispered in my ear as we joined the post ID checker, pre x-ray belt line.

"We never should have gotten involved with someone like Raven." I wrapped one arm around Elizabeth's waist and rammed my other hand into my pocket. Neither actually hid how badly my hands were shaking.

"It worked," Devon said. "Raven didn't almost get us tossed by security, you did. So just relax. We'll be napping on the plane in no time."

"But she—"

"Mr. Adams didn't mention that you have a fear of flying, Bryant," Cindy said.

"I have a feeling there's a lot my dad forgot to mention."

With Cindy standing so close, I couldn't even tell the others that Raven might be the crack in the dam of secrets that could ruin the lives of everyone in the world.

6

W hen flying internationally, if the chaperone your dad hired decides to upgrade all of you to business class, you go with it. That way, you can pretend to sleep while actually panicking about the fact that you've quite possibly destroyed both the magical and non-magical worlds in comfort.

During take off, I was still super worried about Raven outing the death of the Ladies to everyone in Beville/having added a code to Devon's and Elizabeth's passports that made them look like criminals so they'd be arrested the moment we landed in Athens.

By the time we'd gotten solidly over the ocean, I realized that, like it or not, I was going to have to find a way to preserve the secrecy of the magical world to:

1. Make sure Manhattan didn't end up looking like a casualty of the latest, large-cast superhero movie.
2. Not let wizards decide to sneak into human politics and slowly take over the world.
3. Keep Beville from becoming a subterranean tourist trap.
4. Avoid being locked in a secret government facility before finishing high school.

Sometime after the last round of snacks but before the plane actually started to land, the first awkward steps of a semi-ludicrous and potentially catastrophic plan started to form.

Of course, I couldn't say anything because Cindy was sitting in the seat right behind me, and for all I knew super hearing was on her special skills list right next to translator and driver.

"You feeling better?" Elizabeth rested her head on my shoulder.

"Umm." I tried to think of a way to tell her my plan without using any words like *magic, seizing control of the government,* or *uprising.* "Yeah. We're really doing this. It feels good to be on the move."

"I hope we can find a second to see some of the sights."

I could hear Elizabeth's smile in her voice.

"If we don't, we'll just come back another time." I shifted so I could wrap my arm around her.

"I'm a soon-to-be emancipated minor. I don't have money for vacations."

"Completely untrue. You're a soon-to-be emancipated minor with a boyfriend who has a father who would gladly pay for the trip as long as he approves all sight-seeing expeditions."

"I'm not dating you for your dad's money." Elizabeth leaned away enough to look into my eyes.

"And I'm not dating you because you're the most gorgeous girl to have ever lived. But those are the packages we came in."

Elizabeth leaned in and brushed her lips against mine. "Your dad paying Nikki to deal with all the legal stuff is a really great boyfriend bonus."

"Yeah, Nikki can be useful."

And just like that, the wheels in my head were spinning like a whirling dervish as we touched down in Athens, Greece—stop one on our quest to save the books.

Even though I was exhausted, hungry, and desperately in need of a shower, a weird kind of energy filled my body as we collected our luggage and got in line for customs.

I had plans. Big, save the world kinds of plans, and I was one cup of coffee and some decent cell service from starting on the project that would save the world.

Dogs sniffed around the customs line, and a little pang zinged through my chest. I wished we could have brought Sniffer McDeadDog with us. The kid deserved some globetrotting. I smiled as the dog came closer to us and sat down, staring right at Devon's suitcase.

"What a good boy." I beamed like an idiot.

The guard said something I couldn't understand to Devon.

"Sorry?" Devon said.

"You, come with me." The guard reached out and grabbed Devon's arm. "Bring your bag."

"What?" Devon said.

"Why?" I said.

"This boy is a minor under my care," Cindy said.

The guard examined our party. "All of you come."

He didn't loosen his grip on Devon's arm as he stormed a path through the rest of the crowd waiting for customs, leaving us to scramble along in his wake.

"I sometimes forget how inconvenient air travel can be." Eric frowned as the guard hauled Devon to a section of tables off to the side of the space. "So much security packed into one tiny place."

"I don't mind being patted down." Devon spread his legs and lifted his arms for one guard to pat him down while another searched his backpack and a third unzipped his suitcase. "I don't know what your dog scented on my bag. I mean, I live with some rare breed canines"—not really an adequate description of Lola's guards, but whatever—"but I don't think any of them went near my suitcase."

The guard searching Devon's rolly bag flipped open the top and started digging through Devon's socks, pants, and toiletries. Everything looked normal until the bottom layer where the security guard reached a metal tube, a blue and orange foam dart blaster, a tub of gray capsules, a shiny jacket, and a metal disk the size of a tea saucer.

I don't think I've ever mentally sworn so much in my life.

"What is this?" The guard lifted the metal hilt.

I held my breath, waiting for the red glowing sword to blossom to life and drive through the guard's face as she squinted into the dangerous end of the tube.

"It's for school," Elizabeth said at the same moment Devon said, "I like to photoshop," I added "LARP!" and Eric sighed and looked to the ceiling like he'd given up all hope.

"It's a LARP school project, and we're using photoshop," I said.

Devon and Elizabeth both looked to me with fear in their eyes like I'd just stepped into a shadow monster's lair without any hope of using magic.

"We're in a drama club back home, and one of the projects we're working on is Live Action Role Playing, LARP, as a way to get really into character and develop traits that fit our roles." The words spewed out of my mouth. "We're going to be missing some school, and to make up for being gone, we're doing extra credit by taking pictures as our characters during our trip. We couldn't bring our whole costumes because the luggage weight would have been way too much, so Devon's going to photoshop in a light saber for his character. The foam blaster and jacket are for me. I'm portraying a futuristic cop, but obviously real-looking weapons are a huge no-no."

"And her?" The guard pointed to Elizabeth.

"Alice in Wonderland," I said. "The disc is a saucer for a teacup at the Mad Hatter's party."

The guard pointed to Eric.

"Don't involve me in this. I'm merely here as the tutor," Eric said.

"I'm the chaperone," Cindy said.

"What are these?" The guard held up the tub of gray capsules.

"Stool softeners," I said. "Devon's a nervous traveler. Can't let nerves hurt the bowels."

Deep pink tinged Devon's cheeks. "I have a temperamental stomach."

"Right." I dug my hands into my pockets, clutching my magical phone and wondering how much damage I would be doing to the fate of the world if I had to use magic to escape the Athens airport.

"Be sure to respect the monuments and temples in your photoshopping," the guard said. "They weren't built for tourists to play in. They were built to honor the ancient gods."

"We will be sure to respect all the things," Devon said. "Promise."

The guard muttered something in Greek I'm pretty sure translated to *stupid American tourists*. She tossed Devon's stuff almost into his suitcase and handed him the unzipped mess. "Enjoy your time in Athens."

"Thanks." Devon took his suitcase and knelt on the ground, shoving what had been neatly folded clothes into a wad so he could zip his bag.

"Mr. Adams didn't mention any photo project to me." Cindy took Devon's backpack from the other guard.

"Dad's never shown much interest in my homework," I said. "As long as I get A's he doesn't actually ask."

"Right," Cindy said. "Well, if I can get a list of your lesson plans tonight, I'll look around and see what nice photo ops we can squeeze in."

"I think Eric can get the schedule to you." I looked at Eric, because clearly as the *tutor* he should be the one who had that sort of information.

"Absolutely," Eric said. "I haven't made a schedule for tomorrow yet. Young Bryant tends to become violently ill at the drop of a hat. I wanted to see if he was capable of leaving his room before making any firm plans."

"I'll locate the nearest hospital, too," Cindy said.

"Thanks." I glared at Eric's back as the guards led us to a special place where we could cut part of the line since they'd gone through the trouble of tearing apart Devon's bag.

"I'm not sure if I should be mortified or impressed," Eric murmured when Cindy had stepped forward to have her passport stamped.

"That you're going to have to turn in a written schedule to Cindy the chaperone?" I whispered back.

"That you managed to tell an absurd yet somehow very convincing lie."

7

G etting rental cars sucks. Driving through a city way older than your country is cool. Finally getting to hop into a hot shower after being in recycled air for so long you might be patient zero for the plague that starts the zombie apocalypse—priceless.

I tried not to let myself think too hard about the epic disaster I might be causing as I messaged my dad.

Landed safe. At the hotel. Also, would it be okay if I asked Nikki to help me with a project? Nothing big, I swear I'm not in any trouble. It's more like an academic theory I want to run past someone who knows about law.

I set my phone down, assuming Dad wouldn't answer since it was the middle of the workday in Manhattan.

I started looking for my toothbrush, and my phone dinged.

Glad you got in safe. As long as it's purely academic, I'm happy to have you chat with Nikki. She's an excellent resource. I'll call her tomorrow and tell her to expect you to contact her.

I let myself feel a moment of triumph and began to set my phone back down before it dinged again.

If you're considering law as a career, I have a friend in the department at Yale. We should drive out and have lunch with her when you get home.

I rubbed my hands over my face. My fingers grazed my hair and, even though I know I couldn't *feel* the purple, it reminded me I still had the do of someone way cooler-with-a-hint-of-punk than I'd ever be.

I pulled my shirt on and tucked my thumbs through their little sleeve holes before I could catch a glimpse of my scarred hand and add that to my freak out over the pile of ways magic had left its mark on my body.

"Bryant," Elizabeth called before knocking on the door, like she knew a random knock would make me panic but her voice would send me to the gooey place where I'm not really capable of worrying.

"Coming." I grabbed my boho scar-covering scarf, crammed everything I needed into my pockets, and ran to the door.

I'll be the first person to shout to the whole world that my girlfriend is glorious, but there was something about her standing in a hotel hallway in an ancient city wearing a pale blue cardigan that made me wonder if maybe Elizabeth wasn't human at all. Maybe she was a goddess and I'd just always been too smitten to see through her ruse.

"Are you ready to go? I'm starving." The goddess reached for my hand and led me out for a night in Athens.

———

I'm not a travel writer. I'm a barely competent wizard who's trying to preserve magical knowledge and maybe not have world order crumble if I can swing it.

I'm not qualified to tell you about the economics that made it so Athens is filled with graffiti right next to, or even on, fancy marble buildings that are way older than anything in Manhattan. I don't know enough about art to tell you why some of the graffiti should really be considered street art and is so cool there ought to be a way to move it into a big art gallery.

I have no clue why the plaza with the big fountain was important, what the random super-old columns in the middle of a field were for, or what the street we walked down to find dinner had been before it was taken over by gift shops and restaurants that catered to tourists.

But, as a person with a reasonable amount of experience with magic, I can tell you that walking through a chilly evening holding the hand of the girl you love, listening to the people you pass speak in a language you don't understand, all while surrounded by architecture so foreign to my Manhattan-raised bones I might as well be in a movie—that is a truly magical experience.

Cindy got us a table on the sidewalk with one of those weird little gas torches in the middle to keep us warm, and by the time we'd eaten, all of us were laughing while gazing up at the ruins of the Acropolis high on the hill with lights beaming on them like it was the end of a quest in a video game.

Eric and Cindy discussed our schedule for the next day while I snuck bits of my meat to the three stray cats hiding under the table and decided I wouldn't mind traveling overseas more often.

The happy adventurer daze carried me all the way back to my hotel room where I was ready to tumble into bed and dream of bringing Elizabeth back to Athens someday when we were old enough that my dad wouldn't be able to demand we have any chaperones. I was just about to crawl in between my blissfully not over-starched sheets when a knock sounded on my door.

I rammed my feet into my shoes while grabbing my phone from the nightstand.

"Who is it?" I called. I didn't sound at all calm. Apparently, I had burned through all my acting skills at the airport.

"Your tutor," Eric said.

"Right." I tried to tuck my phone into my pocket before remembering I was wearing pajamas. "Sorry." I kept the phone in my hand as I opened the door.

Eric, Elizabeth, and Devon waited in the hall. Eric pressed a finger to his lips and led them all inside, then clicked the door quietly closed behind them. He murmured a spell at the door and I felt a whisper of magic fly past me.

"Do you think we're going to be attacked?" Devon sat on my bed. His pajama pants had pockets, and there was no mistaking the presence of his sword's hilt.

I suddenly felt a lot less weird about gripping my phone for dear life.

"I have no reason to believe we'll be attacked," Eric said. "However, with the unexpected added complication of a chaperone, I thought it best to make sure she didn't hear any voices coming from Bryant's room."

"When did the whole chaperone thing happen?" Devon asked.

"When Dad agreed to pay." I ran my hand over my hair, remembered it was purple, and cringed. Not that purple isn't a great color for hair. I just wasn't the kind of guy who could pull things like that off. "Sorry, I thought he didn't mean it."

"It'll be fine." Elizabeth eased my phone out of my death grip. "One human chaperone doesn't even rank on the list of top twenty problems we've encountered."

"It does cause a rather large headache for the tutor who is supposed to have a lesson plan," Eric said.

"Sorry," I said again.

"So what's the schedule for tomorrow, Teach?" Devon asked.

"We have a rather long day visiting the Acropolis Museum and the Acropolis itself," Eric said. "Both of which are located conveniently near the only wizarding contact I have in Greece. I'm hoping once we're thoroughly ensconced in the history of ancient Athens, Cindy will allow us to wander away."

"And what's the lesson plan from there?" I asked. "We don't know where the woman who was shipping the books to New York to be sold might actually be."

"I've informed Cindy that Bryant's father arranged this trip in the hopes of Bryant gaining a deeper understanding of non-U.S. cultures. To instill the greatest appreciation in Bryant, we're going to be following his interests," Eric said.

"What does that mean?" I asked.

"Get ready to lie some more, because you're going to be in charge of convincing Cindy to drive us wherever we need to go next," Devon said. "It's a perfect plan. What could go wrong?"

"Thanks." I punched Devon on the shoulder.

"Best to get some sleep. We're beginning our studies early in the morning." Eric muttered another spell at the door before slipping back out into the hall.

"It's almost like he doesn't want me to know that one," I whispered.

"Is it weird if I sort of hope the books are hidden near Mount Olympus?" Elizabeth sat on my bed next to Devon.

"Is it weird if I hope the books are on a beach?" Devon asked.

"Not unless it's weird that I hope we find them tomorrow and get to play tourist for a few days while Nikki figures out how to get them through customs." I sat beside Elizabeth.

"Am I the only one who feels less prepared to fight bad guys here than in Manhattan?" Devon asked.

I looked to Devon, searching for a crack in his usual bravado.

"Nope," Elizabeth said. "I'm telling myself it's the language barrier and lack of home-field advantage."

"Sounds good." Devon stood up. "We'll just go with that and hope Eric's one Greek contact happens to know someone who's been hoarding a mound of priceless books. See you kids tomorrow."

He winked at me before slipping through the door, leaving Elizabeth and me alone.

My heart fluttered in circles in my chest as she reached up and touched my forehead. Then I remembered my purple hair again and winced.

"Do you think it would be better or worse if I just shaved my head?" I asked.

"I like it purple." Elizabeth gave a sly grin. "You're a rebel. Why shouldn't you look like one?"

"But—"

"I have black streaks, you've got scars and purple hair. Think what a perfect pair we make."

A pair. Like two halves of the same thing. Like two pieces of a really easy-to-solve puzzle. Like a couple drawn together by fate herself.

"Yeah," I said. "It's not so bad." And then I leaned in and kissed her.

8

As a native New Yorker, I do my best to avoid tourist hotspots. Times Square, Rockefeller Center at Christmas, the zoo on free days. I just don't go near them. Heading to the Acropolis Museum reminded me why.

It's not just that there's a ton of people all wanting to be in the exact same five-foot square to get the best picture. It's the school groups with the teacher walking backward, not caring if she steps on you, just as long as none of her students go AWOL. And the mom who forgot that if she didn't pack a juice box, her kid was going to have a meltdown, and now the kid's realized there's no juice box in sight so its DEFCON five tantrum time.

Then there are the retired dodderers who can't seem to remember that anyone could be on a schedule, so they just meander while somehow blocking everyone around them from actually moving at a pace suited for getting anywhere within a reasonable timeframe. The social media influencers who are going to spend twenty minutes in everybody's way taking the same picture over and over again. The ones who talk super loud like they want to prove they have a voice even though they don't speak the local language. The people who drank too much the night before and look like they might spew on your shoes if you step too near them.

And, worst of all, the chaperone your dad hired who decides she'd like to see the same museum you're going to, making it impossible to give her the slip.

"Do they sell coffee here?" I whispered to Elizabeth as the entrance attendant scanned my ticket.

"I really hope so." Elizabeth spoke through her yawn.

The ticket taker eyed my hair for a moment before letting me through the turnstile.

I puffed my chest out, attempting to look like a badass as I sidled through the barrier, trying not to let the rotating bars knock into me in any unfortunate places.

"So, Bryant, what would you like to see first?" Eric didn't bother hiding his frown as he glanced from me to Cindy, who looked like a kid in a candy store as she stared through the glass floor to the excavated ancient settlement beneath us.

"I don't know." I bit my cheeks to keep from smiling. "You're the Greece expert. What are the most fascinating bits of the museum?"

Eric's eyes darkened from their normal creepy bright blue to an angry dusky blue. "This expedition is to be led by my students' interests. Take a look around and see what strikes your fancy."

"This is pretty neat." Devon headed away from the mini replica of the Acropolis and to the glass walls filled with artifacts.

I kept close on Devon's heels, hoping that, if we moved fast enough, we could ditch Cindy right away and head straight to Eric's contact.

But Cindy was not to be dissuaded so easily. We hadn't even made it to the end of the hall before she caught up to us, giving a little wave as she kept to her side of the exhibit.

"Should I text my dad and ask him to tell her to leave us alone for the day?" I whispered to Eric. "I mean, Dad knows we're supposed to be meeting people Cindy shouldn't know about."

"The problem is the address," Eric said. "She'll want to follow us. To know where to pick us up."

"Would that be so awful?" Devon said.

"I think we can all agree the time will come when we can no longer tolerate Cindy following us." Eric led us up the glass steps to the next level. "When we are forced to part ways with Bryant's chaperone—"

"I think she's really here for all the teenagers on this trip," I said.

"—the last thing we'll need is for her to show up at the door of my contact looking for answers," Eric said. "There are very few I trust in this world, and I will not betray Zoe by leading a human anywhere near her doorstep."

"So let's give Cindy the slip and catch up to her at the hotel," Elizabeth said.

I started looking around the gallery for an easy exit that wouldn't require magic or cause any security footage that might come back to bite us in the butt.

"Stay near the stairs," Eric said, "when Cindy wanders to the far side of the gallery, we'll causally walk back down to the lobby and be on our way."

"I love a good meander." Devon headed toward a statue of a woman who had lost both her arms, though I couldn't tell if time or violence had harmed her.

"It's actually a really cool museum." Elizabeth held my hand as we wandered to a statue that gave us a great view of Cindy coming up the stairs and heading right to where she could keep an eye on me.

"The statues are cool." I actually looked at one of their faces for the first time, and a weird shiver shook my spine. Not like fate had come for me, or the museum held some sort of magic my body was sensing. The shiver was a pure human reaction to remembered terror.

The cut of the statue's chin, the pure white of her stone hair, all of it just screamed *Lady* in my brain.

I wanted to crack the statue apart, destroy the piece of ancient art just to prove it wasn't really a Lady and they hadn't come back from the grave to kill us.

"You okay?" Elizabeth squeezed my hand.

"I don't think I'm a fan of all-white art," I said.

"They didn't used to be like that." Elizabeth pointed to a sign in front one of the other statues.

That woman had bits of color in her hair. Not coating it, just in the crevices of her curls.

"A long time ago, most of the statues had bits of color," Elizabeth said.

I tried to picture it. Not being surrounded by white statues that gave me flashbacks to some pretty traumatic near-death experiences, but instead, having vibrant color filling the room.

"I wish they were still that way." I studied the lines of a man's stone beard, deciding where I would add pigment.

"Time wiped it all away."

"I wonder..." I looked back to the lady with the color creeping out of her curls. She had color in her eyes, too. There were even places where it looked like there should be vibrant hues on her dress.

"Yeah?" Elizabeth prompted.

"I wonder if it's all a metaphor." I rubbed the center of my forehead with the knuckles of my non-Elizabeth claimed hand.

"I think it's really a statue." Elizabeth nudged me with her elbow.

"I know that. I just mean, what if the Ladies, like *capital L* Ladies, used to be all vibrant and lifelike, too? What if they were like us when they started? Full of hope. Wanting to save knowledge. Wanting to create a peaceful and prosperous life for the people of Beville. And then their humanity got drained away as magic leeched the color out of them so when we finally met them they were no better than bleached stone."

"I don't think their humanity got syphoned away." Elizabeth twisted our wrists so she could kiss the back of my scarred hand. "I think they got greedy, and they forgot it was their job to protect the people in their care. Being in power makes some people want more power, and the Ladies fell so deep into wanting to stay in control, they forgot about everything else."

"I don't want to end up like them." The truth of my words stung in my chest like someone had popped the balloon that held my thin resolve to stand at the center of the web of fate as we put right the wrongs the Ladies had started. "Someday, years from now, when I'm dead—hopefully of natural causes—I don't want some teenage kid looking at my life and wondering how I got to be so evil. I don't want to be in anyone's nightmares. I don't want to be so hated people won't even be mad or sad that I'm gone."

"That's not going to happen, Bryant." Elizabeth took my face in her hands. "You are a good person. You would never let that happen."

"But what if the Ladies started off as good people, too?"

"This isn't going to work." Devon stepped up next to us, stopping me before I could confess my half-formed plan to Elizabeth.

"You as the third wheel?" Elizabeth said. "It wouldn't feel right without you around."

"Ha." Devon flicked one of Elizabeth's curls. "We're not going to be able to ditch Cindy. Not when she glances up from every plaque she's reading to make sure she still has eyes on Bryant."

"Do I call my dad, or do we try and magic our way out of here as subtly as possible?" I asked.

"Neither," Elizabeth said. "Get Eric, and head out front. I'll meet you there in five minutes."

"Why?" I caught hold of Elizabeth's hand. "What are you going to do?"

"I'm going to abuse the girl code all women must obey and beg her to come help me in the bathroom," Elizabeth said. "I'm probably going to get some nasty karma for this."

Elizabeth let go of my hand and headed toward Cindy. She glanced over her shoulder and winced before leaning close to whisper something to our chaperone.

"Let's grab Eric," Devon said as Cindy led Elizabeth toward the bathroom. "Don't want to waste Elizabeth's violation of the girl code."

9

If wandering around the city the night before had felt like we'd left New York a world away, following Eric through the winding streets around the base of the hill where the Acropolis itself stood seemed like we'd fallen into a different time.

In the little neighborhood built of uneven alleys and super old houses, where there were stairs set into the street so there was no way a car could follow you, it sort of felt like we'd stepped into a fairy tale.

A clowder of cats lay in a sunny patch between houses, not even bothering to look up as Eric stopped beside them, examining the sapphire blue door of the yellow house on our right and the blood red door of the pale blue house on our left.

"Hmm." Eric tented his fingers under his chin.

"What?" I asked.

"Don't tell me we're lost," Devon laughed.

"Not lost," Eric said. "Simply still searching."

"Is there anything I should be looking for?" Elizabeth kept hold of my hand as she stepped closer to the yellow house, studying the trim-like graffiti someone had painted along the bottom of the wall.

"Use your gift as well as you can," Eric said, "but I'm afraid I don't know what to tell you to look for, only that I shall know when I find it."

"Do you have an address?" I asked. "I could look it up."

"Zoe never gave me her address." Eric headed down the narrow street, ducking below branches that would have dripped with fruit during the summer. "I don't believe she ever intended for me to visit her."

"Are you telling me we're going to drop in on someone who doesn't actually want you visiting them?" Devon asked.

I ducked below the branches, almost tripping over a cat who'd decided that while I was bent double was the perfect time to wind between my ankles.

"We are in pursuit of a great and noble cause," Eric said. "Is one unexpected house call too great a price to pay for saving the books?"

"No." Devon dodged around Elizabeth and me to walk beside Eric. "But it does change my expectations for how knocking on the door is going to go. I mean, the whole Raven thing worked out well in the end, but if this is going to be the same sort of deal, I'd like to be ready in case screaming and spell throwing start to happen."

"It's not at all the same." Eric stopped at a fork in the road, taking a moment to study each path before heading downhill. "There are no previous entanglements between Raven and me."

"Wait"—Elizabeth dragged me along with her as she ran a few steps to walk right behind Eric—"are you telling me we're paying an unexpected call on your ex?"

"Not an ex," Eric said. "A former entanglement."

A mixture of laughter and exasperation sparkled in Elizabeth's eyes. "This should go well."

We headed down another set of stairs where each cat in the clowder—and yes, that really is what you call a group of cats—had claimed a different step.

Mwarr. The cat who had tried to trip me earlier darted right under my foot as I went to step down. I wobbled and would have fallen and smooshed a cat if Elizabeth hadn't grabbed my arm.

"Careful, kitty." I tried to step around the cat, but it dug its claws into my shin and gave an awful *yowl*. "I didn't step on you! Why would you hurt me when I didn't step on you?"

With another *yowl*, the cat headed back the way we'd come, stopping at the fork in the path where Eric had chosen to go down. The cat turned to make eye contact with me and yowled again.

"Eric, can cats be like Lola's guards?" I said slowly.

"That really looks like a normal cat," Elizabeth said.

"Okay, but can a normal cat be magical?" I said. "Like a familiar, or a guide to lead you on a side quest in a videogame?"

Devon climbed back up the steps to stare at the cat.

The cat yowled again.

"That is a little weird," Devon said.

The cat hissed.

"I have heard rumors of select felines being trained as companions with skills far beyond that of a normal cat," Eric said, "but I've never seen such a thing put into practice."

"Okay." I nodded like I could somehow take that as an affirmation I hadn't lost my mind. "I think we should follow the cat and see what happens."

"Because the cat seems to know more of where it wants to go than Eric?" Devon asked.

"I mean, yeah," I said. "That, and it just feels right."

"Then we'll follow the feline." Eric looked to the cat. "Lead on."

The cat gave a satisfied little *merp* before walking down the path Eric hadn't chosen.

"I don't want to be the naysayer," Elizabeth said.

"If there are shadows creeping in around us, please just tell me." I held her hand tighter, determined not to allow any monster to rip her away from me.

"No beasties." Elizabeth stepped in front of me as we reached a road too narrow for us to walk side by side. "I just wonder if following a cat to see someone who probably really doesn't want to see Eric isn't some sort of a trap."

"Oh, it very well could be," Eric said from the front of our feline-following parade. "But it would be a trap of magical making, and that would definitely lead us closer to the right direction."

"So, the good kind of trap," Devon said. "Sounds great."

The cat/possible bait for a magical trap led us onto a wider street, up an alley between houses I wouldn't have been brave enough to cut through on my own, past a café where a couple sat outdoors sipping wine and staring up at the hill where the Acropolis lay, through another alley, and out into a court-yard surrounded by four houses.

The cat turned to give us another *merp* before heading toward a house with a violently pink front door.

"Looks promising," I said. "Not pure white. No weird markers."

"I'd prefer Elizabeth's assessment." Eric crept closer to the door.

With a final *yowl*, the cat walked into the bushes and disappeared from view.

"It looks like a house." Elizabeth tipped her head to the side. "A cool house, but there's nothing strange about it."

I agreed with the cool house bit. Aside from the bright pink door, the place looked like somewhere you'd find a Greek grandma busy making you dinner. You'd sit around a lace-clothed table with fresh-cut flowers in the middle and be overfed while she told you stories of all the young men who flirted with her when she was a girl.

"Once more unto the breach." Eric knocked on the door.

"No *cliaxo*?" Devon whispered.

"It might not be Zoe's house," Elizabeth said.

"And if it is," Eric said, "I don't want to give her any reason to turn us away."

We waited a full minute before Eric raised his hand and knocked again.

The moment his knuckles touched the pink wood, the door swung open with a *squeak* straight out of a horror movie.

"Lovely," Devon said.

I watched Elizabeth as she peered through the door. She furrowed her perfect brow but didn't look scared.

I turned my gaze to the inside of the house. It was a little darker than the bright morning suggested it should be but otherwise looked like we could walk into my Greek grandma food fantasy—a pretty painting on the wall, a carefully swept stone floor.

"After me." Eric stepped through the door.

I held my breath, waiting for disaster to strike as Devon followed.

The house didn't grow teeth and eat them, so I wrapped my arm around Elizabeth's waist, keeping her close to my side as we crept through the doorway together.

I dared to take another breath. The faint scent of old books mixed with the aroma of something baking.

Devon looked to me and opened his mouth to speak just before everything went to Hell.

With a jolt like I'd been launched out of a cannon, gravity shifted, and I fell toward the ceiling.

I tried to keep ahold of Elizabeth, twisting in hopes of my body cushioning her fall, but the new freaky gravity had different plans for her.

She tumbled sideways, landing on the pink door with a *thump*.

The air I was going to use to shout "Elizabeth!" was knocked out of my lungs as I hit the ceiling. I tried to push myself up to my knees, but my brain's understanding of gravity wasn't meshing with the reality of my situation. I swayed and flopped sideways like a dying fish.

Devon had fallen to the far end of the entryway and was trying to stand on the painting of flowers that hung on that wall.

The only one who hadn't been cast aside by the laws of physics was Eric. He stood on the normal floor, not even fighting as the stone twisted and curled as it wound up his legs and wrapped around him like cartoon bandits were going to tie him to the train tracks.

"Well done, Zoe," Eric said once the rock ropes had stopped moving. "I expected security from you, but training the house to have more than one response to unwanted visitors is quite impressive."

I looked at the doorways around us, trying not to vomit from the super weird vertigo, waiting for Zoe to saunter out and purr at Eric that she'd been waiting for him to arrive.

"Zoe," Eric said, "I know we didn't part on the best of terms, but I'm not here for a personal call. I've come to discuss some very important business. I need information."

"Based on this greeting, I really don't think she's going to want to tell you anything." Devon had managed to get to his feet, clinging to what had become his wall for support.

"She won't want to give me information," Eric said. "I would never be naïve enough to believe that. But once she hears who I'll use the information to eliminate, that might be interesting enough to entice her."

"Entice me?" A woman stepped through one of the doorways. Her black hair shimmered around her shoulders, and her green eyes shone with loathing as she glared at Eric. Though she had an accent, her words were perfectly clear as she stalked closer to him. "I have you trapped in my house. I have your friends, too. I can't think of any pleasure in this world that would keep me from hurting you, or a prize that would be worth my helping you."

10

"Zoe, it's a pleasure to see you again." Eric smiled.

Zoe took two steps forward and slapped him across the face.

"Come now," Eric said, "you can't possibly hate me more than you loathe anyone else in the world."

She slapped him again.

"What did you do to her?" Devon asked.

"None of your damn business." Zoe rounded on Devon.

"Okay." Devon nodded, paying for moving his head with a stumbling wobble. "I don't doubt you have every right to slap him."

"I'm looking for books." Eric pulled Zoe's focus back to him.

"I'll kill you before I let you near my books," Zoe said.

"I don't blame you," Eric said. "After what the Ladies did to you, I don't think a person with any empathy would speak ill of you for hoarding your collection away from the world."

"Do you want me to believe the great Eric Deldridge can feel compassion?" Zoe pursed her lips. "I'm not that foolish. Hunt for books somewhere else. You aren't welcome here."

"It's not your books I'm interested in," Eric said. "And if I succeed in my mission, the Ladies will fall. Their time in power will be over. So which do you prefer? Petty vengeance for a love affair that ended badly, or a hand in the destruction of a regime that stole everything you truly cared for?"

Zoe chewed the inside of her lips before speaking. "There's not a book in the world that can end the Ladies' rule. Whatever spell you find, they'll have something more powerful. Whatever weakness you think you've discovered, they will find a way to trap you. I would have thought you were smart enough to know that, Eric."

"A single book could never topple the Ladies," Eric said. "But a few thousand books, stolen from their Library, hidden away for years…if someone were to find that trove of knowledge and expose that the Ladies had concealed the theft for decades, all the people of Beville would rise up. And with the wisdom of the lost books on the people's side, even the might of the Ladies would crumble."

Zoe lifted her hand. For a moment I thought she was going to slap Eric again, but she just fiddled with the pendant on her necklace. "Even if you were right. Even if there were such a masterful thief and the books really had been saved from the Ladies, none of the books I have would help you find the missing volumes."

"As I've said, I have no intention of going anywhere near your books. I'm simply seeking information."

"My father didn't steal the Ladies' books, and neither did I."

"If you wouldn't mind reaching into my right pocket. There's a picture on my phone. I want to see if you recognize the place or perhaps even the handwriting."

With a twist of her finger, the stone coils around Eric shifted, leaving his pocket exposed. Zoe pulled out Eric's phone, then stretched the bindings so she could press his thumb to the scanner.

"This?" Zoe turned the phone enough that I managed to get a glimpse of a torn shipping label.

"Some of the books were mailed to New York," Eric said. "That is the information from the box."

"So you have nothing?"

"There's got to be the name of a city," Eric said.

"Yes, and?" Zoe said.

"How many wizards and witches are there in Greece?" Eric said. "One thousand, maybe two?"

"Not quite two," Zoe said.

"That's a fairly small community, all things considered," Eric said. "I simply want to know if any wizards live near the city from which the box was shipped. A name would be lovely. An address, most appreciated."

"You're a fool." With another flick of her finger, Zoe shifted the ropes enough to shove the phone back into Eric's pocket.

"Do you want me to beg?" Eric said. "Do you want me to tell you I'm sorry for being a cad who broke your heart?"

"You give yourself too much credit." She clenched her fist, tightening Eric's bonds.

"Don't hurt him." I raised my hand to start a spell, but the gravity on the ceiling/my floor doubled, pinning me to the ground.

"Nothing I say will make a difference to you." Eric's words came out strained. "You wouldn't give me water if I were dying of thirst. I understand that, and most would even say I deserve it."

Zoe gave a bitter laugh.

"But what the Ladies did to you, to your father…" Eric dragged in a breath. "Your vengeance against them is worth far more to you than your loathing of me."

Zoe waved a hand, and the stone bindings froze.

"You're looking for Meteora." Zoe looked down at her hands as she spoke, like she didn't want to admit to herself that she was helping Eric. "I don't know the names of any people, but I did visit there with my father when I was young. The area isn't only sacred to the unmagicked. The keepers of our books used to live up there, hidden amongst the rocks and monasteries. When the airport came, the books moved to Athens, but some of the bookkeepers stayed behind.

"They were old men when Father and I visited them. They stayed in their home, studying the few books they'd kept for themselves. If I had to guess, all that's left in that place are the bones of old men who died hunched over dusty volumes."

"Where in Meteora are they?" Eric asked.

"I don't remember much." Zoe furrowed her brow. Her gaze traced the lines on her palms like she was looking over long-forgotten terrain. "We walked through the woods to get there, and I was afraid. I begged my father to carry me, but he said I had to make the journey on my own feet. There was a path, and light all around me. But shadows lurked, too. Shapes I tried not to understand. There was a building perched high up on the stone. It's not on any map. They designed it that way, a secret not to be shared or easily discovered. I'm honestly not sure I could find it again."

"That's all right," Eric said, his voice lacking its usual bravado. "You've given us more than I have any right to ask for."

"I have," Zoe said. "And if you die chasing your dream of dethroning the Ladies, I won't feel even a prickle of grief."

"That much, I am sure I deserve." Eric gave Zoe a nod.

A sudden feeling of overwhelming awkwardness sent heat to my cheeks. Not because I was still pinned to the ceiling in a super uncomfortable position. It felt like I was spying on them. Seeing Eric in an intimate and vulnerable way that I had never wanted to see him. And that was completely apart from the fact that I'd only ever known him when he was with Lola. Well, maybe not *with*, but the *we don't talk about it but it just sort of is* equivalent.

"Would you like me to tell you when our task is complete?" Eric asked. "Knowing the women who killed your father have been washed away might allow you some closure."

"Closure is a myth," Zoe said. "My grief doesn't end, and neither will my watch. Still, tell me if you survive to see the Ladies burn. My father never got to finish his work. Once the Ladies are gone, I'll do it for him."

"As you wish," Eric said.

"Now get out of my home before I decide to kill you and let your apprentices finish your task." Zoe stormed away.

The door closed with a *click*, and gravity went back to normal. I fell with a shout and hit the ground hard enough for stars to swallow my vision.

"Ow." I rolled onto my back, wondering if I should do a healing spell just in case any of the twenty-odd bones that felt broken actually *were* broken.

"That went well." Devon stood and brushed himself off while Elizabeth came to steady me as I wobbled to my feet.

In my defense, I had fallen much farther than they had.

"We should go." Eric shook his shoulders, and the stone ropes that had bound him shattered and fell to the ground.

I watched in awe as the floor reabsorbed the debris.

"Can your house do that?" I asked.

"I hope to never find out." Eric opened the door and stepped back out into the courtyard.

I herded Devon and Elizabeth in front of me as I scampered outside before gravity could go all weird again.

Eric looked around the tiny square for a moment.

"Are you going to tell us?" Elizabeth asked.

"Once I know which direction we should go, I will certainly enlighten you." Eric studied the way we had entered the square.

"I mean about Zoe," Elizabeth said. "What happened to her father?"

"Her father was the official librarian of Greece." Eric stared at the pink door as he spoke. "It's a small collection, but valuable nonetheless. As much as I hate to speak ill of the dead, her father was an optimistic fool. He brought some of his precious books to Manhattan, hoping to compare them with the Ladies' texts."

"Let me guess," Devon said, "they killed him and kept his books?"

"Right in one." Eric led us down a narrow path, heading toward the Acropolis hill.

"No wonder she wants revenge," I said.

"It's her place, both as a daughter and as the new librarian of Greece," Eric said.

"She's the librarian?" I turned to look back at the house with the pink door.

"Indeed," Eric said, "and you've just been inside the library."

———

When we met Cindy back at the hotel, she was so freaked out about having lost us, I didn't even have the heart to tell her it wasn't really her job to follow us around all the time. So, I just gushed about my newfound fascination with religious structures built on top of rocks and asked if she could drive us to Meteora.

Elizabeth picked a new hotel for me to book, Devon picked where we should eat dinner, Eric brooded his way through it all. Really, it was almost like we were on an actual educational tour of Greece.

But I couldn't get the cycle of worry in my brain to stop.

We were getting closer. I could feel it. Like the strings of fate that had been wrapped around my being were tightening their hold, determined not to let me go before I found the books.

When I finally got back to the hotel after dinner, I typed out my message to Nikki.

The request was absurd. Any decent lawyer would have laughed and said *No, you nerdy freak. I want nothing to do with your shenanigans. Even a pair of natural 20s couldn't persuade me to help you.* But before I'd brushed my teeth and hopped into bed, I'd gotten a message back.

Hi Bryant,

Sounds like an inventive project. Let's start by making a list of specific items you want to address. What are your top concerns? Once we get those hammered out, we can get into building a more detailed structure.

Nikki

Top Concerns

- *Magic must remain hidden from non-wizards for the safety of all*
- *No noticeable spells in human territory*
- *No telling humans about magic*
- *Freedom of knowledge must be established*
- *The Library of Magic will be open to visitors, free of charge*
- *Penalties for injuring people or property with magic , be set*

Other crimes that need set penalties

- *Buying and selling wizards*
- *Kidnapping wizards*
- *Death matches*
- *Grave robbing for the purposes of bone magic*
- *Grave robbing in general*
- *How TF are we supposed to enforce the laws if there are no cops, jails, or anybody in charge?*

11

There are a lot of things in life growing up in Manhattan totally prepared me for. Dodging through tourists. Eating sketchy food made in carts where there's clearly no way for the food preparer to wash their hands. Navigating broken subway systems. Judging when a street performance is going to drift into railing against society so you know when to run for it.

What Manhattan didn't prepare me for—long road trips.

Greece may not look huge on a globe, but if your driver insists on going the speed limit even though there are no cops in sight, it's still big enough to make it a four-hour car ride between Athens and Meteora. Which is just as bad as trying to get from Hell's Kitchen to Brooklyn when the MTA decides not to run...I'm almost kidding.

For the first part of the trip, Cindy taught us all a few words in Greek.

Δεν προσπαθώ να είμαι αγενής, απλά είμαι αδέξιος.

Which gave me a totally new appreciation for the Phoenician alphabet.

Then, Elizabeth read us some facts about the soaring monasteries of Meteora.

The more Elizabeth told us about the monasteries, the more ravenous the worry gnawing at my stomach became.

The regular, human monasteries had been built on soaring columns of rock starting in the 11th century. The monks had used ladders and scaffolds and nets to get to their homes perched high above. The pictures on Elizabeth's phone were amazing and awe-inspiring and...if human monks managed to build in such hard to reach places, where had the wizard bookkeepers built?

Elizabeth laid her hand on my knee as she read to us about the raids on the monasteries during the 17th century, like she knew my mind had started to creep to the panicky place where remembering to breathe took a lot more effort than normal.

By the time we got our first glimpse of the soaring monasteries, I was basically convinced I should become a hermit and live in a cave on the side of one of the stone pillars because there was no way we were going to find the secret hidey hole of the probably deceased bookkeepers. But there was something soothing and empowering about the monasteries floating high up near the sky.

That's when I decided I would be a real asshat to give up and hide, because if 11th century monks could build those monasteries without the help of the internet or magic, then I needed to buck up and find the damn hidden books.

We got into our second hotel and I took a moment to hide and check my email for a message from Nikki.

> Bryant,
>
> *If your primary concern is maintaining order, you need to consider retributive vs. restorative justice. Take a look at both options and see which you think works better for your world building.*
>
> *I'd love to see your campaign notes when you're done. I used to dabble a little in my pre-law days.*
>
> Nikki

Retributive or restorative.

The two words swirled around in my head as I devoured some really good food for lunch.

A cat wound around my ankles in the restaurant as I ate, but I think it only wanted a bit of my cheese, not to answer any philosophical questions or even give me directions to the bookkeepers.

Retributive or restorative. Two little words that could remake the world.

"You okay?"

I blinked at Elizabeth and realized I had somehow daydreamed my way from being inside a restaurant to walking down the street beside her.

"I'm fine." I kissed the back of her hand and wrapped my arm around her waist.

"When Zoe told us the bookkeepers had a hidden place here," Devon said, "I had sort of hoped there wouldn't be quite so many good places to hide."

Devon was right. The stone columns stretched out to the side of us as far as I could see. We could spend years hunting through every crevice and not find anything.

"Our first order of business is to get rid of the chaperone," Eric said. "Once we no longer have a human pretending not to follow us—"

"Don't diss the humans," Devon said.

"—we'll begin our search in the only way possible—asking the locals," Eric finished.

"You're kidding, right?" I dragged Elizabeth forward a few quick steps to walk beside Eric so I could actually watch his face for any hints that he was joking.

"Not at all." Eric raised an eyebrow at me. "This is a very serious matter, Bryant. We are talking about the accumulation of centuries of knowledge. I would never be so crass as to joke about it and would hope for better from you as well."

"Who's on ditch-Cindy duty?" Elizabeth asked before I could say I knew damn well the fate of magic rested in our hands, thank you very much. "I took care of it yesterday."

"I can do it." Devon reached into his pocket.

For one terrifying moment, I thought he was going to pull out his glowing sword, but instead, he pulled out his foam blaster.

"Right over here, if you will." He stepped into the little space between two restaurants like he wanted to look over the dinner options on the menus out front.

Cindy kept walking toward us, looking at the buildings like she wasn't stalking us.

Devon let out a long breath and pulled the trigger. With a little *dhoomp*, a tiny gray thing shot out of the blaster and hit the sidewalk.

"What are you—"

My question was cut off by Cindy's squeal as she tipped forward, leaving her shoe stuck to the sidewalk behind her.

"I think we should call that the Cinderella maneuver." Devon led us down an alley and out onto the next street over.

"How did you do that?" I asked.

"Remember two years ago when the props shop figured out how to fill blood capsules and shoot them out of foam blasters for the barricade scene in Les Mis?" Devon asked.

"I remember my mom banning it," I said.

"Well, I got ahold of one of the guys who figured the capsules out, asked him how it was done, and made some tiny doses of the sticking potion." Devon beamed as he winked at me. "Thus the sticky blaster was born. It's not as showy as the water gun technique, but I figured the capsules would be safer for air travel."

"Devon, I mean this with absolutely no derision," Eric said, "I am thoroughly impressed."

"Thanks," Devon said. "I'm pretty proud of the sticky blaster concept. Now let's hope we can get back to New York without me needing to use any of my other toys."

"Wouldn't that be living the dream?" There was a tiny touch of worry in Elizabeth's voice as she laughed.

"Where are we supposed to find a local who might know about the"—I stopped myself from saying *magical bookkeepers* as a group of tourists passed by—"what we're looking for."

"By reading the signs," Eric said.

Reading the signs.

I started searching the sidewalk for any hint of a stray cat wanting us to follow it. Or a door appearing where it shouldn't be. Or words shimmering into being at the exact right moment.

"This should do." Eric stopped in front of a building with wide widows.

A sign hung in the glass.

Monastery Tours! English speaking guides! Snacks and bottled water included!

"Oh," I said, "that kind of sign."

Giving me a pitying frown, Eric pushed open the door to the little shop.

The scent of some really good kind of food that I couldn't quite pinpoint, but definitely made me want to curl up in front of a fire binge eating bread, filled the air.

The man behind the counter said something I couldn't understand before smiling and starting again. "Are you looking for a tour?"

"At the moment, we're just shopping around." Eric stepped forward with a smile. "We have some rather unique interests and are hoping to find a guide with knowledge to suit."

"Ah, Americans." The man gestured toward my purple hair. "I should have known."

"Thanks?" I said.

The man didn't acknowledge me. "Our guides are all very knowledgeable on the monasteries and the history of the hermits in the area. If you are more looking for the geology, we have a tour that examines the rock pillars—"

"We're more interested in the myths of the area," Eric said.

"Myths." The man leaned his elbows on the counter, a slight furrow creasing his brow. "What myths are you looking for? Our history in Meteora is written on the stones you see rising toward the sky. There is no myth involved."

"The stories I've heard haven't been presented as fact," Eric said. "Unless, of course, there truly were men possessing otherworldly powers who were drawn to Meteora. From the tales I've been told, they were rumored to be scholars, keepers of books that held great power."

The wrinkles on the man's brow faded as he smiled. "Ah, I see. Why would you want to hear children's stories when the truth of the monasteries offers more adventure?"

"It's for a school project," Elizabeth said. "We're collecting local legends from all over the world."

"That's quite the project," the man said.

"It's an arts-based school," Devon said.

"Ah." The man frowned like he was just as confused with Devon's lie as I was with how Eric thought we were going get good information from the tour guide. "We don't go near those things on our tours. I can promise you, none of the companies you will find here talk about that. We look at the history of this place. Not strange stories that change with each telling. Sorry. I cannot help you."

"I know it wouldn't be right to ask you for the stories for free." I stepped toward the counter. "But, is there some sort of private tour rate? You could charge us for the whole thing and just tell us the legend here. I mean, I know it's not true, but it would be really helpful for our project." I pulled out my black credit card and slid it across the counter. "It wouldn't take more than a few minutes of your time."

"I suppose not." The man took the card and started punching things into his computer. "The stories used to be told as truth even when I was a boy. They would say there are men in the woods who are not monks. They hide in the forest behind the monasteries, deep in the trees where no sane person would dare go on purpose. But if you were foolish enough to stumble into the territory of the shadow men, you have found a place where no one with a soul belongs."

A shiver twitched up my spine.

The man shoved my card into the scanner. "If you are unfortunate enough to find the shadow men hidden behind the stones and trees, the best thing to do is pray for a swift death."

"The shadow men kill people?" I whispered.

"Some." The man set a receipt on the counter and handed me a pen. "Some are found dead in the woods with no hint as to what killed them. Some are never found at all. The ones that do make it back, they tell stories of horrors hidden in the darkness. Bear marks of the torment inflicted upon them. Strange scars and deformities."

I signed without looking at the total and stuffed my scarred hand into my pocket.

"Wings like a dragonfly growing from their backs, webs of white scars that cover their bodies, images of terrible monsters burned into their minds so they can't close their eyes without screaming from fright." The man looked down at his own hands on the counter.

"But if the shadow men are hidden," Elizabeth asked, "how did so many people end up running into them in the woods?"

"The path that leads into the darkness is said to hold beauty beyond compare." The man shook his hands out and shrugged. "Some found the path by accident and didn't have the strength to turn back. Others went looking for it, wanting to see whatever splendor had lured so many, and foolish enough to think they could resist. When I was very little, my grandmother told me not to worry. The monks of the hidden monastery had learned how to scare the shadows away. I used to believe it was true."

"And now?" Elizabeth asked.

"Now I'm old enough to know a bedtime story told to keep children from wandering into the woods when I hear one."

12

I leaned against the wall in the men's room, trying to get through checking for messages from Nikki quickly enough they wouldn't send Devon in to make sure I wasn't stress puking.

I had a text from Dad.

Check in with your mother, and don't forget you have a session with Dr. Spinnek this week. I expect you to take her call.

I had a text from Mom.

I hope you're learning a lot. Stay safe, and call when you get a chance. Don't forget to message your dad. He worries about you.

I had an email from Nikki.

Hi Bryant,

With the format you're talking about, your best bet would be a council. Think a not-for-profit board but incorporating the best parts of the Knights of the Round Table. Keeping it small would maximize getting things done quickly, but having multiple members would prevent one bad actor from spoiling the system. Laying out duties depending on the council size would help decide who would be best for membership by choosing a candidate for each particular role.

How many are you including in the campaign? Would you like a council seat assigned to each of them?

I'm excited to see your maps when they're ready.

Nikki

Maps. I hadn't even thought of her wanting to see maps.

I dragged my hand over my purple hair, warring between keeping up the story versus calling the whole thing off to protect the truth I was dancing around so hard I might as well have tried out for the New York City Ballet.

I didn't have a clue as to how many council seats would be a good number. Or how council members should be chosen, or…what the hell I thought I was doing lying to a lawyer about creating a hypothetical framework to govern a community of wizards.

"Stupid, stupid, stupid." I knocked my head against the wall behind me.

I typed a quick message to Nikki, tucked my phone back into my pocket, and looked in the mirror. "I am Bryant Jameson Adams, sidekick to the great wizard Eric Deldridge." I fixed my scarf to cover the burn scar that circled my neck. "And I have no idea what fate wants from me."

I carefully removed the look of mingled resignation and angst from my face before stepping back out into the restaurant. Two men sat together off to the side, playing guitar while occasionally singing but mostly just talking and laughing with each other.

Self-loathing curdled in my stomach as I realized I was jealous of the men. Not because I didn't like my life. I just wanted the decisions I had to make to be as easy as what song to play next, not if taxing wizards was a feasible concept and would I get murdered for suggesting it.

"The boys make bets with each other sometimes." Our server leaned close to Devon, tipping her torso in a way that displayed her ample cleavage. "They climb up behind the cliffs and see who can last the longest in the woods alone. They all come home, but the funny part is watching for which ones come out crying."

"Have you ever gone into those woods?" Devon gave the girl a grin as he spoke, like he wanted her to know he knew she was trying to show him how low the front of her shirt was, but he wasn't going to take the easy bait.

"I've been to the cliffs at night but never into the woods." She filled Devon's water glass. "I like an adventure, but there are limits."

I waited until the server walked away to take my seat.

"That's the third confirmation of the story we've received," Eric said.

"No two people have told the exact same story," Elizabeth said.

"But there are enough similarities to make me certain there is something in the woods the locals cannot explain." Eric studied the leftover food on his plate like it might somehow form a map to the bookkeepers' lair. "What awaits us in the woods might not be exactly what we're looking for, but it most definitely seems worth exploring."

"So we go into the woods people have been avoiding at night and see if Bryant gains a pretty pair of dragonfly wings?" Devon asked.

"Absolutely not. Magic has done enough weird things to me lately. You get the wings." I shoved the rest of my stuffed leaf into my mouth.

"Not to mention that wings could be really helpful if they were sturdy enough to hold your weight," Elizabeth said. "Between being able to fly and all your other new toys, you'd be ninety percent of the way to being an actual superhero."

"I guess you're right." Devon tossed a bit of his Souvlaki to the cat begging from under his chair. "A cool name, and I'd be at ninety-five percent."

"Shall we begin our climb now?" Eric asked. "Or do we need to wait for Devon to design his costume?"

"I could finally answer Cindy's voicemails and ask her to give us a ride," I offered.

"And have me goop her shoes on a cliff at night to get rid of her?" Devon asked.

"We'll walk," Eric said. "It will do Elizabeth good."

"Excuse me?" Elizabeth glared at him with a forkful of dessert halfway to her mouth.

"While I have every confidence in the education Lola has been giving you, there are some things only experience can teach." Eric pushed away from the table.

I frantically waved my black credit card at our server like a noob who'd never paid in a restaurant before.

"Think of the shadows, shimmers, and monsters you've seen in New York as the local flora and fauna," Eric said. "You are used to the squirrels, pigeons, and elms of Manhattan. There are some species, like cats for example—"

Devon's begging cat gave a well-timed *meow*.

"—that can be seen both here and in Manhattan, though admittedly in vastly different quantities. Then there are the types unique to our current environs such as a white-toothed shrew, or perhaps a mountain goat. While the aim of our trip is not to expand Elizabeth's education, we would be remiss to ignore the opportunity. Especially as the alternative would require petty deceit or intervention on Devon's part."

"Technically, it's Bryant's turn to ditch the babysitter." Devon pointed at me.

"I don't mind waiting for my turn."

The server scanned my card and I tacked on a tip and signed, all while trying not to think through how much money we'd actually spent in Greece so far.

"Better start walking." Elizabeth pulled on her sweater like she was donning some sort of armor against whatever might wait in the shadows growing outside.

"I may not be as comforting to have around as Sniffer McDeadDog, but at least you won't be alone," I said.

"Ha ha." Elizabeth nudged me with her shoulder before lacing her fingers through mine.

I could tell from the way she held my hand, clutching it as though wanting to make sure that even if the earth cracked open and tried to swallow her she wouldn't lose her grip, that she did not at all like the idea of the magical seer equivalent of finding a white-toothed shrew. Still, she didn't argue as we headed for the road that wound up toward the monasteries.

The setting sun left strange shadows slanting away from the massive stone columns.

I tried not to stare at Elizabeth as we climbed up the steep road. I wanted to know if she was seeing anything lurking around us as the darkness deepened, but I also knew my watching her like she might spook and bolt at any moment wasn't going to help the situation.

None of us really said much until we passed the first monastery.

"Anything yet?" Eric asked as we crammed ourselves against a stone guardrail to let a tour bus pass.

"Not really." Elizabeth chewed her bottom lip for a moment.

I fought away the sparks in my stomach that made me want to have a turn with her bottom lip.

"It's wobbly," Elizabeth said.

"I'm sorry, what?" The sparks in my stomach fizzled away.

"Like frosted glass." Elizabeth tipped her head, examining what looked to me to be completely normal shadows around a strangely twisted tree. "It looks like there might be something moving on the other side of the glass, but I can't tell what it is or if it's really there."

"That doesn't sound so bad." I took a bracing breath and started up the hill. For once, all the others actually followed me.

"Hmm." Eric made that awful noise before we'd walked ten steps.

"What *hmm*?" I picked up my pace, climbing with the determination of a kid at a birthday party trying to get to the front of the food line because he knows full well there aren't going to be enough slices of cake to go around.

"On the one hand," Eric said, "the lack of aggressive presence lurking around us is extremely fortunate. We are on a mission to find a place that could very well be guarded by unknown magic."

I started walking even faster, like I could somehow outrun the needle of fear that wanted to pop my courage bubble.

"On the other hand," Eric said, "we are in a place that has been inhabited by humans for centuries. And not only humans, but humans who are devoted to things beyond the mundane and easily visible. I would find it extraordinarily odd if no shadows or creatures had found their way to this remarkable place, and odder still if none had been birthed here."

"What are you actually trying to say?" By that point, I was jogging up the mountain, dragging Elizabeth along behind me.

"If Elizabeth is correct, and there are shadows kept just out of sight, as though trapped on the other side of a pane of glass, the necessary questions become more difficult," Eric said.

"What's so bad it's been hidden behind glass?" Elizabeth said. "And where does the barrier between them and us break?"

13

The *crack* of the branches beneath my feet was somehow as frightening as the *snap* of stepping on unknown bones in the tunnels on the outskirts of Beville. I kept my shoulders relaxed and didn't let my hands shake. I don't know why, but admitting that being in the forest at night freaked me out seemed somehow worse than being scared under normal circumstances.

Of course, from the way Elizabeth kept flinching, I was probably right to be scared.

The sun had gone down before we'd reached the top of the hill where a sketchy bridge and obscene number of stairs allowed visitors to access one of the monasteries.

In a way, the fact that we were creeping into the woods in the dark was a good thing. No one could see us, so what chance did Cindy have of finding us?

On the other hand, we hadn't seen the terrain in the daylight, so even Eric couldn't pretend he knew where he was going as he led us through the woods.

I gripped a sphere of light in one hand and kept my other raised, ready to shout a spell if anything leapt out of the trees to terrorize us. Elizabeth gripped my arm for dear life as she stared into the shadows. Devon gripped his sticky blaster like he was ready to star in an action movie. And Eric led with a little less confidence than I'd grown used to.

In New York, it always seemed like Eric was just storming through the world, knowing exactly where he was going even when I was pretty sure he was as lost as the rest of us.

Apparently, that Eric superpower didn't extend beyond the Tri-State Area.

"I still don't see anything different," Elizabeth said when Eric paused on the edge of a dark precipice. "There's the same wobbly darkness but nothing beautiful and enchanting to lure us to the shadow men."

"I think I spotted another trail a ways back," I offered. "Or we could go back the way we came and wait to hike around in the daylight. Get the lay of the land, then come find the shadow men at night."

"We're not leaving these woods until we find the bookkeepers' lair." Eric headed left, in the opposite direction of the perfectly good trail I had spotted.

"Whelp, I'm glad I ate a big dinner." Devon followed Eric, staying close on his heels to take advantage of Eric's magically made light.

"I don't like the feel of these woods." Elizabeth loosened her grip on my arm as we picked our way across a patch of rocks jutting up through the dirt of the trail.

"Under the circumstances, I don't know if that's a good thing or a bad thing," I said.

"I think it depends on if we're all still breathing come morning," Elizabeth said.

"Right." I nodded like an idiot. "That would shift the point of view."

The path Eric had chosen—if you can call a thin strip of semi-worn dirt a path—cut farther down the slope, away from the town of Meteora, all the monasteries, and any hope of someone finding our bodies before we'd been eaten by wild animals.

The farther downhill we went, the closer together the trees grew, their thick branches hanging over the path like nature was trying to trap us in some sort of weird wooden cave.

Or casket.

I tried really hard not to let myself think *or casket.*

Something rustled in the trees overhead.

I grabbed Elizabeth, pulling her close to me, ready to shout a shield spell to protect us from whatever monster was attacking.

The rustle of wings and a high squeaking carried to my ears before I could speak the spell.

"Bat," I panted. "It's just a bat."

At the time, it didn't occur to me that it was strange that no one laughed and said *Of course, Bryant* or *Take a breath, Bryant, nothing's going to swoop out of the sky and attack us,* or even better, *Bryant, we're perfectly safe here. There's absolutely no reason to think we'll be murdered tonight.* They stayed silent as we all just turned back toward the not-really-a-path path and kept heading downhill.

Three more bats and one woodland mammal terrified me before a hint of light caught my eye.

I squinted against the glow of my spell, trying to see if I'd lost my mind or if my eyes had gone funny. But as hard as I squinted, the light didn't disappear.

The tiny glimmer wasn't anywhere near us. It was way off through the trees.

"Guys," I said, "I think I see a thing."

"A thing?" Devon asked.

"How descriptive," Eric said.

I tucked my light behind my back, but I couldn't see the gleam any more clearly. "Is that a building?"

"Maybe." Elizabeth let go of my arm and cupped her hands around her eyes to shield them from our magic-made lights. "I mean. It looks like a normal light to me. I don't see anything magnificent or magical about it."

"Then we shall find a path toward the light." Eric looked around for a moment before giving up the not-really-a-path-but-better-than-nothing path we'd been on to bushwhack through the trees.

"Are you sure about this?" I pushed a branch aside for Elizabeth only to have the dumb thing smack me in the face as I tried to duck beneath. I sucked air in through my teeth and touched my cheek. My fingers came away red. "Great. *Sinato.*" I gritted my teeth against the bite of my own healing spell.

"I'm not sure if it would be pure comedy or cruel irony if we die falling over the edge of a cliff in the dark," Devon said.

"I'd call it solid dark humor." Elizabeth flinched, ducking away from me.

"What?" I raised my palms toward the tree branches above us.

Elizabeth screamed and covered her head, cowering as though a thousand bats were attacking her.

"*Primurgo.*" I wrapped my arms around Elizabeth, protecting her from the invisible things as my shield spell blossomed over us.

"Elizabeth, what are you seeing?" Eric spoke calmly even though he'd cast a shield spell of his own to protect himself and Devon.

"I..." Elizabeth's breath came in shaking gasps as she moved her arms away from her face and looked up. "I don't know. It's things."

"More detail." The light in Eric's hand vanished.

I hesitated before letting the orb in my palm fade.

"Not quite human." Elizabeth leaned closer to me, like she really thought I could defend her against the darkness. "Not like Charles. Not people coated in shadow. More like memories. Faded and distorted. But the worst memories.

The things that come back in your nightmares." A tear ran down her cheek. "I think they were people once."

"Ghosts?" Devon reached into his pocket and pulled out the hilt of his sword. "Are you seeing ghosts?"

"I don't know." Elizabeth yelped and pulled herself closer to me.

"What do we do?" Devon said.

"That depends on what we are facing. Have the spirits of the dead somehow been trapped in these woods, or are the woods themselves trying to tell us a tale of their own?" Eric trailed his fingers along the inside of his own shield spell.

"Was I supposed to understand that?" My voice came out all whimpery.

"Elizabeth, do these seem to be the same sort of figures you saw near the monasteries?" Eric asked, his tone calm like it was a simple, academic question.

"Yes, but those were contained and hidden, these aren't." Elizabeth flinched as a weird shimmer zinged across the top of my shield spell like something had just crashed into it.

"Aha," Eric said.

"Tell me you have a plan." I looked to Eric.

"It's more a theory," Eric said, "but it does mesh with the history of this place."

"Do we get to hear the theory?" Devon asked.

"I don't believe what Elizabeth is seeing are individual spirits," Eric said.

"So we're not surrounded by ghosts?" The panic constricting my lungs eased enough I could almost take in what counted as a breath.

"I fear our predicament may be far more troubling," Eric said. "I believe we have walked into a forest filled with phantasms."

"Phantasms are more troubling than ghosts?" I slid my hand into my pocket to pull out my magical phone.

"If these aren't spirits or creatures," Eric said, "then someone or—the more tragic possibility—this place is deliberately manifesting the phantasms."

"You're really not helping with the panic," I said.

"Terrible things have happened near the soaring stone columns. We read the truth of it all over the brochures in town," Eric said. "The tourists don't understand the raw horror of it, but the woods remember. Pain, fear, panic, grief, all etched into the trees themselves. The overabundance of humans at the monasteries would block such things—too much petty worry and greed oozing out of the hordes. The memories the forest holds can't hope to break through. But out here, where people are not meant to be, the trees remember."

"So what exactly is the protocol for dealing with tree memory phantasms?" I asked.

"Keep walking, stay together, and pray to whomever you think watches over you that we will have the fortitude to hear what the woods want to tell us, the courage to push forward until we meet the light, and that the memories held within these woods have not been twisted to a darker purpose." Eric waved his hand through the air, reconjuring his light as his shield faded away.

I shoved my fear down, cramming it beneath my need to protect Elizabeth. "You ready?"

"Sure." She trembled in my arms as her eyes tracked the movement of something I couldn't see.

"I promise, I'll stay right beside you," I whispered. "I won't let anything hurt you."

"Okay." She slipped her hand into mine. "Just don't leave me."

"Never." I let my shield dissolve. "*Heliono.*" My orb of light reappeared in my palm.

Eric kept his pace slow as we headed toward the light in the distance, making sure our little pack stayed close together.

"It's really not fair, you know." Elizabeth's voice wavered as she spoke. "Seers should be given some sort of defense mechanism."

"Want my sticky blaster?" Devon asked.

"Thanks, but that's not what I mean." Elizabeth flinched and tightened her grip on my hand. "I don't think a sticking potion would help with dive-bombing forest memory spirit things."

Eric paused at the top of a rocky slope. He peered into the darkness before leading us sideways, cutting along the incline. "What sort of defense would you prefer?"

"Some built-in badassery to go with being a seer," Elizabeth said. "Porcupines get quills, bees get stingers, even skunks get stink sacks. I should have something."

"Have you ever mentioned this to Lola?" Eric asked.

"Yep." Elizabeth clung to my arm. "We have to move faster. There are more of them here."

"What did Lola say?" Eric picked up the pace, walking quickly enough to knock stones down the slope.

The sound of the rocks clattering away into the darkness felt like we were sounding an alarm, telling everything in the forest that might want to torment, haunt, or kill us exactly where we were.

"That life has never been that kind to seers," Elizabeth said. "At least society has progressed enough that I hopefully won't be institutionalized for being hysterical or burned because people freak out and think I'm a witch. So, that's something."

The ground leveled out in front of us, offering a better view of the light I'd spotted.

A single candle glowed through a window partway up a cliff. As we moved through the woods, the window came in and out of view, but it wasn't until we reached the edge of the trees and stood at the base of the stone pillar that I realized there was more to the structure on the side of the cliff than a single lit window.

A whole two-story building clung to the side of the rock, though how it stayed stuck to the pillar, I had no idea. There were two little chimneys and a set of carved stairs leading up to the entryway. If it hadn't been dark, and Elizabeth hadn't been shaking like she was facing an orc army without even a Halfling-size sword to defend herself, it might have been a charming hideaway in the woods.

But Elizabeth shouted, "Eric stop!" right before he reached the stairs, and all my feelings of awe for the little structure clinging to the side of the rock in a completely illogical way vanished.

The woods seemed to still for a moment, like the trees and their weird memory spirits/phantasm things had all paused to see what had frightened Elizabeth so badly.

"What do you—" I never finished my question.

The air around me seemed to solidify, pressing against my skin. But the pressure wasn't even. It shifted and lurched like I was being jostled in a crowd.

"I don't think they want us to go up there." Elizabeth reached out, running her fingers across something I couldn't see.

14

"Don't!" I yanked Elizabeth's hand back, terrified that whatever it was she was touching would devour her.

"Why are they here?" Elizabeth said. "Why do they have substance?"

"We need to get into that building." Eric slogged toward the steps like he was shouldering his way through Times Square on New Year's Eve.

"The seer just said no to going into the building," Devon said even though he was already shoving his way forward in Eric's wake.

"We are looking for a hidden place that at the very least contains invaluable information." Eric gripped the wall by the stairs and dragged himself forward in a way that would have been super comical if it weren't for the invisible—to me—things holding him back. "The place we are being prevented from going is the most likely candidate for being the place we seek."

"Love it." Devon reached for the wall but could barely graze the stacked stones with his fingers.

Eric grabbed Devon's wrist, wrenching him forward.

"Stay right behind me." I shifted to stand in front of Elizabeth, knocking my shoulder into something that felt like a linebacker. I clenched my jaw against the inevitable bruises and shoved another foot forward.

"They really don't want us to go into that building." Elizabeth wrapped one arm around my waist, keeping herself tucked to my back as I stepped forward. "Bryant, they look desperate."

The night pressed against me as I squeezed between two invisible things. I would have thought I was back in Athens with the weird gravity pressing me to the ceiling, but whatever beings/spirits/woodland memory phantasm things I was shoving between had enough substance that my sleeves shifted on my arms like the material had caught on other people's clothing.

I gritted my teeth and plowed another step forward.

"Has it occurred to you," Elizabeth said, "that maybe we're being kept from getting to the building for a good reason?"

"We must assume the reason is to protect whatever secrets wait inside," Eric said.

"I meant a *good* reason." Elizabeth pressed on my back, steering me a little bit left. I couldn't see why, but my next step was slightly easier. "Like maybe they're trying to protect us."

"What makes you say that?" My voice came out all strained as I pushed through what felt like a wall of rubber to get to the base of the steps.

"If the bodies of the phantasms can make it harder for us to walk, couldn't they do other things to us, too?" Elizabeth said. "If they wanted to hurt us—"

"Let's not give the creepy things ideas." Devon grabbed my wrists while Eric reached for Elizabeth.

I have no memory of being birthed, but Devon dragging me onto the steps was way closer than I ever wanted to get. Something between a groan and a yelp sprang involuntarily from my throat as my body was compressed like Devon was trying to drag me through a tube. As soon as the pressure was gone, I stumbled forward, knocking face first into the rock wall. Dragging air into my lungs, I looked back to try and help Elizabeth, but she was already standing next to me, her hair barely out of place as she stared into the woods.

"I just think some things are hidden for a reason," Elizabeth said. "And if the phantasms are trying to protect us, then whatever's inside could be a lot worse than what's out here."

"If the phantasms you see mean to help us, we will thank them after we've seen what waits inside." Eric started up the steps. "We cannot be dissuaded from our cause."

"Do you really think the things you're seeing want to help us?" I wrapped my arm around Elizabeth's waist, not only because I wanted to make sure the shadows didn't drag her away. I also just needed to feel her safe and solid beside me to maintain my ever-slipping attempt at remaining calm. "You don't normally seem this freaked out by the things you see."

"Of course I'm scared," Elizabeth said. "I don't want those things flying around me, and I like them being solid enough to block our path even less."

"But?" I whispered as Eric reached the door of the building.

"I just can't get it to make sense," Elizabeth whispered back. "If Eric's right and it really is the woods projecting a visual memory, what reason would a memory have for solidifying to block us? And if they're individual spirits, what common goal could they share that would make them stand in our way?"

"I have no idea." I kissed Elizabeth's temple. Partly because I was in love with her and wanted to offer a bit of comfort even though I had literally zero comforting things to say. The other part was me wanting to sneaky smell her hair to give myself an aromatic bravery booster as Eric reached for the latch on the door.

The bar moved up with a sharp metal-on-wood *clack.*

Eric extinguished the light in his palm, and I did the same. He pushed the door open and stepped into the shadows.

I much more reasonably pulled out my normal phone and turned on the flashlight before stepping up beside Devon.

Elizabeth shifted away from me, peering at the shadows Eric had so casually walked into.

"I don't think there are any phantasms inside," Elizabeth said. "At least none that I can see."

"There won't be," Eric said. "I doubt they can exist on consecrated ground."

I inched forward enough to be able to see Eric standing in the entryway, staring up at a glittering mural that looked like it belonged in a cathedral.

"The hidden monastery where the monks learned how to scare the shadow men away." I stepped inside, and the air changed, growing colder and damper within a few feet.

"Well, they're keeping the phantasms out, but what about the shadow men?" Devon shined the light of his phone up at the paintings that looped around the top of the wall.

"This way." Eric beckoned us toward the only other door in the room.

The bolt moved with another *clack,* but the stone of the walls seemed to amplify the sound, making it bounce around the enclosed space.

I held my breath, listening for any hint of angry monks coming to chase us back out into the horde of phantasms.

Nothing.

Making sure Devon and Elizabeth stayed right behind me, I stepped through the door and into the corridor beyond.

A row of doors took up the side of the narrow hall closest to the rock face, and on the other side, a single door opened into a dark room overlooking the woods.

"Where's the candle?" I whispered as loudly as I dared.

Eric pointed forward where another closed door blocked our path.

I shook out my free hand, trying to convince myself I could not only move my fingers, but was also capable of creating a spell to defend us.

Eric paused in front of the door, studying the light drifting through the tiny cracks in the wood. He reached forward to touch the bolt, but before his fingers even grazed the metal, the door swung silently open.

Devon pressed his sticky blaster into Elizabeth's hand and pulled the metal tube of his hilt from his pocket.

"I'm so sorry to interrupt your evening unannounced." Eric spoke calmly and cheerfully, like he'd spotted an old friend in the white-painted, candlelit room beyond, where there was definitely no person in sight. "We're here on some rather urgent business that couldn't wait until morning. If you have time for a quick word, I'd be very grateful for your assistance."

He was so smooth, so unafraid, if I hadn't been on the spooky walk through the woods with him, I might have believed we were just dropping by the monastery for a chat. And that chill-under-pressure definitely ranked in the top ten reasons why I would always be the sidekick to Eric Deldridge, wizarding hero.

Eric stepped into the room.

I attempted to walk with a calm swagger as I followed him. I'm pretty sure it just looked like I was sore from too many squats in gym class.

I glanced around the room. The rock face of the cliff had been used as one of the walls. Candles had been set into the crevices, though none of them were lit. The other three, man-made walls had all been painted the same pure white without any of the fancy murals from the entryway. A single candle burned in the window.

"We're seeking a place that should be near here." Eric turned in a slow circle as he spoke, like he was addressing a gallery full of people instead of an empty room. "I was told by an old friend that I might find the bookkeepers in these woods. You may have a different name for them. Perhaps you call them the shadow men, though I believe that local legend might come from the entities outside."

"Eric," Elizabeth said.

I spun toward her, ready to shout a spell to defend her. But she was still and calm as she pointed toward the corner where a man was slowly materializing out of the white wall.

The man was old with a weathered face and bright white hair to go with his bright white robes.

I fought against my urge to shout a spell to knock him back into the wall as my instincts screamed *Lady*.

"The men you're looking for are gone," white-hair wall-appearer said. "They all died years ago."

"I'm very sorry to hear that," Eric said. "I was hoping they might be able to help me. I'm looking for some very particular books."

The man shook his head. "They are gone. Their home is gone. The path to their home is gone."

"How?" I asked. "What happened to them?"

The man studied us all for a moment before moving.

He took a step forward, and for one awful moment, I thought he was going to attack Devon. But the man just walked through the door and waved for us to follow.

I held back, staring at the place where the man had appeared out of the wall, as Devon and Eric followed him.

The wall was just a wall. No hidden cubby I could see. No marks where he'd done some creepy camouflage thing.

"Where did he come from? Did you see any weird magic?" I asked. "Are your eyes fuzzy? Is he using bone magic?"

"I don't think so." Elizabeth took my hand, leading me after the others.

Electric lights had been turned on in the big room opposite the wall of doors.

Elizabeth and I arrived just in time to watch the man push aside a super old tapestry to reveal a little kitchen, complete with a stainless-steel fridge.

He pulled out four bottles of water, giving one to each of us. "Even when the weather isn't baking you, it's not an easy path to get here."

"Thanks." I tamped down the voice in my head that railed at me for touching single-use plastic and took a drink of the cold water.

"We don't get many visitors to our monastery during the day," the man said. "We get fewer at night. I try not to count the time between those who stumble to our door as they seek the other men hiding in the woods."

"Because they're dead?" Elizabeth asked.

"More than a decade." The man sat on one of the spindly, wooden chairs. "They were nice men, for the most part. We weren't supposed to know what they were doing out in their corner of the woods. But you can only see so many strange things before you start to guess.

"I would watch them sometimes when they were out walking in the woods. They were as friendly as one can expect of recluses. Some of their visitors would end up at our door by mistake. Some of ours would get lost in the woods—it didn't go so well for them. We have stone stairs leading to our monastery, but the path to their home was filled with unnatural things."

"Did you ever see it?" I sat down in front of the man.

"Once." He stared at the wall like he was seeing the path all over again. "One of theirs came to our door. She was badly wounded but insisted there was nothing a doctor could do to help her. I had never been near the other place, even though I'd lived in this monastery for twenty years by then. I'd been told which direction the other place was when I first came here, as a warning not to venture to that corner of the forest. But I couldn't let the woman die, so I went to find the men.

"I walked in the direction everyone had pointed." He tapped his chin like it was a nervous twitch as the wrinkles on his brow deepened. "I hurried through the woods, calling for the men, praying they would find me."

"And did they?" I asked when he hadn't spoken in a few moments.

"No," the man said. "I had almost given up hope. Then faint lights began to glimmer all around me, like the dust in the air had learned to shine. I followed the glow, keeping to the bright path. Up ahead, darkness swallowed everything, like I was staring into the mouth of a great beast. The light around me grew, everything gleaming with more beauty than this earth was meant to host, even as demons I cannot name surrounded me, trapping me in a place I did not belong.

"I was sure it was the end of my life, so I shouted to the other men, trying to make sure they would know to hurry to our monastery and help the woman. One of the men stepped out of the darkness and took my hand. In that moment, all the things I had seen vanished. I led the man here and watched as he used his powers to heal the woman. It was a miraculous thing."

"Thank you for being willing to help one of our kind," Eric said. "And for accepting the differences between us."

"The peace we shared was a good one." The man nodded.

"But what happened?" Elizabeth asked. "How do you know they're dead?"

"One came to visit years ago. He said he was the last. Said the way the path to their home was created depended upon his life. And when he was gone, their home would go with him. He warned me I would hear whispers in the woods. That his fellows had been keeping the trees quiet, but the silence would end with the rest of it.

"It wasn't more than a week later that I woke to find six books by the door. The man left a note. He said it was his time. Asked me to keep the books. Said one day someone would come looking for them, to please keep the volumes safe until I could pass them on. That night when I tried to sleep, the whispers in the woods woke me."

"I'm so sorry." I didn't really know what I was sorry for, but it was the only thing I could think to say as childlike fear filled the man's face.

"I'd grown used to the whispers," the man said. "When she came, she dampened their sound. Made things easier for me here in thanks for my having kept the books safe while I waited for her."

"This *she*," I said, "do you know her name? Or where we could find her?"

"Iliana?" The man finally looked back toward me with a mixture of fear and grief in his eyes that made me want to run. "I don't know where to find her. But now that she knows you're here, she'll come for you."

I set down my water bottle and stood, wondering if the rolling in my stomach was from the man having drugged me or just plain panic.

"How would Iliana know we're here?" Eric asked. "Did you send her a message?"

"No. I don't know how, but she always knows when one of your kind enters our sanctuary." The man stood and went back to the fridge. "But now that you're inside the monastery, the whispers in the woods won't let you out. Don't worry. I have enough food to keep us all alive until she comes."

"And once she gets here?" Devon said.

"I have never been brave enough to ask." The man froze, his back still toward us. "But when the screaming starts, part of me misses the whispers."

15

————

I've been told more than once that my self-preservation instincts need to be honed. I'll panic when things are fine and not even notice when death is flying straight at my face.

However, I can say with complete certainty that when I grabbed Elizabeth and Devon by the arms and dragged them out of the monastery sitting room from Hell, my self-preservation instincts were working just fine.

"Bryant, wait," Eric said just as I was about to throw open the outside door and run down the stairs into the phantasms/shadow people I couldn't see but could definitely feel as I'd shoved my way through them just a short while before.

"Wait to find out exactly what Iliana is going to do to us to make us scream?" I grabbed the door latch.

"I have no intention of waiting here," Eric said. "But if we are going to force our way out of this place, it should be me who leads."

"Right," I panted, letting go of the latch and stepping aside. "I can see the logic in that."

Eric tossed open the door. "*Heliono.*" A glowing orb burst into being in his hand. He strode down the steps toward the things we couldn't see with as much confidence as a varsity quarterback in a JV game.

"*Heliono.*" My light flickered and dimmed in my hand as my magic wavered.

You will not panic. You are not allowed to panic.

The orb buzzed as the light shone bright.

"Let's go." I took Elizabeth's hand and stepped out into the night.

A cold wind touched my cheeks as I walked down the stone steps. I tried to tell myself the sounds I was hearing were only an unfortunate combination of the wind rustling through the trees and my heart thumping so loud I might as well have installed subwoofers in my ears.

But Elizabeth said, "Eric. Eric, I don't know if we can get through," and the fear in her voice shot ice down my spine.

"We don't have a choice." Eric stopped at the bottom of the steps.

The sounds of the whispers surged and fell like waves trying to drag us under.

"Bryant," Devon said.

"Yeah?" I fought against my instinct to reach for my phone, unwilling to let go of either my light or Elizabeth's hand.

"I think this would be the time to freak out." Devon's red sword voomed to life.

"Great. Good to know." I swallowed the knot in my throat before my fear could choke me.

"If we're separated, head back toward the road. And know I will not rest until I've found you." Eric stepped off the stairs.

To my normal eyes, it looked fine. Like he'd just stepped down onto the forest floor.

But Elizabeth screamed, "Eric!" as the air around him seemed to shift and a giant tear appeared on the arm of his coat.

"Get away from him!" Devon leapt off the side of the stairs, slashing his sword at the things he couldn't see. A deeper *hum* vibrated through the glowing blade as it met his invisible foe.

I hesitated on the bottom step.

We needed to escape.

But I had to protect Elizabeth.

I had to help Devon and Eric, who were both fighting like they were penned in by a pack of demons.

But I had to protect Elizabeth.

Devon shouted and stumbled back. Blood oozed from a cut on his cheek.

"Stay right beside me." I wrapped Elizabeth's arm around my waist. "*Aarantha!*"

The wind of my spell surrounded us, the vortex picking up dirt and debris from the forest floor as we stepped down onto the ground.

Elizabeth clung to me as I moved toward Devon.

I kept waiting for something to block my path, making each step forward a fight. But I didn't feel any resistance as I reached out to grab Devon's arm. If I could get him into the funnel of my spell and then grab Eric, I could keep the spell going all the way out of the woods.

Even as my brain formed the plan, I knew I wouldn't be able to maintain the magic for that long.

"Devon!" I grabbed his arm and wrenched him through the vortex.

Elizabeth let go of me to steady him.

"Stay close." I headed toward Eric.

Even if I couldn't keep the spell going for the whole hike back to the road, Eric could. He could keep the wind going. I just had to get to him.

"Eric!" I reached forward, trying to grab his arm as a stream of crimson haze flew from his palm.

The haze didn't rush through the air and dissipate. It solidified, forming the outline of a person.

The phantasm's mouth opened in a soundless scream as it swung its arm down as though preparing slice through Eric's neck.

The haze lengthened, growing around the outline of a sword as the blade neared Eric's flesh.

"No!" I dove forward, out of the safety of my own spell, grabbing the misty form around the middle and tackling a very real-feeling body to the ground.

"*Exci.*" I tried to pin the form down as my spell pummeled it in the face.

The mist that had surrounded its head poofed out in an almost beautiful way.

I rolled to the side, and scrambled to my knees, trying to stand so I could get back to Elizabeth.

A stab of pain cut through my side. Like I'd been struck by lightning, or stung by the world's largest wasp, or stabbed.

I looked down to find lots of blood on my stomach.

"Oh, shit." The pain quadrupled as I realized I'd literally been stabbed. "*Sinato.*"

The agony of my healing spell seared through me, and the whole world went wiggly and dark. I could feel myself tipping toward the ground. I put my arms out, trying to stop my fall, but somehow I hit the ground on the side where I'd been stabbed.

A scream tore from my throat as I rolled onto my back, digging into my pocket for my magical phone, desperate to find a better healing spell.

A horde of people surrounded me, blocking Devon and Elizabeth from view, keeping them from seeing how badly I needed help.

But the figures looming over me weren't made of red mist. They were people with faces and clothes and weapons.

A *rustle* and a faint sound like a long-forgotten scream came from nearby, but I couldn't see who had cried out.

"*Telinto.*" I felt the magic rush from my body, like I'd tried to topple a city instead of casting a simple slicing spell.

The shimmer of my spell flew toward the man closest to me. He grunted and stumbled as my magic met his very real-looking flesh, but he didn't bleed or fall.

He screamed words I couldn't understand, his filthy, bearded face twisting with a kind of loathing I'd never seen before.

"I haven't hurt you." I tried to push myself up, but the pain in my side shocked through my body, making it impossible to stand. "*Primurgo.*" I barely managed to say the spell. Still, my shield blossomed around me, blocking the bearded man's blade.

His face shifted from loathing, to awe, then to fear.

He shouted something to the other warriors.

As one, they all stepped toward me, crowding around like they wanted to squash me to death.

"Who are you?" I coughed, and something that tasted horribly like blood flew from my mouth. "*Sinato.*" The sting of healing came again, but it already hadn't worked once. "Eric." I coughed more blood.

The men, and they were literally all men, loomed over me, pushing against my shield like they didn't care about the horrible way my magic should have been stinging their flesh.

I pressed my hand to the blood on my stomach, making myself breathe instead of scream in pain. The world wobbled for a moment, but when I could see clearly again, the men were still standing over me.

"What do you want?" I asked.

One of the men pulled his spear back and stabbed at my shield. A horrible *hum* vibrated my bones, but my spell held.

Another man, this one wearing armor, slashed at my shield with his sword. Metal met magic, and the man let out a ferocious scream as my shield flashed.

And that's when I realized none of the men matched. It was like my mom had decided to do a Shakespearean play, but the costumer didn't know what concept Mom had chosen. There were old school warriors, a guy who looked like he could be a Victorian duke, and a guy who looked like he was trying to be a 90's PI.

"Why are you all here? Why is she making you do this?"

The 90's dude raised his pistol and pointed it at me.

"I'm not here to hurt anyone. I'm trying to help find the books."

Books.

It was like the trees had started whispering the word.

Books. Books. Books.

The shapes of the men around me shivered and reformed.

Books. Books.

"We want to protect them." I tried to take a breath and gagged on my own blood. "Someone stole them. We have to find the…"

Everything started to fade into darkness. I thought it was the end.

"…the books."

I would die in the woods in Greece. Eric would have to tell my parents. Cindy would have to arrange to ship my body home.

But death didn't come for me, and the darkness didn't swallow me whole. It shifted and twisted, turning into a different scene.

Green leaves hung from the trees like we'd leapt through time to the beginnings of summer, and the Monastery glued to the rock face disappeared. The whole stone column vanished like I'd moved to another part of the forest.

A light, like glowing shimmer powder, filled the air as the men who had tried to kill me faded away, leaving a girl my age standing on the gleaming path, speaking to an older man.

I couldn't tell what either of them was saying, but I could read the look on the girl's face. She thought the man was lying to her. She was suspicious and livid.

The man kept his voice calm, but his eyes were filled with authority tinged by fear.

The girl shouted something at the man and turned away. As she stalked past me, she muttered in perfect English, "His lies will get him killed someday."

The scene twisted, the glow twirling around me, blocking everything from view before a new scene reformed.

The older man limped toward the darkness at the end of the gleaming path, pausing for a moment before stepping into the black and out of sight. The darkness did nothing to dampen his terrible scream of pain.

I tried to push myself up so I could go see if the man needed help, but I couldn't get my body to move.

I'm sorry. I couldn't even make myself speak the words.

Another, younger man stepped out of the black. Blood coated his cheeks and hands. But there was something about his face that seemed familiar even through the gore.

Thaden.

Terror joined the pain still zinging through my stomach as Thaden walked past me and faded into the darkness.

The glow that filled the air shifted, dimming as everything went bone-chillingly cold. The light vanished, and my teeth started to chatter as the ground beneath me turned to ice.

A *crunch* of frost under feet came from beside me. I looked up to find the girl from the first scene standing next to me. But she wasn't a girl anymore. Time had passed since she'd shouted at the man.

She looked around the woods for a few moments before calling out.

I held my breath, waiting for someone to answer. The forest stayed silent without even the wind or phantasms whispering through the trees.

She called out again as she walked toward the place where Thaden had been in the scene before. Moving slowly, she crept through the spot where the darkness should have eaten her.

She buried her face in her hands before letting out a horrible scream. Lightning streaked down from the sky, striking the ground around her. She let her hands drop and looked back to where the man had stood years before. "I'll find them myself. Rot in Hell, cowards."

The trees shifted, moving me back to the forest right beside the monastery. The mismatched men surrounded me again, their weapons raised, their gazes locked on my face.

I opened my mouth to try and talk, but my body didn't seem to be able to rally the strength to speak.

The 90's-looking dude pressed his palm to my shield. "They were never here." He spoke with a British accent. "They decimated the keepers in their search. But the books you seek were never here."

How do you know?

I wanted to ask the question, but the world started fading. No monastery, no trees, no creepy mismatched phantasms, no beauty from the shimmering path made of light. Just darkness creeping toward the center of my vision as everything faded to black.

"You've died for nothing," he said.

You're wrong.

16

You're wrong.

    You're wrong.

The words kept churning through my head over and over as the blackness spun around me like I'd fallen into a bottomless pit.

You're wrong.

There was pain in the blackness. A sharp, white-hot pain in my stomach.

I hoped the others were alive and Eric would heal me. Or, if they were dead, I hoped their deaths had been less painful than mine.

You're wrong.

You're wrong.

Eventually, the spinning changed into a sort of bouncing that made the pain in my stomach worse. Then the blackness became less complete as sound broke through my shroud.

Panting. Footsteps, panting, and a little cough like someone was choking on tears.

Elizabeth.

I tried to get my mouth to form the word, but all I managed was a weird cough.

"It's okay," Devon said. "You're going to be okay, Bryant. Just hang on."

Devon sounded so confident I didn't mind when the blackness started to swallow me again.

I knew that dude was wrong.

I may not be the most knowledgeable world traveler, but here are some tips for creating a joyful international escapade.

- Don't go into hidden monasteries at night.
- Don't forget to run as soon as a monk materializes from a wall.
- Don't get stabbed by a forest phantasm.
- Don't wake up on the side of a cliff with the taste of your own blood still in your mouth.

I mean, maybe those are just things I personally don't enjoy, but if there were a way to leave a negative review for a morally questionable monk hiding in a forest filled with tree memories of death, I would have some nasty things to say about that whole night.

On the plus side, I finally managed to make my eyes flutter open to find Elizabeth kneeling beside me, holding my hand, Devon alive and with his face already healed, and Eric looking more worried than disappointed. So, it could have been worse.

"Careful." Elizabeth wrapped her arm around my back as I sat up.

The terrible agony in the side of my stomach from being stabbed had morphed into a clenching pain like I'd gotten a cramp from running for too long.

"I'm okay." I managed to speak without coughing up any blood.

"Shit, Bry." Devon rubbed his hands over his face. Some of the dried blood on his cheek flecked away. "I really hate it when you do the near-death thing."

"I'm not such a big fan of it myself." I tried to laugh. It came out more like a death rattle.

"We should keep moving." Eric stood, brushing imaginary dirt off his pristine clothing.

"He needs to rest," Elizabeth said.

"I agree," Eric said. "But he'll rest better at the hotel, and the more distance we put between us and that vile monk, the better. I'd prefer to be far from here when Iliana comes."

"Are you sure?" Devon grabbed me under the arms and hoisted me to my feet.

"A woman who managed to manipulate phantasms to trap people in the monastery until she could make them scream?" Elizabeth wrapped her arms around me, holding me steady as my legs wobbled. "I don't want to wait in the dark for her to show up."

"But we need to talk to her," Devon said. "If she knew the bookkeepers, she could be the next step in finding the books."

"I agree," Eric said. "We will find Iliana, but we will not wait near the woods she's contaminated. I will not give her that advantage."

"I hope we can find some food in town." Devon started down the steep slope of the road.

"Let me help you." Elizabeth kept her arm around my waist, helping me balance as new shocks of pain zinged through different parts of my body with each step. "We don't even know if Iliana has any more books than the six the monk gave her."

"But we're not the only ones to have thought the books stolen from our Library ended up here," I said.

"What do you mean?" Eric asked.

"Thaden was here." I started to take another step down, but the rest of them had frozen.

"What?" Elizabeth said.

"Thaden was here. I assume he was looking for the books. I don't know why else he'd show up in a forest in Greece to kill someone," I said. "And there was a girl looking for the books, too."

"What are you talking about?" Devon wrinkled his brow as he studied me, like maybe I'd lost my mind when I'd been stabbed.

"When I was on the ground, coughing up blood, and the weird whisper phantasms looked like real people, I saw where the entrance to the bookkeepers' lair was," I said. "Thaden killed a guy and walked away, and a woman visited twice. I know she was looking for the books, so I think it's safe to assume Thaden was, too."

Everyone stared at me.

"Am I the only one who saw this?" My shoulders crept toward my ears as a need to hide from their gazes tightened in my still-throbbing stomach.

"You were the only one who was dying," Eric said. "The phantasms may have recognized you as one on the brink of joining their ranks, balancing on the bridge that joins our world and theirs."

"That's not good," I said.

"You went down, and then you got really rigid and started twitching." Elizabeth's fingers dug into my recently stabbed side. "I didn't know if you were having a seizure or being tortured by something I couldn't see."

"I'm sorry." I kissed her temple, pretending her gripping me as she remembered being terrified of losing me didn't feel like she was shoving a hot poker into my flesh. "I didn't mean to scare you."

"Don't apologize." Elizabeth thankfully eased her grip as she started walking down the hill, guiding me along with her. "It's not you who needs to be sorry. It's Iliana the psycho witch who decided using phantasms to attack people was a good idea. She's the one who's going to be sorry."

"If she's that determined to murder wizards who show up at the monastery, she must have a good reason." My sentence was punctuated with odd grunts as my organs rearranged themselves back into their pre-stabbing positions. "What better reason could there be than the books everybody's been going into the woods to try and find?"

"Great," Elizabeth said, "then I don't even have to feel guilty for wanting to track her down tonight. Eric, can you get ahold of Raven from here?"

"I'm sure I can," Eric said.

"Have her find us a witch named Iliana," Elizabeth said. "Hell, have her find every witch who's ever been named Iliana. Bryant's dad can pay her for her work."

"Elizabeth," Devon began.

"Do not tell me to calm down, Devon Rhodes." Elizabeth's voice had a dark quality to it that was both terrifying, because she sounded like she would be willing to burn Iliana alive, and exhilarating, as she would be doing the burning on my behalf.

"Okay, no calming down." Devon held up both hands. "Just remember to bury your rage enough that you won't be caught unawares if Iliana comes to find us first. Also, maybe don't let Cindy see the murdery vibe, either."

Elizabeth took a deep breath. "I watched my boyfriend bleeding out on the ground, and there was nothing I could do about it." Her hands started to shake. "I've gotten used to seeing horrible things and not being able to do much to defend myself from them. But what Iliana set those phantasms up to do to us, what they've done to other people...she's a murderer. And we're going to make her pay."

"Indeed, we are," Eric said.

"Good." Elizabeth started down the hill again.

It took me a while to figure out what words I wanted to say, and then a little bit longer to be brave enough to say them.

"I love you," I whispered, counting on Devon and Eric to at least pretend they couldn't hear me. "And I'm sorry for all the terrifying things you have to see."

"It didn't even help." Tears glistened in Elizabeth's eyes. "I knew we were walking into shadows, and it didn't help anything. I should have been the one to get stabbed. Seeing is the only thing I'm good for."

Fear that I somehow hadn't felt when I'd been stabbed shot through my whole body. "That's not even a little true."

"Yes, it is," Elizabeth said. "Otherwise, I wouldn't have felt so helpless."

I tried to think of comforting words to say as we made our way into town.

No, not comforting, that wasn't what I wanted to be. I wanted to be honest about the real value she held, make sure she understood that her bravery, and intelligence, and relentless determination had saved us all more than once. But I couldn't think of a way to say it that wouldn't risk sounding patronizing.

"You should clean your clothing." Eric stopped in front of the door to our hotel.

"*Nudla*." With a *hiss* and a *pop*, the blood and dirt disappeared from my clothes. "*Nudla*." I cleaned what I could only assume was my blood off Elizabeth's sweater.

"We should rest," Eric said. "I'll send a message to Raven. Hopefully, she'll have some information for us by the time we wake up. Then we can be off to our next destination."

"Iliana is supposed to be on her way here," Devon said.

"All the more reason to move quickly," Eric said. "I would very much prefer to search Iliana's life for any sign of her knowing the whereabouts of the books before she gets home from her mission to murder us."

"Great idea." I nodded. "First, we sleep."

We all entered the lobby and headed toward the polished wooden staircase that led up to our rooms.

Elizabeth kept her arm around my waist as we reached my door, and a little bit of joy flitted circles in my chest as I wondered if she'd insist on coming into my room so she could sleep in my arms and feel that I was safe and breathing.

"A moment, Bryant." Eric stopped right beside my door.

The flitting stopped.

"Get some rest." Elizabeth brushed her lips against my cheek and headed toward her room at the other end of the hall.

Eric didn't speak until Elizabeth had closed her door. "I know what you did."

I froze as my mind raced back through the woods to the monastery, back to town, and into a bathroom where I'd sent a potentially catastrophic email.

Nikki.

My newly healed stomach clenched itself into a super painful prune of fear.

"The blow that nearly killed you was meant for me," Eric said.

My stomach expanded out of its fear-prune state only to start shaking around my gut in weird, nervous embarrassment. "I mean, the thing was swinging for your neck. I had to do something."

"No Bryant, you didn't. In fact, many wouldn't have. You could have stayed in the safety you'd created for yourself and hoped I would see the sword in time to defend myself. But you didn't. You put your life at risk specifically to protect mine." Eric held my gaze for a long moment. "I am very grateful."

"Oh." Heat burned my cheeks. "It's no problem. It's not like you haven't done the same for me."

"But I am the teacher. I hold a burden of care when it comes to the life of my apprentice. You have no such obligation."

"Yeah, I do." I patted Eric on the arm. "It's called having friends. *Cliaxo.*" I ducked into my room before I could say anything that would make my embarrassment complete enough for my face to actually catch fire.

I dug my fists into my eyes for a few seconds, letting the spots dancing in my vision block out the images the forest had shown me.

There was something about it that didn't make sense, but I couldn't quite figure out what bit of the puzzle I'd put in the wrong place.

I tried to sort through it as I changed out of my clothes. My shirt and sweater both had holes slashed through them. I thought about searching the phone for a mending spell, but honestly I didn't want to wear either of them ever again. I wadded up my stabbing attire and shoved it into the trashcan.

I didn't check my phone for a message from Nikki. I didn't even shower. I just climbed into bed and lay staring at the wall, trying to put the pieces into an order that made sense.

17

Fact one: The books used to be in the Library in Manhattan.

Fact two: The books were stolen from the Library a long time ago.

Fact three: There used to be men who lived in the woods in Meteora. They had books, but NOT the books from the Ladies' Library.

Fact four: Zoe now has the bookkeepers' texts in her home/library in Athens—except for a few the bookkeepers kept for themselves then gave to the monk who gave them to Iliana, the woman who made the forest phantasms all evil and murdery.

Fact five: Thaden came to Meteora—probably looking for the books from Manhattan once he found out they'd been stolen.

Fact six: Phantasm vision lady wanted the books from Manhattan but they were not in the woods.

Fact seven: I'm still massively confused.

I stared at the notes I'd written on my napkin while Elizabeth and Devon tried to run interference with the now very angry Cindy while Eric paced on the street outside the dining room window, talking on his phone to who I really hoped was Raven.

Fact eight: Vision lady and Thaden both found some evidence that made them believe the books were in Meteora.

Conclusion: At least we're not the only people to think the books are in Greece.

Post-Conclusion Statement: None of this actually tells me where the freakin' books are.

"Isn't that right, Bryant?" Elizabeth said.

I clapped my hand over the notes on my napkin and looked up. "Yes, absolutely." I had no idea what I was agreeing to, so I kept my gaze locked on Elizabeth so I could real smile at her instead of trying to fake smile at Cindy.

"It was such an amazing time," Elizabeth said. "The history behind the monasteries is so fascinating. I don't remember the last time I felt so immersed in history."

"Yeah, it was like I was being sucked into a vision of another time." An involuntary laugh rumbled in my throat as I appreciated my own grim joke.

"Well, I'm happy to drive you wherever it is you want to go today," Cindy said. "And since your phone seemed to have such problems yesterday, I'll make sure I stay nearby so you can get a ride back whenever you're ready. After all, your father is paying me to make sure you get where you need to go, and to translate for you. I can't translate if I can't find you."

A little, tiny pebble of guilt sank in my stomach. Cindy seemed nice enough, and I couldn't blame her for being miffed that the rich guy's teenage son was making it impossible for her to do her job.

At the same time, it's not like I was running away with my friends to drink Raki. I was on a mission, and the knowledge of generations of wizards hung in the balance.

"I'm not used to having access to a car," I said in a way I hoped sounded self-deprecating instead of condescending and ungrateful. "Back home, I take the train or walk most places. Sometimes, I take a cab if I need one. But a driver? I've only ever had one pick me up when Dad wanted to send me somewhere specific."

Cindy's shoulders relaxed a little. "Well, since there's no public transportation to run you where you want to go, and you can't read the signs to try and find your own way, how about you let me do what I was hired for? I promise, you'll learn a lot more if you aren't spending half your time wandering around lost."

I wasn't sure I completely agreed with the sentiment, but I gave her a nod anyway. "My legs are too tired to do much climbing today anyway."

"So you want to go back up to the monasteries?" Cindy asked.

"No!" Elizabeth, Devon, and I all said at once in a way no one could deny was completely suspicious.

"Bryant's monasteried out," Devon said.

"Too much iconography for me," I said.

"Then where to next?" Cindy sipped her coffee. "Do you need any help with your photoshop project for school?"

I glanced out the window. Eric was still pacing on the street.

"Eric's working on it." Devon swept in and saved me. "He's talking to some of his contacts about where our next stop should be."

"Great." Cindy sounded like she did not at all think the situation was great. "A spontaneous European trip. What a thrill."

I slid my written-on napkin off the table as we all went back to awkwardly eating our breakfast.

I set my napkin on my leg and scrunched in one more line of writing.

Fact nine: Zoe's dad became the librarian for Greece. If the bookkeepers had ever known where the stolen books were they would have told him. He wouldn't have gone to Manhattan, and he wouldn't have died.

I crossed out my old conclusion and wrote in:

New Conclusion: Whoever sent the package from Meteora left us a bread-crumb trail leading to stabby near-death and failure.

I shoved the napkin into my pocket.

I almost died because we were tricked into coming here.

My breakfast turned to lead in my stomach as I remembered the searing pain of almost dying less than twelve hours before.

"You okay?" Elizabeth squeezed my hand.

"Yeah. Just tired." I threaded my fingers through hers, needing to have something to hold on to so I wouldn't start screaming at the top of my lungs. "I might sleep on the ride to wherever we go next."

Devon cleared his throat and nodded toward the door as Eric strode into the dining room like he was first in line for a Black Friday sale.

"We're going to Crete," Eric said. "Get your bags. We can book a ferry on the drive south."

"Okay." I stood and headed for my room before Cindy could argue.

———

Normally, in regular life and with magic stuff, I try to pull my weight. But since I had been stabbed and nearly bled to death the night before, I didn't feel too bad about falling asleep in the car and not waking up until we were all the way back in Athens.

I probably could have slept even longer if Eric and Cindy hadn't been grumbling at each other in the front of the car.

"We don't need to be on a tight timeline."

I think it was the unfamiliar snappishness in Cindy's voice that dragged me out of sleep.

"We can contact Mr. Adams, ask him if he prefers we fly," Cindy said.

"The flight would get us in later than the ferry," Eric said. "We're taking the boat."

"Why are you in such a hurry?" Cindy asked. "We can get an early flight out tomorrow."

I shifted to sit up, realized I'd been leaning on Elizabeth's shoulder, saw the drool-covered napkin she'd draped over her shoulder, then died a little inside as embarrassment surged through me.

"Perhaps I've misunderstood," Eric said. "I was under the impression your job was simply to be the driver and translator. Has something in this arrangement changed?"

"I can't be the driver if you all keep running away so I can't find you," Cindy said. "I also can't be the translator if you hide from me."

"No one's hiding," I said.

Elizabeth gripped my leg, apparently not so disgusted by my drool she never wanted to touch me again.

"Exactly," Eric said. "We are following Bryant's academic interests."

"Bryant," Cindy said, "exactly what academic interest has us racing to a ferry right now?"

"As I've said—" Eric began.

"I asked Bryant." Cindy turned off the highway and onto a road with a sign that seemed to imply we were heading toward the water. "So, Bryant, what about Crete sparks your interest?"

"I..." My heart started racing. I looked to Elizabeth, but she just stared at me wide-eyed and desperate. "Well it's really about"—I glanced toward Devon, but he was already shaking his head in defeat—"I've heard the food's good."

"That's it." Cindy pulled into a curbside parking spot, squeezing between two cars with a slickness I don't think even a Manhattan cabbie could have managed. "I was sent here by Mr. Adams, who happens to be my boss, as in the one who makes sure I have health insurance, to be sure that his son was moved safely from place to place while visiting a foreign country. Now, I don't care if Bryant is interested in art, mythology, foodie culture, or rescuing stray cats, but I did not graduate from an Ivy League school to be duped by this lame ass shit. So, what the hell are you all planning, because this is clearly something Mr. Adams has not sanctioned!"

"*Fransencio*," Eric said.

Cindy's head dipped forward, and she gave a weird little giggle.

"What did you just do?" My hand shook as I reached forward to touch Cindy's shoulder.

"Get your bags. We can walk from here." Eric opened his door and stepped out of the car like everything was normal.

Devon climbed out his side of the car and onto the sidewalk.

I froze for a second, torn between trying to shake Cindy out of her weird spell-induced stupor and running before her mind cleared and she, very justifiably, flipped out at us. The sound of the trunk slamming shut was enough to send me scrambling after Devon. "Eric, what did you just do?"

Eric handed me my backpack and rolly bag.

"Eric," I said, even as I put on my backpack like I was obviously going to follow him whether or not he answered my very important question.

"What did you do?" Elizabeth stood on the street-side of the car, arms crossed as she glared daggers at Eric.

"She'll be fine in a few hours," Eric said. "She may have a headache, but it will buy us time to get to the ferry without interference. I think we can all agree carting Cindy along has been a failed experiment."

"Is she going to remember where we're going?" Elizabeth asked.

"Yes." Eric set Elizabeth's bags in front of her. "Wiping her memory is beyond my skill."

"Then we'd better hope she doesn't come after us." Elizabeth put on her backpack.

"Wait. We're not actually leaving her here," I said as the others all started walking toward the ferry sign.

"That's exactly what we're doing," Eric said. "Now hurry, or we'll miss the boat."

The three of them all kept walking down the sidewalk.

"But we can't do that." I didn't move. I couldn't get my feet to follow them.

"We can, and we are." Eric stopped and turned to face me.

"No," I said. "We can't just leave a lady passed out in a car in a foreign country."

"*Oxailoc*," Eric said.

The locks on the car doors *thumped* closed.

"We must be on our way," Eric said.

"And if a cop comes to see why she's sitting in a car?" I asked. "Or when she wakes up and has to call my dad to tell him she lost us? I have the credit card, not her. What's she supposed to do?"

"That isn't our problem," Eric said.

"But it should be!"

I hadn't even noticed the lady walking past with her kids until she grabbed both of them by the backs of their coats to hurry them away from me.

"She hasn't done anything wrong." I dragged my bag closer to Eric so I wouldn't scare any more small children. "We can't just leave her here. It's wrong."

"Her inconvenience is nothing compared to the suffering the people of Beville have endured," Eric said. "She will have a bad afternoon. We have suffered for years."

"But she has nothing to do with it!" I whisper-shouted. "She hasn't hurt anybody, or sold anybody, or kidnapped anybody. She hasn't even been mean. The only thing Cindy's guilty of is trying to do the job my dad hired her for."

"That job interferes with our aim," Eric said.

"And?"

"Interference is intolerable. We must find the books. I will not allow a human to stand in our way." Eric turned and headed down the street like he'd made a judgment call and the conversation ended there.

"You don't get to do that." I cut around and planted myself in front of him, chin high, shockingly little panic flying through my chest.

I looked between Devon and Elizabeth, waiting for one of them to yell at him for daring to place humans below the books. But they both just stared silently at Eric. Their hurt made everything worse.

"You don't get to trash people's lives because of what you've decided is important." My anger brought heat to my face. "Cindy is innocent. And if you hurt her, you become the bad guy."

"My moral status matters little. There is nothing more important than protecting the books," Eric said. "We have to find them. We have to return the knowledge of ages to its rightful place. Nothing can be allowed to stand in our way."

I let out a breath, and it was like a part of me flew out of my body and something heavier, more mature, took its place. "I bet Thaden said the same thing. And the Ladies. I think it would be impossible to count how many people started off wanting to help and ended up ruining everything because they didn't think about what they were sacrificing to win. You don't get to hurt innocent people. We aren't the villains. I won't let you make us the villains."

"Then stay," Eric said. "Stand beside the car and wait for her mind to clear. And when we lose our chance at rescuing the books, be comforted that you did the right thing."

He stepped around me and strode down the street like he was going to leave without us.

"Eric, stop," I shouted.

I was a little surprised when he actually stopped.

"I'll call my dad," I said. "I'll beg for some favors and make sure Cindy is safe. But you can't keep doing this. You can't keep putting people in danger for what you think is right. Because someday, I won't be able to agree with you. And once you go that far. You might as well be Thaden."

Eric flinched like I'd actually attacked him.

"If you fall that far, none of us will be able to follow you."

Eric stayed frozen for another moment before walking away, following the picture signs that herded us toward the ferry.

I looked back at the car and Cindy staring out the window like a toddler watching a Disney movie before following Eric.

"Bryant." Elizabeth tried to take my hand, but I just kept walking.

"Bry." Devon gripped my shoulder, keeping pace as I followed Eric.

"I will not serve the next Thaden." Heat burned my eyes as I spoke. "I'm not going to sacrifice innocent people for what we've decided is right. If we can't build a system that helps people instead of tossing them out of our way and hoping they survive, I want nothing to do with magic."

"You're right." Elizabeth caught up to me and slipped her hand into mine. "If we're no better than the Ladies, then everything we've done will have been for nothing."

"I don't think Eric sees it that way." My throat was so tight, my words came out raspy.

"Then we'll make him see it that way," Devon said. "If we're supposed to be the good guys, that means it's our job to save people. It means we don't abandon our friends when they get lost."

"What are we supposed to do?" I asked.

"Try and reason with him," Elizabeth said. "Convince him he's better than Thaden could ever have been. If that doesn't work, we lock him up until Lola can figure out how to knock some sense into him."

18

The ferry wasn't too crowded. Elizabeth had booked us seats inside, but I managed to find a quiet place on the deck where I could call my dad. You know, to try and explain why we had ditched Cindy in her car and ask if he could please pull some strings to make sure she stayed safe.

I contemplated being a complete coward and just texting, but it was super early New York time and I didn't want to risk Dad missing my message because he was asleep. Cindy deserved better than that.

"You can do this." I shook out my shoulders like I was about to walk into a fight. "You can do this."

I punched the button to video chat with my dad. I don't really know why, but being able to see his face while I told him how badly things had gone somehow seemed easier.

My phone made a series of weird dinging noises before Dad answered.

"Bryant?" His hair was all messy, and his eyes were only half-open. "Bryant, whass wrong?"

"Nothing," I said. "I mean nothing that bad."

The light shifted as Dad sat up and got out of bed. "Just tell me what's going on."

"Cindy got suspicious about the whole"—I glanced around the deck to make sure there was no one nearby—"magic thing. She started asking too many questions, so we had to leave her behind."

"Leave her behind?" Dad's eyes shifted from sleepy to alert, and he started pacing in front of a pale-painted wall. "What do you mean *leave her behind*?"

"She's super loopy and sitting in the rental car near the docks in Athens. It's not her fault, but you may want to send someone to check on her."

"Come home right now." The path of Dad's pacing expanded. "This is a failed experiment. If you need to study in Greece, it will have to wait until your mother or I can accompany you."

"But Dad—"

He paced past a grandfather clock, and my brain screeched to a stop.

"Dad, why are you in Mom's apartment?" My whole body went sort of numb.

Dad froze. His eyes got wide for a split second before his face went suspiciously calm. "Nonsense. I'm at home, Bryant. I'll book you a ticket—"

"You're sleeping at Mom's!" I shouted loudly enough for one of the ship dudes to peek around the giant tube-ish things on the deck to glare at me. "What the hell, Dad?"

"Bryant, I am not going to allow you to pull me off topic. You, Devon, and Elizabeth are getting on the next flight home."

"I can't come home until our work is done." I held the phone close to my mouth and shouted. "Hope you're getting a good night's sleep, Mom!" into the microphone before hanging up.

I stared at my phone, considering throwing it into the water. Anger, a weird ickyness, and utter disappointment swept through me so quickly, I was too exhausted to throw the phone by the time it started ringing as Mom called me.

I turned my phone off and shoved it into my pocket.

I didn't have time to delve into the possible long-term ramifications of my parents having a slumber party while I was out of the country. I mean, I couldn't deny the obvious. As soon as things went bad between them again, my life would become a nightmare of them not speaking to each other for years, all while sending aggressive messages through their lawyers and passive aggressive messages through me.

"I'm almost eighteen." I dug my knuckles into my eyes. "Once I get to eighteen, it won't be my problem anymore. Except for every holiday and major life event. Oh, this is going to end badly."

With a giant blast from its horn, the boat pushed away from the dock, and we officially left Chaperone Cindy behind.

"You don't get to brood, Bryant." I squared my shoulders and headed toward the cabin. "You're saving the magical world. Teenager-from-a-broken-home brooding will have to wait."

The door to the cabin was heavy enough I had to ram my shoulder against the metal to swing it open, which was harder than it looked since I had to step over a six-inch lip on the ground while doing the pushing, which was way more than my overwhelmed brain could handle and resulted in my stumbling into the cabin while the crewmen stared at me like I was probably drunk.

Giving a little wave and an apologetic smile, I made my way around the rows of seats to the booth Elizabeth had booked for us. There was enough seating for six, which only made poor Chaperone Cindy's absence more noticeable.

"How did it go?" Elizabeth asked.

I opened my mouth to tell them exactly what had happened, decided I didn't have the energy to deal with it, and said, "Dad wants us on the next plane home. I said no. I don't know if my credit card will still be working by the time we get to Crete."

"We'll find a way around it," Eric said. "We could try and persuade Raven to help us keep your card open."

"Great." I sank down into the spot next to Elizabeth. "I can't wait to see what Dad's legal team does with that."

"We can worry about money later," Elizabeth said. "What did Raven tell you about Iliana? Why are we going to Crete?"

I perked up, and thoughts of how badly my parents were yelling at each other over whose fault it was that I'd found out about their sleepover, or whether they'd skipped the blame game to jump straight on to buying tickets to Greece so they could haul me home, slipped away.

"Iliana Dorinda Drakos has a registered address in Crete, and her web traffic seems to confirm that location," Eric said.

"And?" I leaned across the half-circle table to get closer to him.

"She frequently travels to the mainland of Greece," Eric said. "Though once she's on land, Raven cannot track where she goes."

"That's it?" Devon said. "That's all we know?"

"It's a great deal more than we knew last night." Eric pulled out his phone and opened an email before passing it to Devon. "We have an address. We'll start our search there."

"She doesn't look like the *murder you in the woods* type." Devon passed the phone to me.

I looked down at the picture that filled the screen. My brain did a little skip step, like it wanted to be sure that, after all the trauma of the last twenty-four hours, I was actually processing what I was seeing properly. It was the girl from the woods, but older. Closer to my mom's age than mine.

"This is Iliana?" I tipped my head and squinted at the screen, making triply sure I was right.

"It is," Eric said. "There were three other Ilianas who pinged as possibilities in Greece, but one was too young, one too old to be traveling, and one seems to have emigrated to England a few years ago."

"She was in the woods," I said. "She's the girl who was looking for books, *the* books. She still hadn't found them by the time the last of the bookkeepers died."

"That doesn't mean she hasn't found them since," Elizabeth said.

"No." Devon stared at his fists on the table. "But if she hadn't found the books before she forced the phantasms to fight for her, what sort of magic is she capable of with basically unlimited knowledge backing her?"

"No way to know until we find her." Elizabeth leaned on my shoulder.

I'd forgotten I'd been the only one to sleep on the road trip. I wrapped my arm around her, holding her close, ready to keep her steady if she nodded off.

"She might not have even found the books." Elizabeth nestled closer to me.

"She did." Something in my chest clicked into place as I said the words. Like there was a key of certainty fate had been waiting for me to find. "The magical world is too small. For her to have been looking for the books. For her to have set a trap in Meteora where the books were mailed from. No one was even supposed to know the books had been stolen. Ginger William the black-market book dealer couldn't have stumbled onto a completely unrelated woman in Greece who just so happened to like to mail packages from a place Iliana was determined to protect. It would take too many coincidences."

"I agree," Eric said. "Each person who knows about the books, that they're missing, who stole them, where they are, is another gap in defending the secret. If there were that many gaps, I would have heard whispers of a trove of hidden books long before we took the Library from the Ladies."

"At least we have a who." I rubbed my free hand across my forehead. "Now we just have to figure out the where."

Somehow, that didn't make things any less daunting.

I kept one arm around Elizabeth as she drifted to sleep on my shoulder, trying not to wonder how easily Raven could dig into my life as I read through all the information on Iliana.

She was only thirty-five.

She'd been born in Greece, but lived in Canada for a while.

There were pictures of her in New York City. From the clothes, it looked like she'd been there about ten years ago.

Then she went back to Greece and had been living on Crete ever since.

No job listed, but the house in her name was nice enough she'd either inherited it or had money coming in through a nefarious trade like selling priceless books on the black market.

There were no papers filed saying she had married or had children.

It was more information than we'd ever had on Thaden, the Ladies, or Kendrick, but it still didn't seem like enough.

I scrunched my eyes closed and went back to the top of the document from Raven.

Why did Iliana go to New York City? Why did she leave? How did she find out the books were missing, and what led her to Meteora?

I formed the list of questions in my mind, but a little voice in the back of my head screamed it was all useless. Whether we found Iliana or she found us first, there would be no time to ask questions about the why of it all. She'd already tried to murder us in absentia. She would try to kill us again.

And we would fight her.

Hopefully, we would win, which would mean she'd probably be dead. And I would never know the truth of why a girl from Greece had grown up to create an evil enchanted forest.

19

Nikki,

Let's say we're taking the laws we've written out and presenting them to the body of people we're intending to govern. How does that work? Do we just show up and say, "Here are some new laws. I have six council positions available. Who do you want to vote in?"

Bryant

I read the message through four times. Each email had been getting harder and harder to write. Not because I didn't have questions, but because phrasing them in a way that wouldn't make Nikki develop a Cindy-like suspicion became more difficult as we got down to the tiny details.

I added, *Some of the people involved like to argue over petty things, and I want to make sure they don't have a reason to hold the action up.*

"It's the best I could grab."

I tapped *send* and shoved my phone into my pocket as Devon handed me a wrap. I was still trying to avoid reading the dozen or so messages from my parents where neither of them mentioned what had happened but both seemed to be very concerned with how I was doing and when I'd have time to talk.

"Thanks." I'd been left to stand with our suitcases while Eric tried to arrange transport, which I hoped made him regret ditching Cindy, Devon went to find food, and Elizabeth went to buy a guidebook, which I know sounds weird but was actually really important.

"Is it lazy if I really hope the books are near a port?" Devon said. "Or at least an airport?"

"I'm sure they are. They'd have to be. How else could you move thousands of books?"

I ate my wrap, watching the other people on the dock being herded into cabs. Some of them were tired, others excited, a few super angry about something. But I was willing to bet none of them were in the process of overthrowing an evil regime and forming a new government.

My phone dinged with a new email from Nikki.

Hi Bryant,

The player in me says you're the DM, you make the rules.

But if you want to go for realism and practicality, it would depend on how you'd taken control of the area. If you've won a battle, then as the conqueror, you have seized the right to lay out a new code of law. If you're trying to peacefully change things, you would have to put your constitution out there and let the people vote.

In my experience, taking the area by force would move things along more quickly.

Nikki

A squirm of existential dread wriggled in my stomach, making me question if eating a wrap was actually a good idea.

"Are you going to tell me?" Devon asked.

"Tell you?" My voice wobbled.

"I'm your best friend, Bryant. Elizabeth may be the girlfriend. Eric may be the wizard extraordinaire. But I'm the guy who's known you since forever. So what's going on?"

"Aside from being stabbed and ditching Cindy?" I took a bite of my wrap, like chewing could somehow save me.

Devon frowned at me in a disappointed parent kind of way.

"What?" I asked with my mouth full.

"You managed to lie to airport security. That doesn't mean you can lie to me."

"I mean"—I took a moment to actually swallow my food—"Dad had a sleepover with Mom."

"What?" Devon laughed.

"And I've been talking to—"

"I've found us a car." Eric strode up to us. "It's a long ride, but I've promised to tip well."

"We can try my card." I shrugged.

"I found a guidebook." Elizabeth appeared next to me.

"Perfect timing." Eric bowed us toward our new ride.

We climbed into the black car, and the driver, who looked weirdly similar to my favorite cabbie in Manhattan, pre-charged my card, which thankfully went through, which probably had a lot to do with the fact that my parents were worried I was traumatized by their weirdness, which I totally was, but that had nothing to do with why I was still battling the existential dread monster as we pulled away from the docks and onto the road. The *oh no, I may have waaay overestimated my ability to deal with helping the world instead of just leaving chaos in my wake* feeling was still very much present and interfering with my ability to eat my wrap.

But I couldn't say anything because we had a driver, who definitely spoke enough English to understand words like *magic, revolution,* and *lifetime of therapy bills.*

So I spent more time trapped in freakin' transit, not really able to do anything but enjoy the scent of Elizabeth's hair slowly filling the car while being amazed that an island could be so damn big.

———

I f Athens was something out of another world, Chania was something out of a romance novel, with a fancy harbor, which looked weirdly similar to pictures I'd seen of Venice, surrounded by lights and shops even though it wasn't the height of tourist season. There were musicians playing outside restaurants, and men selling flowers. There were restaurant hawkers trying to lure us in, and cats roaming everywhere.

The driver dropped us off at our hotel so we could leave our bags before finding the bad guy, which was not a practicality I had ever had to consider in Manhattan. Then we walked through the harbor district to get to Evil Iliana's house. And ginger librarian William's story about meeting a woman in Greece, having a nice meal with her, and then having her steal the light and sound from the night almost made sense. You've already slipped into a Rom Com setup—might as well add magic. That's just good marketing.

Elizabeth held my hand tight as we weaved away from the harbor and onto less well-lit streets where tiny little restaurants hid between houses.

A very daring part of me wanted to whisk her into the shadows and kiss her until we both forgot about magic, books, and the fate of wizard kind.

But taking time off to make out with Elizabeth while violin music drifted through the windows of a tiny restaurant would have meant risking Iliana murdering us while Elizabeth and I were swirling in a land of bliss and love.

I made a mental note to definitely bring Elizabeth back someday, when our lives weren't in danger, and didn't argue as we left all traces of restaurants and romance behind.

After my legs had gotten tired, but before I'd worked up the nerve to ask Eric if he was lost, he gestured to a bright white house at the top of a hill.

The place was beautiful in a way that didn't seem to fit the old city vibe we'd just left behind.

The walls had been smoothed with concrete and painted pale white. There were two balconies set with chairs so Evil Iliana could have her fiendish friends over to stare at the water far below. A waist-high concrete wall topped with a wrought iron fence, like Iliana had been preparing for the zombie apocalypse, surrounded the grounds, even protecting what would have been a nice garden in the summer and a pool large enough to swim laps in.

"Selling books that should belong to other people may be an awful thing to do," Devon said, "but it looks like a bangin' way to make a living."

I glanced down as a faint *mew* sounded by my ankles.

A little tabby cat blinked up at me.

"Hey, kitty." I looked back to the house. There weren't any lights on inside. There wasn't a car in the driveway either. "Do you think she's already up north trying to kill us?"

"We can hope," Devon said.

"Something doesn't seem right," Elizabeth said.

"Like *seer* doesn't seem right or like *this is way too convenient* doesn't seem right?" I slipped my magical phone out of my pocket.

"Both." Elizabeth walked toward the gate that led to the driveway.

Meow! A new, gray cat stepped on my foot as though wanting to be really sure I knew he was there.

"Sorry, I don't have anything for you." I gave the cat an apologetic shrug before following Elizabeth.

"Do you see any spells?" Eric tented his fingers under his chin. "Any hint of shadows or bone magic?"

"There's something around the front door." Elizabeth tipped her head as she stared into the shadows, letting her curls tumble across her shoulders in a way that made me forget to breathe until a *yowl* yanked me back into the brutal reality of impending larceny.

I looked down to find that the tabby and gray cat had been joined by a massive ginger. "Hey fellas. You're all so pretty."

"There's going to be more than a simple incantation to protect the door," Eric said. "You don't enchant a forest to snare those who might seek information you're protecting only to leave your home open to attack."

"So what's the plan?" Devon gripped his foam/sticky potion blaster in one hand and the tube/hilt of his glowing sword in the other.

"I've no idea." Eric furrowed his brow.

"Well, that's not comforting," I said.

A tiny *mew* sounded by my feet. I looked down to find two little kittens had joined the three other cats.

"So cute," I cooed like a goober, trying to decide if risking ringworm was worth snuggling the tiny calico kitten as she rolled onto her back and showed me her stomach.

"I've told you before," Eric said. "It's never my goal to comfort you. My aim is always to keep you alive."

"Consider me not comforted," I said.

"I think it would be best if Elizabeth and I try to approach the house first." Eric paced in front of the gate. "Once we are sure of the house's safety, the two of you can join us as we search for more information about the books."

"What?" Devon said at the same moment I said, "No way in Hell."

Eric held up both hands to silence us. "As we are traveling into unknown magic, it makes the most sense to leave part of our party on the outside in case rescue becomes necessary. That requires Bryant and me to move separately. Since we will be stepping into spells that could quite possibly involve bone magic"—a shock of dread zapped up my spine—"having Elizabeth with me will ensure our best chance for success."

"She is not going in there without me," I said.

"I believe Elizabeth has autonomy and can go wherever she chooses," Eric said.

"Wait a minute, that's not what—"

"I should go in with Eric." Elizabeth laid her hands on my chest. "He's right. This is how I'm supposed to be helpful, and I'll only be like a hundred feet away."

"But—"

"I'll be fine." Elizabeth kissed my cheek. "Someone has to save Eric from Eric."

"Just be careful." I pressed my lips to her forehead. "If anything happened to you, I think I'd literally lose the ability to breathe."

"You'll catch up to us in a minute." Elizabeth gave me a smile that made the air rush out of my lungs like they were trying to prove that she literally did control my body's ability to consume oxygen.

"What about me?" Devon said. "Should I just chill out here with the cats until you get back?"

"Bryant is staying out here to provide assistance should Elizabeth and I encounter trouble," Eric said.

"And that leaves me...?" Devon glared at Eric.

"Staying with Bryant in case he becomes the one who needs saving," Eric said. "We can't leave him alone."

I was about to snap at Eric for being rude, but Devon stopped glaring at Eric and looked at me.

"Fair." Devon shrugged.

"I..." I deflated a little. "Okay."

"Then in we go." Eric stepped closer to the gate, raising his hands as though testing the air for tension. "Stand back, if you would."

Devon grabbed me by the scruff of my sweater and pulled me away.

I shuffled my feet, making sure I wasn't stepping on the cats, but still a chorus of angry *meows* surrounded me.

"Sorry, sorry." I looked down at my feet to make sure I hadn't hurt any of the five cats only to find three extra cats I'd never seen before. "Why are there so many of you?"

A tiny little black cat gave the sweetest *mew* in response.

"We've got to help these cats," I said. "They look so sad and lonely."

I looked away from the cats as Eric began his spell.

"*Numbare fungilo lui confello. Cliaxo entrunto krifundia!*"

He finished speaking, and an oddness flew through the air. Almost like a ringing I couldn't quite hear. Or a breeze too soft for my skin to feel through my clothes.

"Are you supposed to know that spell?" Devon whispered to me as the gate swung silently open.

"I hope not," I murmured.

Eric swept his hands through the air again before beckoning Elizabeth to follow him.

She gave me a little wave and a smile before stepping through the gate.

"Should we hold the gate open?" Devon whispered.

"I don't think so," I said.

Before I had a second to consider why I didn't think we should keep the gate from closing behind Eric and Elizabeth since I had no freakin' clue how to do the spell he'd used to open the gate, the metal swung shut and closed with *clang*.

Elizabeth flinched, so I knew the sound had carried to the inside of the compound as well. But Eric didn't seem bothered as he stalked slowly toward Evil Iliana's house.

Merwrrow one of the cats at my feet said.

I looked down to find the eight cats had turned into something closer to fifteen cats.

One of the kittens batted at my shoelace.

"If I'm not disowned when we finally get home, do you think I could convince my dad to save the cats here?" I looked back toward the house as Elizabeth took Eric's arm, leading him around one of the paving stones in the walkway.

"Do you mean, like, all the cats?" Devon asked. "Because that might be a stretch even for your dad. I mean, look at them."

I glanced away from Elizabeth to find that closer to twenty cats now surrounded Devon and me.

"Do they not have animal control in Greece?" I asked. "Or a trap and spay program?"

"I don't know the local laws," Devon said. "Look it up after we rescue the priceless books."

"Right." I focused my attention back on the house where Eric and Elizabeth had gone, not to the front door, but to a window on the far side of the entrance. I chewed my lips as Elizabeth slid the window open. "Do you think the owner of the neighborhood cat rescue died and these guys have come to us for help?"

Mew. The tiny little sound came from near my feet as an itty-bitty kitten bumped her head against my ankle.

"I have no idea, dude." Devon took a step closer to the gate.

"But we've got to do something for the cats. I mean, look at them. They need us. They're coming to me for help."

"You probably still smell like dinner."

"I'll find them something to eat once we—"

I never finished my thought.

I was too distracted by the now obvious fact that what the cats wanted to eat was us.

20

It was the tone of the next *mew* that gave me my first warning. What had been an adorable sound that made my insides gooey and my paternal instincts kick in had suddenly become lower and gruffer.

I tore my gaze away from Eric closing the front window of Evil Iliana's house, and looked down to see what big kitty had made such a sound, expecting to find a chonker of a tabby glaring up at me.

I was sort of right.

There was a tabby glaring up at me, but he was not an adorable chonker. He was the size of a Labrador and drawing back his lips to show me his over-sized teeth.

"Devon." I gripped his sleeve.

"They're almost in," Devon said.

The other cats started to grow, like they were weird monsters evolving in a video game. Their coats shimmered as their muscles bulged and their bones grew.

"Devon." I shook his arm.

"We can save the cats later," Devon said.

"Devon!" I shouted just as the monster who had been an itty-bitty kitten less than a minute before hissed and launched himself at my side.

"Shit!"

I guess Devon had finally noticed that we'd been surrounded by an über clowder. He grabbed my shoulder, pulling me back as the cat sank its claws into my hip.

"*Primurgo!*" I screamed the spell, but it didn't do anything, probably because I was more focused on the searing pain in my hip than on enunciating the spell.

Another of the feline-ish monsters reared back to pounce on me.

Devon shot a sticky pellet at it.

"You can't do that to a cat!" I pressed my hand to the blood leaking out of my hip.

"It's a demon, not a house cat!"

Three of the demon cats launched themselves at us at once.

Devon stickified one, I shouted "*Stasio*" and trapped another, but the third leapt up and got me, sinking its claws into my ribs as its fangs dug into my shoulder.

"Why?" I knocked the monster off me as Devon grabbed my non-bloody arm, dragging me toward the gate.

The clowder yowled in creepy unison as he touched the metal, but the gate swung open without us having to do any sort of spell.

I watched all the monsters rock back on their haunches as though preparing to pounce, but I wasn't dumb enough to watch them surge forward, choosing instead to just assume they were going to murder me at any moment as we tore up the driveway.

The painful heat of my wounded hip made my stride uneven as we sprinted toward the house.

Devon was right ahead of me, glowing sword in one hand, sticky blaster in the other.

"*Lobula!*" I tried to block the cats/demons because, even though they wanted to eat me, I didn't want them having to chew Devon's sticking potion out of their fur.

I heard a growl of displeasure but didn't look back to see if the cats were still following.

Devon veered toward the walkway, aiming for the window Elizabeth and Eric had crawled through.

"There's a bad stone!" I shouted a moment too late.

Devon stepped onto the stone Eric and Elizabeth had avoided.

For a split second, I foolishly thought everything was going to be okay, but then a sharp *crack* cut over the *yowls* of the demon cats.

The ground didn't rumble or shake. Chunks of it just started falling away, forming a ravine-style moat around the house.

Not thinking about the probability of our demise, I grabbed Devon around the middle and leapt across the still-growing gap. My toes barely caught the edge of the ground on the far side, but I flung our weight forward, toppling both of us onto the grass.

I lay on the ground panting for a few heartbeats.

"Thanks." Devon pushed himself to his knees, reclaiming his weapons from where they'd fallen.

First, I heard a *yowl*. Then a *hiss*. Then I sprang up just in time to see the cats from Hell pouring around the sides of my blocking spell and charging toward the gap in the ground.

"Run!"

Devon raced toward the window where Eric and Elizabeth had disappeared.

I tore after him, but too much of the ground had fallen away, leaving no path to the window.

Panic flew through my chest as I looked to the door. There was a spell on it. I knew there was a spell on it and was very confident in my inability to break through the spell before being eaten.

I looked toward the next best option, the window on our side of the front door. It was closed and I assumed locked, but the alternative was being eaten by cats.

"*Abalata!*" The black mist of my spell pooled in my palm. I threw it forward with all my might, aiming for the window.

The impact of spell on glass reverberated up my arm, but the window didn't shatter, just formed a spiderweb of cracks.

"Guard my back." Devon turned toward the window while I faced the chasm and Hellcats.

"I don't want to hurt you!" I screamed at the first demon cat that leapt across the gap. "*Conorvo.*"

The tabby shrank as it soared over the crevasse, landing as a less terrifying, Maine Coon-sized cat so it's teeth and claws sank into my thigh instead of my hip.

"Stop biting me. *Stasio!*" A barrier shimmered into being, caging in the fluffy monster.

Three more cats growled as they leapt across the ravine.

A new spell was already forming on my lips when Devon grabbed me and yanked me backward, pulling us both through the remnants of the window.

Ignoring the pain of landing on a bunch of broken glass, I fixed my gaze out the window. "*Milkawa.*"

The ground outside the window twisted and grew, forming a spire of dirt and stone that blocked the opening.

"Bryant." Devon gripped my non-maimed shoulder. "Are you okay?"

"Yeah." I wobbled my way to my feet while getting as little glass embedded in my palms as possible. "Did you get bit?"

"No." Devon looked toward the window where the monsters yowled and growled as they scratched at my dirt barrier.

"*Sinato.*"

Devon breathed through his teeth as bits of glass fell from his skin as he healed. "You should do yourself, too." He shook out his hands and picked up his blaster and sword.

"Can't." I looked down at the blood seeping through my clothes. "I don't know if the demon cats have venom."

"Right." Devon furrowed his brow as he looked from the blood on my leg to the blood smear I'd left on the floor. "Let's get to Eric and Elizabeth."

I took the lead, crunching my way across the glass on the floor. "How did you break the window?"

"Sliced through it with my sword."

"Nice." I peered out into the hall, expecting to find Eric and Elizabeth, but the corridor was dark and empty. "We made a lot of noise."

"We didn't have a choice." Devon's sword voomed to life.

"But why didn't Eric come see why we were screaming?" A cold trickle of fear wound its way from my neck to my gut. I opened my mouth to call for them but hesitated before whispering to Devon, "I don't want to be responsible for our deaths by calling for them like we're written to be the first to die in a horror movie."

Devon let out a long breath. "Right. We'll just look for them."

The clamor of the demon clowder followed us into the dark hall.

Honestly, if the demon cats hadn't been a thing, the house would have been a great vacation rental. White tiles, an open floor plan for the kitchen and dining area. A glass banister along the steps that led upstairs.

"Do you know any tracking spells?" Devon asked once we'd made a lap of the ground floor, passing through a living room with an epically large TV and finding no trace of Eric or Elizabeth.

"Nope." I eyed the steps to the second floor. "Should you wait down here?"

"Because separating has already done us so much good in this place?"

The yowling and growling outside paused.

"Let's go." I headed toward the stairs, my years of plotting how to survive the zombie apocalypse telling me in no uncertain terms that if we had to fight the demon cats again, higher ground would totally be helpful.

Devon reached the stairs first and started climbing. I let him get three steps up, just far enough for me to follow him without feeling like I was trying to crawl up his butt, lifted my foot to step up onto the first stair, and then it happened.

The steps tipped and smoothed, and then just vanished.

"Devon!" I lunged forward, trying to grab him, but he was already falling into the darkness below. "*Frico.*" I focused on Devon's belt with all my might. My magic latched on to the leather, yanking it toward me, but the stairs shimmered back into being before I could pull him up.

I didn't even hear a *thump* of him hitting the underside of the stairs. He was just...gone.

I stood there, staring at the steps for a moment, like if I didn't move Devon would just magically reappear. Only magic doesn't work like that.

My breath seemed to rattle in my ears as I looked around the empty house.

"Okay." I spoke to myself, because that somehow made it less scary. "You're cornered in a house that's booby-trapped like an old school Christmas movie. But you still have options, Bryant Jameson Adams. You can A) Walk up the stairs and hope you get trapped wherever Devon is and hope you both end up not-hurt enough to find a way out together.

"B) Scream for Eric and hope he comes to save you. C) Try to get out of the house, past the demon cats, and hope you can find someone other than Eric who can help you, except that would make you an awful person since you'd be leaving your girlfriend, best friend, and sometimes asshole-ish mentor behind."

I couldn't handle any of those options. I couldn't leave them behind. I couldn't dive after Devon.

"I'm not supposed to be the one who's left on their own," I whispered. "I'm not the one who stages rescues. I'm a walking master of destruction. I don't save people. I just wreck things."

A weird sensation filled my chest. Not the usual panic, fear, or self-loathing. I poked the wounds on my leg and shoulder, trying to figure out if maybe I'd been poisoned, before realizing what the feeling was.

I felt confident. I felt sure of my ability to contribute to our cause in a meaningful way. Because if my time in the magical world had prepared me for anything, it was causing major structural damage.

"Hope you've got insurance, Iliana. *Aarantha.*" The vortex of my spell started out as a funnel surrounding only me. I pushed my hands out to the sides, spreading my spell wider, letting it tear the paintings from the walls.

With a *screech*, the TV ripped away from its brackets, joining the debris of my twister.

I shifted closer to the steps, letting the TV smash through the glass banister of the staircase.

"I'm coming for you, Devon. *Kunga!*" My spell pummeled the side of the steps, but the white concrete didn't shatter.

"*Kunga!*" A dark crack split through the white, but it wasn't enough.

I stepped closer to the stairs, holding my fingers out in front of me like they were some sort of knife. "*Caruson.*"

The heat of my spell vibrated my fingers as I sliced through the wall like I was wielding Devon's laser sword. Before I'd even finished the lopsided circle I'd been trying to slice free, the force of my vortex ripped the chunk of wall away.

"Devon!" I shouted over the rumbling of the wind and the crashes of debris smacking into the walls. "Devon!"

I forced my spell forward, leaning through the hole I'd created. "Devon."

A dark space waited under the stairs.

"*Heliono.*" A sphere of light appeared in my hand. I leaned farther into the opening in the wall. There was no cupboard under the stairs where Devon had been locked. The actual space under the steps was bare. "Devon!"

I leaned my entire torso through the hole, ready to crawl into the dark space to search for him. Just before I was going to climb into the dark, I bothered to look down and saw there wasn't actually a floor below me. Just a ten-foot drop and a clear prison where Devon had been trapped.

But Devon wasn't on his feet trying to break out. He was suspended midair, lying facedown, like he'd fallen into a mold of clear gelatin and been trapped.

I took a few deep breaths, trying to convince my body that panicking was not, in fact, a helpful reaction.

"I'm really sorry if this goes badly. *Abalata.*" The black of my spell pooled in my palm. I aimed right above Devon's shoulder and threw the black as hard as I could.

The goop of Devon's prison cell shuddered at the impact, but none of it broke away.

"*Exci.*" The force of the spell pummeled the ooze, but the cube stayed intact.

I didn't want to slice into the goop in case it went wrong and I ended up decapitating my friend. I couldn't jump down and try to rip him out by hand in case I ended up stuck so I couldn't free either of us.

"This is such a bad idea." I pulled the force of my funnel into my hand. "Such a bad, bad idea."

The *crash* of falling debris shuddered around the room as I aimed the vortex down toward Devon.

The tip of the funnel met his gelatin mold prison from Hell, and...yeah.

Goop everywhere.

Flying through the air. Covering the underside of the stairs like a food fight straight out of a lunch lady's nightmare. Splatting against the walls with squelching and flooping sounds gross enough to put me off gelatin for life.

Swallowing the sour in my mouth, I pushed the spell down a little farther, letting the vortex burrow closer to Devon. I squinted through the mass of transparent debris, waiting for a glimpse of goopless Devon.

His leather belt, where I'd tried to catch him before, emerged first.

Focusing with every bit of concentration my poor overstressed brain could manage, I fixed my gaze on his belt again. "*Frico!*"

A strain like I was trying to lift a car pulled on my whole body. Every muscle trembled, and a scream tore from my throat.

With a sickening *squelch* and a massive *pop*, Devon squeezed free from the most disgusting cage I've ever seen, soared toward me butt-first, and crashed into my chest, sending us both sprawling onto the living room floor of Evil Iliana's newly wrecked home.

21

"Ow." I coughed out the word.

Devon groaned and slipped/rolled off of me to lie facedown on the floor.

"Are you okay?" My arms shook as I sat up.

"What the hell just happened to me?" Devon panted, not even attempting to move.

"I don't think you want to know. But we have to find Eric and Elizabeth." I stood and surveyed the damage I'd done to the house. The bits that had been covered in drywall had patches torn away. Half the TV had been lodged in the wall beside the front door. The other half seemed to be mixed in with the wreckage that littered the edges of the room.

"Elizabeth!" I shouted. "Eric!" Neither of them answered me.

"What happened in here?" Devon stood, wiping chunks of goo off his sleeves. "What am I covered in?"

"Elizabeth!" My legs wobbled as I circled the room, searching for a place where Eric and Elizabeth might have been trapped.

There was nothing. I mean, lots of wreckage, but not another goo cube prison.

"Elizabeth!" I opened the fridge door and peeked behind the oven.

"What are you looking for?" Devon asked.

"I have to get upstairs." I bolted back to the steps I'd mostly trashed, dragging a cast-aside stool from the breakfast bar along with me.

"But if they'd tried to go up the stairs, wouldn't they have fallen through like me?" Devon grabbed his own stool.

"Not if Elizabeth saw the trap." It wasn't until I'd climbed up onto the bar stool and started scrambling onto what was left of the stairs that I realized I hadn't heard the demon cats yowling in a while. I froze for a moment, torn between finding out if the cats had combined their powers to morph into one mighty demon feline and getting upstairs to hopefully rescue Eric before I had to find out.

Elizabeth.

It didn't matter if the demon cats got me if I couldn't save Elizabeth.

Slicing my hands on the smashed remains of the banister, I pulled myself up and hobbled at top speed toward the second-floor rooms. I darted into three bedrooms, scanning the spaces, hoping for some clear sign of where Eric and Elizabeth might have gone wrong in their search of the house.

The second to last door led to an office that opened up onto a balcony.

Outside the window, the glow of the harbor district reached toward the water. The sight was beautiful, and massively marred by the stone and dirt spire blocking the center of it.

But more importantly, a desk waited off to one side of the room. Not like an evil villain desk. A normal desk with a computer monitor so large there was really no reason a regular person could need it, a stack of papers in a white wire tray, and a flat desk calendar. There was even a little blue coaster waiting to hold Evil Iliana's morning coffee.

I crept toward the desk, testing every step for a trap.

"Do you think she has information about the books on her computer?" Devon asked.

"It seems like she uses it for work." I leaned closer to the desk, resisting the temptation to reach out and wiggle the wireless mouse to see if the screen would light up.

"I bet we could get Raven to connect to the hard drive." Devon took a step closer.

I reached out and grabbed his arm before I really knew why. I blinked for a second, trying to figure out what had made my heart leap into my throat like a sword had been swinging for my neck.

A tiny clump of mostly-blond-but-a-little-black hair stuck out between two tiles on the floor.

"I need you to cut there." I pulled Devon back and pointed to the spot. "Don't cut too deep. Elizabeth is down there."

"So, no pressure then." Devon flicked his wrist and his glowing sword voomed to life. He shook out his shoulders and widened his stance before touching the tip of his blade to the ground. The contact made a *crackle* that would have been really satisfying if Elizabeth's life weren't on the line.

I held both my hands in front of me, ready to shout a spell and rip the section of floor away.

Sweat dripped down Devon's brow as he cut a wide circle. His arms were starting to shake by the time he made it most of the way around.

I held my breath as he sliced through the last few inches of floor.

"*Frico!*" I leapt aside as the section of tile and concrete soared toward me.

"Holy shit." Devon gaped down into the gap he'd made.

The cell was deeper than the space between the ceiling on the first-floor and the floor on the second-floor should have allowed. The compartment was filled with the same clear goo Devon had been trapped in. Elizabeth and Eric floated inside.

"Stand back," I said. "This part is gross."

I formed a vortex and let it suck out the gelatinous ooze.

Devon gagged and stumbled to shelter behind me before I'd gotten deep enough to see the back of Elizabeth's sweater. The weight of the spell pulled against me as I ripped her free, but I only glanced toward her long enough to be sure she was breathing before pushing the funnel farther down.

Devon jumped forward, tossing his nasty coat over the keyboard as the vortex got so filled with slime it started spraying out, covering everything in the office. It splattered across the balcony windows, smacked into the walls with enough force to leave dents, and flooped to the floor with oddly moist sounds that will haunt my nightmares forever.

Finally, I saw it—the front of Eric's coat. "*Frico.*" Using the last bit of energy I had, I tore him from his prison. The vortex goop all splatted to the ground in one squelching *plop* as I fell to my knees, trying to convince my lungs they could still pull in air even though my whole body felt on the verge of collapse.

"Eric"—Devon grabbed Eric's hand, yanking him to his feet—"you need to call Raven."

"Raven?" Eric swayed as he looked around the goop-coated room. "I thought I told you to stay outside."

"Shit happens," Devon said. "Call Raven."

"Bryant." Elizabeth crawled through the slime to reach me. "Bryant, you're bleeding."

"What?" I looked down at my body. Beneath the layers of clear sludge, new blood was still oozing from my cat wounds. "Oh yeah. I couldn't heal them. I don't know if the demon cats have venom."

"Venom?" Eric looked to me, his phone held up to his ear.

"You heal Bryant. I'll talk to Raven." Devon lifted Eric's phone from his hand. "Hi, Raven, this is Devon. The one who bought all the cool toys. I need some help, and we're willing to pay."

"What wounded you?" Eric knelt beside me, his face twisting in disgust as he wiped the goo off my arms.

"The *not cat* cats." I blinked, trying to decide if the room had started swaying because I was dying or if I was just that tired.

"*Not cat* cats?" Elizabeth took my hand, drawing me back to the immediacy of our problems.

"The cats outside," I said. "They got bigger, and evil, and then they attacked us, so we bolted for the house, but now there's a ravine, but we would have had to come in eventually because you got stuck in gelatin jail."

Eric furrowed his brow and started muttering fancy words while hovering his hand over my shoulder.

"I don't have a jump drive." Devon spoke into the phone as he pulled his coat off the keyboard. "Well, I wasn't expecting to have to hack into anything."

A horrible, mind-numbing burning filled my arm. I gritted my teeth against the pain but couldn't stop the groan that rumbled in my throat.

Eric moved on to the wound in my hip.

"Just create a new login?" Devon started tapping on the keyboard.

"I love you," Elizabeth said as the awful burning spanned from my hip to my knee.

I tried to stop the groan in my throat to say *I love you, too* but only managed to make a sound like a pained goat.

"Thank you for saving us." She kissed my goopy cheek.

"How long is this going to take?" Devon said. "I know I'm not actually doing the hacking."

"That should be it," Eric said. "But you've lost a lot of blood. You'll need food, drink, and rest."

"Should we take him to a hospital?" Elizabeth asked.

"And have them ask how he lost blood when he has no visible wounds?" Eric said. "He'd be subjected to more testing than we have time for."

"I am grateful," Devon said, "but we really have to get out of here."

I don't know if the demon cats could understand Devon's words, or if it was just one of those weird magical coincidences fate likes to throw my way, but right after Devon finished his sentence, a shrieking *yowl* split the air.

"What was that?" Elizabeth asked.

"Demon cat." I struggled to my feet, the floor slipping beneath my trembling legs.

Elizabeth stood beside me, wrapping her arm around my waist.

"We need to search the house," Eric said. "I found no sign of the books. But there must be some—"

Another *yowl* cut through the night, and a chorus of screeching demon cats joined in the call.

"I've gotta go." Devon hung up the phone.

The clacking of rock striking rock came from outside the full wall of windows that led to the balcony.

"Do we try for the front door?" Devon raised his sword.

"We go out here." I headed toward the balcony door.

"We have to keep looking," Eric said.

"Trust us," Devon said. "We don't."

"Eric, take the back, make sure they can't follow us." I raised my hand toward the window. "Stay close. I don't know how long it will hold."

Two pairs of glowing eyes peeked up over the edge of the balcony. The cats spotted me and yowled their triumph to the clowder.

"*Exci*." The force of my spell smashed through the window. I ran forward before the glass had finished hitting the ground.

One of the demon cats leapt onto the balcony, ready to attack.

"*Kunga*." I couldn't allow myself to feel guilty as my spell knocked the demon cat over the balcony railing. I didn't have time. I fixed my gaze on the spire of rock and dirt. "*Telinto!*"

The force of the spell leaving my body knocked me back, but Elizabeth grabbed me, hauling me forward as the spire toppled like I'd chopped down a tree.

"*Exci*."

The glass railing of the balcony shattered just before Elizabeth and I reached the edge.

I've gotten us killed. We're going to fall into the crevasse and die. The horrible thought swirled through my head as Elizabeth and I jumped.

The coward who will forever live deep in my soul screamed for me to shut my eyes as I fell, but I had to protect Elizabeth, so I dared to look down.

The spire had toppled across the crevasse, giving us a bridge to the gate and the road beyond.

My feet slipped as we landed, but Elizabeth gripped my waist, not letting me fall.

One of the demon cats on the far side of the gap growled and sat back on its haunches, waiting for its moment to strike.

I took a breath, rallying the strength to do another spell, but a little *dhoomp* sounded from behind me, and a pellet of grayish goo flew past my shoulder and hit the demon cat in the face.

The cat gave a pathetic *merp* and rolled onto its back, swiping its paws over its face, trying to remove the goo in a way that would have made me feel guilty, but if it's okay to defend a village from a dragon, it's okay to defend your friend from a demon cat.

At the far end of the tumbled-down spire, the dirt crumbled beneath my feet.

Elizabeth jerked me forward and onto solid ground because she's a total badass.

There was more dhoomping, and Eric was shouting spells behind us. But by the time I managed to turn around and look, they'd both made it over the bridge.

Eric had both hands raised as he began to cast a spell. Devon stood beside him, shooting goo pellets at the demon cats who tried to attack.

It was before my knees gave out but after Eric's green barrier had started to shimmer into being that I decided I really missed Manhattan and was very ready to go home.

22

Things I didn't expect to learn while in Greece.

- Washing weird stasis cell gelatin goop from your hair takes an oddly long time.
- Not all cats are friendly.
- Having a hacker on payroll is super helpful.
- My girlfriend is amazing. I already knew it, but her saving me—again—emphasized that fact.
- I may not be the best, most competent, daring wizard the world has ever seen, but I am actually capable of rescuing people if there are no other options and you don't care about structural damage.

Bryant,

I've started compiling the document, and, with the legal language and technicalities, it's already over sixty pages.

Do I need to pare it down? You don't really need all the jargon for your purposes.
Nikki

Nikki,

I want the full document to be loophole free. I don't care how many pages it takes.
Bryant

I sat on my bed in my hotel room in Chania. We'd gone back to wash the goop off while we waited for Raven to do her *non-magical but seems like magic to someone who doesn't know how it works* computer hacking thing.

By the time I'd managed to scrub the gelatin from my purple hair, had a minor freak out when I remembered I still had purple hair, thrown out my goop-covered clothes, realized my suitcase was way more empty than it had been when we'd landed in Greece, had a moment of existential crisis about how much clothing I was sending to a landfill, and finally went to join the others in Eric's room, they were all sitting around his desk completely calm, clean, and eating dinner out of takeout boxes.

"No huge news yet." Devon didn't even look up as I walked into the room. "Raven's been sending information over as she finds it, but most of what she's dug up so far is boring and non-magic related."

"Like what?" I sat on the edge of the bed nearest the desk.

"We know she has an accountant, a landscaper, and her cleaning lady emails her a lot." Elizabeth passed me a box of food. "We also know she really likes online shopping."

"New document." Devon tapped to pull something up on his phone screen. I stood and peered over his shoulder.

"It's a spreadsheet." Devon opened the file. "Holy shit."

I opened my mouth to say something, but my jaw just hung loose. I couldn't do anything but stare as Devon scrolled down the list of hundreds of book titles, before tapping on the next tab over, which held hundreds more.

"How many tabs are there?" Eric asked.

"About twenty," Devon said.

The tabs across the bottom were marked with titles like *Bone Only, Elite, New York, London,* and *Do Not Sell.* Some of the titles were highlighted, like Iliana had marked the books that had already been sold.

"Well," Elizabeth said, "at least we know for sure she's the one with the books."

"Does Iliana send all her expenses to her accountant?" I ran my hands through my purple hair.

"I don't know," Devon said. "But we can look."

"Check that and her credit card for any recurring payments," I said. "That many books are going to have to be stored in some kind of warehouse, and that would mean rent or a mortgage."

"Smart." Devon started a text to Raven.

"Yeah, well, Dad used to interrupt a lot of coffee dates to yell at his under-lings about their mismanagement of rented space," I said.

"What exactly does your dad do?" Elizabeth asked.

"Make lots of money?" I opened my dinner and was grateful to find none of my food was leaf wrapped.

"What do we do if we find the warehouse?" Elizabeth asked.

"Seize control," Eric said.

"Sounds great," I said. "Just as long as there aren't any cats."

I munched away on my flakey, cheesy pastry as we waited for Raven to send more information. It felt like we were wasting time. Like we should be running for our lives, tearing through the night to find Iliana, or sleeping.

"I must say, I'm proud of you, Bryant." Eric turned in his chair to look at me.

"Whaa fur?" I tried to ask with my mouth full.

Eric didn't even raise an eyebrow at my lack of dignity. "You've saved my life before, in the Battle of Beville, last night in the woods, but tonight was different. Taking on the responsibility of helping someone who is helpless requires courage. You displayed enormous bravery."

I swallowed hard. "Right. Well, I couldn't just leave you, so it's not like I had a choice."

"What I don't think you understand, Bryant," Eric said, "is that a great many people would see a choice."

"We have four abnormal recurring payments and none of them are for a warehouse," Devon said. "Two for different boat docks, one to a woman's name, and one to an inn."

"Please tell me some of those payments go to the same location." I gripped my food box so hard it wrinkled.

"One of the docks, the lady, and the inn are all in the same place." Devon turned around, beaming. "I don't want to push things too fast, but I think Raven might be the love of my life."

"Perhaps you should spend more than an hour in her presence," Eric said.

"Don't need to." Devon grinned. "Some chemistry can't be denied."

"And that's my cue to book us transport." Elizabeth got out her own phone and started working.

Eric pulled out his phone and started reading through the list of books like a guy who was dying of hunger and found a pho place with an extensive menu.

I just kept eating, trying to convince my stomach that it had room for food despite the overwhelming sense of gratitude filling my chest that my friends were alive, not only because they were my friends, but also because I didn't have to be in charge of figuring out how to get us to Iliana's weird dock.

I'd made it through my cheesy pastry and moved on to little balls of I don't know what before Elizabeth started making calls, Eric started pacing, and Devon sat beside me to pick at what was left of my dinner.

"There's no way we're going to get to sleep here tonight is there?" I whispered.

"Don't worry," Devon said. "We can sleep in the car."

I managed to be brave and not whine as we all grabbed our bags and headed down to wait for a cab in the middle of the night. I even pretended to be excited about the boat Elizabeth had somehow found to ferry us around Crete in the dark. I didn't wince as I handed the boat captain my dad's credit card even though the man had a gleam in his eyes like I'd just paid for his next vacation. I didn't refuse to board the boat when I realized it was a glorified speedboat with no place to sit out of the wind.

But when the boat started bumping through the water and chilly winter mist soaked my sweater, I lost my ability to cheerfully blunder through this adventure hoping we'd end up with the books instead of ending up dead.

"Got any discreet warming spells." Elizabeth took my arm, wrapping it around her shoulder.

Holding her close eased me away from the verge of having an exhausted breakdown.

"*Relanto*," I whispered.

The cold wind warmed, making the air feel more like summery bliss and less like wintery death.

Elizabeth kissed the side of my neck, right beneath my ear.

Warmth that had nothing to do with magic spread through my chest.

"You really are a hero, you know." She nestled closer to me.

I wanted to say something brave like *I'd fight an army of evil cats for you* or romantic like *If I'd lost you, I would have lost my heart*. But it was Elizabeth, so I couldn't stop myself from telling her the truth.

"I don't feel like a hero." I looked over my shoulder, making sure Devon and Eric wouldn't be able to hear me from their seats in the little niche in the back of the boat. "I feel cold and wet and exhausted and weirdly homesick for New York."

"Me too," Elizabeth said.

"What?" I leaned away from her enough to be able to look into her eyes.

"I know I only lived there for a few days, but all I want is to be back in my bed at the Consortium. I want to wake up knowing where I am even if it means having Sniffer McDeadDog hovering over me when I open my eyes. I want to sit at a table in the restaurant, having muffins and coffee for breakfast. I know what we're doing is important and has to get done for the good of all wizard kind, but I just want to go home and sleep for a week."

A genuine chuckle shook my chest. "I thought it was just me."

"Nope." Elizabeth reached up, brushing a bit of my purple hair away from my forehead. "But I don't think being tired and wanting to go home stops you from being a hero. I think it makes you more of one. Because you stay. You keep going even when you don't want to. That takes a lot more courage than living like Eric and being so in love with danger you don't even realize how much you're risking."

"I really do love you, Elizabeth Wick."

"I love you, too." She leaned in and kissed me.

It didn't make me forget how tired I was, but holding Elizabeth in my arms and knowing she thought I was strong enough to keep going made a little voice start speaking in the back of my mind.

You're brave enough to do this.

Fate put you on this boat for a reason.

You're a strong enough wizard to see this through to the end.

By the time the sun began to rise and our destination came into view, I almost genuinely believed I was the hero Elizabeth thought I was. Or at least I could be close enough not to be ashamed of sucking at saving the magical world.

I'd barely been paying attention while Elizabeth had been working out how to get us to the dock where Iliana paid monthly rent for boat space, so I hadn't realized we were going to be landing at the base of a massive gorge.

With the way the rising sun cast shadows across the slice through the earth, it was easy to think we'd found a path to a shadowy underworld.

If it hadn't been for the little village at the base of the gorge, I would have completely believed that headless Thaden and the Ladies had risen from the dead and were going to pour out of the darkness with an army of shadow monsters.

I fixed my gaze on the little cluster of buildings, trying to take comfort in the fact that, if those little houses had been around for years and years with the gorge right nearby, odds were good a Hellmouth wasn't going to open today just because we'd shown up.

But as I studied the little pastel painted buildings, a touch of dread settled in my stomach. There were no warehouses in sight. No giant buildings where Iliana could store the thousands upon thousands of books she'd hoarded.

As the boat stopped at the dock, I could see signs for inns, signs for food, signs for places to buy t-shirts during tourist season, and not one stinking hint of where the freakin' books might be.

23

The sunrise shifted the angles of the shadows in the gorge, making it look less like a pathway to doom and more like an entrance to another world.

I gripped my coffee cup with both hands, trying to anchor my mind to the little inn/café where we'd managed to find breakfast instead of the dark patches in the gorge and what monsters might hide just out of sight. I could hear the rumble of Devon's voice. He was out by the front desk of the inn, being charming as he plied the innkeeper for information about Iliana, the nice woman we'd met in Chania, who'd raved about this spot and told us we *just had* to come.

I couldn't see or hear Eric. Of course, that wasn't surprising as he'd gone for a pre-breakfast stroll around the little village to work up an appetite and hadn't come back to Iliana's favorite inn and café.

I wanted to be strolling, or at the very least not sitting at a corner table in the tiny dining room gripping my coffee for dear life, but Elizabeth and I had been assigned the *look normal* part of the plan.

We were just travelers. We were only looking for breakfast. We were in no way suspicious. And we most definitely were not looking to steal some already stolen books from the lady whose house we had just trashed after she tried to murder us.

I gripped my cup tighter, resisting the urge to check under the table for demon cats.

"Eat, Bryant." Elizabeth nudged my leg with her knee.

"Right." I pried my hands off my coffee cup and went back to munching on my cream-filled breakfast pastry.

"Relax your shoulders," Elizabeth said. "You look like you're waiting for a fight."

"I am," I whispered.

"Our server doesn't need to know that."

I glanced over to the corner where a guy, who I assumed was the innkeeper's son, glowered at us.

I exhaled and forced my shoulders to relax, then gave Elizabeth a smile I hoped looked flirtatious instead of evil. "How long until we worry?"

"Another ten minutes." Elizabeth looked back to her guidebook.

"I can do ten minutes." I took a bite of my pastry. I have no idea if it was good. My nerves had stolen my ability to taste.

"It's a pity we're not here at the right time of year to hike the whole gorge." Elizabeth pushed the guidebook closer to me. She leaned her shoulder against mine, offering me something to focus on besides wondering if Iliana had found Eric, if Devon's charm was actually going to be enough to get the innkeeper to talk, and how fast my dad could track my credit card transactions here and if he would hire mercenaries to drag me home.

"Do you like hiking?" Elizabeth asked.

"I don't think I've ever tried it." I sipped my lukewarm coffee.

"It's like walking but harder." She winked at me.

"I'd probably fall to my death."

"I'll catch you."

She looked at me with her perfect, sparkly eyes, and I forgot about everything.

"Yeah," I breathed, like a total goober, but she's in love with me so she just smiled and kissed my cheek.

"Thank you," Devon said, loud enough for me to clearly hear. "You have no idea how much I appreciate this."

He strutted back to our table with a gleam in his eye like he'd just picked up two tourist hotties in Times Square.

"Good news." Devon slid into the seat opposite me. "Our lovely hostess recommends we buy a few nice bottles of wine from the little shop down the street to leave for Iliana as a thank you."

"Right." I gripped the edge of the table to keep myself from leaning forward in excitement.

"How long until she gets the wine?" Elizabeth kept a finger in the guidebook to hold her place.

"Iliana usually comes twice a month to go hiking in the gorge." Devon took a sip of his coffee, wrinkled his nose, and set his mug back down. "She was just up last week, and she's not booked to come back for another ten days."

"That's all right," Elizabeth said. "It's wine, not fruit. Wine can keep for much longer than ten days."

I shoved the rest of my pastry into my mouth.

A little voice spoke in my head, sounding like an enthusiastic train as its words rumbled all the way down to my chest, making me feel something shockingly similar to hope.

You're almost there. You're almost there. You're almost there.

A bell *tinkled* on the front door of the inn. I slipped my hand into my pocket to grab my phone at the same moment Devon reached into his own pocket to grip the hilt of his sword.

"A fresh round of coffee, if you could." Eric spoke from the tiny lobby/front room of the inn.

There was something about the tension in his voice that kept me from relaxing my grip on my phone.

He strode into the dining room, subtly glancing to each of the corners before sitting in the last chair at our table.

"Did your walk help you work up an appetite?" Devon slid his hand back out of his pocket.

"No," Eric said. "But as the time for breakfast is nearly gone, I will have to make myself eat anyway."

"So nothing...satisfying about your stroll?" I said as casually as I'm capable of, which was still obvious enough to earn me raised eyebrows from everyone at the table.

"The views are magnificent, but I didn't find any inspiration," Eric said.

We all slipped into silence as we worked our way through breakfast.

I wanted to be planning, or searching the village, or digging to try and find an underground lair.

But the plan we'd agreed on when we'd been dumped on a chilly dock by our boat captain, who seemed to laugh with glee as he sped away like my father's credit card had fully funded his retirement as payment for a few hours' work, didn't allow for any of those things.

Iliana paid people in this village on a regular basis.

Iliana might have paid them to tell her if anyone came poking around the village and seemed suspicious.

If we were lucky, Iliana was still in Meteora, trying to find and kill us.

Iliana getting tipped off to the fact that we were here would bring her sweeping in, ready to slaughter the people who'd escaped her phantasms. Letting her go to her trashed home and then come here to check on the books would give us more time to search.

Our half-assed plan? Pretend we'd met Iliana at a restaurant and she'd told us about the beauty of the gorge. We'd followed her travel wisdom. Hurray for Iliana the travel guru.

Henceforth, tearing through the village in search of the books was a big ole' no-no.

I finished my second pastry and considered ordering a third. Not because I was hungry, just because eating gave me a non-suspicious activity to do.

"I'd like to go for a hike after breakfast," Elizabeth said.

"While the gorge is beautiful," Eric said, "I think we should explore the village to see what's available for our visit."

"But I really want to go hiking." Elizabeth pushed the guidebook across the table.

Devon leaned close to Eric, and both of them read the page.

Eric tented his fingers under his chin, and Devon pursed his lips.

Elizabeth pulled the guidebook toward me and tapped on a section that had been printed inside a little gray square.

The gorge's history is as fascinating as the natural wonders of its rock formations and plant life. In the eighth century, more than four thousand people sheltered deep in the gorge as they hid from Turkish invaders.

In the 1890's, when the rest of Greece fell under the rule of the Ottoman Empire, only the gorge remained free. During World War II, the gorge served as a primary escape route for allied troops.

That one place has sheltered so many across its well-documented history can't help but make you wonder how many others have secretly sought refuge deep within the gorge.

The answer? We'll never know.

As you hike through the gorge, taking in the one-of-a-kind scenery, try to imagine where so many fugitives, refugees, and exiles found sanctuary between the rocky cliffs.

Legends have long told of hidden caves and gullies that protected the people of the gorge, but beware: the rangers will fine anyone found off the designated trails.

I read the passage twice before my heart picked up its pace like I'd already started climbing.

"I think hiking could be fun." I took Elizabeth's hand, threading my fingers through hers. "Help us work up an appetite for lunch."

"Indeed." Eric finished his cup of coffee and stood.

"Oh, like now?" I pounded the rest of my coffee, straightened my scar scarf, and grabbed my sweater from the back of my chair.

"Fate does not favor the hesitant." Eric strode out of the dining room. "We'll be back for lunch. Thank you again for your hospitality."

I tried to match his determined stride as Elizabeth, Devon, and I followed him. It came out more like an awkward scamper, but the innkeeper still smiled and waved at me as we passed her and stepped out into the bright morning.

The air had turned from misty and miserable to crisp and refreshing while we'd been inside. The sun gleamed in the sky like she was urging us on to triumph.

We're almost there.

"Elizabeth," I whispered as we reached the edge of the village, "you're a genius."

"Don't compliment me until we find something worth the climb," Elizabeth said.

If I were smarter, I would have taken that as a warning.

I didn't think much about the steepness of the hill leading out of the village—I'm from Manhattan. I live to climb stairs.

But then we got to the top of the hill and I realized we weren't actually at the gorge, we had to walk two miles uphill to get to the *actual* gorge that had somehow mysteriously protected so many people.

Fine. Whatever. Two miles isn't a big deal. I'm used to walking all over the city.

Then we got to the bottom of the gorge proper, and I realized how tiny and incapable I was. The gorge reached a solid fourteen miles above us, and each of those miles would be climbing uphill.

I whimpered as we began the trek, my legs already screaming at me for being a stupid, cocky, hiking noob. After the first twenty minutes, I pulled out my phone to search for a spell that would make walking easier. It was the only thing I could do to keep myself from crying as my legs began to shake.

Elizabeth stopped every hundred feet or so, staring around us for a few moments before climbing some more. Eric whispered spells under his breath. I didn't know what he was trying to do, but I could feel the ambient magic radiating off of him.

Devon slowed his pace to walk with me at the back of the group. "If the books really are hidden in some cave, how do you think they got here?"

"Lots of donkeys?" I winced as my calves seized up like they wanted to be super sure they made their displeasure known. "Honestly, they were probably—"

A ringing from my pocket cut me off.

Eric glanced back to glare at me as I pulled out my non-magical phone.

Two horrifying words showed on the screen.

Dr. Spinnek

I let out a string of curses that made Devon snort.

"What?" Elizabeth glanced back at me, not glaring but with her brow locked in a thoroughly furrowed position.

"I forgot I have phone therapy." Giving in to the anxiety sinking into my chest like poured cement, I pressed the answer button. "Hi, Dr. Spinnek."

"Bryant," Dr. Spinnek said in a cheerful *not at all suspicious that I literally almost died twice in the past two days which would add up to five recent near-deaths if you counted all the almost dying from the week before we'd left Manhattan* way. "I'm so glad we're able to chat even though you're traveling."

"Yeah," I said, "it's great."

"How has your trip been so far?" Dr. Spinnek asked.

Aside from ditching my chaperone in a morally questionable way, all the near-deathness, and having a newfound fear of cats, great!

I swallowed the honest answer I wanted to give and said, "Going really well. I'm learning a lot."

"I'm glad you're learning," Dr. Spinnek said, "but you sound a bit tired. Wanting to take in as much as you possibly can is understandable, but sleep deprivation takes a real toll on mental health."

No, lying to the people you're closest to about maybe the best/worst thing you've ever done, all while trying to find books so you can steal them from a murderer, takes a toll on mental health.

"Well, I'm hiking right now," I said. "So I probably sound more tired than I am."

Elizabeth stopped and took a few steps toward a crack in the side of the gorge. The space only reached back about fifteen feet, shallow enough that bits of moss had grown in the farthest shadows.

"...will make a huge difference," Dr. Spinnek said.

"I'm"—I tried to make my brain remember what Dr. Spinnek had just said. "I'm so sorry, could you say that again?"

"I said eating well and getting enough exercise to help you sleep soundly will make a huge difference in how you perceive your trip when you look back on it."

Elizabeth moved on, walking at a slower pace as she studied the cliff face.

I squinted at the stone, trying to see what Elizabeth was seeing. There were a few trees growing out of the side of the cliff in a gravity-defying way, which was cool, but not really the magical hiding place we were looking for.

"Bryant," Dr. Spinnek said, "I hate to take time out of your trip, but I really think you should pause for a moment so we can chat without distraction."

I can't pause to chat without distraction. We don't know when Evil I've-almost-killed-you-twice Iliana is going to show up.

I took a deep breath and told the best almost-truth I could. "I'm sorry, Dr. Spinnek, I'm just having problems with my parents and I'm not sure I'm ready to talk about them yet."

I looked to Devon who made a *I mean, it might work* grimace before following Eric and Elizabeth across a little log bridge over a creek that sparkled in the sun.

"What sort of problems?" Dr. Spinnek asked.

"I was sort of homesick, so I called my dad for a video chat," I said. "It was stupid early New York time, so I woke him up. He'd been sleeping at my mom's."

"Oh," Dr. Spinnek said.

Elizabeth turned around to look at me, her eyes wide with shock.

"Yeah," I said. "That happened. I don't know if I'm really ready to talk about it."

"It's alright to need some time to process," Dr. Spinnek said.

Elizabeth mouthed *wow* and kept climbing.

The path on the other side of the river wasn't the packed dirt we'd been climbing before that I should have known enough to be grateful for. Our new trail was covered in loose stones that twisted under my feet.

"Let's set aside your parents for a moment," Dr. Spinnek said. "Your father said you were traveling with your friend and girlfriend. How is that going?"

"Great!" A bit of the cement left my lungs as I managed to answer one question with complete honesty. "Being with them is great."

Trees grew across the path up ahead, leaning low enough that Eric had to hunch over to get under their branches without messing up his ever-perfect hair.

"Having these memories with them is wonderful," Dr. Spinnek said. "Is Elizabeth doing well?"

"Yeah." I ducked under the trees, forgot to breathe for a second as I entered the gully on the other side, remembered my therapist was on the line, and took an awkward gulping breath before continuing. "I think the trip is good for her, too. Getting out of New York has been great for all of us."

Eric looked around the gully, then started along the path again, but Elizabeth didn't follow him. She sort of drifted to the side, like she was on a path I couldn't see, which with Elizabeth was entirely possible.

"I'd like to give you a little project, Bryant," Dr. Spinnek said.

"Uh-huh." I followed Elizabeth, keeping ten paces behind her so I wouldn't distract her from whatever she was seeing.

"Normally, I'd say you need a notebook, but since you're traveling, keeping notes on your phone will work fine," Dr. Spinnek said.

"Great," I said.

Elizabeth reached a sign that read *Most Dangerous! Rock slides!* She stepped around the sign, continuing toward the cliff face.

"Every morning, I want you to take a moment and write down your emotional goal for the day, and three things you can do to help yourself achieve it," Dr. Spinnek said.

"Alright." I crept around the warning sign and took a few quick steps, halving the space between Elizabeth and me.

"In the evening, I want you to look at that goal, and honestly ask yourself if you used all the tools you have to keep yourself happy, grateful, calm—whatever your goal for the day might have been," Dr. Spinnek said.

"I like having tools," I said.

Elizabeth paused for a moment before heading toward two boulders that looked like they might have been two halves of one boulder before they'd fallen in a *most dangerous* rockslide.

"That's good," Dr. Spinnek said. "What we're trying to do is create an emotional tool belt for you so you know how to handle any situation you encounter in a healthy way."

"Wouldn't that be magical?" I said.

Elizabeth tipped her head to the side. Her curls tumbled over her shoulder in a perfect little cascade. She touched the boulder, trailing her finger along a slice in the stone.

"That is the magic we work toward when we commit to giving therapy a genuine try," Dr. Spinnek said.

"That's what I'm doing," I said.

Elizabeth stepped between the boulders and out of sight.

"So, what can your emotional goal for today be? What thoughts do you want use to propel yourself forward?" Dr. Spinnek asked.

"Well, I—"

A flash of light, a rumbling *crack*, and Elizabeth's scream drove every thought from my mind.

24

"Elizabeth!" I didn't even feel my phone fall from my hand.

I couldn't see her.

She'd slipped between the two boulders before she screamed.

My heart didn't beat as I dove through the gap. I was numb. There was no sound, no feeling. Nothing in the world existed but getting to Elizabeth.

I reached a little clearing on the far side of the boulders. There was dirt and rocks on the ground, a few scrubby little plants struggling to survive, but no Elizabeth. No monster. No blood. Just a strange shadow that didn't seem like it belonged.

My ears started to work again as I heard a muted scream.

I looked up.

Elizabeth floated twelve feet off the ground, struggling against bonds I couldn't see, lying on her back like someone had lifted her out of bed.

The sight of her still breathing and fighting was enough to allow air back into my lungs.

"Elizabeth!"

She gave a louder muffled scream in response.

"Bryant!" Devon shouted behind me.

I made myself look away from Elizabeth, scanning the trees around the clearing before studying the ground.

Something magical had hoisted her up there. Some spell or trap.

"Bryant, are you hurt?" Devon rammed into my shoulder as he ran into the clearing.

I grabbed his arm before he could move past me.

"Shit," Devon said. "Eric, we need help."

I hated it. I hated that I needed Eric's help, but as Elizabeth struggled, hanging in the air, I would've taken help from the Ladies if it meant getting her down safely.

"Hold on, Elizabeth." I forced my voice to stay steady and sure. "We are going to get you down. You're going to be okay, I swear to you."

Devon's sword voomed to life.

I whipped around as rocks *clacked* under footfalls behind me.

Eric stepped out from between the boulders, frowning as he looked from the clearing to my girlfriend hovering in midair. "Well, Elizabeth, it seems you were right in wanting to go for a hike."

"What?" I shouted.

"Elizabeth wouldn't have stumbled into a spell unless someone had placed one here." Eric frowned as he studied the cliff face. "Why would one risk placing magic so close to where humans tread if there weren't an exceptionally good reason?"

Elizabeth squeaked another scream as she began gliding toward the rock face.

"*Frico.*" I focused on the back of Elizabeth's sweater. My spell yanked on her, bouncing her in the air, but she still kept floating toward the cliff.

"To use such a spell, the reward must be worth the cost." Eric picked his way out into the clearing.

"I don't care about the cost," I said. "Help her."

She was only ten feet away from the rock face. I didn't want to know what would happen when she reached the stone.

"I am helping her," Eric said. "I need to think. I need to know what sort of magic we are facing."

Elizabeth screamed something that sounded like she was trying to speak, but I had no idea what she was saying.

Seven feet.

"You're running out of time," Devon said.

"I'm trying not to make things worse," Eric said.

Five feet.

"I'm so sorry." I took a deep breath. "*Eshan.*"

I focused on her waist with every fiber of my being as I stretched my hand toward her. I'd never tried the spell before. I didn't know to expect the crackling heat on my palm, or the nauseating tugging on my skin as the magic flew from my hand like my flesh was unwinding. Like the glowing gold cord was a bit of magical fishing line made of my own body I'd just cast to try and save Elizabeth.

Two feet.

My spell wrapped around Elizabeth's waist. Part of the gold touched her bare wrists. She screamed as my magic made contact with her skin.

"I'm sorry." I pulled back on my hand, drawing the cord between us tight.

A wave of crackling sparks streaked toward her.

She screamed again as the sparks burned her skin.

"I'm so sorry." I pulled back harder, dragging her away from the cliff. Tears burned in my eyes. I knew the pain I was causing her. I knew how the heat was searing her flesh. Even remembering that pain around my neck brought bile to my throat.

I knelt, dragging her closer to the ground.

"Devon, grab her." I spoke through gritted teeth as I pressed the back of my hand to the dirt.

Devon ran forward and jumped up, catching Elizabeth around the middle.

For a moment, it looked like they would both stay in the air.

"*Eshan.*" Gold flew from Eric's hand, wrapping around Devon's middle.

Devon sucked in air through his teeth, but the spell hadn't made contact with any of his bare skin.

Eric pulled Devon down, getting him low enough that his feet touched the ground, then jerked his hand back, breaking the cord that had bound them.

"*Stasio.*" Eric's spell shimmered into being, surrounding Devon and Elizabeth.

Devon kept hold of Elizabeth, pressing her down even as his own feet left the ground. He only rose a few inches before stopping, like his head had hit some invisible ceiling.

I moved to break the spell connecting Elizabeth to me, but Eric shook his head.

"Keep her tethered." Eric stepped slowly forward. "Until we are sure of what this spell is, we cannot risk her being whisked away."

"I'm so sorry." Tears burned in my eyes as I crept slowly toward Devon and Elizabeth. "I didn't want to hurt you. I didn't know what else..." My words faded away as I saw Elizabeth's face.

Tears streamed from her eyes and trickled down into her hair. Pain had formed creases on her brow. Her jaw moved as she tried to speak, but it was like her lips had been super glued together.

"I'm sorry."

"What happened?" Devon said.

"She was walking ahead of me." My voice cracked. "I was on the phone. I wasn't watching. She went through the boulders before me, and then I heard her scream."

"If she chose this path, she must have seen something to lure her in this direction," Eric said.

Elizabeth gave a muffled sound of affirmation.

Eric tented his hands under his chin. "Was the thing you saw beautiful?"

Elizabeth gave a tiny shake of her head. The movement seemed to cause her pain. Fresh tears pooled in her eyes.

"Was it dark?" Eric asked.

She shook her head again.

"Did it look like regular humans had done it?" Devon asked.

Elizabeth nodded.

People. Normal people had left something that made Elizabeth want to come this way. I tried to think back. I'd been talking on the phone. I'd been an asshat who hadn't been paying enough attention.

I'd been too busy looking at the way Elizabeth's hair swished around her shoulders to really think through the groove in the rock she'd trailed her finger along.

"There's a cut, like a hatch mark on the boulders we had to walk between," I said.

Eric paced beside Elizabeth and Devon's cage, his brow furrowed and lips pursed.

"What?" I wanted to step into Eric's path to stop him, but I couldn't risk hurting Elizabeth more by pulling on the bond between us.

"There are choices to make," Eric said.

"Choices?" Devon said.

"I believe I know how to free Elizabeth without killing either of you," Eric said.

"That would be the ideal outcome," Devon said.

"But there would be no covering our tracks," Eric said. "The moment Iliana walked between those boulders, she would know we'd come this way."

"I'm fine with that," I said.

"It will also take more magic than one wizard should channel in a day," Eric said. "I can't afford to face someone like Iliana in a weakened state."

"You also can't possibly be considering leaving Elizabeth and Devon here." Anger burned past the panic in my chest.

"It may be our best chance of reaching the books," Eric said.

"No." Devon twisted to look at Eric. "Don't go down that road."

"Devon, your safety is simple. All you need to do is step away from Elizabeth. We can leave her here. Come back for her later," Eric said. "There would be no reason to create a trapping spell of this magnitude if one's purpose was to kill. There will be something, like the cells in Iliana's house, that will contain Elizabeth. She can—"

"And if Iliana gets to her first?" My anger shifted to a weird white-hot rage that somehow made my voice creepily calm. "If Iliana questions her? If Iliana hurts her? If you're wrong and there is no trapping, just death?"

Eric didn't say anything.

"If you walk out of this clearing, you go alone," I said. "If you abandon the people you're supposed to care about, none of us will follow you. We're done."

"We are here for the books." Eric spread his arms wide. "They are here. I can feel them. The work of centuries, ready to be restored to its rightful place."

"But it wouldn't be," I said. "How many times has Elizabeth saved us? How many times has Devon fought beside us? How many times have I almost died because I had your back during a battle?"

"And I am grateful for all those things," Eric said. "We will come back for Elizabeth."

"If you walk away from one of your own to find the books, then you shouldn't have them." Pain clawed at the sides of my throat. "If you fall that far, you're not any better than the Ladies or Thaden. You wouldn't be returning the books to their rightful place. You would just be the new bad guy in charge of the treasure."

"You don't understand—"

"There has to be more to magic than fighting and hoping you're not the one who ends up dead!" I shouted. "We have to be better than abandoning our friends to get what we want. If that's all you're capable of, then I want no part in the world you're creating. I won't do it. Because I know we can be better than Thaden, or the Ladies, or anyone else who's come before. We can make the world a better place. We can be happy and peaceful. We don't have to sacrifice people to save the day."

Eric crumpled. Not like fell to the ground, but like a tiny bit of the scaffolding that had been holding up the hero's absolute determination that he was right had been ripped away, leaving a mere man standing in his place.

"Do the spell," Devon said. "You may not have our backs. But you know we have yours."

Eric closed his eyes for a moment before nodding.

I didn't want to be done screaming at Eric. In fact, I would have loved to punch him in the face a few times, but he stepped forward and raised his hands, and it was like a subtle breeze suddenly filled the little clearing.

"*Mea brago indulno*"—Eric tipped his head back as the breeze turned into a wind that whipped around us—"*vinesca endrago*"—the light in the clearing faded as a *crack* sounded from the rock face—"*tearinsca falto*—"

I wanted to glance over to the cliff to see what had made the noise, but I couldn't look away from Elizabeth. Ribbons of light had begun to glow around her like I was finally seeing the magic that bound her.

"—*farita entrasco*—"

The ribbons of light stretched, reaching toward the cliff, and the wind grew into a full-blown gale, stinging my face and slicing through my sweater.

I finally glanced at the cliff just in time to see the shining ribbons slip into the stone like there was something inside the rock face trying to drag Elizabeth away.

"—*tarigo erbracina!*"

The wind vanished. The was no sound that came with the ending of the spell, just a moment of stillness before Elizabeth fell to the ground and Eric collapsed to his knees.

Devon still had her around the middle. He held on, softening her fall and keeping her from bashing her head on the ground. "I've got you." He kept her steady as she opened her mouth and gasped in a breath.

I flicked my wrist, getting rid of the tether that had bound me to Elizabeth.

The golden cord vanished, sending a flare of heat to pummel my palm as Elizabeth took a shuddering breath that ended in a sob as she clutched her hands to her chest.

"You're okay." Devon held her, rocking her as she cried. "It's over."

I wanted to take a step forward, but I couldn't make my feet move. "I…"

Be brave. You owe it to her to be brave.

"I'm so sorry." My words seemed hollow and stupid as Elizabeth looked toward me, and I caught sight of the bright red, indented burns across the backs of her wrists. "I'm sorry."

Elizabeth reached for me. Like she wanted me near her. Like she didn't hate me for torturing her with the spell. Being dragged to auction with that curse around my neck had been bad enough. I'd pulled her whole body, dragged her away from the force of another spell. I'd hurt her, and even Lola might not be able to mend the scars.

I took a step forward.

Elizabeth didn't flinch.

"I'm sorry." My feet fumbled on the rocks as I stumbled to her side and knelt to hold her.

"It's okay." Elizabeth buried her face on my shoulder. "I'm okay."

I wanted to squeeze her to my chest, like I could protect her from any more agony just by locking my arms around her. But I didn't want to cause her more pain by holding her too tight.

"Can you get up?" Devon asked. "I don't think we should stay here. I don't know if the spell could recharge or something."

"That spell is broken." Eric's voice sounded raspy and weak enough that I actually bothered to look toward the asshat who'd suggested we abandon my girlfriend.

He knelt on the ground, sweat slicking his brow, the blue of his veins fighting through his pale skin.

"Though I do agree we need to keep moving." Eric planted his hands on the ground, his whole body shaking as he lurched to his feet. "If Iliana set one trap on this path, there will be more. We can't afford to waste time."

"Saving Elizabeth was not a waste of time," I spat.

Elizabeth squeezed my arm before I could start shouting all the names I wanted to call the nasty, abandoning Eric Deldridge.

"I could see something." Elizabeth pressed on my shoulder, using me to steady herself as she got to her feet. "It was like a tiny shimmer on the ground, or a sparkly little rock. It was over there." She pointed behind Eric. "I didn't even get within ten feet of it before I got sucked into that spell."

Eric's head sagged forward.

For a second, I thought he'd passed out, but he just let out a long breath before speaking. "The traps in the house were worrying. Well-disguised and each less visible to Elizabeth than the last. But to set a trap designed to lure in a seer, that leaves us more vulnerable than I had feared."

"Do you think this isn't the way to wherever the books are hidden?" Devon said.

"I'm quite sure the books are this way," Eric said. "I only worry what else awaits us."

"Come on then." Devon lifted Eric's arm, draping it over his shoulder, and wrapped his own around Eric's waist.

"I can manage without assistance," Eric said, his voice wavering in a way that made me sincerely doubt he wasn't about to keel over.

"We're the good guys," Devon said. "We don't leave our own behind, even if they make a shitty mistake. Now come on. Let's go finish this thing."

25

As a general rule, feeling useless is pretty standard for me. But as we crept down the tiny path that cut along the bottom of the cliff face, somehow not being able to help felt way worse than normal.

I couldn't hold Elizabeth's hand, because it might hurt the wounds I'd left on her wrists. I wasn't going to be the one to help Eric shamble down the path, because he could go screw himself for all I cared. We may have needed him to get to the books, but I was not prepared to forgive him. Not by a long shot.

So, Devon had taken up the duty of keeping Le Grand Asshat on his feet while the asshat and Elizabeth examined every stone, twig, and shadow for the next trap. Which was the smart thing to do but made moving along the path a very slow process, so all the hairs on the back of my neck prickled like Iliana was already watching us and just having too good a laugh to be bothered with jumping out to kill us.

We'd given a wide berth to two more sparkly things only Elizabeth could see, skirted around a patch of shadows that darkened the ground even though there was nothing any of us could find that should have been blocking the sun, and fully ignored a cry that was either an abandoned baby or mating animals, before we finally came to a little waterfall cascading down the side of the cliff.

The water looked clean and beautiful. My first instinct was to reach out and touch the pool at the bottom to see how cold it really was, but there was something in the way the water glimmered in the light that made me fairly certain touching the falls would end badly.

"Well"—Elizabeth tipped her head as she studied the water. I looked away before her movements could distract me—"I guess she gave up on subtlety."

"Or this spell is of an older making." Eric stepped away from Devon's support to stare at the pool below the falls.

And, as a mark of how truly hopeless I am, I didn't actually notice how weird the base of the falls was until everyone around me was staring at it.

The water falling from the cliff was a little too beautiful to be normal, but the super weird bit was the fact that the water fell into a ten-foot-wide, shallow pool with no outlet. No stream running out of it. No marks where the pool sometimes overflowed.

"Huh," I said, like the genius I am.

"This is where the path ends." Elizabeth moved like she was going to dig her fingers into her curls before wincing and lowering her arms. "If the books are hidden in this gorge, they've got to be here."

We're almost there!

"So," Devon said, "do we dive in or walk through the stone wall?"

"I say we move the water and see what it's hiding." I stepped as close to the edge of the pool as I could and stared down.

"Move the water?" Devon said.

"I mean, we're way past the point of subtlety." I shrugged.

"I'm afraid I haven't the energy to manage it," Eric said. "You'll have to do the spell yourself."

"I don't remember asking for your help." I flexed my fingers a few times as I stretched my hands out over the water. "*Stilgarna.*"

If you've ever seen a fire hydrant explode, just magnify that amount of water and gushing force by about ten thousand. If you've never seen a fire hydrant blow, then picture all the water from the waterfall and all the water from the pool shooting out toward the middle of the gorge like a badly aimed rocket.

The blast of water knocked over trees, shoved aside boulders that probably hadn't moved in a few thousand years, and washed enough dirt away in three seconds that I'd probably changed the terrain forever and really confused future geologists.

"See anything!" I shouted over the continuing roar of my water cannon.

"There's a gap in the cliff." Elizabeth crept closer to the rock wall. "It's big enough to fit through."

"I'll go first." Devon looped around, her pulling out his sword.

"I can go," Eric said.

"You're barely standing, we need Elizabeth to spot traps, and Bryant's our only functional wizard." Devon's sword voomed to life. "I'm the spare. Don't worry. I know you won't abandon me."

"Devon, you aren't the spare." I took a step toward him, but he'd already slipped through the crack in the rock.

My water cannon wavered as fear filled my chest, not because the spell still actively needed my magic to work, more like the spell was a part of me and my whole being tensed as I waited for Devon to scream.

"First five feet are clear," Devon shouted.

The water cannon restabilized as Eric slipped into the crack.

I moved to scoot around Elizabeth to go into the darkness, but she held a hand up, blocking my path.

"I'm having a really bad day." Elizabeth gave me a strained smile. "Don't make me watch my boyfriend walk into the dark."

"That's supposed to be my line."

"We're a modern couple, remember?" Elizabeth stepped into the slit.

I ran a few steps and darted between the stones right behind her, the terror in my chest that screamed the rocks would close and I'd never see any of them again batting aside my reason.

The rough texture of the stone pulled at the fabric of my sweater as I sidled into the black.

I'd thought it would be like walking through a door, but the stone path was long enough I'd started to wonder if claustrophobia was going to join my list of issues before I managed to make it out on the other side.

The glow of Devon's sword was the only light to be seen. The red gleam cast shadows that towered over us, which somehow didn't feel more comforting than being in the dark.

"*Heliono.*" The glowing sphere appeared in my palm, giving more light to the space, but not offering much more comfort.

The chamber was about fifteen feet wide. Someone had carved stacks of large ledges into the side walls. I hoped the shelves were meant to be stone beds, but they could easily have been made to hold corpses.

On the far side of what I really hoped was a sleeping room, another tunnel led deeper into the darkness.

"Can we cross?" I looked between Eric an Elizabeth.

"A stone please, Bryant." Eric held out his hand.

I looked around the floor, but there were no loose stones I could see.

"From the wall, Bryant." Eric kept his hand raised.

"You could have started there." I turned toward the wall and raised two fingers like I was making my own knife. "*Caruson.*" The magic buzzed through my hand as I carved out a chunk of stone that I really hoped wasn't necessary for the structural integrity of the chamber. The rock radiated warmth as I passed it to Eric.

His legs trembled as he lowered himself to kneel. He took a moment, actually aiming the stone, before sliding it across the floor toward the tunnel beyond.

I held my breath, waiting for spells or spears to shoot from the walls like I'd gone from being a wizard to being a whip-wielding archaeologist.

Nothing happened.

"Elizabeth?" Eric asked.

"Nothing," Elizabeth said.

Eric started across the chamber, Devon keeping close behind with his non-sword hand hovering near Eric's back as though ready to catch the attempted abandoner if he fell.

"*Abalata.*" I let the black of the spell pool in my hand, ready to throw it at whatever waited for us in the tunnel.

Elizabeth picked up the rock I had carved from the wall, tucking it into her pocket before entering the narrow passage.

The light from my spell wavered against the chamber walls as I headed toward the tunnel, keeping to the same path the others had tread, not running from the ghosts my gut seemed really sure were staring at me from the shadows.

The passage sloped down. Not at a severe angle, just enough to make you wonder how deep the person who'd dug the tunnel was brave enough to go.

I studied the walls as we moved slowly farther away from fresh air and freedom. The passage was magic-made. Even if the walls hadn't been so smooth there was no way a human could have done it, I could feel the ambient magic in the air, pressing against my skin.

Who made this place, and why did you have to hide?

I knew I'd never get an answer even as I thought the question. The people who'd dug this tunnel were long dead and the history of magic too buried by violence and secrets.

A gasp sounded from up ahead.

"Eric." I tried to keep my voice calm, but I sounded freaked out anyway.

"He's okay," Devon answered.

Another light joined the glow of Devon's sword.

"Wow," Elizabeth breathed just before stepping out of the tunnel and into the room beyond.

"Whoa." I stood at the end of the passage for a moment, trying to get my brain to process what I was seeing.

A round room was a good place to start. Gold inlay swept through the stone walls, making a massive image of the gorge and the falls outside.

Silver shapes, like oversized steppingstones, had been set into the floor.

Thousands upon thousands of jewels sparkled from the ceiling, their gleam brightening to an unnatural glow as I stepped into the room and added my light to the space.

I wanted to walk along the wall, trailing my fingers across the bits of gold, but the others stood clustered together, so I stepped into the pack before I could start a cave-in by touching the wrong thing.

"This isn't right," Eric said.

"It's amazing." Elizabeth tipped her head back. The jewels set into the ceiling sparkled their dazzling glow across her face.

"But it can't be the end," Eric said. "The books aren't here."

"Right." I looked around the room, searching for the books, feeling like a boob for having momentarily forgotten about the things I'd almost died a few times trying to save.

"I don't think this is the end." Elizabeth took a tiny step away from our group.

I shifted with her, keeping so close my arm brushed against her back.

"Do you see any exit?" Eric said.

"No. It's..." Elizabeth turned in a slow circle. "I can see where magic melded the metal to the stone on the walls. I can see the power it's taking to hold all the jewels in place on the ceiling. It all has a faint glow, almost like a visible hum. But there aren't any cracks in it, no places where a part of the wall should push away."

"Then it's gotta be down." Devon inched a step forward.

Elizabeth furrowed her brow as she studied the floor. "There's nothing joining the magic that formed each of the steppingstones, but they all look the same."

"Then we must take our chances," Eric said.

"What?" I let the black in my hand fade so I could take Elizabeth's arm, drawing her away from Eric.

"One of these stones must open," Eric said.

"Which means touching the others will probably do something that might get us killed," I said.

"Exactly." Eric carefully picked his way across the floor, avoiding stepping on any of the silver stones.

I shook out my shoulders, fighting my surprisingly on-point instinct to flee. "The entrance would have to be large enough for a person to fit through."

"That would be imperative." Eric stopped to study the stone at the center of the room.

"So don't pick a small stone," I said.

"A very wise point," Devon said in a mock Eric voice.

"I've never said Bryant was unwise." Eric moved closer to the left-hand wall. "He, like all of you, lacks experience. That is neither a personal insult nor a permanent state. It is merely an honest fact."

He moved toward the right-hand wall and leaned over a stone that would have been large enough for a person to fit through as long as that person had no fear of covered playground slides.

"This seems to be the clear choice." Eric tented his fingers under his chin.

"But how does it open?" Elizabeth said.

I studied the floor, trying to see why that particular bit of silver on the floor was a clear choice. They all looked the same to me.

"I'm not sure." Eric reached his foot forward like he was going to press the stone with his toe.

"Don't!" Elizabeth took a careful step toward Eric and pulled the rock from her pocket. "Let's try not to get stuck in anymore traps." She bounced the rock in her hand for a moment before tossing it onto the bit of silver.

The rock hit the steppingstone then tumbled aside with a *clatter* that echoed around the room.

I think we all held our breath as we waited for the floor to open up, so we all got to hear the *click* from the ceiling.

"*Primurgo!*" I grabbed Devon and Elizabeth, covering them with my shield spell, extinguishing the light I'd held in my hand.

Pops came from above as a shower of jewels shot toward us and pinged off the floor.

I pulled Elizabeth and Devon closer to me as the hail of priceless projectiles pounded against my shield with enough force to penetrate a human skull.

"Eric!" Elizabeth shouted.

I looked toward him.

Devon's sword gave the only light in the room, but through the shimmering of my spell, I could see Eric's outline—hunched over as his own shield crackled and sparked under the impact of the room's attack.

"It'll be done soon," I called over the noise of the jewels bouncing off the stone, like I actually knew what was going to happen. "Just hang on."

Eric fell to his knees like something had hit him.

My heart tightened and flew up into my throat as the crackling of Eric's shield began to fade. I wanted to help. I needed to help. But I didn't know how to do anything without dropping the barrier that was protecting the three of us.

"Let me out." Devon looked to me.

"What? No!" I tightened my grip on Devon's arm.

"Just let me out." Devon pulled a tea saucer-sized, silver disk from his pocket. "Trust me, Bry."

I let go of Devon and held Elizabeth close to my chest, pulling my shield away from my best friend.

My spell pulsed as Devon pressed a tiny indent on the silver disk, making it grow from the size of a saucer to a full shield. He shouted as he shoved his way out of my barrier and the spell sizzled against his skin.

The pinging of the jewels against the metal rang around the room as he bolted toward Eric. He stumbled, his feet slipping on the jewels, but kept his shield over his head.

A groaning rattled my spine, like I had literally been consumed by my fear and was standing in its rumbling stomach.

Devon screamed and stumbled again. "I'm okay!" he shouted as he knelt beside Eric, holding his metal shield over both their heads.

Eric's shield spell faltered as he slumped toward Devon, who caught him around the middle, keeping him from falling out of the safety created by the Raven-made shield.

26

There are some death-defying situations in life that start to get a little boring because they're just too drawn out. You're there, almost dying, in fight or flight mode. And then you're still there, still almost dying, but there's nothing else to do about it besides what you've already done and your adrenaline starts to fade and suddenly the whole mess is just exhausting.

I was about halfway to exhausted by the time the jewels stopped raining down on us. First, it slowed from a barrage to a patter, and then, with a weird swishing *tinkle*, all the stones that had pelted our shields soared back up to their places on the ceiling.

Devon gave a yelp and a groan as a jewel ripped out of his calf and flew up to join the rest of the stones that had already nestled back into the ceiling.

I waited for a long moment before letting go of the shield spell that surrounded Elizabeth and me.

"Do you need me to heal you?" I looked to Devon as he pressed the indent on his shield to shrink it back to being pocket-sized.

"As long as jewels don't have venom." Devon spoke through gritted teeth.

"*Sinato.*" I bit my lips together, hoping I wasn't accidentally murdering my friend.

Devon hissed through his teeth as my healing spell knit his skin back together.

"Thank you." Eric's voice sounded hollow and husky. "Thank you for protecting me."

"That's how we do." Devon let out a long breath before pushing himself to his feet. "Let's try another bit of floor and see what fun things happen."

"I think you already did." Elizabeth pointed to a silver steppingstone Devon had run across as he'd bolted to help Eric.

The silver had sunk an inch into the floor, leaving shadows around its edges.

"Maybe we should stand together in case I have to make a shield to cover all of us." I reached for Elizabeth.

"Good idea." She held loosely on to my fingers as we wound our way between the steppingstones toward Devon and Eric.

"So, do we just poke it?" I planted myself closest to the sunken stone, ready to cast whatever spell I could to protect us from the next doom that decided to attack.

"I'll do it." Devon stepped up beside me, reaching his toe toward the stone.

"You aren't expendable," I said.

"But you're so good at healing me." Devon slammed his foot down onto the stone and leapt back just before a weird shimmer passed over the silver.

Primurgo balanced on my lips as the stone began to glow, but instead of blasting us with high-end shrapnel, the light faded and the stone disappeared, leaving a hole leading into the darkness below.

I formed a light in my hand and reached toward the opening. The shadows shifted, revealing a worn stone staircase leading down into the black.

"That's not creepy at all." My voice wobbled as I spoke.

"After me, I think." Eric stepped up to the edge of the gap, swaying slightly from the effort.

"You're barely standing," Devon said.

"All the more reason for me to be the first to meet my fate if any of us should fall. *Heliono.*" The light that blossomed to life in his hand was half the strength it should have been, but none of us argued when he stepped onto the top stair. "I think it's only right after the mistakes I've made."

"Death is permanent," Elizabeth said. "Mistakes can be forgiven."

"And atonement carves that path." Eric gave a sad smile before heading down into the darkness. Once his head was below floor level, Devon started down the steps.

My heart raced. I wanted to say something profound and meaningful in case we were all about to die, but I couldn't think of anything as Devon climbed down, leaving the red glow of his sword as my only assurance that he still existed.

Elizabeth squeezed my fingers before starting after them.

I knelt beside the stairs, lighting her path for as long as I could. But her shiny blond hair disappeared into the darkness, so there was nothing I could do but follow.

"You can do this, Bryant." I clenched my jaw as I stepped onto the first stair. The stone beneath my feet stayed solid. "You can totally do this."

I started down the steps, trying not to grind my teeth to the point of cracking them and making a mental note to talk to Dr. Spinnek about relaxing my jaw while under intense stress if I survived the creepy stairs and if she was still willing to schedule me for an appointment.

From above, I'd thought the steps just went straight down, but really it was a wide spiral staircase reaching deep into the earth.

"You can't scare me with going belowground." I spoke to the stone around me. "I've been to the tunnels below Beville. This is nothing."

"Are you okay?" Elizabeth took a step back to look at me.

"Yeah." Heat crept into my cheeks. "Just talking to the stairs."

"Ah. Totally normal." Elizabeth winked at me and stepped forward, shifting out of my view around the spiral.

The temperature of my cheeks still hadn't returned to normal by the time the end of the stairs came into view.

It didn't look like anything special. There was no grand entryway. No singing angels or sparkling lights. Devon didn't whoop in triumph, and Eric didn't say anything snarky.

A desperate disappointment stabbed at my stomach. I shoved the feeling aside and squared my shoulders, ready to give a rousing motivational speech if that was what it took to keep the others going as we searched for the books.

I stepped off the last stair, my mouth already open in preparation for saying something deep and meaningful about the salvation of knowledge, and then I just froze. Like I'd been trapped in one of Iliana's gelatinous prisons.

Books.

Everywhere books.

Thousands upon thousands of books.

Tables laid out with stacks of books. Trunks so packed with books, they couldn't be closed.

Shelves along the walls had been filled with books, and the room stretched farther back than my light could reach.

I stood there, staring as my body went completely numb with awe.

Even knowing what we'd been looking for, I hadn't realized how beautiful the sight would actually be.

I took a step forward, wanting to race into the dark just to know how far back the room reached.

"There are so many," Elizabeth said.

"Who the hell got them all down here?" Devon said.

"We won't be able to move them quickly enough." Eric's hands trembled as he reached for the nearest table. "Even if Iliana doesn't come for days, we won't have enough time to get all the books safely away. We need help."

"We need a shipping container," I said.

Eric picked up one of the books and ran his fingers along the cover. "The most precious wisdom our people possess. Hidden belowground for generations."

"We should take what we can carry," Devon said. "Get it up and out of here while we come up with a plan."

"We can't leave any of the books," Eric said.

"We can't risk ending up with none of them if Iliana decides to get vengeful and destroy them all," Devon said.

Two sounds carried from the back of the space. A sharp, slow clapping and low relaxed laughter.

"How very smart the boy is." A female voice spoke as the *clack* of footsteps on stone came closer to us. "You've come all this way, to try and take my books. I can't let you have them. I would rather they burn."

A flare of fire burst to life, crackling in Iliana's palm. She held the flames in front of her, casting their flickering glow across her face.

I could tell she was the girl from the forest. She had the same features, the same hair. But there was a malice about her the phantasms hadn't shown me. Or maybe she hadn't sunk to that level of evil before she'd gone to visit the bookkeepers in the woods.

"You would burn the books?" Eric stepped forward. "After all you did to find them?"

"You're right." Iliana smiled. "I did find them. I spent years hunting for this place. Tracking the footsteps of a long dead thief to find his lair. If it weren't for me, the books would have moldered down here. I found the treasure. The books are my prize, and I will not let you steal them. Better burned by my magic than ripped from my hands."

"There's something glowing behind her," Elizabeth said, her voice loud enough to bounce around the space. "It feels like death. I think it's bone magic."

Bile stung my throat. She'd used bone magic where she kept the books. It felt like a double desecration.

"A seer," Iliana said. "You really did try your hardest. That should bring some comfort to you before you die."

"There will only be one death here today," Eric said. "And I will not lose one of mine."

"*Erunca!*" I shouted the spell, not waiting for Eric to perform his own. Streaks of lightning shot down from the ceiling.

Iliana raised her hand, swatting the bolts aside in a way I didn't know was possible. But the lightning still touched her skin, and her face betrayed her pain. "How cute. Attack me again, and your deaths will be painful."

I froze, stuck between my need to fight and my unwillingness to be the cause of my friends' suffering.

"*Lobula.*" Eric held his hands to his sides, staggering as the magic of his spell shot out of his palms, forming shimmering shields on either side of Iliana, blocking her from reaching the tables.

"Bryant," Eric said. "If you would."

I stepped forward and everything inside me got creepy calm. Like I was just in the ballroom at Eric's house in Beville, ready for another sparring session, and he'd given the order to begin.

"*Parapus.*" The thin, black lines of my spell soared toward Iliana, clanging against her hand as she batted them aside. "*Exci!*" I shouted my second spell before she looked away from the first.

She coughed and doubled over from the blow. Then her head snapped up and she glared at me. She didn't even mutter a spell, but a stinging radiated through my hand and dragged a scream from my throat.

Devon bellowed as he charged forward, his sword raised.

The stinging in my hand faded as Iliana turned her attention toward Devon.

His steps faltered, but he still swung his sword, nicking Iliana's arm.

"*Kalitza,*" Iliana spat.

Devon screamed and fell onto his back.

"*Abalata.*" I threw the black from my palm, shouting, "*Tudina!*" before the first spell even reached her.

Iliana ducked, and a shield of light blossomed from her arm, protecting her from my magic.

Devon gasped on the ground.

I glanced down. Blood had started dripping from the corners of his eyes.

"Eric!" I shouted. "*Hieata.*" I glanced back toward Devon as Iliana knocked my spell aside.

Eric knelt beside Devon, eyes closed as he whispered.

Iliana looked that way, too.

"*Erunca.*" I tried the lightning spell again. Not because I thought it would work, just to get Iliana to stop looking at Devon.

She used her shield of light to shove my attack back at me. I dove to the ground, reaching for Elizabeth, ready to pull her out of the way of the lightning, but she was gone.

I wanted to call out and see where she was, but I didn't have time.

Iliana snapped her fingers, shoving Eric and Devon aside.

Eric's spell that had been protecting the books flickered and faded away.

Iliana laughed as flames reappeared in her hand.

"*Ilmatiot.*" I hated the feel of the spell in my mouth, hated the fact that I had to use it.

Iliana's breath hitched in her chest, but she still stalked toward me. She inhaled deeply then blew on the flames in her palm, making the fire grow.

"How many books will I have to burn before you give up and die?" She tossed the fire onto the nearest table of books, letting the flames consume the priceless pages.

"No! *Aarantha!*" I formed a vortex, syphoning the flames away from the books and toward the ceiling.

"You are not going to win this fight," Iliana said.

A red light flashed through the corner of my vision.

Iliana saw it, too. She turned toward Devon as he lunged, reaching his sword for her gut. Her shield of light blocked the blow, then solidified and lengthened, her magic forming a gleaming blade of her own.

I hadn't even really registered what was happening before she stabbed Devon in the chest.

27

"Devon." Panic froze my veins as Devon crumpled to the ground. The vortex I'd made vanished, and the flames trickled back down onto the books. I didn't care.

"One down." Iliana grinned.

"Devon!" I scrambled toward him.

Iliana swung her spell-formed sword, blocking my path.

"*Milkawa.*" I curled my fingers toward the ground, begging the stone to grow to my will.

Iliana sliced her sword, aiming for my neck.

I barely ducked away.

I couldn't run. I had to keep her still. I had to get to Devon. I had to protect the books.

I couldn't do all those things. I could barely keep myself alive.

I was failing, and the people I cared about would pay the price.

The air in the room shifted as the flames rose back away from the books, not in a funnel, but as though someone had lifted dozens of torches.

Eric knelt beside Devon, blood on his hands as he forced the fire up with some spell I'd never learned.

"Are you volunteering to go next?" Iliana looked toward Eric, lurching as the stone I'd grown around her feet held her in place. She laughed. She actually looked down at her trapped feet and laughed.

The sound of it brought bile to my throat. "*Erunca.*"

Lightning flashed down from the ceiling.

She knocked my magic toward me again.

I leaned out of the way, already focusing on her legs. "*Turso.*" The streak of white light hit her in the knees. She buckled forward.

That little movement changed the course of the deep green, jagged arrow that flew from her hand.

I felt myself scream as her spell hit me in the shoulder, felt my arm go limp. But the pain couldn't break through the anger that had swallowed my whole being.

"*Telinto,*" I spat the spell.

Blood sprayed from a cut on Iliana's cheek.

"How cute." She flicked her finger toward her feet, shattering the rocks that had bound her. "I had expected more from wizards who came so far to steal my books." A blazing sheet of orange shot toward me.

I dove under a table. The heat of the spell blistered the skin on my arm. I screamed and rolled farther away.

"You really do disappoint me." Iliana's boots crunched across the shattered stone.

I forced myself to my hands and knees.

Eric knelt on the ground twenty feet in front of me, sweating, swaying, and crumpling beneath the weight of his own magic.

Devon lay still beside him. Blood stained his eyelids.

Pain that had nothing to do with my injuries shot through my whole body.

I screamed as I scrambled back out from under the table. "*Frico.*" My spell grabbed onto Iliana's jacket, yanking her toward me. I didn't bother formulating a spell as I swung and punched her hard in the face.

Something stung my side. The warmth of my blood trickled down my ribs.

"*Erunca.*" I grabbed onto Iliana as lightning streaked down from the ceiling.

The spell finally found its mark. The surge of it traveled through my hands, knocking my heart out of rhythm as Iliana tossed me to the ground.

I tried to get up, but my limbs couldn't hold me.

"I'm tired of playing." Iliana raised her hand. Bits of carved, white shrapnel flew from the back wall to land in her palm. She grinned as she blew on them. The bits of bone glowed red.

"*Primurgo.*" The word stole the last bit of air my lungs had to give.

She threw the bones at me like they were nothing more sinister than confetti.

Sparks crackled across my shield, the weight of other, long dead wizards' power pressing against my weakened magic.

Iliana screamed and turned away from me. Blood dripped from a wound in her back.

"Leave my boyfriend alone." Elizabeth gripped a bone-tipped spear whose point had been slicked with red.

"Is it time for me to hurt you now?" Iliana raised her hands.

"No." Elizabeth smiled as she glanced toward me. "It's time to end this the way it all began." She leveled her spear, ready to charge forward.

I wanted to shield her. I would have thrown myself in front of her if I could move. But I had nothing left. No magic. Not even enough air in my lungs to tell Elizabeth I was sorry for failing her.

Iliana shouted a spell I couldn't hear over my pulse thundering in my ears.

Elizabeth staggered before thrusting the spear again.

Iliana laughed as she leapt aside.

Elizabeth didn't cringe. She didn't back away. She was brave and strong and everything I'd loved since before she'd actually spoken to me. Since before it all began. Since the day I started a fire in a stupid scene shop and fate dragged Elizabeth into my life.

She swiped the spear at Iliana's ankles.

I grabbed my phone, pressing my thumb to the scanner before I'd even gotten it out of my pocket. A little icon of cartoon fire popped up on the screen. I tapped the app. A picture of flames appeared, along with a level bar.

I aimed the phone at Iliana's back.

She lifted her hand. Jagged shards of white surrounded her fist as she shifted her weight to aim for Elizabeth.

I dragged the bar all the way to the right.

A pillar of flames roared to life in the middle of the room. There was no screaming. Just fire.

One, two, three.

Elizabeth dropped the spear and backed away from the flames.

Eight, nine, ten.

I dragged the bar to the left, and all the fire, from the pillar that surrounded Iliana to the blaze Eric held in the air, just disappeared.

The room went silent.

I coughed a sob and dragged myself across the ground toward Devon.

Eric sat back on his heels, covering his face.

"I'm so sorry." I reached my best friend's side and clasped his still-warm hand. "I didn't...I'm so..." I couldn't speak through my tears.

"Devon." Elizabeth knelt beside him. "Devon, wake up."

"Elizabeth, he's…" I couldn't make myself say that my best friend was dead.

Elizabeth tore open the front of his sweater and shoved his shirt up.

I started to close my eyes, not wanting to see his wound, but Devon's skin was the wrong color. Something silver covered him, and there wasn't any blood.

"If Raven's armor stopped the blow, why isn't he awake?" Elizabeth shook Eric's shoulder. "Why isn't he awake? Think, Eric." She yanked his hands away from his face.

"She manipulated magic, concentrating the force of it to form a blade." Eric rose back up to his knees, new life filling his eyes as he touched the thin fabric that covered Devon's torso. "Raven's invention stopped the blow from penetrating Devon's body, but the dispersed magic still struck him."

"Okay, so how do you heal from that?" Elizabeth said.

I reached my hand out, laying it on Devon's chest. It didn't move. "He's not breathing."

"The lack of inhalation is a side effect, not the true problem. He is suffering the receiving form of a burn out. Too much magic where it should not be." Eric swatted my hand aside and laid both his palms on Devon's chest. "*Crantella stasina bracenta erbracina!*"

The most radiant glow I'd ever seen floated up from Devon's body like Eric was separating spirit from flesh.

Eric raised his hands, lifting the light, drawing it toward himself. The gleam wrapped around his arms and traveled up his neck before surrounding his whole body. He gasped as the last of the light peeled away from Devon.

Before I could start to panic, Devon took a great shuddering breath.

"Devon." I squeezed his hand.

A weird *hum* pulled my attention from my now not dead best friend.

The gleam surrounding Eric had condensed, forming a solid light like a suit of armor that blocked his actual body from view.

"Eric?" Elizabeth reached toward him.

With a *crack*, the light flashed as it shot into Eric's body.

"Eric!" Elizabeth threw herself toward him as he fell, catching his head before it struck the ground.

Devon squeezed my hand.

"You're alive." I leaned over him.

"What the hell was that?" Devon blinked the blood from his eyes.

"You were a little dead, but you're better now." I laughed, not caring that my tears were literally falling onto Devon's non-punctured chest.

"Go slow." Elizabeth wrapped an arm behind Eric's back as she helped him sit up.

"Thank you, Eric," I said. "Are you going to be okay?"

"A wizard's body can handle more magic than a human's." Eric swayed as he looked to Devon. "I'll have a few bad days. But I'll survive."

"At least you can read a good book while you recover," I said.

"Where's Iliana?" Devon sat up.

I grabbed his shoulder, keeping him from tipping over.

"She's gone," Elizabeth said. "All we have to do now is sort the books and see which ones need repair."

"And figure out how to get all of them back to America." Devon looked to me.

I cringed, remembering my abandoned therapy session, tossed aside phone, and having broken the one rule my parents had laid out for the trip.

"Maybe it's a good thing my parents are having slumber parties," I said. "Nothing like a little emotional blackmail to get someone to pay for international shipping."

"That's the spirit." Devon laughed. "Everything happens for a reason."

And for a little while, I thought he was right. I'd fulfilled my destiny. The four of us were meant to work together because it took all of us to find the books and defeat Evil Iliana.

We were done. Fate could find someone else to twist her web around and leave me alone.

But fate wasn't done with me. Not yet.

28

It was already dark by the time we got back to the inn and I finally ran out of excuses for not calling my dad.

I bounced up and down on the little street that led to the water, like a boxer getting ready for a fight.

"You are not a coward, Bryant Jameson Adams." I took a deep breath and tapped on my phone's now super-cracked screen to call my dad.

He answered on the second ring. "Bryant, where are you? Why the hell did you go to Crete?"

"I guess the credit card tracking is working well for you." I shoved down my anger at being stalked by my own father.

"Bryant, you need to come home right now," Dad said.

"I want to." I looked out over the dark water.

There was no trace of people existing beyond the island. A pang of homesickness joined the fatigue that filled me. I missed Manhattan's light pollution and constant ambient stink. I missed ticket scalpers and sketchy food vendors. I missed angry tourists and packed subways and toxic street sludge.

"You have no idea how much I'd love to hop on a plane and be back in New York."

"Tell me exactly where you are, and I'll find a way to have someone pick you up," Dad said.

"I can't come home yet. I still have something I need to do, and I need your help." I rocked back on my heels. "Do you happen to know someone who could help me get about nineteen-thousand-ish irreplaceable books from Crete to Manhattan?"

———

E xplaining to your dad that you lied about why you needed to come to Greece? Not the best time.

Figuring out how to get thousands of books out of a hidden cave of death? Enough to make your head explode.

Dealing with renting donkeys to haul the books? Stinkier than you'd think.

Finding secure local storage while you wait for the book ferry to arrive to carry your massive shipping crates? Gonna give you an ulcer.

Having both your parents show up to *help*? Adding to the therapy bills.

Having your parents sneak around together while you pretend not to notice? A small price to pay if your dad's footing the vomit-inducing shipping bill.

. Getting books regular humans should never see through customs? I have no idea. Dad hired someone, and I decided not to ask how legal it was.

Packing your almost empty bag to accompany the books home? Priceless.

Having your magical I-never-ring phone ring in your pocket for the second time ever? Gonna make this story just a little bit longer.

I know, shipping the books to Manhattan and restoring generations worth of knowledge to its rightful place should have been the end of the story, but like I said, fate wasn't quite done with me.

———

T he sun was already bright enough to burn the little bit of my pasty neck that peeped up over my bohemian-chic scar scarf by the time the crates were all on the medium-size boat that would carry us to the larger boat that would take us home.

I stood on the dock, holding Elizabeth's hand while Dad chatted with the captain, and Eric intimidated the crew that had been charged with securing the crates.

"I can't believe we're heading back." Elizabeth leaned her head on my shoulder.

"How far behind do you think we're going to be in school?" I'd been avoiding the question for the two weeks it took us to figure out how to get the books out of the cave of deadly wonders and to Manhattan.

"I don't know," Elizabeth said. "But we're going to have nine days on a cargo ship to figure it out."

I rested my cheek against her hair, reminding myself of the primary reason—besides protecting the books—that nine days stuck at sea sounded like a really good idea.

"We're ready," Eric called from the deck.

"Coming," I said.

"The faster we're gone from this place, the better." Eric swept inside what passed as a cabin on the ship.

I could understand his loathing of the gorge. I don't think he'd really gotten over the fact that Iliana had come super close to actually murdering all of us. I'm not sure he ever will.

I didn't blame him. Iliana had given me issues of my own. I'd had two phone therapy sessions with Dr. Spinnek where I meticulously didn't mention the fact that I'd torched a person, and I still didn't really want to look at my magical phone.

It wasn't like I thought it was the phone's fault I'd added to my deeply disturbing body count. If I hadn't been able to use the phone to stop Iliana, the four of us would probably be dead. But I still felt icky about touching it, like a favorite kitchen knife you'd used to stab a murderer who'd broken into your home. Only magical. And one of a kind. And tossed into your path by fate herself.

I let my fingers graze my pocket, checking to make sure I hadn't somehow lost my magical mobile, as Elizabeth led me toward the boat. I pulled my hand away, and a ringtone sounded. Not a normal ringtone. A weird song I had only heard once before.

Elizabeth and I both froze.

The phone rang for a few seconds before Elizabeth met my gaze. "Bryant, why is that phone ringing?"

"I don't know." I didn't even look at my pocket. I kept my eyes locked on Elizabeth's like if I didn't acknowledge my phone, it would stop.

The song ended.

My shoulders relaxed just a touch before the song started again.

"Come on guys." Devon stepped out onto the deck. "Eric's going to lose his shit if we don't start moving." He tipped his head to the side. "What's that?"

"My phone's ringing." I cringed, flexing my fingers as I worked up the nerve to fish out my phone.

"Wait, like, the special phone?" Devon jogged down the ramp to the dock. "Answer it, Bry."

"Right." I reached into my pocket. "That's what one does with phones."

I held my breath as I looked at the screen, hoping against hope it would just go blank and I could pretend it hadn't rung at all.

Unknown Number

My hand trembled as I pressed the answer button.

"Hello?" My voice shook.

"Hi, I'm calling to make sure you've finalized your ticket purchase for The Event tomorrow night," a chipper voice on the other end of the line said.

"The Event?" I said.

"It's not to be missed!" the voice said. "And no one will be allowed into The Event without a pre-booked ticket."

"I'm sorry," I said. "I think you may have the wrong number."

"I don't think so," the voice said. "This number is definitely on my call list, and Mr. McDonald handed the list to me himself."

"McDonald." A chill trickled from the back of my neck to the base of my spine.

"Absolutely," the voice said.

"How did he get this number?"

"That's above my pay grade, sir," she said. "Would you like to book your tickets now?"

"I'll take four," I said. "I'll give you my credit card number."

I pulled my wallet from my back pocket and ran onto the ship, reading the numbers to the woman on the line as I shouldered open the cabin door.

"Perfect. What name should I have the tickets waiting under?" the woman asked.

"Umm." I froze, staring at Eric who glared at me like making the boat wait a few minutes to leave was clearly the most disappointing thing I'd ever done.

"Put them under Mr. Wick."

Eric wrinkled his brow at me.

"First name?" she asked.

"John?" My voice wiggled.

"Perfect Mr. Wick," she said. "We look forward to hosting you for the premier of The Event."

I tapped the button to end the call.

"Who is John Wick and why are Devon and Elizabeth still on the dock?" Eric frowned at me.

"We have to get off this boat." I grabbed Eric's arm, dragging him toward the door.

"Absolutely not." Eric yanked his arm free. "The books are on this boat. We are staying on this boat."

"Yeah but my *phone* rang"—I held up my magical mobile for added emphasis—"with a call from someone who works for *Mr. McDonald* making sure I had my tickets for the premier of *The Event* tomorrow night." I opened my eyes awkwardly wide at Eric as my parents sidled around to our side of the cabin.

Eric tented his fingers under his chin. "We cannot leave the books unprotected."

"We can't ignore a literal phone call from fate," I whispered.

"Bryant honey," Mom said. "Are you okay? You look a little flushed."

"If someone were to find out what these crates contain, it would be a disaster." Eric shook his head. "We've come too far."

"Dad, I want to fly home." I looked to my dad, who had no idea I'd just put an unknown amount of money on my credit card.

"Fly?" Dad wrinkled his brow. "I thought you wanted to ride with the cargo?"

"Yes." My intestines clenched as I tried to come up with a reasonable lie. "But I'm starting to panic about being behind in school. If we fly home today, I can hop right back into class."

Mom pursed her lips and crossed her arms, diving deep into full parental suspicion mode.

"I appreciate your wanting to get back to school—" Dad began.

"Your father and I can tutor you on the trip," Mom cut across him.

"But that's not the same as being in class?" My voice pitched up at the end like I was asking an actual question.

"You'll get individual attention," Mom said.

The cabin door swung open, and Devon and Elizabeth came to stand behind me.

I'm a badass wizard. I can pull this off.

"Ok. So, the man who tried to have me kidnapped is having a party. I want to go and identify him so the *people who deal with those things*," I said like it was code for the magical police that in no way existed, "can get him once and for all. They aren't going to hold him for nine days waiting for me to get back. And if they don't grab him at his party, I don't know when we'll get another chance to finally stop him."

Dad looked to Mom.

"We could get rid of him once and for all," I said. "I'd be free. I wouldn't have to look over my shoulder anymore."

"We cannot abandon the books," Eric said.

"I can stay," Devon said. "I'll keep an eye on them."

"I am not leaving a minor alone on a cargo ship," Mom said.

"I'll hire a plane," Dad sighed.

"Leo, that costs as much as a house." Mom gripped his arm.

"I already own a house." Dad pulled out his phone and walked onto the deck.

Mom buried her face in her hands.

My heart felt like it was going to explode with panic at the mere thought of dumping the money on a private cargo plane.

Elizabeth slipped her arm around my waist like she knew damn well I was about to pass out.

"Well," Mom said. "I guess I should email the school and tell them I won't need a sub for next week."

"If we ever decide to get married," Elizabeth whispered in my ear, "we're eloping before your dad decides to drop that much money on a fancy ceremony."

My panic disappeared in a flush of absolute joy as Elizabeth threaded her fingers through mine, and the medium-size ship finally left the little village at the bottom of the gorge, heading to a place where we could catch our last minute cargo plane to New York.

The next bit of the story is really just blah, blah, blah, boat, blah, blah, sketchy customs official who lets us through way too easily. Blah, blah, blah, flying in a cargo plane is not actually fun. Blah, blah, I bet you forgot about the time the New York City police had pictures of us wreaking magical havoc. Too bad for us, the police didn't forget.

29

B y the time we landed in New York and got to the weird offshoot of customs where people on non-commercial flights are sent to feel special, all I wanted was to sleep in my own bed. I'd dozed on the uncomfortable plane, but between all the traveling and Eric's freak out about having to step away from our precious cargo to go through customs, my whole body felt like it had gotten packed full of sand.

Even my eyes were gritty as the customs official asked me his questions.

"Do you have anything to declare?" The man barely looked at me as he spoke.

"No." I dug my nails into my palms, forcing myself to not wince at the not-quite-a-lie. Technically, Dad was the one with an entire plane full of things to declare.

"Reason for travel?" The man flipped through my passport.

"Vacation." I turned my voice wobble into a pretty convincing yawn.

"Where do you live?"

"Manhattan."

I got through and dragged my rolly bag to meet Mom on the other side.

"Can you come home to rest for a bit?" She pushed my purple hair away from my face.

"I don't think so," I said. "I have to meet *the people* soon."

By *soon* I meant *I don't actually know what time The Event is or where it is, but Devon texted Raven and offered to pay her if she could send us the information because I'm an asshat who didn't bother to ask either of those questions when I was on the phone with the bad guy's sales rep.*

A group of people entered through the sliding doors that were very clearly marked *Exit.*

"I don't think you should go back to school tomorrow," Mom said. "Take a day to rest and catch up on your work. Running yourself into the ground won't do you any good."

"Yeah. That would be nice."

The door people just hovered near the exit, not blocking it, but not seeming to have had any reason to have entered either.

"I could help with unloading the books," I said.

"I want you resting and doing schoolwork." Mom stepped in front of me, blocking my view of the hoverers. "Unloading those books could take weeks. You'll have plenty of time to help."

"With the way the Library's filing system works, it'll be done a lot quicker than you'd think."

"I can't wait to not have a suitcase with me anymore." Elizabeth rolled her bag next to mine and took my hand. "Also a hot shower and one of Lola's muffins."

"I'm sure she's been lonely," Mom said. "Her guards aren't exactly keen on conversation."

Devon set his suitcase next to mine as Dad gave Mom a smile before stopping ten feet away from us to make a call.

"I wonder if we could grab some muffins before we head down," Elizabeth said.

"I'm starved," Devon said.

I was going to say something along the lines of *I three crave nourishment,* but the hoverers moved away from the door, their whole unit coming straight for us.

Letting go of Elizabeth's hand, I took a little step sideways, just enough to keep any spells from hitting her before I knew what kind of wizards had come to attack.

"Elizabeth Wick," was not the thing I expected the lady at the front of the pack to say.

"Umm, yes?" Elizabeth pressed her hand to my back, though which of us she was trying to keep from panicking, I really don't know.

"Devon Rhodes?" A man stepped up beside the lady.

Until then, I hadn't realized the lady looked kind, like a superhero's aunt.

The man's stern expression and harsh voice made me appreciate the lady a lot more.

"That would be me," Devon said.

The man pulled a shiny badge out of his pocket. "We're going to need you to come downtown. We have some very interesting questions for you."

We're going to need you to come downtown. He actually said it like that. Like on a cop drama.

"About what?" Devon didn't even sound shaken.

"You're wanted for questioning regarding a disturbance at a retail location," the cop said.

"Just for that?" I cut in. "Nothing else?"

Devon stepped on my toe. "I don't know what you think I did wrong—"

"Devon, don't say anything without a lawyer." Dad stepped forward and took Devon's shoulder.

"Mr. Adams," the cop said. His knowing my dad's name sent a shiver down my spine. "We'd also like to speak to your son. If we could schedule an appointment for you to bring him down to the station—"

"Why don't I get an appointment?" Devon said.

"We don't have Bryant on camera using an unknown weapon." The cop nodded, and two men with handcuffs stepped toward Devon.

"What do you want with me?" Elizabeth prodded me to move so I stood mashed up next to Devon.

"I'm from Child Protective Services." The lady gave what could almost be considered a sympathetic smile.

"Why?" Elizabeth asked.

Devon pressed a metal cylinder into my hand. I slipped the hilt of his sword into my pocket.

"Your parents have been looking for you," the lady said.

"My parents have nothing to do with me," Elizabeth said. "I'm petitioning to become an emancipated minor. I can live on my own."

"The court has yet to hear your case," the lady said. "A minor leaving the country without parental consent is—"

"You don't have to grab me." Devon glared at the cop who had him by the arm.

"—worrying enough that your parents contacted our office," the lady finished.

"First of all, how did they even know where I was? They have no right to track and harass me like that," Elizabeth said. "Second, I'm not going back to their apartment, and I'm sure as hell not going back to Soaring Horizons."

"Elizabeth, just go with her," Dad said. "I'll have Nikki take care of it."

The CPS lady frowned at Dad.

"What's going on?" Eric strode toward us, his voice almost bored even though there was a pack of cops facing us.

"You," the head cop said, "we've been looking forward to speaking with you as well. Finding your name has been an interesting chore."

"And I'm afraid it will have to remain a mystery." Eric gave them a nod. "Shall we?" He looked to me.

"I don't think we're actually allowed to leave right now," I whispered.

"We don't have time for this," Eric said. "*Fransencio.*"

All the cops' faces went a little slack, and the CPS lady giggled.

"That's not good," I said.

"What did you just do?" Dad said in a cool tone before looking up toward the security camera in what he seemed to think was a casual way but totally proved where I get my awkward-under-stress habits from.

"We need to be going," Eric said. "As it is, we'll barely make it to The Event on time."

"I don't know if I can go," Devon said. "I'm pretty sure I'm being arrested for having a magical sword."

"I'm not going back to my parents," Elizabeth said.

"It'll be temporary." Mom laid a comforting hand on her shoulder.

"No." Elizabeth stepped away from my mom. "I'm not going back at all. Not even for a night. I'm not going to live with them and pretend magic doesn't exist. I can't. I've seen too much, and I can't pretend to be the girl who doesn't know there's more to life than my parents' petty drama."

"Elizabeth is coming with us. Devon?" Eric looked to Devon.

"I don't think I have a choice," Devon said.

"He can't go anywhere," Dad said. "If he walks out of here, I don't think the police will be very friendly next time they find him. My lawyers are good, but resisting arrest is not a charge you're going to want to fight."

"And if I let them take me, how am I supposed to explain what happened when we fought the Lancre?" Devon said. "What answers am I supposed to give them?"

"None, until you've spoken to a lawyer," Dad said.

"I can't tell a lawyer the truth either. Not without betraying the wizards we've been fighting to protect," Devon said. "I think I'm really pretty screwed here."

"I give you both two choices." Eric looked between Elizabeth and Devon. "Stay here, take Mr. Adams's kind offer and allow his lawyers to assist you. Lie as well as you are able, and hope that will be enough. Bryant and I will go tonight and do what we can without you."

"Get to the option that doesn't involve you and Bryant going after Kendrick without us," Devon said.

"Going after?" Mom said.

"We walk out of here," Eric said. "And you accept the fact that a human attempting to live a life that bridges the gap between the normal world and ours is unsustainable. That many secrets and lies are too great a burden for anyone to bear. You have to choose a path. Were it my choice to make, you'd come to Beville. You belong with the magical community."

"Sounds great," Elizabeth said. "I can go to cyber school until I'm eighteen. After that, my parents can—"

I won't type out what she actually said.

"Being a wanted man," Devon said. "Not quite the take on desirable I thought I was going to end up with."

"Devon, absolutely not," Mom said. "You have your whole life to think about."

"I've got some pretty cool friends belowground," Devon said. "I think a little flirting might be able to get me wiped out of every database."

"I won't pretend I have the power to stop you." Mom planted herself in front of Devon like she very much thought she had the power to stop him. "But you are throwing away a very promising future. You're both invested in your lives at school and—"

"And how many people want to run away to a place filled with magic?" Elizabeth hugged my mom. "We actually get to live it. This is what's right for me."

"Shall we?" Eric wheeled his suitcase around the still-dazed cops.

"Bryant, honey"—Mom let go of Elizabeth to grab my arm—"I will not lose you to the underground."

"Of course not." I hugged Mom. "Can you take our bags to the apartment and I'll come get their stuff later?"

"Yeah." Mom gripped me tighter. "You had better be home by morning, Bryant Jameson Adams."

Dad stepped in to wrap his arms around both of us.

"I will." I gave them an extra squeeze. "But maybe look into the cyber school paperwork for me, too."

"You need to go to university," Dad said. "I already have interviews lined up for you at—"

"Let's figure out how to get rid of the purple hair and then I'll apply to college," I said. "After the year I've had, I'll have some really interesting experiences to mostly lie about in my college essays."

"See you at home." Mom laced her fingers through Dad's.

"Love you." I took Elizabeth's hand. "Let's go."

The three of us followed Eric outside.

The biting cold of New York greeted me, slicing through my coat as its own little welcome home.

"Are you really sure about this, Devon?" Elizabeth whispered. "My parents can't get to me after I turn eighteen, but if Raven can't hack you out of this, the police could be looking for you for a really long time."

"I may be able to charm my way out of just about anything," Devon said, "but convincing cops they shouldn't worry about me using a magical sword to stab a guy with venomous fangs in the smart watch section? Even I'm not that good. I knew the risks when I started carrying the sword. That's the problem with being a non-wizard in a magical fight. Your weapons are way more obvious than spells."

"I'm sorry," I said.

"Don't be," Devon said. "Just get the handcuffs off. They do not live up to the hype."

"*Cliaxo.*"

The locks clicked open.

Devon shook out his wrists. "So much better."

A cab pulled up to the curb, and the driver rolled down his window. "I haven't been to this part of the airport in ages." The world's best cabbie gave us a wave.

"How did you know?" I would've hugged him if it wouldn't have been almost weirder than leaving my parents in a pack of dazed cops.

"I called him," Eric said. "Lola's guards are seeing to the books. We are going to Columbus Circle. And, with any luck, order will be restored to the people of Beville before morning and we'll never have to hear the name Kendrick McDonald again."

30

The sweet scent of car exhaust and overcooked hotdogs filled the air as we stepped out of the cab at Columbus Circle. A glorious slosh of freezing sludge lapped into my shoe as a car raced by. An angry tourist shouted at a street musician for being too loud.

I was home.

"I love New York," I whispered to myself as my whole heart filled with such joy, I would have sat down and wept if there had been a semi-clean place to sit.

"Come on." Elizabeth ran back up the stairs to collect me. "We're on a schedule."

"Right." I shook my head, knocking my thoughts into an order that didn't center on how much I loved the chaos and grit of my hometown.

We weaved through the crowd, my purple hair attracting shockingly little attention, and toward the strip of wall where no one ever seemed to look.

"Where exactly are we going?" Devon asked.

"To Beville." Eric glanced causally around before muttering. "*Portunda*."

"Where in Beville?" Elizabeth asked.

"No idea." Eric opened his newly formed door. "All the chatter Raven could find simply said The Event could not be missed."

"Hopefully they meant that literally." I slipped through the door after Elizabeth.

Even though she'd started walking down the tunnel, she held her hand behind her, waiting for me to catch up.

I ran a few steps to reach her hand and kissed the scar I'd left on the outside of her wrist before lacing my fingers through hers.

She gave me a smile that reached her perfect, sparkly eyes as I walked beside her.

My heart swooped around in my chest so hard I almost forgot we were on our way to do deadly and important things.

"Any chance of Lola's guards joining us?" Devon held his sticky blaster up to the dim light of the tunnel's ceiling, checking the...I don't know, but it looked like he was checking something important.

"They're needed to get the books safely into the Library," Eric said. "I think we can all agree leaving the books waiting in a truck is an unacceptable risk."

"There are too many wizards in Manhattan who would kill to get them," Elizabeth said.

"Can they save us at least one crate to file?" I pictured myself dumping a crate of books over the railing on the top floor of the Library and watching the books drift down to their places on the levels below.

Eric raised an eyebrow at me.

"We can always reload a crate to dump." Devon clapped me on the shoulder. "We can make a daily game of it."

"While you're hiding from the law in the basement of the Consortium?" Eric said.

"The Consortium's not a bad place to be," Devon said. "And if things get too dicey aboveground, I'm sure your house could find space for me. You know you love company." He winked at Eric.

"And if we get cornered at the Consortium?" Elizabeth asked.

"We know a back way out." Devon shrugged. "We'll even bring goggles this time."

"On the plus side, life won't be boring." Elizabeth laughed.

I made myself give a few chuckles of support, but I honestly couldn't wrap my head around it.

None of us were going back to school.

It wouldn't be safe for Devon to sit in Times Square trawling for girls.

He and Elizabeth were dropping out of the spring play.

It wouldn't be safe for me to take Elizabeth on dates aboveground for a long time.

Worries about college and job possibilities and how I was going to explain switching to cyber school to Dr. Spinnek all swirled around in my head.

Life was never going to be anything close to what is was before we'd stumbled into magic.

But the thing was, I couldn't find a *but* that made it not worth it.

"Should I bother asking if we have a plan?" Devon asked as we neared the end of the tunnel to Beville.

"We always have a plan," Eric said.

"Find the trouble. Pretend we're going to scope out the trouble so we can form a plan," Elizabeth said. "Forget we were supposed to form a plan and dive into the mess. Sound about right?"

"Yep," I said.

"I do appreciate consistency," Devon said.

"This isn't the time for sarcasm," Eric said.

I was on the verge of saying something sarcastic and funny when a familiar noise caught my ear.

At first, I thought it was a rumble like a subway train racing overhead. Then I noticed the consistency and rhythm. Like people stomping on the bleachers at a basketball game.

"What is that?" Devon handed his sticky blaster to Elizabeth and pulled out the hilt of his sword.

The end of the tunnel opened in front of us. On one side, the stone spire that reached up to Times Square pierced the ceiling. But where we should have had a clear view of the houses on the other side, the area had been blocked off by a white-and-black circus tent someone had erected in the middle of the street.

"They did say we wouldn't be able to miss The Event," Devon said.

"It's strange." Eric took the lead as we headed toward the tent of doom. "On a personal level, I find the lack of subtlety distasteful. But as someone who needs to find Kendrick—"

"Kudos to him for making it easy," Devon said.

"At what point are we going to acknowledge that the giant tent set up by Eric's house is probably a trap?" Elizabeth tightened her grip on my hand like she thought Kendrick was going to try and swoop out of the sky to kidnap me again, and she wanted to protect me because she's the most amazing girlfriend in the world like that.

"I figured we were just going to ignore it," Devon said.

"Trap or not, we can't afford to forgo this chance," Eric said.

"Nope." I slipped my non-Elizabeth claimed hand into my pocket, pulling out my phone. "If fate let the magic phone ring, we answer the this-is-totally-a-trap call."

"Tell me you have someone lurking in the shadows as backup," Elizabeth said.

"I've already told you Lola's guards are unloading the books," Eric said.

"And Charles?" I asked.

A loud guitar lick came from inside the tent.

"Charles doesn't communicate through technological means," Eric said. "He doesn't even know where we went, let alone that we're back in the country."

"Awesome." Devon ran a hand over his hair, somehow making tousled and jetlagged look cool.

The entrance of the tent came into view. More instruments joined the guitar, blasting out music so loud I was worried the vibrations might shake the ceiling apart and send Times Square tumbling down onto our heads.

The same beefy dude who'd been the bouncer at The Game stood at the entrance. He'd traded his awkward kilt and top hat combo for a black-and-white spandex and latex combo that would have totally worked in a production of Pippin.

The tiniest hint of a menacing smile curved the corners of the bouncer's lips when he saw us approaching.

The music paused for a moment, and a roar of joy filled the tent.

"That's probably a bad thing." Fear wiggled its way down my throat to squirm in my stomach.

"Welcome to The Event." The bouncer gave a sanctimonious bow. "I hope you purchased tickets in advance. Our performance tonight is sold out."

"We have tickets," I said.

The bouncer snapped his fingers, and a girl stepped out of the tent, tablet in hand. She wore a glittery body suit, which failed so badly at actually covering her body Elizabeth side-stepped to plant herself between me and the girl.

The worry in my gut paused for a moment to do a happy little jig because Elizabeth wanted to defend her territory, which made me her territory because the most perfect girl in the world had actually claimed me.

"Name?" the girl said.

"Mr. Wick." The joyful dance shifted back into worry as an *Ohh* like people were wincing at someone else's pain came from inside the tent.

"Welcome, Mr. Wick." The light sparkled on the girl's shiny lipstick as she smiled at me. "We have your booth waiting for you."

She bowed us toward the open entrance of the tent.

I could tell the tent flaps had been tied open but could see only darkness inside.

I shook my shoulders out and tipped my chin up, because if I was going to walk into a trap and potentially be murdered in a really horrible way, I didn't want tales of my demise to center around how I'd been a coward as I faced my doom.

"Come along. After the month we've had, I could use a bit of diversion." Eric strode into the darkness.

I held tight to Elizabeth's hand as we stepped into the tent, expecting to be shrouded in black. But as soon as we passed through the canvas opening, dazzling lights surrounded us.

We weren't on the ground anymore. Somehow, we'd entered a box on the highest of the three tiers of the audience. Wooden walls formed the two sides of our box, with black velvet across the back blocking our way out, and the open front giving us a perfect view of the inside of the tent and the things I really didn't want to see.

It was like we'd entered a modern-day version of a gladiator's arena.

Off to one side, a band played on a little platform. On the other side, another platform had been set up with a board displaying betting odds.

But most of the lights were focused on the center of the arena and the two fighters who faced each other on the blood-stained ground.

The crowd cheered as the boy charged the girl, his knife raised.

She shouted something and dove to the side.

The boy's shoulder lurched back like someone had punched him. Blood dripped from his fresh wound, but I had no idea what spell the girl had cast to do the damage.

And suddenly, the cops not handcuffing Eric or me for the trouble at the electronics store made a lot more sense.

The girl attacked first the second time. She raised her fist like she was going to bop the boy on the head, and a rolling wave of light, like sound made visible, pounded from her fist as she leapt high.

The boy staggered but stayed standing and sliced his hand through the air to strike her in the back of the knees.

From the way her mouthed moved, it looked like she was screaming as she fell to the ground, but I couldn't hear her over the pounding music.

The boy smiled as he stalked toward her, raising his arms, asking for the crowd to cheer for him.

The roar from the audience brought bile to my throat.

The boy looked down at the girl. His mouth moved as he began a spell, but the girl sprang to her feet, digging her fingers into the boy's chest like she was going to rip his heart out.

The boy stiffened. His hands started to shake, and the trembling spread up his arms until his whole body was twitching.

"We have to stop her." I stepped toward the railing of our booth. "Eric, we have to stop her."

The girl yanked her hand back, and the boy crumpled to the ground. He lay on the blood-stained dirt and didn't twitch anymore.

The crowd cheered.

"He's dead," Devon said. "He's dead, and they're cheering."

The music from the band swelled as the girl raised her arms high.

She bowed as two men entered the arena to carry the boy's body away.

"What a match!" A horribly familiar voice echoed around the tent.

A spotlight blinked on directly opposite our booth.

Kendrick McDonald stood on a glistening black stage. His black-tipped white Mohawk practically glowed in the light. He wore his black, fur-collared cloak and had added black lipstick to complete the Ren Faire Goth vibe.

"I promised you this would be an event to remember," Kendrick said. "Have I kept my word?"

The crowd cheered.

Kendrick raised a hand to quiet the masses. "And the excitement is only beginning. This night is not merely one of entertainment. The end of an era has arrived. It is time to say goodbye to the fly that buzzes around our ears. Please welcome Eric Deldridge and his crew of interfering, do-good misfits. Tonight, we end their reign of nuisance and see how easily their blood is split. Let's get a round of applause for our guests of honor."

31

A new spotlight flashed on, shining down on our booth, blinding me to the crowd who roared their approval.

"So definitely a trap then," Devon said.

"I didn't know you were this unpopular," Elizabeth said. "An entire tent full of people cheering for your death?"

"People will cheer for anything if you present it with the right enthusiasm." Eric stepped up to the rail and waved at the crowd below.

"So, are we going to try for a plan?" I pulled my thumbs out of the holes in my sleeves, placing my hand scars on full display. I hesitated before taking off my scarf and letting my neck scar show, too.

Maybe I imagined it, but it almost seemed like the pitch of the cheering changed as the audience saw all the spell damage I'd managed to survive.

"We get to Kendrick," Eric said. "Without a ringmaster, The Event ends."

"Better than we usually have," Devon said.

Eric raised his hand as Kendrick had to silence the crowd.

They all went quiet, but in a different, eager sort of way.

"Flies, Kendrick?" Eric said. "You've been defeated by *flies* twice. What sort of wizard does that make you?"

"The sort who will be responsible for your deaths." Kendrick shrugged, the fur shoulders of his cape almost eating his face with the movement.

I don't know if it was jetlag, desensitization from almost dying so many times, or the fact that he looked like a furry puppet, but I just started laughing. Like full on tears in my eyes, belly laughing.

"Bryant," Eric said with a hint of warning in his voice.

"I'm sorry." I wiped my tears away. "Sorry. Keep going."

Eric kicked the waist-high wall at the front of our balcony and it tipped forward, unfolding and lengthening to form a ramp that reached all the way down to the center of the arena.

"You have to teach me that one," I whispered.

Eric raised one black eyebrow at me.

"I don't mean right now," I said.

"I must admit, Kendrick, I didn't think you'd be so bold." Eric strode down his ramp. "Pulling all these people together. Congregating in the open to commit such dark deeds. Do you really believe there will be no consequences for your actions?"

"Let the Ladies come for me," Kendrick said. "I don't fear them."

For the first time, a sound came from the crowd that wasn't excitement. It was like every person had looked to their friends and murmured *he shouldn't have said that* at once.

I squared my shoulders and followed Eric, trying to look like a second who was ready for a duel. Pretending to be a badass got a lot easier when I heard Devon's and Elizabeth's footsteps following me.

"The Ladies missed us at The Game," Kendrick said. "We were already gone by the time they arrived. We slipped right through their fingers. It's been months, and they haven't come for me. Not even a whisper of the Ladies coming to exact their justice. Do you know what that says to me?"

I bit my lips together to keep from saying *They're all dead?*

"That either they are too weak to confront you"—Eric stepped down onto the ground—"or they agree with your cause—creating the strongest possible wizards by letting the weak be slaughtered in battle."

"You must think you're so smart." Kendrick stomped on his stage. His ramp unrolled like a long black carpet.

"Intelligence is one of my finer attributes." Eric bowed. "Would you like to know why you're wrong about the Ladies?"

"No." Kendrick started down his ramp. "I'd like you to be dead so I never have to hear you speak again."

"Are you sure?" Eric said. "It might change your plan."

"At least Kendrick has a plan," Devon murmured.

I glanced toward him, but he wasn't looking at me or at Kendrick. His gaze was fixed on the aisle between the tiers of booths where three people lurked in the shadows.

"I want you dead," Kendrick said. "I want my patrons to watch your apprentice die. The fact that you dragged two humans to the slaughter? That just gives the crowd a better value for their ticket."

Ignoring the fact that Kendrick had almost reached the bottom of his ramp, I looked around the tent. Four shadowy aisles hid eleven fighters.

Twelve against four didn't sound like the worst odds in the world, but they didn't really make me feel any better either.

"Then I will reveal the truth that could have saved you after you're dead," Eric said. "Bryant, try and buy Kendrick and me some time alone."

"Sure." I bounced on my toes. "Sounds exciting. *Milkawa.*" I focused my magic on the nearest aisle where the girl who'd killed the boy lurked in the shadows.

The ground rumbled and started to grow, twisting and morphing to block the entrance, like I'd created a stone door that could rise up from the ground.

As I was marveling at the fact that I'd learned to somewhat control the spell, two of Kendrick's minions leapt over the top, leaving one behind.

"Not a bad start." I turned toward the next entrance. "*Milkawa.*"

Eric began a spell, but the band started playing again, and I couldn't hear anything over the music.

All three of the wizards made it out of the second aisle, but at least I'd made it so more couldn't come pouring in to join the brawl.

Devon flicked his wrist, his sword vooming to life as I sealed off the other two entrances.

A fountain of sparks flew from Eric and Kendrick's fight, but I didn't have time to see why the audience was cheering. Ten of Kendrick's minions were closing in on Devon, Elizabeth, and me.

Elizabeth aimed the sticky blaster and shot one of the boys in his bare chest. He looked down in disgust and tried to wipe the goo away, sticking his hand to his own skin.

"Nice one!" I shouted, not knowing if she could hear me but needing to praise my girlfriend anyway because she's freakin' amazing.

One of the minions raised his hand like he was grabbing a spell out of the air to hurl at Elizabeth.

"*Erunca!*" The lightning streaked down from above, striking two of the spotlights before hitting the minion. The two lights flashed out as the minion screamed and fell to the ground.

Not what I had wanted to happen, but whatever.

A girl dove at me, brandishing a black knife.

"*Stasio.*" The clear cage formed around the girl. She looked like she was screaming in rage, but I'd already turned to my next opponent.

Half of his face had been covered in sticky potion, but he'd been smart enough not to touch it.

"*Abalata.*" The black of my spell pooled in my palm. I tossed it at the gray goo on the minion's face. I hit my mark and the spell stayed stuck to his cheek as I jerked my hand back, yanking him forward. I cringed as he hit the ground hard. "*Stasio.*"

"Bryant!" Elizabeth shouted.

I whipped around, ready to defend Elizabeth, but she'd stuck one of the minions to the ground by her bare feet.

"*Stasio.*" I trapped that one, too.

I spared a glance for Devon, who swung his sword with such speed, the light of it blurred in my eyes and I couldn't get a clear aim to trap his opponent.

A scream from behind me barely carried over the music.

The girl who had killed the knife boy leapt toward me, her hand raised as the weird wavy spell pooled beneath her fist.

"*Exci.*" My spell hit her in the stomach, knocking her off course just enough to let me dodge out of the way.

I caught a glimpse of Elizabeth. She pulled the trigger on the sticky blaster but nothing happened. She'd run out of pellets.

One of the minions raced toward her, knife raised.

"*Frico!*" I yanked the knife out of the minion's hand.

The blade flew toward me. I dodged the knife, knowing full well I had no chance of catching it without hurting myself.

A grunt sounded from right behind me.

I spun around.

The girl who'd killed the boy stared down at the blade lodged in her chest.

"Oops." I raced for Elizabeth. "*Erunca!*"

Lightning streaked toward the girl who'd been charging Elizabeth. She dodged, missing the full blast of the spell, but it was enough to draw her attention to me.

She grinned as she stalked toward me.

Devon raced behind her, running from someone who wasn't the minion he'd been fighting before.

"*Turso,*" I shouted.

White light whipped out, catching Devon's foe. The minion fell to the ground.

The girl who'd tried to stab Elizabeth muttered something as she came closer to me.

"*Parapus!*" Thin, black lines flew from my hand and soared toward the girl.

She sliced her arm down, batting my spell aside.

I backed up a step. The music had started to make my brain go muddy. I just wanted everyone to be quiet while we fought, but that's not exactly a thing you can ask for when you're stuck in a death match.

A giant *crack* sounded from the far side of the arena where Eric and Kendrick fought. The crowd gasped.

"*Hieata.*"

The girl coughed as my spell knocked all the air from her lungs.

"*Stasio.*" I stumbled as the clear cage wrapped around the minion.

I glanced down to see what my feet had gotten tangled on. The girl I'd accidentally stabbed lay dead on the ground.

I yanked the knife from her chest and bolted toward where Devon and Elizabeth stood back-to-back, each facing a minion.

"Leave them alone!" I shouted.

The music stopped.

The sudden quiet rumbled in my ears.

"Go to Eric." Devon passed Elizabeth a fresh clip of sticky pellets.

There was something in his tone that shot fear into my spleen.

I looked toward Eric for the first time.

His face was stained red with blood, and I could tell from the way he had his feet planted he was barely staying upright.

"He can hold on."

A wave of heat lapped toward us from the guy who was facing Elizabeth.

"*Stasio.*" I made the split-second decision to trap him before protecting us. On the one hand, I got him stuck in a cage. On the other hand, his spell stung my skin like I'd swum into a cloud of jellyfish.

I gritted my teeth against my own scream even as Elizabeth's cry dug into my heart. I looked toward the last of Kendrick's minions.

A storm of silver clouds grew above her, flickering with bolts of lightning that glowed electric blue.

A stream of the bolts hurdled toward Devon.

"*Lobula.*" I blocked the bolts' path.

The minion looked toward me. I could see hate in her eyes, but there wasn't any fear. Like Kendrick had somehow drained that bit of humanity from his fighters as he trained them to kill in his stupid show.

"*Stilgarna.*" I felt heavy as I spoke the spell. Exhausted from the cycle of fighting and killing.

A stream of water flew up from the ground, dousing the minion and bringing her own lightning down to strike her.

She fell to the ground, screaming in pain.

"*Stasio.*" I trapped her before she'd stopped twitching.

I scanned our part of the arena. Two dead, seven trapped. The dude with the goo on his bare chest had somehow stuck both his hands to himself and glowered from the shadows.

"*Stasio.*" I locked him away before running to the far side of the tent.

32

The band stayed silent as I sprinted toward Eric. I could see the audience watching me. Some of them looked enthralled, but most seemed disgusted or sad or scared, like they'd realized they'd been watching real people fight and die. None of this was a game. It was a deadly battle we'd been trapped in for months, even if the reality of the blood and pain had been hidden beneath the shining façade of entertainment.

Every part of my body hurt and I wanted nothing more than to curl up in one of the fancy audience boxes and sleep, but their disillusionment gave me comfort and made me run faster, because if they could see how far they'd fallen, maybe they'd want to help build something better.

A massive cloud of deep gray mist formed in front of Kendrick, billowing toward Eric, who had one hand pressed to the blood that leaked from a gash on his cheek.

I opened my mouth to start a healing spell, remembered the *no venom* rule, and stayed silent as I skidded to a stop by his side.

"You made quick work of them," Eric said.

"Yeah, well," I spoke loudly enough for Kendrick and the audience to hear, "maybe Kendrick should have taken a little more time training his new flock of minions. Did you even want them to win?"

"Their fate is not my primary concern." Kendrick's cloud raced toward us.

"*Primurgo!*" I grabbed Eric's arm as my shield spell blossomed over us. "So you're admitting in front of everyone here that you were willing to let all those kids die?" I shouted as the cloud surrounded us.

The weight of Kendrick's spell pressed against my shield.

I took a deep breath, calming my nerves and forcing my magic to hold strong.

"They are a sacrifice I am willing to make to rid Beville of the pestilence of Eric Deldridge," Kendrick said.

"Let me out." Eric spoke softly.

I dropped my shield.

"*Habelo.*" A wave of wind erupted from Eric's hand, blasting Kendrick's cloud away, carrying with it all the debris from their battle in a storm of wreckage.

"Kendrick McDonald," I said, "you recruited underage wizards with the promise of training them to be strong enough to build a better future. Using illegal Lancre, you captured underage wizards and forced them to fight to the death. You have just admitted to willingly sacrificing all of their lives to your vendetta against Eric Deldridge, a man you have only hated since he destroyed your restaurant after you tried to kidnap me."

A blaze of wavering, deep blue light *screeched* like a bird of prey as it streaked toward us.

Eric shouted something I couldn't hear over the earsplitting noise. Purple flames flew from his hands, consuming Kendrick's spell.

Kendrick waved a hand, sending the flames up toward the roof of the tent.

"Kendrick McDonald," I shouted, "will you confess to your crimes?"

"The only true crime is weakness." Kendrick sneered.

The purple flames spread out over the roof of the tent, reaching toward the top tier of the audience. Frightened screams filled the shadows.

"Then you are guilty." Eric held out his blood-coated hands. "*Tudina.*"

Kendrick lunged to the side, a smile twisting his lips.

"*Ilmatiot.*"

Kendrick didn't stop smiling as Eric's spell squeezed all the air from his lungs. He stayed on his feet for a moment, raising his hands as though he thought he could still fight back.

"*Aarantha.*" I formed a vortex, syphoning the purple flames away from the roof as Kendrick fell to his knees. "*Stasio.*" The cage formed around Kendrick as he clawed at his throat. "Let him live, Eric."

"Let a monster live?" Eric asked.

"We have a chance to build a better world. Shouldn't that world be built on justice and mercy?"

The radiance of Eric's flames hovered above my hand.

"What you ask can't be done," Eric said. "To let a monster walk free—"

"He won't walk free," I said. "Just trust me. I actually have a plan. This is our chance to change everything."

Eric held my gaze for a long moment before nodding. He waved a hand, and Kendrick gasped in a breath.

"How shall we change the world?" Eric asked.

The crowd in the stands began to murmur, growing restless since imminent death was no longer a concern.

I froze for a moment, realizing that literally hundreds of people were watching me. Then I heard my mother's voice in my head.

A good production comes down to staging.

"Come on." I headed toward the ramp that led up to Kendrick's stage, waving across the arena for Devon and Elizabeth to join us.

The walk up that stupid ramp was the longest climb of my life. I could feel the gaze of everyone in the place on the back of my neck.

"Bryant, what's going on?" Devon whispered.

"We're forming a new magical government," I said.

"We're what?" Elizabeth slipped her hand into mine.

"Don't worry, it's all very legal. I had Nikki write us up a constitution and everything," I said.

"You did what?" Devon whisper-shouted.

"Kendrick's imprisonment will fall under section twenty-seven, paragraph six," I said. "There's already a criminal indictment procedure laid out."

"What?" Elizabeth asked.

"It's fine," I said. "As far as Nikki knows, she's being paid overtime to help me plan the most detailed Dungeons and Dragons campaign of all time."

"She fell for that?" Devon laughed.

"Lying is a lot easier through email."

We reached the top of the ramp, and the spotlights swiveled to beam onto our backs, silhouetting the four of us across Kendrick's shining stage.

I didn't need Elizabeth's little gasp to know I'd seen the image before. The hero, the adventurer, the apprentice, the seer. The four of us together. All part of the same picture. All necessary to make it to the end of the journey.

I took one more deep breath and turned to face the crowd. Cold dread trickled into my fingers.

"Shall I begin for you?" Eric said.

"Uh-huh."

Eric stepped in front of our group.

"Witches and wizards," Eric said, "too long have you lived in a darkness filled with secrets, lies, and the constant threat of danger. Today we move forward. Today we take the first steps toward a better world. The Ladies are dead."

A rush of gasps and whispers flew around the arena.

"We conquered them and took control of the Library and the Consortium, only to find the books, the very knowledge the Ladies claimed to possess, had long since been stolen from them. We have journeyed across the ocean to reclaim what rightfully belongs to the wizards of Manhattan.

"We have fought, and bled, and killed to give you hope for a future where knowledge is the right of every child born with magic. Where digging in the shadows for scraps of magic is no longer needed. Where hiding from the wrath of dictators is nothing but a grim memory from our dark past. Today, we step into a new world. Join me, for our future will be glorious." Eric turned to me.

"Right." I glanced to Elizabeth and Devon.

They both smiled at me, like they knew I'd be okay.

I looked around the arena. At the bottom, where there shouldn't have been any people moving, ten women stood together. The keepers of the dead, watching me with joy filling their faces.

Tears burned in my eyes as I gave my fairy godmothers a nod.

"Our new society must have a structure that can last for generations. That's what we want, a peace that will outlive us all." I tipped my chin up, letting my voice fill the arena. "There will be laws and consequences for those who break them. Kendrick will be tried and punished for his crimes. A council of six seats will be formed to run our community. We won't be outcasts hiding underground anymore. We will be a magical world, thriving just out of sight."

The people of Beville cheered, and a weight broke away from my shoulders, like the golden strands of fate that bound me had loosened just a bit. Devon clapped me on the back, Elizabeth squeezed my hand, and hope that maybe it really had all been worth it bubbled inside me.

We had reached the brink of a new era of magic. And I, Bryant Jameson Adams, teenage wizard, hopeless geek, and daydreaming misfit had survived to see the start of the most prosperous years Beville had ever seen.

But that's a tale for another time. I'll end my story standing with my friends as the fate of wizards in Manhattan changed forever.

EPILOGUE

Post Credits Scene (You know, like the little flashes of extra story that pop up once they've scrolled past the stars' names in the end credits at the movie theatre.)

I know I said I was done, but I don't think it would be fair to walk away without telling you how things turned out.

Chaperone Cindy got a promotion and is now the assistant to the head of HR for my dad's company. He said her ability to handle difficult people with grace made her the perfect candidate for the job.

Nikki has started DMing her own regular Dungeons and Dragons game. I've played a few times. There are a lot of rules involved.

Dr. Spinnek is writing her first novel. It's about a boy who's a part of a secret society that lives under Manhattan.

Charles and his people gladly took over the role of jail keepers for Kendrick and other criminals of the magical variety. Charles is on the council of six.

The keepers of the dead are still below the Library. I tried to visit once, they laughed, told me it wasn't my time, and sent me away.

Lola sits at the head of the council of six. She's still in charge of the Library, and Sniffer McDeadDog and the rest of her guards do a great job keeping the books safe.

Mom and Dad get a little more complicated. Since I'm gone so much, Mom moved in with Dad *so she wouldn't be too lonely*. They have two separate bedrooms. We all pretend I don't know it's a sham.

Mrs. Mops is really happy living in Dad's giant house where she has lots of places to nap.

Eric is still Eric. He's on the council, sprints around Manhattan seeking adventure, and is the one all the bad guys fear. He's been keeping Charles in business as he rounds up the wizards who have been breaking the laws of Beville.

Elizabeth is still living at the Consortium with Devon and Lola while we all work on cyber school. Nikki managed to get her emancipated from her parents before college applications had to be sent in. She's applying for a double major in musical theater and classic literature with an emphasis on mythology. She's clearly going to get in everywhere she's applied because she's the most brilliant and perfect girl in the world. And she loves me. Which is the best thing that's ever happened.

I'm applying to all the schools she is, but as a political science major. Dad got way more chill about me not going to an Ivy League for undergrad when I told him I want to be a lawyer. He hasn't figured out it's because I'm on the council. I've decided not to tell him that little tidbit. Also, my hair still grows in purple, which is a fun thing I get to deal with. On the plus side, I'm easy to find in a crowd, and Elizabeth swears she thinks it's cute.

And Devon...well, technically Devon Rhodes no longer exists. Raven had to wipe out all digital traces of his name to get him off the police radar. No past. No paper trail. My best friend's life is a completely blank slate. Mom's making him finish high school under a fake name, but he's not applying to college. He's been making a list instead. Pinpointing every place where Lancre might be hunting. Raven's been helping him search and building him all kinds of crazy stuff, and...

That's his story. So I better let him tell it.

ESCAPE INTO ADVENTURE

Thank you for reading The Geek's Guide to Wizarding Mastery in One Epic Tome. If you enjoyed the series, please consider leaving a review to help other readers find Bryant's tale.

As always, thanks for reading,

Megan O'Russell

Never miss a moment of the danger or hilarity.

Join the Megan O'Russell mailing list to stay up to date on all the action by visiting https://www.meganorussell.com/book-signup.

DISCOVER A DARKER TALE IN…

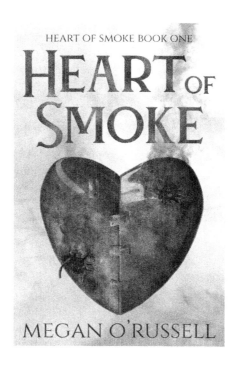

HEART OF SMOKE BOOK ONE

HEART OF SMOKE

MEGAN O'RUSSELL

One will betray her. One will save her. One will destroy her world.

Do the work, steal the goods, keep her sister alive—a simple plan Lanni has been clinging to. With the city burning around her and vampires hiding in the shadows, making it until morning is the best she can hope for.

But order in the city is crumbling, and the thin safety that's kept Lanni alive won't be enough to protect her family. The people who live in the glittering glass domes—lording over the city, safe from the dangers of the outside world—have grown tired of the factory filth marring their perfect apocalypse.

When the new reign of chaos threatens her sister, Lanni faces a horrible choice—accept the fate she was born to, or join the enemy she's sworn to destroy.

CHAPTER ONE

The scent of ash blew in through the window, joining the stench of burning oil that always filled the factory. The foreman had been pushing the machines faster for the past week, so a hint of singed rubber added its stink, too.

I tightened the bandana that covered my face as I waited for the next rack of syringes to rumble down the line.

The outside doors banged open, letting in a fresh plume of smoke.

The foreman greeted the next shift of workers by shouting at them.

I let the hum of the machines drown out his words.

The new rack of syringes slid toward me. I flipped them all into the tray, moving quickly so the heat from the glass wouldn't burn my hands. The belt moved as I patted them all flat, waiting until the last moment to slip one syringe up my sleeve.

The packaging machine ate the tray, hiding the gap I'd created. I reached up to tighten my bandana again, letting the syringe fall farther up my sleeve. I gritted my teeth as the heat stung my arm.

With a rumble, the next batch headed down the line.

Three solid taps on the shoulder and I stepped out of my place, gladly giving my spot to the worker for the next shift.

I stretched my arms toward the ceiling, letting my back crack as the hot syringe slid down to the base of my spine, landing where my shirt tucked into my pants.

I'd only managed to snag six during my shift. Not a great day's work by any means.

Better than any of the others could manage.

"Check out," the foreman shouted, like he thought we didn't know what we were supposed to do at the end of our shift. Or worse, he was foolish enough to think we wanted to stay.

All of us rushed toward the booth. I didn't run. I couldn't risk a sharp ear catching the faint clinking of my hard-won treasure. By the time I joined the line, there were already six others waiting to be checked out by the foreman's wife.

Mrs. Foreman sat in the booth, scanner in hand, frowning at each person who dared ask for their belongings back and to be paid for their time.

Or maybe it wasn't our wanting to be paid for our labor that she found so offensive. Maybe it was our dirty faces and rounded shoulders. Or the stink of sweat and rubber that had gotten permanently stuck in all our clothes. Maybe she didn't like the reminder that her husband's factory really produced two products—syringes and broken people.

I leaned out of line, peeking through the door to the courtyard.

The smoke hadn't fully blocked out the sun, but the ash came down thick. The fires were burning close to the city again.

A knot of panic twisted in my stomach as the line shifted forward. My nerves sent tingles from my fingertips to my toes.

Don't panic. You can't afford it.

I pressed my shoulders back and stood tall, making sure not even Mrs. Foreman's keen eyes could spot the lumps on my back from the pilfered goods.

"Trip Benson." Trip held out his wrist, offering his chip band.

Mrs. Foreman narrowed her eyes at him, like she wasn't sure if he was the same Trip Benson she'd been checking out after his shift six days a week for a dozen years.

"Trip Benson." He held his wrist right in front of her face like he wanted her to lick the tarnished metal bracelet instead of scan the chip it held.

Mrs. Foreman turned in her chair, taking her time gathering Trip's bag and jug, before handing them over and finally scanning his chip.

"Thank you." Trip snatched his things and strode out the door.

I took a deep breath, filling my lungs till they ached, pulled off my bandana, and stepped up to the counter, holding out my wrist.

"Name?" Mrs. Foreman pursed her lips at me.

I leaned over the counter, holding my chip band right under her scanner.

"Name?"

I held her glare even as my lungs started to tense.

Mrs. Foreman made a sound between a growl and sneeze before turning around to grab my bag and three jugs. She lingered, enjoying tormenting me, lining the jugs up perfectly on the counter and trying to balance my bag so it wouldn't tip over. When my lungs had started to burn and my brain had started to scream that I needed air, she finally scanned my chip, transferring over my credits and ration for the day's work.

I grabbed my things, making myself walk calmly to the bare patch of wall where I could set everything down. My fingers fumbled as I tied my bandana back around my face. I took a deep breath, and the familiar scent of the thick fabric pummeled my nose. My head spun as oxygen raced through my veins, leaving bright spots dancing in my eyes. Snatching my things back up, I headed out into the square.

My shoulders relaxed as soon as I stepped outside, though walking through the square between the four factory buildings was hardly more cheerful than working the belts.

Litter and ash stirred with the chill wind that swept between the brick buildings. A crumpled, blue pamphlet rolled across my foot.

I grabbed the paper and tucked it into my pocket as a wave of laughter came from the men smoking in the back corner of the square.

They were right to laugh. There was no use in reading the kep-made pamphlet. Even if I was foolish enough to trust anything the glass guards said, weak words of comfort wouldn't offer me any protection.

I glanced up at the sky. To the east, I could see evening light peering down, but to the west, thick, gray smoke blocked out the sun.

"Dammit." I bolted across the square toward the most rundown of the four brick buildings.

The ash must have been falling the whole day—the thick layer of it muffled my footsteps and puffed up, leaving the ankles of my pants gray.

"Where's your coat, honey?" one of the men in the corner called.

I tossed up my favored finger rather than waste air shouting back.

The men laughed again.

I flinched as one of them dissolved into wracking coughs that made me wonder how much longer I'd have to deal with his daily taunts.

The sound of his hacking followed me into the children's factory.

There were no machines to offer a blissful, mind-numbing hum on the kids' work floor, where they scrubbed and sorted bolts and scraps. Everything had to be done quietly so the teacher standing on the scaffold could be heard as she shouted her lessons to her three hundred students.

I stood on my toes, trying to catch a glimpse of Mari's shiny, black hair.

A kid started wailing in the far corner. The foreman strode toward him, but the teacher didn't pause her lesson on the decimation of the oceans. I tried not to wonder if the kid was wailing because he'd cut himself or because he couldn't stand the misery of knowing that something as beautiful as a sea turtle had once existed and he'd never get to see one in real life.

One of the minders finally caught sight of me. "Mari Sampson."

I gave the minder a nod of thanks as Mari hopped up from her place at one of the back tables and ran toward me.

"Slower, Mar," I whispered, though I knew my sister couldn't hear me.

"I thought you'd never come." Mari grabbed the jugs from my hands, setting them on the ground while I dug through my bag.

"I come at the same time every day." I pulled out Mari's hat, coat, and gloves.

"But some of the other kids have already been collected." Mari spoke so fast she sucked a bit of her bandana into her mouth and had to spit it out before continuing. "I got stuck on bolt scrubbing today, so you'll have to dig the metal bits out for me."

She held up her hands. Scratches deep enough to bleed marked her fingers.

I shoved down my sympathy and held out her coat.

Mari sighed before letting me dress her in the heavy fabric. I didn't blame her for hating the coat. The ratty outer and inner layers hid the dense material that was worth its weight in credits, but knowing you were lucky to have a bit of protection from the lethal sunrays and liking to wear the damn thing were two different matters.

I fastened her coat and held out her gloves.

"My fingers already hurt." She tucked her scratched hands behind her back. "I won't get burned. The sun's almost gone, and the sky's filled with smoke. I don't want to wear them."

"Hmm." I tugged Mari's wide-brimmed hat onto her head and tied the rope beneath her chin. "I heard a rumor that someone's been hoarding peaches. I was going to nab them as a treat for you, but if you don't *want* to wear your gloves—"

Mari snatched her gloves away from me and tugged them on.

Biting back a smile, I pulled my own layers from the bag and dressed myself in a quarter of the time it had taken me to dress Mari. I slung my bag on and passed her one of the jugs, keeping two for myself.

"We're going to jog today," I said.

"Why?" Mari tipped her chin up so I could see her eyes below the brim of her hat.

"Smoke's coming in from the western side of the city."

"Oh, reef bleachers!" Mari cursed, grabbing my hand and running out the door.

I let her set our pace as we headed through the litter-strewn square and onto the street beyond the factories.

The streets themselves had been kept clean of trash—the kep laws made sure of it—but not even the sweepers could keep up with the ash coming down from the sky.

Most of the people we passed had covered their heads, trying to keep the falling grit from settling into their hair. Some held cloths over their mouths or had tied rags around their faces. All of them had the same painful air of resignation. We all knew the city could drown in ash, and there wasn't a damn thing any of us could do about it. But watching hopelessness smother us when the ash was only a few inches thick...it almost seemed worse than letting the whole city burn at once.

I glanced up. The smoke had drifted farther in, close enough to coat the western edge of the city. I ran a little faster as we reached Generation Way, trying not to grip Mari's hand tight enough to make the scratches and slivers any worse.

The thumping of a club's music pounded through the air as we rounded the corner onto Endeavor Avenue. The handful of daytime bars that had been allowed to stay open had all been packed into the same few blocks with the shops that still sold non-essential goods. Cheers came from the nearest bar as a singer started a new song.

Mari took the lead, weaving a path through the customers eager to spend their credits.

Before we managed to break through the shoppers, I caught sight of the end of the line. It already stretched a block back from the tanks.

We dodged around a few of the slower people carrying jugs and claimed a place in line behind a man who stank with a tang exclusive to chem plant workers.

"The line's too long." Mari gripped my hand.

"We'll be fine," I said.

"What if the fires get too close and they call the kep away? What if the smoke stays in tomorrow?" She stood on her toes, trying to see between the adults in front of her. "What if they can't push the fires back?"

"Everything is going to be fine. We got here in time. We'll make it to the front." My guilt at lying to my little sister crashed into the hunger rumbling in my stomach.

"Two tanks," a woman farther down the line shouted. "Smoke's coming in, and they're only running two tanks!"

I caught a glimpse of the front of the line as we all shuffled forward.

The woman was right. They were only distributing from two of the three tanks. The kep had only bothered to send twelve glass guards in fancy black uniforms to deal with the thirsty masses.

"Keep to a single line," a guard shouted. "If you all keep to a single line, we can get you through faster."

We won't all make it.

I turned my gaze up to the edge of the overhang, choosing loathing over worry. Years of smoke and soot hadn't managed to destroy the painting some idiot had had chosen to place over the tanks.

A picture of a happy family and a blooming tree flanked the words *For the Future of Our Children.* Like they cared about Mari's future or mine.

I kept my gaze fixed on the family until Mari started bouncing.

There were only five in line ahead of us.

"Come on," Mari muttered. "Come on." She pressed her cheek to my waist, tilting her hat.

I unfastened my coat and draped the side over her, covering the bit of her neck the hat left exposed.

I glanced west.

The smoke had shifted again. The entire western side of the city would be covered.

One jug. If we can fill just one, we'll be fine.

A grating beep came from the front of the line, near one of the two working green tanks.

"I'm sorry, ma'am. Your chip shows no ration." The guard with the scanner turned away from the rationless woman.

"That's not possible." The woman stepped in front of the guard, holding out her wrist. "I did my day in the factory. They added my ration to my band, I know they did."

"Next."

The chem worker walked past the woman to the other working tank.

"Check it again." The woman shook her wrist at the guard. "I have a ration."

"The factory may have placed the ration on your chip," the guard said, "but water was diverted from this station for the protection of the city. We have to make sure everyone is provided for."

"I'm everyone," the woman shouted. "I need my ration."

"We've had to prioritize, ma'am," the guard said. "You are not in the approved group."

"I will die," the woman said. "You are throwing my life away."

"Difficult decisions had to be made," the guard said. "We thank you for your sacrifice."

The woman threw her jug and leapt toward the guard, reaching for his neck like she thought she could choke him.

Another guard lunged forward, cracking the woman over the head with his club before her fingers had even grazed his fellow's neck.

The woman crumpled to the ground and lay still. She wasn't even breathing.

Mari started to shake as the woman's blood stained the ash on the street.

"Next," the guard called.

I held Mari close, guiding her around the growing red sludge and to the tank. I raised my wrist for the guard to scan my chip band. My heart froze as I waited for the beep.

"Cleared for three jugs," the guard with the scanner said.

The other guard took Mari's jug.

My heart didn't start beating again until he turned on the tap and water started filling the container.

I let go of Mari to open the other jugs.

The guard passed the first back to Mari and had started filling the second before all the keps tipped their heads to the side at once as though listening to a voice only they could hear.

I reached forward, bracing the still-filling jug the moment before the guard let go of it and bolted for the side of the overhang.

Mari squeaked as I caught the jug, managing to keep it upright so it wouldn't spill. I twisted the top back on, taking the second to protect the slim bit of our ration we'd claimed before grabbing Mari's hand.

"Run." I didn't have to say it.

Mari darted for the corner of the overhang as the high whine of the closing gates began. We slipped into the narrow alley beside the tanks before the crowd still waiting in line began to shout.

The water station would be closed while the glass guards hid, or fought the fire raging around us, or whatever it was the kep in black uniforms did when they abandoned their petty attempts at helping the city scum.

Everyone left in line would have to go without.

Thank you for your sacrifice.

Order your copy of Heart of Smoke *to continue the story.*

ABOUT THE AUTHOR

 Megan O'Russell is the author of several Young Adult series that invite readers to escape into worlds of adventure. From *Girl of Glass*, which blends dystopian darkness with the heart-pounding danger of vampires, to *Ena of Ilbrea*, which draws readers into an epic world of magic and assassins.

With the *Girl of Glass* series, *The Tethering* series, *The Chronicles of Maggie Trent*, *The Tale of Bryant Adams,* the *Ena of Ilbrea* series, and several more projects planned for 2021, there are always exciting new books on the horizon. To be the first to hear about new releases, free short stories, and giveaways, sign up for Megan's newsletter by visiting the following:

https://www.meganorussell.com/book-signup.

Originally from Upstate New York, Megan is a professional musical theatre performer whose work has taken her across North America. Her chronic wanderlust has led her from Alaska to Thailand and many places in between. Wanting to travel has fostered Megan's love of books that allow her to visit countless new worlds from her favorite reading nook. Megan is also a lyricist and playwright. Information on her theatrical works can be found at Russell-Compositions.com.

She would be thrilled to chat with you on Facebook or Twitter @Megan-ORussell, elated if you'd visit her website MeganORussell.com, and over the moon if you'd like the pictures of her adventures on Instagram @ORussellMegan.

ALSO BY MEGAN O'RUSSELL

Printed in Great Britain
by Amazon